Y0-BDD-498

FIREWORKS

Three more explosions shook the building. I saw flames leaping from the roof of the failed laboratory. The chopper pad was almost like daylight from the fires.

"What are you going to do?" Anne asked.

"I'm going to give the Russians some more trouble."

I took out the boxes of Crabtree & Evelyn soap. Gift-boxed for Aunt Matilda in Des Moines. The first two were real soap. The third was lemon-smelling. Thermite bomb. I broke open the wrapper of the white shoelaces and took out a lace. It was a one-minute fuse. I stuck it in the bar. I found a lilac bar and shoved in a shoelace. High explosive.

I hugged the wall and went down to the fourth window, tossed it in. I quickly lit the other bomb and tossed it into the open rear of a truck as it came careening by. The building and the truck were soon engulfed in flames. I had established sufficient diversion. When you're hot, you're hot. And I was on a roll.

PINNACLE BRINGS YOU THE FINEST IN FICTION

THE HAND OF LAZARUS   (100-2, $4.50)
by Warren Murphy & Molly Cochran
The IRA's most bloodthirsty and elusive murderer has chosen the small Irish village of Ardath as the site for a supreme act of terror destined to rock the world: the brutal assassination of the Pope! From the bestselling authors of GRANDMASTER!

LAST JUDGMENT   (114-2, $4.50)
by Richard Hugo
Only former S.A.S. agent James Ross can prevent a centuries-old vision of the Apocalypse from becoming reality . . . as the malevolent instrument of Adolf Hitler's ultimate revenge falls into the hands of the most fiendish assassin on Earth!
"RIVETING...A VERY FINE BOOK"
— NEW YORK TIMES

TRUK LAGOON   (121-5, $3.95)
Mitchell Sam Rossi
Two bizarre destinies inseparably linked over forty years unleash a savage storm of violence on a tropic island paradise — as the most incredible covert operation in military history is about to be uncovered at the bottom of TRUK LAGOON!

THE LINZ TESTAMENT   (117-6, $4.50)
Lewis Perdue
An ex-cop's search for his missing wife traps him a terrifying secret war, as the deadliest organizations on Earth battle for possession of an ancient relic that could shatter the foundations of Western religion: the Shroud of Veronica, irrefutable evidence of a second Messiah!

Available wherever paperbacks are sold, or order direct from the Publisher. Send cover price plus 50¢ per copy for mailing and handling to Zebra Books, Dept. 084, 475 Park Avenue South, New York, N.Y. 10016. Residents of New York, New Jersey and Pennsylvania must include sales tax. DO NOT SEND CASH.

THE WIRE WINDOW

FRANK J. KENMORE

PINNACLE BOOKS
WINDSOR PUBLISHING CORP.

PINNACLE BOOKS

are published by

Windsor Publishing Corp.
475 Park Avenue South
New York, NY 10016

Copyright © 1988 by Frank J. Kenmore

All rights reserved. No part of this book may be reproduced in any form or by any means without the prior written consent of the Publisher, excepting brief quotes used in reviews.

First printing: August, 1988

Printed in the United States of America

CHAPTER I

We caught a bubble of hard air and rode up on it and I felt my spine compress down into the seat. Then we fell off the bubble, straight down for maybe a hundred feet and my head hit the canopy. I was fighting the F-14 for every inch of mean sky. Six hundred feet below, the North Sea was a scary mass of mountainous grey waves and surging watery valleys topped by ravaged windswept peaks torn with white foam. The sea was swollen, moving and ugly, driven by eighty-mile-an-hour winds.

We caught another vicious up-draft then slid off it and my head banged into the canopy again. We had dropped two hundred feet and I pulled the F-14 back into the ceiling, now not much more than five hundred feet. I searched the terrible sea once more. Where in the hell was the *Independence?* A rain squall drummed into the canopy and I couldn't see a thing. A gust blew the starboard wing over and I fought the controls again. My eyes dropped to the tapes and feeds for the hundredth time. Jesus!

"Christ, can't you see it yet, Piece?" Harrison "Dilly" Dilworth, my backseat weapons officer. "I'm so goddamn sick, I can't see a thing. Scope's a blur. God. Can't look at it."

Like me, Dilly was a reserve officer putting in a month

at sea. Dilly had a tendency to airsickness and must be having a tough time of it back there. He was logging airtime because he had to. Were the truth to be known, Dilly liked flying his desk out of the Pentagon and going to embassy garden parties where he claimed to cut out the interesting and willing women between thirty-five and forty. He argued they were peaking in their sexual energy and interest at that age. Right now, sex wasn't on his mind.

I thumbed the mike button. "Gun Train," I mumbled, "this is Renegade 206. I can't find you. Where in the hell am I?" For the past forty-five minutes I had been working through a series of radars and controllers on the *Independence*. They had gone silent for the last ten minutes.

There was a rattle and howl in my earphones. Then the controller's voice. "This is Gun Train Strike. We have you on search radar, you are about ..." A voice interrupted.

"Piece? This is Magic. You are about eight miles out. Maintain that heading. You have to be just about over the *Sullivan*. Should be under your port wing. What's wrong with your RIO? You should have us on his scope, easy."

"He's sick as a dog. Can't look at the tube."

I stuck the wing down and there she was. A tin can wallowing through sixty-degree rolls from port to starboard, her bow lifting out of the banks of huge, rolling waves before plunging back into them. She was plowing doggedly into the wind as grey as the heaving sea around her.

"Yeah, I got her, Magic. Right below."

"Stay with it kid. You're just about home."

"How's the deck?"

"Still a mess. They haven't got the tanker clear of the pendants. Landing gear gone. Fell onto the deck. Hook fouled on the wire. Tank ruptured. Gas all over the god-

6

damn place. The last F-14 tangled with the island, chopped a wing and knocked off some of our navigational aids."

"Wonderful."

"How's the gas?"

"What gas? The whole panel is showing red. Christmas tree down there."

"You're going to have to make at least one pass, Piece."

"Swell."

It had been a busted exercise from the start. Our squadron commander, Magic Carlson, had sent six F-14's up in dirty weather to practice mid-air refueling. Anyone can refuel in good weather, Magic reasoned. But a combat situation doesn't always happen in cooperative weather. So you learn to refuel in ugly stuff. Right? Makes sense. But the skies deteriorated faster than the weather guessers predicted and we found ourselves in a full-blown North Sea gale. Planes were scattered all over. The tanker couldn't find us in the howling soup and was ordered to return to the *Independence*. The nearest divert field was five hundred miles away. Without gas no one could make it. The mission was aborted and everyone was called back.

But things had gone sour on deck. Trouble comes in bunches. The tanker waiting to intercept us on the way back couldn't get off the *Independence*. The catapults went down. Bugs and glitches were showing up in ships' radar after the overhaul in Philadelphia. Then the returning birds were having trouble getting back down on the pitching deck tossed by the mountainous seas and freaky cross winds. The last two down, the tanker and an F-14, had trouble, and crews were still struggling to clear the deck. We were the last aircraft back and I was running out of gas.

Finally, up ahead, I made out the *Independence* through the murk and blast. She was belting stolidly into the heavy

7

seas in the middle of her escort of two light cruisers and three destroyers. Four thousand yards to starboard and five hundred off the stern, the inevitable, grubby, rust-streaked Russian trawler kept pace with the fleet. She was taking a hell of a pounding in the huge seas.

"I see her, Piece," Dilly moaned through the intercom. "How's the gas?"

"We'll get down okay."

But I wasn't so sure. I kept my eyes glued on the total-izer that read the fuel in the main feed tank for each engine. I was sure that each of the five tanks that service the main tanks were dry.

Down below the dark, grey *Independence* was driving into the heaving sea. She was virtually new, rebuilt from its recent overhaul in Philadelphia. Now she rose and fell in the awesome seas, in the flying foam and spindrift, plunging into it, throwing huge waves off her bows, a small grey brick determined to stay afloat in the surging, howl-ing North Sea.

"The tower has a visual on you now, Piece," Magic said into my earphones. "It's up to the Paddles to get you down now."

"How's the deck?"

"Haven't heard anything. Don't know. I'm in with all the radar." I heard him blow out a breath. "Owe you a drink, Piece."

I didn't like the sound of his voice. The commander had ordered the mission and it went sour. He was worried. He wanted his boys back.

I checked the tapes again. We had less than six hundred pounds in the main feed tanks and the tapes were going down. The telepanel was red. Those tapes were rapidly heading to three hundred pounds, and at that point there were no assurances of any fuel left at all. I had a minute, maybe two and no more. I was starting to sweat.

We were four hundred feet off the starboard beam of the *Indépendence,* throttled down, barely maintaining airspeed, hanging on the blades, gear and flaps up, staying as slippery as possible. I did a one-eighty off the bow and had a look at the deck coming back down the port side. Couldn't see too much. Shreds of low-flying clouds came tearing by. We were still bouncing all over the sky. More goddamn rain.

The crews were frantically moving the busted tanker over toward the elevator but she was still in the landing area. I saw two limp cross deck pendants. I would have to get the hook into the number-one wire. The engines chugged.

Tapes dropping fast. I called the Boss.

"Boss," I thumbed forward the mike. "I'm abeam, I'm out of gas. I've got to land."

"You'll have to go around again, Piece. I've got no deck for you." The air boss was firm. He must be at least a senior commander. He was probably standing there in his plexiglass box five stories up on the island watching me wobble three hundred feet over the port beam. He was waving me off. Still too much clutter on the deck and only a couple of wires for me to set the hook into. Maybe just one.

"Boss, I read under four hundred pounds."

"Roger. Understand. We have to strip some pendants. We got fuel spilled all over the deck. We got crippled planes all over the place. You have to go around again."

"Boss, I see the deck. It's clear. I'm goin' for the number-one wire."

"Piece, make another pass."

"Don't have the time, Boss. The deck is clear. I'm comin' in."

"Make another pass. That's an—"

I pulled the dodge that every pilot in the fleet has used at one time or another. "Boss, you're breaking up. Can't read you. I'm coming in, Boss. Clear the deck! I'm rolling into the one-eighty. It's trick or treat. I'm coming down."

"Piece! Make another go!"

"Boss, I'm going dirty up here. Clear the deck! I'm abeam. I'm coming down. I'm landing this pass." I rolled off the one-eighty, the engines were chugging.

We were committed. Screw the boss. I was into the final turn, six thousand yards from the deck. I was slowing from two-thirty mph down to about one-fifty. I would consume two miles in a minute.

"Piece, I'm getting sick." Lieutenant Commander Harrison Dilworth again. Tell me about the hot pants matrons at the garden parties, Dilly. When do they peak sexually? Another downdraft was sucking us into the drink. Funny what you think about in situations like this. I was repressing reality. But my whole life still hadn't passed before my eyes. Good sign.

"You have your mask on Dilly?"

"Godamnit Piece, get this thing down. I want to get out of this airplane. Jesuschrist, I'm getting sick again. Piece! Fuck the air boss! Fuck the bastard. Get this thing down! Oh God . . ." He was heaving again.

We were turning through the ninety degrees to go to position, and up in his goldfish bowl the air boss would be finally convinced we were coming in. He would grab his PA mike and start screaming, "Clear the flight deck! We have an emergency in-bound! Stand by Crash and Salvage. Clear the flight deck. Stand by medics!" Horns and loudspeakers would be going off all over the place.

People would be ducking into shelters. We were getting taped, filmed, and audioed.

I was lining up the F-14 with the stern. I was totally absorbed with the cockpit now, watching gauges, throwing switches. I put the throttles on APC, automatic control, to free my hands and eyes for other jobs.

"Okay, Dilly," I said, "we're on APC, I'm flying with one hand. The stick and the throttles are looking good on automatic. If we flame out, stand by to eject on my call, pal. I've got my hand down on the ejection handle now, Dilly. Only on my call, babe. You got it?"

I swung out of the turn a half mile off the *Independence*'s stern. Fifteen seconds to touch down. I lined up in the groove, would fly the meatball, the optical system, for the last ten seconds. We were closing the ship at 120 knots. Gear still up. I couldn't believe the huge seas below us. We hit another rain squall. A wind shear drove us down to four hundred feet above the raging sea. I struggled to keep the wings level.

Something gurgled in the rear seat.

Two thousand yards off the pitching stern of the *Independence* and the landing signal officers were screaming into their radios. "Get your gear down! Get your gear down!"

"Not yet, boys. Too much drag. Got no gas. I'm staying clean."

We were closing at two miles per minute, just seconds to touch, and I grabbed the gear handle, then the flap handle. Gear down, flaps out, hook extended, we wobbled down toward the *Independence* in a monstrous North Sea gale. The engines took on a new sound. They were winding down.

"Wind down," I said into the mike.

I was fighting to keep the nose at about a fifteen-degree

11

angle of attack for maximum lift. The freaky gusts were pushing us every way but the right way.

"Eighty percent RPM." No climb in them.

We were drifting closer to the wavering stern of the carrier. God, we might make it.

Engine RPM surged once, then died.

"Flame out," I transmitted to the waiting world.

We were now dead in the air forty feet up and sixty feet off the pitching stern. Still we had a chance. We floated closer. The stern was clear. Everyone had taken to cover. Lord, we just might. Then a cruel, battering gust held us up like a great fist and seemed to hold us frozen in mid-air. I watched helplessly as the stern drifted away in the boiling sea.

We would hit about three feet down the ramp, crumple like a broken accordion, explode, and then fall into the slowing, turning screws below. No way we could make it now. I said to myself, "Relax, kid, why die all tensed up?"

There were more gurgles coming from the rear seat.

But the mysterious ways of the fickle finger of fate that drove that terrible wind into us now threw down its hold card. It shoved some huge, monstrous wave under the bow which, in turn, forced the stern down. So the deck seemed to be falling away as we settled closer, giving us more air on which to slide forward toward the ship. That huge rogue wave that picked up the *Independence*'s bow had dropped the ship's rear end maybe fifty feet. So we ghosted silently above the stern by twenty feet. We were over the deck and home.

It was not really a landing. It wasn't even a controlled crash. We were fresh out of airspeed. I stalled the F-14 about fifteen feet above the deck and we fell the rest of the way. We came down like a ton of bricks well short of where I would have liked to. With a sharp crack, the nose tire blew right away and we plunged forward up the deck toward the first and probably only pendant.

I held the stick in my lap trying to keep the nose up and hook down, held my breath, raced up the deck, felt the hook bite into the wire and the plane began to slow. God! Then the entire nose wheel assembly collapsed and we were grinding forward nose on the deck, throwing up a shower of sparks and clouds of grey gunk. We missed a puddle of spilled jet fuel by three feet and continued to slide along the deck. We tore by the outstretched wing of the crippled tanker by ten feet, but the pendant held. Finally, the F-14 came to a shuddering stop, canting abruptly in toward the island as the hook tore loose under the strain. I hit my head on the canopy again. Helmets were really a good idea.

The deck crews were on us the second our forward motion ended. They sprayed the nose with foam. They chocked the two remaining wheels. They tied the plane down. I was getting frantic signals to chop the throttles, but they had been history fifty feet off the stern when we flamed out. Two trucks were lumbering up to tow the F-14 out of the landing area. They had no way of knowing we were the last ship in. Guys were piling out of the crash truck. One went under the nose and popped the canopy.

The boss was screaming over the loudspeakers. "Get that aircraft secured. Check for fire damage. Medics!" Sounded real pissed.

"You okay, sir?" It was the maintenance chief. He was bald, had a broken nose, needed a shave, had a scar that ran from his jaw to a corner of his mouth and he was missing half a left ear. He was beautiful. He loosened my restraint harness. I was sucking deep breaths of fresh sea air and getting drenched in the rain. Loved it. I lifted up my face and felt the cool drops slide down my neck. I opened my mouth to the rain. Hadn't done that since I was a kid. Rain is really wonderful. Wonderful when you are back on deck. Everything was beautiful. Marvelous! Dear God, we were down and alive. I was shaking. Tried not to show it. Be cool. Hero down from the terrible sky. Piece of cake if you're smooth. Fighter pilots talk that way.

I got out on the wing and looked around. The huge waves were as high as the flight deck. Surging, rolling toward the stern. Rain, foam, spume, spindrift slanted down on the deck. Crews struggled in foul weather gear. Everything was soaked. Roar, howl, whine and shriek. I had a silly smile on my face. Couldn't keep it off.

"Your RIO doesn't look so good, sir," the chief observed.

I looked back. Dilly was still slumped in his seat. He looked dazed and pale.

"Better get the medics over before you pull him out, chief."

"Yes, sir."

I got off the wing and looked at the sea. I couldn't believe I had flown over that watery insanity, so huge, angry, driving, roaring, threatening. But I was on deck and it couldn't get me now. I felt the steady motion of the ship as she plowed into the gale, all of her birds back and safe.

A medical team was up on the wing and working on Dilly. Someone had a stethoscope out and was checking his chest.

"You had better get over to Flight Deck Medical, sir," the chief said.

"Oh, hell. I'm okay." Not so okay. My legs were shaking. Aftershock.

"Sir, you're bleeding."

14

"What?"

"Your right eyebrow. Looks swollen and you're bleeding from it, sir."

I reached up and touched my eyebrow. My hand came away with blood. I didn't even know when it happened.

We headed toward the island and the little room where the emergency medical team was waiting. Two doctors and two nurses were inside. There was a compact examining table in the middle and the walls were covered with glass cabinets filled with medical stuff. The nurses were temporary. Not regular crew. Two-week training session for them. They were getting some experience today.

"Up on the table, Lieutenant," the doctor ordered. He was short, grey haired, and exuded confidence. Seemed a little bored. He loosened my torso harness and opened up the G suit. "Color's good," he observed absently. He put his hand on my throat and checked for pulse. He frowned, then studied his watch for thirty seconds.

"You're beating no more than seventy a minute. How can you do that after landing? You're too slow."

I shook my head. "I'm up, Doc. For me, that's fast. Normally, I'd be in the low sixties. At night, at rest, I'm in the low fifties."

"You a runner?"

"Yup."

He nodded. "That explains it."

I could see a medical team had Dilly on a stretcher and was taking him off to sick bay.

"How is he?" I asked, inclining my head to the departing stretcher crew.

"Awful pale. Pressure's up. He should be okay. I just checked with Commander Pearson. He thinks it was motion sickness brought on by terminal fear. They are going to run some tests. I'll be going down to help."

15

He grabbed my jaw and turned my head to the left and right. Took a good look at me.

"You're okay. You're a tough kid." He turned to the two nurses who were standing by. "Looks like he banged his head. Pressure bandage should do it. Clean him up and get rid of him." He went after the stretcher crew.

One nurse was in her forties, plump and with those wise women's eyes. The other was in her mid-twenties, with light-brown hair, willowy figure, clear skin, and bright brown eyes. The young one moved first.

She put her hand on my forehead. Her mouth opened. Nice pink lips. Her tongue ran out between her teeth. She tilted up her chin. Lovely jawline and throat. I could smell soap, maybe shampoo.

She got out a basin, splashed some liquid in it. The old nurse leaned back into the bulkhead, folded her arms, and watched.

"How did you do it?" the young one asked. She was wiping my face, eyes big and concerned. Tongue still out. It made me nervous.

"No idea."

"You hit awfully hard. We knew it was an emergency landing what with the loudspeakers going off and all." She continued swabbing me down. She had a sexy Deep-South drawl.

"What was the problem?"

"Ran out of gas."

"In this storm? God!"

I nodded.

She smiled now. Glorious. "Well, you're back and that's what counts."

She ran the cloth around the back of my neck and up into my hair, then put her left hand on my shoulder. Lot of pressure.

16

The old nurse exploded. "Jenkins, stop fooling around that boy. Get the bandage on! We have work to do!"

Jenkins shot her a look. She went to a cabinet, tore a bandage from its paper packet, pressed it into my eyebrow, and tilted her head to one side. She nodded. Then she took a towel and blotted my face and hair. She put the towel down, stepped back, and fluffed my hair with her hand the way they do.

"You're fine," she said. Her clear brown eyes got into mine and a lot of subliminal transmission went on. "For now," she added.

The old battle-ax's face had softened a lot. "Come on, Mary," she said quietly. "They need us in sick bay." They left me sitting on the table. I sat there a couple of minutes slowly settling down.

"How are you doing, Lieutenant?"

It was Commander Clarence "Magic" Carlson, standing at the door to the Medical Assist room, arms folded and with no smile. The commander was about five ten or eleven, mid-thirties, thickly built, with an open, uncomplicated face, brown eyes and hair, ruddy complexion, thick mustache. Nothing remarkable, but if you were to see him in civilian clothes walking down a street and asked people what he did for a living, one out of ten might say "pilot" or "flyer." One in twenty, the really perceptive ones, would answer, "Fighter pilot."

"I'm okay, sir."

"You flame out?"

"Yes."

He nodded. Still no smile. "Get your gear stowed. Get cleaned up and report to my stateroom." He turned abruptly and walked off.

I went back to the pilot's locker room and took off my torso harness, G suit, stowed the oxygen mask and helmet,

17

put on my rumpled khakis and went to my stateroom on the 03 level.

No windows, fifteen by twelve feet of two bunks, an island of lockers, cabinets with two built-in desks, stainless steel sink up against an interior wall. Charlie Pisano was in the lower bunk in just a pair of shorts. He put down the book he was reading. Charlie goes five nine and a hundred sixty pounds, half of it body hair and nose.

"The story about," he said, "is that you blew the air boss off and came in when he waved you around."

"About right." I stripped down to my shorts, put a towel around my neck, and headed for the door.

"It's your ass, man, blowin' the boss off like that. I mean it was Prentice, man, he's all book."

I nodded.

"You flame out?"

I nodded again.

"And you put the fucker on the deck. Walked away." He shook his head.

I looked at Charlie.

He blew out a breath. "Nobody real can do that, man." He puffed out his cheeks, thinking on it. "It's your ass anyway. No way they are going to let you blow off the boss with everybody listening. They are going to eat you alive. Feed what's left to Congress. Shit."

Charlie is from New York, so he thinks like New York. Somehow he got into the Academy. Somehow he passed his courses. I don't know how. Charlie has a totally Machiavellian view of the world. It's all con and calculation. Charlie believes that only he who understands the rules of the game is in a position to cheat. He is a natural sociologist, so he studies human social organization with a view to first comprehend it and then manipulate it. Charlie is not only New York but he's Italian, so it's a genetic thing

18

with him, too. He understands the Navy already. He will certainly be an admiral one day. He's a fair fighter pilot.

I opened the door.

"Piece," Charlie said quietly, "I saw it, man. If I hadn't seen it, I wouldn't believe it. Nobody can do that after a flame out. But you did it and in this shit weather. Two other guys wiped out and they had engines. They got no right to screw you now."

That was the first moral judgment I ever heard Charlie make. Fundamentally, he's value-free.

He picked up his book and started to read. I couldn't see his face. "You're some fucking pilot, Piece. They got no right. I mean, nobody can fly like that. Bird, maybe."

I took a shower, put on some fresh khakis, and fifteen minutes later knocked politely on Magic's door.

"Enter," he said. His cabin was just slightly larger than mine. Only one bunk, same cabinets, lockers, sink, desk, no ports. He stayed at his desk. I came to attention and saluted. He answered the salute. We were very formal. No nicknames. We were into the normative order, rules, and regulations. The system. The Navy. The book. I was a deviant. I must be sanctioned.

"The air boss waved you off. You disobeyed and landed. He gave you an order." He was looking steadily at me.

"At ease, Smallpiece," he said.

I unfroze.

"What's your story?" he asked.

"I knew I had only enough gas for one approach. I wasn't even sure of that. We were below three hundred pounds. We flamed out just short of the stern."

He nodded. "I saw it. I was in the tower."

"If we went into the sea, that sea, we would be finished." I took a gulp of air and went on. "I didn't see how they could get a hilo off to fish us out. Anyway, the canopy on that F-14 hasn't been working right. I didn't trust it. I didn't think it would sequence properly in a low altitude ejection. I figured our only chance to stay alive was to make for the ship."

He nodded again. Put a pencil in his mouth.

"The way it worked out," I continued, "we are alive because I came in. Had I done what the boss ordered me to do, Dilly and I would be feeding the fishes by now."

He pursed his lips. "Did you report the canopy problem to the maintenance chief?"

"Several times."

"It's on the postflight reports? In writing?"

"Yes, sir."

He nodded. "I know of at least two guys who bought the farm when they went in and the canopy wouldn't jettison." He looked up at me. "But you're right, if you ejected into that sea, you would have never come back even if the canopy worked as advertised."

The MC loudspeaker broke into the silence. "Lieutenant Smallpiece will report to the captain on the bridge on the double."

Carlson got up. "He's a little late. I thought he would be on the horn before this. You know the captain?"

"No, sir."

"Damn good man. He'll listen. But Air Boss has been raising hell. He's talked to the captain already."

I said nothing.

"Okay, Piece, let's go." He used my combat nickname. He bought my story. He was coming with me to the bridge. It would be two of us against the Naval Establishment.

On a fighting ship the stairs are really ladders slightly off the vertical. You go up hanging onto chains on the sides. You bump your head a lot on low overhead stuff, mostly pipes and conduit. We worked our way up to the bridge. I had never seen it before.

It was smaller than I thought it would be. Maybe forty feet across the front, all three-by-four windows. Once I had been on the bridge of a huge oil tanker and it seemed as big as a football field.

There were eleven or twelve people scattered around the scopes, navigation gear, communications equipment, and the like. Nobody noticed us. The helmsman was peering steadily ahead into the pitching seas. The navigator, a junior captain, was whispering an order. I heard a muted "Aye, aye, sir."

The captain was seated in the captain's chair on the port side. It looked like a barber's chair. Directly behind, a Marine corporal stood at ease. He was wearing a side-arm.

We marched directly to the captain and saluted. He replied smartly but stayed seated.

"Lieutenant Smallpiece reporting as ordered, sir!" I belted out the sir.

The captain got out of his chair and stood in front of me. Small man, not more than five eight. Hair almost totally white, crew cut, ruddy face, Anglo features, sharp, intelligent eyes. He was fit and trim, not more than a hundred and fifty pounds. He wasn't smiling. He studied me. I was frozen into attention. He didn't put me at ease. I studied the horizon even though there wasn't one.

I let my eyes drop a moment. The captain was carrying a folder. I saw my name on it. It was my service record. God!

"You ignored the air boss's order and landed." He had a very deep voice for so slight a man. He could have gone into radio or TV.

"And don't give me any bullshit about his transmission breaking up. I heard the tape."

"Sir!" I exploded. I have found that by just bellowing "Sir!" at a senior officer bent on chewing your ass, it sometimes pleases them, and they don't chew so hard.

"What happened, Lieutenant?" Wonderful voice. Therapeutic.

I took a deep breath. "No gas, sir. We read about three hundred and fifty pounds. I figured no more than fifteen to thirty seconds of power left. No way we could make another pass. It seemed that the ship was a better possibility than the ocean, sir."

I heard the radar beep, some electric motors softly humming, twenty or thirty windshield wipers clicking steadily. Something buzzed. Someone was talking over a radio in a subdued voice. Nothing else. Twelve men on the bridge and not a sound. Only the howl of the North Sea gale outside. Everyone seemed to be frozen. Motionless. I watched the rain driving into the big, square ports. Saw the bow dig into a wave and throw it off.

"Flame out?"

"Yes, sir."

"The air wing maintenance officer reports you had totally dry tanks, not even fumes. He further indicates you had trouble with the canopy. Even on a calm sea you might have gone down with the aircraft. That right?"

"Yes, sir."

He paused for a moment. "Commander Prentice has just talked to me."

Here it comes. Charlie would bust a gut laughing. After a ritual trial the guilty man was promptly hung. The Establishment was gathering itself for the coup de grace.

The captain blew out a breath and studied my face.

"Sir."

"The commander says he was wrong in ordering you around. The deck was a mess and you could have killed yourselves had you missed the pendant, but there was no hope for you in that sea. None. The commander says you made the right decision and he made the wrong one."

I couldn't believe it. "Sir." More like a gasp than a proper sir.

"It wasn't easy for him to say that. A decision had to be made in seconds. I agree with him. You saved two lives and the taxpayers an expensive aircraft."

"Sir."

"At ease, Lieutenant. Your ass is out of the woodshed."

Was I wrong? Did everybody unfreeze? Did I catch a smile on the senior navigator's face? Two or three men coughed at the same time. The helmsman had a grin from ear to ear. The Third Officer of the Watch and the quartermaster were talking quietly on the starboard side, both darting thinly disguised glances in my direction. Magic was leaning up against a port window, easy smile on his face.

The captain got back into his chair. He waved the folder in front of me. "Fascinating. You're not an Academy man."

"No, sir." I tried to look apologetic. Ashamed.

"Harvard, was it?"

"Yes, sir."

"Played football? Baseball?"

"Yes, sir."

"You were in some kind of special naval training program there. Took air training as a undergraduate? Never heard of such a thing."

"Experimental program, sir. Twenty of us. We had flight instruction, special courses within the regular undergraduate curiculum. We were commissioned and got our wings at the end of four years."

23

The captain scratched his jaw and shook his head. "Never knew about that program."

"Didn't work out, sir. Not too many survived the four years. They gave the program up."

"How many got their wings?"

"Four, sir."

"How old are you?"

"Twenty-seven, sir,"

"Hum. You were on the *Kitty Hawk* after you were commissioned?"

"Yes, sir."

"Service record says you tangled with Nate Reardon. They took you off flying status for a while."

"Yes, sir."

"I knew Nate in the Academy. He was the biggest horse's ass I've ever met. He's out of the Navy now and not by his choice."

I nodded.

"Record says you were assigned to Naval Intelligence. Then it gets a little vague."

"Sir."

"Secret stuff? Can't talk about it?"

"Yes, sir,"

He accepted that. Nodded.

"Then you left the Navy and went to Yale and got a Ph.D. Started teaching at Spaulding University a couple of years ago. What do you teach?" It seemed like he had committed my whole service record to memory.

A phone rang somewhere and was quickly answered. The Officer of the Deck and the navigator were quietly discussing a course correction. I wondered where all this was going.

I shrugged. "The application of mathematical models to social theory. Axiomatic theory. The miniaturization of theory. Systematic paradigms. Computer applications. Man-machine interface."

The captain rolled his eyes, "Jesus Christ. I don't even know what any of that means."

"It's fairly exotic stuff, sir."

He nodded and inclined his head toward Commander Carlson. "Magic tells me you were his student at the Fighter Weapons School in California last summer. Top Gun?"

I couldn't keep a smile off my face. Rueful smile. "No, sir. Second Gun. Honorable mention. Also ran."

"Magic says you hadn't been in a F-14 for eight months when you arrived out there. I guess you were teaching that stuff at Spaulding. He says if you had another week you would have been Top Gun and in two weeks you would have blown every instructor out of the sky."

I looked humble and flashed my boyish, wistful smile. The captain continued to study my face. I don't think he bought the smile. Finally he said, "Do you know the Secretary of the Navy?"

I sucked in a fast breath. "No, sir."

"Never met him?"

"No, sir."

"Any of your family know him?"

"I have no family, sir. No, sir."

Another phone buzzed. The sky seemed to be lightening. Rain wasn't as heavy. Deck was steadying.

"The secretary seems to know you. His office called twice when you were in the air and once after you got down. They want to talk to you."

"Sir."

"No idea why, Smallpiece?"

"None, sir."

25

"Neither have I." He scratched an ear. "You're not in trouble?"

"I don't think so, sir."

He turned to the Marine guard. "Tell the radio people to return the call." The Marine went off to the captain's-at-sea cabin just off the bridge. It's a place where captains go when they want to rest, have something to eat, talk in private, think, write a letter home, but still stay close to the action.

The Marine returned almost immediately. "They're already linked up, sir."

"Okay, Smallpiece," the captain said. "you can take the call in my cabin. He pointed in the direction the Marine had come from. "Close the door."

I shut the door and saw the phone lying on the closed day bed. The room was not more than ten by eight with a small desk and chair, sink, and head in a tiny, curtained alcove. There were three wall phones and a lot of heavy intercom. The desk had a photograph of a pleasant, fif-tyish woman and four smiling blonde girls about college age. Couldn't tell one from the other.

I picked up the phone and said, "Smallpiece."

"Just a minute, Lieutenant." It had to be a junior aide. Now I would get a middle level aide. I would be run through the ranks so that I would learn to appreciate power and authority, order and hierarchy. Charlie Pisano under-stands things like this.

"Lieutenant Smallpiece?"

"Speaking."

"This is John Willard."

I sucked in a breath. It was the Secretary of the Navy. How do you address the Secretary of the Navy? Your Na-viness? Your High Navalness? Exalted Shipworthiness?

I settled for, "Yes, sir."

26

"I hear you had something of an adventure today. North Sea kicking up, running short of fuel. But you got back. Congratulations. I can't wait to see the film and tape." He sounded like he could be an announcer, too. Deep, modulated baritone.

"Yes, sir."

"Well, you are wondering why I am calling. There is somebody here who wants to talk to you, so I'll put him on and end the mystery. Good speaking to you. I hope to meet you someday."

The phone rattled as it exchanged hands.

"Smallpiece?"

I knew the voice right away. Judson Kirk. President of Spaulding University and erstwhile, shadowy figure connected to Omega One, an unknown, totally invisible, buried and possibly nonexistent intelligence unit reporting only to the President of the United States. Or so I've been led to believe. I think I'm part of it. It is an intelligence operation of the last resort, hence the Omega from the last letter of the Greek alphabet. The One I wasn't sure of, but more than once, I wondered if I was the only one the One referred to. After an adventure in the Bahamas last fall, Kirk had recruited me into Omega One, but no action had come from it. He continued to function publicly as the president of Spaulding and I went to class and mumbled something about system theory and mathematical application.

"You had us worried for a few hours."

"I had me worried, too."

"Uh huh. Got a job for you, Smallpiece."

"Can I talk?"

"Yes."

"We have a Russian trawler about half a mile off the stern and they aren't fishing."

"This conversation is being scrambled twelve ways to midnight. No way they'll understand."

"Omega One?"

"No. We are loaning you to the English."

"What?"

"You are being detached from the *Independence* immediately. You are to go to London and you will be contacted there."

I exploded, "Why me for christsakes? I like it here. I like F-14's. They got a great bunch of guys here. Even the goddamn chow's good! It's fun!" I was cross, petulant. My lower lip stuck out. I had totally repressed the morning. Never happened.

Kirk was typically unflappable. "You'll have to give it up, my boy. Why you? They have some very special requirements. Height and weight parameters, somebody who is fluent in Russian, somebody who knows some higher mathematics and who can hold his own in physics. Somebody who has covert intelligence experience. Somebody who can handle himself in a bar fight or back alley. Maybe somebody who can kill somebody. When they ran all that through their computer, they came up dry. So they asked us. We ran it through ours, and came up with you."

I sucked in a breath and blew it out. "No way I can get out of this?"

"Of course. You can refuse." He paused a minute. "Smallpiece, the English went to the President. It was on that level. He came to me. I get the feeling this is very important and our English cousins have a very serious problem. They need someone very, very good."

"I should be flattered?"

"You should be. Yes."

"You have no idea what it is all about?"

"No."

"You have any sense of time on this?"

"None, but they want you in London tomorrow."

"Where?"

"Check into the New Piccadilly. You'll be contacted there."

I waited a full thirty seconds. Kirk said nothing.

"Okay."

"Good boy!"

"You got anything else wonderful to tell me?"

"No, that's about it."

"Well, I'll see you when I see you. London, New Piccadilly, tomorrow?"

"That's all I have. Put Captain Schroeder back on the phone. The secretary will want to talk to him. Good luck."

I laid the phone back on the day bed and went out on the bridge. The captain was in his chair, studying a report. "They want you back on the phone, sir," I said. He handed the Marine corporal the report and disappeared into his cabin. He closed the door.

"What the hell is going on, Piece?" Magic asked.

"I don't know, but I'm being detached from the ship."

"Because you didn't kill yourself back there?" He was incredulous.

"No. It has nothing to do with that."

He waited a minute. "I saw your service record, too, Piece. I know you did some sort of intelligence work. They got you back on that?"

I shook my head and searched my squadron commander's earnest, concerned face. "Really can't say. All I know is that I'm off the ship." We both looked through the ports. Didn't talk. The seas were slowing. Waves were smaller.

The captain was back. He looked at Magic. "You're dismissed, Commander, and thank you."

29

Magic didn't hesitate, flung a salute at him, about-faced, and stalked out the port entry. The captain turned to me. "The secretary gave me verbal orders, but a coded message will come through within half an hour. You know the essence of it. Tomorrow at zero seven hundred you will fly an F-14 directly to England and the Naval Air Facility at Mildenhall. You will turn your aircraft over to a senior grade lieutenant, name's Wild, Adam Wild. You will sign for its release. Then you will find public transportation to London. You are to wear civilian clothes. What you will be doing there, I have no idea."

I nodded.

He put out his hand and smiled. "Just when I was beginning to like you, too. Well, that's Navy life. *C'est la vie.*" He hesitated for a moment. "Look, I have a small farm near Arlington. I really love it. You know, split rail fences, horses. You're not that far away at Spaulding. I expect to spend August there. I'll give you a call. Maybe you can spare a weekend. I've got four daughters and they'll all be home."

I smiled, nodded again.

We shook hands.

As I turned to go, the captain said, "You know, Piece, the Navy is more understanding than you think. It's changing. We can even forgive Harvard and Yale. Wouldn't hold it against you too much. Ever think about making a career of it? We could use a pilot like you."

I couldn't hold back a genuine grin. "Yes. Thank you, sir. I will. I like this ship." I left the bridge. The gale was blowing itself out. The ceiling was lifting, the wind was down, and I could see the stubby Russian trawler keeping pace three quarters of a mile off the starboard beam.

* * *

At zero seven hundred and three minutes, the port catapult fired the F-14 into the still, calm, early June air. I felt the familiar, momentary sag as the initial heave of the catapult fell off and the power of the jet turbines had not yet been fully established in the forward drive of the fighter. But we now were on our own and I pulled up into a leisurely, arcing curve back toward the *Independence* and leveled off at five hundred feet.

The sky was a brilliant cloudless blue and the calm, tranquil sea sparkled from an infinite wash of tiny watery prisms glinting in the light of a glorious sun. The *Independence* plowed purposely through it, a small bone of white water pushing off her bows and a great wake spreading off her stern. The escort had gathered in, two destroyers a half mile off the bows, the two cruisers a quarter mile abeam, the last destroyer a mile dead astern. The Russian was where he belonged, about four thousand yards to starboard, three hundred back.

I radioed the Russian using their North Red Star identification on the frequency they would generally be using. We heard them talking every day and it was not about fish. I got a raspy reply.

"Yes? Who is this?" Typical Russian, crude and direct.

"Renegade 302. I'm right over you."

"You are the American aircraft? You speak Russian?"

"You guys speak English. Why can't we speak Russian?"

"What do you want?"

"I want your captain. Get him."

"He's having breakfast. This is not regular. Not procedure."

"Move your ass. Get the captain before I report you to the KGB."

31

"I don't know."

"What's your captain's name?" He hesitated. "Come on, I just want to talk to him."

"Wait."

It was a new voice. "Who is this? Identify yourself."

"You the captain?" Talking to Russians is like filing a claim with the Veterans Administration twenty years after the war.

I droned on. "Renegade 302. I'm off the *Independence*."

"I know the squadron designation. What is your name?"

"Lieutenant Colin Smallpiece, United States Navy."

There was a pause.

"You are the one whose code is Piece?"

"I am the one whose code is Piece."

"You got back all right? You were low on gas. The Boss told you to go around. We lost you in the overcast and rain."

"I got back. Who am I talking to? Or is that a big Soviet security secret? Have to clear with the KGB to say your name?"

"I am Vladimir Kulikov, captain of this vessel."

"Glad to meet you, Vladimir. How's the fishing?"

I was drifting off ahead of the fleet, now three miles back.

"Fishing is good. You speak an excellent Russian, Piece."

"Thank you. How did you guys make out in the blow yesterday?"

"Not so good. This is not a young ship. One man broke his arm. Something fell on him."

"Bad break? What did you do for him?"

"He's in a splint, but we have no doctor."

"We have a lot of good docs on the *Independence*.

First-class equipment, too. You want some help? I know Russians are not supposed to need help, but maybe you really do."

More pause as the wheels went around. Ideology versus reality. State policy versus pragmatic solutions at sea.

"I don't know. He's just eighteen. His arm will never be right again unless he gets proper care. You have something in mind?"

"We could get him off in a chopper."

"You could do that?"

"The captain would have to authorize it, of course."

No response, then, "See what you can do." Another pause. "Where are you? I don't hear you anymore."

"You on the bridge, Vladimir?"

"Yes."

I was lined up pretty good on his bow, about three miles off. I dropped down to fifty feet and inverted.

"Take out your glasses. Look dead ahead and low."

Pause. "Yes. Wait. Ah. There you are. I see. My God! You're almost in the sea!" There was some heavy breathing and a gasp. "My God! You're upside down!"

I looked "up" and saw a blur of waves about ten feet below the canopy. I shoved up the throttles. The North Red Star was coming fast.

"What are you doing?" Vladimir was screaming. "Get away. Turn over! Crazy Americans. You'll hit us! My God! My God!" Funny how the Russians go to religion when there is no other way out.

Russian trawlers are used to being buzzed. It's our favorite outdoor sport and the brass doesn't chew us too much for it. The new wrinkle was that I was talking to him and I was inverted. That was unusual. I kept the F-14 low on the water and raced toward the trawler. One hundred feet off his bow I shoved the stick forward and shot over his funnel by five

33

feet. Might have blown away a few of his antenna wires. I looked down and saw the deck filled with men gaping up. There would be considerable noise, blast, and heat down there. Much consternation, too.

With the Russians you have to give with one hand and take from the other.

I rolled the F-14 over, did a one-eighty, and got up to five hundred feet. The trawler had wandered two hundred yards off course.

"Happy fishing Vladimir," I said. "I'll see about getting your man some medical help. Farewell, comrade. Don't think too badly of me."

I didn't wait for a reply.

I called Gun Train Tower.

"What the hell were you doing blasting the trawler?" It was Magic, and properly aggrieved. "What was all that talk about? All we heard was Russian."

"They got a guy on board with a broken arm. Sounds like a bad break. See what can be done to take him off and get it fixed. Okay, Magic?"

"The old man won't like the fly-by and inverted. Christ!"

"He's probably still in the rack."

"He'll know about it."

"Got to make tracks, Magic. I'll get in touch."

"Okay, Piece. Take care, kid."

I pulled the F-14 up to twenty thousand feet and watched the *Independence* and her small fleet shrink into the horizon. And then they were gone. I flew over a bright blue sea. The sun beat through the canopy. I felt warm and drowsy. The F-14 bore steadily through the quiet air toward England and I didn't know why or what for.

CHAPTER II

The cab dropped me off at The New Piccadilly Hotel, and it had gone through a substantial face-lift from the dumpy middle-class hotel I knew from the past. Nine rusticated Roman arches with large extended keystones faced the sidewalk on the first two floors. Six freestanding Ionic columns lined a deeply recessed third-floor cut-back and supported a massive entabulalture running across the entire top face of the building. It was Italian baroque, in the style of Christopher Wren, with a frivolous, airy exuberance not found in the glass-and-stainless-steel functional boxes built today.

A tall doorman with a top hat and some sort of black-and-white formal outfit solemnly took my two bags and we went through the revolving doors into an elegant, understated foyer with diamond-shaped black-and-white floors, and square white-and-gold pillastered columns along the sides. The lobby was small by the standards of hotels in large American cities but quietly done in cream, gold, and white, and with a new oak trim. Large bouquets of fresh flowers were everywhere. The concierge, at his desk on the right, was holding up a map of London for an elderly American couple who were seriously nodding at it. She was wearing white shoes and he a rumpled pearl-grey, double-knit jacket with metallic threads, Hawaiian shirt, and camera. Midwest. Peoria.

There was a clutch of bright, busy young people behind the desk on my left, wearing the same black-and-white uniform. They were all under twenty-five, and the girls had that delicious peaches and cream complexion of the English. They had been picked very carefully by someone conscious of image.

I walked up to the desk and got a brilliant smile from a handsome blonde.

"You have a reservation for Ralph Bostwick?" I asked.

The smile never left her face while she consulted her file.

"Ah! Here it is." I got busy with her eyes. Male and female. Call of the wild. The Game. The Chase. Yin and yang. A month at sea didn't hurt. Her eyes widened when she got the full blast of the old frosty blues.

She fussed about some. Was that more color creeping into her cheeks? Still had my touch. No ring on her finger. Maybe.

"Yes. Er. Ah," she began, holding out a card. "Would you sign here please, ah, Mr. Bostwick?" No smile this time. She kept her head down, and her fingers were busy with a lot of cards and paper.

I signed.

She hit a small bell.

"You are in 340," she said, "center, front." Her eyes fluttered into mine. I had been at sea too long. F-14's are okay, but they are of little comfort in bed on cool June nights. I nodded. She pulled in her lower lip and bit it.

A bellperson arrived, picked up the keys, gathered up my duffle and the soft-sided wardrobe bag with bulging pockets. I kept the smaller "carry on" hanging from my shoulder.

"This way, sir," he said, and moved toward the solitary elevator. We passed ten or twelve Japanese businessmen seated in a corner lounge, and no one was smiling. I have often wondered what the Japanese did for fun. The elevator was small but was made to appear larger with mirrors. I waved at the blonde as she turned and caught my eye. Her head went back down, no response.

My room was halfway down a wide hall that was not nearly as posh as the lobby. But then, they never are. He spent some time explaining the security system on the lock. Very complex, I was sure I would never manage it on my own. We went in, and he put the luggage down on a rack, put the lights on in the bathroom, pulled open the drapes, and took a dollar in American as he left.

I sat down on one of the two twin beds and looked around. Class all the way. The room was in two levels, the upper was set off by a black wrought-iron fence and had a Queen Anne desk and table, four matching straight-back chairs, and a well-stuffed loveseat in a rich cream brocade. Color TV was tastefully hidden in a corner. The lower level had the beds and another soft chair. The walls were done in blue wallpaper, had some sort of sheen, and were accented with prints that didn't bother you. By the door, on the right as you came in, there was a fully stocked, refrigerated liquor cabinet in simulated wood grain. The bathroom looked marble, but I suspected a clever plastic. It had a large chrome heated towel rack.

I checked the liquor cabinet, found a supply of Whitbread's ale, a chilled glass, and went to the upper level and turned the loveseat toward the windows. I poured the ale into the glass, put my feet up on the windowsill, and carefully considered the network of scaffolding on a building undergoing extensive repair halfway down the street. I kicked off my shoes, worked on the ale, and worried about the workmen on the scaffolding who were flying about like insane acrobats. I knocked off another Whitbread's and studied my watch. Somebody should be checking up on me. There was a knock on the door. Ah!

There were two men, both about five ten, medium builds, clean-shaven, conservative dress, nice smiles. Nothing to distinguish either of them. Perfect spies.

"Ah, Mr. Bostwick," the one with the sandy hair said, "I hope you are settling in. Had a good flight, did you?" Very English.

"Yes. Quite good."

Then I got the first line. "I'm Chalmers," he said, and pointed to his companion. "This is Cyril Hastings."

I gave them my prescribed response, "You would be from Empire Copper?"

We shook hands and I said, "Please come in."

They selected the upper level and sat at the table.

"Can I get you anything?" I asked, holding up my bottle of Whitbread's.

"Does look inviting," the one with the brown hair and dark-blue suit said. He was answering to Hastings at the moment.

"Two?" I asked. Chalmers nodded.

I poured two more ales, handed them over, and pulled the loveseat around and faced them.

"We hear they literally plucked you off the *Independence,*" Chalmers said.

I nodded. I didn't know who they were or how much they knew. Let them come to me.

They studied me and we smiled at each other and pulled on our Whitbread's.

"Looks like you keep fit," Hastings observed.

"Try to run and work on the weights when I can."

"Difficult to run on an aircraft carrier I would expect," Hastings put in.

"Well, there's about four and a half acres of deck to run on. It's manageable when the wind is down. I've heard of a couple of cases where guys have been blown off the deck in a stiff wind."

"Oh, my." They had worried, concerned faces. We put away some more ale and smiled. The clock ticked away.

"Smallpiece," Chalmers said, and set his glass down on the table. Finally he looked like he was going to say something. "We have seen something of your record, sanitized and laundered by Washington and then by Whitehall, I expect." He ran his finger along the edge of his glass and looked at me. "We know about Tripoli, Bierut, Teheran, Baghdad, Managua, Havana." He paused, then went on. "You seem to leave a lot of dead people lying about."

I caught his pleasant brown eyes and held on. "Yes, well, that was generally what those men had in mind for me."

He smiled and nodded.

"You don't use firearms, we've been told."

I nodded, too.

"You used your hands on those men?"

I shrugged, "Maybe half. Sometimes you have to take their guns away from them, if you can. If the situation requires it, I'll use their weapons on them if I have to. Depends."

Hastings gathered his hands together, fingers touching just at the tips. He looked almost clinical.

"Do you like doing what you do?" he asked.

I produced a moderate sigh. Smiled. "I'm a college professor. I like students, mathematics, logic, and the theory of science. I'm also a reserve naval pilot. I like the combination. Not a bad life for me, right now."

39

"But the intelligence work?"

"I have done it because I was asked. I think I'm reasonably good at it, but I can't say I like it. No."

Chalmers raised an eyebrow. "But then, why do it?"

I studied his face. Open. Honest. Sincere. Interested. Bullshit. The guy's a spy. He can make his face do anything.

"I don't know. I just do it."

We all went back to our glasses. Nobody had fallen off the scaffolding yet.

"What do you think you will be doing ten years from now, Smallpiece?" Chalmers wondered. Some sort of projective technique, I supposed.

I checked the ale in my glass and smiled again.

"No idea."

I poured the last of the Whitbread's from the bottle into my glass. Nice foamy head. I looked at Chalmers, and gave him my half-wit smile.

We had a nice silence going now. I raised my empty bottle and inquired with my eyes.

"No. No, thank you," Hastings replied.

They stood up. Chalmers took an envelope from his pocket and tossed it on the table. "There are two thousand pounds in there," he said. "If you need more you will know who to contact."

I was standing.

Hastings handed me a card with an address in Whitehall.

"Be there at ten-thirty tomorrow morning," he said.

I smiled that I would. We were all smiling again. Spies have at least twenty different kinds of smiles, maybe twenty-two or -three.

"You two have any idea what they want me for?" I asked.

Chalmers shook his head. "None at all."

I walked them to the door.

"Did I pass?" I asked.

Chalmers blew out a breath. "Oh yes, you passed, Smallpiece. You look and talk like you should be in your third year at Cambridge, but you're a cold piece of work. I think you did all the things your record says and I thought it was all a lot of Yankee PR fluff."

I opened the door. We shook hands. Practiced our smiles.

"What happens now?" I asked.

"You're appropriate as far as we are concerned, Smallpiece. But we were just a preliminary screening. I suspect you will get a more thorough going over tomorrow."

They closed the door behind them.

They were a couple of middle-level M15 types sent out to see if I had horns. Basically they were there to drop off some expense money and to let me know where I was to report tomorrow.

I checked my watch. Three-thirty. Still a lot of time before supper to wander about London and see some of the old sights. So I left my key at the desk and got a georgeous smile from the blonde. She was warming up. Better than maybe, now.

There was the threat of rain, but in London that is not news. I went right on Shaftesbury Avenue then left on Charing Cross. Traffic was very heavy but what can you expect in the center of London? Noise and bustle everywhere. Motorcycles by the hundreds nipping through the famous London cabs that were mostly still in their basic black but a few were tan or almost gold. The air was redolent with leaded gas exhaust. The English have done a marvelous job on their waterways, but they haven't confronted automobile pollution or the catalytic converter.

After an hour of idle wandering, I found myself at the British Museum, a low white building that looks a bit scruffy on the outside, but the exhibitions are first rate. They have the best Egyptian collection I have ever seen. I browsed around for a few hours and departed with the crowd at closing time. I checked the menu posted outside the restaurant of the Kenilworth Hotel a few blocks from the museum. It was French and the prices were reasonable. Did I have lunch? Didn't think so. I went inside.

It was an attractive room with a low ceiling, thickly carpeted, subdued, and dimly lit. Privacy was achieved through the use of richly grained five-foot-high walnut partitions and leafy green planters. I took a seat at a table set for two. The muted tones of a piano drifted from a corner.

I ordered the veal marsala. Had a martini, which is very rare for me. The service was excellent. The wine steward, the waiter, and bus boy were courteous and attentive. The food was superior. I was equally generous with my smiles and expansive with the taxpayers' coin.

I walked out into the London dusk with the streetlights glowing in the twilight and the traffic now polite and orderly. I let the crowds carry me along Oxford Street, the shoppers now gone, but the young holiday crowd was out. More Japanese again, but the Americans outnumbered them. We were into the brightly lit theater district with the garish signs and the punkers.

It was quieter at Waterloo Bridge and wisps of fog lifted from the river, making soft halos around the the streetlights. I watched the Thames flowing to the sea. The Romans had seen it, too. A tug hooted somewhere. The gulls wheeled and called. A rusty freighter silently plowed to the sea. Where bound? Night came in with the fog. I thought of Sherlock Holmes and Fu Manchu and Jack the

Ripper. Lord, it was foggy London Town in June but Kelly McGillis didn't run from a misty corner, put her arms around me, and whisper that a giant bald-headed man with an Oriental symbol branded on his forehead was trying to kill her.

I eventually returned to the quiet lobby of The New Piccadilly and found the lovely blonde gone. I went up to my room, spent five minutes figuring out the lock system. Took a shower, listened to the soft natter of the traffic outside. There were no sirens. I was asleep in five minutes.

The address Hastings had given me led to a five-story, grey-stoned Victorian building in Whitehall with large bowed glass windows, potted geraniums, and a green-and-white-striped canopy that led from the massive oak entrance down to the sidewalk. The building was protected by a six-foot cast iron fence rooted in a bed of ivy. It looked substantial and well maintained. A discreet brass plate set into the stone on the right side of the doors read, "The Union Jack Club." The doorman, in a long red coat with brass buttons, tipped his right hand to me. It was a soft military salute. He had no left hand.

The lobby was cool and dark, paneled in oak and richly carpeted. A massive, curving staircase wound up from the right, around the back, and continued on up and left. I walked to the center of the lobby and looked overhead and saw the staircase spiral on through the floors ending in a stained-glass skylight in the roof. The staircase could not be replaced today. The skill and craft in the carving and joinery had been lost. Anyway, they don't make trees like that anymore.

A man was seated at a small period desk on the left with a brass lamp and green shade. He was busy writing

43

and took no notice of me. Hanging on the walls were large, heroic canvases of long-past land and sea battles. The mood of the place was military, varnish and wax, efficiency and order, history and the past, class and wealth. Rank has its privileges. It was all very English. There was nothing remotely like it in Washington. I thought of the austere, spartan captain's cabin on the *Independence*. There is still a lot of Puritan in American culture.

People moved through the lobby going up the stairs or down the halls on either side. Conversation was subdued and quiet. About a third were in uniform, Air Force, Navy, Army, all English and all ranking officers. A woman, an Army major, went by talking to a middle-aged man in civilian clothes. He was nodding earnestly, in total agreement. She gave me a good look as she went by. I flashed her my boyish grin. The man at the desk finally looked up and saw me. He was wearing a black patch over his left eye.

"Can I help you, sir?" he asked.

"I was told to be here at ten-thirty," I replied.

"And who were you to meet, sir?"

"I was not told that."

"Ah." He consulted a notebook on his desk.

"Would you be Lieutenant Smallpiece, sir?"

"Yes."

"Just a moment, sir."

He picked up his phone and spoke into it. He nodded. "Someone is coming down for you now, sir."

"Thank you."

No more than a minute later, a man, about twenty-five, came down the stairs. He spotted me right way. He carried a cane and had a slight limp.

"Lieutenant Smallpiece?" Earnest, bright face. He wanted to please.

44

"Yes."

"This way, sir." We went up the magnificent staircase and then left on the second floor. The walls were filled with the portraits of military men, more battle scenes, and romanticized sea fights. Halfway down the hall we stopped, went through a door and into a small room furnished like a living room. A middle-aged woman with blue hair sat at a desk, authentic Chippendale, and was speaking on the phone.

She smiled, put her hand over the phone, and said to me, "You can go right in, Lieutenant." They all had given it the American pronunciation, not the English "Leftenant." She pointed to a door set in the paneling. I opened it and went in.

It was a large corner room at least thirty by forty feet, oak paneled, as was the entire building it seemed. Tall, narrow windows on the two outside walls, heavy green drapes, now pulled open. The windows along the front were bowed. A large, sculptured white marble Victorian fireplace was set along an interior wall that was entirely bookcases, floor to ceiling. Again, the room was furnished as a residence, in period pieces largely. Chippendale, Queen Anne, Hepplewhite, and they all went together. There were two large Oriental rugs with a cream background, and on the walls, the usual military paintings. Campaigns in Africa, Asia, America. The sun never sets.

Three men were seated when I came in and got immediately to their feet. They were dressed in civilian clothes but nothing could hide the military background. They were all in their sixties and were giving me a very hard study. No smiles.

"Ah, Smallpiece. Good of you to come." He was perhaps sixty-five, slender, brown hair without a touch of grey,

45

aquiline nose, firm mouth. Hawk-faced. He held out his hand and I took it.

"I'm Fitzworthy," he said, "Royal Navy." He would be an admiral. He turned to the two others. "This is Robert Harkness." I shook hands with Harkness, white-haired, ascetic face, could have been a monk. "He heads up our intelligence services in the Soviet Union and the Iron Curtain countries."

I had recognized the third right away. Medium height, slender, dark-blue suit with a subtle grey stripe, aristocratic face with brown, wavy hair, large forehead, intelligent, penetrating eyes, straight nose, mustache, thin mouth that was relaxed in an easy smile. He could be David Niven's twin, but he wasn't. He was Roger Halliburton, MP, and next to the Prime Minister the most powerful figure in the UK. There are those who would argue he was the most powerful.

"I'm not sure if you have ever met Mr. Halliburton," Fitzworthy continued.

"No," I said, "but I know who he is."

Halliburton nodded. The smile wasn't so easy as it looked.

They had been seated around a low table in sea-green leather chairs to the right of the fireplace. A silver service was on a low circular table with four tea cups and saucers.

"Tea, Lieutenant?" Fitzworthy asked.

"Thank you."

We sat down. I took the fourth chair. Fitzworthy got busy with the cups. They were looking at me.

I sipped and smiled. They made polite noises. Somebody mentioned the weather. There a couple of coughs. One "Hummmm."

We smiled some more. Just like spies.

"You have an unusual name, Lieutenant," Fitzworthy

46

observed, settling back into his chair, holding his cup and saucer neatly on his crossed knee."

"Yes, sir."

"Your Secretary of the Navy only sent us an abstract of your service record and some educational background. I'm afraid we rushed him some. We don't even know where you were born."

"Rockport, Maine. Sir."

"I see. Hummmm. Ah." He was struggling. "The name Colin Smallpiece has appeared down through the generations in the Royal Navy. It is a very distinguished name. Any connection there, do you suppose?" He was looking at me very sharply.

I put my cup back on the table. "My father was Colin Smallpiece. He held the rank of commander in the Royal Navy. He and my mother were killed in a traffic accident in Vermont when I was six months old. My grandfather, also Colin Smallpiece, held the rank of admiral in the Royal Navy. He is now retired and lives in Cornwall."

The atmosphere in the room changed instantly. All three simultaneously produced sighs, then smiles, and the mood of the room went from the strained formality of an obligatory cocktail party to the locker room of a football team that had just pulled the game out.

"Jove!" Fitzworthy exploded. "Collie Smallpiece's grandson! Knew it!" He folded his arms and thrust his chin out.

"Jolly good!" Harkness slapped his knee.

"Incredible! Smashing!" Halliburton had lost a lot of cool.

"It's in the blood," Fitzworthy explained to Harkness. "You can't deny the blood. The Navy is in the blood. Look at him, a navy man and a pilot, just like his father

47

and his grandfather. It's in the blood. Can't be denied! Bloody sociologists!"

Clearly I was bonded into the group.

Body language. Everyone had settled back into their chairs, crossed their legs, easily sipped some tea. Fitzworthy snorted and blew his nose loudly into a giant handkerchief. "Ah!" he happily announced.

There was about ten minutes of small talk, smiles, a few jokes, and some tea drinking. They still were looking me over very carefully. They asked a few polite questions about my family in America, my education, that sort of thing.

Halliburton sobered them down. He looked me directly in the eyes and held on, "We have a very serious problem and we need a very special man. It will probably involve penetrating the Soviet Union. It is a high-risk mission and the probability of success is low. The probability of danger, possibly death, is high."

I used my usual noncommittal nod.

Halliburton leaned forward and rubbed his hands up and down his thighs. "Your record looks very good, extraordinary really. But there are one or two things we would like to see for ourselves. We feel we must put you through a bit. Ah. Er. See how you handle yourself in physical situations. That sort of thing." His eyebrows shot up. "You can refuse, of course. It can stop here."

I effected my usual shrug and wagged my head. I had no idea what was going on or why I was here. "I might refuse, but let's see what you have in mind."

"Good. Capital," Halliburton said. "Fitz will take you to the mat room."

They all stood up. There was more smiling and the shaking of hands.

"Please come with me," Fitzworthy said, and I followed

him through the door and out into the hall. We went up the circular stairs one more flight, then down a hall to the right with more romantic scenes of the Empire and the glory that was England. He opened a door and we were in a small locker room.

"You can change here," Fitzworthy said, "put on those things and hang your clothes in the locker. Then go through there." He pointed to a door at the far end of the locker room. "Meet you in there." He disappeared through the far door.

I put on the "things" which were a T-shirt, running shorts, sweat socks, and tennis shoes. The T-shirt had a small American flag embroidered on the upper left side. I hung my clothes in the locker and went through the far door.

The room was perhaps fifty feet by fifty feet, thirty feet high, and the floor was covered by a soft mat. No windows, bare walls.

Fitzworthy was talking to a group of men, saw me, and detached himself. "Ah," he said, "that was fast. Come over."

I joined the group but my interest was centered on one man. He was dressed as I was except that his T-shirt had a Union Jack. He was about six feet, very thick in the upper arms and shoulders. Probably went about two thirty-five. I had a few inches on him, but he had the weight. It was clear that I had to fight this guy. I wasn't introduced.

He had hot black eyes, and a thin film of perspiration was on his forehead. We looked at each other and I shrugged, raised my eyebrows, grinned at him. No grin back. The man didn't like me. Was it because of the small Stars and Stripes on my shirt? There had been no introductions, but the man knew I was an American. Ah so!

We had, perhaps, some national pride going here. Very clever these English.

"There will be no names or ranks," Fitzworthy was saying, "this will be a no-holds-barred fight. Anything goes. You are to put your man down as if you were to kill him. You will not do that, however. If it looks like someone is about to be seriously hurt, I will shout 'stop.' If you don't stop, these two gentlemen will see that you do."

The two gentlemen were grim-faced, short-haired, well-built athletic types in sweat clothes. There were two other men in the room. One was tall, short hair again, and was powerfully built. He had a military aura and he was looking me over as if I were a prize horse he might buy. I guessed he was an Army man and possibly a specialist in hand-to-hand. The other was middle-aged and had a stethoscope sticking out of his jacket pocket.

"All right, you two," Fitzworthy called, "come over here and face each other. When I count three, go at it. Do you understand? Any questions?"

I looked into my opponent's eyes and smiled. He glared back. A hot head. Might use that. Everyone backed away to give us room. Fiztworthy said, "One, two . . ." On the two, I had put all my weight on my left foot. "Three."

As the "threeeeee" trembled off into eternity, I had my right foot off the ground, behind his left leg, came forward with it hard. As he toppled backward, I got my right hand under his left leg and lifted him higher. His back came down on the mat with a considerable thud. It was a graceless fall. Ungainly. Awkward. It was a no-class flop.

He was up instantly. "He moved before he should have!" he protested. Surprising high voice.

Fitzworthy looked pained, but the hand-to-hand guy was shaking his head. I moved faster.

"Let's go again," I suggested. But I had put him down and he knew it.

Fitzworthy was grim. He motioned us to line up again and counted slowly, "One, two, three."

Before my man moved, I stomped his left foot very hard. I wanted him to experience a moderate amount of pain and to occupy his mind. Then I gave him a head fake and he jumped back and showed fear. I turned slightly from him, as if going away, but then went for his head with my right arm, pulled him in, and got my hip under his body. I lifted him up and then flung him down with a hard body hip throw. I was on top of him with my right arm around his head.

I looked up at Fitzworthy. "I could break his neck right now or I could choke him or I could shatter his windpipe with the edge of my hand."

There was a pregnant silence in the room.

"Let him up," Fitzworthy said.

I did as I was told.

"Another try?" I asked.

Fitzworthy seemed pained.

My opponent didn't look at me, but he was on his feet. Fitzworthy didn't look at me, either. The hand-to-hand man was smiling.

For the third time we were toe to toe.

"One, two, three."

I went immediately for his throat with my left hand, and again he backed up. Losing becomes a habit. An attitude. He now expected to lose. But, my motion was continuous from throat to waist and I was into him with a bear hug. I picked him up, slammed him onto the mat, and came down hard on top of him. I heard the breath go out of him. He groaned.

Again I looked up at Fitzworthy, who had gone a little pale.

"You want any more of this?" I asked. I helped my man up. Patted his backside. Brushed him off. He was beaten and bent over, holding his left side. The doctor was attending him.

"Look," I said to Fitzworthy, "I know the English sense of fair play. Officers and gentlemen, right? I don't know who your man is, but I don't think he has ever killed anyone with his hands. If you have anyone that's a real test, get him in here. Otherwise we are all wasting our time."

We had some more silence. The doctor was pressing the man's chest, asking where it hurt.

"I think we may have a couple of broken ribs here," the doctor said to Fitzworthy, who gestured abruptly to the door. The doctor helped the man out.

Fitzworthy was grim. I think he wanted me to win because of the mission and possibly the Smallpiece name. But then national pride got in the way. I made their champion look bad. But the guy was bad. Really bad.

Fitzworthy blew out a breath. Sighed. He studied the floor for thirty seconds.

"Get Flynn," he said finally to one of the men in sweatsuits.

Flynn came into the room at six six and probably two hundred sixty pounds. He had a T-shirt with no Union Jack. He wore a long pair of shorts that almost came down to his knees. They were either long short pants or short long pants. His accessories were black socks and grey tennis shoes. Flynn was not into fashion. He would be into street fighting.

He had red hair that was almost shaved at the temples, a flattened nose that had been broken a dozen times and hardly elevated from the face at all. His eyebrows looked like they had been stitched together by a mad surgeon and his mouth was permanently turned up at the corner by a scar that ran from his throat to his chin and into the mouth. The scar gave Flynn an eternal, insane grin. Flynn could be killing you and you would think he was smiling.

His face and tatooed forearms were darkly tanned, while his chest and legs were absolutely white and totally smooth and unblemished. He had powerful, sloping shoulders, a heavily muscled barrel chest, and massive legs that were as thick in the calves as the thighs. I had never seen hands on a human being that big. His body was one continuous, unbroken vertical line from shoulders to feet. He was built like a tree trunk. Oak tree. English oak.

He looked at me and smiled the way I had smiled at the other man. I smiled back. The man was a fighter, probably fleet champion for years. When he wasn't fighting for the Royal Navy, he was amusing himself in bars— Singapore, Manila, Calcutta, Cairo, Casablanca, Cape Town. Places like that.

Flynn had me by fifty pounds and three to four inches. He was enormously powerful and his ruined face told of hundreds of street and bar fights. He might be ten years older than me and would be slowing up. I had speed and might possibly match him in strength. But I had never come up against anyone like him. He was a huge, monstrous man and there was a happy gleam in his eyes. He was fighting again and before very important men. I doubted if Flynn had ever lost a fight before.

Two things would happen to me during this fight. One, I certainly would have a dialogue with Sergeant Norbert McCorkle. I knew that would happen. Secondly, I might have a hyperdrive episode and I didn't want to. If I did, it meant I feared for my life.

I met Sergeant McCorkle about four years ago in Camp Perry in Virginia. It was part of my spy training. I had successfully completed a course in hand-to-hand at Parris Island, and with five others was sent up to Camp Perry to continue on in a special program called "Multiple Armed Adversary Combat" or MAAC for short. The idea here was to learn how to take out men who had guns on you—multiple armed adversaries. They told us the grim odds from the very beginning of instruction, but if you are going to be shot anyhow, here's what you might do. Maybe it will work. What have you got to lose? You're going to be dead anyway.

McCorkle was a career Marine, a professional fighting man who wore his wide-brimmed campaign hat square on his head. He was made of wire and leather. He frightened everyone, even his commanding officer. Nobody got in his way and nobody knew how to kill a man faster and more efficiently, with just his hands, than Sergeant McCorkle.

From the first day of the training program McCorkle picked me out for his goat. He constantly rode me for the whole five weeks. "Come on, lady, get into it.... What are you waiting for, Smallpiece, go after his balls.... Jesuschrist, Smallpiece, you're supposed to break his arm, not go dancin'! Maybe you do want to go dancing with the guy! That what you want, Smallpiece? Throw the fucker. Throw him. You're supposed to break his rib cage. Get your fingers into his eye. You take the goddamn weapon away from him by breaking his thumb. Bend it back, it snaps. It's easy. Sweet Jesus, I think maybe he's got it ..."

Toward the end of it, he challenged me in front of the squad. He hit me with a sucker punch, put me down, called me names, and for a moment I lost my cool and got angry. Still on the ground, I grabbed McCorkle's leg, pulled him over, got my foot into his back, and flung him seven feet through the air. Broke his elbow. Separated his shoulder. They took him off in a stretcher and he looked back at me. He was smiling!

"Finally got to you, huh, Smallpiece? I knew you would be something if you ever got mad." They carried him off with his broken elbow. McCorkle seemed quite content, almost happy. I think he had planned the whole thing.

McCorkle had become a part of me. He resided in my unconscious, sunk into my brain, and was buried deep into my personality. An irresistible force like McCorkle was hard to deny. A part of him fused into me, became me. In the stress of those intelligence missions, he would surface and speak.

In Tripoli or Baghdad, he would come up into my conscious mind and rationally analyze the situation, explain alternatives, suggest combat strategies. We talked and argued. McCorkle became my consultant in intimate violence and when I needed him, he was always there. He was my superego of deadly force.

I am the only one who believes in the hyperdrive. I know it happens to me, but when I explain it to others, even doctors, they think I'm imagining it. After all, they say, it happens only during crises, during intense emotion, in situations of hyperactivity and acute stress. Nothing like that can really happen to a person. No way. Some people probably thought I was crazy. So, I don't talk about it anymore.

I first experienced the hyperdrive (I had no name for it then) when I was fourteen years old, in June, in Rockport. I was home from Phillips Academy for a few weeks before flying to England, to Devon, to spend my summer as I always did, with Uncle Phillip. I had come out of the movie theater in Camden, it was ten-thirty at night and I went into the alley by the theater to get my bike that was chained to the bike rack. Four punks were trying to steal it. They cornered me. I recognized them. Fifteen, sixteen-year-olds, drop-outs, misfits from broken homes, kids with police records and already deep into failure. They were the current crop of adolescent smart asses, village toughs. They were looking for some action. They found me.

Small towns are gold fish bowls. Everybody knows everbody. I knew I was in trouble.

"Give us the key, Smallpiece, and maybe we won't beat you up."

"No."

"Then we'll beat the shit out of you anyway and take the key."

"No."

They came toward me, silhouetted against the streetlight. I retreated into the alley. The rat pack followed. I heard them breathing. I smelled them. Saw their heads hunched down in their shoulders. Adolescent gargoyles. For the first time in my life I felt physical fear. Fear that I would be badly hurt, and with it, anger.

Then they froze and didn't move. And the cars in the street were hardly moving. Sound was deep, sonorous, like a record running down. Everything had stopped. Nothing moved. I didn't know what was happening. But there they were like threatening statues, rooted, fixed, immobilized in the night. A rigid tableau of frozen aggression. I didn't wait to figure it out. I stepped into the first punk and slammed a hard right into his jaw. I could still move! He fell in slow motion. I hit the next one in the stomach and as he caved in, I caught him with two strong left jabs. I kicked the third in the legs, got him in a head lock and threw him into the alley wall. The fourth started to run,

56

but he hardly moved. I tackled him and pounded his head into the pavement.

When I had my bike unlocked, sight, sound, and motion had returned to normal. The cars moved briskly up Main Street. Horns sounded clear and sharp. I looked down the alley, two were sitting up. The moans and gasps were normal. Everything was quite normal. I was normal.

I rarely experienced it after the initial episode in Maine, just four or five times in prep school and college. But the intelligence missions I was sent on, the MAAC training, all brought me into violent, life-threatening confrontations and it was the hyperdrive that got me through them. It gave me two to three times the speed of my adversary. I saw punches coming in slow motion. I got out of the way. I could even dodge a thrown knife if I had twenty feet. Guns took an eternity to clear a jacket or holster. I retaliated with a blinding speed my opponent could not adjust to.

Eventually, I tried to explain it to the navy neurologists and they listened gravely and nodded and took notes. Then they gave me tests, probed and pinched, wired me, and shot electric currents into my brain. They looked at meters, studied computer printouts, and when they were done they told me it didn't happen. All in my mind, they said. They made jokes about it. Called it "Smallpiece Syndrome" or "Neurological Hyperdrive." I think they read a lot of science fiction. They assured me I wasn't crazy, that I really thought it happened because, in stress, everything is magnified. I was overwrought, perhaps, because of the things I had to do.

The psychologists suggested I take it easy. Maybe I had seen too much violence. Too many missions and too many dead men by my hands. On the edge perhaps? Why not go to graduate school? Use that super IQ, get a Ph.D. and go academic. Forget Tripoli and what I did there. So I did.

Now I was looking into Flynn's smiling, ravaged but contented face, and Fitzworthy was going over the rules again.

"Don't try to box that man, Smallpiece. If he connects with one punch, you're out of it." McCorkle. I knew he would talk.

"Maybe. I don't know. Let's see what he can do." You understand, I don't move my lips or actually speak. It all goes on inside. I'm not crazy. I know McCorkle isn't really there. I'm pretty sure about that.

Fitzworthy said, "Three."

Flynn had small, very blue eyes. They never left my face. We circled each other. It looked like he wanted to box and be a gentleman for a while. He probed with an exploratory left. I tucked my head down and easily brushed it off.

He shuffled in, left arm extended. I ducked to his right and pounded two hard, straight left jabs into his eye. He backed off.

"Well, now," Flynn smiled, "what have we here?" I think he had set me up for that. He wanted to see what I could do.

While Flynn was admiring my left, I pumped a hard right into his chest and that stopped his forward motion. Again the smile and a condescending nod. Sort of a salute. I flicked a few more lefts at him. We circled again. His arms seemed to be dropping and I stepped in, blocked his left arm, and hooked a strong right into his eye. It drew red right away but suddenly a cloud of sparks exploded in my brain. His right had come out of nowhere. He opened up the cut in my eyebrow. I backed off, lightheaded.

"Are you satisfied now?" McCorkle nagged. *"If you*

58

stand toe to toe with this man you will be pounded in a bloody rubble in ten minutes. You'll have a face like his. You want that, Smallpiece? What about all those girls you have plans for? Girls like your face. Now.

"Okay. Okay."

"You know what to do."

"Yeah. Okay. Shut up for christsakes."

"I'll shut up."

"Well, do it!"

"All right." He always has to have the last word.

I resumed my boxer's stance. Flynn was a mountain above me. He still seemed slightly amused. Time for me to go to wit and skill. I stepped toward him with my left foot, then I turned quickly away but kept my head facing Flynn. I let some fear into my eyes. He shuffled forward and believed the body fake and the fear. I turned and pumped a very hard right into his gut. It hurt and Flynn bent over. I brought my right knee up under his chin and straightened him up. He was bleeding from the mouth.

Flynn was no longer amused. It was a bar fight now. He was embarrassed in front of all that rank. I'd use the emotion but now I would let him come to me. He knew I could hurt him. But there would be no spectacular body slams now.

I threw another punch and Flynn blocked it. He flicked a right and grazed my temple. I faked a left jab and it appeared we were gentlemen boxers again. Flynn shuffled in, determined to pound me into the mat. No more games. I had my scared look on again, and backed away. Flynn came to me. I spun on my left foot, half turned, and kicked out my right leg with all my strength and caught him flush on the jaw with my foot. It has to be done with great speed and power. No arm could deliver a blow like that. His head

59

snapped back. He stood there flat-footed, openmouthed, and swayed.

Flynn was out on his feet and bleeding from the nose and mouth. Only his strength, his iron will and pride kept him up. His arms had dropped. He didn't move. The force of the kick would have broken a lot of jaws and killed some men.

I looked at Fitzworthy. "You said to put the man down. You want him down?"

He hesitated for a second, but his eyes said yes.

Now I was the one who hesitated, then I moved. I didn't like it a bit. I liked Flynn.

I stepped into Flynn, who continued to sway defenseless in front of me, and hooked two savage body blows into him with all the strength I had, a left and a right. The old one, two, right into that massive chest, over the heart. He gasped, sucking air. His eyes rolled to the back of his head. Finally he began to sink. His legs had buckled. He sagged down toward the mat like a great majestic oak slowly beginning its fall. I got my arms around his waist and eased him down to the mat.

I turned to Fitzworthy, who looked stunned, mouth agape, not at all the way an admiral should look. "What's his rank?" I asked.

"Chief," he mumbled.

"You okay, Chief?" I asked Flynn, who now sat spread-eagled on the mat. His color wasn't bad and his eyes were open. They just weren't aware of the world.

"Chief?" I rubbed his neck. "You with us?"

"Coo."

"Come on. Look at me. You're okay."

I rubbed his face with a wet towel.

"Come on, Chief. Snap out of it. How do you feel?"

"Blap."

60

"Look at me, Chief. What's your name?"

"Alice."

He rubbed his eyes. Shook his head. I worked on his neck. Everybody else watched.

"What's your name?"

He sucked in a great breath and blew it out.

"Michael Horatio Flynn." He recited it slowly, like a schoolboy.

"What's your ship?"

"*Endeavor.*"

"What happened?"

"I just got fuckin' decked. I think."

The doctor was back and was fussing around him, checking his heart, then his blood pressure. The two men in sweat shirts helped Flynn up. The hand-to-hand man wasn't smiling anymore. He seemed pensive and thoughtful, then he went to a door. I caught his eye and he threw me a very precise, English military salute. I responded. He nodded and opened the door.

The doctor and the two men supporting Flynn went out another door, leaving Fitzworthy and me alone in the room.

Fitzworthy was shaking his head. "I can't believe it," he repeated. "I can't believe it. Flynn was a legend in the fleet. You put him down in less than a minute. If I hadn't seen it, I wouldn't believe it. The size of the man!"

I waited a minute, letting my breathing go back to normal.

"You have anything else for me, Admiral?" I asked.

He looked up, still far away. "Oh. Yes. Seems damn silly now. But they will want to know." He pointed to another door. "Through here," he said.

It was a weight room. One of the men in the sweat suits was standing by the bench press

"We want to see how strong you are."

I shrugged. "Why?"

"Physical strength is essential on this mission."

I loosened up a bit, shook the muscles out. Got on my back and bench pressed up to 475 pounds. I quit at 500, didn't want to bust anything. On the power clean lift I went to 275 and then on the stand-up military press I took it to 300 pounds. I might have gone further but Fitzworthy was satisfied.

He was smiling again.

"What next?" I asked.

He grinned. "A shower and then lunch."

"Capital," I said. When in Rome.

CHAPTER III

I never thought I would like a purple carpet, but I liked this one. We were in the dining room in the Union Jack Club, Halliburton, Fitzworthy, and Harkness. Like everything else in the club it was posh, elegant, and very English. But there were no grand military scenes on the walls, only the magnificent raised panels in quarted oak, set in heavy stiles, with a rich, almost three-dimensional patina. Even admirals and generals like to eat without having to contemplate someone gloriously dying for king and country at the Khyber Pass. Four great brass chandeliers hung from the ceiling, and there were three fireplaces with massive oak moldings and brass wall sconces with sparkling crystal globes. Heavy, intricately carved booths lined two walls. The room made you want to lower your voice like in church.

There were fifty or sixty diners, close to half in uniform. I saw five women, three in uniform. The place still was a men's club, but struggling. Tables with snowy white cloths and fresh-cut flowers were well spaced and we sat in an honorific corner booth out of the way. We were getting a lot of polite, covert, English-style glances. Who is that young chap with Halliburton, Fitz, and Harkness? Must

63

be somebody's son. Too young to be anybody. What are they up to?

I had a steak, baked potato, and a salad that had a lot of stringy, hairy stuff on top. It wasn't much. Great steak though, must have come from Cornwall. There was the usual banter at the table with a lot of names I didn't know. But they kept me into it with questions about the carrier, F-14's, Spaulding, my classes, and the like. They even got into American football and were interested in my Harvard days. Oddly, nobody smoked. Unusual for Europeans who are not into health and fitness like Americans. Now and then each one would look away and his face would go grim. Then they would take a big breath and get back into entertaining the guest with forced smiles.

We were having coffee, and I pushed my chair back and checked the room again. Very quiet, very proper, very English. The service was the best I had ever seen, but many of the staff were missing hands or eyes, and some limped.

"Obviously this is a club for senior military officers," I said to Fitzworthy.

"Yes," he blotted his mouth. "For over a hundred and fifty years. Not all in this building though. We got this place in the fifties. Close to a lot, War Ministry, that sort of thing."

"The people who work here are former military people?"

"Oh, yes. All of them."

"With service-incurred injuries?"

"Yes. Many, but not all."

"But some are in their early twenties."

"Falklands."

I nodded. "Of course."

I looked at Halliburton. "I get the feeling this is more than just a social club."

I got a blank stare from his David Niven face. "Why would you say that?"

"I don't know. Just a feeling. I think this is also something else. I noticed two Marine guards at the third-floor landing, and there was a velvet chain across the opening."

"We do use it for a few other things." Harkness, the intelligence boss, answered easily.

A waiter drifted over with a small silver plate and Halliburton signed something. He looked up at the waiter and said, "Tell Major Compton everything was just fine. First rate. My compliments."

The waiter beamed and limped away.

He turned his attention back to me. His fingers drummed the table, his mind still apparently on my comment about the Marine guards. "Perhaps it is, Smallpiece. But we shall see." He blew out a breath and gravely regarded me. "We still have more business for you this afternoon. I hope you do as well as you did this morning. No one can believe you put Flynn down, let alone in less than a minute."

"How is Flynn?" I asked.

"Oh, he's fine. His pride's hurt, of course. He wanted to know who you were. He thinks you're Superman or something. We told him your name and he actually smiled. Seemed his father served on the same ship as yours. He knows the name."

I finally asked, "Well, what do you have for me this afternoon?"

"Oh," Fitzworthy grinned, "we want to see what goes on in your head. We know who you are physically."

"Psychologists?" I frowned.

"Oh, no. Nothing like that. Bloody half-wits, if you ask me. We want to know what you know."

"About what?"

He produced a conspiratorial smile. Put his right forefinger vertically across his mouth. "You'll see." He looked at Halliburton. "Perhaps we should get on with it?"

"We shall see you later this afternoon then." Halliburton extended his hand. I took it. He had a firm grip. "Come along with me, Smallpiece," Fitzworthy said. I waved a reluctant farewell and we mounted the magnificent staircase again and went up to the third floor this time. Fitzworthy was breathing heavily.

The Marine guards snapped to attention and Fitzworthy waved a card at them. A small sign read, "Private. No Admittance." There were another pair of guards midway down the corridors on both the right and left of the stairs.

"Down this way." He indicated left and we stopped before the third door on the right. No pictures on the walls, no lovely oak panels, just green paint and varnished wooden floors. It was absolutely quiet, as if the entire floor was sealed. Maybe it was.

Fitzworthy opened the door a crack. "I'll leave you now. Good luck." He opened the door and I stepped inside.

It was a windowless room maybe fifteen by twenty feet with bare walls. There were four easy chairs, looked like leather, centered around a low, square table. In the middle of the table there was a small bouquet of silk flowers. The room was lit by eight wall fixtures with brown parchment shades. There was a ventilating grid in one corner. The room was cold and austere. It had but one function. It was a place where people could talk privately.

My entrance was observed by three people who occupied the chairs and who remained seated, two men and one woman.

"Please sit down," one of the men said. "There will be no introductions." He held his hands out apologetically. He spoke in Russian. He was pattern bald, had a beard, dark-brown eyes, and it seemed that he would normally smile, but the situation prevented it. He looked like an academic to me.

The other man was short and round, with curly light-brown hair, black-rimmed glasses, and he clutched his hands in his lap. He had a deep scar that ran from his right eyebrow halfway through his cheek. The scar tended to pull his eye down so that he appeared to be about to wink and share a conspiratorial joke. He seemed the most relaxed of the three.

The woman was young, in her mid-twenties, and was looking at me as if I were a small, squirming, distasteful thing under a microscope. She was curious, but totally detached. She had lovely, thick blond braided hair that was coiled around her head, Scandinavian style. She wore glasses and her eyes seemed blue. Beautifully arched, dark eyebrows. She had a nice straight nose that tipped up at the end, but her mouth was compressed and showed nothing. There had to be lips there someplace. She was fair but had rough skin with pimples around the chin. Can you have acne at twenty-five? I think she must have been quite tall, maybe five ten, but it was hard to tell. She had to be forty pounds overweight. She wore a frumpy blue dress with little flowers. No style at all. She looked like Miss McGilicuddy, my Sunday School teacher, from Rockport. Unlike Miss McGilicuddy, who blushed a lot, this one fixed me with a cold, clinical stare.

I dropped into the empty chair and grinned at them. Muttered something about it being a lovely day outside. It was raining. I spoke in Russian because that seemed to be how the situation was defined. I nervously reached into

67

my pocket and pulled out a pen and promptly fumbled it to the floor. I flashed another half-wit grin, bent down and picked up the pen and spotted the wire running from the bottom of the table, directly underneath the fake flowers and into the top of the table leg. There would also be a bug in the ventilator grill and probably a couple in the parchment shades. I got back up and put the pen back in my pocket.

"I hope you enjoyed your lunch," the bearded man said. He had a concerned smile.

"Yes, very much," I replied. The other man seemed to be relieved that I enjoyed my lunch, too. The woman couldn't care less. She never took her eyes off me. Who was cat? Who was mouse? Why did I feel that she was the significant personality in the room? Maybe because she was a woman. No, it wasn't that. I've been known to ignore women. She was fat, but she had charisma.

"You have traveled to the Soviet Union?" the bearded man asked.

"Yes."

"Often?"

I thought for a moment. Squinted my left eye. "First time, I think I was eight. I've lost track since then."

"Why so many trips?"

"My uncle. He was fascinated with everything Russian. I made trips with him during summer vactions up until, oh, five years ago."

"Why did the trips stop?"

"Well, I was getting on with my education. Had a more complicated life by then. He died three years ago."

"I see."

I shrugged. She didn't have a bad face. Double chins. But why carry so much weight?

"Do you know Leningrad?"

"Yes."

"How well, would you say?" The bearded man was carrying the conversation. The other man and woman were listening.

"Quite well. Yes."

"What is Saigon?"

"In Leningrad?"

"Yes."

"A café."

"Where is it located?"

I rolled my eyes heavenward like a kid in a spelling bee. "On the corner of Nevsky and Liteiny streets."

"How many tables are there?"

"No tables. There are counters running along the walls. You stand up and eat at the counters."

"Do they have waiters or waitresses?"

"Neither. It is a help-yourself place. Cafeteria style."

"What do they serve?"

"Oh, coffee, *pirozhki*. Things like that."

"What is *fartcovshchik?*"

"It's a slang term for a black market place. A place to get drugs, where Russians can buy things stolen or bought from tourists. It's a place where you can get things the government stores don't have. No questions asked. Capitalist place, lot of private enterprisers. Generally, the government pretends it's not there. Every major city has them."

"What about *Barakholka?*"

"It used to be a flea market on the outskirts of Leningrad. Black market place."

"Have you ever been there?"

"No. I heard about it, but I think the authorities closed it up."

"What is the most popular sport in Leningrad?"

I stroked my chin. "I guess it might be a toss up be-

69

tween ice hockey and soccer. Probably ice hockey. Yeah. Definitely ice hockey."

"What is the team called?"

"*Ska.* Sporting Club of the Army."

"Have you ever been in Leningrad on the twenty-first of June?"

"Yes. I think so."

"Why is the twenty-first of June significant?"

"It's called the 'white night.' It's daylight almost all night long because the city is so far north. It's a holiday time and young people go to the river and there is music and dancing. They're celebrating the end of the school year. Everybody sort of lets down after the long, cold winter. It's like a carnival. I remember meeting a great girl there when I was still in college. Sonia? Really built. Free spirit. Man, that girl!"

I sneakily checked the fat girl's face.

The men looked interested, the woman, bored.

The bearded man then took me through Moscow in much the same way. How to get from here to there, the obvious places. But then he asked me about the jokes that made the rounds at cocktail parties, or the special places where you could buy a stolen battery for your motorcycle. Again, he got me into the underlife of Soviet society, that part you can't find in the tourist brochures or the travel books.

I didn't mind it. It was question-and-answer for fifteen or twenty minutes. It was clear what he was after. He wanted to hear my accent, listen to my accounts of Soviet life. Could I pass as a Russian? I thought I did okay.

He seemed to have run out of gas. He looked to the man with the scar who had pulled himself to the edge of his chair. He pushed his glasses back up on his nose and couldn't keep a small smile of anticipation from his mouth.

The bearded man, his job done, settled back in his chair, crossed his legs, and studied the far wall. The fat girl hadn't moved and still found me fascinating. It is not nice to be regarded as a bug.

"I understand you know some physics and mathematics," the man with the scar said, keeping his small smile under control. He had a soft, conversational voice. He spoke a standard Russian. I couldn't place his accent. Maybe the south.

I nodded pleasantly. Waited.

"Have you followed the SDI debate?"

"Star Wars?"

He shrugged. "Do you call it that?"

"I don't call it anything."

"Do you think it feasible?"

I pulled a face. "Anything is feasible. It depends on how much time and money you have."

"How much time do you think it would take to make SDI operational?"

"Which system?"

"Tell me about the systems."

I shrugged again. "There seems to be two possibilities, ground-fired missiles, interceptor rockets, guided from hardened ground-based radars. The missiles might be similar to the present Spartans with nuclear warheads. They would be really big bang defensive devices."

"They would have to be nuclear?"

"Probably, but not necessarily, there could be non-nuclear versions using terminal homing devices in the interceptor. They would be more sophisticated than the nuclear warheads. More precise, more surgical in concept."

He nodded and stroked his chin. "I see. What about the other system?"

71

"Space based. The defensive devices would be fired from satellites in space."

"Firing nuclear warheads or more conventional explosives using homing devices?"

The fat girl's mouth had opened. I saw a line of even white teeth.

"Possibly, but you read and hear more these days about neutral particle beams or chemical lasers." I grinned. "Death-ray stuff."

"I see." Again the small smile. The room was so quiet, the bugs would have no trouble picking this up. It would sound like a recording studio. I was beginning to feel warm.

"What do you think the principal problems are with a ground-based system?"

I scratched my head. "You understand, I'm not an engineer or a physicist?"

He nodded.

"I think the basic problem is software. We're pretty well along in hardware, that is, missile design, warheads, computer hardware. Computers are going to have to manage the battle. They will process the raw data from the sensors. They will direct the missile firings, determine the source of the attack, compute the trajectories, distinguish between authentic warheads and decoys. That and a lot more."

"I see."

I was warming up to it now. "An SDI battle management system will be the most complex software system ever devised involving perhaps a hundred million lines of computer code assembled by thousands of programmers. There will inevitably be errors, mistakes in the code. Not all circumstances will have been anticipated in the program. And how are you going to know it works? The thing

72

cannot be tested until there is an attack. The complexity of the software really boggles the mind."

He nodded.

"You mentioned neutral particle beams and chemical lasers as space-based weapons in an SDI system."

"Yes."

"Which, do you think, has the greatest possibility of success?"

"Probably NPB."

"Why?"

I leaned back in the chair and put my hands in back of my neck and shot a quick look at the girl. A little bit of pink tongue showed between her teeth. "They are atomic particles, accelerated to a high speed in charged form by electric fields in an accelerator. Currently, I believe, they produce particles of energy, in a solid cone angle, corresponding to acceleration by a few million volts of electric field. In the future, as both theory and technology proceed, the hope is to produce a hundred million electron volt energies. At that energy level, a particle beam device would be effective."

"I see," he said, resting his chin in his right hand. "But, at present, the energy levels are still quite low to make an effective neutral particle beam device for an SDI system?"

"I believe so, yes."

"How long, do you suppose, it will take to produce energy levels up to a hundred million electron volts?"

"Ten to fifteen years, I would think. And even then the new technology will probably not be able to put more than ten percent of the primary energy into the particle beam itself."

"What sort of technology would produce that kind of power?"

"Probably nuclear."

He nodded.

"So the country that could produce a device capable of accelerating a hundred million electron volts in a neutral particle beam would be way up in the SDI race?"

"You mean now? The present?" I asked.

"Around now."

"But there has been no theoretical development for that and certainly no technology, even experimental technology. At least nothing has been published." Then I added, "That I know of."

"Of course." He studied me for a minute, then asked, "Are there any other problems with an NPB system?"

I raised my eyebrows. "A hell of a lot. There would be the usual target acquisition and tracking problems. Software problems. Then, too, the magnet used to point the beam would also have to neutralize it, so that the beam would not be deflected by the earth's magnetic field. It would have to be very heavy."

"But a particle beam accelerator is still far off in the future?" He was repeating himself.

"There are presently accelerators, but nothing that could produce an operational NPB for an SDI system. Not now. Probably not for fifteen years."

He nodded and shot a glance at the man with the beard. For the next fifteen minutes he raised a series of questions in theoretical physics and I stumbled through some answers. He produced a pad and wrote some equations on it and I worked out some solutions. There were more questions. Finally he looked at the girl and she nodded. Had I passed or failed?

The two men had settled back in their chairs, she continued her unblinking, cobralike stare.

"What are the Russians doing with particle beam technology?" she asked.

"How the hell would I know?" I was getting nettled. Her stare was getting to me. She really had very nice eyes. Why would she let herself go like that?

She remained unflapped. "Tell us what you do know. Guess."

"I think they are probably working on powerful accelerators like everybody else. But I don't believe they have demonstrated the feasibility of the propagation of a particle beam for any meaningful distance. I doubt if they have moved very far on it."

"Kirov mean anything to you?"

"Certainly means a lot in Leningrad. There's a theater named after him, a stadium, a park, a factory, a street. I think he was a local Communist hero."

"Anything else?"

I blew out a breath. "A class of nuclear-powered guided-missile cruisers. Pretty new."

"What do you know about the Mig-29?"

"It represents the Soviet transition to a new generation of more capable combat aircraft. It has a true look-down/shoot-down radar so they can engage low-flying aircraft or cruise missiles. I'd stick with the F-14 or F15E, if I had a choice."

"Who is V.G. Kulikov?"

"Don't know." I grinned. No response.

"What do you know of the Victor III class of Soviet submarines?"

"Armament, torpedoes, SS-N, fifteen. ASW missiles. Propulsion, nuclear. Became operational around 1978 or '79."

"The T-54 or 55 tank?

"Weighs about thirty-six tons, goes about 50 km an hour, fires a 100 milimeter shell.

"How many tanks do the Russians have?"

"Right now?"

"Yes."

I looked her hard in the eyes. She didn't blink. "Maybe fifty thousand."

"The United States?"

I pouted. "Maybe fifteen."

I settled back in my chair and crossed my right leg over my left knee. Her mouth was relaxed. Full lips. Naturally red. Now they compressed into a thin line as she returned her attention to me.

"What would be the Russian equivalent for the English word, fuck?"

"I beg your pardon?" I almost fell off the chair.

"You heard me."

"Iebatsia."

"Cock?"

"Khui."

"Shit?"

"Gavno."

"Cunt?"

"Pizda. Look, you want me to run through a bunch of naughty Russian words? Save some time."

"Go ahead."

I started off with the common four letter words, graduated to the more complex. When I got into the beastialisms and more kinky perversities she began to go a little green. She no longer reminded me of Miss McGillicuddy.

"All right," she said, "you have demonstrated you can swear like a Russian. That's enough." She drew in a deep breath and gathered her hands in her lap.

Both men had got their hands into their faces trying to

hide the half smiles. Still the old double standard. She flashed the bearded man a look that could kill.

Now we had a good silence going so I put my grin back on.

The fat girl renewed her consideration of the witness in the dock, then she bent forward. She had a sheet of paper in her hand. She put it on the table. Equations.

"What do you make of this?" she asked.

I studied the equations. I was at it for minutes. I felt my heart beat pick up. My hands started to sweat.

"Who worked this out?" I asked the girl. My voice didn't sound like my voice.

"It doesn't matter now. Do you know what it is?"

I stared into her glasses. "I lost it halfway through. I just don't have the mathematics. I've wondered about it. I thought it might work out this way. Somebody has actually done it. Forgodssakes. It comes out negative doesn't it? I mean, eventually, you have a negative result?" I forgot that she was a fat girl with a bad complexion. I think she forgot that I was a bug. She had color in her face and excitement in her eyes.

"Yes. It comes out negative. A reverse universe. Conventional physical realities invert." Her eyes had gone very wide. "It's incredible that you could suspect that with just the one formula."

My mind was rushing on. "If it is negative, then it would be theoretically possible to engineer an accelerator that could produce two hundred-million-volt levels. Even more. An antimatter accelerator. My God."

"Yes," she said. She settled back in her chair. "But, of course, it's all theory." She patted her dress, knees together.

I looked at the numbers and symbols again. Jesuschrist. I was lost in it. Five minutes, ten minutes went by. I came out of it and found her looking at me. I shook my head and smiled. Real smile. I scratched my head.

Then I noticed the men were gone.

"It was time for them to leave. You were deep into the formula. They asked me to say goodbye." She was speaking in English. Upper-upper class.

"Oh."

She checked her watch. "It's time to leave. You have an appointment."

"Okay." I was back to my basic American.

She took a thin briefcase from the floor and stood up. She was tall but dear Lord she was really fat. We walked down the hall, past the Marine guards. She held up a card for them. We got a smile and brief salute. She stopped before a door and unlocked it. There was a metal panel on the other side with what appeared to be a small computer keyboard built into it. She pressed her hand into a small glass plate beside the computer unit and fingered some keys. The panel slid back and we entered the elevator.

Inside, there was another computer keyboard and she punched a few more keys. The door slid back. She hit a few more keys. There was a soft alarm buzz and a panel lit up with the word "Overload."

"Oh, damn," she said, her face drawn into a frown. "I forgot to put you in. What do you weigh?"

"About two ten."

She hit a few more keys. There was a quiet hum. I felt vertical motion for no more than two seconds. The door slid back and we were out into a hall that was brilliantly lit. No more Union Jack Club decor. Half metal walls, light green, then frosted glass. Two men in shirt-sleeves were talking as we went by. I was getting a good look. The girl opened a door and we went through.

78

The room was about forty by fifty feet and full of computer hardware. Discs whirling, motors humming, air cooled to the exact temperature. Place looked like something out of a Star Wars movie, panels, colored lights, dials. A couple of printers were grinding away. No windows. Just five or six people, four men, two women. No one looked at us.

We went quickly through the room. She opened a door and we were into a small conference room furnished with an oiled walnut table and six matching chairs with black vinyl cushions. The almond walls were bare. There were three computer terminals on a white counter at the far end of the room. There were six telephones, in a variety of colors, mounted on the wall near the computers. One was red. Light diffused evenly from a translucent ceiling. No windows, the place was antiseptic.

Halliburton, Harkness, and Fitzworthy were seated at the table. The girl and I sat down. The table was bare. Nobody smiled.

Harkness, the master spy, turned to the girl. "How did he do? Sounded awfully good, we thought."

"His Russian was excellent."

"What about the others?"

"They both approved. No problem there."

"Do you see any problems?"

"Yes."

Harkness frowned. "What?"

"He's too young."

"Well, we knew that. The makeup people can handle it."

"Maybe. He's really very young."

I was getting steamed. "I'm twenty-seven. I'm older than you."

She shot me a pained look.

79

"He's obviously American."

"How could you tell?" Fitzworthy asked gently.

She almost pouted. "Brash, arrogant, condescending." She flashed another look at me. "But, he is bright."

"For christsakes," I exploded.

"See what I mean?" she said. "He doesn't act like a Russian. He doesn't look like a Russian. He's built like an American. He should be playing for the New York Bears."

"New York Giants," I patiently corrected.

"What?"

"It's the Chicago Bears."

"I don't understand."

"You think I would play for the Bears, for godsakes?"

"I don't . . ."

"I'd never play for the Bears. How could you think that?"

"What are you talking about?"

"For christsakes. The Bears! Never in a million. . . . Redskins maybe."

"That's enough, Lieutenant," Halliburton shut me up. I glowered at the fat girl. The Bears!

"He'll have to be coached," Harkness suggested.

"Maybe," she said.

"Maybe is right," I exploded. "Now what is this all about? I've been pulled off the *Independence,* no more fun flying F-14's, I've had to fight two guys, I've been brain-picked for two hours and I have been called brash, arrogant, and condescending. My country of origin has been called into question. You tell me I might get killed on some kind of intelligence mission, that I probably will. I want to hear something. I want to hear it now."

I folded my arms across my chest in a brash, arrogant, and condescending manner. I tried to catch her eyes but she was looking down at the table, a little flush in her fat cheeks.

Fifteen seconds of nothing, then Halliburton said, "You are quite right. We owe you an explanation. All of this, now, is totally confidential. Your President has told the Prime Minister that you are absolutely secure."

I never met the President. How would he know if I was secure?

Halliburton looked at the girl. "He seems to have anticipated the device."

"Yes," she said, looking up, "it was really quite incredible considering the formula he saw. He doesn't have all of the mathematics, but neither do I. But he already concluded the theoretical possibilities of an antimatter accelerator."

"That's what we thought, too."

Halliburton took a deep breath, produced a massive sigh, gathered his hands together on the table, and gravely considered me. "I can't pretend to remotely grasp the physics, the mathematics, or even the engineering of it. But it came to the government's attention that a neutral particle beam component of an SDI defense system was theoretically possible."

He paused to see if I had his attention. He had. "The idea had originated with a brilliant Cambridge professor. Twenty-eight years old, if you can believe it. He had worked it out mathematically and theoretically. He and two colleagues wanted the government to fund the experimental engineering. I spoke to the chaps myself. Took their ideas to three physicists in this country and four in the United States. Everyone was intrigued.

"The Prime Minister spoke to your President and promptly got some additional funding and a lot of specialized equipment. We set up a laboratory on an old, abandoned U.S. landing strip from the last war. That was three years ago.''

He looked at me and his eyes were growing worried. He shook his head, ran his fingers through his hair. Studied the wall.

"To simplify and get on with the essence of it, they succeeded brilliantly. They produced a prototype NPB accelerator that had astronomical energy-producing levels.'' He looked at me again. His hands were shaking.

"It meant, of course, that a major component, perhaps the most essential component of the system had been achieved. We felt that the West could have a reliable SDI system operational within three to four years. The balance of strategic nuclear power had shifted dramatically to our side.''

I had never heard so profound a silence. It was as if no one was breathing. The girl was running her finger, back and forth, along a stretch of grain in the wood. Her mouth was open. Fitzworthy looked stricken. Harkness, the spy, revealed nothing.

"Sounds pretty good for our side,'' I said.

Halliburton fixed his troubled eyes on me. "Not so good," he said slowly, "the Russians have it. Stole it.''

"My God.'' What else could you say?

"When?''

"We think four or five days ago.''

I let it sink in. "I'm to help get it back?''

"Yes.''

I was stunned. "But how? Surely the laboratory was secure? How could they have gotten to it?''

"We think, possibly, one of those three young men, perhaps the one who originally worked out the physics and the engineering, went over to the other side.''

"You don't know that!'' the girl screamed.

Harkness pulled in a deep breath. "No. We don't know for certain."

"Why would you suspect he went over?" I asked.

"He disappeared the same time the accelerator pod did."

"Any number of things could have happened," the girl interjected. "He could have even been killed trying to protect the pod. He could have been forced to go with them."

Harkness raised his sad eyes to her. "We don't think so."

"Why don't you?" I asked.

"A number of reasons," he went on. He folded his arms over his chest and spoke to me. "We have intercepted a number of Soviet messages. We have broken their code. They refer not only to the device but to a passenger."

"I see. Where is it now?"

"On a submarine, in the Baltic."

"On its way to the USSR, of course."

"Yes. But we have a bit of luck on that. We think we know where they're going to take the accelerator pod and the scientist."

I sucked in a breath. "Where?"

"We think somewhere just beyond the Finnish border. Up north."

"And I'm supposed to go up there and get it back?"

He blew out a breath. "Essentially, yes." His fingers drummed the table. The girl looked devastated.

"By myself?"

"We aren't sure about that. Possibly."

I nodded. Nobody said anything.

I looked at Harkness. "If the thing is still on the submarine, it seems that we can't move for some time. Your idea is for me to penetrate the place the accelerator is being sent to? After it arrives, right?"

He nodded again and went on.

"Four to five days should clear up what we must do. At least that." He looked me directly in the eyes. "We have excellent intelligence on this. We will know where the pod is and we will be able to place you right there."

Halliburton blew out a breath. He seemed to have aged ten years. "We will know a lot more in a few days, but you have the essence of it. It is a dangerous mission with not much chance of success." He looked down at the table and spoke to it. "If you won't do it, or if you fail, we are considering an air strike. The shift in the balance of power is that great. We simply cannot give the Soviets that weapon."

Nobody talked. Nobody moved.

I found the girl looking directly at me. The color had drained from her face.

"That could start the next World War," I said.

"Yes, it very well could."

My turn to suck in a breath and blow out a sigh. "Give me a chance first," I said.

Somebody coughed. Somebody blew his nose, probably Fitzworthy. Somebody sucked air through his teeth.

"Good chap." Halliburton.

"Splendid, old man." Harkness.

"In the blood. What would you expect?" Fitzworthy.

The fat girl considered me with her great eyes and pale face. She said nothing. She got up and silently left the room.

I got a pat on the back from Halliburton. He went, too.

"We have three, maybe five days and we'll know where the pod is," Harkness said. "We also have something of a plan and we have already moved some people into place."

I nodded.

"Fitz will tell you what to do over the next few days."

I nodded again.

"Thank you." Harkness said softly, and left the room. Fitzworthy blew his nose. Snorted.

"No sense you hanging about London. Why not go down to Cornwall and see your grandparents?"

"I might do that."

"Let's see," he paused. "They should be getting ready to go to Scotland for the Highlands ball that they give every year at this time. You just might get to go to it."

"I just might," I agreed. "The girl," I went on, "what is she in all this?"

Fitzworthy idly traced a finger along the edge of the table. "I shouldn't say too much, at this stage." He looked up suddenly. "She's very bright you know. She works for Harkness. Seems to know everything. It was the mathematics and physics that got her into the research group working on the pod. She kept her eyes on things for Harkness. The others never knew, of course. And she did her job on the development end of it."

"She seems very intense."

"Oh, yes."

"I don't know her name."

"No."

"Does she know mine?"

"No. But she knows your grandparents very well. We thought it best to keep your identity confidential at this point. Of course, we weren't sure until this morning ourselves."

"It seems strange that so young a girl would be working

85

so closely with three of the most influential men in England."

"Not so strange. You're not much older and you're working with us, too. It's talent, strength, and intelligence that we need."

"Have you seen the pod?"

"Oh, no."

"And they expect me to run away with it?"

"You won't run."

"Why not?"

"I haven't seen it, but I know it weighs eighty-six pounds."

CHAPTER IV

I checked my watch for the tenth time and swore under my breath because I didn't want to offend the cabbie. We were stuck in early-morning rush hour London traffic, headed for Kings Cross station and the 8:32 for Plymouth. My watch read 8:15 and we hadn't moved for five minutes.

I had taken Fitzworthy's advice and checked out of the hotel with all my luggage. It would be three to four days, Harkness estimated, before his people would have a clear fix on the pod and where it was headed. I sensed that a great deal of preparatory activity was going on, but there wasn't much that I could do. When they wanted me to move, I would be told. What I was to do, and how I was to do it, was still a mystery. But a retrieval scheme was hatching among the creative minds of Harkness's people. Where did the fat girl figure in?

There was some movement in the traffic ahead, but the two drivers in the cars immediately in front of us were slow moving off. My cabbie muttered something, moved sharply to his left, got two wheels up on the sidewalk, and pulled around them. We blew through a narrow opening between a truck and a red Austin, swung around the repair work going on in the middle of the road, and shot clear of the slow-moving tangle of traffic.

"Kings Cross," he announced a few minutes later and pulled up before a scruffy building that didn't look much like a railroad station. I shoved some bills in his hand, got my stuff together, and ran to the entrance. There was a knot of porters professionally observing my departure from the cab. One detached himself from the group. He was dark, swarthy, and had a pockmarked face. He went one twenty wringing wet. North African.

"Can I help you, sir?" He had a good smile.

"Yeah. I'm going to Plymouth."

"You have tickets?"

"No."

"Oh." He looked worried.

He picked up my two heavy bags and rushed through the doors. "Follow me, sir. It will be close. An adventure."

He was small, but he was strong and fast. He got me to a ticket counter. Thank God, no lines.

"First class to Plymouth," I said, and shoved some pound notes under the grill. She was agonizingly slow and kept an absurd patter going with the clerk in the next booth. I was an annoyance.

"Please," I said to her, "I might miss my train."

She languidly let her eyes drift over me. "You'll make it, love, they're always a bit late in going off."

I got my ticket and change and we were off rushing again. I had no idea where we were going, but grimly stuck with my man. If he had the size, he would make a great blocking back. We were getting a lot of amused glances as we flew about this way and then that. At last, finally, a platform and a long blue-and-silver train with a shiny, streamlined dark-blue-and-yellow engine.

There were whistles and clatter and people with gaping mouths and amused smiles. Children laughed. Bloody cheek. The train was moving and we raced along the platform toward the first-class cars. We legged up to them and, still at a full gallop, I flung open a door, tossed in my bags, shoved a five-pound note into his shirt pocket and leapt aboard.

The compartment was something out of a Hitchcock movie and the Orient Express, must be fifty years old, all glossy wood and deep-green plush seats, not like the open airline cars that BritRail goes for these days. They must have got this car out of a museum for the summer tourists.

Six eyes were trained on me, all female. A fiftyish, handsome matron and two college-age girls. American. Blue jeans, running shoes, little white cotton blouses, healthy faces, short hair, one red, one honey blond, no makeup, long glittering pendant earrings, open mouths, even white teeth. Orthodontics, conspicuous consumption, social class, honorific status. Sociologists understand all of that in a simple smile.

"Just made it," I smiled. It was my shy, boyish grin.

"Yeah," the redhead said.

I stashed my luggage in the bins and dug a paperback out of my carry-on bag. The train was picking up speed, the big diesels smoothly pulling us through outer London now. I couldn't get over the antique car and the wonderful woodwork. It looked like the seats had just been recovered.

The two college kids were still openmouthed and the mother would look over at me from behind her book. They were silently talking about me. Women can do this. I know they can do it but most men have no idea. They would be deciding if I looked interesting, what kind of a guy I was, where I was going, how old I was, did I have a girlfriend, would they like to be my girlfriend. Stuff like that. All of this was going on in their heads. They have to look at each other in order to communicate. The two girls would silently turn and face each other and exchange information, then they would look at me some more. I'm used to it. Get a lot of it at Spaulding. I understand women. Particularly when they are five or under.

We were up to sixty or seventy miles an hour and out into the suburbs, heading south. I was somewhat uncomfortable with the three women. I wasn't dressed properly. I had rushed out of the hotel and knew I was in for a three-and-a-half-hour train trip to Plymouth, so I dressed comfortably in Navy khakis, running shoes, and a Spaulding sweat shirt under a leather flight jacket. Normally I would be in jacket and tie. You don't go through Phillips Academy without learning that a necktie is the single most important item of apparel in a gentleman's wardrobe. At Spaulding, the rumor was that I slept in a tie. At Phillips, I knew of some football players who tried to wear neckties under their jerseys. Coach was wise to it, and made them take the ties off. Guys got really upset. Talk about in-group norms.

I settled back in the seat, picked up my book, but looked out at the lovely English countryside. I forgot the girls and their big eyes and silent talk. Let them have their fun. I even forgot the pod, the Russians, and World War III.

I had never met my grandparents. Fitz didn't know that. I never knew my parents, either. I knew who they were, of course. Hard not to know that. My mother was Catherine MacRae of the Rockport MacRaes. She won two gold and one silver, swimming for the United States team in Melbourne in 1956. She met my father there. He had something do with the English team. I have seen photographs of my mother. She was beautiful and, after the Olympics, she had Hollywood offers. But instead, she got married to Colin Smallpiece, the dashing flying officer from the Royal Navy. It was in all the papers, American/Brit romance. I read the clippings my aunt had saved. I
90

think the English press made more of it than the American.

I arrived into the world in 1961 and six months later there was the automobile accident in Vermont. I remember nothing of it of course, but my grandparents came to the funeral and immediately returned to England. I was raised by my mother's brother and sister in Rockport in the ancestral MacRae fifteen-room house with its ten pine-filled acres on Penobscot Bay. They were both crazy.

Neither was married. My aunt was a bibliophile and insisted I learn French and German and, along with the languages, the histories, the literature, the grammars, the philosophies, the cultures. I think I had read every important book in the nearby Camden library before I was twelve.

My uncle retired early from the Navy as a junior commander. I think he was asked to leave or was so sufficiently discouraged by his lack of advancement that he left on his own. He was a survivalist before they became an ideology and a cult. Because his life had been less than satisfactory, he was determined to rectify his own fault with me. At eight he had me running six miles a day. At ten he had me working on the weights and taking boxing lessons, then it was the martial arts.

By the time I was ten I had learned to survive for weeks on deserted Maine islands with nothing to eat but what I could scrounge. I had to hike twenty miles through virgin woodland to a point he had marked on a map. I sailed open sloops in gale-tossed seas down to Newburyport when I was eleven. I grew tall and tough, lonely but independent. The psychologists call it autonomous.

Mattie Jackson saved me from my crazy relatives. She was the housekeeper. She was middle-aged, too heavy, too religious, uncomplicated, caring, and very black. But Mattie loved me. She took me to church, a blond white kid among all those black people. But I belted out the hymns with the best of them. When my uncle went too far with his survivalist schemes, Mattie stood up to him.

"What you mean makin' that chile go out in the woods like that with no jacket and no food? Snow on the ground. He's just a baby. Makes no sense. I ain't gonna let you do that, Commander. Now you let that boy come into the kitchen and warm hisself."

And he would back off. I think he was frightened of her. When Mattie got mad, everyone backed off. She gave me love and warmth. Mattie saved me from my crazy aunt and uncle. When things went wrong, Mattie would gather me into her great bosom, put her arms around me, and tell me everything was going to be all right. And it was. I'll never forget that big kitchen and the wood stove and the smell of cinnamon and cookies, homemade doughnuts and hot cider and Mattie standing there. Smiling.

I was twelve when my uncle and aunt died within a few months of each other. Mattie drifted off south to a relative in trouble. I was already enrolled at Phillips. The Camden lawyer who handled the estate wrote to Uncle Philip in England, and from that time on I spent my summers in Devon.

Once, when I was twelve, I wrote my grandparents, and later at fourteen. Both letters were returned unopened. I never knew why. Uncle Philip was a quiet, gentle, introspective man who ran a small, unprofitable publishing house. He never mentioned my grandparents and never took me down to Cornwall to see them, although they were only forty miles away. I had the feeling that my grandfather disapproved of Uncle Phillip almost as much as he disapproved of me. Looking back at it, I think it was because Uncle Phillip was shy and scholarly and in the publishing business and not the Royal Navy where all Smallpiece men should properly be. But why would he turn a small boy away?

"Why so serious?" the honey blonde asked. "You were really far away."

"Oh. Was I? Didn't realize."

"Yup."

The car was getting warm with a soft June sun beating down on it. I took off the flight jacket and tossed it on the seat beside me.

Their eyes widened. They spotted the faded "Spaulding" on the sweatshirt.

"You from Spaulding?" the redhead asked.

I nodded.

"Wow. Must be a brain. But you're not a nerd." Tentative grin.

"Hope not."

"We go to Lafayette."

"Oh."

"That's a small college in Pennsylvania."

"I know it. Good school. I was up there last October." Two simultaneous "Wows!"

I nodded, smiled.

"We beat you guys in football," the honey blonde said.

"I know. Lafayette has a good team."

"You play?"

"I'm not a student. I'm on the faculty."

Two brows wrinkled, two mouths turned down as one. "Come on. You're a student."

"Nope, faculty."

They looked at each other and shared an intimate communication. Voiceless, of course. I was putting them on. The redhead shrugged. "Where are you going?" she asked.

"Cornwall, to see my grandparents."

They both nodded, still not buying my faculty story. The mother had put her book down and was watching.

"I'm Betsy Wilson," the redhead said, then inclined her head toward the older woman. "That's my mom and this is Gloria. We're roommates."

"Colin Smallpiece," I said, and shook hands with all three. "Where are you heading?"

"Penzance," Betsy said.

"You'll like it, not too many pirates left, though."

"What?" Gloria asked, brow wrinkled. She didn't get it.

"Nothing." Mrs. Wilson got it, and smiled and went back to her book. We had gone through Reading, would stop next at Westbury, then Taunton, then Exeter. Could be in Massachusetts.

We got into the old naval city of Plymouth at 11:45 and I said goodbye to the girls, they would stay on to the end of the line. The blonde wrote down my name and address in Spaulding. They would come down for the Lafayette game in October. They would look me up. I would take them to dinner. They had glowing eyes.

I rented a late model Jaguar, in classic green, from Hertz, on the taxpayers' largess, and took A386 north, skirting the edge of the great moor, all three hundred sixty-five square miles of it, with its mysterious stone circles, prehistoric markers, evil mists, and great prison. I was headed for the Atlantic coast and it looked like some forty miles on the map the rental people had given me.

The air was delicious with the scents of thick golden gorse and wildflowers—jasmine, myrtle, violets, sweet roses, and honeysuckle. I worked my way seaward along worn ancient tracks four and five feet below fuchsia hedgerows guarding the green fields on either side. I drove mechanically, my mind constantly drifting back to yesterday.

What was there about the fat girl? Certainly not her double chins, pimply face, and inner-tube waist, although she had fine shoulders and a lovely neck. Her eyes were beautiful, if sad and troubled. But it was more than that. It was both enigma and intelligence. I wanted to reach into that mind and the mysteries there. She was a paradox and riddle. Frumpy with her goofy dress, and yet charismatic and compelling. Why was I getting steamed over a fat girl who thought I was some sort of American thing? Forget it. Drive the car. I was in Cornwall, but still she was a challenge and that troubled me.

Cornwall is a storied land of wraiths, spirits, and ancient magic. Up ahead there would be Tintagel and its romantic ruin, a tumble of stone facing the sea—where King Arthur ruled. And down in the fog-bound coves, somewhere, I was certain, I could find the lost city of Lyonesse. I knew it was there to the pure in heart. There were no Russians, accelerator pods, or space wars here. Around the next turn, beyond the leafy bower and the wild roses, I would stumble into Brigadoon and be gloriously lost to the world forever.

I pushed the Jag on.

But I couldn't escape yesterday and Halliburton's chilling words. *"If you won't do it, or if you fail, we are considering an air strike . . ."*

And my reply, *"That could start the next World War."* Jesus.

Eventually, somehow, I found myself on the A39, headed south, away from Tintagel and poetic romance, toward Wadebridge. I made a right at the stone marker the gas station attendant had told me to watch for and once again the Jag pitched and rolled over little used country lanes.

Then I saw another marker, sticking up in the gorse. It read, "Smallpiece Four Miles." It had been in the ground for decades, perhaps a century. My throat constricted and went dry. What the hell is going on?

It was a hamlet, nothing more than a cluster of five or six cottages, a store that would sell everything, an inn, "Sail and Spar," an ancient stone church in the squat English Gothic with its inevitable yard and mossy, tipping markers. In what appeared to have once been a livery or stable, there was now an automobile repair shop. Through the doors I saw a farm tractor with its hood off.

I pulled the Jag into a small parking lot beside the inn and got out. Still no sight or sound of people. Ah there! Some rattle of tools in the auto repair shop. I checked my watch. Three thirty-five. The sun was warm. I looked about. Maybe this was Brigadoon. Wildflowers, thatched cottages, raspberries for the taking, a patch of nodding yellow daisies, hedges of fragrant primrose. The tiny make-believe village, soft and yellow in the mid-afternoon sun, quiet and secure, dappled in shade from the great oaks overhead. *Smallpiece!* I was sweating.

I went into the Sail and Spar. Cool, dark, honest, and totally unselfconscious. Four or five men were talking at the bar, they looked to be fisherman, maybe one farmer. It was a small bar, couple of tables, all dark wood, great fireplace in the corner, low-beamed ceilings, wainscoted walls, half wood, half plaster. There were three small whiskey casks on the ten-foot bar, prints of old sailing ships on the rough plaster walls with lots of brass plates, old photographs of smiling young sailors from World War II. A village public house that had not changed much in one hundred years.

They stopped talking when I came in. The bartender

looked me over carefully. They don't get many strangers who pass through the time warp into Brigadoon.

"Day, sir," the bartender beamed. Red-faced, sandy-haired, missing two front teeth, but peace and contentment were in his eyes.

I smiled. Looked about at what the men were drinking. There would be no cold lager here.

"I'll have a pint," and I waved my hand toward the other men's glasses.

"Yes, sor."

He drew the pint and placed it before me. I put a pound note on the bar. He let it lay. We smiled at each other.

"Could you tell me where I am?" I asked.

"You're in Smallpiece, sor."

I nodded. "I thought so. Wasn't sure. Lovely place."

"Yes, sor."

"Could you tell me where Admiral Smallpiece lives?"

I got another good look. "Just follow the lane through, it ends about a quarter of a mile and you are there. Can't miss it."

"Thank you." I knocked back a third of the glass. Wiped my mouth with my hand. "Tastes good." The bar was completely quiet and the customers were watching the show.

"You know the admiral, sor?" he asked, busily wiping the bar.

"We've never met."

He looked me squarely in the face. "We don't get many people through here, but I'm pretty good at figuring accents. Now, I must confess, you've got me puzzled, sor. You're not midlands, you're not Scotch, Welsh, or Irish. You're a hard one to figure, sor. You look like Cambridge or Oxford but you don't quite sound like them."

"Try Rockport, Maine."

97

"Rockportmaine? Never heard of it." He had a half grin.

"America."

"Oh, you're a Yank. But you don't talk like one, either."

"Is the admiral in, do you know?" I asked, changing the subject.

"Oh, he's in, but he will be leaving for Scotland tomorrow for his big bash. Does he know you're coming, sor? He's a hard man to get to see, if he doesn't know you're coming."

"Perhaps I should phone."

"There's a public phone by the store next door, sor." He got out a pad and pencil, wrote something down, handed it to me. "His number, sor."

"Thank you." I dialed the number he gave me in the red booth in front of the store. There were two rings.

"Smallpiece residence." It was an ancient, quavering voice.

"Is the admiral there?"

"Who is calling, sir?"

"Can he be reached?"

"Not at the moment, sir. May I have your name?"

"My name is Smallpiece."

I heard nothing for fifteen seconds. "Would you repeat that, sir?"

"My name is Colin Smallpiece. I'm the admiral's grandson from America. I'll be over in forty-five minutes."

More silence. Some gasping. "Oh, er, ah, hummm, sir. I don't know what to do. Really, sir . . ."

"I'll be there in forty-five minutes. That is all you have to tell him. Goodbye."

I went back to the bar and the buzz stopped again. Two

more people were there. The show went on. I got a big, gaping smile from the bartender.

"Do you rent rooms?" I asked.

"Yes, sor."

"I will want to change and take a bath." A shower was out of the question.

"You won't want the room for the night, sor?"

"I don't think so."

"Just for a change and a bath?"

"Yes."

"Pound would be all right?"

"Fine."

He found a key with a tag that read 424. "Head of the stairs, sor. Can't miss it." I wondered where the other 423 rooms were.

I went out to the car and brought the heavy soft-sider in and went up the creaking stairs. Four twenty-four was just off to the right. The floor fell away a good six inches from one wall to the other. Big four-poster bed, heavy Victorian dresser and wardrobe, one unsteady chair, white-washed walls, no pictures. White cotton curtains softly stirring by the open casement windows, geraniums in pots on the sill. Clean and very old.

I found the tub next door. It had feet. I had a shave and took my bath in lukewarm water. Toweled off and got out my blues. Paid a fortune to a Washington tailor whose firm had custom made naval officers' uniforms since 1825. It fit like a glove and not a wrinkle in it. I ran a tissue over the wings just in case they weren't shiny enough. Then I gathered up my gear and went back to the bar. I checked my watch. Still had a half hour. Did I hear a gasp?

"Got any single malt whiskey?" I asked. My heartbeat was up. I knew it was up. Why?

He beamed. "Right out of the peat bogs, sor. Get it special." The room had added four more. Three women, one man. Everyone was over fifty. Again, the profound silence. But it was more now, a hush.

The bartender poured my Scotch neat. Three fingers. Ice was a sacrilege. His eyes never left my face.

I sipped it. Soft and smooth, warm going down, purred in your stomach. I smacked my lips.

Still the silence and the audience was totally fixed on me.

The bartender was struggling to say something. "Sor," he said, "beggin' your pardon, sor, but would you mind sayin' your name?"

I didn't hesitate. "Colin Smallpiece."

Three sighs, a couple of nervous coughs, a few murmurs, much shuffling of feet.

"You're his grandson, then? From America?"

"Yes."

"Coo."

I knocked back the Scotch. One woman had her hand to her mouth.

"You favor your father, sor. You looked familiar from the start. The uniform did it."

I nodded.

"We're glad you come home, sor."

"Yes, thank you." I checked my watch. Checked my shoes. They were still on. Checked the sun. Still working nicely. Studied the Scotch, still some left. What the hell was going on with me?

"Will you have another, sir?"

"Thank you. Yes." Might help.

He poured. I pushed a few notes toward him.

He pushed it back. "Your money's no good here, sor."

"Why not?"

He drew in a breath. "Just not, sor. You come home, sor. You're a Smallpiece come home and that's all of it."

"Thank you."

I drained the Scotch, picked up my bag, waved and got back into the Jag and followed the narrow lane out of the village. For a moment it broke free of the trees and hedgerows and, three hundred feet below, I saw the little harbor. Past another small copse, the track rose onto a plateau of grassy hummocks along the top of the cliff. Suddenly everything was all sun and sky and sea. Off to my left, I could see the great headlands curving into the misty distance and down below the savage, brooding cliffs, with lonely stretches of beach disappearing into the surf and rocks.

The track dipped into a tangle of trees again. On my right, there was an old eight-foot brick wall. It ran along a few hundred yards where the road ended in a turnaround. There was an open iron gate in the wall supported by two mossy square brick columns. The name "Smallpiece" was carved in a marble plaque set into the brick. I turned in and followed a gravel path. My hands were wet.

The drive mounted through a small wood, broke into a meadow, and beyond I saw cultivated fields. The drive split in two. I went right and, past a stand of hardwoods, I saw a very blue, ten-acre lake down in a little valley sprinkled with towering oaks. The opposite hillside was covered with pine. Planted. Not native. Now I was into the park, at least six or seven acres of lawn and at the top of the rise, nestled in a hollow, was the house or a settlement. The gravel drive followed the tree line and then swung in front of the house. I parked the car on a cobbled court large enough for thirty cars.

I got out and looked at a hundred and eighty degrees

of glistening, tranquil sea. Overhead the sky was a great, inverted, flawless blue bowl. No clouds at all.

The wind blowing in from the Atlantic through the trees was the only sound.

From the drive the house appeared to be a tiny medieval village with steeply pitched slate roofs punctuated with dormers, bold chimney stacks, and half timbered second floors pushed out here and there from the roofs. From where I stood on the court, the main portion of the house might have been an ancient castle, or monastery. But now all that was left of it was the old stone of the first floor. An architect had skillfully blended the ancient flint walls into a new house. I looked at it, but saw nothing.

I hardly noticed the place. I slammed the car door shut and moved quickly to the front door. My heartbeat was over a hundred. I hadn't come close to that when I dropped the dead F-14 onto the pitching deck of the *Independence*. What was it with me? I had difficulty swallowing.

I rang the doorbell. My hand was shaking.

Fifteen seconds. Thirty seconds. I rang again. Again.

The door swung open. He was over eighty, slight, stooped, thin white hair, slightly palsied, in great distress.

"I am here to see my grandparents," I said.

His eyes rolled into mine. "Oh, sir. I really don't think. . . . You see, sir . . . I can't . . ." He was in agony.

"What is your name?" I asked gently.

"Gibbons, sir."

"Gibbons, you can either take me to them now, or I will find them. What will it be?"

He waited ten seconds, took in an enormous breath, and blew it out. He squared his slight shoulders. "It's not right," it tore out of him. "It's not right at all. I don't care. Come with me, sir."

102

I noticed very little. Large entryway and foyer. Light streaming through tall windows with small diamond panes of leaded, colored glass behind the stairway, tans, beiges, clears. Down a wide hallway, portraits on the walls, he stopped before a pair of double doors. He waited.

I opened the doors and stepped inside. Closed them.

He was standing before a window, back to me, looking out.

She was seated in a chair, facing me, wiping her eyes. She had been crying.

"He hasn't gone yet," he said. "What is that old fool doing?"

She saw me and stood. Her hand went to her throat.

I walked to the middle of the room.

"Collie," she said quietly. "He's here."

"Eh? What?" He turned.

He was smaller than I thought he would be, five eight or nine. Slender, straight, not an excess pound. He clutched a cane. Sandy hair, parted in the middle, white bushy eyebrows, generous nose, firm skin, large white mustaches, his mouth was working. It was his eyes, large, fierce, alive, utterly determined. They shone from his face like piercing psychic windows revealing the strength, the will and power of his mind. Windows to the soul. He stood there with his eyes and swayed on his cane.

The tears had flooded down her cheeks. "Oh, Collie," she gasped. "It's him. Colin. Dear Lord. The face. It's him."

It all tore loose in me. No control left.

"Grandmother," I said. My voice broke.

She took a step toward me, opened her arms. I took her in mine. She kissed me. Put her hands on my face and sobbed. I patted her back. She patted mine.

I looked at him. "I had to come, sir."

He said nothing. His mouth was working again. I couldn't read him at all.

She gently pushed me back. Even in her seventies, her beauty was still there. She was as tall as he, with thick light-brown hair, widely spaced clear blue eyes with that insight and awareness that comes to women with age. Intelligence, charm, grace, character, breeding, and a beauty that still withstood the years. All there. She dabbed her eyes and looked at me with glory in her face.

She sighed and took my hand. Led me to the couch. "No," she smiled, "stand there. Let me look at you."

She couldn't stop the tears or hold back the smile.

My grandfather hadn't moved. His eyes flashed up and down, taking me in. The uniform was a masterstroke.

"Flyer?" he asked.

"Yes, sir."

"What?"

"Fighters."

"Harumph." He really said, "What else?"

He took a tentative step toward me like a mechanical man.

I held out my hand. He searched my face with wonder and took my hand. His eyes were filling. He gasped something. And then I had both arms around him, clapping him on the back. They were both a shambles now. I was doing pretty well.

"He's Colin, he's all you," my grandfather said to her, snorting into a handkerchief.

"But not in the eyes," she said, "he's you."

"Maybe."

"Turn around, Colin," she commanded.

I did as I was told.

"Lord, the size of him," she said. "Smallpiece men are not tall. Never have been."

"MacRaes were very tall people," I said. No sense backing away from it. I wasn't all Smallpiece.

That sobered him. He took a chair and I sat on the couch next to my grandmother.

"Raise you papist, did they?" he asked, his face had gone grim.

"No, sir. Presbyterian actually."

"I was told she was Catholic."

I shook my head. "Protestant."

He blew out a breath. "Thank God for that." He screwed down his eyes. "You much on religion?"

We were into politics and religion right away. "No, sir. Not very much."

My grandmother was looking troubled.

"It's the trouble with the world today," he exploded. "Religion. Where are all your trouble spots? Eh? Ireland, Lebanon, India, Pakistan, Ceylon. Religion! Bloody priests and holy men ..."

"Collie," my grandmother interjected, "the boy doesn't need a lecture. Not now. Now hush."

I looked at my hands. Ten fingers, still there. Shoes looked good, too. What a lovely smile she had. He was checking his hands also. Must be a genetic, Smallpiece thing.

He subsided. Looked at me with confused, sad eyes. "I've been a fool about you," he said. "Old, bloody fool. Seemed too late to change things, now." We both went back to our fingers again.

There was a comfortable silence in the room. I could see the blue ocean through the windows. They kept looking at me.

My grandmother clapped her hands together. "How long can you stay. Oh please, a few days at least!"

"I think probably." I nodded.

She shot to her feet. "Oh, how wonderful! You can come to Scotland with us! Oh, my! Let me see. I'll have Colin's room prepared." She put her hand to her chin, eyes happy, cheeks flushed. "And I must tell Cook." She started checking things off with her fingers. "Oh, dear! Excuse me." She fled from the door.

He followed her with his eyes out the door. Shook his head. "It's been years since I have seen her so happy. Now she can fuss over her brood. Women."

I nodded. Women.

"You're not married?"

"Oh, no."

"Good."

"One day though."

"Oh, certainly."

He studied me some more. "Why are you in England?" He settled back in his chair. He was relaxing, letting go.

"I've been flying off the *Independence* for about a month. Having a little holiday."

"Navy and fighters," he mused. "Like me, like Colin. Makes you wonder why."

"Yes, sir."

"Annapolis, I suppose?"

"No, sir. A.B. Harvard, Ph.D. Yale."

He was incredulous. "You're not a career man?"

"No, sir. I'm on the faculty of Spaulding University."

"You're a bloody don?"

"Also a reserve fighter pilot. They say I'm quite good." I was desperately trying to preserve something of value.

"Teacher?" He wore an expression like you do when you find you have eaten half a worm. I tried to look embarrassed. Unworthy. A failed sailor.

Gibbons teetered into the room. He looked at my grandfather. He was quite uncertain.

"You have a phone call, sir."

"Who the bloody hell?"

"Admiral Fitzworthy, sir. He said it was urgent."

Grandfather exploded a breath. "If Fitz says it's urgent, it's urgent. Probably can't get to Scotland." He looked at me. "I'm glad you came. I'm a damn fool. Tell you about it someday. Maybe not." He stumped out.

Gibbons was about to follow. He looked at me. "Was it all right, sir?"

"It was fine. You did just the right thing."

"Not much choice, had I?"

"No, I guess not."

"You're staying, I hear, sir."

"Yes."

He paused. "Sometime later sir, er, ah, Cook, Tim the gardener, a few others. They knew your father, sir. They would like to meet you, if it's not too much trouble."

"Anytime. It would be my pleasure."

"Thank you, sir." He beamed and closed the door. I sighed and leaned back and put my head on the soft top of the couch. I closed my eyes and settled down. Didn't even study the room. Didn't care. The place was filled with Oriental rugs, carved chests, velvet couches, a spectacular fireplace, gorgeous woodwork and paneling and, surprisingly for an old house, full of air and light. Lovely, very English, a very English country house, very upper class.

I have never felt upper class, or middle or lower, for that matter. I have always felt unstratified and out of the social hierarchy. In this regard, I am not very English. After tea, the English love class next. I ran my fingers over my closed eyes. Blew out a breath. I had done it. Why had I done it?

My grandfather came back ten minutes later.

He was serious and pensive, thoughtful.

"You know Fitzworthy, I understand," he said carefully.

"Yes," I said with equal care.

"He told me a few things about you."

"Oh."

"You put Flynn down in less than a minute."

"Yes."

"Nobody can do that to Flynn."

"Must have been an accident. He slipped. Freak thing."

"Fitz didn't think so. He says you are very strong, speak Russian, know a lot of physics and mathematics. You are also a terror with your hands. Actually, his word was 'unreal.' He says you are here to do a job for us."

I nodded. "It looks that way."

"He couldn't say much."

"No."

"You can't, either?"

"Shouldn't, even if you are my grandfather and an admiral."

"Quite right."

"Fitz says there is considerable danger, risk."

I nodded again. "Probably."

"He did say that you had done this sort of thing before."

"Yes."

"You are more than a professor, then?"

"I suppose so, yes."

He sighed and looked at me with very sad and serious eyes. A little of the fire had gone out of them.

"I have a message for you. I was told to say that it seems to be going where they thought it was going. They think they will be ready for you in two days."

"Thank you."

"You still have time to come to Scotland with us? We fly up tomorrow. Fitzworthy might be there. He will be if he can." He was almost pleading with me and an hour ago he tried to send me away.

"I'd love to go to Scotland with you, Grandfather."

"You will say nothing of this to your grandmother."

"No."

He looked helpless. "Serves me right, for what I've done." He studied his hands. I looked through the windows and the late-afternoon sun had turned the sea to bronze and the grass and trees to green-gold.

Later they made me tour the place, two hundred and sixty acres of Cornwall that had not changed in over a hundred years. Stables with three fine horses, formal gardens and informal gardens, a small orchard, the lake with stocked trout, a few fields of corn, a small herd of cattle, the famous red "rubies" of Cornwall. They grew most of their own food. It looked very well managed.

They apologized for not dressing for dinner and were serious about it. We ate informally on a small terrace with a quarry tile floor, surrounded by a three-foot boxwood hedge with shiny, olive-green leaves. We sat at a wrought-iron table with a glass top and on chairs with floral cushions. A soft wind drifted up from the sea, spiced with honeysuckle. The bronzed ocean never moved. My grandmother could never stop smiling. She seemed to have lost twenty-five years in three hours. We were served by two elderly servants with shining eyes and anxious to please.

For dinner it was fresh Cornwall asparagus and hollandaise, then poached scallops, then a rack of lamb with a soft Riesling and tiny French beans, new potatoes, and for dessert an apple crisp floating in home-grown cream so thick it would not pour. You spooned it. Coffee was hot and black. We watched the sea turn from bronze to hammered silver as the night wore on.

My grandmother took my arm and we went into the living room and talked until almost midnight. Eventually I kissed her good night, shook hands with my grandfather who cuffed me on the back. They walked me down the hall on the second floor and I went into my father's room. It looked to the sea.

It was still a boy's room full of ship models and airplanes, a great oak bed, bookcases, work table, desk, square, utilitarian furniture of no particular style or period, unpretentious and functional. There was a window seat below three large casement windows facing the sea and a telescope on a tripod pointing out. On the walls, on the desk, on the dresser, everywhere there were photographs of groups of boys in athletic uniforms. Which one was he?

"You come home, sor."

His room. I ran my hand over the desk. How many times had he puzzled over a math problem on it? On the work table I saw bits and splatters of paint from a model project. Was it a ship or a plane? How many times had his eye drifted to that bubble, a flaw in the glass, on the window, the third pane from the bottom?

"You come home, sor."

I got into bed. Tossed and turned. Why had I come here? The search for some primordial genetic link? Why had my throat gone dry and my hands sweat and shake? Was some cosmic biology playing out here? Like a salmon who has to swim back to where he began. Or was it cosmic sociology and the mystic power of consanguinity, the blood linkage, the clan, the social and biological continuity with those who came before me? Some unconscious, deep-seated search for origins? My autonomy was fast fading. Who am

I? For the first time in my life, I felt intimately a part of a human group, that I belonged in this house and was a part of it.

"You come home, sor."

There were friendly ghosts everywhere. I lay in bed and tossed and couldn't sleep. I checked my watch. Two hours had gone by. It was no good just lying here. I put on my robe and went out into the dimly lit hall.

I walked downstairs in the great, silent, rambling house. The walls were filled with portraits of men in the uniforms of the Royal Navy. The uniforms and the men spanned two centuries.

"That was my father."

I turned. It was my grandfather in his robe and leaning on his cane.

"Couldn't sleep, either?" he asked.

"No."

He pointed to the portrait on the wall. A man in his forties, mutton chop sideburns, fierce, uncompromising military face.

"He commanded a destroyer flotilla at Jutland. Lost an arm."

"Ah, now," he stopped again. "This is Percival Smallpiece. Admiral of six ships of the line, at the Nile, with Nelson.

Halfway down the stairs, he stopped and pointed with his cane. "This is one you might find interesting. Captain Robert Smallpiece, he captured the Massachusetts privateer, *Rattlesnake,* 1871 I think it was. Pesky bugger, kept sinking our shipping. He commanded the *Assurance.* Forty-four gun frigate.

I looked up into Robert's peaceful face.

"The *Rattlesnake* was an undersized frigate of twenty

guns," I pointed out. "The *Assurance* had twice her armament. And she still made a fight of it."

He cleared his throat. I went on. "Her second mate was Murdo MacRae. Twenty-three years old. He died in the hulks of scurvy and malnutrition."

He sighed. "That was war then."

He found a wall switch and the small lights above all the portraits came on. We walked down the main first-floor hall.

"Robert Smallpiece," he said, pointing to a stern figure with intense eyes. "He commanded H.M.S. *Dreadnaught,* 1907 to 1910."

We moved on.

"Clarence Smallpiece, he died with Nelson on the *Victory* at Trafalger, 1805."

"George Smallpiece, captained the *Duke of Wellington,* 1853. She had two thousand horsepower. We were going to steam then."

"Jamie Smallpiece, midshipman, went down with the-sloop-of-war, *Curizer,* in 1804. He was sixteen."

He stopped before a handsome, smiling young man in civilian clothes. "Reginald Smallpiece. Made a fortune shipping slaves into Savannah. Died at thirty-one. Black sheep. He was shot."

"Firing squad?" I asked.

Grandfather sighed. "He bedded someone's wife who was a better shot than he was."

"Why would he be here among all these Royal Navy men?"

Another sigh. "Good and bad in all families. He had style. Give him that."

We held up before another portrait.

"Ramsey Smallpiece. Commanded the *Ajax,* one of three light cruisers who drove the German pocketbattleship *Graf Spee* into a river in South America, 1940, where she scuttled. Got through the war fine. Died in a yachting accident in 1953. My brother." Then he added, "Makes him some sort of uncle."

We stopped before a young flying officer pictured on the deck of an aircraft carrier. We looked silently into his confident face. In the background, on the deck, there were single wing planes with five-bladed propellers.

"Your father on the carrier, *Ocean*. He had just been commissioned. They were off to Korea, 1952."

I nodded.

He turned to me. "You care for a drink?"

"Good idea."

We went to the far end of the hall, turned left into one of the "cottages." It was either a study or a drawing room or a library—one wall was floor-to-ceiling bookcases. Leather furniture, Oriental rugs, big desk, several chests, no portraits but original seascapes. I sprawled into a deep chair. He splashed a good three fingers of something amber into cut crystal glasses. Held up a siphon bottle of water. I shook my head.

I sniffed the glass.

"Bourbon?" I asked.

"Right from Kentucky. I love it."

Fifteen minutes later I was back in my room and asleep almost right away.

CHAPTER V

It wasn't an airport. It was a closely mowed strip of grass, about fifty yards wide and a quarter of a mile long, that ran right off the edge of the Cornwall cliff. If you were a duffer, it would be paradise. No way you could go wrong, except lose your ball four hundred feet down the cliff into the surf and rocks.

It was ten-thirty in the morning, the weather still held clear and we bounced up in the blue family Jag to the waiting airplane, its metal propellers glinting in the morning sun. The dew was still wet on the thick turf. My rental Jag was already on its way back to Plymouth driven by Tim the gardener and a helper who followed in a truck.

There were six or seven other airplanes on the strip, all single engine and deserted. There was a lone brick shed, big enough for one single engine craft. I presumed for emergency repairs. Nothing else but a listless wind sock on a fifty-foot pole that hung straight down. The pilot was standing by the starboard wing smoking a pipe, which he knocked out on his heel when he saw our car.

It was a recent Cessna 310, I thought, with twin Continental engines, probably fuel injected, about two hundred horsepower. Maybe five place. Our driver unloaded our luggage from the trunk and, with the pilot's supervision, stowed it aboard.

My grandmother was ecstatic. "Isn't it a lovely day, Colin? You brought us good weather." She looped her arm around mine and shielded her eyes from the sun. The brilliant sea was full of glittering diamonds. A freighter plowed silently toward the horizon. Closer to shore, a brightly painted purse seiner was preparing to drop its nets in the soft swell.

"Ready when you are, Admiral," the pilot said to my grandfather. He was over fifty, lean and stringy, Harris tweed jacket, light-brown hair and a creased, deeply tanned face with canny blue eyes that were taking me in. He wore a tartan tie.

My grandfather took him by the arm and gently propelled the man toward me. "Kenneth," he said, "want you to meet my grandson, Colin. He's from America."

He turned to me. "Colin, this is Kenneth MacKenzie. The MacKenzie. He owns this toy." The MacKenzie stuck out his hand. Firm grip, wide smile. The Mackenzie would be head man among all the Scotch MacKenzies.

My grandfather nodded toward me, "His mother was a MacRae." He said it quietly. I couldn't read him.

MacKenzie's grin grew even larger. "A MacRae?" he said. "MacRaes fought with the MacKenzies, during the time of the clan wars, against the MacDonalds. We called the MacRaes 'MacKenzie's Shirt of Mail.' " I was a buddy for life. He had a soft Highland burr.

We clambered into the Cessna.

"You want to co-pilot, Colin?" my grandfather asked.

"Rather not. I've had enough for a while."

He seemed relieved.

"Colin, you come back here with me," my grandmother called, patting the seat across from her. So I settled down

115

next to her while my grandfather got into the co-pilot's seat and belted up. MacKenzie flipped switches and fired up the port engine right away and then the starboard. They idled smoothly and sounded new, gurgling contentedly at about a thousand RPM. He brought up the avionics, adjusted his altimeter, checked his instruments, brought the RPM over a thousand and we swung over to the middle of the strip. We looked at the sea, dead ahead, off the cliff.

He set the brakes, ran each engine up to fifteen hundred and checked the prop governors, then up to two thousand and studied his magnetos. He craned his head forward. Must be looking at alternator and gyro suction output. He pulled the throttles back to idle.

He moved the fuel selector to the inboard tanks, switched both fuel pumps on. Thumbed the idiot light button and got a green panel. He opened the cowl flaps, adjusted our trim, and gave my grandfather a thumbs-up signal.

My grandfather took the controls.

"I hate this part," my grandmother said, and reached over and took my hand. "I think we are flying off the ends of the earth."

My grandfather had the throttles and shoved them forward. The Continentals howled and the Cessna shook. He let the brakes go and we fled down the soft strip of grass. The wheels got light and the wings built lift. He eased her off the ground in fifteen seconds. We shot over the cliff, the surf, and the rocks below. The wheels went up and the flaps slid back. He was into the blue line climb speed and he built altitude and we swung higher over the peaceful Atlantic. Cornwall faded behind in the morning mists. My grandmother opened her eyes and smiled.

We were on our way to Scotland, about three hundred

sixty air miles away, to a place called Loch Sunart, off the Sound of Mull. "Flying is the only way to get there," my grandfather had said. "Railway or car would take days. It's lovely. But it's nowhere." We would make it in under three hours.

The Cessna built altitude as we headed north over the Bristol Channel. We would pass briefly over the westerly tip of Wales and then over water again, Cardigan Bay.

We were going to one of the five or six major social affairs in the UK, the "Loch Sunart Ball." It had been sponsored by Smallpieces for three generations and was held in a restored castle on the loch. It was literally a gathering of the clans, with a few favored English, to celebrate the end of winter and the coming of summer. "Too bad the Queen can't come," I had said somewhat facetiously to my grandmother.

"Yes," she had replied with a small frown, "but she's in Australia and can't make it this year. She's been to the last three, though. Too bad, she really has a good time."

The Continentals droned happily away. We were over water again. My grandmother had her eyes closed. Minutes slipped away. Then an hour. Off the port wing, I saw an island and checked my map. We were eight thousand feet over the middle of the Irish Sea, had to be the Isle of Man lying emerald green in the glittering sea.

Why was the fat girl on my mind? Why did three powerful men listen to her? She had excellent shoulders, very wide for a women. Lovely neck. But then, there were the double chins, the rough, pasty skin, and the thick, rolling waist. Where was the goddamn accelerator? What was I doing here?

The Cessna sliced through the smooth morning air and we were over the western fringes of the Highlands, sea to the left, soft green hills and mountains on the right. Then

117

it was Oban and Loch Linnhe, the southwesterly terminus of the Great Glen, the sixty-mile watery cleft that begins with Loch Ness, then Loch Lochy through to the Caledonian Canal, and finally into Loch Linnhe.

MacKenzie throttled back over the Isle of Mull and lost altitude. We were at three thousand feet over the Sound of Mull and, down below, a glorious patchwork of islands, serene lochs, gaunt mountains, and soft velvety glens underneath the ridges. Here and there, I could see whitewashed crofters' cottages and tiny patches of cleared land.

There was a village off to port, that might be Glenborrodale, then two islands and a stretch of loch, must be Sunart. MacKenzie was throttled down now. I heard a whine as the flaps came out, then the gear went down. We banked back over the peaceful loch. It looked totally deserted. He was setting up to land. Three hundred feet over the blue loch and we were getting some turbulence. We whispered over an ancient castle with a crenellated lookout tower placed at the end of a promontory thrusting out into the loch. Five or six ocean-going yachts were anchored in a small cove, mostly sail. Then we were over brush and bracken, settling down and the wheels touched. Scotland.

He reversed the props and we slowed. It was another grassy landing strip, but this one was filled with aircraft. At least thirty, from an ancient single engine to new Lears, all lined up in a neat row a hundred feet off the strip. MacKenzie taxied to the end of the strip, pulled up beside a glistening twin engine Piper, and chopped the throttles.

A 1967 Ford Country Squire station wagon, complete with simulated wood grain sides, was waiting to meet us. We clambered out and I helped unload our luggage.

MacKenzie stuck out his hand, "Glad to meet you, Colin. I'll be off now, but I'll see you tonight."

"Thanks for the ride," I said. He had a word with my

grandfather, waved, and made off for a thicket of pine and a hedgerow at the far end of the strip.

"Where's he headed for?" I asked my grandfather as we moved toward the station wagon.

"You can't see it," he said, "but beyond the trees is a meadow filled with tents. There are no accommodations really around here, so over the years the families have stored tents here and we put them up for them. We built some permanent bath facilities, so it's something of a campground. Some have been here a week already, fishing, looking about. Some of the Americans have large tents for fifteen or twenty people. All clan, of course."

The driver, a grizzled, baldheaded old Scot, with tufts of red hair sticking out from his tam-o'-shanter, loaded our gear into the wagon. His shapeless corduroy breeches were stuffed into thick rubber boots that came up to his knees. He was not much on conversation. He had a job to do.

The wagon pitched and yawed over the rough track. We dipped into a soft glen of oak and holly, crossed a rough wooden bridge over an easy flowing burn, then mounted up through a hillside purple with waving heather. My first sight of the house was four massive chimneys, then a steeply pitched hip roof of rust-colored tiles. The house grew out of a knoll of flowers, so many and with so much color, that I could only catch a glimpse as we drove by.

The house was very old, brown, red, and rust-colored brick, with rough vertical half timbers showing in the mortar on the second floor. A entire row of eight or nine small casement windows lined the second floor, under wide eaves. A wing thrust out from the right, breaking the roofline with a perfect triangle with four on four windows in the center. The first floor was all brick and set behind a generous overhang, now in shadow from the mid-afternoon sun. It was a lovely Scotch house thoughtfully set down in a knoll on the heather-covered hillside, in a glorious patch of wildflowers, facing the loch and the timeless castle.

We were met at the door by the smiling housekeeper and I presumed her husband. A boy of sixteen or so took our luggage and disappeared into the house. The living room was large, with a gallery and a wooden balustrade running along the second floor. At the far end there was a huge fireplace, set in a carved, wooden alcove under the gallery. A series of raised panel wooden arches led to an interior hall. There must have been ten deer heads on the wall along with three or four large portraits, three women and a young man, in kilt. They were dressed in the style of the twenties. There were Oriental rugs on the floor topped by two lion and tiger skins.

I found my room on a second-floor corner looking out on the loch and three ridges of distant hills beyond. My grandfather had gone off almost immediately to see how preparations were going for tonight. My grandmother was conferring with the housekeeper. Some houseguests that were expected had not arrived as yet. She seemed slightly concerned.

"You will not be able to speak to your grandfather, Colin," she explained. "He will be quite impossible until tonight. You'll have to be on your own for a while, but it's lovely here. You'll be fine." She kissed my cheek and patted my hair like women do. "Oh, I'm so glad you're here." And then she went off with a list in her hand to see the housekeeper.

Three-thirty in the afternoon. Where was the accelerator? Maybe Fitzworthy would have something to say tonight. When would I be sent off? How would I get the damn thing out? How could the English be so dumb to let the Russians walk off with it? Who was the fat girl? Why was she on my mind?

I was fidgety and restless and there was the loch and the Scotch hills out there. I could use a run, so I put on my running shoes, cotton shorts, and old sweatshirt with the sleeves cut off. There had to be ancient trails winding through the glens and over the high moorland. The house seemed empty when I went outside, down the drive, into the lane, and back toward the air strip. I walked down to the castle through the bracken and broom and stood at the edge of the loch. It seemed like a lake, two or three miles wide, but there was a cut in the distant hills, where the loch eventually reached the sea.

The castle with its six-story crenellated watch tower stood at the end of a man-made narrow causeway two hundred yards out into the still loch. It was totally surrounded by water. The twenty-foot drawbridge was down. It was an ancient Scottish keep, designed to protect the local people from Viking predators or the ravages of nearby clans. It was over a thousand years old. Three generations of Smallpieces had slowly restored the moldy pile of stone back to its original shape and condition. It was now a tourist attraction and in all the guide books.

It came sheer out of the loch with two squat, crenellated, rounded corner towers on either side of the drawbridge. They had narrow, slitted openings to permit the defenders a field of fire. The watch tower rose from the rear. How many men and how many carts of earth and stone had it taken to make that causeway a thousand years ago, I wondered. How many years to build the castle? How many Scots had died on its battlements?

There was a chill in the air and a wash of clouds was building in the west. I looked at the keep, and the loch and the low-lying hills. Nothing had changed in a thousand years. There was a path that wound to the left along the shore. I stretched and loosened up for five minutes, tossed my towel on a bush, then took off at an easy gait and followed the trail.

The path wound through golden broom and gorse, mounted up into the grassy rises and high moorland. I ran through a small copse of larch and then up a narrow, steep incline and along a ledge overlooking the loch. Down below, to my right, was the castle and causeway, now a half mile away. Up ahead, three successive ridges rose in the distance, all reaching down to the loch as it wound its way to the sea. Beyond the ridges, a bald four-thousand-foot peak still had winter snow at the summit. Sea gulls wheeled and called overhead. It was a wild, windswept land of gaunt peaks, rocky ledges and ridges, serene lochs, peaceful bays, and mysterious, wooded glens down in the valleys, under a huge, open sky.

I was following a narrow track up a steep, rocky gorge with heavy lugged tire tracks pressed into the soft earth and mud. The track came to a rise about a hundred feet ahead and disappeared. I heard a dog barking. Over the rise came a small knot of busy sheep. They filled the track, so I hopped on a rock to let them pass. A tall girl with a shepherd's staff followed the herd. She had long, dark curly hair that came halfway down her back and she looked at me with an easy smile, with no fear or uncertainty. She shouted a command at the dog who promptly ran to the head of the pack, rounded them off, and stopped them.

"You've been runnin'?" she said. "You got a good sweat."

"Aye," I said, falling prey to her soft burr.

"You're not from the loch," she observed.

"No. I came for the affair at the castle."

"Oh," she nodded. "You know the laird?"

"Smallpiece?"

"Aye."

"My grandfather."

She nodded and smiled.

"Do you live about here?" I asked.

She tossed down her staff, climbed up on my rock, sat down, and gathered her knees into her arms. Her dark hair blew in the wind. She had blue eyes and color in her cheeks. Handsome, not pretty. She had a strong, intelligent face. There was no hesitation at all.

"Aye, close enough."

"Is it a croft you have, then."

She shook her head and and pushed the hair away from her eyes. "No, it's a proper farm. My father fishes and my brothers work the farm."

"And you?"

"I go to university. Edinburgh."

"And what do you study there?" I was sounding more Scotch all the time. She didn't notice.

"Veterinary medicine."

I nodded my head in understanding.

"When you finish, you'll come back here?"

She was looking me very steady in the eyes. She shook her head and smiled.

"Oh, no. There is not much here for me, although I love it. Young people leave the Highlands and go off. Youth is our principal export."

"Where would you go? Canada? Australia? The States?"

"Oh, not America," she said with conviction. "It's all drugs and crime and easy fun. I went to New York last year. The underground is filled with scribblin', paint, and terrible people. The streets are filthy, and everyone seems to be running someplace. They don't teach them anythin'

123

in the schools. All of the women go to work and leave their wee bairns wi' somebody else. I couldna live there."

I said nothing.

"I've got to go now," she said, getting down from the rock. The dog, who had been resting with his eyes fixed on her, got to his feet, circled the flock, and began to bark and nip at the sheeps' heels. The herd moved down the track.

She turned back to me, a lovely wind-blown Highland girl, sure of herself, with confidence in her eyes. "Isn't it a grand view from here?" she smiled, waved, and moved down the track. The wind took her hair and she just shook it free.

I followed another path back to the loch and ran through a pine grove with gorgeous air, over some primitive wooden bridges that spanned crashing torrents spilling down from the gaunt, rocky uplands, into a glen of birch and hazel, and then along the banks of the loch back to the castle.

I had run a good eight or nine miles, my muscles were relaxed, and I was confident and optimistic. Runner's high they call it. There were no Russians or neutral particle beam accelerators. I was back in some forgotten, misty land cut out and reamed by timeless glaciers, and where the sea crept inland and drowned the valleys. It was a hawk's lair of lofty crags and lonely hills, of ruined castles rising out of eternal lochs and fairy folk—demons, hags, water horses, gnomes, and devil dogs. I thought of the girl in the mountain pass with the wild black hair, calm eyes, and roses in her cheeks. There were no Russians at all. None.

Still caught up in the reverie of the run, I trotted back to the castle and splashed some loch on my face and dried off with the towel I had tossed on the bracken. I wrapped the towel around my neck and headed for the house.

There was a chill in the air as I wound my way back up the drive, past the hillside of waving flowers. There was a car parked in the court, a tan Bentley. I went up the stone steps, opened the door, and walked inside. Two leather suitcases were in the hall. I looked into the room with the gallery and the sightless deer. A woman stood by the window and turned to me.

She was in her early to mid-forties, about five six. She had thick, soft golden hair cut short, not much below her ears, and was carefully made-up, but understated. White blouse, light-green cardigan sweater and a tweed skirt, hose, and flat brown shoes. But it was her face that drew you, sensitive, lovely, aristocratic with large blue eyes and dark, arching eyebrows. Superb figure. She was just about all a woman could be in her prime, and she stood and faced me with very wide eyes. Her mouth was slightly open. Those eyes never left my face.

Predictably, I became an instant shambles. Groped. Flushed. Maybe, if I fainted, but I didn't know how. Older women with wise eyes do this to me. Beautiful, makes it worse. I have never had a worse case of acute self-consciousness in my life.

"I've been running," I said. Great opening line. Really impress her with my wit. I should have said, "I've been playing in my sand box."

"Yes, I can see."

"I'm a little wet." My hands fluttered helplessly.

"Yes."

I was struggling. She could see right into me. She was a glory.

"Running is good for you."

125

"I've been told that. Yes." She was being understanding and patient. She would ask me what grade I was in.

"But you have to wear running shoes," I gravely informed her.

"Yes." I was now three years old. Four tops. Not even in school.

I wound my battery-powered watch. I couldn't keep my eyes away from her. She had moved to within a few feet of me. Eyes still fixed on me. Mouth still open. She wore a subtle perfume. I was in orbit. Free fall. Might explode.

"I know you," she said.

"Oh, er, mam, er, ah. Don't think so. I would know that. Really would."

My grandmother came into the room. Saved by good old granny.

"Kate," she said with a smile. "Where have you been? I started to worry."

Kate turned to her. "Oh, some last-minute shopping." She went back to me. My grandmother was at her side. They unconsciously reached out and took the other's hand.

My grandmother studied us for a minute.

"Do you know who he is?" she asked.

"It's Colin, of course." She turned to my grandmother. "Fiona, you never told me."

"I wanted it to be a surprise. He came to Cornwall yesterday with no warning. Just came in."

She hadn't really heard her. "His son. From America. It has to be. It's incredible." She ran a hand through her hair. She found a couch and sat down, pulling my grandmother with her. They both looked at me. I stood and checked on the deer. One winked. God!

"What do you think?" my grandmother finally asked Kate.

"The size of him."

126

"Yes."

"Colin's eyes?"

Kate stood up and put her hand on my jaw and turned my head. "Yes, she said. "The Smallpiece eyes, but not with that fierce intensity." She held her head to one side. "No, they are more gentle."

Christ, I had enough of it. I looked her directly, fiercely into the eyes. Gave her the old Smallpiece eyes. Full of intensity. A real blast.

"Mocking maybe. A little amused," she said after a moment.

That tore it. They didn't have the courtesy to talk about me in their silent, women's language. They were doing it out loud, right in front of me. It was the worst possible thing women can do to me. A nightmare. I flushed again and felt the heat come into my cheeks. I was completely, totally, absolutely helpless. Return of the blob.

"Isn't he the handsomest thing?" my grandmother asked. They both sat there calmly on the couch with their hands in their laps and looked. I was fixed into the floor.

"That is not quite the right word, Fiona."

"I don't understand, Kate."

"He's kin. Your grandson. You don't see him quite the same way other women would. He's good-looking all right, but he's more."

Oh, God. Sweet Jesus. Right in front of my face. I was pudding. This is how they really talk. I wanted to run, but my feet were rooted to the floor. Fixed or rooted, same effect, I couldn't move.

Kate looked at me. "Oh, dear," she said, "I think we've embarrassed him. He's gone awfully pink. He looks like a boy, but I think he's a man."

"Oh, my," Grandmother said, and stood up and patted my hair. "Run along, Colin, and take your shower. You'll be fine." Thank God. I was excused, dismissed, sent to my room.

I walked out like a robot in a 1930's movie, stopped at the door, and turned around. I was churlish.

"What do I wear tonight?" I asked, working at a scowl. I was trying to salvage a bit of dignity, but I asked a boy's question.

"Your uniform, of course. It's been sponged and pressed. It's all laid out in your room, Colin."

I nodded. I was still flushed. I was five years old. They knew it. They were smiling their wise women's smiles.

"Now tell me about the girls." My grandmother turned to Kate and they were into some women's babble and I was out of it.

At nine o'clock it is hardly dusk in northern Scotland. We were walking down the drive to the castle, my grandparents and Kate Cameron. I knew her name now. They had a country estate across the loch many years before the Smallpieces acquired the castle, and six hundred and fifty acres around it. This part of Scotland had been traditionally dominated by Camerons, MacLeans, MacMasters, MacDonalds, and MacGillivrays. The clan MacRae was thirty miles to the north, near Gleneig, off the Isle of Skye.

Kate had two daughters who were late, but on their way. She also had a husband who was in Washington having trouble with the difficult Americans. I think he had a title.

The women wore white evening gowns with clan tartan draped over their left shoulders and gathered together by silver brooches at their waists on the right. I recognized the predominant red and green of the Cameron. My grandfather and I wore narrow tartan sashs over our shoulders. "Mine's honorary," he explained to me. "Macken-zie. Yours is MacRae." I pointed out to him that I was out of uniform with my sash. "Can't get in the place without a tartan," he laconically explained.

In the highland gloaming we walked down the drive and turned toward the glassy loch. I heard the whine of a generator and saw a van parked deep into a hedgerow. It was a nondescript grey and a half dozen antenna sprouted from its roof. One telescoped thirty feet into the air and aimed a three-foot dish to the south.

"What's that for?" I asked my grandfather.

He gave it a good look and scratched his jaw. "I don't know," he said. "Maybe Fitzworthy. Probably."

A stream of people were out on the causeway, headed for the castle, now lit with floodlights in the slowly gathering dusk. All of the women wore white, and clan tartan over their shoulders, three-quarters of the men were in kilt. Children were miniaturized versions of their parents. We joined the slow-moving procession, walked the causeway, over the drawbridge and got a good going over by four kilted guards as we entered the castle courtyard. The stark watchtower loomed overhead in the rear. We followed the line through the open doors into the great hall.

It was about the size of an average high school gym, but the resemblance ended there. Solid, massive grey wood beams, tree trunks, spanned the width of the hall thirty-five feet up. Great trusses were pinned and dowled into them and supported the roof which angled up toward the ridge pole, lost in shadow. A dark wooden gallery, ten feet out from the stone walls and twenty feet above the floor, ran around the two stone side walls and met over the entrance that we had come through. Thick stone columns rose from the flagged floor, every twenty-five feet, to support the gallery and the crossbeams. Soft light still diffused through the narrow slits in the walls along the gallery where defenders could launch arrows and, later, musket balls, at the enemy.

At the far end of the hall there was a raised dais and, in the center, a yawning blackened fireplace with a huge fire, flames six feet high, roaring and cracking and throwing trembling shadows on the rocky walls. Overhead, on poles anchored into the wooden gallery, the coats of arms of the clans hung in large, brilliant, silky banners on either side of the hall, a glowing, fluttering canopy above our heads. There were fifty on each side of the hall. The color was incredible. The sense of clan and history and Scotland was overpowering.

Crossed claymores and pikes glittered in the firelight on the stone walls. The place was filling up. Tables had been set on the galleries, underneath them and along the periphery of the great hall. The center was clear.

My grandfather led us to a table near the dais. He took me by the arm and pointed to the roof. "When my father began to rebuild it," he said, "there was no roof, half of the watch tower was gone and so was the north wall. For centuries the local Scotch had carted off the stone to use as ballast in their ships. For fifteen years my father collected the old stone, or found suitable replacements. Then he had the scholars and architects research the old libraries and documents for sketches and plans. It was twenty-two years after he began the restoration that the first stone was set in place. We've been at it ever since."

My grandfather was getting a lot of waves and shouts of greeting. Kate and my grandmother seemed to know everyone, and I was the object of much discreet observation with my U.S. Navy uniform. Everyone was standing. Waiting for something. Conversation was subdued. Finally, it fell off altogether. There was three minutes of nothing, then I heard the pipes.

They came through the doors of the great hall in columns of four wearing the tartan kilt of their clan, with bonnets and black velvet jackets with silver buttons, dress leather sporrans, plaids fastened on the left shoulder with silver brooches, knee-length stockings or white gaiters. And the tartans! The plaids! Dark blue and lighter green of Campbell, the green squares and overlapping red lines of MacDonald, the red stripes and yellow and black of the MacLeod of Lewis, the yellow and red of MacMillan.

The drumbeat was awesome and the pipes skurled out their martial, mystical call. Forty pipers stood in the great hall and filled it with the strange, magical music of the Highlands. The clans had gathered once again, but now in this ancient keep rising out of a tranquil loch, they came in peace and celebration and not war. Eventually, the pipes wound down and there was silence. The audience remained standing. Waiting. There would be more.

My grandfather mounted the dais and then a small podium and in quiet tones welcomed his guests. He mentioned briefly the names of those who had participated in former celebrations, in previous springs, but who had died this past year. He gave one final word of greeting and called on Reverand Macpherson, who spoke the invocation in Gaelic. We bowed our heads. He retired. And the pipe band played a few more stirring pieces, and my throat tightened. I had bought it all. No objective sociology left in me. The audience still stood. From somewhere there came a shout. "Mac Ghille Aindrais!" And the crowd shouted it back. "Mac a'bhaird!" The crowd hurled it back. "Canonach!" Again, the audience flung it back.

"What are they doing?" I asked my grandfather.

"They are calling the names of the clans in Gaelic."

"Are there any MacRaes here?" I asked.

"No. Not this year."

"What is the Gaelic for MacRae?" I asked.

"MacRath."

When they got down to the M's, after MacQueen, I shouted "MacRath!" and got a thunderous return. The shouting and roaring continued. I was into it. There are no Russians out there. No accelerator pods. This was really Brigadoon.

"Well, finally," Kate said, "here they come."

I looked over to the doors and saw two young women headed our way in the flickering light of the tapers mounted on the stone columns. The first girl had seen her mother and waved. She made her way among the tables and the roaring crowd, beneath the fluttering clan banners and through the standing pipers. Nothing seemed quite real. It wasn't.

She was an attractive brunette, dressed in the classical white evening gown complete with tartan over her left shoulder. But her gown was strapless and the tartan couldn't hide the fullness of her breasts, her narrow waist, and full hips. She embraced her mother, then my grandfather and grandmother. It was warm and genuine. They all went back many years. There were hugs and kisses, coos and ahs.

"Where is Anne?" my grandmother asked.

"Oh, she saw some MacDuffs and stopped to talk. She'll be along."

Her eyes found me.

"Oh my," she said, "what have we here?"

Attractive was not the right word. Glamour, style, sophisticated, contemporary, aware, sensual, calculating, intense sexuality all does it better. She radiated female. She would gather men like adolescents gather pimples. She was ready when she was twelve.

Kate introduced us. Her name was Sable. She was skilled at eye contact and never backed away. I flashed my half-wit grin and she ran her tongue between her teeth. Ah so.

"Oh, here comes Anne, finally." Kate said.

Through the pipers and the roaring crowd, I made out a figure coming our way. Big blond girl. She tripped. Looked up. The fat girl! She was twenty feet away and saw me. She did a perfect double take and then, instant fear. For a moment, I thought she might turn and run, but then she came on. Again there were the embraces and hugs with my grandparents and finally her eyes came into mine.

"Anne," her mother said, "this is Colin Smallpiece. He's from America. He's Fiona and Poppie's grandson. Bit of a surprise for everybody."

I held out my hand. "Glad to know you, Miss Cameron."

Instant relief replaced instant fear.

Someone in the crowd shouted "Uallas!" Wallace. And the response came roaring back with cheers and handclapping. The Scots had run the alphabet. All of the clans had been accounted for. Again they subsided into silence with everyone still on their feet. Then the pipers played "Auld Lang Syne" and we gathered hands and sang in the Gaelic. I faked it.

For the Scots it was a new year and the renewal of friendships and ancient memories. Their lovely voices, men and women, filled the ancient hall with their love of the land. Eventually, the pipes finally whispered into silence. The pipers moved off on their own. The ceremony was over. For thirty minutes the old keep had become a sacred place, a kirk, a church, and Scotland was God.

Everybody found somebody to kiss. I looked for the fat girl but she had her cheek pressed up against my grandfather's. Why did I look for the fat girl, when the sexpot was at my side? But Sable had slipped into me and wound her arms around my neck. She pressed her soft and experienced mouth into mine and I felt the pressure of her hips. I went from the sacred to profane fast. I had my arms around her, pulled her into me, and gave her as good as she gave me.

"Well now," she said, "I'll see you later." But there was a shadow in her eyes. Something about me troubled her.

I saw Fitzworthy coming our way. He was dressed in black tie and had a wrinkled tartan sash over his shoulder. I found his eyes and got a slight negative shake of the head. Nothing yet. Now platoons of waiters were carrying huge trays of food onto the tables that had been set down where the pipers had stood. Suckling pig, racks of lamb, sides of beef and venison, red lobster piled high by the barrel, smoked salmon, bushels of shrimp, great crystal bowls of fresh-cut fruit, strawberries, and frosted silver bowls of whipped cream. Hot breads, rolls, tubs of butter. Blazing white tablecloths and candles. And still more came.

Fitzworthy said, "Why not try the bar, Colin. I think you will find something interesting."

"Good idea." What could be interesting? But I could use a drink.

I made my way through the crowds at the groaning tables and found the bar. Forty feet of alcohol on rough planks in just about any form human ingenuity can create. Nine men in white jackets were working frantically to satisfy the thirsty Scots. And there, behind the barmen, supervising the bar, was six feet six inches of Michael Horatio

Flynn. He saw me instantly and his eternal lopsided grin got even larger.

"Good to see you again, sir," he said. "Much happier circumstance, if you get my meaning, sir."

I smiled and stuck out my hand and he took it.

"No hard feelings?" I asked.

"Oh none, sir. I was due for it. I'm gettin' on. You did for me proper."

"What brings an Irishman to a clan affair in the Highlands?"

"Born in Glasgow, sir. More Scotch in me than Irish. The admiral asked me to come and keep these sailors honest. Said you might be here."

I nodded.

"Get you a drink, sir?"

"Scotch. Neat." He spoke to a barman and I got my drink.

A voice behind me said, "Think I might have one of those myself."

It was the tall, hand-to-hand military type who was in the mat room that day. He was a captain of Marines and in dress blues. He had calm grey eyes, regular features, and an unforced smile. He looked like a fighting man who would be where he was supposed to be and do what he was supposed to do.

"Ian Llewellyn," he said, holding out his hand.

"Colin Smallpiece." I took his hand.

"Navy pilot," he said. "American. Surprising."

I nodded. Produced a grin, wondered what surprised him. I used the same approach on him I had on Flynn.

"How come a coal miner like you is up here among the sheep herders and fisher folk?"

"Admiral's orders." Flynn passed him a Scotch.

"I see." What I saw was that Anne Cameron, Ian Llew-

135

ellyn, Michael Flynn, Admiral Fitzworthy, and myself, who were caught up, one way or another, with the accelerator pod, were now together once again. It seemed more by design than chance.

I studied Llewellyn over my glass and he studied me. We were both wondering what role the other was to play in the forthcoming game.

I took him by the arm. "Come with me," I said, "I'll introduce you to some friends." We returned to the table. The party was now in full swing. An eight-piece band was up on the dais and belting out some popular tunes. Couples were dancing. There was a fight at the end of the hall. The booze was flowing. My grandparents were circulating. Kate Cameron was dancing with a kilted Black Watch major. Sable was at the end of the table with three young men, a MacInnes, a Robertson, and a Farquharson. Her eyes flicked to me. Anne was talking to Fitzworthy. I introduced Llewellyn around and he drifted back down to Sable. Where else? Fitzworthy wandered off.

"Dance with me, Anne Cameron," I said.

She had lovely light-blue eyes. Sable's eyes were like computer screens that were blank until a button got punched, then they lit up and calculated. Anne's eyes seemed endless and full of turmoil and mystery.

"Why?" she asked.

"Why what?"

"Why do you want to dance with me? Sable's been watching you all night."

"I didn't ask her. I asked you." I held out my hand.

She got up and we moved to the floor. I put my arm around her and it was like holding two inner tubes. She tripped, but I held her up.

"I can't dance," she said. "This is ridiculous."

I got my arm under her and pulled her in. She was

wearing a white gown buttoned up to the neck with puffy little sleeves. It would be quite appropriate for her first Communion.

I danced, she tripped. Not much conversation but her eyes were good although she didn't give me much of them. I did see a lot of her thick, long lashes. The band took a break and we walked back to our table. I held her hand, but she snatched it away. Llewellyn had chased off the boys and had Sable's attention. Anne shot me a quick look, no smile, waved at a clutch of girls and went off to them. I watched her go. She was a bundle of incredible contradiction.

My grandparents returned and insisted I be introduced around. So I spent a half hour with them under the fluttering banners and the light of the tapers in the ancient hall. I excused myself and made my way to the entrance of the watch tower and found the circular stairway lit by modern electricity. I worked my way up the six stories and walked out on the battlements and saw the loch shimmering in the half moon. I could see the distant hills and a wash of stars. Same view a thousand years ago. I heard the music from below, but it was soft and far away. I studied the loch and thought about Anne.

I heard a rustle and saw movement. Kate Cameron.

"I saw you go to the stairway." she said. "Isn't it lovely up here?"

"Yes."

"And the party?"

"I've never seen anything like it. Another world."

"Yes." Lord, she was beautiful in the moonlight.

"You've upset Sable. I've never seen her like this."

I shook my head.

"Oh, you wouldn't know why," she went on. "Sable collects men. She sees, conquers, discards. I don't know

137

why. She has very strong physical, ah, needs. You bother her, I think."

"Why?"

She shrugged her shoulders. "I don't know, maybe she senses a strength greater than hers. Or maybe she is really drawn to you and feels she can never have you. I really don't know. It's very unusual."

I shook my head. What could you say?

"You danced with Anne and not Sable. That was unusual, too."

"I like Anne, but I don't understand her."

"Who does? She is the most intelligent person I have ever known. I don't know what goes on in her head. Nobody does. She's been a mystery since she was a little girl. She's extraordinarily private. She works for the government, but I have no idea what she does." She shook her head and smiled at me. Her mouth remained slightly open.

"Why does she let herself go like that?. The weight, her skin, the goofy dresses?"

She blew out a breath and produced a small gasp. "I don't know why. I've been at her since she was fifteen and can't get anywhere. It's not that men aren't interested in her. They do come around. I think she finds them superficial and can't keep up with her intellectually. I really don't know."

"Have you spoken to anyone about her. I mean, tried to get some help when she was younger?"

"You mean doctors? Psychologists?"

I shrugged. "Maybe."

"She would outwit them all in five minutes. Her intelligence is frightening."

I nodded. Lord, she was lovely. She was studying me.

"You're more composed than you were this afternoon."

"Beautiful women rattle me for a while. I'm okay with one, outside."

She was quite close and shivering. I could smell her perfume and her skin was flawless and so white in the moonlight.

"Put your arms around me, Colin."

I did.

She had her arms around me and her hands ran up my neck and into my hair. I held her and kissed her cheek. She trembled. Her eyes were closed and she held onto me. Two minutes, then she pushed me away.

"Oh, dear God," she said softly, "you took me back thirty years. It was like yesterday and I was with your father for a moment. I loved him so."

My father.

She pushed her hair back and smiled.

"Thank you," she said.

She went back to the stairwell and looked back at me. Hesitated.

"You are the son I never had."

She disappeared down the steps.

I was alone again in the watchtower with the eternal loch and hills. Five minutes later I was back in the great hall. Sable was dancing with the Farquharson. I went back to the bar and ordered another Scotch. Flynn was gone. There was another fight and I heard a woman say, "The Macdonalds and the Mackenzies, what else? It never ends." I went back to the table but Anne wasn't there. Fitzworthy was.

"We fly to London in the hour," he said quietly. "Leave everything here, but change out of your uniform. It's on."

Brigadoon vanished before my eyes.

CHAPTER VI

Harkness was being very patient. He rolled his eyes and spread his empty hands, palms up.

"You're out of your goddamn mind," I exploded again.

"We really have no choi—"

"She can't walk twenty feet without falling down!"

"The mission goals have been . . ."

"She runs the hundred in two days for christsakes."

"We realize you never worked with anyone else . . ."

"Going over a five-foot fence is high adventure for her."

"Yes, but . . ."

"She'd bust the fucking fence!" I rarely use profanity. I did now to the chief of Britain's intelligence operations in the Soviet Union and assorted satellites. He continued to be very rational. Very English.

We were in my sleeping quarters on the fifth floor of the Union Jack Club. Bed, desk, small chest of drawers, one chair, one closet, translucent ceiling, tiny john with shower, no windows, everything off-white and plastic.

We got into London at eleven last night, Anne, Fitzworthy, Llewellyn, and Flynn. Anne and I were taken directly to the club and assigned quarters on the fifth floor. I didn't know where Flynn or Llewellyn went. I slept there. They brought me breakfast on a cart. I ate by myself. I

140

was free to walk in the halls but nowhere else. They gave me a pair of white coveralls. Visiting hours were between two and four.

Harkness arrived at eight-thirty, and told me Anne Cameron was going into Russia with me. I was still trying to cope with the idea.

I looked Harkness dead in the eye. Conjured up some Smallpiece intensity and fierceness. "What are the odds we can pull this thing off?" I asked.

He rolled his eyes some more. "Who knows? No one can say."

"Say something. Ten to one. Twenty to one?"

He blew out a breath. "Maybe."

"Odds are we won't make it. Right?"

He nodded. He looked pained. Unhappy. Frustrated.

"Odds are we'll get ourselves killed. Right?"

No response.

"You want to get that fat girl killed, Harkness?"

"Of course not!"

"It's damn impossible, that's what it is."

He sighed. "The mission goals have been changed. We no longer think we can retrieve the pod. It must be destroyed. Only the girl can do it."

That quieted me down.

"Why?" I asked.

"It is not a pure prototype of the accelerator. For security reasons, we built an explosive device into it. The device is triggered by a combination of numbers punched into a panel on the pod. Anne Cameron developed the device, knows how to arm it and time the detonation. It's all very complex. I don't claim to understand it. But only she can do it. Works on some system of random numbers. She knows how to handle them. Nobody else does."

I stared at him.

141

"There's something else," he said. "Moscow is sending two specialists up there to see the pod and get a preliminary report from the accelerator scientists who will be studying it. One of them is a woman. When we make the switch, one will have to be a woman."

I let it all sink in. I didn't want to see her at risk.

"Why do you think the pod can't be retrieved?"

Harkness spread his palms out to me again. "Maybe it can be. We would have to penetrate the camp, find the pod, eighty-six pounds of it, and then move it ninety miles to the Finnish border. All the time we are surrounded by KGB and the Red Army who don't like the idea."

I looked at the wall.

"It just seems much more in the realm of possibility to get to the pod and destroy it. We can make another, and the Russians will have lost the one they took."

"Anne is the only one who can do that?"

"She is the only one who can code in the commands to the internal computer in five minutes. She wrote the program. You could do it with a four-hundred page field manual in maybe three hours. Maybe."

He was looking intently at me

"You know the significance of it all, Smallpiece?"

"A girl's life is a small price for the risk, you mean? The global balance of power and all that?"

"Yes. I mean just that."

I rubbed my hands together. Studied my palms. "Does she know?" I asked.

"Yes."

"She's willing?"

"Yes."

"Hesitate?"

"No."

"She'd risk it with me?"

142

"Yes."

"I don't like it. Don't like it at all."

"Of course. Who does?"

"Did she have any concerns?"

"Yes."

"What?"

"You. She didn't think you wanted her into the operation."

"She was right." I got up and paced in my cell. Rubbed my hands together. "Did she say why she thought I might object?"

"No. Not directly. She realizes you have extraordinary athletic and adaptive skills and she has none. That she could slow you up. While she never said directly, I suspect she regards you as a chauvinist who thinks women can't do anything of significance but replace the population." He paused for a moment. "There is something else, I don't think she likes you . . ."

"Wonderful."

I heard a clock ticking. There was no clock in the room. Symbolic clock. Goddamn psychic symbolic clock.

"What happens," I asked, "if I refuse?"

Harkness took a breath and examined his knuckles.

"She goes in with Captain Faraday."

"Who's Captain Faraday?"

"Chap you put down on the mat three times."

I searched his eyes for bluff and deception and found nothing. But he's the head spy. He can do anything with his eyes. He had choir boy eyes. Singing choir boy eyes. Nothing more innocent than that.

"You'd send the fat girl into Russia with that clown?"

"Yes."

"You're bluffing, Harkness."

"Try me."

143

"You send her in with him and she's dead."

I was getting more of the choir boy face. He had the hand. I heard the clock again. Blew out a breath. No choice.

"Okay," I said, "She goes."

He seemed to collapse a little and found something interesting in the floor. He looked up. "I don't like doing this . . ."

"But somebody has to do it. Right?"

"Yes. Somebody has to."

"Okay. I need some answers to a few questions. You ready to answer?"

"If I can or should."

"What's Flynn and Llewellyn doing in this?"

"They're back-up if you should need a small force to help get you out. Fifteen of the best trained hand-to-hand, small arms fighting men in the UK. They are going into Finland as agricultural experts, animal husbandry specialists, to see how the reindeer are coping with acid rain. Industrial civilization. That sort of thing. They will be simply on stand-by if you need help getting back over the border. Or any other eventuality."

"Why Flynn? He's Navy."

"Volunteered. He likes you. Don't ask me why."

"He doesn't know where, when, why, or how?"

"Of course not. He just knows it's high risk. Fitzworthy must have told him enough to whet his appetite. Flynn likes a fight."

"The *swat* team isn't here? In the club?"

"No. But they are highly trained and ready. When you come out, they will be in the general area and you'll know how to communicate with them."

"What do we do now?"

144

"We have about forty-eight hours here to get you ready for insertion."

Spy talk.

"How do we get inserted?"

"Helicopter."

"Where do we get inserted? Who inserts us?"

He wasn't amused. He blew. I'd seen that face before. "Look, Smallpiece, I know you come from a distinguished Royal Navy family, that you're a hot shot fighter pilot, that you've forgotten more mathematics and physics than I'll ever know, and that you can kill almost anybody with your hands. I know all that. I also know Anne Cameron and have a deep affection for her, even though I don't understand her. Her father is probably my best friend. I don't like sending you and that girl into this. I know what you're getting into. I know the odds. But I must. Do you understand that? I must! I'd send you both to hell if it would get that damn thing back!" His voice cracked.

He was pumped.

"Okay. Okay. What's going to happen over the next forty-eight hours?

He settled down.

"We have a program for you and Anne Cameron that will give you about fifteen hours' sleep for the next two nights. Other than that, you'll work around the clock."

I nodded. "One final question."

"All right."

"The day I passed my Russian final and we met up here in that sterile conference room?"

"Yes."

"There was mention made of the young Cambridge genius who mathematically discovered the theoretical basis for the accelerator."

"Yes."

"He got you people interested, put together the funding, and developed the prototype."

"Yes. Alan Vickers."

"That's his name?"

"Yes."

"At our meeting, it was suggested that he might have gone over to the other side."

Harkness sighed. "There is mounting evidence to indicate that he did. We know that he is now in the camp with the pod. We know the Russians are keeping him in a kind of house arrest in that camp. There is some collaboration. We think he paved the way for its removal from this country. Very possibly assisted in it."

"He's a traitor, then?"

"Yes. You could say that."

"Anne Cameron didn't think so. She thinks Vickers is either dead or coerced and taken off by force."

Harkness gathered his hands together and studied the off-white wall. "Anne is brilliant and enormously talented. She was my personal link between the engineering team and the government. She did a considerable amount of the basic research. She is also very loyal to the people around her. I don't think she could emotionally accept the fact that Alan Vickers defected and took the accelerator pod with him. But we think he did."

"She was very insistent, I thought."

He continued to look at the wall for a few seconds and then he turned to me. "This is a very critical issue here, Smallpiece, and you have quite accurately sensed it right away. When it comes to Vickers you must use your own judgment in the field. You cannot go to Anne. Her view is colored and to a degree emotional."

"You mean she might act like a woman?"

"In this particular matter, yes."

146

"You a chauvinist, too, Harkness?"

"No. I don't think so. I know her and her situation better than you."

"You going to talk about Vickers in our briefing sessions?"

"I don't plan to. He is, to a degree, irrelevant now."

"If I can get him out, do I take him out?"

"Oh, yes."

"What if he doesn't want to go?"

"Use force if you have to, and if it doesn't jeopardize the mission."

"And the mission is to get the pod out if we think we reasonably can, or blow it up if we can't?"

"Yes."

"What if the fat girl doesn't like me using force on Alan?"

For a moment he got testy. "Why do you insist on calling her the fat girl, Smallpiece? She has a name." He exhaled with some effort. "That is a field situation. Use your own judgment at the time."

"Does Vickers understand the self-destruct system?" I asked.

"No. It involves a lot of computer theory and innovative hardware and software. That is what Anne was working on. Vickers is strictly theoretical physics and basic engineering. His concern was the acceleration of energy levels. He was completely unconcerned with the internal security device."

"He couldn't activate the self-destruct system then?"

"No more than you."

Harkness got up. "Does that take care of your questions?"

"For the moment."

He checked his watch. "We will have a general briefing

on the mission in the conference room in forty-five minutes."

"I'm not going anyplace."

Harkness moved to the door. I stretched out on the bed and picked up yesterday's copy of *Isvestia*. Required reading. I looked at him over the newspaper as he opened the door.

"Harkness," I said softly, "would you have sent the girl in with that guy?"

He allowed half a smile. "That is something, Smallpiece, that neither you nor I will ever know." He closed the door.

Forty-five minutes later I was in the conference room with Anne, Llewellyn, Harkness, and Fitzworthy. Llewellyn wore civilian clothes, the two goats were in white overalls. A slide projector was on the table and a screen had been pulled down at the far end of the room.

Harkness spoke. "Captain Llewellyn is here for simply a broad overview of this operation. We will speak only in general terms at the moment."

Anne sat across the table from me. Her pimples had wandered from her chin up to her left cheek. Her hair was in a long braid which she had pulled over her left shoulder in front. She would not look at me. I was apparently not in the room. Lord, she had eyes, that girl.

Harkness took a deep breath and plunged into it. "The mission is essentially to retrieve a device, developed in this country, but which is now in Soviet possession. The device is in a research facility approximately eighty air miles due east from the Finnish border at this point." A highly detailed map of the northeast quadrant of Finland flashed on the screen.

He ran his pointer up along the Finnish-Soviet border. "The closest sizable Finnish town is Kuusamo, up here, but we will put you down in Livarra, here, which is quite close to the Soviet border.

This is a very lightly settled area, as you can see, a few small settlements, some campsites, largely pine and spruce forest on either side of the border. You'll note there are many rivers and lakes. It's wild, rolling country. Some swamp. The Soviet research facility is quite isolated. So they have relatively few security concerns. At one time the place was an agricultural experiment station. Then it was used for biological warfare research. Two years ago it was set up for particle beam research, which has a relatively low priority in Soviet weapons research and development.

"Our plan is a relatively simple one. We know the Soviets are going to send two Moscow experts up to the camp early Thursday morning. One is a weapons research specialist with a great interest in SDI development, Dmitri Lushev. He holds the rank of major in the Aerospace Forces. The other is Olga Yefimov, KGB. She follows Dmitri around. He apparently is fascinated with the West, is something of a man-about-town and Olga keeps an eye on him. They will be going to the camp in Finland almost directly from Paris. Brief stop in Leningrad. We think Lushev has been trying to buy some French computer components which will go by way of Italy, then Hungary, and eventually into the Soviet Union. Photos of Dimitri and Olga briefly flashed on the screen.

"Our intelligence is that they will arrive here at Kalevala in the Soviet Union and then helicopter the remaining distance, about a hundred and ten kilometers to the research facility. Our plan is to divert the helicopter across the Finnish border, at this point, near Livarra, have it put down, and switch Smallpiece and Cameron for Lushev and Yefimov.

"You are wondering, of course, how we will manage

149

this. The helicopter pilot is ours. He will fake engine trouble, set the craft down and Captain Llewellyn's men, who will be in position, will take the Russians into custody. Smallpiece and Cameron then continue on to the camp.

I was watching Anne. She was intent on the screen. She had her hands in her lap and they didn't move.

"You are also wondering," Harkness went on, "how we can manage all of this in a foreign country. The Finns have a general idea of what we are about. They don't like that research camp so close to their border and apparently there were one or two incidents during the time when the Russians were using it for germ warfare research. Something leaked and the Finns caught it. Some cows and reindeer got sick and had to be destroyed. Relations are not very good along the border there.

"So the Finns are simply looking someplace else. They don't want to know anything. They won't interfere. Llewellyn's men go into the country as a visiting team of agricultural specialists. They will keep a low profile up there, poke around and look legitimate and just be handy if needed. They are back-up if the situation requires them."

Harkness went back and forth on the general theme for another fifteen minutes, showed a lot of slides of lakes, rivers, and pine forest and then he dismissed Llewellyn. No mention had been made of a major technological breakthrough in particle beam accelerators. Llewellyn now knew that two of us were going in, but he didn't know why or what for. He would be ready to help out if we were having trouble at the border coming back.

We then saw slides of the Soviet research camp taken by an American reconaissance satellite. It had incredible detail. There were three buildings in the shape of H's, all interconnected because of the snow which falls in September and continues into June. The camp was located on a

150

large lake and had two belts of barbed wire, in the cleared area, about three hundred yards from the buildings. We saw a helicopter pad with two choppers on it, a motor pool, and the usual vehicles. There was only one gate that opened to a meandering dirt road cut in the pine-spruce forest. The place looked like Stalag Seventeen.

"Okay," I said, "we know how we are going to get in. How do we get out?"

"Moscow gets you out," Harkness replied. "The camp commandant will get a phone call from Moscow, one of our people will have tapped the line. He will be ordered to prepare the pod for shipment to Moscow and that a helicopter will arrive in two hours. You two and the pod will be on it."

"Why should he go along with that?" I asked.

"The commandant is Constantine Voroshilov, a career army man with a spotty record. He drinks and womanizes. His future is on the line. He doesn't want another muckup. He'll require written orders and they will arrive on the helicopter. He will be talking to a man who sounds just like C-in-C A.I. Koldunov. We think Voroshilov will fall for it. He'll have to sign for the pod's release on the proper forms and everything. He's not too bright."

"What if he doesn't?"

"We have two fallback plans, but I would say you are going to have to become fairly adaptive. They say you're quite adapative, Smallpiece."

"Sure."

Following the travelogue on the wonders of the lakes and rivers of the Soviet-Finnish border and the flora and fauna of the region, we had lunch. Anne and I were required to have lunch together in the conference room and talk in Russian. She had a salad and I had steak and beer. Who was she kidding? We talked about the Nevski Pros-

151

pect in Leningrad, the Bolshoi, the Pushkin Art Museum in Moscow, and that led to Soviet realism and from that to literature. Finally it got into contemporary philosophy and we stopped eating. She bought Sartre and the existentialists. We were deep into the concept of freedom when the bell rang. She really had an incisive mind and she never lost her cool. I don't give a damn about Sartre one way or the other, but her eyes!

After lunch we had a lecture on what was going on in Moscow society and what the current antiestablishment jokes were, what the soccer and ice hockey teams were doing, what was showing in the theaters, what was in good supply and what was not. In short, we had a briefing on the current state of Soviet popular culture.

We were measured for uniforms.

Then a James Bond freak, with enormous enthusiasm, showed us two over-the-shoulder traveling bags with false bottoms, just about an inch. In the hidden compartment, we would have maps, medicines, mosquito repellent, fish line and hooks, compass, a lethal pill in case things got too rough, high energy emergency rations, deep woods survival stuff. He thought it was marvelous.

James wondered if we had any suggestions. I thought about it, wrote a list and gave it to him. His brow wrinkled.

"Interesting," he said. He ran a finger down the page. "That we can do. Hummm. The soap? Hummm."

"Put them in Crabtree & Evelyn boxes. You know, the quaint, charming kind."

He shook his head, but said he would do it. I also requested a heavy hunting knife, but that could be visible. He told us that Russians, returning from the West, load up on items not easily found in the Soviet Union. So we could carry just about anything that didn't look like the spy or survival stuff in the hidden compartments. I suggested a couple of Swiss army knives, gift-boxed, an electric shaver, Swedish high potency vitamins, three bottles of Chanel for my girlfriends. Anne had a list, too.

The makeup person blew into my cell in a flutter. He had pictures of Lushev in his hand. He took one look at me and said, "They want me to do this to that? It can't be done. It shouldn't be done."

He put his hand on my chin and turned my face this way and that. He studied me for some time. More time than he needed.

"I'll get ill," he said. "Positively sick."

Lushev was thirty-five, with jowls, two chins, and receding hair. He dyed my hair dark brown and shaved my hairline. Then he made up heavy brows to glue over mine, shoved sponge up under my cheeks to fill them out, made little rubber bags for under my eyes, put plugs up my nostrils, yellowed my teeth, and stained me grey. I was much too tall. Perhaps they could shave my feet.

He moaned and groaned. He would stop and step back. Put one hand on his chin, rest his elbow in the other. Tilt his head. Ah, better. He seemed satisfied. He handed me a mirror. "What do you think?" he asked.

"Jesuschrist. I look like Jack Nicholson. Worse than Jack Nicholson."

"I love Jack Nicholson."

He took the stuff off and went out glowing.

Anne refused to have her hair cut. Flat out. Since it was highly doubtful that anyone would know Olga in the small research camp, they decided to let it go. She was a blonde anyway. Since women's faces change so easily with makeup and hair style they were not too concerned about her. She was sufficiently styleless and dumpy anyway to pass easily for a Russian woman.

153

When Anne saw my new hairdo she took a deep breath, her eyes went wide, and she looked away.

"I thought you might like me better this way," I said. "I look like Jack Nicholson."

"Don't be ridiculous. It's awful."

"You don't like it?"

"Of course not." She still wouldn't look at me. "My God," she said quietly, and looked at her hands. They were shaking. I wondered if this was the first time she really considered what we were into. I didn't like to see her hands twisting like that. She should be holding hands with a young MacDuff in the moonlight by a quiet loch. That half-wit, with the magical secret compartment, had held up the red poison pill for her to admire.

What was I doing here anyway? Five days ago I flew an F-14 out of a North Sea gale onto the deck of the *Independence.* Got a lot of pats on the shoulder for that. Hot pilot. All I had to worry about was Dilly and his airsickness. Now I was taking a fat girl who couldn't walk straight into Russia to get her killed.

I told Anne to go back to her antiseptic sleeping capsule and get some rest. Screw Harkness and the insertion program he meticulously planned tonight. We were dead anyway.

I had a terrible dream. I took thirty-six Russian slugs and was still on my feet. Anne was dead but still bleeding. I carried her to the pod and her lifeless hand punched out the code on the panel, but she was bleeding so hard her blood fouled the keys and the pod wouldn't explode. I looked down at her and she was a husk in my arms, a dried-up mummy with long blond hair. I woke up and gasped.

I didn't eat breakfast.

A communications man went over the seven different ways we could contact the *swat* team.

The makeup person came back and spent an hour and a half teaching me how to put my new face on. I could manage it. He was grouchy and churlish. Would hardly speak to me. Must have had a spat. He put the stuff in a box and left.

We had a final fitting for the uniforms.

We were scheduled for a lecture on survival in the Finnish pine forest. I cut it, and went for a swim in the club pool. Twice, guards challenged me but let me through. There would be phone calls. I think I looked pretty wild. Nobody wanted to tangle with me.

I swam steadily for an hour. Up and back. Up and back. Up and back.

Harkness was waiting for me in the locker room while I dried off and changed back into my white coveralls.

"What do you think you're doing, Smallpiece?" He was quite put out. "You're flying out at seventeen hundred hours. You haven't completed the briefing. We insert tomo—" He checked himself, but he had said it.

"Fuck the briefing."

He glowered.

"I'm going to be inserted into the Soviet Union tomorrow, right?"

"Yes."

"You insert a light bulb into a socket. You insert a key into a lock. You insert batteries into flashlights. Generally, things you insert are not alive. They are passive things. You don't insert living people. I think your language is both symbolic and prophetic."

We walked back to the conference room in silence.

"You didn't eat your breakfast," he said.

"No. You eat yours?"

155

He hesitated. "Come on, Harkness. Did you?"

"No."

"Well, there you are."

"What's bothering you, Smallpiece? None of this behavior is indicated on your psychological profile."

"What's bothering me, for christsakes? Jesuschrist. What's bothering me?" I looked him directly in the eyes for fifteen seconds. "You know much psychological bullshit, Harkness? I mean the jargon, the processes? Freud? Psychobabble?"

He shook his head.

"I'm in conflict, Harkness. That's bad. I'm pulled in two directions at the same time by two equally powerful needs. I want to save the Western world and I don't want to kill the fat girl. I can't do one without negating the other. Probably, all I'll manage is to get her killed. So I'm frustrated. When people are in conflict they tend to be moody, introspective, quick to anger, irritable, truculent, uncooperative, and oftentimes disrespectful of authority."

"I see."

"No, you don't see. That's psychological garbage. But it's partly true."

"You are not concerned for yourself?"

"Sure I'm concerned for myself. You think I want to return to the nitrogen cycle at age twenty-seven? But I can manage this thing on my own. Always have." I was rubbing my palms together. They got hot.

"It's that goddamn tub of lard. She trips every twenty feet no matter what. Sure as hell, she's going to get killed. Her head's full of computers and philosophy and daffodils on a hill. I really don't know what it's filled with."

I stood up. Paced. "She has lovely, innocent, troubled eyes. She's fat, she's got pimples, but I like her. I don't think she has ever knowingly hurt anyone in her life. I

156

want to hold her hand and walk with her in Scotland. Instead, I have to . . ." My voice broke and I was shaking. What the hell was going on with me. I had just said what was going on with me.

Both of us were breathing pretty hard.

"You still going?" he asked.

"She goes, I go."

"She goes."

I nodded.

"How's she doing. She won't talk to me."

"All right. She doesn't understand your behavior. It bothers her."

"Bothers me."

"You won't go to any more of the sessions?"

"I don't need any more. Keep her at it, though."

"You won't go to Finland together. She goes out earlier."

"Good."

At four-thirty they took me to Heathrow in a beat-up van. I was dressed like a rumpled businessman with a Jack Nicholson hairline. I flew Finnair to Helsinki in about three hours. Two men met me at the airport and took me and my baggage through the usual airport maze ending up before a twin engine private plane with the engines slowly turning over. Conversation was confined to "We turn left here." I flew to Kuusamo which has commercial airline service. I was met again, waited until dawn, and then flew single engine to Livarra. We landed on a small, grassy strip cut out of the pine. Anne and Llewellyn and his band of cutthroats were already here.

We would get inserted at about 09:45 hours.

Operation Midnight Sun was off and running.

The gave me a code name. Merlin. For magician.

CHAPTER VII

I stood along the edge of the landing strip with my two bags and watched the plane flutter back into the sky. All I could see around me was a skyline of jagged triangular pine and a ridge poking up beyond the trees about half a mile away. The silence was total and oppressive. There was no movement anywhere. Where to go? What to do? Wait. Let them find me.

I saw something in the solid belt of pine across the strip. A figure. The figure waved and came toward me. Big man dressed in camping attire. Very big man. Flynn.

He couldn't control his grin. He looked me over and lost his grin.

"What did they do to your hair?" he asked.

"Died it brown and shaved back the hairline."

"Doesn't look like much."

"I'm supposed to look like a Russian."

"Oh, well, that's why."

He picked up my gear and I kept my shoulder bag with the James Bond fake bottom.

"Where's the girl?" I asked.

He pointed into the woods from which he had come. "We have a small caravan in there on a dirt road. Quarter of a mile in. She's there."

158

"How is she?"

"She's fine, sir. She looks like a Russian, too."

We walked across the wet grass and into the trees. You could smell the pungent resins and it was dark and damp. The sun glistened on the wet branches. Shafts of misty phosphorescent light broke through the overhead and lit up patches of earth in bright greens, browns. It was a primal conifer forest. Mosses, ferns, and lichen. There were little purple flowers with thick, waxy leaves growing out of the spongy humus. Virginal. Flynn led the way over a trail of brown pine needles with my bags. My shoes were wet already.

We stopped before a small camper, the kind that folds out into a tent from a box with wheels. The heavy dew was dripping off the canvas in small rivulets. Five or six men were giving me a careful look. A couple wore hip waders for fishing. Hats full of flies. Fighting men trying to look harmless.

Llewellyn came out of the camper. He wore fake glasses, a necktie, and knee-high rubber boots with his pants stuffed in. I think he was trying to look like a zoologist. He looked like a tough hand-to-hand man trying to look like a zoologist.

He gave me a good look but didn't say anything about my Jack Nicholson forehead. "The chopper is due in three hours. How long will it take you to look like a Russian?" he asked.

"Probably six," I said, "I'll get ready inside. You guys all ready?"

"We're ready."

Anne came to the canvas flap that served as a door on the camper. She was in uniform and it looked good on her. She had her hair in braids wound tight on her head.

She nodded when she saw me. Her mouth didn't move. New batch of pimples. I could believe she was KGB.

I smiled back. My good guy smile. My confidence-building smile. I picked up the bag with the makeup and uniform and went inside. There were two full bunks on either side of the narrow aisle. Waterproof tarps were on the beds. Automatic weapons, Uzi submachine guns, three high-power rifles with scopes, pistols, ammo, trench knives, and a case of grenades were on the tarps. I pushed them aside and opened my bag and got out my uniform. Anne hesitated for a moment and then went out to Llewellyn who was looking at a butterfly, professionally.

I got into my uniform and carefully put my makeup on. Took close to an hour. Then I walked outside and got a lot of smiles. My Russian hat was so wide it was a small umbrella. The pants had legs twice the width I normally wear. I felt like a barrel. I clamped my thumbs into my belt and strutted.

"How do I look?" I asked Anne.

"Like you play for the Chicago Giants. You look too American. Slouch."

I slouched. "Like this?"

"Maybe." She shrugged.

"It's the New York Giants and Chicago Bears. We did this before." She considered me.

The minutes slipped by. I walked around their little camp. Followed the dirt road a quarter of a mile.

"Where does it go?" I asked Llewellyn.

"There's a river about half a mile from here. Some government campsites. Back over that ridge that you can see from the strip is a small settlement on a dirt road. This is a remote area. Genuine wilderness."

"I wonder what people do for a living?"

"Not much," he said.

160

I checked my watch. "I think we had best get out on the strip. If he's on time, we have half an hour."

"Righto."

Llewellyn got his men together and we moved off. Two of his men carried our bags. Anne was ahead of me. She stumbled on the trail twice. Out on the fringe of the strip the men went immediately to their assigned positions. Everyone was in the shadow of the pines. We waited.

The appointed time came and went. Fifteen minutes. Half an hour. We studied the sky and pointed our ears.

"Anything could have happened. Engine trouble. They never made it out of Leningrad. The pilot got caught. Anything." He checked his watch. He wanted some action.

Forty-five minutes and holding. Anne was very quiet. When wasn't Anne very quiet? Did I hear something? I looked at Llewellyn and he nodded.

It was a chopper and out of the east.

"Be alert," Llewellyn shouted. "On my signal!"

It came in at three hundred feet, hovered over the strip, and settled down. A big, ominous dragonfly. The rhythmic whooshing of the blades made speech impossible. The tall grass was whipped into a frenzy as the wheels touched and the turbines wound down. It was an MI-24, code name, Hind, speed 320 km an hour. Carried about twelve men. Had a big red star on the side. I didn't like it. Foreign looking. Russian.

A door swung out and the pilot climbed up the fuselage and popped an engine panel. Two figures tentatively emerged from the interior then dropped to the turf. The man stretched and looked around. He had a uniform like mine. The woman stooped down and picked a flower.

The pilot was talking to them and pointing to the line of pine on the opposite side of the strip. They drifted to the other side of the chopper, Llewellyn's men were out of the shadow, over to the helio, two went around either side, two went under it.

Fifteen seconds later everybody was back, the two Russians were handcuffed, arms behind their backs. Llewellyn signaled "mission accomplished" by pumping his right arm up and down three times. Anne and I were out of the woods and into the chopper. I didn't even look at the Russians. Anne tripped going into the aircraft and I caught her from behind and shoved her inside. Somebody tossed our bags in. I threw the Russians' stuff out. Llewellyn was at the door with a big grin and handed me an envelope. Lushev's orders.

The pilot was back. He gave us a quick smile and a thumbs-up gesture. We sat down and belted up in two canvas seats. The turbines howled and we lifted off. The men were waving, but then we were over the pine and I lost sight of them. We gained altitude to about a thousand feet and headed east.

The chopper had been badly used. The seats were torn, paint scraped, metal dented, inspection panels yanked out and never put back, wire and cable joined crudely and left to hang. Two windows were cracked. I had been told about Russian maintenance. Well, it flew.

Anne sat in her torn canvas seat and studied her hands. I studied the terrain. Low-lying, undulating country. Pine, spruce forest wastes as far as you could see. Some ridges, maybe three hundred or four hundred feet. Rivers and streams, lakes everywhere. Gorges cut out of the rock over the millenia. We were over a stretch of rapids. Then I saw a small settlement by a bend in the river. Ten or twelve wooden houses, boats pulled up on the shore, dirt roads, three trucks, pine and spruce stretched in undulating waves into the horizon.

We must be thirty or forty miles into the Soviet Union.

We passed over an oddly shaped lake. It was quite large, maybe three or four miles long, two miles wide, and shaped like a figure eight. It was a lake in two parts, intersecting in a narrow gorge topped with a thick overlay of pine and spruce.

The pilot swung south so that we would come into the Soviet research camp heading north. More lakes and streams and a lot of swamp. We had been in the air for half an hour, then he curved north and lost some altitude. We were down to three hundred feet and over a big blue lake glimmering in the sunlight. I saw the three buildings in the shape of an H and all connected. It was just like the satellite photographs, the motor pool, the chopper pad, a couple of soccer fields, the two barbed wire fences, the dirt road, and the infinite pine forest.

The turbines throttled back and lost their howl. We settled down and the wheels touched. The pilot was killing switches and buttoning up. The door was opened and a Soviet soldier thrust his peasant face up at us. "Welcome to Research Facility Kirov," he said with a smile. What else?

I helped Anne out of the chopper. That might not have been good Soviet form, but she could have easily gone sprawling.

There was no reception committee. A young lieutenant in a field uniform stepped up and saluted. I returned it crisply. I tried to look superior and sinister while slouching. Anne quite properly returned his salute as she had been taught.

I had a look around. Single-story unpainted barracks-type buildings with the exterior walls set back six feet to allow covered walkways and easy access through the winter snows from building to building. All of the H's were connected.

163

The place looked well managed. Some off-duty men were playing on the nearby soccer field. A knot of noisy children were doing the same thing. Must be the scientists' kids, I guessed. Grass was cut. There were a few flower gardens and some esthetically placed small groves of pine. The lake was gorgeous under a clear sky and brilliant sun. A boat was out and two men were fishing. There was an old-fashioned, high wing float plane anchored off a small point.

The laughter of the children floated up to us and a gentle breeze carried the fragrance of the pines. The flowers nodded in the sun. Welcome to Camp Potawatame. It looked too good. Nobody paid any attention to the big shots from Moscow. Seemed contrived. Pastoral. Idealized. Planned.

"Your luggage will be taken to your quarters," the lieutenant said.

"Fine."

"You had a good trip?"

"Very smooth."

"And Leningrad?"

Was he asking me about the weather or the cultural life? "Well," I smiled, "you know Leningrad."

"Yes. I am to take you to the commandant."

I nodded.

"May I have your shoulder bags taken to your quarters, sir?"

"No. I have orders, reports, confidential material here. You understand?" I patted the bag and smiled. He smiled back. Men of the world.

We followed him up a well-raked path with stone borders. We admired the flowers. I commented on how healthy the children seemed. We were under one of the protective roof overhangs now and clumped along the wooden walkway. Went through a door into a hall with plywood walls, we were in the center bar of the H. Then we went through one of the inclosed passageways that connected the buildings. We had entered the middle H, went through the center bar of this one, too, and were outside once more, under the wide eaves, our footsteps sounding hollow on the wood floor. Again, no paint but the wood had silvered. We walked all the way down to the end and through a door into an orderly room.

It had the usual cluttered desks, duty rosters, bulletin boards, filing cabinets, telex machine, beady-eyed sergeant, bored clerks, and ringing telephones. The military from one country to another tend to copy each other. Consequently, among all armies, everywhere, there is a generic orderly room. They are interchangeable. Only the uniforms differ.

The lieutenant knocked at a door. We heard "enter" and we walked in. It was a large corner office and better than I expected. Bookcases that were almost completely filled, mostly with scientific journals. Four windows. Lovely view of the lake. Worn rug. Plywood walls, one had a big four-by-four ground plan of the camp, with a room by room, area by area detailing of the functions of the buildings. An office with a red star read "Commandant." Another said "Commissary," and another "Laboratory A." Functional, military camp-style office.

Behind the desk was a tall, smiling man, mid-forties, with slicked-down brown hair, fair skin, bright, intelligent brown eyes, aquiline nose, and an extended hand. It was a professorish face and not unkindly. He was in fatigues and wore no insignia of branch, unit, or rank. He had a good smile but he did not have good teeth. Crooked and yellow. He smoked and had nicotine-stained fingers but he seemed very glad to see us. I shook his hand, nicotine and all.

"Colonel Boris Nikolay," he said.

"Lushev," I said. I pointed to Anne. "Olga Yefimov."

"Please, sit," he said, waving us to two wooden chairs placed before the desk. He was giving Anne a very careful look. He sat at his desk, elbows on the arms of his chair, his hands slightly coming together at the fingertips. The smile could have been painted on.

The man at the desk was not Constantine Voroshilov, the commandant we were told to expect at the briefing. Could be any number of legitimate reasons, of course. My apprehension increased.

"Good trip, Major?" he asked.

"Yes. Very good."

He nodded agreeably.

"You are a little younger than I expected."

I shrugged.

"And you are here to make a report on our recent acquisition."

"Yes."

"May I have your orders?"

I handed over the orders Llewellen had taken from the Russian. He studied them for just a moment then put them down on the desk. "They seem to be in order," he smiled.

"I understand, Lieutenant, that you have recently been to Paris." He was looking at Anne.

"Yes," she said. She wasn't generous with her smiles with him either." But she was KGB. They are humorless.

"What were you doing in Paris?"

"My assignment was to assist Major Lushev in some purchases."

"What kind of purchases?"

166

"That is classified information. I am not at liberty to say." She fixed her blue eyes on him and didn't blink. First class job. Should have made him feel like a snoop. You don't want to get the KGB mad at you.

"Of course." He turned back to me. The phone rang. He picked it up. "Yes. Yes. Thank you."

He sighed. A pleasant, contented smile. An everything is in order smile. Bureaucrats smile like that.

"Major, would you mind going to the door and tell me what you see in the orderly room. If you would."

What the hell? I got up and opened the door. Fifteen men were there with Kalishnakovs pointed at me. I blew out a breath and closed the door and sat down. Nikolay caught my eye and grinned. Then he brought up his right hand and placed it on the desk. His hand held a Tokarev 7.62 pistol, four and a half inch barrel, black plastic grips. Plain, simple and functional. Ugly gun actually. Not beautiful like the Colt 45 or the Walther P 38. But an ugly gun will kill you as dead as a beautiful one. Anne gasped.

He turned to Anne. "Miss Anne Cameron." He looked at me. "Lieutenent Colin Smallpiece, United States Navy."

I blew out a slow breath.

He was still smiling. "We knew you were coming for a visit, Lieutenant, before you did."

I blew out another breath. Took another. Settled down. "How?"

"We have penetrated the fifth floor of the Union Jack Club for some time now. It was an excellent plan and had we not known about it, you very well might have gotten away with it. That idiot Voroshilov would have helped you put the accelerator in the helicopter."

I was looking crestfallen while memorizing every detail on the ground and building plan on the wall. Ah, there was the armory. It was in this building, opposite side and end. Some laboratories were in this building as well. Keep him talking. Recoup. Respond. React. Plan.

"Who were the Russians on the helicopter?" I asked.

He looked positively smug. "Bylova and Kozlov? Lovers. Troublemakers. They would have defected to the West, anyway. We helped them. The English got them and we got you. Unfair exchange."

He was having a good time. Played with his pencils.

"I would imagine there is considerable consternation in Whitehall and Washington around now," he added.

"Suppose."

"Is Alan Vickers here?" Anne asked in a quiet voice.

The smile became paternal this time. "Yes, Miss Cameron, and you shall see him soon. One or two things first, though." He pressed a button. Two hefty Soviet-uniformed females came in. They looked at Anne. One could have played for the Bears.

"Miss Cameron, if you will go with these women for just a few minutes, and then you will be returned here."

Anne looked at me. "It's okay," I said in English. "Probably a search and some new clothes."

"Very good, Lieutenant" Nikolay maintained his parental smile. He seemed proud of us.

Anne left with the two women. She was biting her lip and had lost some color. Pimples seemed bigger than ever. Nicolay's eyes followed her out the door.

"She is very bright, we have been told," he added conversationally.

"Oh yes. Very bright." Would there be catwalks up in the attics, I wondered. The roofs were quite steep in order to shed the snow. I noted that there was an access panel cut into the office ceiling.

"She designed the self-destruct system and programmed it, we understand," he said.

168

"You got me there, comrade." How would he know that? According to Fitz, only Vickers and two other engineers knew she was working on the system. I continued to let my eyes drift over the locations and functions of areas in the buildings. Where was north? Important to know north. I was like a bird, once oriented to north, even in a cave, I knew my way out. Sixth sense of some sort.

"Lovely lake. Do you swim in it?"

"Oh, no. Much too cold." He shook his head, frowned.

"It's beautiful. Fishing good?"

"Excellent. We have fresh fish every other day. You will have some tonight, I believe."

"What do they catch?"

"Mostly salmon, some bass, trout."

I squinted through the windows. "Which way is north?"

"That way." He pointed. That's what I thought. He's giving away a lot. He's got us, me, by the balls.

They brought Anne back in. She was wearing olive-green coveralls. She was flushed and her eyes were on the floor. She had been given a very complete search. They had taken out her braids and her lovely blond hair fell loose to the small of her back. She felt humiliated and wouldn't look at anybody. She was very far from the castle on the loch and her Cameron sash. God, she was. Her hands helplessly twisted in her lap. No tears. She was tough. I could count on her.

My turn. Two men came in and I went out to a primitive bathroom down the hall and I got a very complete body search and a pair of coveralls. They handed me a bar of brown soap and told me to wash my face. I took out all the plugs, sponge, fake eyebrows and scrubbed the stains and dyes off. Felt better right away. The makeup hurt. I even got some brown color out of my hair. Still had my Jack Nicholson hairdo.

He studied us with wide eyes and an open mouth. Anne to me, back and forth.

"You're both so young," Nikolay exclaimed. "Not with us. Old men. No fire, no creativity in the system, no youth. We stifle innovation. You invent, create, discover, and then we steal it from you, like the accelerator. We have to steal from the West to keep up. We just can't innovate. Why? And they send children to get it back. It's too much for me." He shook his head.

Big speech. He looked a little uncertain. I think he thought he had said too much.

"You KGB?" I asked.

"Not quite." He went no further.

He pressed a button on an old-fashioned intercom. "You'll see Alan Vickers now, Miss Cameron," he said.

He looked down at his desk and twisted a pencil. He looked up and the smile was gone. "You should know," he said, "that you must be regarded as spies and as enemies of the Soviet state. Your situation is not good." He gestured to the guards to take us away. They tossed our shoulder bags on the beat-up leather couch. So much for James Bond and his magical suitcase.

So much for glasnost.

If I was right, the lock-up should be in this building near the commissary. They would have built some very strong storage rooms for their food and supplies. Strong enough to frustrate hungry soldiers bent on a midnight raid on the pantry. We clumped back back down the protected wooden sidewalk, entered the center bar of the H, then turned right on the top left leg and stopped before a heavy door. The guard unlocked it, and shoved me in. Anne followed. I had been right.

It was a storage room with no windows. Twenty by thirty feet with heavy wooden walls. One naked electric blub in the ceiling. Three cots. One occupied. A thin man, wiry sandy hair, beak of a nose, bruised lips and frantic eyes. He struggled to get up from his bunk.

"Alan!" Anne moaned, and was into his confused arms. She kissed his cheeks, patted his back, held his battered face in her palms. She hugged him. Now she had tears. So that's the way it is. Should have guessed. Harkness and all that damn oblique talk of loyalty and emotional bias. They were lovers. You do tend to get loyal and emotional when you are somebody's girlfriend.

Vickers was having some trouble comprehending it. He had also been beat up a few times. Nikolay wasn't such a kindly professor after all.

I let them catch up on old times and had a look around. I punched the wooden walls. Solid. I looked for hidden cameras and bugs. Nothing. The camp was too deep in the northern wilderness for sophisticated devices. No need. No trapdoor in the ceiling, either.

In a half hour, they were hugged and talked out and looking at me.

"Why did they beat you up?" I asked.

"They accidentally touched a few keys and started a preliminary sequence in the self-destruct device on the pod. They asked me about it. But I didn't know anything. They used force, but I still couldn't tell them anything. Anne set the programming up."

"You told them about Anne?"

"Yes." He looked alarmed. "I had no idea she would end up here. I thought she was in London." He was talking to the floor.

"Are the Russians concerned about the self-destruct system?"

"Yes. They think it might be sequencing now. They don't know. They want to stop it."

171

Not good news for Anne.

I took a good look at him. Not a strong face. Probably very bright. He did get the accelerator started. Showed initiative. I gave him that.

"If we can get out of here, Vickers, escape some way, do you want to come with us?"

"Of course. Yes."

"You defect? Go over?"

"No. Not voluntarily." He looked away.

A triumphant gasp from Anne. "I knew it!"

What did she see in the guy? He was a wimp, even if he did discover the negative equation. Maybe I was jealous of him and his relationship with the fat girl. Jesuschrist.

I lay down on my bunk and considered the ceiling. Catwalks up there, connected the whole complex. How could we get up top? Then, we would have to get to the laboratory and steal the pod, slip through the guards, sneak over to the chopper pad, grab one, load everything on board, keep the fat girl from falling into the lake and Vickers from wandering off, then fly away. Take some doing, planning.

I planned. There was some banging in the hall outside and a squeak in the lock as the bolt was withdrawn. The door swung open and two soldiers came in pushing a crude cart. The cart had bowls and a steaming porcelain pot with big chips, a dented metal pitcher, glasses, wooden spoons, and a platter with big chunks of black bread. One man ladled soup into the bowls.

I studied it all. Made some judgments. I could take both of them, but then, outside the door, I noted two guards with rifles. It would get messy but with the right plan, maybe. You have to take what they give you.

The soup smelled good. They put the steaming bowls, the glasses of hot tea, and the chunks of bread on rough

172

wooden trays, and put a tray on each bed. We got pleasant smiles. They wished us a good lunch, we wished them a good day. They almost bowed out. Good jail. Excellent management.

"Are they always this nice?" I asked Vickers.

"No," he said and didn't elaborate.

Anne wasn't bothering with lunch which surprised me, but I tucked right in. Good soup, cabbage and potato and I think a bit of reindeer. Bread was even hot. No butter. They forgot the napkins.

Vickers just stared at his tray. Lovers don't have much appetite I have been told for food. It was then that I noticed a bit of paper sticking out from underneath my bowl. I slid it out and opened it. A note, it read, "Don't despair. Tonight."

Well now.

I showed the note to Vickers. "You ever get any fan mail like this?"

His eyes widened. "No."

Anne had a look. "What does it mean?" she asked, voice low, trying not to hope too much.

I scratched my head. "Maybe the fifth floor isn't the only place that's been penetrated."

We spent a bit of time just looking at each other.

"What do we do?" Anne asked, turning to me.

"We don't despair and we wait for tonight," I said.

I stretched out on my bunk, put my hands behind my head, and returned to the buildings and ground plan. There had to be catwalks! I reviewed the locations of the critical places. If there were no catwalks we were sunk. However, in the spy business, we are taught that if at first you don't succeed, try, try again. But try something else. I forced myself to think of alternatives. I put four plans together. The hours slipped by.

173

Anne was asleep in the far bunk. Her mouth was open. She looked like she was twelve years old. Vickers was staring at the ceiling, too. I got up and caught his eye. I beckoned to him and sat down on the floor as far from Anne as possible. I patted the floor next to me. Vickers sat down and ran a hand through his hair.

"They had something on you, didn't they?" I asked.

"What do you mean?" He drew in a sharp breath.

"You were being blackmailed. They threatened to go public unless you cooperated."

A sigh. He was resigned. Defeated. "Yes."

"You gay?"

"Yes."

"They set you up?"

"Yes."

"Took pictures."

"Yes, they took pictures!"

"Quiet. Take it easy. You see the pictures?"

"Yes."

"How many?"

"For God's sake do you think I counted?"

"A dozen? Two dozen?"

"Does it matter? A dozen maybe."

"You come back with us and it could still hit the fan."

He produced a long, lingering explosion of breath. "I don't care anymore."

"If you don't care, why did you go over in the first place?"

Another sigh. "I was stalling for time. Maybe I could figure out the self-destruct system. Escape. I was in shock. Needed to think." He looked over at me. His eyes were in agony. "I made a disastrous mistake. What's one man?"

I sighed. "Yeah, what's three people?"

I checked my watch. "What time is dinner served?"

"Around six."

"Do you know who set you up, Vickers?"

"Oh yes. It was Roger Henderson." There was no hesitation. Clearly he had thought about it. Arrived at a conclusion. No doubts at all.

"Who's he?"

"He's with Harkness's staff. Very high up."

"He's gay, too?"

"I thought he was."

"He had Harkness's complete confidence? He knew everything that was going on? What you were doing? What Anne was doing? All of the security arrangements? Breaks in security? Changes in security? He knew about me?"

"I would think so. Yes."

"You're sure he set you up."

"God yes! He was there!"

I thought of Anne. "You attracted to women at all, Vickers?"

"Sometimes. Not often. I'm really gay."

"Does Anne know about your, er, primary sexual orientation?" I sounded like a goddamn San Francisco social worker.

He bristled. "Of course not."

"Vickers," I said slowly, "we were set up, too. The Russians knew we were on our way here before we did. The commandant, or the man acting like one, said the Union Jack Club had been compromised. The Russians knew all about it and had a man there. Henderson, do you think?"

"Of course."

I went back to my bed and considerd the ceiling again.

I may have dozed off later in the day. I heard the familiar rattling in the hall, muffled voices, a crude laugh then the lock squeaking. The door swung open and the

175

waiters pushed their cart in. I saw two Kalishnakov assault rifles poking through the doorway. Their hands gripped the stubby pistol stocks, fingers on the triggers.

It was indeed salmon. A five- or six-pound salmon boiled alive with its eyes still on. It was on a wooden platter. We were given three hot glasses of tea and great chunks of black bread. No plates, no napkins, no tableware.

"I'll be back in fifteen minutes to clean up," the small waiter said. He was balding, about twenty-six or twenty-seven, with black eyes, a nervous smile, and body odor. He was a private soldier and a soprano.

"We will not despair." I said with a smile.

"That is good," he said. "I will be back. Enjoy your meal."

"How do you eat this thing?" I asked Alan.

"With your hands. This way." He took the fish with both hands and gently broke it apart. He picked up a piece with his fingers. "That's it," he said.

So we sat on the floor and picked up bits of salmon with our fingers. Anne finally went at it. We had picked it clean in ten minutes. In fifteen he was back. The Kalishnakovs still poked in the door.

"Excellent," I said. "Compliments to the chef."

He fumbled around with the platter.

"Tonight at twelve-thirty. Be ready." Sotto voice.

"I need a few things." Equally sotto.

"I don't know."

"Try."

"What?"

"Two flashlights, fifty feet of strong rope, a folding shovel, a box of matches."

He dropped the platter and made a good show of swearing and picking up the fish bones.

"It will still be light. There is no night up here. The suns never sets. You will not need flashlights."

"Humor me."

"I don't know."

"Get them."

"I'll try."

He wheeled the cart out.

There is not a great deal that three people can do in a small wooden room, particularly when they want six hours to go by instantly. I tried to sleep. I think I did. The hours dragged. At ten-thirty I was pacing. Anne and Alan watched. I was checking my watch too often. The leader should be calm and inspire confidence in the troops.

There were a few things I needed to go over.

"Where is the pod in relationship to where we are now?" I asked Vickers.

"We are in the central building. You know they're built like an H?"

I nodded.

"Most of the labs are in this building, barracks and apartments are in the two outside buildings."

"Right."

"To get to the laboratory, where the accelerator is, we have to go down the outside hall, back into the center part of the H, and out again to the top left end of the opposite arm of the H."

"In other words, it's right across there." I pointed.

"Yes."

"That's good."

I had their attention. "Now, I think our friend, who doesn't want us to despair, is going to take us to the laboratory where the pod is located."

"But he is going to help us to escape," Anne said.

"That's right. But he also wants us to accomplish our

177

mission, and that's to activate the self-destruct system. Then we escape. We are here to do the job we were sent for. You both understand that?"

Two nods.

"I'm pretty sure the laboratory will be bugged. This room isn't, because it's not important. The lab is important. So don't say anything until I do, and then you're going to have to be smart enough to pick up and reinforce what I'm saying. Go along with me. You understand?"

"No." Anne said it, but Vickers looked uncertain. too.

I turned to Anne. "If I ask you how long it will take you to neutralize the self-destruct system, you tell me about an hour. Okay?"

"But it can be done in a few minutes, once I read how the random number sequences are going and begin the override."

"You know that, but the Russians listening, they don't know that. I'm stalling for time. I need an hour."

"What for?"

"I'm not sure. I'm not sure of a lot of things. We're going to have to be very loose and adaptive in that lab. You're going to have to follow my lead. We're going to be playing a kind of game."

"If people are listening, why won't they come and get us?" Anne asked.

"They might. They might not. Depends. I'm not sure."

"I don't like this," Anne said with despair in her eyes.

I patted her shoulder. "Don't despair, kid. Remember the note." She nodded.

"There may be some violence," I said.

She looked uncertain.

"I may have to do some things," I said. She looked away. Vickers looked at his shoes.

Twelve midnight.

Fifteen minutes past.

Jesuschrist.

There was a rattle in the lock, the door swung open, and he came in carrying a canvas bag.

"You got the stuff?" I asked.

"Yes, all of it."

"Let me look." It was all there. "Okay, let's go."

He went first. We followed.

We went out under the roof eaves. We were in shadow, but it was still twilight, a deep dusk. Land of the midnight sun. Eternal soft summer light. No wind, no breeze. Very quiet. Not even a dog barked. No guards that I could see. We stayed close to the walls, clothed in shadow, four wraiths, moved down to the center part of the H and went inside and across, just one dim light, then out and up again. Silent. Empty. We stopped before a door and our man had a key. The lock turned and we melted inside. She didn't trip once. Two dull lights burned in ceiling sockets. There was a trapdoor. Thank you most kindly. The windows were boarded over and covered with a dark-green canvas.

The place was full of equipment. Looked like a Star Wars spaceship, gauges, dials, motors, a dozen computer screens, mysterious finned devices everywhere. But my attention was on the pod. It sat on a bench and looked like a big, ribbed watermelon, rounded at the ends, with a ceramic surface. In each of the rounded ends there was a depression of five inches. They were receptacles for interface connectors. Must be over two hundred pins in each receptacle.

Anne pulled open a panel door on the top which revealed a miniaturized computer keyboard. Two red lights were flashing. The pod rested on two flat horizontal bottom members with holes drilled at the ends. Nobody had spoken.

Over the interface receptacles there were two handles.

179

I reached out, grabbed the handles, and lifted the eighty-six pounds.

"What are you doing?" the small man hissed.

"We are getting the hell out of here and fast," I replied.

"But we have been told the destruct system is operating. It should be neutralized. Now. Here."

"We can do that on the chopper. We take it back with us. That's what we came for."

"How do I know it won't blow up in two minutes, or on the helicopter? No, we neutralize it here."

Anne and Vickers stood silently by, watching me with pale, strained faces.

"It can be done on the helio, why wait around here?" I asked.

"No, here. I won't move until it is done. The helicopter pilot will not move until I say so. Do it here. Now."

The guy was a Russian plant. They were trying to get Anne to cancel out the self-destruct with ruse and trickery. Tomorrow it would be force and violence.

I blew out a slow breath. So be it. I put my right foot on his left foot and got my left hand very quickly over his nose and mouth. I pulled him up with my right hand, holding his head in the crook of my right elbow, and sharply twisted his head three-quarters of the way around. He struggled, but he was not very strong. I heard the head separate from the spinal column with a sickening crack. His body continued to agitate for a moment, but then went limp. I kept my hand over his mouth but I spoke in his squeaky soprano voice.

"You really must understand this. It has to be done here. Then we go. Only then."

I let his body slip down. He was grinning at me with
180

his chest on the floor but his head was twisted around and his sightless eyes stared at the ceiling.

"How long will it take you to work out the neutralizing sequences?" I asked Anne in my own voice.

"About an hour if everything goes right." She gave a good steady response. Remarkable really, with a grotesque corpse leering up from her feet.

"All right! All right! But do it," I hissed in the dead man's voice.

Anne's hands were moving over the keys. There were the characteristic computer clicks. I hoped the bugs were picking it up. Vickers had found a pencil and pad. "Why?" he wrote.

"Russian ploy to get us to neutralize the pod," I wrote quickly. "They think it's going to blow."

He nodded.

"How is it going?" I asked her.

"Fine. It just takes time. I'm into the second random sequence now."

"Must you have absolute silence for the last fifteen minutes before you introduce the final commands for neutralization?" I asked.

She picked up right away. "Yes, the reprogramming is audio sensitive. The whole sequence of neutralization can be erased by any sound above a whisper. I'll tell you when we get to that."

"Can't you speed this up?" I used the dead man's voice.

I picked up the pad and pencil and wrote. "I'm going to the armory. Keep some sort of patter going. The computer clicks are effective. Keep at it."

They both nodded.

I used the dead man's voice again. "What's happening?

All three red lights are blinking. What are you doing?" I put a little panic into it.

"That means the first phase of neutralization has been completed. Stop pestering me. You're making me nervous. If I make a mistake, I'll have to do it all over again."

She was peevish, complaining, and female. The Russians would love it. She should go to spy school. Probably went to spy school. She had natural talent for this sort of work.

Vickers stood by silently, his face pale and apprehensive. He was the problem, the girl was doing fine. She was scared but functioning well. He was scared and immobilized. Have to watch Vickers.

I pointed to the trapdoor and then to me. Anne nodded. Vickers blinked. A lab table was directly under the trapdoor. I put a stool on the table and got up on it. I put my hands on the plywood access panel and pushed up. There was some resistance. I pushed harder and it lifted up. I gently shoved it to one side, resting the panel on a beam and got my head up through the opening. It was pitch-dark up there. I cast my light about. A six-foot-wide catwalk ran down the center! It disappeared beyond the length of the flashlight beam. I threw the coil of rope up on the catwalk and hoisted myself up.

I could stand easily without stooping. The ridge pole was two feet over my head. Hairy wooden beams angled down, black with dust. The roof shingles were grey with age and water streaked. I headed back down the catwalk, and stopped over the intersecting center bar of the H. Outside, a couple of platoons of Russians would have their eyes glued on the laboratory, rifles and automatic weapons on the ready. Straining their eyes for movement in the perpetual twilight.

I followed the center corridor intersection, then turned up on the left leg of the H. The lab where Anne and

Vickers now waited was directly across from me. I must be somewhere over our cell. I could see openings where other access panels had been fitted into the ceilings below. I went quickly and quietly. Stopping every thirty feet to listen. The catwalk was thick with dust. I could see my footprints where I had just walked. The stale air smelled of ancient wood.

I found the last access panel. It should be right over the armory. I listened for a good two minutes and heard nothing. I lifted the panel out very carefully and laid it down on the crossbeams. I cocked my head, listening again. Nothing.

I tied my length of rope around a roof beam and dropped it down. Listened again. I grabbed the rope and let myself down and hit the floor softly. Froze for a minute. Looked around. Pitch-black. There were no windows. I flicked the flashlight on briefly. Not the armory! Small office. Shit!

I swept the office with my beam, then off. Eight by ten. Battered desk. Shelves with wooden boxes. Not much else. There was a door. I tried it. Locked. Christ! I had another look. Chair behind the desk. Six or seven clipboards with lists. Wooden pegs on the wall. Couple of jackets, foul weather slicker, key ring. Key ring!

The door opened. I was into the armory. No windows. Racks of rifles, six light machine guns, three heavy machine pistols, assault rifles, rockets, metal ammo cases stacked six feet high, two feet wide. I was looking for dynamite sticks or plastic explosive and rope fuse. The place smelled of oil and metal. There were grenade cases on shelves, recoiless rifles mounted on tripods, antitank rocket tubes. No plastic. No dynamite sticks. I did find coils of rope fuse.

Then pay dirt! Small casks of what might be black blasting powder tucked into a corner and hard to see. Labels

183

said they were. I found a bayonet and punched a hole in the lid. Blasting powder! It would do nicely. But how long should the fuss be? I had no idea what the rate of burn would be. Timing would be critical.

I cut a short length of fuse and went back to the office. I lit it and timed it. It sputtered, flamed, and smoked. But I got the burn rate. Dangerous thing to do, but I had to know. Back in the armory, I shoved an end of fuse down into a cask of black powder, piled two other casks on top of it, sprinkled some powder about, and ran the fuse back into the office and up into the attic. Then I cut what I hoped was the proper length of fuse with the bayonet and wedged it into a crossbeam back in the attic. I went back down to the armory, found a sack, and put in two more casks and a length of fuse and then went back up. I hauled the rope back. The whole thing had taken twenty-two minutes. I retraced my steps in the ancient dust back to Anne and Vickers.

I tied the rope around a crossbeam and lowered myself down into the lab. I gave them a thumbs-up gesture, and said loudly, "You must be getting close to the audio override."

Anne picked it up right away. "Yes. Very soon now. Complete silence or we do it all over again."

"Please be careful," I bleated in the dead man's voice.

I gestured for them to go up into the attic. I steadied Vickers on the stool and he struggled up. There was no way Anne would make it that way. I put the stool on the floor, squatted down, and she straddled my shoulders, my head between her legs. I stood up and she went right up into the opening. She wasn't that heavy, but I was pumped full of adrenaline. Vickers hauled her the rest of the way.

I piled the two casks in the center of the lab and heaped a lot of combustibles around them. Then I ran a fuse from the casks up into the attic. Anne grabbed it. I looked

184

around for a final check. Then I hefted the pod over to the rope and tied it fast. Back in the attic, I swayed the pod up and then over onto the catwalk. I poked my head down into the lab. The casks were ready and waiting, the fuse snaking across the tables and up next to me.

Anne and Vickers were watching, waiting.

The Russians were listening to the silence. Looking at their watches, waiting for the fifteen minutes to be up. Maybe smiling. They had been very clever. The whole thing had gone their way.

I lit the fuse. It sputtered and flamed and started licking its way to the casks below.

"Follow me. Be very quiet." I picked up the pod. Three amber lights were blinking at me. "Vickers first with the flashlight. Then me. Anne, you follow. Put your feet exactly where mine have been. You got it?" Maybe she wouldn't fall through the ceiling. Fifty fifty.

She nodded.

"Vickers, go straight down and follow the footsteps you see in the dust. Stop at the intersection."

We moved off. Vickers stopped where he should stop. I took his flashlight. "Be back in a sec," I grinned and went back to the armory. I lit the fuse and returned.

"Okay, straight ahead," I said to Vickers. "You won't see any footprints now. Be very quiet. We are heading for the commandant's office. He should be in it. Listening."

He set off, his flashlight sweeping ahead over the time- and dirt-blackened beams, our feet raising clouds of fine dust on the catwalk. We went down to the end, about a hundred and fifty feet from the lab. I put the pod down and checked my watch. We heard voices below. I laid down in the dust and gestured for them to follow. I heard Nikolay.

"How much time left?" he asked someone.

"Seven or eight minutes."

"But we'll have it!" he chortled. "This was the best way. Why hurt the girl? I told you."

Vickers was laying down facing the laboratory. The wrong way. I gestured for him to turn around and for he and Anne to cradle their faces down, into their arms. We were breathing dust. Our faces and clothes were black with it. It was an unforeseen bonus. Natural camouflage in the eternal dusk outside.

"Soon now," I heard from below.

Soon now, I thought to myself. Anne had her head up. I pushed it down.

Then it came. An awful, ear-splitting roar from the lab and a gush of concussion that swept through the attic and blew dust everywhere. The whole building shook. Shingles blew off the roof. For a second I had a glimpse of the lake. We were covered with clouds of swirling dust. I pushed my face into my coveralls in order to breathe.

There were shouts from below and confused orders. Doors slammed, more shouts, footsteps pounding on the wooden walkways. I looked back and saw flames leaping up from the lab revealing the stirring black figures around me. Anne was sitting up. Looking around. I think it was Anne.

Then there was an enormous explosion as the armory blew and the wooden structure shook again and the roof seemed to sag. We got another blast of dust and stale air. Time to go. There were more explosions from the armory.

I moved to the access panel, opened it, and dropped the rope down into the commandant's office.

186

CHAPTER VIII

We looked like three chimney sweeps who had had an excellent week. Three more explosions shook the building. Rockets. Through the window I saw one oscillating on an insane course into the lake. We stood in the eternal northern twilight and heard shouts, engines racing, doors banging, more explosions. There was a lot of frantic action out there.

"What now?" Anne asked softly.

The commander must have quick and ready answers. No hesitation or indication of weakness or uncertainty. Decisiveness is the key.

"We swipe a chopper and split." That should inspire anyone. Concise, clear, and simple. "I'll take a quick look outside."

I went out the door and saw the flames leaping from the roof of the failed laboratory. They had a garden hose weakly playing on it. Hardly any pressure. No way they could hold the fire back in this old, dry, wooden building. It was a fire waiting to happen.

There was another explosion from the armory. More shouts. More brattle.

I took a quick look out at the chopper pad. It was easy to see in the light of the flames from the armory. I could see figures completely lining the pad every ten feet, weapons thrust forward, on the ready. They looked like the old British square, Kitchener and the Sudan, like the glory and empire decades so vividly hanging on the walls of the Union Jack Club. A mouse couldn't get through.

Go to plan 356. Plan 356B. The float plane still swung on its anchor off the little point below. Do you suppose it could fly at its age? Give it a try. Nobody was paying it any attention. They were concerned with the helicopters, maybe the motor pool.

I took another look. The chopper pad was almost like daylight from the fires and the constant twilight. Trucks and jeeps were going everywhere. We would head for the old float plane. If it didn't have a motor we would melt into the pine forest and become adaptive.

Back into the office. All I could see was their eyes.

"The choppers are out. Soldiers all over the place. We'll try that old float plane out on the lake. If it won't go we'll have to take our chances in the woods. Lay low and figure our next move. Okay?"

"What plane?" Vickers asked.

"I'll show you outside. Let's go."

"I found these," Anne said, holding up our shoulder bags.

"Our stuff still there?"

"I think so. The bottoms are intact."

"Great."

We went outside, keeping close to the wall and down the steps in the front. The fire from the lab was spreading forward.

"That's the plane." I pointed. "Take the pod down to the lake. Keep into the brush and work your way around to the point. Go down that gulley there. Rest in that clump of pine. You are so black nobody will think you're alive."

188

Another rocket wobbled across the sky and fell into the lake. A truck slammed up to the chopper pad with more men. They tumbled out and took position. An ant wouldn't make it through now. Another rumble from the armory. That wing of the H was totally in flame.

"What are you going to do?" Anne asked.

"First, I'm going to give the Russians some more trouble. Then I've got to figure a way to float the pod out to the plane. Get going."

They picked up the pod and wobbled off into the gulley. I couldn't see them. I opened my shoulder bag and took out some boxes of the Crabtree & Evelyn soap. Gift-boxed for Aunt Matilda in Des Moines. The first two were real soap. The third was lemon smelling. Thermite bomb. I broke open the wrapper of the white shoelaces and took out a lace. It was a one-minute fuse. I stuck it in the bar. Then another lemon bomb. I found a lilac bar and shoved in a shoelace. High explosive.

I worked my way toward the first building, quite close to the chopper pad. Everything was still a Chinese fire drill, a circus, demolition derby, Keystone Kops, five women trying to change a flat tire in the rain. I was close to the inner leg of the first building. I hugged the wall and went down to the fourth window. Broke a pane of glass. I lit the two thermite bombs and tossed them in. Should be the kitchen.

I ran back to the front, trying to look invisible, buried myself into a spruce, and waited. Both bombs went off and the kitchen was burning, flames licking out of the windows already. More trouble for the Russkies.

But what to do with my HE? A truck came careening down the path. I quickly lit the bomb and tossed it into the open rear of the truck as it came by, tearing for the chopper pad. It slammed to a halt before the huge MI-6 helio, a Hook, that could carry seventy soldiers. Two men hurried out and then the rear end blew, shoving the truck over onto the side of the MI-6 and then its tanks went up. Truck and chopper were now engulfed in flames and the Keystone Kops went into their routine again. Another rocket shot into the lake twenty feet over the pad. I had established sufficient diversion. McCorkle would approve. When you're hot you're hot. I was on a roll.

How could I float the eighty-six-pound pod out to the plane?

If I had a couple of life jackets, that might work.

If you were a life jacket, where would you be?

Down by the lake. On the dock.

Out in the open?

Probably in a box with a lid.

Would the box be locked?

No. People who need life jackets are generally distraught and have no keys.

But Russian soldiers love to steal.

Why would they want to steal life jackets?

Fuck the Army.

True.

Take a chance?

Right.

I drifted down to the lake and waded into the icy water over to the dock. I kept down below the brush. They were all very busy up there. The building with the kitchen was doing nicely. But the armory had had it. It was just burning now. The chopper pad had a great deal of action. The MI-6 was over on its side, its great blades pointing oddly to the sky.

I was in the water, worked my way to the box, knelt up on the dock, and found two moldy life jackets in the bottom. The good ones had all been stolen. These might do for the pod. There were also living things in the box. Slimy and wet. I didn't look. I went back.

I found the two of them out on the point with the pod. It took some looking. They were pressed into some young evergreens. The float plane was about a hundred and fifty feet off the point, swinging easily on its mooring, effervescing in the light of the fires. It was a very old, canvas-covered, radial engine metal prop, probably American. I guessed an old Stinson from the forties or fifties. Now it had a red star on the side.

I tied the two jackets together and floated them. Anne steadied them as I placed the pod in. The jackets would float the pod adequately. I put the canvas sack with the rope, flashlights, folding shovel, matches, and two shoulder bags on top and waded in. There was a roar from across the cove and a shower of flames and sparks shot into the sky. Something went in the kitchen.

"Okay," I said, "it's cold but it's not that far off. You two get into the rear and we'll play it by ear."

We waded in. The bottom fell away gradually. Anne and Vickers began to side-stroke toward the plane. I got my feet off the bottom and frog-kicked. The pod was about a third in the water but the life jackets were holding. The water was very cold. Halfway there now. the old aircraft still glowing in the light of the fires. Finally we got to the floats. I was shivering. Vickers was up but Anne was having trouble.

"Hang onto the pod," I told him. He did.

I moved over to Anne, wrapped my arms around her thighs, and shoved up. I went down four feet, but half of her was over the pontoon and she struggled up the rest of the way.

The fires were still doing very well across the cove. I had the door to the Stinson open. Vickers and Anne strug-

191

gled up and into the back. I wasn't sure if there were seats or not. Probably not now. Then I straddled the pontoon and hefted the pod onto it. I power clean-lifted it onto the front seat and secured it with a seat belt. No wonder they gave me the strength tests.

Now what to do? Free the aircraft from the mooring right away or try the engine first? Six of one and half of another. If we had no engine and the plane was free, the wind would push us to the opposite shore, away from the Russian camp. If I tried the engine and it wouldn't go, what would we do? We would have to make for the shore anyway.

I opted to check out the cockpit and try the engine before freeing the plane. I got over onto the left float, opened the door and up into the seat. I couldn't believe the condition of the dash. It had been Russianified. It was full of gaping, empty holes. Sightless eyes. No airspeed, no RPM, no altimeter, no mags, no oil pressure, no radio. It did have compass, fuel, and temperature. The dash looked like a frozen spaghetti dinner had exploded on it. Wires, tape, cable running in and out of the empty holes. Russians make Italians look like Germans.

"Doesn't look very good, does it?" Anne asked from the backseat. She and Vickers had lost some soot. But we still looked like something out of the Black Lagoon. We were not as homogeneous or uniform, but more striped now. Variegated.

How do you start this thing? Sometimes you have to crank them. I put the switch on. Hit what appeared to be the starter button, couldn't be anything else. The prop swung but the engine didn't pick up. I tried again. Nothing. Starter sounded good. Prop swung with vigor. What's that other thing? Could it be a choke? Do you have to choke or prime these things? I pulled it in and out a couple of times. Set it halfway. Hit the button and the engine fired right away and settled down in a rattling idle. Coffee grinder. But she held.

I hopped out and cast the mooring free. Immediately the wind starting pushing us to shore. I ran the throttle about a quarter up and we pulled forward. I kicked right rudder and we moved away from the camp, deeper into the lake. I ran the engine up some more. It sounded really bad, like the pistons were rattling a quarter of an inch in the sleeves and the bent and twisted valves were seating into an inch of carbon. Each.

I swung the ancient craft around. Up ahead we could see the blazing camp, not as intense now. The center building was gone. It was burning itself out.

"You all belted up back there?" I asked.

"Yes."

"Okay. Let's see if this old bird has any fly left in her."

I shoved the throttle all the way. Too fast. The engine sagged. I backed off and ran it up gradually. She took and roared into life. The old craft surged into the wind, the camp directly in front of us. We were building speed. But it was too slow. The ancient radial just didn't have the torque anymore. It sounded awful.

Ah now. The wings were starting to build some lift. The floats were coming free of the water, showing less spray. Finally, they were clear. A foot off the water and the camp dead ahead. I kept the stick almost neutral. Not forcing lift. Let her fly herself. Ten feet now. Three hundred yards from the camp. I eased her into the eternal day. Twenty feet. Fifty.

There were little flashes of light up there. Small arms fire. Rifles and sub-machine guns. Then tracers floated up toward us. Heavy machine guns. Two of them. We were flying into a converging cone of fire. Then we were into

193

it with marginal airspeed. With an F-14, I could have stood her on the wing and whipped around before they could bring their guns to bear. In the clattering Stinson, I flew into their fire and saw the tracers bite and pound into the pontoons and up along the wing, punching holes in the fabric. Pieces flew off. The plane shuddered under the impact of the incoming fire as it tore and ripped into the ancient canvas body and up along the wings. A wire popped. We seemed to stagger in the air. Held up by the punishment we were taking.

I heard a moan from the rear. But we were beyond the fire now and I pulled around in a gentle 180, came back over the lake and headed west at five hundred feet, not much above the hills. I could still see gun flashes but we were out of range.

"How is it back there?" I shouted.

"Alan's hit! Oh, dear God . . ."

"Bad?"

"I don't know."

"Better check."

I got up to what I thought was seven hundred feet. Lakes below, small streams. Left window was streaked. Fuel read just half. Thought it was more.

"How is he?" I shouted.

"I think it's bad." Her voice broke.

"What's bad?"

We were getting some turbulence. I let her flop around a bit. She rose up on a bubble, then down. The coffee grinder seemed content enough.

"How is he?"

"There are two holes in the leg. Bullets went right through, I think."

"Bleeding a lot then. Put some pressure above the leg. Stop the bleeding."

194

Fuel down to a quarter of a tank. We had been in the air ten minutes. Both tanks had been hit. We'd never make Finland. Christ, I was running out of gas again. I started to look for a lake. Enough of them down there.

"He's hurt in the chest, too."

"Bullet?"

"Yes."

Oh boy.

We had five minutes to get down. The gauge was going down that fast. Up ahead I saw that odd lake shaped like a figure eight with the gorge and tree cover over it. Good as any. Maybe better than any.

Three minutes and I heard the first engine stutter.

"We have to land. No gas," I shouted. "Get strapped in. Get him ready."

Down to three hundred feet, I curled the Stinson in over the water, throttled back, dropped the flaps, settled down, down. Kissed the water, real smooth. I shoved up the throttle and raced toward the gorge before the engine quit. We roared down the lake toward the gorge, up ahead now and very clear in the half light. The floats were sending up geysers of water. We shot by a sandy beach. There it was, a rift, a split in a hill, joining two lakes by a narrow band of water fifty feet wide. It narrowed in the gorge. I sped toward it, kicking up spray, the engine hesitated, we were losing power. Gorge dead ahead only fifteen feet wide. We were considerably more. The engine sagged, picked up again. Everything was getting very tight. We were under the pine and spruce overcover. The engine quit when we were thirty feet from the narrow gorge.

We drove into it and sheared off six feet of wing on both sides. We wrenched to a stop, the seat belts holding us in. Then I felt a blinding pain in my right foot. The pod, eighty-six pounds of it, had slid out from under the seat belt and crashed down onto my foot. I sucked in a breath and bit my lip. Let the dust settle.

I killed the switch. We were wedged into the gorge under fifty feet of tree cover. No way we could be seen from the air. I tried to move the toes on my right foot, but there was too much pain to tell.

When you're hot you're hot. There's another side to it. When you're cold you're cold. I was forty miles from the Finnish border with a fat girl who trips every twenty feet, a seriously wounded man, an eighty-six-pound weapon of war that was technologically as significant as the atomic bomb was in 1945, and I had one good leg. Things had cooled down considerably in half an hour.

I turned and looked back. Anne was working over his chest. He was slumped over. Very pale beneath the grime.

I opened the door and got out on the float. We were wedged deep into the gorge. High rock walls towered on either side. Overhead, a pine-and-spruce bower. I dropped down into the water. It was three feet deep and I waded out of the gorge onto the small, sandy beach where the stream flared and widened. I fell down. The foot would not hold me up.

Wonderful.

Anne followed me. "What's wrong with your foot?" she asked. No expression in her face.

"How's he doing?" I countered.

"Two bullet holes in the leg. A ricochet in the chest, I think. It's still in there. He's blowing a pink froth out of his mouth."

I shook my head.

"What's the matter with your leg?"

"Pod fell on my foot."

"Is it broken?"

"I don't know. Hurts. Won't take my weight."

"Get your shoe off."

"Why?"

"Now is the time to look at it before the swelling starts. If something is broken we can tell now."

If it is, I wondered, what can we do about it.

I took off my shoe sitting on a rock. Didn't look too bad. I tried to wiggle my toes and had some movement. Considerable pain, too. Anne took my foot in her hands and pressed. Really quite gentle hands, but competent. She squeezed all over. I sucked in some breath.

"Hurts?"

"Hurts."

"Where?"

I pointed. She pressed. I hurt.

"I can't feel any broken bones."

"Good."

"Why not keep it in the cold water. Hold down the swelling."

I got up and moved toward the plane stuck between the cliff walls, water swirling gently underneath the pontoons. I limped. I managed.

"Where are you going?" she asked.

"Alan. I want to have a look at him."

I hopped up on the plane, using my left foot and staying off my right as best I could.

He was propped up in the rear seat. He had a bad hole in his chest. I was less concerned with the leg. He was conscious.

"Bad show," he said. "Banged up a bit." He was being very English.

I got out one of the shoulder bags. It was mine. I located the hunting knife, ripped out the false bottom, and brought out the waterproof, transparent case. I found the medical kit, cleaned up the chest wound, and put a gauze dressing over it. Taped it down. Same for the legs. They were torn up badly and the flesh around the wounds was grimy with dirt and dust. I did what I could do.

He looked awful. Eyes dull and pain-wracked. Pink spittle gathered at the corners of his mouth. I took out a morphine syringe and gave him the full load. It eased the pain in just minutes.

I took my knife and slashed a hole in the back of the rear seat. Then I gently eased his legs through the opening. At least now he could stretch a bit. He seemed to be sleeping. I propped up his head with a front seat cushion. He would be dead in three days. Four on the outside.

Anne watched it all silently. Her lovely blond hair was streaked with dirt. Her face pallid, eyes red and strained. No tears, no breakdown. God, that girl held so much inside.

"Why don't you take a bar of soap from my kit," I said. "And go through the gorge. I think there may be a bit of beach there. Take a bath. Wash your coveralls. Cleanup. I'll start a fire. Stay under the tree cover. Not much more that we can do for Alan."

"That's why you put the plane here? So we can't be seen?"

"Yeah. In a half hour you'll hear them all over the sky."

She nodded and went into my shoulder bag.

"Anne." I stopped. "We're okay. We got the pod and we got away."

She didn't answer but rummaged through my bag.

"Lemon is thermite and lilac is high explosive. The rest is soap." I was grinning at her. She found a bar of soap.

"No towels. We're roughing it. You'll have to put your coveralls on wet. But they'll be clean. I'll get a fire going and you can dry off."

Not even a wan smile

She went off. I found some dry sticks and pine needles. Made a fire under the spreading evergreen cover. In a half hour she was back dripping wet, but she smelled good. She was carrying two white, wet lumps. I handed her a bar of concentrated chocolate. "Dinner," I smiled. She took it.

"Fire feels good," she said, and took a bite. "How can I dry these out? Bra and pants." She held up the wet lumps.

"Oh," I said. "We'll rig up some sticks next to the fire." I cut a few thin limbs from a nearby spruce and shoved them into the sand near the fire. She spread the bra and pants out on the needles for maximum exposure to the heat. She pushed her hair out of her eyes, knelt on the sand, and looked over at me.

"It's pretty primitive, but we can manage. If you like, you could dry your coveralls off the same way. I'm going to build a shelter up there." I inclined my head toward the little beach.

"Maybe later," she said.

"He's sleeping." I nodded toward the plane.

"How's your foot?"

"Better," I lied.

"I could never imagine you being hurt and dependent," she said, and looked into the fire.

"Here," I said, "put this mosquito stuff on. They come in clouds up here. It's great stuff. Just a little around the forehead and neck and they won't bother you."

I tossed a few more sticks on the fire. She got close and let the heat get to her coveralls. I went off and cleaned up, too. That was the first time she had ever indicated she even thought about me. Even now, she had never called me by name.

A Russian chopper came over forty minutes later.

* * *

She slept in the Stinson. I made a lean-to of spruce and pine up on the beach, but under the overhead, and crawled in still wet.

Twice I got up to check on Vickers. The morphine kept him asleep. Four days, no more.

Five times I heard Russian helicopters.

I slept fitfully. Anne was awake each time I went over to look in on Vickers. At six in the morning, with mists rising off the lake, I dug into our emergency case and took out the hooks and fishing line. Time to replenish our food supply.

I turned over some rocks down by the water's edge and found all kinds of crawling things. I baited the hooks and limped down the beach to a big boulder and a swirling pool of black water next to it. My foot had swollen during the night. But the pain was no worse.

I tossed in the line, and the weights carried the hooks down. Ten feet of water. Should I move the bait or let it lie? Was anything down there? I jiggled the line. Fifteen minutes and no luck. I tried more shallow water and had a strike right away. Good size, too. I hauled it in. Five-pound salmon!

I gutted the fish and went back to the dead fire, found some dry needles, cut some fuzz sticks out of dry pieces, got the fire going. Then I cut some young limbs from a spruce and ran one through the salmon. I stuck one end in the sand and let the flames work on the fish. Now and then, I turned it.

I took a high potency vitamin capsule.

A Russian chopper roared overhead at five hundred feet. It thundered and shook the ground. I had a good look at it through the overhead. It was a huge MI-26 Halo, capa-ole of carrying eighty-five men. It would appear they were dropping squads for a ground search.

Anne came out of the Stinson and waded over to the fire.

"What was that noise?" she asked.

"Russian chopper. Big one. They're looking for us."

She had her hair in loose braids. It was fuzzy from the dampness. Her eyes had dark hollows underneath. She seemed calmly desperate. Was she on the edge? Didn't think so. Not yet.

I handed her a capsule.

"What is it?"

"Vitamins."

She nodded. Went back to the stream, cupped her hands in the water, and swallowed. No hesitation. She planned on survival. Life force. Good sign.

"What kind of a night did he have?" I asked.

"Bad. He's hurt very bad." She shook her head. Picked up a twig and worked a pattern in the sand.

I nodded.

"You better have something to eat." I found a big, broad leaf from some sort of bush and put a piece of salmon on it. She took it and ate with her fingers.

"How far are we from Finland?" she asked.

"Thirty-five, forty miles."

"He can't even sit up,"

"No."

"How's your foot?"

"Better."

"Can you walk thirty-five miles carrying eighty-six pounds?"

"Not yet. Have to give it some time."

"How much time?"

I shook my head. "I don't know."

201

"It seems absolutely impossible." Her eyes were frantic

"Nothing is impossible." Pollyana. Look on the brigh side. Every cloud has a silver lining. Boswell's Doctor Mer ryman. Think like that.

Another Russian chopper came over the far end of th lake, headed east. She didn't even look at it.

She turned and looked at me with her eyes really get ting into mine. "You really think we can do it, don't you?"

"Yup. I do."

She shook her head. "You're something. I think yo do, too."

I threw a few more small logs on the fire. Driftwood.

"What can we eat? We will be finished with the emer gency rations in a day or two."

"Plenty of food out there. Fish, birds, reindeer, rabbit fruits, tubers. Food's no problem. Plenty of water."

"What's the problem then?"

I smiled over at her, stuck a tender green shoot of some thing in my mouth. "We have three problems. Vickers i in a bad way, can't be moved, and the Russians are be ginning a ground search. Number two, we got eighty-si: pounds of dead weight to move through wilderness ove thirty-five miles. Number three, at the moment, I hav only one foot."

"You didn't mention the fourth problem."

I wrinkled my brow and chewed on the green shoot "Don't know that one."

"The fat girl who can't walk twenty feet without fallin, down."

"Harkness told you that?"

"Yes."

"You're in the best shape of anybody."

No reply. She started braiding three strands of gree shoot.

I changed the subject. "When did you find out you were going to Finland?"

"When we got back to the club, after the party on the loch."

"Harkness told you then?"

"Yes, he and Henderson."

Ah! Hah!

"How did Henderson feel about your going?"

"He was much more enthusisatic than Harkness. Harkness knew you wouldn't like the idea."

"So Henderson pushed it and that was just a few days ago, after the pod had gotten into the camp, and they started kicking Vickers around."

"Yes."

I nodded. It was beginning to make more sense.

She looked over at me and started to work on another grass braid. "Why did you kill that man? I couldn't believe it was happening. So fast. Awful. You seemed to have almost planned it." She shuddered.

"The Russians planted him to get you to neutralize the pod. They were convinced the self-destruct was operational and counting. They beat up Vickers and couldn't get anywhere. When the man wouldn't go for the chopper right way, I was convinced."

She worked on the grass braids. She had lovely hands. A woman's hands. She didn't belong here with death all round.

"I didn't know your name was Smallpiece, but they let me see part of your record. No one could believe the violence. I believe it now."

I looked away.

Her eyes were very wide. "Do you like to do it?"

"I have to do it."

That was no answer and she knew it.

203

I got up and waded over to the Stinson. Vickers was still asleep. There was dried pink spittle at the corners of his mouth. I checked the dressings on his thigh. Sniffed the wounds. Rotten flesh and spreading. I changed the dressings. Cut some fabric from the seats and made wash cloths and towels. I cleaned him up some more. At least we had plenty of soap.

Eight in the morning and the sun was strong. It would be a warm day. There were only a few fair weather cumulus in the sky and the lake was a deep, glinting blue saucer surrounded by mounting tiers of spruce and pine. The air had a woodsy fragrance and there was no sound but the birds.

I wanted desperately to get moving, but my foot wouldn't hold me up much over a hundred yards. Action types have a real problem with inaction. We were stuck here, and the Russians were all over the sky. How many search parties had they put in the woods? I looked about for Anne and saw her walking down from the little beach. Her coveralls were open three buttons down. I saw a white strap underneath.

We went back to the fire. I handed her a silk map of the area that had been part of the emergency kit, a compass, and one of the Swiss army knives.

I opened up the map and showed her the figure-eight lake.

"This is where we are. Over here, to the west, is Finland. We will have to go this way." I ran my finger to the west. "There are a couple of lakes in the way. But there's a river here and a small village, only ten or twelve huts. We passed over it on our way to the Russians. I saw some boats. The river flows toward Finland, maybe twelve or fifteen miles almost due east. If we can get a boat, maybe we won't have to walk all the way."

204

Her eyes widened.

"But there seems to be a considerable distance from here to the village," she said.

"About seven miles as the crow flies. Trouble is, we aren't crows."

Another helio swept over the lake. Low and throttled down. They circled over the far end and came back. Then they flew east. Good sign.

The sun got hotter and dried things out. Her coveralls were still dust-streaked. Her neck and ears were grimy.

"Look, Anne," I said, "we are going to be here a while. If you want to wash out your stuff again, you can. The sun is out and there is a bit of breeze. Take some soap, walk around the bend, and wash out everything again. Hang it up to dry, but watch out for the Russians. Take a bath. I'll keep my eye on Alan."

She considered it. "Okay."

Cleanliness is next to godliness, and in the woods cleanliness is hard to come by.

I tossed her a couple of washcloths cut from the seat fabric. She drifted down the beach and out of sight behind the pines.

I found a straight, two-inch round piece of wood that might make a crutch. I spent the next two hours whittling and shapping a piece to fit under my arm. Not bad. It took the weight off my foot. The swelling had gone down.

Alan was conscious. I gave him another morphine shot. You could smell his leg in the growing heat of the cabin.

Anne came back with her coveralls clean and dry, her neck and ears glowing. Her golden hair caught the sun. She let it run with the breeze. I was sitting on a rock finishing up my crutch. She understood what I was doing right away.

205

"Good idea," she said. She held out her hand, palm up. "What are these?"

I picked one of the berries up, sniffed, then ate it. "Looks like blueberries, but they're only native to North America. Something like them."

Her eyes went wide with pleasure. "There's a whole meadow filled with them back there!"

"Lot more than that out there," I smiled.

"How's Alan?" The smile faded.

"About the same."

She nodded.

"I'll pick some after lunch."

"Good."

I caught a pike for lunch and roasted it over the fire. We had two concentrated fruit bars for dessert. She checked on Vickers.

"His leg smells bad," she said, and looked down.

"I know."

"Nothing we can do?"

"No."

She let out a sigh. "He was conscious," she said. "Quite rational, really. Wanted to talk. Seemed better."

"I gave him some morphine."

"Oh."

"He's not better."

No reply. Her hands were twisting in her lap. A fish jumped in the lake and startled her.

"You got your map, mosquito repellent, and knife?"

"Yes."

I tossed a square of cloth from the back of the pilot's seat. "Why don't you go off to that meadow and get us some berries for supper? If you hear a chopper, get under a tree or a bush fast. Okay?"

My idea was to keep her busy and not thinking to

much. Conquer the small tasks. Achieve something. What could we do anyway?

She ran a hand over her forehead. "All right. You'll be here?"

"I'm not going anyplace, babe."

Her brow wrinkled for a moment, and then she set off. I smoothed and fine-whittled my crutch. Dug out a hole in the bottom of the curved part that went under my arm to take the pole. I used the Swiss Army knife.

"Smallpiece?" Vickers from the Stinson. It was a cry more than a call.

I waded over and got up into the cabin.

"How ya doing?"

"Get me out of here. I want to see the sun." Thin voice. No strength. I had to bend down to hear him.

"I don't think that's a very good idea. You shouldn't be moved."

His eyes had gone dull, lifeless, and were sunk deep into his head, now shrunken, brittle, wasted. He had no color at all. Grey. His lips were cracked and dry. "Get me out. Please."

I considered it. He was dying anyway. We were doing all we could.

"You sure?"

"Yes. Please."

I got my arms under him and lifted him out. Not easy with one foot. I propped him on a float, got into the water, and carried him to the beach, over to the ashes of the fire. I put him down by a rock, resting his back against it. Not good for a man with a chest wound. He didn't seem to mind.

"Where's Anne?" he asked in his tired, frail voice.

"She found a meadow of berries."

He smiled. "Good. Good. That's good."

207

He looked around. Craned his head up. He nodded. "They can't see us here?" The morphine really had him.

I nodded. "Right."

He coughed. Not really a cough. He didn't have the strength to cough. It was a weak hack, a sputter. It brought pink froth to his mouth. He wiped it away on the back of his hand. Studied it. Turned his head to me."

"I'm dying," he said.

I just looked at him.

"I'm holding you up."

I had my eyes on the lake. Very blue. Peaceful.

Another weak hack. More spittle. He put his head back and squinted at the pine spruce bower overhead. He never saw it. He came back to me.

"You've got to kill me, Smallpiece."

I sucked in a breath. Shook my head at him. Ran my tongue over my lips. I studied him. I knelt beside him. He was right.

"Do you know what you're saying?"

"Yes. I've thought about it. All night. I'm done for. You know it. I can see it in your eyes. Sadness, but you know."

"But Anne . . ."

"She doesn't want to believe it. Can't."

"I don't know . . ."

"You must. Please. The pain."

"I really . . ."

"Anne. You're her only hope. If you . . ."

"I'm not sure . . ."

"You have to get her out of here."

"I really . . ."

"Please. Anne. Plea—"

My fist was already driving into his jaw. His head snapped back onto the rock. He was unconscious instantly.

208

With my left hand I pinched his nostrils tight. I clamped my right hand over his mouth. The autonomic nervous system took over and he struggled for breath. Body over mind. He was surprisingly strong for a man in his condition. The struggle lasted thirty seconds. He slumped back. I did not take away my hands for two minutes. I checked for pulse. None. I listened for heartbeat. None. He was dead.

I knelt on the sand beside him. "Jesuschrist," I said, and repeated it two more times.

Two MIG-31's drifted over at a thousand feet, heading to the Finnish border. They were throttled way down.

I found the folding trenching shovel and went up the beach and stared to dig on my knees. In an hour I was down deep enough.

Anne saw me and started to run. She dropped the berries. She saw Vickers sprawled up against the rock. Head thrust up, eyes closed, mouth open. She stooped down and knew.

She turned to me. I had never seen eyes like that. Wide and terrible and full of hurt and pain.

"You killed him?"

I looked helplessly at her.

"Yes."

She gasped and her mouth worked and her terrible eyes burnt into my soul.

"He was my brother!"

And she came at me with both hands and I toppled backward on my one leg and felt pain in my foot again. I fell down, moaned, and pulled my knee up toward my chest, lying on the sand, next to Vickers's grave.

CHAPTER IX

The pain eased. I stretched my leg out.

She looked at me with her mouth open, breathing heavily. The anger and horror in her eyes were replaced by something else. I couldn't read her. Regret? Ambivalence? Realization?

I rolled over and struggled to my feet. Hobbled across to Vickers, still lolling against the rock, his arms outstretched. I hadn't noticed the small trickle of dried blood in the corner of his mouth. I gathered him up and, with some pain in my foot, carried him to the hole. Anne backed away. Her face was white. I laid him down by the grave and got down into it. Then I took him in my arms again and lowered him into the sand. I grabbed the rope that was secured to a nearby tree and pulled myself out.

I went over to one of the wings that had sheared off when we drove into the gorge and cut off a piece of canvas sufficiently large. I lowered myself back into the grave and pressed the shroud around the body and pulled myself out again.

I turned to Anne.

She came over, somewhat hesitantly, and looked down. I stepped back and walked down the sandy beach about a hundred feet. Sat on a rock and considered the peaceful blue lake and the pristine pine forest rising from its shores. No clouds now. Late afternoon. The lake was a flawless image of the sky. Everything on the land had gone bronze.

Not a bad day or place for a funeral. Cosmic place.

She still stood silently at the grave, a rumpled, dumpy figure in her shapeless Soviet coveralls. Her golden hair shielding her face as she looked down. The girl always seemed to carry some secret sadness. She started shoveling sand.

I let her work at it for fifteen minutes and then went over and helped her. I knelt and pushed sand into the grave. We filled it together. No talk. In ten minutes the job was done. I walked on it, packing it down, smoothing it out with my hands. Alan Vickers, who discovered an equation that might have made him one of the significant physicists of this century, lay in a sandy grave beside a nameless Russian lake, with just a sister to mourn him. But a lot of people have died with less than this.

I went back to the Stinson and looked for a beat-up harness that I had seen stuffed down beside the rear seats. It was an old, torn backpack. Civilian, not military. The aluminum frame was bent, it was missing a lot of straps, but the heavy shoulder harness looked serviceable. I had to carry the accelerator out on something. I tossed the pack down on the sand, sat on a rock, scratched my chin, and tried to figure how to do it.

Anne had found a few flowering plants and had dug them into the grave. She was on her knees smoothing out the sandy earth when the chopper came in very low over the gorge. She stood up, frozen by the grave. She almost seemed to be protecting it. I rushed over and pulled her down by a thick clump of young spruce. We rolled into it in a busy tangle of arms and legs.

The chopper was a hundred feet over the lake and just

a hundred and fifty feet off the stream as it meandered out from the gorge. The helicopter moved closer, its whirling blades churning up the lake's calm surface. It did a slow, ominous three-hundred-sixty-degree turn. Stopped, swung, and pointed at the gorge again. I saw the sunlight glint off the windshield and the two intent figures inside. The chopper inched forward, nose down, tail high, biting into the air with the tilted blades. It stopped. They were checking the gorge. I don't think they could see the Stinson. Too low.

They stayed there for maybe a minute just looking, slowly turning.

Then the craft rose and went down the lake and lowered over the far end. It swung around easily again. Looking. Finally, It rose and flew east over the jagged horizon of pines. Silence returned once more and so did the realization of our problem.

"We get out of here tomorrow morning when there is enough light," I said, and went back to the Stinson. I hoisted myself up on the right float, opened the door, and worked the pod out of the cabin. I lowered it to the float, dropped into the water, and carried it to shore. I knelt and eased it onto the sand. I did everything on my left foot.

Anne walked over and looked at the pack and the pod.

"You can't possibly think you could carry the accelerator out with that thing? On your one foot?"

"I'm going to try."

I went back to my problem. Engineering a broken, worn-out backpack to carry an eighty-six-pound compact weight. I would need a lot of rope.

Anne sat on a nearby rock and considered the lake. Now and then she would look over to see what I was doing. She would run her hand through her hair and shake her head. A female gesture. Normally, it would give me pleasure.

I took out the fish line and baited it.

"Why not try getting some supper," I said. "Pike bite pretty good down by the reeds in the shallows. Salmon seem to like it around the big boulder over there by that dead pine."

Eye contact for just a moment. Nothing there. But she took the line and went off and I went back to my problem. I cut some rope, straightened the frame, tried a few things. Laid the pod into the frame, then I bent it closer, tighter. I hefted the pack and pod together. Didn't rattle too much. Seemed secure. I bound more rope around it. Then on my knees, I shrugged into it. I used my crutch to get up. Eighty-six pounds were now on my back. I practiced crutching around. Jesus.

Do it!

Dusk drifted in and the birds quieted down. The eternal twilight settled around us. Land of the midnight dawn.

Anne caught a big seven-pound salmon. She cut some fuzz sticks and got a fire going. Then she gutted the fish and skewered it on a green stick. She learned fast.

I practiced walking. Tied a few more ropes here and there. Developed my crutch technique. I must not put weight on my right foot. I had to learn to depend on the crutch.

The fish was good. Roasted to perfection. We ate fruit bars from the emergency kit. The twilight wore on and the deep silence of the northern wilderness settled on us. Two Russian helicopters came by.

I had assembled all our gear. Made a pack for Anne out of the two shoulder bags and the canvas sack. I cut more canvas off the Stinson, folded them into squares, and put them into Anne's pack. At ten-thirty, in the ever-present dusk, I washed my face, brushed my teeth, and felt the beard stubble. I was losing my high forehead. The brown dye was out of my hair. I was looking more like myself. But I only had one leg.

"I'm turning in. We should get clear of here by six," I said to her. I headed for my lean-to of pine and spruce.

"You staying with the plane?" I asked.

"Yes."

"I don't know if that's a good idea."

She said nothing.

I went up to my shelter, an A-frame of small spruce and pine trees that I had cut and laid along a ridge pole and bound onto the limb of a big spruce. I crawled inside, the air was pungent and rich with pine resins. Smelled like Christmas. I lay down on a soft bed of needles and new growth boughs and checked my watch. Eleven o'clock at night, dusk outside, but darker here inside my piney burrow. Sleep came hard. I kept seeing Vickers' wasted face. A jet came over quite low. Eleven-thirty. I heard something stirring outside, and my hand went to the handle of the survival knife. Six-inch blade.

It was Anne.

"Move over," she said.

There were too many old ghosts in the ancient Stinson. She opted for life.

I moved over. She wedged in beside me.

I could smell the soap in her hair. She kept well over on her side, almost into the spruce.

We were both asleep in fifteen minutes. I awoke in the morning to find her arm draped over my chest and her face buried into my neck.

We finished the salmon for breakfast. I walked through the place. Everything of value was in our packs, including the rough washcloths and towels I cut from the plane's

214

seats. I had given Anne a compass and map from her emergency kit to carry in a pocket. She had a Swiss army knife. She knew the direction we would be taking.

I got into my pack and felt the enormous weight of the pod on my shoulders. Anne stood silently by Vickers's grave. I moved off slowly up the rise, taking my time, learning to use the crutch. I waited for her. Looked at the old Stinson buried into the walls of the gorge. Then at the small grave and at the sad figure by it. She seemed to take a deep breath, turned away, and came up the rise. I moved off and into the wilderness.

Rhythm was part of the answer. Left foot out, down on the crutch, take a breath. In with the good air, out with the bad. Foot, crutch, air. Foot, crutch, air. Then take a look. Go around that tree. Watch out for that root. Foot, crutch, air. Don't think about the weight. Move on. Only forty miles as the crow flies. You're not a crow.

We were out in a small meadow of wildflowers.

See? We were doing nicely.

I looked back at Anne. Her hair was working loose of the braids. She kept pushing it back.

Foot, crutch, air. We were back into the forest, heading almost due west. I was beginning to feel it in the right armpit as the crutch pushed into it.

After half an hour, I called a halt. I sank to my knees and worked out of the harness. Anne slipped out of her pack and had a good look at me.

"How is it going?" she asked.

"Fine. Really good."

"You would never say, anyway."

"No. Really."

I got out some airplane canvas and wrapped strips around the crosspiece on the crutch. Then I made several loops of the stuff to slip over my shoulder and under my arm.

We were deep into the spruce-pine wilderness, heading west. We might have gone half a mile.

"You okay?" I asked.

"Good as you," she replied.

I blew out a breath and got back into the pack, up on my feet, back on our way. Wonderful, I thought.

Foot, crutch, air. Don't think about anything but maintaining the essential rhythm. Balance and rhythm, that's the secret. In and out of the trees. Branches reached out for us. Held us back. Roots grabbed at our feet. Trees so thick we had to backtrack and find another way.

An hour and a half. A mile from the Stinson? Were we walking a circle? Was it just over that rise? No. My infallible sixth sense kept us glued on a course due west. I called a halt again, and slumped down onto the humus, looked overhead at the conifers reaching to the sun.

Anne was trying to do something with her hair. She had several scratches across her face. No complaint from her. She kept looking at me.

I dug out two concentrated chocolate bars. We chewed them silently, getting some quick energy back into the bloodstream. I lay on my back, arms outstretched, easing the muscles. Right foot felt great. Everything else was in agony. I rolled over on my stomach and looked around. We were in a sea of pine trees. Nothing differentiated. Nothing stood out. I checked my map. Checked the compass heading. I knew we were here and going to there. You could get claustrophobia in a place like this. We were in an ocean of trees. We were in the bottom of an ocean of trees.

Left, crutch, air. Left crutch air. It's all a matter of rhythm. Keep your right foot off the ground. I was breathing through my mouth, taking huge gulps. I could feel my strength running out of the pores with my sweat. I teetered forward.

The deer saved us. Probably reindeer. We came across a trail and it went directly west. No more bashing our own path. I followed it. Course of least resistance. We had been out four hours. I began to stagger. Bounced off a couple of trees.

"Take it easy, Smallpiece. You got a lot of mileage ahead of you." McCorkle. He finally had to get into it.

"Who told you to come up?" I asked.

"The girl is having a rough time of it back there," he said.

"Since when do you speak for someone else? You are an abberation of my superego. A psychic phantom. An illusion. I make you up."

"Better knock off for a while. Eat another chocolate bar. Take a breather."

I crashed into a boulder. Staggered upright.

"Good idea. Chocolate bar."

"Now you're using your head."

"Okay. Okay."

" 'Bout time."

He always has to have the last word.

I fell down by a small stream.

I got out of my pack and felt like I could jump over a one-foot hurdle. Anne was sitting on the ground, leaning up against a tree. Her face had disappeared under her hair again. She shoved it back and took great gulps of air. I gave her a chocolate bar. She offered me no gratitude.

I put my face in the stream and had a long drink. Cold and clear. Best water I ever had. She did the same. I checked my map. Why did I check my map? I had no

217

landmarks to sight on. The compass told me were heading west. Deer know where to go.

I struggled into my harness. Anne looked at me.

"Do you know why you do this?" she asked. Voice low, husky. Eyes went right into me.

"Tell me."

"Challenge."

"Right."

"You can't ever let anything conquer you. Beat you."

"You got it, babe."

"The forest is challenge. The pod is challenge. The Russians are challenge. Your foot adds interest."

"I'm having fun?"

"In a way."

"Like Hillary and his mountain?"

"Exactly."

"Bullshit."

I shrugged into my hair shirt.

"Come on, kid, we're on our way again. Gonna have some more fun." I held up her pack. She got into it.

Left, crutch, air. Left, crutch, air. It's all a matter of timing, you know. Rhythm. Little guys with timing and rhythm can hit a ball out of the park. Big guys press, lose their timing, and fall on their face. Timing and rhythm. She thinks I think it's a game. Some dames. Where did she get that idea?

I fell on my face into a bush. Lost my timing. See what I mean?

Then I began to hallucinate. There was water up ahead, I could see it through the goddamn spruce. Mirage. Deserts always have mirages. Thirsty men on the desert see mirages all over the place. But this was no desert. We were in the Russian pine forest, headed for Finland, in order to save the Western world.

218

No mirage. We had made the lake!

Eight miles through the wilderness carrying eighty-six pounds on one leg. Challenge she said. That was garbage. It was an operational exercise. I fell down thirty yards from the lake. Fell on my left side. Right foot was doing great.

I was out of the harness. Anne struggled up and I helped her out of her pack. Her hair was all over her face. She had cuts and scrapes. She was beautiful. I hugged her. She let herself get hugged. We put our faces in the water and drank. I rolled over and looked at the sky. I checked my watch. Five in the afternoon. I lay on my back and got my breathing in order. Anne sat propped against a tree.

The longest journey starts with the first small step. Ancient Chinese proverb.

I got my strength back. We recovered. Anne caught a salmon. I made an evergreen shelter again by lashing small spruce and pine to a ridge pole with one end on the ground and the other supported by two crossed shear poles. I made a fire in front. We ate the fish and had two more fruit bars. Anne cut some green, new growth for a mattress and put down a square of airplane canvas. Kept one for a blanket.

The Russians were still overhead, but we were too deep into the trees to be seen. We were on a very long lake that ran north and south. We would have to detour eight miles to walk around it. We wanted to go west, but due west was directly across the lake. Half a mile, maybe a little less. The more I looked, the more I didn't want another walk. The half a mile across the lake was beginning to look smaller. Could we float the pod and swim it? What was the water temperature? Forty, forty-five degrees? How long can people swim in forty-five-degree water and stay alive?

219

Anne was picking junk out of her hair.

"It has to be cut," I said.

"What?"

"Your hair. It gets in your way. It impedes function. It has to be cut."

"No."

"Anne, you can grow new hair when we get out. Long hair and dead is not in your interest."

She looked helpless.

"I can cut it. I do my own."

"What?"

"I cut my own hair. Always have since I was twelve. We have scissors in the emergency kit. I'll do a good job. We may have a swim tomorrow."

She pointed across the lake. "Over there?"

"Maybe. We have to think about it."

She grabbed a hank of hair. Made a hopeless face. "It's really a mess."

"Let's cut it. Now." I went to the shoulder bag, got out the scissors. "On that rock, over there." I pointed.

"I don't know."

"When we get out of here, you can grow hair down to your ankles."

She moved over to the rock, it was a chair-height rock. She shut her eyes. I took out the scissors and chopped a couple of inches below her ears. Then I shaped it using the scissors and sometimes the very sharp Swiss Army knife. She kept her head down, eyes closed. She was trembling.

With no comb, I had to run my hands through her hair, fluffing it, shaping it, tapering it. I was totally immersed in the job. Took maybe twenty minutes. She still had her eyes closed.

I put my hand under her chin and raised it up. Her

220

eyes opened. I stepped back. The change was substantial. I sucked in a breath. What was essentially a survival decision had profound esthetic consequences.

She studied me, trying to read my expression. Wondering.

I held out the stainless steel signal mirror from the emergency kit. She took it and looked. She looked a very long time. Turning her head to the right and left.

"It's very different," she said.

"Yeah."

"Do you like it?"

"I do. Big change."

She studied herself some more. She was very serious. Eventually, she smiled.

"I like it. I really do."

That was the first big, genuine, unrestrained smile I had seen from her.

"But it needs a good wash." She found a bar of soap, went down to the lake, and lathered up. She dried out with a homemade towel. Held up the mirror, ran her hands through her hair, fluffed it up. Another smile. For a moment, I thought of yesterday afternoon. We were far away from yesterday afternoon.

"You don't think I look like a boy?" she asked.

"Nobody could ever think that."

The eternal evening wore on. I sat on the edge of the lake and looked at the finger of land that pushed out toward us from the opposite shore. It was a small headland with a hog back rising about three hundred feet out of the lake, pine covered. How far away? Half a mile? Maybe less. Easy swim in temperate water. My shoulder ached and I had difficulty lifting my arm over my head. The muscles were still in trauma from the insane trek through the bottom of the pine forest. No way I could do another eight miles tomorrow.

"You think we could swim that?" Anne had silently come up and sat down beside me.

"What do you think?" I asked.

"Doesn't look that far."

"What kind of a swimmer are you?"

"Very good. I'm a floater." She bit her lip. Studied her hands.

"Water's very cold."

"Yes."

"Think you could make it?"

"You would make a raft for the accelerator?"

"Yeah."

"We'd have to push it. Stay in the water?"

"I think so."

She blew out a breath and studied the headland lying so peacefully in the tranquil lake. "You couldn't take another hike in the woods. You became a little crazy in there. Started to fall down." She shook her head.

"I know."

"And we would be going in the wrong direction. Not west."

"That's right."

She looked again. "I could make it."

"I think so, too."

"What would we do when we get across?"

"Rest up a bit." I dug the map out of my pocket and laid it on the rock and put my compass beside it. "There's a village about eight or nine miles southwest from that headland." I ran my finger down to it. "There's also a road. Here."

She nodded and put her finger on the village.

"I saw some boats pulled up on the shore. There's a

river here, and it goes west. If we can get a boat and go down the river, we would knock another ten miles off. We drift and I don't have to carry that damn thing. We ditch the boat here, where the river bends south, and hike another six miles through the jungle to the border. About here."

She studied the map. "You would have to carry the pod from the headland to the village?"

"Yes. But we could rest up over there for a few days."

"The Russians will be looking for us."

"Chance we have to take."

She sighed. "It doesn't really look that far away."

"I know. The more you look at it, the closer it seems."

The sky had gone grey and had the look of rain. I tossed the last remaining square of canvas over the lean-to. Then I took the four feet of serrated wire from the emergency kit and cut down some trees with four-and-five-inch trunks, hacked off the limbs with the survival knife, and then cut five-foot lengths. I had enough for a raft to float the pod.

It began to rain and we got into the pine shelter. It was about ten at night, but the sky had a soft luminescence and I could see the headland through the mists across the lake. Anne came in with the signal mirror, and sat up drying her hair. She had finally got all of the trail junk out of it.

She looked at herself in the mirror, mouth open, running her tongue along her teeth.

"I really like it," she said, and tilted up her chin, turning her head left and right. Her mouth was still open as she studied herself. Then she lay back and folded her arms behind her head, looking up. The soap was floral scented. Didn't know which flower. Jesuschrist. I was acutely aware of female. Gorgeous profile.

I rolled over and listened to the rain hit the canvas. She

223

had a face designed for short hair. Some women don't. Her eyes were large and the brows seemed darker and more fully arched. Her eyelashes were very thick and dark. She had her mother's eyes. I never noticed the curve of the upper lip before, and the pimples were going. Her skin was clearing. Salmon and fresh air were working wonders. Or was I in the Russian wilderness too long and anything was looking good to me? She was a beautiful girl.

I fell asleep marveling at women, their faces and their hair. Too much for me.

We finished the cold salmon for breakfast and I tied the raft together with rope. The day was clear and the woods were filled with sparkling diamonds from last night's rain. You could smell the lake—early-morning lake, musty and alive.

The raft floated with the pod. I secured Anne's pack to it and stuffed the whole thing with pine boughs. From the air, it would seem like a bush washed loose from the shore.

It looked like we were going for it.

"Still want to give it a shot?" I asked her.

"Yes."

"How long will it take you to set the pod to blow in two hours?" I asked.

Her brow wrinkled, and she turned to me. She no longer hesitated on eye contact. "Why? What do you mean?"

"Let's have an answer."

"It will take me five minutes to set it. Why?"

"Let's say we don't make it. Let's say we get killed, drowned out there. The pod drifts around. Eventually somebody sees it. We lose it to the Russians again."

She nodded. "Yes. Of course. Two hours you said?"

"We couldn't survive out there for two hours. We have to reach that hogback in one hour."

I took the canvas off the pod. She reached underneath

224

and the panel lid popped back. She studied the three LED readouts. Hit a key. Got a blue light. Watched the numbers again. Hit three keys. The blue went out and two ambers came on. The LED's went into slow motion. One stopped entirely. Now she was holding a key down and punching others. All of the lights were out. The numbers slowed even more, then stopped. The whole thing looked dead. She slowly hit eight keys. I counted and three red lights came on. The numbers started to roll again.

She turned to me. "It's done. It blows in two hours."

"How long to cancel out?"

"One minute."

"Okay kid, into the drink."

We waded in. The longest journey begins with the first small step. Yeah, I heard it before.

God, it was cold. We had our shoes off and stuffed into the raft. I pushed it away and floated. Now the cold hit me in the chest. I sucked in a breath. God!

I looked at Anne and nodded.

We were afloat, over our heads. I kicked the raft ahead of me. Frog kick. Anne was pushing easily beside me. What kind of a girl does stuff like this? She hadn't complained once and I killed her brother.

In with the good air, out with the bad. No crutch this time. But rhythm was still part of it. Frog kick, breathe. Frog kick, breathe. God it was cold. One hundred yards out and the hogback looked closer. No currents blocked us or pulled at us. It was just the cold. We had to conserve our strength. Keep our energy expenditure down. Don't thrash around. Slow and steady does it. Frog kick, breathe. Did it yesterday. Do it today.

Three hundred yards out. I could see individual trees now, and the top of the hogback seemed to have patches of rock showing through.

Halfway. Point of no return. No way back. Frog kick, breathe. I shoved the raft ahead of me.

Oh, Christ! Chopper. Drifting right over the lake.

"Get into the pine cover. We have to stop."

Anne nodded. We waited.

I checked my watch. We had been out fifteen minutes. I didn't know what the water temperature was. If it was forty degrees, we could last maybe forty-five minutes. Forty-five degrees, maybe an hour. If it was fifty degrees, possibly an hour and a quarter. We were young and healthy. No way this water was fifty degrees.

The chopper drifted overhead and moved down the lake. Got lost behind the pine horizon.

We waited, losing too much time.

"Let's move," I said.

My legs were getting numb and my hands were getting blue.

I kicked and we moved.

Hypothermia. Low blood temperature brought on by exposure to extreme cold. Symptoms? Shivering, numbness, marked muscular weakness, drowsiness, confusion, disorientation, unconsciousness, death.

I was numb and shivering. Anne's chin was quivering. Frog kick, breathe, shove. Damn, I could see birds in the trees along the top of the hogback. Two hundred yards. Push. Kick. Why?

I didn't want to kill the guy.

She must know I didn't want to kill the guy.

How did I know he was her father?

What was her name?

I should know her name. Shouldn't I know her name?

Nice out here. Peaceful.

Nice lake.

Rest, maybe.

"Get off your ass, Smallpiece, and swim." McCorkle. I knew his name.

"You back? I thought you died yesterday."

"Push this raft. You want the girl to do it all? You a girl?"

"Trying to get my goat, McCorkle? Call me girl? Old trick. I'm wise."

"Move it, lady."

"Okay. I'm movin' it, for christsakes."

I kicked, I pushed. Legs wouldn't work. The girl. How's the girl? "Hey, kid? you doin' okay? You look blue, kid. Blue girl. Never saw one of those before. Nice. Blue girls. What will they think of next?"

"Colin, get your head out of the water!" The blue girl was pulling my head up. "Look, we're almost there."

I felt something under my feet. Muck, soft stuff.

She was pulling me.

"I can't lift you. Get up. Get up!"

Nice here. Why get up?

"You the blue girl?"

She was tugging me, grabbing.

"Please, Colin. Get up!"

She was not the blue girl. Anne was her name. You think I didn't know that? Christ!

"Okay. Okay. You're as bad as he is."

I was on all fours, crawling up on the shingle, free of the lake. I headed for the tree line just like a rabbit for cover.

She was pulling off my coveralls. Rubbing my arms, chest.

"Colin, are you all right?"

"Only hurts when I laugh, babe."

"Get up. You have to move."

"Okay." I was starting to think again. I was sitting on

227

a shingle beach. I was in Russia trying to save the world. I stood up. Wobbly.

Anne was into the tree line. She was making fuzz sticks. She had a fire going. I was still pretty slow. I picked up a few dry pieces and tossed them on. Sat down. Felt the warmth. I was stripped but for my shorts. She wasn't blue anymore and she was wearing a bra and pants. We stayed by the fire and thawed out.

"This is getting too much," I said.

Anne nodded. "You started to go out there," she said.

"I know."

"Who's McCorkle?"

"Marine sergeant. Guardian angel. Figment of my imagination."

"He got you mad. Made you swim."

"Yeah. That's how he works. He's a sonofabitch."

I was warming up. Anne had her color back.

I was thinking. "How come you made it better than me?"

She smiled. Nodded. Looked at me. "You know how much body fat you have?"

"Yeah, I had the tank test. Why?"

"You're all muscle mass. No fat."

"Right."

"I'm a fat girl. Remember? I have more insulation. The cold got to you faster and you were working a lot harder."

"You saved my life."

She smiled. Seemed to like the idea.

"I think you saved mine, back there at Camp Kirov." She sobered down. "I know what they would have done to me the next day."

Now the sun was getting to us. Delicious warmth. Then I saw the pod on the raft. I checked my watch. An hour and three quarters! Jesus! It would blow in fifteen minutes.

We were still not thinking too well.

I shook Anne by the arm.

"Hey kid, we better neutralize the pod. We have fifteen minutes. Hope you remember how."

We got back to the accelerator on the run. Not a panic run, but a run nonetheless. She punched some keys. Lights blinked, LED's went insane, Anne smiled.

"Done," she said, and I hoisted it up and into the tree line.

"Kinda close. Forgot all about it."

We dried our coveralls out by the fire and let the sun help.

We drowsed and recovered.

"It looks sort of like half a loaf of bread," Anne said, pointing up at the hogback. "It's a sugar loaf. See the icing on top?"

"Yeah. The trees are thin up there. Must be rock. Might not be a bad place to camp for a while. We could see in all directions."

"Can you get the pod up there?"

"Sure. Want to give it a try?"

I broke up the raft by saving the rope. Watched the pieces float away. I got back into the harness and felt the familiar weight of the pod on my shoulders. I would have to go easy on my right foot. But no pain today. Cold reduces swelling.

We went up the hogback laterally, taking our time. The pines and spruce at the base were very tall. We worked our way up. In fifteen minutes we had reached the top. It was mostly rock. Solid. Some of the taller trees along the sides and rocky ledges were no more than fifteen or twenty feet overhead. The top of the hill, Anne's sugar loaf, was

229

somewhat caved in, depressed, dished. In the dish, topsoil had formed over the centuries and young evergreens, pines and spruce, were growing there, but most of the surface was rock without vegetation. Empty and open. Windswept. The front, facing the lake, was fairly sheer and, down below, maybe three hundred feet, we saw the shingle beach and a fringe of tall pines growing out of it. It was a rocky headland, a promontory, jutting out into the blue, untroubled lake.

Unlike the frontal cliff face, the hill shallowed down gradually behind us. We had a three-hundred-sixty-degree view of the lakes and the ocean of rippled pine that stretched in ragged layers to the horizon.

I sat on the rocky edge of the front face, and looked out at the far shore, where we had begun our swim. The lake was a brilliant blue and mirrored the puffy cotton ball clouds in the sky. A soft wind sifted through the trees. The quiet spoke of eternity. Were there cities? We were back ten thousand years. Anne rested her arm on my shoulder.

"It's lovely," she said.

"It's Russia." The place was magical. But a chopper might be just over the nearest line of trees. Looking.

I made another pine lean-to, right in the middle of the grove of young trees up the rocky summit, invisible from the air. We settled in. Some sort of crisis seemed to have passed. We were out of the Russian camp. We had the pod and were working our way back. They killed one of us. We got one of them. We were sort of catching our breath, regaining our strength for the next part. Whatever that would be.

We went back to the beach, walked a few hundred feet, found a dark pool of water by some rocks. She caught a five-pound salmon. We found some fruit that tasted lik wild raspberry. We picked a quart and put them in one of the towels cut from the Stinson's seats. Containers, we didn't have.

We ate the fish and fruit for supper.

Day faded to dusk.

We sat on the granite outcropping. Listened to the silence. I leaned against a tree.

"I like it here," Anne said.

"What do you think we ought to do now, Anne?" I asked.

"Recoup," she said.

"Here's looking at you, kid." Why was I sounding more like Humphrey Bogart each day?

CHAPTER X

It rained all night and most of the next day. It rained on and off for the next six days. It kept the Russians out of the sky.

I put two canvas tarps cut from the Stinson up on the ridge pole over the small pines. I placed two more trees across the front of the lean-to. We slept under the third canvas, a make-do blanket. But we were dry and warm under it. Body heat. We were so totally exhausted, so punished from the hike and swim, we didn't move. Couldn't move. Drained. We crawled in, got under the tarp, and were asleep when our heads hit the pine boughs. I didn't realize it was raining until morning and I saw the leaden skies and grey lake.

What do you do to keep busy and productively occupied on a wet, rainy, windswept hilltop in a pine forest, on a small projection of land, in the middle of a lake, surrounded by Russians who wish you no good? You make a bow and arrows, that's what you do.

In the list I had given to the James Bond freak, I asked for six arrow heads and two bow cords. The arrowheads were blue steel, razor sharp on the two wings, ending in a deadly point. The arrows would be forced and twisted into a ribbed socket on the heads, then glued and bound with thread.

I had found a small hardwood tree that might produce an adequate bow. I didn't know what kind of wood it was, but the limbs were both dense and supple. I cut a length with sufficient thickness. Then I searched for pieces that were straight and thin enough for the arrows.

I sat in the entrance of the lean-to and whittled away with the survival knife and shaped the bow. I began with the handle then cut deeper into the wood for the flatter, curved arms of the bow. I was at it all the first day on the sugar loaf.

We had finished the cold salmon and the rest of the fruit. Anne took one look at the sky, pulled the tarp over her head, and went back to sleep. Both of us still drained and shaken from the physical ordeal of the past three days. A cold, wet mist drove in from the west, but the pine lean-to with the tarps over the ridge pole kept us warm and dry.

The bow was beginning to look like a bow and the wood seemed sufficiently flexible. By mid-afternoon, I was using the smaller Swiss knife to fine-cut and smooth. Anne was stirring finally. The sky seemed to lighten and I could see patches of blue to the west. I went back to cutting the notches for the bow string. Had to be careful on this. Not so deep as to weaken the tips but deep enough to firmly hold the cord under the stress of the bowed wood.

I heard an explosion of breath. An agonized wail.

Anne was crying. Deep sobs. Wracking sobs.

I turned to her. She was sitting up, clutching a rumpled piece of paper. She was in torment. Tears streaming unchecked from her eyes.

She looked at me helplessly, eyes wide, agonized.

"What is it?" I asked.

233

I crawled back to her.

She silently handed me the paper, folded her arms into her chest, bent over and sobbed.

It was a penciled note.

Anne dearest,
No hope for me. Can't last two days. Morphine helps. Terrible pain. C has to do it. I'll ask him. He must. He can get you out. Goodbye. Sorry.

Alan

"Where did you find it?" I asked.

"In my shoulder bag, just now."

She was wiping her eyes. Taking deep breaths. Running her fingers through her hair. Her frantic hands shook.

"He asked you to do it?"

I nodded. "Yes."

She shook her head.

"And I came at you that way! Why didn't you say?"

"Would you have believed me?"

She shook her head again. Ran a hand along the side of her cheek. Wiped away the streaming tears.

"I don't know."

I waited. Tried to say something.

"It didn't seem important at the time. We had to get out of there. It was just a matter of time for him. He knew it. I knew it. You knew it, but couldn't face it."

I picked up her right hand.

She dabbed at her eyes with her fingers. "Yes."

She reached over and shook my arm. "I'm so sorry, Colin."

I nodded.

"The way I acted." She shook her head.

"He was your brother. There are no clear rules anymore. You reacted naturally."

Another explosion of breath. She studied her hands.

She saw the bow. Tried to brighten up. Went after her eyes again.

"What are you making?" She took a deep breath. Steadied down.

"Bow and arrow."

Her brow furrowed.

"Can you do that?"

"I have the cord and arrow heads from the emergency kit."

"Why?"

"Wolves, Russians, bear, deer. I feel more comfortable with something in my hands In a situation like this."

She nodded. Dropped her hands to the tarp and held them.

She was settling down. Saw the rain dripping through the trees guarding the front. "How long has it been raining?" she asked.

"Most of the night, I think."

"We seem pretty dry."

"Yup."

She blew out a breath and stretched back, holding up her head with a hand, elbow bent on the pine boughs. She was quietly regarding me.

We had an easy silence going now. There had been a healing.

"I'm curious about something," I said, working on the bow, not looking at her.

"What?"

"Your brother's name was Alan Vickers, yours is Anne Cameron. Why don't you have the same family name?"

She smiled, laid back, and put both arms under her

235

head and looked at the ridge pole. Drew up a knee. "My mother married Robert Vickers when she was quite young. He died when she was pregnant with Alan. A year after Alan was born, she married Duncan Cameron and eventually Sable and I arrived on the scene."

"But why didn't Alan take the Cameron name?"

She rolled over and propped her head on her hand again. She was smiling.

"My father is the Duke of Dumfries. Royal line and all that. Alan could not take my father's name or title. No blood connection. So he remained a Vickers."

"I see. You're titled then. Royalty?"

"Yes."

"That's a bunch of nonsense."

"I knew you wouldn't like it."

She smiled. "Did you know your grandfather is Sir Colin Smallpiece."

"Nope. Don't give a goddamn about that. Ancient, goofy English stuff. Ought to be done away with." I went back to my bow.

"You know my grandparents very well, don't you?" I asked, sighting along the bow. Rubbing it down with a piece of stone.

"I love Poppie."

"How come? What's the connection between the two families? Smallpiece and Cameron?"

"They have known each other through the generations. Country places on the loch. There's a lot of Royal Navy among the Camerons. Not like Smallpieces, of course, but what family is? You people bleed navy blue."

"My father knew your mother."

"Oh, yes."

Some mysteries were beginning to be less mysterious. "Did you and your mother know about me in America?"

236

"She knew, but there was never any talk about it. I had no idea at all."

I put the bow down and crawled back. She didn't back away from eye contact at all anymore.

"Let me tell you something," I said. "I've never understood it. It was clear my grandfather never approved of my father's marriage to my mother. When my mother and father died in an automobile accident, my grandparents came to the funeral and went right back to England. Never looked at me. Never acknowledged that I was alive. I was six months old. Later, when I was old enough to understand, I was told about it.

"When I was twelve, I wrote to them and never got an answer. I would spend summers in Devon with my uncle Philip, but we never went to see my grandparents." I blew out a breath. 'I was getting a pretty heavy case of rejection, but I never knew why. Do you know why?"

She sat up, crossed her legs lotus fashion. Very serious face.

"My mother."

I shook my head. "Why?"

"Your father and my mother were engaged. Katherine MacKenzie and Colin Smallpiece. Everybody knew they were to get married. It was an understanding between the families and my mother and your father. Childhood sweethearts. Your grandparents were delighted. I think everybody was. And then your father runs off with this beautiful American girl, Olympic swimmer, and everything fell apart. My mother sort of went into shock and then married Robert Vickers too quickly. On the rebound, I guess. Your grandfather's hopes were dashed. He really loved my mother and wanted so much to see his son married to her."

237

I blew out a breath. "So that's why he didn't want to know about me. Or have anything to do with me."

"I would think so. Poppie can be very stubborn."

"He sure can be."

"But it's over now. He was bursting with pride when he introduced you at the ball. I'd never seen him like that."

"Yeah. I hope so."

"One other thing, Colin," her eyes were very large. "Had the marriage between your father and my mother happened as planned, then neither you nor I would be here now. We wouldn't exist."

I blew out a breath. Nodded.

I went back to my bow. "But we are here now," I said. "And we have a problem."

She dropped back down and studied the ridge pole. "That we do."

I spent another half hour rubbing down the bow. I tested the flexibility by bending the arms back. Looked good. The bow would probably be dried out, cracked and checked in a week, but in a week I didn't plan on being in Russia.

The rain finally let up and we got out of our pine burrow. Shafts of sunlight were breaking through the clouds and lighting up patches of the pine forest below and across the lake. We had eaten the last of the concentrated emergency rations. From now on, it was survival from the forest, scrounge what we could. Make do.

"How do you want your fish tonight?" I asked. "Baked, boiled, or roasted over an open flame?"

"Roasted might be nice for a change."

"Want to go shopping for berries and I'll see to the fish?"

"Splendid."

We went down the sugar loaf and out along the shingle beach, worked our way down the shoreline. Anne went into a meadow to see what she could find by way of fruits and berries. I drifted into the treeline and continued on. I thought I had seen some birds from our hilltop vantage.

It was dusk now and I heard the cackling and cooing of birds. Around a bend I saw a sizable gathering of large birds, might be sandhill cranes up north for the summer. They stood in a shallow, reedy pond, gathered compactly. Sandhills are naive birds and were talking to each other. They paid me little heed as I quietly approached.

I had a throwing stick in my hands, about three inches thick and about two and a half feet long. I eased up on the birds gradually and they continued their natter and gossip. When I was close enough, I threw the stick at them with a lateral, spinning motion. There was a lot of noise and clack and the birds took to the air, but two were down. I wrung their necks and brought them back to shore. In a half hour, I had them gutted, plucked, headless, washed and skewered on a green pole.

Anne was coming out of the meadow with her cloth filled with berries. She saw the birds.

"Roast bird tonight," I said.

"What kind of bird?" She seemed suspicious.

"Some sort of crane. They eat real good."

"You sure? I have to admit, the fish were beginning to get boring."

Roast bird-in-the-wild is excellent. We ate them on the sheer rock face overlooking the lake. Berries were dessert. We had to go back down the lake to wash up. Eating wild bird can be messy. I reminded myself to cut a couple of four-inch-round pieces of pine, about five inches long, hollow them out for cups, glasses. We drank from the lake by cupping our hands.

We spent six days on the sugar loaf getting my foot back in shape, recuperating from the march and swim, finishing the bow and arrows. Preparing for the next move to the village and the boat. The days were grey and misty. A cold wind drove out of the west. We explored, gathered fruits, berries, tubers, caught fish and birds. I even snared a rabbit. We lived off the land and were dry in our hilltop bower. I tried to jog and felt no pain.

The choppers were still overhead, but no longer seemed so frantic. We almost knew when they were going to appear.

As the days wore on, Anne underwent a change. Her skin cleared and tanned. Her eyes seemed to get larger, and she was starting to get to me as a woman. I didn't understand it. I looked at her a lot. How she held her head. How she laughed. What she did with her hands. She had beautiful hands. Something else. She was changing, physically changing right before my eyes. I resolved to watch for it each day. Maybe it was me. Stir crazy, randy in the woods. But every day I saw it more. I couldn't believe it was happening. But it was. And I wanted her.

McCorkle warned me off one night.

"Stay away from her. This is not the time or place."

"I know. God, she looks good. Did you see her eyes?"

"I saw them. I know. She's beautiful. Keep away."

"Yeah."

"Remember Kristin? You got involved."

"Why bring her up?"

"You may have to kill this one, too."

"For God's sake. That was different."

"You may . . ."

"Why?"

"Who knows why? The mission may require it."

"She's on our side for christsakes."

240

"The mission comes before anything else. You know that. Stay away. Don't get involved. Not yet. Don't have your judgment impaired. That's all I say. Not yet. Stay away from her."

I stayed away. But I watched and she had changed some more and I got scared.

Fifth day on the hilltop. I was firing practice arrows into a plump, thick spruce. Anne came up from the lake. She had been washing again, brushing her teeth. She continued to metamorphose. Christ. It's impossible. Couldn't be me. But I saw it every day. I'm trained to observe. It wasn't me. It was her. And it was impossible.

She was draping her stuff on the trees to get what there was out of a weak, watery sun. I can't go on this way. Got to find out. Must ask.

"Anne," I said casually in my most matter-of-fact voice. "Are you taking any pills. You got any stuff in that shoulder bag of yours?"

"I take those high potency vitamins like you do." She seemed puzzled.

"Anything else?"

"Why?"

I had run out of patience "Come on! Yes or no. Anything else?"

She went into the lean-to and came out with her shoulder bag. She reached in and held out a packet of pills. "I take these."

"What are they?"

She glowered at me.

"They prevent me from having a problem a woman doesn't want to have in the woods. In a situation like this."

I shook my head. "I don't understand."

241

She frowned. "Sometimes, Colin Smallpiece, you are a consummate ass."

I gaped.

"They prevent my period, you half-wit!"

"Oh."

I recovered. "You've got to stop taking them right away, Anne. Right away. Now. You must stop. Now."

"What on earth for?"

"Side effects. They have terrible side effects. Must have something to do with the fish, the stress, the air. I don't know. All I know is, you have to stop. Maybe it's not too late."

"What are you talking about. You're frightening me, Colin."

"You must have noticed. How could you not notice?"

"Notice what?"

"How could you not know? When it's happening to you? I see it every day. It's more noticeable every day."

"What's more noticeable? Please tell me. I don't like the way you look. Really, what? You have me worried now."

I took a deep gulp of air and swallowed. She didn't know. I had to tell her. "Anne, it seems impossible I know, but you, er, ah, you. For christsakes, Anne, you're growing!"

"I'm what?"

"You're growing. At least four inches in a week. I've seen it happen before my eyes. Has to be the goddamn pills. Some sort of weird chemistry. This situation. Iodine in the fish. I don't know. Fall out from Chernobyl."

Her mouth fell open. She was in shock. She couldn't understand the enormity of what I had said.

"You think I'm growing? Gaining height?"

"No doubt about it. I've seen it."

"Like a child?"

I nodded. Licked my lips. "Yes. That's right. Seems impossible. Has to be the pills."

I have never heard a woman laugh so hard, so honestly, so long or so loud. It vibrated off the hill and went all the way to Lenigrad, Moscow even. She held her sides and still laughed. She had tears in her eyes. She shook with laughter. Almost rolled on the ground.

What do you do when you tell a person they are undergoing physiological disaster and they laugh at you. What is the appropriate response? I had no idea, so I did nothing. Probably blinked. The girl was a medical freak and she laughed. In a week, she would be seven feet tall. Could play for the Lakers.

"Oh, Colin, you're wonderful." She came over and kissed me on the cheeks, hugged me like I was a child. Patted my back. Smoothed my hair. She wiped her eyes and knelt down to where I was sitting. Looked me in the eye.

"I'm not growing, Colin."

"But I can see. I . . ."

"I'm losing weight. I look taller, that's all."

"Yes, but . . ."

"With all of this exercise and fish and upset and turmoil, the pounds have been torn off. I've lost over twenty pounds, maybe more. I'm just not dumpy anymore, Colin. I'm five feet nine inches. I'm beginning to look it."

You ever see one of those cartoons where a light bulb goes off over some idiot's head when he finally gets it? A dozen bulbs just exploded over my head. I got the idea.

"Oh. Yeah. Might be. Sure."

"You were worried."

"Sure. Of course. I thought you were some goddamn medical catastrophe."

243

"You've lost weight, too."

"I suppose."

"It just doesn't show on you so much." She smoothed my hair some more, like they do.

She ran her fingers over the hair that was growing back over the Jack Nicholson hairline. "Thank God," she said. "You have such lovely hair."

The sun was breaking through the clouds. From the west the sky was all blue. The low pressure system that had us for close to a week was blowing east.

"Let's go down the back of the hill, Colin. The weather's clearing. There are some meadows back in there. Maybe we can find some berries."

"Okay. Good idea. I'll take my bow. Maybe I can get some supper."

I took some practice arrows and three steel-tipped ones and put them in my canvas quiver. Anne had a square of canvas for the berries and we went down the easy incline at the rear of the sugar loaf. The sun felt warm on our faces and we worked our way down the hill and into the pine forest beyond. I took a few shots with my practice arrows at trees that looked like bears. Killed both trees.

We picked our way through the pine and spruce for half an hour, crossed a clear stream. Had a drink.

Anne found a meadow of berries.

"I'll work around over there," I said, pointing to a small rise.

"Why?" She was busy with the berries.

"Might find a deer."

"You wouldn't shoot a deer."

"I crave red meat."

"I don't. Shoot a rabbit, maybe."

"I could hit a fly easier."

"Don't shoot a deer, Colin."

244

"Pick your berries. I'll try to get some supper."

I threaded my way through the meadow and into the shadowy forest. I worked around the rise for fifteen minutes and couldn't even find a fly. Plenty of mosquitoes, but the repellent kept them away. I started to circle back.

I heard a scream.

Anne. Back at the meadow.

I ran.

Another scream.

Through the pine, I saw them. Three men. Soldiers. One had his arms around her waist. Another was at her coveralls and was tugging them down by the shoulders. I could see the white straps underneath. A third was smiling nearby, leaning against a tree trunk. He would have his turn, later.

I went into the hyperdrive right away. Everything was now frozen. The men moved in slow motion. I saw his hand move toward her breast. Saw him turn slowly to the man leaning against the tree trunk. Then the laughter, low, sonorous, beating into my ears like a bass drum, steady, rhythmic, echoing.

"Take the one against the tree trunk, Colin." It was McCorkle, speaking now as he always does when the hyperdrive comes and death often follows.

"When he goes down, they will lose their interest in the girl."

I moved to the edge of the trees, still in shadow. His hand was reaching out. They were grinning. She was arched back. I heard the scream, punching slowly into my ears in the strange, slow, half world of the hyperdrive.

I fitted an arrow to the bow. Pulled the cord back into my nose. Sighted down on the grinning man by the tree. Let the arrow release. I heard the low twang, hum. Saw it fly, in odd suspension, across the fifty feet of meadow, straight and true. Saw it bury deep into his chest. Saw the expression of amazement. Saw the horror of realization when he looked down. Saw him try to pull it out. Then he slumped to his knees and then the man with his hand on her breast turned around. They both looked about and fear had replaced anticipated pleasure.

"Move off a bit. Get the one in front of her. You have their attention now."

I drifted ten feet to my right, still in the pines, still in shadow. They didn't know where I was. Didn't know what was happening. The man in front of Anne had stepped away, giving me a clear shot. He was looking up the meadow when the arrow left the bow. Too high! Too high! I aimed for his heart, but the arrow took him in the throat. He twisted around trying to get free of it. Staggered. Sank to his knees, hands to his throat, working to get rid of the awful thing. He broke the arrow off, leaving a four-inch stump sticking out. The blood was pouring out of the wound. He thrashed about in slow motion agony as the life poured from his throat. He was on the ground, still writhing, twisting.

The last man held Anne around her waist. He stood behind her, using her as a shield. I couldn't get a shot at him. I didn't want to, anyway.

"You can take the bastard with your hands, Colin."

I walked out of the pine cover into the meadow. He saw me. I dropped the bow. He grinned and shoved her away.

He was a big man. About six four and two hundred forty pounds. Half was beer belly. A barracks fighter, brawler. He had a stupid, ugly face. He came at me in the sun splashed meadow, innocent with wildflowers and berries. He was profane, a corruption of this pure place.

"You are going to die, prick," he said.

Even in the heavy, beating cadence of the hyperdrive, I heard and understood.

"Three will die," I said. "You are the last. Give me about a minute."

He bellowed like a bull. It was the intimidating roar of the beast, the chest-pounding gesture of the gorilla, an aggressive display calculated to produce fear, to frighten.

I waited for him in the berry patch.

He swung at me by way of England.

I raised my left arm and blocked it.

I ducked under his arm and drove a hard right into the beer belly. It sort of exploded.

He staggered among the wildflowers.

I jabbed a left into his eye. His head rocked back. I hooked a right into his chin. He sagged.

I turned him around and got my left hand into his collar and my right into the seat of his pants. I drove his head into the nearest tree. He was down and out. I snapped his head around and heard it separate from the spinal cord.

I was back in the world again. Anne was moving at normal speed. The birds were calling, clouds moving, flowers nodding as they should. All was well in the world again.

She collapsed into me.

"You're fine. You're okay." I kissed her forehead. Hugged her.

She clung to me. I could feel her heart beating right into my chest. Rapid.

I walked her across the meadow. Sat her down. She was coming back. She had seen me kill a man in the laboratory. Saw the tracers coming at us in the Stinson. Buried her brother in the little beach by the cove. She had seen a lot.

She had her knees drawn up and was pressing her forehead into them. I patted her back.

247

"They're dead. Gone."

She nodded into her knees. No tears.

"You okay?"

"Yes."

I patted some more.

I felt her suck in a breath.

Two or three minutes. I patted. Waited.

"I was so scared, so frightened. I screamed."

"I heard it."

"I never screamed before in my life."

"Good thing you did."

She looked up. "Soldiers?" she asked.

"I'll check."

"You be okay here?"

"Yes."

I went over to the bodies. They were all wearing coveralls. No insignia of unit or rank. Odd. I went through their pockets. The two with the arrows had nothing. The third had a big roll of bills and a key. I looked hard at the key. It was fastened to a metal ring through which a loop of hairy twine secured a rumpled tag with the number 42 written on it. An ignition key!

I pulled the bodies into the tree cover about a hundred feet. They all had dog tags. Russian.

I went back to Anne and showed her the key.

"What does it mean? A car?"

"I think so."

"Where?"

"Let's take a look."

I pulled her up. She was still shaken. Still pale. She had forgotten her berries.

"Who were they?" she asked.

"I think they were prisoners. Soldiers in the stockade."

I think they may have escaped and were on the run. Maybe stole a truck, something."

We went farther into the pine forest, west toward the road I had seen on the map. In ten minutes we found the jeep. It was at the end of an ancient track, hardly anything at all. They had left the jeep and went into the woods. What were they looking for? They had found Anne.

"Looks like we may have come upon a quick way to the village," I said.

She nodded.

I checked out the jeep. Looked fairly new. Two caps were in the backseat. I tried the engine and it fired right away. Idled smoothly. Gas gauge read empty! I killed the engine. The tank sounded hollow. I removed the cap. Couldn't see anything. I tried rocking the jeep and listened. I heard some sloshing. Something was down there. I was having a string of very bad luck with gas tanks this month.

"The gauge reads empty, but there's still some gas left. Take a chance?"

"What do you think," she asked.

"What do you think," I threw it back.

"I think it's time to leave," she said.

"Me too."

We went back to the sugar loaf and struck camp. Not much camp to strike. I made up Anne's pack and hoisted the pod up on my shoulders. I felt the familiar weight, but I had two feet under me and I was strong. The rest had put some spring back into my legs.

We stood on the granite outcrop and looked down at the lake, blue and peaceful in the evening sunshine. The breeze drifted through the pines. Our lean-to was still intact. Anne looked about. What was going on in her head?

"I wish I had a camera," she said.

"What?"

"A camera."

"What for?"

"To take a picture. It's a lovely spot. We spent six days here."

"You're a spy for christsakes," I exploded. "You've penetrated an unfriendly country. You almost got raped down there! You want to take a picture! Jesus!"

"I liked it here. For a lot of reasons."

I tugged her arm. We went down the sugar loaf. Anne looked back three times.

I loaded our gear into the rear seat. Backed the jeep around, and followed the old rutted track back to the road. Then we waited for dusk about two hundred feet into the pine from the dirt road that led to the village. We had wild berries and cold crane for supper. At 9:30 an old truck with rattling stake sides went east, leaving a cloud of exhaust behind. At 10:15 a newer truck, a dusty pick-up, went west to the village. The road stopped there. At 10:30 we rolled onto the road and turned west. It was cut out of the pine, wide enough for one vehicle. I wondered what would happen if two met head on. I didn't bother with the lights. No need. Land of the midnight dawn.

CHAPTER XI

We ran out of gas in a quarter of a mile.

Now I knew why the jeep was where it was. They ditched it.

The engine just sputtered, caught for a second, then died. We rolled to a stop. I pulled over into the pine, but it was doubtful if another vehicle could get by.

"Beautiful. What is it with me and gas tanks?"

It was about time for Anne to say, "What do we do now?"

She surprised me. "I think you better get the pod out and hide it in the woods."

"You're right."

I got the pod out and hid it in the woods.

I got back in the jeep muttering.

"Somebody might come along and help," she said optimistically.

"Like a truck full of soldiers?"

"What would a truck full of soldiers be doing out at this time of night?"

"What would anybody be doing out at this time of night?

The pines and spruce reared up in the dusky glow. A pale half moon shone in a cloudless sky and all you could see were the ubiquitous conifers and the dirt road stretching to infinity. There was no Spaulding University, there was no England, no United States, sports cars, beaches with tanned, long-legged bosomy girls with interesting eyes, white teeth, and easy smiles. All there was in the universe were Russians, helicopters, and pine trees. And us. And we ran.

Do we sit or move? That is the question. If we sit, maybe somebody would help us. On the other hand, maybe somebody would arrest us. If we move, we are back on the trail with an eighty-six-pound monkey on my back. Let's compromise, we sit for two hours and then walk if nobody comes along. Okay? Makes sense?

We talked. Anne asked me about Spaulding and what I taught there. I told her about paradigms, system theory, man-machine interface, and the miniaturization of systematic social theory. She was interested and asked good questions.

I asked her about Harkness and how she got tangled up in the spy business at her tender age. She was not in the spy business. She was quite firm on that. She was an engineer, a computer specialist, interested in some mathematics, particularly probability theory. Yes, she did go to Russia for Harkness, five times, no more, brought some reports back, made some contacts. It was a favor to an old family friend. Yes, she did carry a pistol. Only once though. Anybody could do that. Yes, she did have a code name and a control. It was nothing. She was certainly not a spy.

How come she got picked to interview me for the penetration job, I wondered. She wasn't sure. Maybe because she knew the pod about as well as anybody except Alan. Or, because she spoke Russian and had a sophisticated sense of the Soviet military establishment. No, she was not a spy. She was very clear on that. Maybe because

Harkness trusted her. Maybe because my name was Smallpiece and might be related to the Royal Navy Smallpieces. Who knows?

How did I get all those muscles, she wondered. Worked on weights, I said. How did I learn to kill people so easily? Wasn't easy, I said. Just looked easy. She wondered how I knew the big guy was going to swing at me before he did. Luck, I suggested. She didn't believe it was luck. Luck didn't put Flynn down. She said she knew I would come and get her from those men. She was scared, but not that scared. I asked why. She said she wasn't sure why, but she knew I would come. She asked me if I had a girlfriend back home. I said I didn't think so. She said she thought I really had a girlfriend. Probably more than one. The talk was insane, but I loved the quality of her voice and the upper-class English accent.

I heard a motor. It was behind us.

"Put this cap on," I said to Anne.

"It's dirty."

"Put it on anyway. Try to look like a soldier. Spies know how to do stuff like that."

"I am not a spy!" she snapped.

A truck rattled up in back of us and stopped. It was the one with the flapping sides and in gross defiance of emission standards in Panama, El Salvador, Mexico, even Russia.

Anne stayed put, I got out.

A grizzled old head with a leather cap and a broken visor stuck out of the door. The head had five days of white stubble on the chin, a generous peasant nose, heavily pitted, and small bright eyes that were almost lost in a mass of wrinkles and creases.

"Good evening, comrade," I said.

"Good evening, shit," the head said. "Why are you here? You're blocking the way."

"We have run out of gas."

"The Army pisses gas."

"I think they forgot to piss this time."

The bright, beady eyes in the sea of wrinkles looked me up and down.

"Where are you going?"

"To the village."

"Why?"

"Well, actually I can't say. Army business." Jesus, what an answer!

"Bullshit," he said. Couldn't blame him. I couldn't believe me either.

His eyes squinted down at me from the truck window. "What's your name?" he asked. He shoved his cap back. Rubbed his nose. Spit.

I had to give him a name. "Dimitri Lushev."

"Lushev. Lushev. Your father works at the lumber mill, right? You're his kid in the Army?"

"Yes."

"Yeah. I know Josef. He holds his liquor. He told me about you."

I nodded.

"Who's that with you?"

"Recruit."

"Hey, recruit. Come on over."

Anne got out of the jeep with her hat on and stood about twenty feet away.

"Damn," he said, "they take boys in the Army that young?"

"What's your name, old-timer?" I asked. "So I can tell my father."

254

"Yuri Timoshenko. Everybody knows old Yuri around here."

"Can you spare us some gas, Yuri? I have money."

"You mean you won't give me some damn piece of army paper?"

"Cash. I need to move."

He got out of the truck. He was no more than five feet tall. He gave Anne another look. Scratched his head. Had another spit. Groaned. Stretched up. Groaned again. He was having back trouble, he said. He told me not to get old.

"How much you need?"

"Just enough to get to the village. My father will meet me there."

"What you got in the jeep?"

"Pump parts."

His eyes squinted. "Pump parts, huh? Bullshit. Little moonlight requisition, huh, Dimitri? Pump parts, shit."

"Maybe."

He took a hard look at me. Ran a hand over his grizzled jaw.

"What do I care? Where do you think I get this gas? Fuck the government. Fuck the Army."

There is more independence of thought in the Soviet Union than most Americans realize.

He had a fifty-five-gallon drum in the truck, hose and siphon. He drew off three gallons, put a funnel in the jeep's gas tank and poured. I paid him from the roll I took from the dead man. He complained about his aching back again.

He took another look at Anne. A long look.

The jeep started nicely. I killed the engine.

Yuri was back in his truck.

"Hey, Dimitri," he called.

I went back to the truck.

"You steal that jeep?"

"What do you mean?"

"Look kid, there is no Lushev who works at the mill."

"Well, I ..."

"You want to sell that jeep, kid?"

"Maybe."

"You're going to the village?"

"Yes."

"Know anybody there?"

"No."

"You need some help? You on the run?"

"Maybe."

"You're not in the fucking Army, are you, kid?"

"Well, you see ..."

"You run off maybe? Army after you? Police? Government?"

"Maybe." I was getting good at definitive answers. Really had old Yuri fooled. Snake bit, he was. Fuddled.

"I got no time for those bastards. You just bought some army gas, kid."

"Yeah. Well." I was tired of sputtering. The old man was always two steps ahead of me. He read me right away. We needed help. I trusted him. Had to take a chance.

"We are in a little trouble, er, just what are you, Yuri?" He grinned. Spat.

"What am I? What am I? Shit, kid, I'm a thief, smuggler, blackmarketeer. Come from a long line of thieves. Only line of work I know. You need it, I can get it."

I let all of that sink in.

"How come you're telling me this? How do you know I'm not the police, KGB, something like that?"

He grabbed his generous nose. "Here," he said, tap-

256

ping his nose. "I can smell 'em. No, you're something else. Your girlfriend, too."

"What?"

"You think I'm blind? An old man who can't get it up anymore? That's a hell of a lot of girl you got there. No way she can hide those big tits behind that coverall. You two are on the run. I know it. I don't like the Army or the government any more than you do. Maybe we could do some business."

We were both looking at each other very hard in the light of the misty half moon, making tough decisions. I was running out of options. He didn't look KGB or police. He looked like what he said. The vibes were good. I had to take a chance.

"We want to go to Finland," I said.

"Hah!" he exploded. "Thought maybe. It can be done." He scratched his jaw and took off his cap.

"Cost something."

"All right."

"Go to the village. Last house on the right by the river. That's my mother's. Tell her Yuri sent you. Tell her I got a full tank. She will know what that means, sort of a code, password. She will know you're all right. Stay in the house until I get there. Don't go out."

"Right."

"Good. You got any money, kid?"

I showed him the roll.

"You won't need the jeep in Finland," he said.

"You get us to Finland and it's yours."

He started up the truck. "See you later, kid. She's a ooker. Some knockers." The truck rattled off down the oad. A thick cloud of hydrocarbons engulfed the jeep. We acked and coughed.

Anne had heard all of it. She buttoned the coveralls

257

tighter around her throat. Folded her arms. Looked at the trees. Didn't look at me. Looked annoyed.

"You trust him?" she asked.

"Yes. Do you?"

"I think so."

"We go to the village? Find his mother? She must be ninety."

"Yes."

"He knew you were a girl."

"I heard."

"He did."

"He was coarse and crude." She fumbled with the buttons around her collar.

"He thought you looked good."

"Let's go."

"You've slimmed down."

"Colin, Please!"

"You have."

"Apparently not enough."

"Looked good to him."

I got glared at.

I went back to the woods and retrieved the pod, stowed it in the rear seat again. We rolled down the dirt road in the valley of silent pines. Two-thirty at night and the sun was out. Why was I here?

The village was a subdued huddle of fifteen or twenty unpainted huts lined along the river. They had steep wooden roofs, thin chimneys, and small windows. In the village center, there was a store, two-story affair, probably a post office, maybe a café. It had a solitary gas pump. Not a light showed in any window. Beyond the row of silent houses, the river glinted in the nighttime sun. It was about a hundred fifty feet wide and the water was moving. It had a gentle, insistent rustle.

I went to the last house and pulled up to a small barn in the back, close to the river. No sound anywhere. No dogs. I heard the river splashing over some nearby rocks. Whispering along the shore. Heard a fish splash.

"Let's take a look at the beach." I pointed toward the river. "Check out the boats."

There were no boats. Nothing. What the hell? The shore was empty as far as I could see.

I sank down on the shingle beach. "I know this is the village and I know I saw boats from the chopper."

"You checked it on the map?" Anne sat down beside me.

I was in turmoil. The boats were our only way to the border without a twenty-mile hike through the pine. I couldn't understand it.

"I'm sure this is the village. I know I saw boats. A dozen at least."

"We'll just have to wait for Yuri." She shrugged her shoulders.

"Something is wrong here." I shook my head.

"Did you mention anything about boats to the old man?"

"No. I'm sure I didn't." I flung a stone down the beach. Stupid move.

"Who is that? Who's out there?"

That tore it.

"Don't say anything," I whispered to Anne. "Lay out flat. Maybe they won't see us." Maybe the Wizard of Oz will send us back to Kansas.

I heard footsteps on the turf, then a rattle on the shingle.

"Who's there?" An old woman's voice.

We lay frozen.

Oh, Christ, she was almost on top of us.

"I see you, come on, get up. You want me to have Boris Gordeyev on you? You want that? Get up. Now!"

I got up. Anne, too.

We saw a small figure, entirely in black, babushka tight over her head. She pointed a stick at us.

"What are you boys doing here?"

"We came to look at the boats, Grandmother."

She came closer. Peered up into our faces.

"You are not from the village."

"No, Grandmother," I said. "Where are the boats?"

She spit. "Who knows? The Army came and took them away. Two days ago. Bastards. That's what they are." She put the stick in my face again. "Why are you boys here? You should be home with your mothers. Safe. Out of trouble. In bed."

"Yuri sent us, Grandmother."

"Yuri? What Yuri?"

"Your Yuri. He said to tell you his tank is full."

A dry explosion of breath. "Ah. Yuri." She craned her head up at us. "Come closer," she commanded. I saw nothing but the babushka and a potato of a nose. She had also given her fine nose to Yuri.

"Come in the house," she said and wheeled around. We followed her to the house with its unpainted wooden sides and steeply pitched roof. There was a bit of ginger bread scrolling by the eaves. It was about the size of two-car garage in an affluent American suburb. We went inside. She pulled a cord and the solitary light went on.

Living room with plain wooden furniture, probably locally made, functional, unstained and unvarnished. Couple dozen awkward, formally posed, self-conscious photographs of departed kinsmen on the wall. Some went back to the turn of the century. Three icons. Three large wooden chairs with pillows, small floral design in the fabric an

…oilies. Old-time crank phonograph. Curtains heavy with …ce over the small windows that were three deep to the …utside. Huge white porcelain wood stove, round and dec…rated with flowers. Wide board wooden floor with rag …ugs not unlike those I saw among the mountain people …f the Blue Ridge. Three glass kerosene lamps. No books. …lo TV. No magazines. Good-looking shortwave radio. Jap…nese.

Through a curtain, I saw the kitchen. There was an…ther small room, furnished as a bedroom. A very steep …et of stairs, not much more than a ladder, went up through … square opening in the ceiling. Must be a sleeping loft …p there.

There was a bouquet of spring flowers on the table in … jelly jar. Whitewashed plaster walls. Low ceiling. The …lace looked like it had been scrubbed with a hard bristled …rush every day.

It was an elf house.

It was spotless.

It looked like home.

Anne was smiling.

The babuska was under five feet tall, with hands like …mall tree roots, and a face rutted and creased like a coun…y schoolyard after recess. After it had rained. Out of that …in, two small bright eyes took us in. And a gasp issued …om the toothless crease of a mouth. She was looking at …nne.

"You're a girl!"

"Yes," Anne acknowledged.

"So tall," she said with wonder. She turned to me.

"Giants. And fair. They say there are giants in the …uth. And fair."

She reached out with her gnarled claw and touched

261

Anne's cheek. "Ahhhh!" So soft." She shook her whit head. "I remember once ... yes ..."

She cocked her head to one side. "Why do you hav your hair cut like a boy?" She looked at Anne's coveralls "Why do you dress like one?"

"Well, I, ah, you see ..." Anne began.

"Such beautiful hair. So fair. Women should have lon hair and not look like a man." She paused, studying. "Bu it becomes you. You are beautiful. Yes, it becomes."

She remembered her manners. "You will have som tea."

She went into the kitchen and poured water from pitcher into a small samovar.

She served the tea in glasses and set out huge slices c black bread and a crock of jam. It was our first glass c hot anything in over a week. It tasted wonderful. I worke on the bread and jam. Grandmother watched and grinnec

"You are married?" she asked.

"Well, er. Ah." I said.

"Soon? You look right for each other."

I nodded.

"Why are you interested in boats?"

"We want to go to Finland."

She nodded.

I had three glasses of tea and half a loaf of bread. Ann was careful. Two glasses of tea. Half a slice of bread. N jam. I think she was on a diet.

We heard a truck motor. Screech of brakes. Yuri fle into the room like a black bat. "We have to get that jee out of sight!" he exploded. "Where are the keys? Tha bastard Boris ..."

He snatched them from my hand, ran from the hous We heard doors swing on rusty hinges, then the jeep m tor, more rusty hinges and he was back in the room. H

mother had a glass of tea waiting for him. He knocked it
back in three swallows, belched, sagged into a chair, wiped
his mouth on his sleeve and regarded us with eyes just
like his mother's. They looked more like brother and sister
than mother and son. Like they should be in the woods
and only come out when the moon is full. They must have
very small relatives in Ireland.

"Yuri," the old woman cackled, "where did you find
these beautiful children?" She clapped her gnarled hands
together, mouth twisted in a grin, eyes bright and happy.

"Out on the road, Mother. They ran out of gas."

"They're so tall, and the hair." She looked at Anne.
"What is your name, girl?"

"Anne." I sucked in a breath so fast and loud that
Anne looked over at me. "I'm sorry, Colin, I couldn't lie
to her. What does it matter?"

Clearly she wasn't a spy. The first rule in the spy book
is "Never tell your name. never." And she blurted it out
right away. She wasn't a spy. Harkness was an idiot.

"Anne? That is not a Russian name. No, I don't think
so. But Anna might be."

"Why are you dressed like that, Anna?" the old woman
asked.

"We have been in the woods. It is best to dress like
this in the woods."

"But why would you be in the woods? That is no place
for a girl like you."

Anne's hands were beginning to twist. She didn't want
to lie or be evasive with this old woman who had opened
her house to us.

Yuri's mother was clearly disturbed by Anne's coveralls,
now ripped and smudged from ten days in the wilderness.
Suddenly, she clapped her hands and shouted, "Yuri, you
remember that foreign woman who lost her suitcase? She

263

was big and had a lot of nice things. Go up in the loft an
bring it down. We'll get this girl looking the way sh
should."

Yuri looked at me and I looked at Yuri. He rolled hi
eyes. I nodded. We understood each other. He went up t
the loft. We heard him banging around. He emerged wit
a relatively new woman's leather bag. He put it by hi
mother's chair.

"Would you like a bath, Anna? Just a wooden tub, bu
I can heat the water for you on the stove. Would you?"

"Oh my, yes. It would be lovely. Could you?"

"Come with me," the old granny grinned and grabbe
the bag. The two women vanished into the small bedroom
A curtain was drawn.

Yuri shook his grizzled head and smiled. He lacked tw
front teeth. "Oh, she's happy. Someone to fuss over, an
a girl. She only had boys and I'm all that's left of the lot.'

I nodded.

"Finland, is it?" he asked.

"Yes."

He screwed his eyes up and studied me. "Something i
going on around the border the past week. Patrols ar
increased. Helicopters all around. Jets flying up and dow
the border. The government seems worried about som
thing. Like they don't want somebody to cross over int
Finland."

"Might be us."

He was giving me a steady, curious look.

"Why would that be?"

I had to level with him. He was a thief and a smuggle
but he was a Russian. There is a fundamental nationalis
that goes deeper than current governments and ideolog
Russians have it. Love of Mother Russia is stronger tha

pique with the state. He might hate the government, but he would die fighting an enemy on Russian soil.

But I took the chance.

"The KGB stole a piece of military hardware from the English. The girl and I were sent to get it back. That's why there is so much activity along the border.

"Why the girl?"

"She helped develop the device."

He blew out a breath, whistled. "She can do that?"

"She's an engineer."

"Ah!"

"Yuri, we're here to get what is ours. What she helped design and construct. What the KGB took."

"I can understand that."

"You'll help us."

"What do you want?"

"A boat to get down the river, that's all. We'll manage the rest of the way."

He smiled, pulled out a pipe, stuffed it, fired it up, and sat in a cloud of the smoke. "Boat's no problem. The Army took all of the village boats away. Now I know why. The pricks. We'll be lucky if we get half of them back."

"You can get us one?"

"Easy, by late this afternoon. Won't be much. But it's a one-way trip."

I was delighted. It seemed so easy.

"How are you going to get through the wire?"

"Wire?"

"The border is sealed off by two hundred yards of cleared land. There are four rolls of very heavy, thick barbed wire across it and in the middle is a fifteen-foot electric fence. Patrols come by at different times. How are you going to get across that?"

I think I dozed through that lecture in the training sessions.

"I don't know. I'll manage it when we get there."

"I think, my young friend, you had better manage it now."

"Can it be done?" I asked.

He puffed and smiled. "Of course it can be done. We do it all the time. I have a loft full of goods that came in from Finland, through the wire. Calculators, TV's, cosmetics, records, videos, films, books. Whatever people want, we can get."

Yuri's vocabulary had gotten more sophisticated and his rough, woodsy, peasant style had faded away. He was more than just a coarse, grizzled, bumpkin out in the middle of the night to steal army gas. He would have made a great spy. He was a great spy.

"How can we get through it?"

"There are several holes in the wire. Not really holes, but the wire has been cut and then tied back. We have jumped the electrical fence with a shunt, a bridge. You'll have to meet a man up there. I can arrange it, and he will guide you to a hole. A window in the wire." He chuckled. "Window. That's good."

"You can do that?"

"I do it all the time. It's my business. I'm a professional thief and smuggler." He looked at me through the pipe smoke. "Costs money."

I tossed him my roll of bills.

"That's all I have and the jeep is yours."

Yuri ran his practiced thumb over the edges of the bills. Squinted. Calculated costs. "It will be all right," he said.

We shook on it.

"You will go down river this evening. Looks like you'll go through the wire the following night or the next. You

266

will have to hike through through the forest first. Seven or eight miles. If it rains, so much the better. I'll see to it."

I nodded.

Anne came through the curtain and Yuri and I were reduced to a gaping, speechless shambles. She wore a black skirt that came down to her ankles and a coarse white peasant blouse with a wide round collar that exposed most of her shoulders and clung to her full breasts with just a suggestion of soft cleavage. She was gorgeous. Her belly was flat, hips full and rounded, shoulders wide and firm. There were hollows in her flushed cheeks that made her eyes seem even larger. Small tipped-up nose, full lips, oval face set on a curving neck and a radiant smile that took your breath away.

"Now that is a woman," Grandma said, and cackled from her pipe.

Anne fell into a chair. "A tub. I never knew a bath could feel so good."

"It sure looks good," I managed.

"Oh my, yes." Yuri agreed.

"You got anything for him. Yuri?" Grandma asked.

"Oh sure. But it won't do for him what you did for her."

He found an old grey shirt and a pair of rumpled woolen trousers that came down just five inches above the ankles. Showed the nice white socks off, though.

The day came over grey and cloudy. Yuri disappeared. The two women laughed and talked in the little kitchen. It went on for hours. What would a young, titled English girl have to talk about with a wrinkled, eighty-five-year-old peasant crone from the northwest Russian wilderness? They were women. And women know mysterious things that men don't know. They talk about those things with

267

each other. It transcends cultures, time and space. It is best that men do not try to understand those things because they will never know. I could have predicted it.

Yuri was back and gave me a conspiratorial wink. Things were arranged, the wink said. He inclined his head to the kitchen and the women's voices, raised his eyebrows. I pulled a face. He nodded. Women. He understood there were things he could not understand, too.

The hours drifted by.

Anne came into the living room with a shawl and a bubushka over her head, just like Grandma.

"We are going for a walk to the post office. You want to come?" she asked.

"Sure." I was feeling a bit claustrophobic in the twelve by twelve living room.

The center of town was about a hundred yards down on the dirt road. We passed five huts not much different from Yuri's. Tiny, wooden steeply pitched roofs, unpainted, small windows. The wooden siding was set in a peculiar herringbone pattern. Some huts had simply vertical boards. A few had been painted. I saw a couple of battered pickup trucks and one ancient passenger car. The whole town had been gouged out of the pine which rose from a shallow ridge behind the houses. The river flowed swiftly on the other side. It was a village whose original economy was based on trapping and fishing but was now changing as the lumber mill, six miles to the east, expanded and filled with bureaucrats and strangers from the south. So Yuri had bitterly explained.

The post office proved to be a general store, café, bar, and community center. It was all contained in a two-story building in the herringbone pattern, painted a brilliant blue with white trim around the windows.

Yuri picked up his mail, three or four letters, three

eight by ten brown envelopes, and a magazine. Business correspondence, I presumed.

The café-bar occupied a corner with five rough country tables and accompanying chairs, and the inevitable round Russian wood stove. It had small dusty windows without curtains, an eight-foot ornate bar, highly carved, and a large silver samovar. Behind the bar there was an eight-foot dull mirror with a massive gilt frame. Both bar and mirror, I suspected, had been trucked out of Leningrad decades ago to lend a touch of elegance to the place.

It was a village gathering place full of loud voices and laughter, coarse jokes and insults from the men, quiet conversation from the women who looked deeply into each other's eyes. More mystery. You could buy a glass of hot tea and a little pie stuffed with some kind of meat mix, or a sweet cake. Anne and I got a lot of attention. She kept her babuska on and her shawl over her shoulders, but she stood taller than most of the men. She stayed with the women. That was the way it was here. The world of men and the world of women.

We were Yuri's friends and that was enough to break down barriers. I had the feeling that everyone knew of Yuri's business and everyone gained from it. A radio here, a German razor there, French perfume, Italian shoes. Clearly he was a popular man and had something to say to everyone. He was a back pounder and told a good joke. He had an easy smile and waved at everyone. In the U.S., he would be a congressman.

I had a glass of tea at the bar served by a plump, black-haired, brown-eyed girl with a clear ruddy complexion and a bosom that would not be intimidated by her bodice.

"You are Yuri's friend?" she asked, and wiped the bar.

"Yes. Just visiting."

She nodded and went no further. Apparently, it was not

good form to question Yuri's friends too deeply on where they were from or why they were here.

She reached over and wiped the bar near my glass of tea. She virtually fell out of her bodice. I got a steady look from the clear brown eyes and a shy smile.

"You live in the village?" I asked.

She continued her vigorous wiping. I got some more eye contact. "Yes. Up above, with my mother. We run the café."

"I see."

"Not much to do in a small village," she said sadly.

"I suppose not."

"Not many boys my age."

"Oh."

"They are country boys. Crude. Only have one thing on their minds."

"I suppose."

She really had interesting eyes. I think she was rubbing a hole in the bar.

"Not that I mind. If it's the right boy." If you know what I mean, she was saying.

"Of course not."

She filled my half glass of tea.

Anne was looking over at me. She seemed to have lost interest in the ladies. She seemed cross with me. Grieved. Put out.

"Would you like a sweet cake?" the barmaid asked.

"That would be nice."

She put the cake on the bar. No dish or napkin.

"Thank you." I gave her my shy boy smile. My non-crude, city boy smile.

Anne was glaring from underneath her babuska.

I heard a car's brakes outside, doors slam and three Red Army men came through the door. One lieutenant

270

and two enlisted men. They stood at the doorway and looked around. No one paid them any heed. The conversation was as loud as ever. They found a table in the corner. The girl with the magical bodice served them tea and a smile. Flashed another at me.

The lieutenant was giving me a going-over. I got the barmaid talking again. She attacked the bar with her cloth once more. Varnish was gone in the one spot. The lieutenant got up and went over to Anne who continued to smolder in my direction. I took in a quick breath when he pulled up a chair and sat down next to her. The two men, a sergeant and a corporal, sat at their table, drank their tea, and appeared to have no interest in the room at all. Got out their cigarettes. Russians smoke a lot.

The lieutenant was smiling. He was in his mid- to late-twenties, stockily built, around Anne's height, going bald with a blue beard that he had to shave twice a day. He had poor teeth, a thin, tricky, used car salesman's mustache, and a way with the ladies.

Anne shot a glance at me and took off her babushka and shawl. The lieutenant promptly spilled his tea and the two soldiers got interested. Conversation tended to go down as the locals had a look at Anne. This was not good spy procedure. The secret of a good spy is not to be noticed. She was getting a lot of notice.

The barmaid with the independent bosom gave me another glass of tea and some more action with the eyes. She reached up to pin her hair back. She was perspiring under her arms. It wasn't that hot in here.

I got some more tea. I was floating with it. The air was blue with cigarette smoke. The girl with the bodice was telling me that she would be finished around six and would be happy to show me the sights. I think the bodice was the best sight in town.

271

The lieutenant was talking to Anne. He was really going on. Anne seemed no longer quite so interested. The babuska was back on, as was the shawl. She wasn't smiling. I caught her eye. He had a hand on her knee for just a moment. His interest in Anne was apolitical. It was hormonal. She was not happy.

He was drinking vodka and on his third.

His hand did not leave her knee.

Anne's eyes found mine and stayed there. They were no longer petulant or accusative.

Oh boy.

The last thing I needed was to take on the Red Army. The situation called for the fox and not the lion. Brains over brawn. Cunning over strength.

He waved over the black-haired girl. Anne shook her head. She was turning down the vodka. He pouted. Kept his hand on her knee, upper knee, heading toward the thigh. Her eyes were getting desperate. Harkness had a very poor spy there.

Time to move. Time to practice cunning and ruse over strength and brute power. He looked pretty dumb. He had to be dumb. Smart guy wouldn't buy it. The three vodkas would help.

I was counting on two things. Small town curiosity and that you could sell this airhead the Brooklyn Bridge if you had the time.

I walked over to the table.

"Can I buy you a drink, Lieutenant?" I asked.

"No. No. Thank you." He returned to Anne. His wave dismissed me.

I bent down. "It is important that I talk to you at the bar right away. It isn't right what they are doing to you." I had whispered it into his ear and went back to the bar. He looked over and I raised a glass of vodka to him and

272

smiled. He was uncertain, then he said something to Anne, and came over. He was not happy. He looked over at Anne. She was looking at us. Her face was hoping that I wouldn't kill him on the spot. That this was not the time and place to kill anybody. I knew that. She think I didn't know that?

"What is it? What do you want?"

"First, I want to guy you a drink."

"I don't want a drink."

"I don't think it is right for an officer in the Red Army to be made a fool of."

His brow beetled. "What do you mean?"

"Please accept the drink, Lieutenant."

I gestured to the girl with the complete bodice to fill his glass. She did.

"Where are you from, Lieutenant?" I asked.

"What does it matter? Minsk. What do you want?"

"Lovely city. Never been there, but I have been told."

"How am I being made a fool of?" He was distressed with me.

I looked him directly in the eyes. "Did you notice that when you sat down at her table everybody stopped talking. Particularly the women. They were looking at you. Did you notice that?"

He shook his head. Thought about it. "Well, yes, maybe they did."

"They were watching you."

"So?"

"Did you also notice that the woman had very short hair. Cut like a man's hair?"

"Well, yes. It's short, but very attractive. How does that concern me?"

"Did you notice that she was quite tall?"

"Yes. I imagine she would be."

"She is taller than most men here. As tall as you."

"Some women are." His eyes squinted at me. "What are you getting at?"

"I just don't want to see an officer, a member of the armed services made a fool of. I just don't like to see that. You defend the motherland." I shook my head sadly. Had a swallow of tea. Nibbled my sweet cake. Looked sad, troubled, patriotic. He was hooked.

"What in the hell are you getting at?"

"You may find this hard to believe."

"Believe what?"

"It is hard for me to say this. You won't accept it."

"What for godsake?"

"Not easy. You'll think me a fool."

"Say it, you idiot!"

I shook my head again and produced a sigh. "She looks like a woman. But she's a man."

"What?"

"I know. You can't believe it. Fools everybody. There's a kind of man who dresses up in women's clothes. I can't remember what they call them."

"A transvestite?"

"Yeah. That's it. He's one. A transvestite." I struggled over the pronunciation. Shook my head again. I was a naive but good Soviet citizen.

He looked over at Anne. "I can't believe it. I saw her breasts."

"He shoves them up with some sort of belt inside. The rest is rubber. He works in the costume department in the Leningrad ballet. He knows how to do things like that. Lot of strange types work there."

He shook his head.

I plowed earnestly on. "Everybody around here knows him. He was born in the village. It's sort of a village joke.

274

You saw how everyone quieted down and you saw the man's hair cut. See how everybody is looking at you now? They know.''

"I can't believe this.''

"Don't blame you. He knows all about makeup, things like that. It's a big joke in the village. Everybody looks forward to when he comes back for a visit. Watch some poor bastard make a fool of himself getting horny over a man. Big joke around here. You were feeling up a man's knee.''

He was beginning to sweat.

"Don't let them see you getting upset. They like that. Part of the show.''

"Shit.''

"One other thing, he's married, has two kids. His wife is very jealous of him. She knows what he does. She drives a truck. Very big woman. She sees you sitting with him she might just go after you. You could have your hands full with her, I'm telling you.''

"Fuck.''

"If you ask me, I think the guy is a fruitcake ready to go over. I think he's looking for the right guy.''

"Ahhhhhhhh . . .''

"Yeah. Well, I thought I'd better tell you. You look like a good guy.''

"Hummmm. Ahhhhhh.'' He was looking around helplessly. Starting to sweat good now.

"Right. I understand. Hard to believe. You'd expect that sort of thing in a city, but not a small town. See how everybody is looking at us with their eyes down? Pretending not to look. But they're smiling.''

I played on his paranoia. And they were shooting covert looks our way. Conversation had dropped down. They were wondering what Yuri's friend could be telling the lieuten-

275

ant that would have him sweating and coming apart in public. Interesting stuff in a small town. They would talk about it for weeks.

"Country bastards. Fuckin' pricks."

"I'd get out of here if I was you. That wife of his might come in here looking for him. I sure wouldn't want a six-foot woman coming at me. You don't want that kind of trouble. Wouldn't look good on your record."

He slammed his drink down, breaking the glass. He had everyone's attention. Looking at him.

He walked, almost ran, to the door and curtly beckoned his men to follow. I heard the jeep start and move off down the road, out of town. Conversation picked up again. Interaction in the little village café assumed its accustomed flow. All but Anne, whose mouth fell open, and Yuri who had watched the entire affair. The hot pants barmaid came by and I reached out and pinched her at the lower end of her ample ass. She turned around with a "why you little devil" smile. Batted her eyes.

Anne, in turn, rolled hers and went back to the ladies. She kept her babushka on and pulled the shawl around those marvelous shoulders. Yuri kept looking at me and scratching the stubble on his jaw. I think he was considering asking me to go in the smuggling business with him. He didn't ask.

The day wore on. The boat arrived in a truck around three in the afternoon. We had a lovely supper with Grandma and Yuri, some sort of stew, hot bread, potatoes. The women cleaned up. The kitchen was filled with their laughter. Nice sound. Yuri and I talked. The hours slipped by. Time to go.

I put the pod in the rowboat. It was about ten feet long, ancient and without paint, had a couple of oars, couple of slow leaks. The sky was overcast and there had been showers all afternoon. The darker the better.

Yuri had studied my map. He had marked the spot where the guide would meet us and take us to the wire, the border.

We stood on the shingle beach in the gloom, the river tugging the boat, the two gnomes in their dark clothing and potato noses looking up at us with their bright eyes. There were no smiles. We were back in coveralls, scrubbed clean.

Yuri put out his hand. I took it.

"Maybe one day you'll be back," he said.

"Yes, there is a hill back there, by a lake. Anne would like to see it again."

"That would be good," he said.

"We would have proper passports and the blessing of Moscow."

He nodded.

The two women, so incredibly unalike, embraced. There was some sniffling.

Anne got into the boat and I pushed off. They stayed on the shore watching until we drifted around the bend. Their hands went up in a final, silent, wave.

"They were so nice," Anne said.

We had known them less than twenty-four hours. How can two woodsy elves who looked like they had wandered off a *Star Wars* movie set get to you like that? Anne was blowing her nose and I kept checking my shoes, clearing my throat. Ridiculous.

CHAPTER XII

I got the boat out into midstream and allowed the current to take her. If our calculations were correct, we would be on the river for no more than five hours to go the ten miles before it turned south and eventually found its way through Finland into the Gulf of Bothnia. Yuri had agreed the boat was our best means of travel given the weight of the pod. The dirt road ended in his village. Truck and automobile travel stopped there. The boat would be a risk from the ever-present choppers, but it was a risk we had to take. It was camouflaged with pine boughs and we would try to stay in the cover of the overhanging pines along the shore.

We were now better equipped for a trek through the pine forests. Yuri had found Anne a serviceable backpack. We had food for two days, a hand axe, two canteens, a pair of binoculars, two warm jackets, primitive cooking utensils, two towels, and three plastic tarps to replace the canvas I had cut from the Stinson.

The shoreline glided silently by, the pines and spruce rearing solidly along the misty banks, the sky overcast and threatening rain in the northern half light. The river was deep and powerful. There were no rapids, Yuri had pointed

278

out, but an occasional rift of white water where the bottom shoaled.

I sat in the middle thwart, looking forward, and guided the boat with the oars. The pod was up under the bow and Anne sat at the stern. She had her hands on the gunnels and was watching the shoreline.

"How did you get that pest in the café to leave me alone?" she asked.

"I reasoned with him."

"He looked like he was going to get sick."

"He might well have."

"Come on, Colin. What did you say to him? You were very calm about it, I must say. At the start, I was afraid you were going to hurt him."

The truth she would never hear from my lips.

"I told him you were married to a KGB who was six foot five and very jealous. Also very influential. Sent a lot of people to work camps in Siberia."

"You're serious?"

"Yup."

"He believed that?"

"When it comes to KGB and Siberia, Russians lose their sense of perspective."

"I guess so."

An hour slipped by and we had made good time. I looked back at Anne and she had slumped down into the bottom and was resting her head on her pack. I could see her white throat, flawless and smooth, her head was back and her eyes were closed. The boat gently rocked in the current. We had had little sleep the past two nights.

The girl was still a mystery. I recalled her fixed, cobra-like stare at the screening interview in London. Then the alarm on her face when she saw me at the ball in the ancient keep on the loch. How she bit her lip when the Russians threw us into that cell in the camp. But that was all. Solid and capable. And how steady she was when we worked the ploy in the laboratory, and the efficient way she staunched the flow of blood from the chest of her brother. How she pulled me, out of my mind with hypothermia, up on the shore of the lake. How the fat girl had turned into a beauty that stunned.

Chopper ahead! I heard it before I saw it. I guided the boat into the shore, spread the pine boughs out in the shadow of the overhang. The chopper beat down the river. The whirling blades thumping, echoing, bouncing sound against the shoreline. It was fifty feet above the water. It appeared to be a Hip, MI-8 with a troop carrying capacity of twenty-six. It beat purposefully down the river and was lost around the bend. I waited until I couldn't hear it and then rowed out into deep water.

The current took us and we nosed downriver again. I checked my watch. Four-thirty in the morning.

"Did you think Sable was attractive?"

"Your sister?"

"Yes."

"Sure. Of course. Came on too strong. Too heavily made-up."

"You really think so?"

"Yes."

"Do you think I look as good as she does?"

"Better. No contest. I liked you better at the party."

"How could you? I was so fat. I stepped on your toes when we danced."

"How the hell can I say? Just was. Something about you."

Two rocks coming up to starboard. Nasty beggars, half submerged.

"I can't believe that. Men have always fallen all over her."

Her hand dropped into the water. She let the current take it.

She shook her head. "I can't believe anybody would find me more attractive than Sable. It has never been that way."

I studied the river ahead. We were into some soft white water. We surged through it. I maneuvered away from some rocks. Then we were past them and were nosing forward again. Ever-present pines sliding by on either shore. Misty ghosts, holding out their arms.

"You really think so?"

"What?"

"About Sable and me."

"What about Sable and you."

She blew out an exasperated gasp. "What we have been talking about. You said I was more attractive than Sable."

"Sure. You are."

Watch the rock! Keep your mind on the river.

"But you said you liked me when I was fat. At the party."

I shook my head. Swung the boat around some suspicious shallows. We were through it. "Jesuschrist. I've always liked you and was interested in you. How do I know why? Just was. Now you got Sable beat ten times past Sunday. No contest. What the hell were we talking about?"

White water coming up. Shoaling fast. Not bad. We're through.

"Hard to believe after all those years."

"Better believe it, babe."

Pause. Small voice. "I've always liked you, Colin."

"You had a damn odd way to show it."

Another pause. Smaller voice. "I was afraid of you."

That got me turned around.

"That's goofy. Dumb. What did I ever do to make you feel like that."

She was looking directly at me. "You did nothing. It was just you. Me. Your looks. Your build. Your intelligence. Your ability. I can't believe you. You were just too much man for me. You don't look real, Colin. You don't act real. I still don't know what you are. I don't know what you think about. You're scary, Colin. What you did to those men."

I shook my head. I didn't know what was going on.

"I don't think you have any idea of the impact you have on people. You seem to be totally lacking in self-awareness."

What is that out there? Dark shape. Log. Nothing.

"Jesuschrist, Anne. We are trying to make the wire on the Soviet border and you're going into psychoanalysis. Gimme a break, kid."

I took a deep breath and turned back to the stern. She doesn't know what I think about? Who in the world knows what she thinks about? Maybe I was afraid of her, too, when she was a fat girl with a poor complexion and intense blue eyes full of charismatic mystery. When she hits London and the sophisticated set sees her, it's going to be "so long, Smallpiece."

I began to pick up landmarks that Yuri told me to look for. Two dead pines out on a little promontory. Ten minutes later a big boulder on the left bank, fifty feet into the river, a jog to the right, then a couple of miles of straight river. Up ahead I could see a low-lying ridge, bald on top. The river went left. Our boat journey was over. Time to go overland. I rowed into the right bank.

We pulled the boat one hundred feet into the pine, and I looked for the trail. It was seven thirty in the morning and the sky was getting lighter. It took twenty minutes to find it. I hoisted the pod on my back. Foot felt good. I had cut two hefty hiking poles. Very handy to knock branches out of the way, probe into soft patches, lean on, scare bears, things like that.

The trail twisted up and into the pine. We were into rolling, ridged country now. The trail was manmade and very old. Probably it was originally a trapper's trail, now smugglers used it in the clandestine traffic between the Soviet Union and Finland.

We wound up through the pines and spruce, the humus soft underfoot, the sun breaking down through the branches and setting a patch ablaze with light. The air was sweet with pine and we hiked steadily up, the pod resting easily on my shoulders, with two good feet under me and the pole poking into the black earth before each foot. We worked deep into the silent forest. Anne walked easily behind. Then, for a change, I put her into the lead and followed. She sifted through the small pine valleys and outcrops with the precision of a woodland Mohawk and I wondered where the awkward fat girl went, or had she ever been?

In three relatively easy hours, we arrived at our destination, a small lake with a waterfall flowing over a rocky ridge and tumbling in free fall twenty feet into a pool. The place could take your breath away. The ten-acre pond was almost a perfect circle, fringed by tall spruce and pine. The ridge rose sheer out of the pond about a third of the way around. Down from the ridge, running a hundred and fifty feet, just above the water line, was a great, smooth ledge of rock. It ran in fifty feet and flowers, blues, yellows, and pinks, poked up from small, pitted depressions in the surface. Pines sprouted along the ridge top, and some rooted into the rocky ledges and strata that projected from the ridge.

The sky had turned a clear blue and the lake was a quiet, tranquil mirror, reflecting identical placid images of sky, ridge, and trees. We had stumbled into some small, deep forest. Valhalla, Olympus, Acadia, Shangri-la, Eden. It was a place of nymphs and fawns and golden butterflies. It had an inner, secret quiet and we felt we were the first humans to discover it.

Two hawks wheeled in the sky.

I rigged a tarp over a ridge pole that I shaped from a small fallen spruce. I limbed it clean with the hand axe and supported the narrow end into a crotch on a tall pine. We had a shelter. The floor was soft with brown pine needles. Anne added some new growth pine bows. Then she made a fire and we had the stew Grandma had packed in a jelly jar.

We would wait here for the guide who would take us to the border. Yuri could not say exactly when. Tonight or tomorrow night. Perhaps even later. The weather would be a factor. The worse, the better.

I checked the map on which Yuri had marked a five-hundred-foot hill with a bald rocky top. You could see for miles, he said. It should not be a quarter of a mile beyond the ridge and waterfall. I decided to have a look.

"You want to take a hike to the top of a hill?" I asked Anne.

"What do you want to do that for?"

"Because it's there for christsakes."

She looked at the small perfect lake, the ridge, the waterfall, the golden butterflies chasing each other over the quiet water.

"No, I think I'll stay here. It's lovely. How long will you be?"

284

"It's right back of the ridge. Not far off the trail. Maybe an hour."

She smiled. "Have a nice walk, Colin."

"You sure? You don't mind?" I was thinking about the episode in the meadow of wildflowers.

"No. It's all right. I'm fine. Really."

I grabbed my hiking pole, jumped up on the rock ledge, and found the trail winding up over the ridge. I looked back. Anne was sitting cross legged, very erect, studying the waterfall. She didn't move. I photographed the scene in my memory. I would never lose it.

Up past the ridge, I found the stream that fed the waterfall. It followed a rocky bed out of the forest and noisily surged and gurgled over the ridge down into the lake below. I knelt for a drink. It was surprisingly warm.

The trail mounted up and through the trees and then I saw the hill with its bald, rocky summit. The trail wound right. I would have to go left and find my own way through the heavy spruce and pine to the top. It was ten minutes of bashing up through the piney rise when I discovered I had left the binoculars in Anne's pack. Sonofabitch. I had to go back.

I worked my way down the trail again, past the busy brook, carefully down the ridge, and out onto the rock plateau. Where was Anne?

I heard a splashing. Laughter. Saw glistening movement by the waterfall.

Anne. She was under it.

I watched from the shadow of the trees. She held her face to the falling water. Shook her head. Pushed off into the lake. Swam back under the fall. There was a shriek of laughter. She sank below the surface and then shot up into the shining, watery cascade. Her skin sleek, wet, glowing. A water sprite. Not of this world. She held her face up into it again. Gasped. Wiped her eyes. Shook her head. She splashed and played for a few minutes more. Not to have watched would have been a sacrilege.

She worked her way back along the shore and then up onto the rock ledge. I retreated further into the shadow. She came across the ledge carefully, bending slightly over, leaving wet footprints, her breasts quivering with the movement. She took the towel off a rocky outcrop and began to dry off.

I held my breath. Frozen. Transfixed.

She wrapped the towel around her waist. Ran a hand through her hair, as gold as the evening sun. She turned and looked out at the lake, and up at a sudden flight of birds, hand over her forehead, shielding her eyes from the sun. Then she abruptly swung around and saw me against the trees.

She made no movement.

Our eyes locked.

Her mouth opened.

Neither one moved.

In an instant we had entered the most fundamental of all male-female relationships. It was the cosmic moment that all of the cosmetics, padded bras, perfumes, rouges, plunging necklines, eye liners, bikinis, miniskirts are designed to ultimately contrive. From the first flirtation to the final orgiastic thrust, she must draw him to her. It is the primal sexual strategy of the female. It underlies all that she does to attract him. He must come to her. She pulls him. In the final confrontation, she may send him off, deny him, if she so chooses. That is her decision, but her physical attraction brings him to her. Her sexual beauty arouses him and causes him to act. It has been going on since the beginning of human time.

The Smallpiece theory of human sexuality has the male

playing the critical role. His arousal and capacity to perform is essential. She may be sexually passive, but ideally not for a glorious and mutually satisfactory coupling. Hence, females concentrate on the strategies of attraction. Males concentrate on the strategies of response and pursuit. That is why the mother of a newly born daughter will ask, "Do you think she will be pretty?" While the first question a fraternity brother will ask his roommate late Sunday morning is, "Did you score?"

A lesbian can submit to a man in disgust and yet get pregnant. She plays a passive sexual role. A male homosexual remains limp and unresponsive before an aroused but confused female. No fitting together. No intertwining of male and female. No coupling. No pregnancy. Nature's magnificent design is frustrated. It is a perversion of cosmic biology and purpose. A pathology.

So he must act, driven by her beauty, her femaleness, her difference. At that moment we were simply another tiny episode in an ageless biological drama.

All of that was in her eyes.

They said, "I am ready. I want you. Come to me."

She stood on the clear expanse of rock with a small shadow of water gathering from her feet. She stood with her weight on her right leg, the left slightly bent at the knee. The towel, a sarong, was tucked high along her waist but angled below the navel and soft, flat belly, low around her rounded hip. Her breasts were high and round and soft.

Her eyes never left mine.

She had sent the cosmic message.

Female flame to male moth.

I stumbled to her as the design requires.

I put my hands on her shoulders. The towel fell. She retrieved it. She handed it to me.

287

"Do you want to?" she asked.

I ran the towel over her forehead and the glistening beads of water. I tapped it against her eyelashes, intertwined and shining with the wet. I brushed it against her cheeks and upturned mouth. Then I dropped the towel and gathered her into my arms and her mouth was warm and soft and working on mine.

I had shed the coverall before we got to the shelter, and then the shoes and everything else. We were lying on the pine boughs. She hovered over me and cupped a breast with her hand, put her right hand behind my head and drew me to her.

"Kiss me," she said softly.

I felt the nipple harden in my lips. She gasped, a small vocalization. My hand ran down, across her waist and over her hip. I pulled her into me.

There is a time for lovers to speak to each other. It is after the sweating, the touching, the juices, the wet, the driving at each other, the discovery of the secret places of the other, the possession, the gasping, the vocalizing, the rolling, the frenzy, the rutting, and the final explosion of the life force. Then all of the tensions are over. The ultimate physical communication of man and woman has been realized, consummated. Then you can talk and the psychological intimacy can begin.

We lay in the shelter, on our backs, shoulder to shoulder, my left hand in her right. We studied the ridge pole and the shadows of the trees as they moved in the breeze.

I propped myself up on my elbow and looked at her face. I ran a knuckle under her chin and along her forehead. After the sexual possession, for a while at least, you feel that you own the other. My index finger traced along

288

her nose. She looked across at me and smiled. She reached over and tugged the pelt on my chest. Fell back again. She smiled at nothing. Something.

"Anne?"

"Hummmm?"

"Can I ask you a question?"

"Of course."

"Personal one. You might not like it."

"Ask."

"Do you know now that you are a beautiful woman?"

What a glorious smile. She stretched. "Yes. I know that now. You made me feel beautiful."

"Okay, you are. So why did you let yourself get fat?"

I have never been known for tact.

She rolled over and propped her chin in the cup of her hand. She considered me. She shook her head. "I've always had a weight problem ever since I was a little girl. I was tall, fat and clumsy."

I nodded. She went on. "You've seen my mother and sister. All the time I was growing up, I heard how beautiful they were. How attractive."

She rolled over on her back and talked to the ridge pole. "But not me. I was too tall. Everybody worried about how tall I was getting. They worried about my weight. Now and then, I would hear conversations about me, my mother and a friend, my mother and your grandmother. Do you know what they called me? 'Poor Anne.' It wasn't just Anne, it was always 'poor Anne.' "

I leaned over her and took a pine needle from her hair.

"I guess I never thought I was in their league as far as appearance went. So I never tried to be. I was intelligent. Everybody knew that. Top of my class. Always. Cambridge was delighted I decided to go there."

She was on her stomach now. "I loved scholarship and

289

ideas, physics and mathematics and literature and philos
ophy. I got caught up in it. I never worried about how
looked. After a while I didn't care if I didn't look as goo
as my mother and sister. I accepted 'poor Anne' at tha
level. I excelled in academics, and the honors that i
brought, and I knew some boys. I slept with a few and
was disappointed in sex with them."

She smiled and turned to me. Ran her hand in back o
my neck and into my hair. "Not like you, Colin. Oh God
not like you."

I smiled. Took her hand and kissed it.

"Why did I get fat? Natural tendency to weight and n
great incentive to worry about it. I guess I'm into an ab
stract world of ideas more than a world of cosmetics
dresses, and men."

I was running my index finger along the curve of he
jaw. She took my hand and kept it.

"You know the story of the ugly duckling?" I asked.

"That's me?"

"That's you. You just never took a good look at your
self. It was always there. You never let yourself come out.'

"I guess so. I didn't care that much. I was satisfie
with what I had done with my life. I didn't mind if Sabl
got all of the attention. She thrives on it. It really didn'
matter."

"And then Harkness got you into the spy business?"

She punched me. "I'm not in the spy business. But
liked the errands he sent me on. It was exciting and se
cretive. I liked being Lady Anne and the Scarlet Pimper
nel at the same time. I liked being in on major events an
things my friends had no idea about. And I was prett
good at it. I was pleased that important men like Harknes
and Fitzworthy listened to me and took what I said seri
ously."

290

I nodded and kissed her cheek.

"But you're not the dumpy girl with the bad complexion anymore. Not an ugly duckling. Certainly not 'poor Anne' anymore. That has to matter to you now."

An explosion of breath. "Oh yes. Now it does. I'll watch myself from now on." She smiled over at me. "If I was still the clumsy, fat girl, would you have made such passionate love to me as you just did?"

My turn to search the mysteries of the ridge pole. "Probably. You were always interesting, even if you looked like a Sunday school teacher with a healthy appetite. But out there, on that ledge of rock, no man could resist you. You're a beautiful woman, Anne."

She smiled and rubbed my chest.

"You're a beautiful man, Colin."

I flustered immediately. "Not the right word. Men aren't beautiful." I shook my head. "I don't know what the right word is."

She had a hand in my hair. "You're a contradiction, Colin."

"Yeah, I know."

"Not the way you think."

"No."

"No man who looks like you should be able to do the terrible things you do."

I frowned.

"You idiot," she smiled. "You look like an angel, but you're a one man army. A wrecking crew. When I'm with you, I feel incredibly safe, even here in the Russian wilderness."

Her hands were running along my shoulders, down along my arms, up into my hair. Her lips were slightly parted. She had her eyes into mine. They stayed there.

291

She wrapped both arms around my neck and pulled me down.

"Do you think . . ."

"Good idea," I said.

As the evening wore on, we had several more good ideas. Eventually, we took a break for a late supper. I tottered out of the shelter and looked for wood. Anne started the fire and I got out the freeze-dried packets of trail food that Yuri had provided for us. They were of Swiss manufacture and, freely translated from the French, were named "Camp Mate." Anne chose Camp Mate "Beef Stroganoff with Noodles—Servings Two," I had "Spaghetti and Meat Balls—Servings Two" and for dessert we had "Chocolate Mousse—Servings Two."

You cooked it all by pouring the contents of the foil envelopes into boiling water and waiting a little while. It all sort of looked the same. Grey. Lumpy grey. Mousse was the lumpiest.

"How's the Stroganoff?" I asked.

"Like straw."

"Spaghetti's straw, too."

"Check the mousse."

I checked the mousse. "Turnip."

Conventional wisdom has it that anything tastes good on the trail. Don't believe it. Label said it had lots of vitamins and basic nutrients, that's why we ate it.

"Should have been labeled 'Servings Half,' " I said.

"Servings None would have been better."

The half twilight deepened and the birds quieted down.

"Do you think he will come tonight?" Anne asked.

I checked the sky again. The pale half moon was still there.

"I doubt it. He will wait for rain. The poorer the visibility, the better off we'll be."

292

She nodded.

The following day was clear and bright in the morning. But clouds built up during the afternoon and a soft rain began to fall around five o'clock. He came in around six. I heard him scrambling down the ledge.

He was a tall, very thin man with a week of black stubble on his face. Mid-thirties, hawk nosed, deeply tanned, a recent scar on the left cheek and a patch over the left eye. He had a leather cap with a stubby visor, heavy blue woolen shirt, thick black pants held up by suspenders, and serviceable trail shoes with lug soles. He looked of the woods. He had no pack. He wore a long hunting knife in a sheath attached to his belt.

He saw me standing by the shelter.

We looked each other over. We had some codes to exchange.

"Much fishing?" he asked.

"Pond's fished out," I replied.

He nodded. "Yuri thought it might be."

"How's Yuri?"

"Tank's full."

I nodded.

"Leonid," he said. "You look like what he said you'd be."

Anne came from the shelter. She smiled at him. "Oh, yes," he said, "And she looks like what he said she'd be."

We shook hands in the fashion of the West.

"How long will it take?" I asked.

He looked at Anne.

"She will be fine," I said.

"Maybe," he said. "If the woman holds up, five hours."

"She'll hold up."

"We'll see."

Anne was treating him to a frosty stare.

293

"We go now," he said.

We broke camp. I got into my shoulder harness with the pod. He looked at me critically. Adjusted the straps. Felt around my shoulders. He nodded. He spent some time with Anne until he was satisfied.

"How much does your pack weigh?" he asked.

"Eighty-six pounds."

He pursed his lips. "You will have some work to do tonight."

"Yeah."

"The woman goes in the middle. Stay close to me."

He set off up the ledge and moved fast. Anne was on his heels in the soft, wet light. She had her pole and used it. He kept the fast pace for half an hour. Broke off from the trapper's trail, going west, and into a new one. Anne stayed close. We were deep into the pine wastes. The branches bit into our faces. We tripped over roots, sunk into patches of humus, labored up steep rocky rises where the trees thinned out, and then down into mossy valleys with the pungent smells of earth, pine, and water.

He called a halt in half an hour. We sank down. Drank from our canteens. I was soaking.

"Only a swallow," he cautioned. He looked at Anne and wiped his forehead with his sleeve. He nodded. "She's a good one. She'll be all right." He smiled at Anne.

We worked steadily west. Leonid slowed the pace down and took more frequent rests. Anne was having a tough time now. Did she seem pale in the moonlight, in the eternal twilight? I was beginning to wobble under the weight of the pod. I found myself relying on the pole Almost leaning on it.

Four hours in the spruce-pine sea.

Leonid was eyeing Anne. "How are you doing?" he asked.

"Fine," she nodded. She was spread-eagled against a tree. Mouth open.

"She's got some sass," he said to me.

"Wish I had a little more," I said.

"Eighty-six pounds?" he asked.

I nodded.

"I didn't think anybody could do that," he said. "Yuri said you would. He was right."

In another hour I was starting to crash into trees. Started to stumble. Fell four times. McCorkle kept his mouth shut.

Leonid called a halt.

"We are about fifteen minutes from the wire. Are you all right?" He was looking at me and not Anne.

"Fine."

"We go slow now. And we make no noise. Take a drink."

It was 12:30. We sifted slowly through the trees, rising gaunt and ragged over our heads. We were into mist and ground fog. Leonid stopped every few minutes, cocking his head forward. Listening. Then we moved on. It began to rain. I was grateful.

There was soft light up ahead. An opening in the wall trees. We crouched forward and lay down. The wire!

Through the mist and gloom we saw a two-hundred-yard wide scar cut into the pine, twisting sharply up from a bend on our left and running along an incline on our right. It got lost around the hill. Four heavy rolls of barbed wire snaked along the scar fifty feet apart. In the center stood a fifteen-foot-fence, threatening and ominous with electrified wire. Ten-foot fences of barbed wire ran on either side of the cut, the top three feet angled outwards toward us.

It looked more like it had been designed to keep people in rather than to keep people out.

Leonid checked his watch. We waited. Ten minutes. Twenty minutes. I heard a motor. Around the bend on our left, in the middle of the scar, a jeep with four men. It ground purposefully up the sloping rise and disappeared down the other side. We waited until the sound of the motor had gone.

"Follow me. Stay right behind me," Leonid whispered.

We scuttled down to the first fence. He stopped six feet from it. Studied the ground very carefully. Feeling with his hands. He swore. He turned back to us.

"The bastards put the mines back. They found the hole."

"What?"

"The entire cut is mined. We find the mines and take them out, then we cut the wire. This is my hole. I know how I arranged the earth after I took the mines out. I place small rocks and pebbles in a certain way. The pattern is changed."

He took out his hunting knife and went back to the fence. Looked at the ground again. Then he carefully inserted his knife down. "Ah!" he said. "They're down there. The bastards!"

I felt the world sinking away.

All of this time. All of this effort.

"What happens now?" I gasped.

"We go down the wire about three hundred feet. I have another hole."

"So close together?" I asked. I was incredulous.

"Would you think two holes in the wire would be that close if you were guarding the border?" He grinned.

"Maybe not."

We went down to the left, keeping inside the trees.

296

Leonid stopped again and went to the first fence. He studied the ground. Felt with his hands. He was back, grinning.

"They didn't find this one. We go. Wait here until I give you a signal." From somewhere in his shirt he found a pair of heavy leather work gloves and put them on.

In the gloom, I saw him slowly pull a section of the fence away. And then he was into the first roll of wire. He pulled a section aside. Then the second. I could hardly see him in the rain and mist.

He was back.

"You must put your feet exactly where I put my feet. You understand. Most important. Mines are everywhere."

We nodded.

Through the mist and gloom, I could see the tiny spaces he had pulled aside in the wire. Windows, Yuri had called them. Little windows in the barricade. Wire windows to Finland and the free world.

God, let's go. We were down at the fence. Leonid wiggled through the opening. We followed. Then the first roll of wire. Anne snagged her pack. They were off our backs and we were dragging them. I reached up and freed it. Crawled through. We were in the middle of the cut. Tree stumps everywhere. Did I hear a motor?

Leonid produced some wires with alligator clips. He clipped them onto the fence in three places. Then he rolled a section back. Another window. He waited a moment. Nodded.

"Now be careful of the bridge wire on the ground. Don't pull it off as you go through. Lift your packs over it."

Anne went through, hunched over, carrying her pack in her arms. Keeping her eyes on the bridge wire.

I picked up eighty-six pounds of pod in my arms, bent my back over, saw the wire, put one foot over it and then the other. The pod slipped out of my arms onto the ground. I couldn't hold it. Missed the shunt by three inches! Jesuschrist. It was a motor.

We went through the two other rolls of wire. I snagged the pod on one and myself on the other. I had a minor pain in my right arm and felt a warm trickle of blood.

A jeep came chugging down the incline not more than four hundred feet away. We had the last fence to go through.

"Don't move. Hunch down," Leonid said. "Pretend that you are a tree stump. Make yourself small. Don't look at it. Look at the ground."

I made myself into a tree stump. I looked at the ground. I willed myself to root into the ground. The rain splashed down my neck. The motor grew louder. It was abreast of us. It continued to drone on. It was moving away down the hill. It was gone. I blessed the rain, mist, fog, and general gloom. Never will I think ill of them again.

Leonid had the last hole in the fence open. We went through!

He had a smile on his face. He walked us to the tree line and into them. We slung our packs.

"Those bastards have extra patrols now. They must want you pretty bad. Planes up and down the border. I never expected two patrols within fifteen minutes."

He clapped me on the back. 'You're through."

"Finland?"

"Not yet. You're still in the Soviet Union. Work to the west. Use your compass. You will come to a fence. It will be full of holes. Nobody repairs it. When you are through that fence, you will be in Finland. I've got to go now and put the fence back so the holes will not be seen."

We shook hands and he melted back toward the first fence. He pulled the wire back and secured it. Then he moved off to the first roll of wire.

We drifted into the pine again. There was no trail. We picked our way. Got slapped in the face by wicked branches. We had no poles to poke the ground or shove the branches away. We inched our way through the piney gloom.

In ten minutes we heard shots. Automatic rifles. The flat whack of Kalishnakovs.

"What is it?" Anne asked.

"They spotted him."

"Do you think he got away?"

"They're still at it."

"Because of us."

"If he made the woods, he'll be okay. No way they could keep up with him there."

We still heard the fire. Automatic fire. They were spraying. Didn't have a target. That was good. Then the fire stopped suddenly. That was bad. Fifty-fifty.

"I think he's in the woods. If they caught him in the cut, they wouldn't still be firing."

Four-thirty in the morning and the watery sun was in the sky and we were still in Russia. We punched through it. No trail. We picked our way. I fell down twice. I didn't have much left.

Then it was the fence! The Finnish border. Old, sagging, chain link with a rusty, token strand of barbed wire at the top. We walked alongside it. Found a ten-foot section that was bent and twisted almost to the ground. We went over it and into the gloom beyond. We walked mechanically for another fifteen minutes. No talk. Heads down, and then there was the barest outline of a path, a track. I fell down on it and crawled over to a tree. Propped up against it. Anne was down beside me. I put my arm over her shoulders. We took deep breaths. Got my head into hers.

"We got the thing out, babe. Jesuschrist." I used English.

She nodded.

"Sonofabitch."

I worked out of my harness and took Anne's pack off. I lay back on the soft turf still sucking in great breaths of free air.

She started to sob. And then it turned into a good cry. I pulled her into my neck. And the tears got me wet. She's something. She held the woman in her off until now. She deserved a cry. I held her close.

Finland.

CHAPTER XIII

We awoke six hours later all wrapped up in an untidy bundle of intertwined legs and arms. I had no idea of going to sleep, we just lay back for a few minutes on the pine needles and gentle turf, thinking we would be up and at it again. But a combination of enormous relief from having made it through the wire and our physical exhaustion from the ordeal of the all-night trek, simply was too much. We were off in minutes. No choice. The body took over.

The sun was high in the sky. My watch said 1:36. We were into the afternoon.

I dug into Anne's pack and found the last of Grandma Timoshenko's elf bread. I cut it in half with my heavy knife.

"It's hard, but it's strength," I said to Anne.

The bread took a lot of chewing. We washed it down with the tepid water from the canteens. Fifteen minutes later we were ready for the trail, back into our packs. I had cut two more hiking poles.

"Which way, fearless leader?" Anne asked.

I checked my compass and the map.

"There are no landmarks to triangulate from, but I think we came in not too far from the landing strip. Maybe six or seven miles below it. It's a guess, of course." I pointed with my finger. "We should be about here, I think. There ought to be a road maybe three miles west. That should be it, about here on the map."

Anne nodded. "What about Llewellyn?"

I shook my head. "He could be anywhere. I have a telephone number. That's all. We need to get to a phone for a couple of reasons."

Anne studied the track. "Which way?"

"Left," I said. "It goes west and that's for us."

We followed the track, towering pines overhead. Patches of blue sky beyond. I thought I heard a chopper. We ran into several forks but stayed on the main path. As we hiked along, the track became more defined, used. We were moving toward people, civilization.

In an hour we had arrived, out of the dense pine, onto a dirt road, a dusty slash hacked out of wilderness. My compass read it ran generally north–south. Which way now?

I looked at Anne. She shrugged her shoulders.

The fearless leader pointed south.

A chopper drifted overhead and we both automatically ducked for cover. It was low and I had a good look at it. It had Swedish markings. Odd. Why would the Swedes be flying the Finnish border?

Fifteen minutes later a bus came by filled with teenage kids. Camping gear was lashed to the roof. Little flags flew from staffs on the fenders. We stopped and waved frantically, hoping for a lift, but the bus roared by and we got a lot of return waves from the kids and a cloud of exhaust.

A dusty Volkswagen camper rattled by going in the opposite direction. We got a another wave. Then it was a truck with a solitary driver. We waved some more. He looked stolidly ahead and bit his cigar. Grouch. We plowed

302

ahead. It was getting warm. We were out of water. Then we heard another engine behind us. A small Mercedes truck. We stopped. Waved. The truck slowed.

He had a round head, balding blond hair, glasses, thin, tipped-up nose, generous smile, faded plaid shirt. Suspenders. One of life's innocents, content but always a little amazed. He rolled the passenger window down. Grinned. Licked his full, wet lips.

He spoke to us in Finnish.

We shook our heads.

"Do you have English?" I asked.

"Of course," he grinned. "Who doesn't?"

"Can you give us a lift?"

"Where are you heading?"

"Nearest town, village. Need to make a phone call."

"Five miles ahead. Hop in. You can toss your packs in the back."

Two jet fighters came low overhead, throttled way down. Norwegian markings. I watched them disappear over the pine horizon. More mystery. Swedes and Norwegians patroling the Finnish border.

We tossed our packs in the back, along with five or six large sacks of grain. We clambered into the bench seat, Anne in the middle.

He never lost his grin. "Looks like you have been in the woods awhile. Been camping?"

"Yeah," I said.

He got the truck moving. "I'm Hekki Pietlila," he said, holding out his hand. I took it, then Anne. His hand was soft and wet.

"My name is Smedley Largepart," I said. "My companion is Hortense Hotbox. We're students." I got a sharp jab in the ribs from Anne. I was giddy, carefree, out of my mind with relief. Loved those Norwegian fighters even if I couldn't figure out what they were doing here.

Hikki's head bobbed up and down. He was in his early forties, fairly thin, maybe average height. He had watery blue eyes behind steel-rimmed glasses. Automatic grin still working. He was anxious to please. He had three ball-point pens sticking out of his shirt pocket. He was a Finnish nerd. Classic type. Didn't know they had them in Finland. Maybe they were becoming a race.

"Your pack looked very heavy," Hikki observed, holding onto the wheel with both hands, eyes grimly fixed on the road. He had ordered us to put our seat belts on.

"Rocks," I said.

"Oh?"

"We're geology students. The University of Newcastle upon Tyne. England. Near the Scotch border. I have some rocks in that pack that will revolutionize the conventional theory of Finnish stratigraphy in the Kuusamo gorges."

He nodded his head with great enthusiasm.

"Oh, my. You're English students then?"

"Yes. We love Finland."

He pumped up. "We have only four million people, but we are the fifth largest country in land area in Europe. We are Lutherans."

"We are Protestants," I said, ingratiating myself.

"That's good, too," Hekki slowly agreed. Clearly Lutherans were better than Protestants, but Protestants were better than nothing.

"Did you know that the sun never sets above the Arctic Circle and in Rovaniemi, from early June to early July. In Helsinki, we have twenty hours of sunlight in the summer."

"Yes. We noticed that. It's wonderful."

Hekki had a good sweat going and gravely worried

304

about the road ahead. He was grinning and sweating. He wiped his glasses that were fogging.

His face lit up. "My farm is just up the road a mile. Would you like a glass of fresh milk? Coffee? Maybe a wash-up? Would you?" His puppy-dog eyes were pleading.

Anne's smile said yes.

"If it wouldn't be too much trouble," I said. I could phone from Hekki's. "Coffee would be marvelous."

He continued to do twenty-five miles an hour down the empty road. We passed one or two small farm holdings, a couple of cars going in the opposite direction. Hekki waved at both and got a reply. Then he slowed before a driveway on our left. Hekki pulled in.

It was a substantial place, a large, rambling, planked wooden house. Steeply pitched matt black roof in the Finnish style with four chimneys, all suede black. Four good-size dormer windows looked out from the roof. There was a small pillared portico over the front door. Flower-pots. Geraniums. Behind the house, I saw a barn and several outbuildings and two cleared fields with neat rows of small, green plants. The inevitable pines loomed behind the cultivated area along a two-hundred-foot ridge, maybe four hundred yards away.

We wound up a curving drive around an acre of grass with strategically placed clumps of white birch. There was a small wood on our left, mostly thinned-out spruce and pine, and beyond it a low rock wall guarding a meadow. Two hundred feet below the meadow, strategically near the house, I saw a long row of neatly stacked firewood. Beyond the rock wall and meadow, on our far left, the dense pines began.

It appeared to be a well-managed, prosperous farm. Nothing needed paint or repair. Everything was in order. Hekki ran a tight ship. He stopped before the front door.

305

The drive curved away to the left and ran behind the house.

"Please come," Hekki beamed. "You can leave your packs in the truck. They are perfectly safe."

I pulled both packs down. Hekki stuck his lip out. He was hurt.

"Valuable rocks," I grinned. "They'll make me famous."

Hekki raised his eyebrows and we went inside. We dropped our packs in the entrance hall. I had a surprise. I had expected heavy, old, well-used Victorian pieces handed down from one generation of Pietlilas to the next. But Hekki had discovered the IKEA catalogue and everything was contemporary Scandinavian. Beiges, whites, and wheats were the prevailing colors. Furniture was low slung, fabrics rough and pebbly, lot of white plastic laminate over particle board in the four-foot bookcases and low tables. Wood was unstained in rubbed, low lustre varnish.

The rooms were light and airy, modern and comfortable. The old floors had been sanded and were almost white under the high-gloss finish. Off-white, knobby rugs covered most of the floors. Impressionistic prints hung at strategic points on the walls. I liked it. Anne was smiling. Free at last. Anything would look good.

A gun cabinet stood in a corner, rubbed limed oak with glass doors and two drawers at the bottom. I saw three shotguns, and two hunting rifles and a smaller caliber rifle. Maybe a twenty-two. The larger rifles looked to be military rifles that had been remanufactured for civilian use with checkered pistol grip stocks and long, reblued barrels. Mausers maybe, with no clips. Mild-mannered, bookish, nerdish Hekki was a hunter.

"Please sit. Or would you care to wash up? Anything. You are my guests." He grinned from ear to ear.

We stood about uncertainly.

"A bathroom is through the hall, on the right. And there is another at the top of the stairs." Anne headed upstairs.

Hekki propelled me into the living room with a Jotul woodstove sitting on a rock platorm in a corner. "Please," he said, "sit, sit. You look exhausted. I will make some coffee."

So I sat and looked around. From the front windows, I looked out across the wide lawn. There was a thin line of birches on the left and I thought I could see two or three horses in the field beyond.

Anne was back with her face scrubbed. There were three or four deep scratches on her cheeks and forehead as branches had whipped and torn at her during the night. She smiled at me. Patted my arm.

"I need a bath," she said. "But this will do for now."

She looked around. "Isn't it nice? Who would have expected this up in the Finnish wilderness?"

I nodded. What was keeping Hekki? Where was the phone?

Then he appeared wheeling a serving cart with a pot of steaming coffee and some little sweet cakes. His grin was out of control. He almost drooled. He seemed to be playing house. He had put on a jacket for the occasion and had slicked his occasional hairs down.

"You live alone?" I asked.

He nodded and frowned. "Yes. Yes. No woman would put up with me, I'm afraid."

"You have a lovely home," Anne said, accepting the cup of coffee.

"Thank you. I work hard at it." He blotted his mouth.

I sipped my cup of coffee. Lord, it tasted good. Hot and black.

There was some more small talk.

"Can I use your phone?" I asked. "Reverse charges, of course."

"Certainly," Hekki grinned. "Hope you have better luck with it than I have. It isn't working well. I've called them. But you know ... " He raised his eyes.

I nodded that I knew about phone companies, too, and got up.

"In the hall," Hekki pointed, "back toward the kitchen."

I found the hall toward the kitchen. The phone was on a small IKEA table in white laminate. The phone was dead. I tried jiggling it. Nothing.

"You didn't get through?" Hekki asked.

"No."

"Well, no matter. I can drive you into the village as soon as you are ready."

"Fine."

I heard a chopper going by overhead.

Hikki grinned and blotted. Couldn't keep his eyes off Anne. I sipped my coffee.

"I saw Swedish and Norwegian military aircraft this morning," I said. "Isn't that unusual? What were they doing?"

Hekki pulled a face. "Who knows? Joint maneuvers, I was told. Damn nuisance, if you ask me. They are up there all the time. Wake you up at night."

I nodded."

"Think I might use your bathroom," I said.

He beamed. "Please." He turned to Anne and I went upstairs.

I looked out of one of the dormers.

Two cars had pulled up on the dirt track that divided Hekki's front lawn with the pasture on the left. One was a Volkswagen van. People inside. I could see their heads. A man got out of the van. He was wearing blue coveralls. Dull, slate blue. He went back to the second car and talked to the driver. They were looking at Hekki's house. They were joined by a third man. They all considered Hekki's house. They all wore coveralls in dull colors. One man wore a cap with a peaked visor. He carried a rifle. It had a large magazine that curved foreward. It was Kalishnakov.

Another car pulled into the track. There were three cars and they were all full of men in coveralls.

I went downstairs and took a look at Hekki's phone. I pulled at the wire that went into the small, gray junction box. It came free. The ends had been neatly cut.

I went back into the living room. Hekki was standing, looking out of the windows. He was still sweating, but no longer smiling. He took one look at my face and shoved a hand into his jacket.

I went into the hyperdrive immediately, and Hekki stood there with his sweating face, pulling a huge six-shot revolver free of his jacket, in Technicolor and slow motion. He swung it majestically on me, his lips were pulled back, he no longer looked like a nerd. I saw the flash and heard the dull roar. But he was way too high and then I was into him, driving him onto the wall, the way an offensive guard is told to take out the opposing lineman. Lot of leg action. I stuffed Hekki into the wall. An impressionistic print fell down. Taking its time. Hekki began his unhurried, graceful descent to the floor. The pistol danced free and lazily skittered away.

I looked through the windows and saw figures moving through the birches along the pasture. They must have heard the shot. Anne was looking at me in frozen alarm. I heard her voice. She was pointing back at Hekki. He had crawled to the gun cabinet and was opening a drawer. I picked up the revolver, pointed it, pulled the trigger, another leisurely explosion of orange flame with a dull, reverberating roar. Half of Hekki's face drifted away in slow-moving chunks. Messed up the off-white wall.

I came out of the hyperdrive right away with the immediate threat gone. Out of the window I could see darting figures among the birches a hundred yards away. Now they had stopped. Wondering about the two shots.

I took the two Mausers down from the gun case, and shotgun. The top drawer was loaded with ammo. I kept the Mauser with the scope and fed shells into a clip. No movement outside. There was some discussion down by the cars.

"Take these rifles and the ammo out back. Find a place in a depression. Get your pack out there, too. Fast. Now."

I got five seconds of very serious blue eyes. Steady eyes. She didn't hesitate. She had a Mauser and a shotgun and a box of shotgun shells and disappeared down the hall. I heard a door bang.

The discussion was still gong on by the van. One man had a walkie-talkie to his ear. The boss. The officer in charge.

"Get the son of a bitch." McCorkle.

"You think I don't know that?"

"Well, do it for christsakes."

"I require no instruction in basic field tactics."

"Move!"

He had the last word. Always does.

I sighted down the scope and got him clean in the cross hairs, squeezed the trigger. Whack! The man spun around and went down clutching his chest. I had the bolt out and rammed another shell into the breech. Sighted down on the man who was standing next to him. He was wildly

310

ooking around, not diving for cover. Whack! Not clean in he chest. Probably in the shoulder, but he would lose nterest in events around him for a while.

Anne was back. She had a net shopping bag and was tuffing it with ammo boxes. She was very calm about it. At the supermarket. She went into the kitchen.

I heard a burst of automatic fire and the windows disappeared. Kalisnakovs. A whole bunch. I ducked across he hall into the dining room. Drew a bead on a figure in he birches, squeezed, fired, the Mauser drove back into my shoulder and the figure went down.

I saw Anne out of the corner of my eye. "Get your pack outside." She nodded and disappeared.

We were taking a steady pounding from small arms fire now. Holes appeared in Hekki's lovely white walls, making little puffs of smoke. Some fire was now being directed into the dining room. Windows were gone and the lovely china in the open cupboard was being systematically reduced to shards and splinters. There was a lot of chunks of KIEA particle board all over the place. Stuff can't take rifle fire. The curtains were in shreds. We had to get out of here. The small-arms fire was incessant. I was on the floor. There was buzzing and snapping overhead. Slugs were smashing into furniture, whining off the cast-iron stove. Glass shattered somewhere.

Anne was down on the floor, crawling back in. She had Mauser with her, cradled in her elbows. She knew the look.

"Everything out?"
She nodded.

There was a pop, and a hole opened up in the wall a oot over her head, spraying her with white powder.

"Keep down," I shouted. We waited. Looking at the loor.

311

There was a lull in the fire. I could hear a helicopter hovering overhead. From the gaping holes where the living-room windows had been I could see it, no more than a hundred feet over the van. Big Swedish chopper. They took no fire and gave none. Just stayed there. Looking.

I found another shadow in the birches. Whack! The shadow went down. That drew an immediately, angry automatic-fire response. I could hear slugs whacking into the walls all around me. I crawled back into the kitchen. Anne was kneeling by the kitchen door. She still had the second Mauser. It had a clip, the bolt was shoved in, and the safety was off.

I could hear a lot of fire up front and the house was shaking under the impact. It stopped suddenly. Then there was a tremendous explosion on the second floor. The ceiling over us cracked opened and a chair fell through from upstairs, followed by a dresser, another chair, a rug got hung up. Couldn't make it through. Swayed there in the dust. Two beams broke off and came falling through. That brought the rug down. We were covered with fine dust. The ceiling was swaying. The whole goddamn house was coming apart.

Bullets buzzed and thudded around me. Ricochets whined. Holes appeared above my head and spurted little puffs of white powder. Assault rifles hammered into the house on automatic fire, seeking targets of opportunity. Me. I lay flat on my stomach and looked at the crumbling hall ahead where the pod wobbled uncertainly on the floor. What was I doing here? I am a very good F-14 pilot. I am happy teaching full-bodied, bright-eyed Spaulding maidens the marvels of a miniaturized social theory, paradigms and higher level mathematics that they do not understand. Why was I here deep in the Finnish wilderness, getting shot at by Russians and ordering a beautiful girl of noble birth out of the kitchen door with an armful of rifles? Made no sense. None at all. Challenge, she would say. Maybe.

I crawled back into the hall and grabbed my pack with the pod and pulled it through the kitchen. There was another violent explosion, this time in the living room. A great cloud of dust blew back on us and the whole house shuddered. Something was burning. I saw black smoke and flames. More incoming automatic fire. A line of holes sprouted three feet over our heads.

"What is it?" Anne asked.

"Antitank rockets, recoiless rifles, boozakas, something like that. We got to get out of here. This house is going to go!"

We were out into the back of the house. A hundred feet ahead was the barn, doors open, tractor in the dim light. On our right a thin line of birch trees about fifty feet from the barn.

On the left of the barn there was a low rock fence. Beyond the fence, a shed and then open fields. Between the house and barn there was a dry drainage ditch, bridged by two culverts. Fifty feet from the house, again on our left, there was a long row of stacked firewood, about a hundred feet long and six feet deep, five feet high. Hekki was planning on a tough winter. The firewood was in front on the drainage ditch. Beyond the ditch was another shed and beyond the shed, along the back, were the fields with the neat rows of green things.

The house shuddered as another rocket slammed into it. A chunk of roof slid to the ground and then one of the black chimneys was down, raining bricks all around us.

"Where are the rifles and ammo?" I shouted.

"Down in the ditch! Follow me!" She was screaming

above the bedlam of exploding rockets and vanishing house.

She ran, hunched over, to the culvert on the left and dropped down into the ditch, now dry and grassy, behind the long row of firewood. We ran along the ditch about a hundred feet from the house. I dragged the pod along with me.

We lay in the ditch, taking deep breaths, looked back, and watched the house being systematically reduced to rubble by the rocket fire. The roof was gone. It was a single-story house now. Soon it would be a pile of smoking dust.

Okay. What do we have? Regroup. Think. Plan. We have two-bolt action military rifles in good shape with plenty of ammunition. We have a big shotgun, probably twelve gauge, with enough shells. We got ourselves a ditch with good cover and a big bunch of wood near it. We also have some high explosive bombs, courtesy of the James Bond freak, still in our shoulder bags. There are two of us. We also have eighty-six pounds of dead weight to move around. The dead weight was why we were here. The dead weight was the mission.

On the other hand, they have twenty or thirty guys with automatic weapons, recoiless rifles or some kind of anti-tank rockets. And they wanted us bad. They were quite determined.

One more thing, we must not get ourselves killed. Challenge, she said.

With the house now in flames or blown into rubble, they seemed to have lost interest in it. I grabbed my Mauser, went up the drainage ditch, and had a look through the woodpile. I found a crack in the logs that gave a reasonable field of fire. I was looking down toward the dirt road that we had turned off from into Hekki's drive. But I couldn't see it. Directly in front of me was a small, cleared meadow. It ended about two hundred fifty feet in a low rock wall. Off to my right, about a hundred yards or so, was heavy pine. Ahead and to my left, I could see a bit of Hekki's drive through some thin birch and spruce. The drainage ditch ran about two hundred yards to our immediate right and into some heavy forest. That seemed to be our way out. But in the last hundred yards it seemed to level off. We would be easy to hit, particularly lugging the pod. Directly behind us, about ten feet from the ditch, was a shed.

Through my crack in the woodpile, I could see some movement in front of what had been Hekki's house. I had a couple of shots but I didn't want to give our position away. They might think we had gone up with the house.

I checked the shoulder bags and found three soap bars that were bombs with fuses.

I motioned Anne up to the woodpile. She scrambled up with her Mauser.

"They don't know if we died in the house or not. They're uncertain about it. Keep your eye peeled on them. You can spot them through cracks in the woodpile. Move up and down. See what you can see. If they come at us, fire at them. Load your shotgun. You know how?"

She nodded. Bit her lip.

I inclined my head toward the shed. "Looks like a work shed of some sort. I'm going to see if I can improve these bombs."

"All right" was all she said. She was very pale. She broke open the shotgun and fed in two shells. Old-time, double-barreled job.

I loaded all the clips we had and laid my Mauser up on the ditch, near the shed.

I took the shoulder bag and crawled out of the ditch

and slithered through the door of the shed. Anne was peeking through the fence about twenty feet down the woodpile. The firing had all but stopped. I looked around.

It was a work shed. Couple of chain saws, riding lawn mower, small, old rusty plow in a corner. Filled with generations of farm junk. Ah! Work bench. Good! Cans of rusty bolts and nails. Excellent! I found three cans about the size of coffee cans in the U.S. and poured in some nuts, bolts, nails, anything hard and hostile that I could find. Then I stuffed in the three soap bars and shoved in the shoelaces, the fuses. I poured in some more nails and hardware, then stuffed in some oily rags to hold it all together. I punched holes in the lids, ran the fuses through, then forced the lids back down. I had three effective hand grenades.

I was back in the ditch.

"What's going on?" I asked Anne.

"The Swedish helicopter is back. See?" Off to the right, over the dense pine wood, I saw it hovering. Two hundred feet up. What were they thinking about all this? They could see the house in ruins. Could they see us in the ditch. Did they know one was a girl? It swung away and was gone.

I saw movement over on the left of the house as we faced the meadow. They were trying to turn our flank. If they moved through those birches and set up, they could fire down on us from behind the woodpile. They could see right into the ditch.

I grabbed a tomato can, some matches, and ran back down the ditch toward the house. I got out at the culvert and crawled on my stomach to the barn and worked my way around to the open doors.

Three men, setting up a light machine gun. Very busy. Very intent on their work. Good concentration. Fifty feet away into the birch. I cut the fuse down to fifteen seconds, fired my match, lit the fuse. Waited ten seconds. Stepped out from behind the door. They were still intent on their gun. I held the bomb in both hands, took a short drop with a quick release. Good spiral. I hit my man on the numbers. I dropped to the ground immediately. Waited. One second. Two. Nothing. Fuse go out? Boom!

Nails and junk thudded into the barn door. Then I was out and into the ditch. Scratch one light machine-gun team.

I knew it couldn't last. Too many of them.

I turned to Anne. "Set the pod to go in ten minutes."

Her mouth fell open. "You mean it?" She read failure in my face. The challenge lost. All this way and now, lost.

"I mean it."

"How long will it take you?"

"One minute."

"Do it."

A rocket blew out ten feet of woodpile on our right near the remains of the house. They knew we were here. Wood and big splinters filled the air. They make nasty wounds, splinters. Tear you apart. Hard to get out. Awful pain.

She punched keys. Lights blinked. She had tears in her eyes. The tears fell onto the panel. She said nothing, but keyed in the sequences. We had failed. We hadn't brought the pod out. We were destroying it. So close.

Another rocket blew twenty feet of woodpile away on the opposite side. Bastards!

"Done," she said.

I checked my watch. "She goes at 4:12?"

"Exactly."

"Okay," I said, grabbing Anne by the arm. "You go down the ditch and into the woods now. You got it. Now. Take the Mauser."

317

She was very firm into my eyes.

"No. I stay. I don't go until you do. Don't argue, Colin I mean it. You want to stay here and argue? We have nine minutes left. I know what you intend to do. Stand them off. Get me some time. I stay."

Another great chunk of woodpile rose into the sky. This time in a slow motion. I was into hyperdrive. My psyche was saying I was in a life-threatening situation.

"Okay," I heard myself say. "Stay in the ditch. I'll be back in a few minutes."

I went down the ditch back toward the culvert and the smoking ruin. I took another bomb and the rifle. I had seen the flash as the rocket left the tube. Long throw.

I was into the smashed firewood, near the remains of the house. What was left of Hekki's woodpile was taking a lot of automatic fire. I crawled out of the ditch and found cover near the ruins. I looked into the birch and saw heads moving, saw the tube. Saw the man sighting down and then the belch of flame as the rocket streaked out. I saw it curve in toward the woodpile, fifty feet from Anne, and then the explosion and chunks of wood sailing slowly across the sky. Everything so slow. So predictable. Like a movie. Wasn't a movie.

I had the match out, lit the fuse, waited, heaved it with all my strength into the trees, saw it deflect short of the target. Then they looked up. The bomb went off and heard a scream. There was confusion. A body reared up and I put a bullet into his chest. Bolt came smoothly back cast out the spent shell, shoved a new one into the breech Wonderful action, the Mauser. Probably the best ever. sighted another figure crouching, and fired. There was shout and a cry. No sense pushing my luck, I was back into the ditch. My corner of the smoking ruin was being smashed, racked by concentrated automatic fire.

I shoved in a fresh clip and waited in the culvert. I saw a head rear up in the trees by the drive and took a shot. Missed. I ducked as more incoming whipped overhead. A ricochet whined into the barn. It was getting awfully hot here.

Then the shed where I had improvised the bombs blew apart. Great chunks lifting into the air. I looked for Anne but she was up against the woodpile, with the Mauser, sighting down and firing! I saw her shoving the bolt forward. Pieces of shed dropped around her. She continued to work the rifle. I saw it kick into her shoulder. But the Russians still had a rocket firing. Another stretch of woodpile flew apart. I could see the flash where it was fired from. Then a Russian reared up. Hit in the chest and fell partly over the rock fence. I saw another fall. I looked to Anne, but she was down in the ditch, reloading a clip.

Out of the dense pine wood over on the right, I saw black figures dart from tree to tree, rock to rock. They fired short bursts. Uzis! Assault rifles. A grenade exploded among the rocket crew. A silent cry welled up in my throat. Llewellyn's men had found us! The big Swedish chopper still hovered overhead.

Now the Russians began to fall back in good order toward the fringe of birches lining the drive. The English commandos were taking a deadly toll as they relentlessly swept from the wood, across the meadow, over the rock wall. They fired with incredible accuracy. I screamed, "Come on, you black-faced bastards. Come on!" But the rocket fired once more and a section of woodpile flew apart.

Anne? Where was Anne? There in the ditch. Near the pod. God, she was down on her back, arms spread out.

The pod! I forgot the goddamn pod! Time was slow for me. The hyperdrive! I checked my watch. Forty-five sec-

319

onds and the pod would blow. I ran down the ditch to the still girl with her arms flung out, face to the sky. She was so pale. I gathered her up and flung myself down the ditch. Small arms fire still whacked into the shattered fire wood. Thudded into the earth. Whined off rocks. I held her and raced on.

I heard the rocket coming. Knew it was coming. Heard the terrible explosion behind me. Felt the awful pain stab into my back, knocking me down in the ditch. Waves of grey covered my eyes. I fought to stay conscious. Terrible pain in my right foot. I struggled up and then over the ditch, clutching the girl, and ran, limped, hobbled toward the English. A bullet plucked my left sleeve. Then a giant figure, had to be Flynn, came up from a rock. My right foot was not holding me. I was down on my knees. Flynn was running toward me.

"No. Go back!" I shouted, but he came on.

I was down again, holding her, nothing left in my right foot. Flynn was ten feet away when the pod blew and the concussion picked me up and threw me into him. We all went down. The pain in my back took over. Dominated me. I had no will. I couldn't move. I couldn't breathe. Things went grey as I lay there, face stuffed into the turf and then the grey started to break up. Then everything was gone.

I was alive.
I was in an airplane.
I was lying down.
Something cool was on my forehead.
I remembered. I remembered I failed.
I kept my eyes closed and got myself together.

I opened my eyes and saw Flynn's ugly face bending over. "Sister," he shouted. "He's coming round."

She had a kindly, middle-aged, professional face. She put her hand on my forehead. She smiled.

"Of course he's coming around. What did you expect? He has a heart like a clock."

She looked at me again "How do you feel?" she asked.

"Great," I said. "Wonderful"

I looked at Flynn. "The girl?"

"Fine, sir. Took a knock on the head, that's all."

"She here?"

"No, sir. Only the dead and wounded, sir."

"Dead?"

"We lost two, sir."

I swallowed and nodded. "You're here, Flynn."

He grinned and held up his left arm. The sleeve had been cut off and it was bandaged around the bicep.

"Ten stitches. A scratch. I got the bastard."

"Where is she?"

"Stayed with the Leftenant. She's fine, sir. She was very upset to see them carry you off like that. Very upset, sir. She sort of went wild for a minute. Very determined to come along. But she's fine, sir. Now."

"Where are we going?"

"Home. To hospital."

"How long?"

"Hour and a half, I think."

I looked at the nurse. "My back?"

"Three broken ribs. Didn't even come through. You have a broken bone in your foot, too."

"Doesn't hurt."

"We have given you something." She patted my shoulder.

I nodded. "Send the pilot back. I must talk to him."

"Well," she said, brows beetling. Most irregular. "I
don't know about that."

"It's urgent. Very important security matter. I must
make a call."

She looked at Flynn, then back down at me.

"Better do what he says, sister," Flynn said. She went
off. The pilot came back. He was unhappy.

"Can you patch through a phone call? It has to do with
the fuss we have all been through. Very important. It's
your ass if you refuse, buddy."

Smartass Yank.

He eyed me for ten seconds. He made up his mind.
Nodded curtly. "I'll try," he said.

I gave him Harkness's special number and my code.
Merlin. Merlin, the failed magician. He went up to his
office.

Ten minutes later he was back trailing some wire, a
headset and a mike. "Go ahead," he said. "He's on."

"Okay," I said. "Everybody disappear. Go." They went
off reluctantly. He would probably listen up front. But I
made the effort.

"Hello," I said.

"Merlin?" It was Harkness. Pretty good voice quality,
considering.

"Yup."

"We had a very brief signal that you were out and the
pod was destroyed."

"Yeah. Sorry, we had it out, but couldn't hang onto it.
Too many Russians."

"It was an incredible achievement."

"I'm not calling about our incredible achievement. You
know we were blown before we left London?"

Pause. I heard a deep breath. "Yes."

322

"The two humpty dumps on the chopper. Not Lushev and Yefimov, right?"

"Yes."

"You got a mole in your bedroom, Harkness."

"What do you mean?"

"I mean the Russians knew everything. They even put in a special order for Anne so she could kill the self-destruct. They were in a panic over that. We obliged."

"How do you know this?"

"Vickers told me. He was set up. He was gay and they arranged a photo session. He told me who arranged it all."

"Who?"

"You remember who pushed to have Anne sent on the mission? You were not so sure."

"Yes. You don't mean to suggest ..."

"Rodger Henderson."

"I can't believe that."

"He's the mole. You've been penetrated. He's been inserted. You understand, Harkness?" I used spy-speak so he would understand and not be confused with the king's English.

Silence. "We'll check into it."

"Don't check. Get him. Give me five minutes with him. Save him for me."

"You're hurt. I'll take care of it. We'll look into it."

"He's the mole. Get him. Sweat him. I mean, don't piss around on this, Harkness."

I heard a sigh.

"You're all right?"

"I'm okay."

"I can't believe you did it."

"We didn't."

Pause.

"But you destroyed it."

323

"We didn't get it out. Ten minutes more and we would have had it out. I blew the job. You should have sent Faraday."

I hung up. Puffed out a breath. My back hurt. My foot hurt. I wondered where Anne was.

We were on the ground in an hour and a half. Doctors and nurses everywhere. They got me and Flynn into an ambulance. He insisted, and he is a force.

I was in a room by myself. They wheeled me into X Ray. I got my picture taken a number of times. I had two nurses. Very pretty English girls. They washed me. They kept looking at each other. Silent female talk. They stayed with me half the night. They patted my hair and fussed.

"Do you want your beard off?" the redhead asked.

"Oh, sure. I forgot about it."

She took most of it off with electric hair clippers. Then she lathered me up and used a straight razor with swift, sure, professional strokes. The brunette watched, arms folded. They both stepped back.

"What do you think?" the redhead asked the brunette.

She stepped back. Put her hand to her chin and studied. Turned to the redhead. "Robert Redford?"

"More like Clint Eastwood. Much younger. Better."

"Sort of a combination, but he's himself, too," the brunette added.

They both nodded.

It was dark outside. Really dark. I looked at the dark. Two weeks in Finland. A two-week day. I had forgotten about the dark. I liked it. Two more nurses took over, as nice as the first two. Both were blondes. All four talked and looked at me. What the hell? I love English girls.

In a half hour they were back with basins and towels.

"What's this for?" I asked.

"Wash, you were filthy."

324

"I had a wash."

"You're getting another. They had to miss something."

They stripped me and went to work. Very thorough. Very complete. Missed nothing. Nothing. I mean nothing.

"I think maybe you better stop now," I said.

"Nonsense, I'm not half done."

"I really think you had better stop. I really . . ."

Her eyes got wide. "Sally," she said, "take a look at his."

Sally's eyes got wide too. "He's some rip, he is," Sally said. "Broken ribs, broken foot, tears and scratches and he's got love on his mind."

For christsakes.

What did they expect?

CHAPTER XIV

They came in on little cats' feet at 9:30 the next morning, Curly, Moe, and Larry. Perhaps more conventionally known by those familiar with the UK power elite as Robert Harkness, spy master, Alistair Fitzworthy, who runs the Royal Navy, and Roger Halliburton, who covertly runs England. They brought two huge Marines and stationed them outside my door. "No one," Fitzworthy commanded. "No one."

They seemed rumpled and tired. The redhead was plumping my pillows, the brunette was tucking in a sheet and the blonde was rubbing down my shoulders. I was radiating cleanliness after four hand baths.

All three girls recognized Halliburton.

"Very good," he said, turning to the redhead. "Your patient seems to be very well taken care of. Very well indeed. You will have to leave him for a little while. Does he require any immediate attention?"

"No, sir." the redhead said in a small voice.

"Then thank you very much. We won't be too long and then he'll be back in your excellent care." He gave them a tired smile and his droopy David Niven eyes melted them.

The girls filed silently out. The blonde gave me a small wave and smile. The bold one. She washed me twice.

It wasn't three weeks since I walked into that room in the Union Jack Club. Now they stood, shifting about uncertainly like schoolboys in trouble. Harkness carried a briefcase. Fitzworthy had a leather case slung over a shoulder. Halliburton carried nothing.

He was the first to speak. He seemed to be struggling. He cleared his throat. "Want to say old chap, er ..." His eyes fluttered to the ceiling. He was like a kid in a spelling bee and the first to go down. "Ah, extraordinary achievement. What you did. Still can't believe .... Frankly, I had my doubts ..." He fell back to cliché. "The nation is deeply grateful." He looked to Fitzworthy for help.

The older man put his hand on my shoulder. "You did all that was expected. More. Much more. You destroyed one. We can make another. They can't. No man could have done more. I don't think any man could have done as much. Incredible, really." Halliburton nodded.

Harkness was looking at me as if I were something under a microscope. White-haired, ascetic, monkish, withdrawn into himself, driven by something. "Probably the most extraordinary mission in my tenure of office."

He reached out and patted my arm. Mechanical pat. He would have no children. Probably no wife, few friends. He was a celibate bishop of spies. The pat, the physical contact, was an extraordinary concession to weakness. He was essentially asexual. Would prefer binary fission as a method of reproduction. But it was impractical among humans. Painful. He probably read a good deal on the current state of cloning theory.

"What about Henderson?" I asked.

He hung his head. Dropped his eyes. Took a deep breath.

"You were right. It didn't take much. He broke in fif teen minutes. He had been working for them for abou two years." He sighed and ran a hand through his whit hair. "We have major problems now. It will take a yea to get everything sorted out." He thrust his jaw out. "We' do it." He was a perfectionist who had made a mistak Reminded me of somebody. Who?

"Were there others?"

He nodded, looking at his hands.

"Four more. That's the lot. We have them all. They'r talking. We're learning a good deal."

I shrugged my antiseptic, gleaming shoulders. "Wel at least that's something."

Fitzworthy pulled up some chairs. They sat down. Har ness got out a pad and slim silver pen. He would tak extensive notes. Fitzworthy took a tape recorder out of h leather case and switched it on. Halliburton would fi everything important into his memory.

I looked at Harkness. "Where is Anne Cameron?" asked.

"London. She is being debriefed."

"How is she?"

"She's fine."

"No injuries? She was unconscious the last time I sa her."

"She is really quite all right. The medical peop checked her out completely."

"You've seen her?"

"We all have. Most of the night."

"I want to see her."

"Soon, old man. Soon. You've both been through great deal. She's sleeping."

"Girl looks damn marvelous, Smallpiece," Fitzwort exploded. "Couldn't get over it. Hardly recognized h

Lost weight chasing about in the woods, I expect. Hummm. Ah."

I looked out the window. Bit more than that. I had a memory of her at the woodpile, pulling back the breech of the Mauser. Stuff raining down all over the place. She just sighted down and pulled the trigger.

"What we need now," Harkness said mildly, "is a detailed recounting of all of the events from the time you got on the helicopter in Finland to the moment you lost consciousness when the pod exploded."

"But you got most of that from Anne."

"Yes," Harkness said. "Now we want to hear it from you."

I took a deep breath and plunged into it. The camp, the ploy in the lab, Vickers and Henderson, the catwalks, the explosions, the escape in the old float plane and Vickers's death. I said nothing about my part in it. Then the trek to the lake, the icy swim to the sugar loaf, the jeep and the village, the two *Star Wars* gnomes, the boat, the river, and the hike into the pine and then through the windows in the wire. Finally Hekki, the farm, and the desperate fire fight with the Russians. Then Llewellyn and the Seventh Calvalry's last-minute rescue. The destruction of the pod. My failure.

My voice got strained with that. I had a hard time with it. Failed the challenge. Myself. Had to talk to Anne. I broke into a sweat on it. Couldn't look at them.

Harkness looked at me with total understanding. Almost compassion.

"Take it easy, old man." Halliburton said, putting a hand on my shoulder.

"Lord. It was an amazing achievement. You should get the Victoria Cross," Fitzworthy said. "Look into that, Halburton."

329

A minute or two of strained silence while I collected myself. They looked at everything but me.

Harkness consulted his notes.

"Vickers died then, the next day, of his wounds?" The man has an instinct. He knew something.

I took a breath.

"No."

That brought all three around.

"I killed him."

Harkness didn't blink. Halliburton was struck dumb. Fitzworthy blew his nose.

"Why?" Harkness asked.

"He had a day or two at the outside. His leg was going to gangrene. Spitting blood. He couldn't be moved. He asked me to do it. Pleaded. He left Anne a note saying he would. She discovered it a few days later in her kit. He was dying. It gave us perhaps two more days to run to the border."

"She told us nothing of that," Fitzworthy said.

I blew out a breath.

"I'm telling you now. I had no idea he was her brother at the time."

"Would it have made a difference?" Harkness asked mildly.

"No."

He nodded. He consulted his notes.

Halliburton and Fitzworthy were busy with their hands.

Harkness went quietly on in his surgeon's voice. "You have not mentioned your right foot. It was severely strained. You couldn't walk on it. Yet you made the eight mile march to the lake, in a dense pine wilderness, on an improvised crutch, carrying an eighty-six pound weight on your back. That right?"

"Yes."

Another pregnant pause.

"Why didn't you report that to us?"

"Wasn't critical to the intelligence of the mission or the result."

He studied his goddamned notes some more.

"You did not mention killing three Russian deserters who were trying to rape Anne Cameron."

I looked him directly in the eye for fifteen seconds. Nobody blinked. Halliburton and Fitzworthy had lost interest in their hands.

"What the hell difference would it make now, Harkness? You want the gory details? Really important for your notes? Posterity needs it? Going to save it for your book?"

"You did it with a bow and arrow you constructed?"

I looked out the window some more. I wanted to see the girl.

"Two. I killed the third with my hands. You want to know the technique?"

"It simply confirms what she told us."

Fitzworthy sighed. "Jove."

Halliburton just stared at me.

Altogether, it took an hour and a half. Harkness would interrupt for clarification. He would nod, go back to his notes. Halliburton just looked and remembered. Fitzworthy seemed to be at a cricket match. He cheered now and then.

Harkness eventually seemed satisfied. Snapped shut his black, leather-bound note book. I had a few questions of my own.

"When did you know we had gotten out of the research camp?" I asked.

Harkness answered immediately. "Next day actually. Satellite photographs showed two-thirds of the main building destroyed and a truck and big helicopter burnt on the landing pad. We also saw that the float plane was gone. Had to be you. We assumed, however, that you had blown the pod right there."

"You should have seen the smiles on the faces of the photo reconnaissance officers when they put their pictures up on the screen," Fitzworthy added.

"Then, too, we knew you were out there in the wilds someplace because the Russians were putting everything they had into the air to find you."

"Why the Swedes and Norwegians?" I asked.

"We went to them and told as much as they needed to know. Had to. They didn't like the idea of such a major shift in strategic military balance going to the Russians. So, if the Russians were going to load up the border to keep you in, they wanted to be there to help get you out if they could.

"After a week, we all knew the border was going to be where things would start. It was a Swedish helicopter who first saw the action at the farm, radioed Llewellyn, picked him up and put his men down where they could help you."

I nodded. Scratched my head.

"How come Hekki got to us so fast?" I asked.

Again Harkness responded immediately. "The Russians finally realized they were not going to find you in the wilderness, so they decided to make their major effort at the border.

"That whole area in Finland is salted with either out-right Soviet agents or Communist sympathizers. They have a lot of safe houses around. They knew exactly where you crossed over the border because they spotted your guide where the wire was breached. So they sent squads, dressed as civilians, through.

"They were patroling the roads with three or four people like Hekki hoping to spot you. Then get you into safe house, call in the troops, and hustle you back over the border at one of the breach points.

"For a while it worked according to plan. Hekki got you into his farm, made his call, and the Russians arrived. They just didn't count on any resistance. You held out long enough, with the help of our Swedish friends, for Llewellyn to get to you."

I nodded and listened.

"The Russians had eighteen dead on the field," Fitzworthy said. "Llewellyn is reasonably sure his men accounted for ten or eleven. They had thirty-five in the action."

There was a slight pause as everybody did a small subtraction problem.

I nodded again. "Then what happened?" I asked.

"After the Swedes took you and the wounded out, we talked to the Russians. It was all over. They accepted it. They had a helicopter there in minutes, took back everything, dead, wounded, and living, weapons, spent cartridges. Cleaned it all up. Nobody wants to say anything about it. It never happened."

"What about the locals? They must have heard it?"

"Maneuvers. Got out of hand. A farmhouse burnt down. That's all. Poor Hekki went up with it."

"I imagine Moscow is very displeased."

Harkness nodded and produced the slightest of smiles. We hope so. They lost the pod. Two English agents took eighty miles to the border. Breached the border. And they got badly mauled in a fire fight, primarily by a man and a woman. I imagine more than one head will roll in the Kremlin."

The talk was winding down. They had enough for now. Their faces and body language said they were getting ready to leave.

333

I got another pat from Fitzworthy. "You'll be out of here in a day or so. Doctors say you're an ox."

"Good."

"Your grandparents will be in to see you this afternoon I think."

"Okay."

"They have been quite concerned."

"They don't know where I've been?"

"Your grandfather knows you've been on an intelligence mission. I think he suspects where. But they know you're back and safe."

"What about Anne's parents?"

"They know she's fine. I believe they have seen her briefly. They know of Alan Vickers's death, but we couldn't say very much at this time. She seemed to understand."

I was getting a very steady look from his bright blue eyes. If he had a white beard he would be a perfect Santa Claus. "She's a beautiful girl, Colin," he said. "She was very concerned about you. Really went after Harkness for not telling her where you were."

"Yeah."

"You two went through a lot. Amazing."

Harkness, the grey eminence, was at the door. He stopped and looked back.

"I was wrong about one thing, Harkness," I said.

"What was that?" I had his attention.

"Anne Cameron. Very steady. I have never seen anyone better when the chips were down. Man or woman. No one. The mission would have been a total bust without her."

He nodded. "She said the same of you."

They stood at the door, Curley, Moe, and Larry, and jostled each other. No one was sure who was to go first. Harkness dropped his case. They all went out as a lump.

334

of arms and legs, jammed into the doorway. There were a couple of grunts.

The wide-eyed, starched white triplets trooped in with basins and towels. Christ, not again.

I gave them my best glare.

"Alice, is it your intention to give me another bath?" I asked.

"Yes. It's time." She was rolling up her sleeves.

"Alice, I'm a good deal bigger and stronger than you."

"I've noticed." They hovered uncertainly at the foot of the bed.

"You get within my reach and I'm going to haul you right into this bed. Right now. In front of Audrey and Karen. You get my meaning, Alice?"

"You wouldn't dare."

"Try me."

"You'd get in terrible trouble."

"You're worth it."

She studied me critically. Head going from side to side.

I threw down my final bluff. "And if those two try to stop me, I'll grab both of them and have all three of you in bed. It'll be an armful of nurse, sister, matron, whatever, but I'll manage it. I can be a very determined fellow when I want to be."

I had their attention. I gave them my best leer.

"You couldn't. Not all of us."

"Bit crisp and starchy, but I would. Hell of a lot of action. Three girls bouncing all over the bed. Bit untidy. Arms going this way and that. Aprons flying off, those neat uniforms up to your ears, hats in the air, shoes sailing about. Legs all over the place. Boggles the mind. Lovely."

They were looking at each other. Talking in their silent language. Weighing the possibilities.

"You couldn't get all of us," Karen reasoned. "Damned impossible. Even for you."

"I'll get each of you. Give you twins."

"Coo."

There was more exchange of silent, female talk.

I threw down my final card.

"If Matron comes in and sees you three in bed with me, thrashing around in a frenzy. Attacking me like that. It will look very bad for you. Cost you your jobs."

"Attacking you?" Three open mouths.

"I'm a patient. Broken ribs. Broken foot. Sick man. Set upon by sex-starved women. Scandal. Awful." I shook my head.

Karen, the adventuresome blonde, said, "Might be interesting, even so. Chance of a lifetime."

Alice tossed her towel onto a chair. She had conceded. "It might have been at that," she smiled.

"Okay," I said, "you're safe for now."

"I may not want to be safe in a few days when your ribs have set." She grinned and plumped my pillows. The redhead, Audrey, was waving a towel at me. It was a bluff.

I love English girls.

After a week up on the loch, I was going up the wall. My ribs felt fine. The bandage was off, but my foot was still in a cast. I hobbled about on a cane. Spent a lot of time in the old keep. Struggled up to the top of the watch tower. Fished a lot from an old rowboat with Jamie, the caretaker. I couldn't row. Not that I really enjoyed salmon anymore.

I was grouchy and curt.

Even my grandparents began to avoid me.

I couldn't locate Anne. Harkness was avoiding my call.

I was going into myself. Introspective. Couldn't run or sweat. All I could do was worry, complain, and hate Harkness.

I was a pain in the ass.

Anne's mother helped. She came by on the fifth day. I was in the big living room. The one with the lion and tiger rugs, the grand piano, the gallery, the great fireplace in the alcove, and the huge portraits of unknown young people from the twenties. The room was a stage set for a Noel Coward drawing-room play. Where were the beautiful, witty, charming people?

Kate Cameron would have fitted in perfectly.

When she came in from the hall, I was dumb, speechless with the resemblance to Anne. Same eyes, same nose, royal head, magnificent neck and shoulders. I was on the sofa, with my bad foot on a table. I grabbed my cane and struggled up, but she pushed me down.

A second look told me she seemed a bit pale. There were shadows under her eyes. She seemed nervous, eyes were too bright. For a moment I panicked. She had bad news about Anne. Then I remembered. She was Alan Vickers's mother. She had been told. Of course. She was quietly grieving for her lost son.

She kissed me on the cheek and sat next to me. Gave me a good going over. I probably blushed. Didn't give a damn. She took my hand.

"You've seen Anne?" I asked.

"Yes."

"Where is she?"

"Right now? I'm not sure."

"But she was all right?"

"Yes. She looked marvelous. Positively marvelous. All of that weight's gone." She looked over at me. "She had

337

scratches on her face. Just like yours. You were together, I know. Something for Robert Harkness."

I just looked at her. No response.

"I know about Robert and what he does," she said.

"Your grandfather hinted that you and Anne had just done something quite outrageous. Something very good for the country, the West. It was dangerous and you were hurt."

She smiled and patted my hand.

"But you don't know where she is now?"

She shook her lovely head. "No. Probably something for Robert again, I expect."

God, the bastard wouldn't. He would.

She was seriously studying me. Still had my hand.

"Anne couldn't tell me too much about what you were doing for Robert Harkness. Russia, I think. They told me about Alan. He was part of it, too. Somehow. I don't know."

She looked away.

I checked my shoes.

Then she took a breath and brightened.

"She had a wonderful tan. Her skin was so clear. You must have been outside a good deal. But she had scratches, insect bites." She put her hand on my cheek. "Just like you."

I said nothing.

"Anne spoke about you. She's very private. Keeps it all inside. You never are ever quite certain what goes on in her head."

I nodded at that.

"When she talked about you, she smiled all the time. It was wonderful to see. She's never been like that. So animated. Vibrant. Vital. She positively glowed."

I wasn't sure where this was going.

She got me into her eyes. Hesitated for a moment. "I shouldn't ask, but do you, er, care for Anne, Colin?"

338

I nodded.

"Yes."

She smiled at that. Relaxed.

"You are concerned about her now?"

"Yes."

"She told me that you saved her life."

"She saved mine."

"She never said that. My Lord, what was Robert Harkness putting you through ..." She was twisting her hands.

"She did."

"I see." She smiled now and squeezed my hand. Looked at the walls and was lost in thought. She seemed happy and content enough. She considered the portrait of the handsome young man in kilt, leaning against the piano.

She turned to me. "You've been a bear around here, I'm told. Snap at everybody. Would you like to get away for a while? Change of scene for a bit?"

"I've been thinking the same thing."

"Can you sail?"

"Sure."

She nodded enthusiastically. Had my hand again.

"In the Hebrides, there are a cluster of islands in the Sound of Harris, south of Lewis and off North Uist. One of those islands is called Lochinver and the Camerons have been going there for generations. We have a small house with a magnificent view of the sea. It's a wild place, not many trees, but with steep cliffs and waving grass and a million sea birds.

"My husband and I thought we would be spending a few weeks there this month, but we can't. We must be in Prague for that time. We have a lovely boat nearby, new, American made, I think. Thirty feet and all ready. But there's no one to sail her now. Why don't you go out there, Colin? Sort things out for yourself for a week or so?

And perhaps you won't bite people the way you've been doing. Will you think about it?

I didn't have to think about it. "I'll go, and thank you."

For that, another kiss. "Oh, how wonderful! Will you be all right with that awful cast on your foot?"

"It comes off in a few days. I'm really getting VIP treatment. They're sending up some medics to take a look at me and put on a lightweight cast in a day or two."

"Wonderful." Lord, her eyes were just like hers.

The U.S. Navy medical team arrived in a van two days later. An orthopedic surgeon, an X-ray technician, and a corpsman. They tried not to be superior or snide regarding the cast the English had put on my foot. The doctor found my ribs healing nicely but I was not to try lifting weights. The lightweight cast they put on my foot was so thin I could wear running shoes. I was not, however, under any circumstances, to run. They wished me well.

Old Jamie took me in the ancient Ford wagon up to the Isle of Skye in an incredibly roundabout way. There were few roads and a lot of water to get around. It was grey and much of the day it rained. I said goodbye at Uig in the north of the island and caught the ferry across The Little Minch to Lochmaddy on North Uist. It was a terrible trip, in a small gale, and everybody was seasick, even some crew.

I stayed in an ancient inn in Lochmaddy, with cold hot water and a lumpy, damp bed. Early the next morning, I found the boat, new and glistening, in a slip off the stone quay. She could sleep four, had a closed head, shower, complete galley, and was beautifully fitted out. The harbor master knew of my coming, so I stowed a few provisions aboard, fired up the Japanese deisel, and chugged out of the harbor.

It was an absolutely gorgeous day. The sky was a brilliant deep blue without a cloud, and the easy sea rippled and sparkled in the sunlight. Once clear of the harbor,

340

ran up the main and the working jib, set her off the wind and killed the engine. The sloop heeled into it. I felt the familiar strain build on the rudder and pointed her higher into the crisp wind, and worked my way out of the bay to the north and the Isle of Lochinver. She was a lovely sailer, full keel and stiff to the wind.

Anne's mother was a marvel. She should have been a psychologist. She knew exactly what I needed. I could feel the tension pour out of me with each glorious mile as the sloop beat northward. I waved at the purse seiners. Got waved at back. Saw a few sails on the horizon. Couple of green, rusty deep sea trawlers went stoicly by. More arms waving. No more Russians. I forgot my failure. Thought about Anne Cameron and what mischief Harkness had sent her on. Thought more about her eyes. Worried about where she was. When would I see her?

I took off my shirt, stripped to the waist, put my feet up, leaned back on the cockpit cushions, and held her tight to the wind. The starboard rail was buried in the sea and swished by.

I raised Lochinver in the mid-afternoon. Ten miles long, five across at the widest part. The north side had steep two, three hundred feet of sheer cliffs with great fleets of seabirds wheeling about. Puffins, I thought. It was rumbled, textured, knobby, virtually treeless, and windswept. I found a small village and tiny harbor on the south, tucked in between two small headlands, forming a natural harbor. There was the inevitable stone quay. Four or five brightly painted thirty-foot fishing boats swung at their moorings. Seven or eight moorings were empty.

I sailed in with no motor. The wind almost astern, on an easy run, main almost at right angles with the boat, jib flopping about with no air. I came about at the quay, lost speed, and simply drifted in. I had the bumpers out, and tied up.

341

Kate had not been very clear on where the place was located but the postmistress was very specific. She also ran the general store, so I bought some more stuff, loaded the boat, and beat down the coast. I found the little protected cove and the white single-story house with the thatched roof up on the cliff. I put into the dock and tied up. Settled in.

For five days I wandered the grassy hills and rumpled valleys. Got used to the total silence and ever-present wind. Biked into town. Had some drinks in the little bar at the inn with the local fishermen. Some had seen me sail the sloop into the harbor, come about, and drift neatly onto the quay. That marked me a sailor, a colleague, a peer, in spite of my strange Anglo-American speech.

When the weather went sour, I read and kept warm with the peat fire in the blackened fireplace. I found some tools and fixed some doors and windows that wouldn't close. The days drifted. I wondered about Anne. But I wasn't hung up on my failure so much.

I lay on the hillock in the grass in the afternoon sun and watched the Coast Guard helicopter thump overhead. I was used to them now and no longer ducked. It was quite low. It dipped down over the sea and headed back toward the cliffs. The birds all took flight and the air was a squawking bedlam. The chopper sank down below the cliffs and settled on the shingle beach. I was down the hill and running easily. Foot felt fine.

The chopper's big door swung open, a man carried two bags out and helped her out. A woman. Then the door shut and the turbines whined and the helio rose back into the sky and swung south.

She saw me and started to run. She fell on the shingle and got up. I slid down the path on the cliff. It had to be her. God, it was. Then we were into each other. Hugs and little joyous bleats, pats on the back and then, finally, the hungry kisses.

She looked wonderful. Golden hair, still very short, pendant earrings, pearl necklace, a beige suit, silky pleated blouse, open, round collar. She could have been going to a cocktail party. She wasn't the same girl in the dumpy coveralls who hiked the pine wastes. But the face was the same with the huge eyes and arching brows and wide, flat, hollow cheeks.

She pushed me back. "God," she said, "you look bloody marvelous." She reached into my hair. "It's almost grown back, and the beard is gone." Her smile dazzled the sun.

I picked up her bags and we followed the winding path up to the house.

She stopped at the door and looked to the sea and around at the grassy, windswept hills. She pulled in her lower lip and bit it.

"Oh, it's so lovely. We spent part of our summers here since I was a little girl."

She ran a hand through her hair and looked at me. We stood in the doorway grinning at each other. And then I had her in my arms again. More hugging and kissing. Happy sighs. Lord, it felt good. I could feel the tensions slipping away, fading by the second.

I asked the question. "Anne, where have you been?"

"Chattanooga."

"What?"

"Chattanooga." She was smiling.

"Tennessee?" I couldn't believe it.

She nodded.

"Yup."

Must be, she was picking up some Americanisms.

"Why? How come?" I still wasn't sure.

"The whole laboratory has been moved. The Americans re doing their basic particle beam research there." She raised her eyebrows, sighed. "So it was decided that we should move our entire operation over. Since security had been breached in the UK, both governments decided to airlift everything over there."

I nodded. "So you've been helping to set it up?"

"Yes. It was all very hush hush of course. They hustled me off right from Finland. I couldn't phone. Just saw my mother briefly. You were in hospital, but they said you were all right. I couldn't write." She had both arms around my neck and pulled me in. "I was so worried about you."

She took my hands and stepped back. "How I've missed you, Colin Smallpiece!" She shook her head and smiled. Her eyes were filling up.

"And you're real. You look as good as I imagined you would."

I wrinkled my brow.

"I wasn't sure if it was a dream and I was making you up."

"I'm real enough," I said.

She fluffed my hair and studied me with half a smile.

"You have had a lot of people worried about you, Colin," she said, the half smile fading. "Your grandparents, my mother, Harkness, even Flynn."

"I'm okay."

"They say you went into yourself, got introspective, wouldn't talk." She was looking seriously at me. Held a hand over her eyebrows, shielding her eyes from the sun. "You think you failed the mission, don't you?"

I looked away. Out to the sea birds. I didn't have an answer.

"You do, don't you, Colin?"

I didn't say anything. I did fail. I knew I failed.

"What was the primary goal, Colin?" she asked.

I hesitated.

344

"Come on," she said. "What was the primary goal?"

"The intention was to bring the . . ."

She put her forefinger across my lips.

"Shusssh." She asked it again.

"What was the mission goal, Colin? The primary goal? Tell me. Why did we go? Say it. Say it!"

Her hands were on my shoulders. Her eyes were burning into mine. I couldn't get away from them. Why was I getting frantic?

I looked at the birds some more.

I gasped.

"Blow the goddamn thing."

"All right. But what was your goal, Colin? Your own personal goal? What were you trying to do?" She paused. "Say it, Colin!"

I checked out the birds again. Nice clouds. Fair weather cumulus. Eight-knot wind. Lovely sea. Lord, her eyes.

"Bring it back! Bring the goddamn thing back!" I ground it out between my teeth. I went back to her eyes. She knew, she cared, she understood.

Why bring it back? Because the sonofabitch was there. That's why. Challenge. She was right. Me against the universe. Want a mountain moved? Colin Smallpiece, Ltd. Specializing in windmill tilting. Want to save the western world? Here's my card. No job too big. Civilizations partially restored. Don't expect perfection. But I'll do it with style. Panache. Might not do it right.

My face was burning. She was getting into a secret psychological place. Didn't want her there. Private. But she knew. Absurd sense of perfection. No such thing. A concept. Not a reality. All empirical triangles are flawed. Perfect triangle exists only in the mind. All phenomena are less than perfect. I am a phenomenon to others. I am flawed. Accept it.

"Challenge?" I asked. "Me and Hillary? Ridiculous sense of the perfect?"

"Yes."

She nodded, put her arms around me, and spoke into my neck. "And what did you do? Did you bring it back? Did you?"

"I lost it."

She pushed back from me. Tears in her eyes. She was furious.

"You brought it back! You romantic idiot! You got it to Finland on your back. Eighty miles and you got it to Finland! Nobody can believe that."

"We lost it." I was petulant. Stubborn, too.

She was around my neck again and talking into my neck.

"Yes, we lost it to thirty-five men with rockets and automatic weapons. You got eight of them. You, both of us, did all that was expected of us. So much more. Did you know that Halliburton is trying to get you some kind of medal? Something special. I don't know what."

She roughly shoved me back. Pushed a hand through her hair, then across her eyes, taking away the tears.

"You going to let this go, Colin? Are you going to stop eating yourself because you are a man and not Jesus Christ? Are you? Are you?" She was shaking my arms. Crying.

I gathered her in.

This was a lot better than Finland and the pod. I let it die right there.

"Yeah, babe. I'm going to let it go. I don't give a damn about Finland. I got you. You're something. You really went after me." I blew out a breath. "You're right. We got ninety-five percent of it. Could have had it all, if Llewellyn could have made it half an hour earlier. We did all we could. We got it there. We did okay."

Her eyes were serious.

"You mean it? You are going to leave it alone now."

"Yup."

Glorious smile. I got hugged some more. She is one strong and determined woman.

She tossed her high heels to the ground. Took my hand.

"Come. Up this way."

She led me around the house and up a vague path in the broom and gorse. Up to a hilltop of waving grass and three ancient, gnarled, windblown, twisted trees. The view was spectacular, panoramic, with the deep blue ocean, peaceful and glistening in any direction. Five hundred feet below I saw the boat tied up at the dock and the pebbly beach with the white combers piling in from the Atlantic.

She stepped down into a small, grassy dimple about fifteen feet across and smiled up at me.

"This is my special place. I came up here as a child and it was a castle. It was any place I wanted it to be. Then later, I would read up here and dream. It's my place, Colin. I wanted you to see it."

"Sure beats pine trees."

She took my arm and we watched the sea birds calling and dipping off the cliffs. She had my eyes briefly and then looked away.

"You think we got bonded in Russia, Colin?" she asked, but wouldn't look at me.

"I think so, babe." She looped her arm around mine and pressed in.

"We have some time to sort things out now?"

"I have all summer, until the end of August. Have to be back at Spaulding around the last week."

"Me, too. I told Harkness I was done with it until the fall."

"Good. The conniving bastard."

"He likes you."

"Harkness doesn't like anybody."

"Then, he likes you as good as he can like anybody."

She leaned against me. I could smell her perfume.

"Nice boat you have down there, Colin."

"Good sailor. Stiff to the wind."

"You want to go sailing, Colin?"

"Not now. Tomorrow maybe."

"Oh, yes. Not now."

She had her jacket off.

"We could work up and down the Hebrides. Tomorrow, that is."

"We could," she agreed.

She unbuttoned my shirt.

"Do you know the Hebrides?" she asked.

"Not this far out."

"Lovely little fishing villages. Tigharry, Balivanich, Cregorry, Daliburgh. We could see them all."

She was into my arms again. Lord, the perfume. The soft cheeks. I nibbled an ear. Guzzled her throat.

"Tomorrow, babe."

"Right."

" 'Course, we could stay right here. In Brigadoon."

Praise for *Inherit*

"A complex, hard-SF tale of nanotechnology and life extension...this futuristic thriller, which contains provocative speculations about the effect of extreme life extension on society, is an enjoyable and challenging piece."

—*Publishers Weekly*

"Brian Stableford has triumphantly created his own niche of hard biological SF, containing the genre's most intelligently imagined marvels and nightmares."

—David Langford

"Stableford delivers fast-paced adventure, and each of his characters comes to life....Entertaining."

—*Booklist*

"*Inherit the Earth* is a gripping multilevel thriller of the Biotech Utopia. Set in a future transformed by the fires of biotech and environmental destruction, this is a quest for the ultimate prize: immortality itself."

—Stephen Baxter

"The excellently drawn characters of *Inherit the Earth* dance through a plot that never gives them a chance to catch their breath."

—David Drake

"Stableford combines the virtues of traditional SF with cutting-edge scientific extrapolation; fearsomely intelligent and compulsive."

—Paul McAuley

Inherit the Earth

Brian Stableford

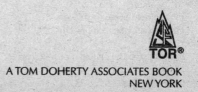

A TOM DOHERTY ASSOCIATES BOOK
NEW YORK

NOTE: If you purchased this book without a cover you should be aware that this book is stolen property. It was reported as "unsold and destroyed" to the publisher, and neither the author nor the publisher has received any payment for this "stripped book."

This is a work of fiction. All the characters and events portrayed in this book are either products of the author's imagination or are used fictitiously.

INHERIT THE EARTH

Copyright © 1998 by Brian Stableford

All rights reserved, including the right to reproduce this book, or portions thereof, in any form.

A much shorter and substantially different version of this novel entitled "Inherit the Earth" appeared in the July 1995 issue of *Analog*.

Edited by David G. Hartwell

A Tor Book
Published by Tom Doherty Associates, LLC
175 Fifth Avenue
New York, NY 10010

Tor Books on the World Wide Web:
http://www.tor.com

Tor® is a registered trademark of Tom Doherty Associates, LLC

ISBN: 0-812-58429-5

First edition: September 1998
First mass market edition: July 1999

Printed in the United States of America

0 9 8 7 6 5 4 3 2 1

For Jane, and all those who toil in the forge of the will

Acknowledgments

I am grateful to Stanley Schmidt, the editor of *Analog*, for buying the shorter version of this story, thus establishing its ideative seed and its commercial credentials. I am grateful to David Hartwell for suggesting that I rewrite the final section so drastically as to obliterate any lingering similarity to the ending of the earlier version, thus proving my versatility. I should also like to pay my respects to Eric Thacker and Anthony Earnshaw, who provided their illustrated novel *Wintersol* with a dedication that would otherwise have been ideal for this book: "To the meek, who will only inherit the Earth by forging the Will."

PART ONE

Paranoid Fantasies

Silas Arnett stood on the bedroom balcony, a wineglass in his hand, bathing in the ruddy light of the evening sun. He watched the Pacific breakers tumbling lazily over the shingle strand. The ocean was in slow retreat from the ragged line of wrack that marked the height of the tide. The dark strip of dead weed was punctuated by shards of white plastic, red bottle tops and other packaging materials not yet redeemed by the hungry beach cleaners. They would be long gone by morning—one more small achievement in the great and noble cause of depollution.

Glimpsing movement from the corner of his eye, Silas looked up into the deepening blue of the sky.

High above the house a lone wing glider was playing games with the wayward thermals disturbed by the freshening sea breeze. His huge wings were painted in the image of a bird's, each pinion feather carefully outlined, but the colors were acrylic-bright, brazenly etched in reds and yellows. Now that the gaudier birds of old were being brought back from the temporary mists of extinction mere humans could no longer hope to outdo them in splendor, but no actual bird had ever been as huge as this pretender.

Silas frowned slightly as he watched the glider swoop and soar. The conditions were too capricious to allow safe stunting, but the soaring man was careless of the danger. Again and again he dived toward the chalky cliff face that loomed above the ledge on which the house was set, only wheeling away at the last possible moment. Silas caught his breath as the glider attempted a loop which no bird had ever been equipped by instinct to perform, then felt a momentary thrill of irritation at the ease with which his admiration had been commanded.

Nowadays, a careless Icarus would almost certainly survive a fluttering fall from such a height, provided that he had the best internal technology that money could buy. Even the pain would quickly be soothed; its brutal flaring would merely serve as a trigger to unleash the resources of his covert superhumanity. Flirtation with catastrophe was mere sport for the children of the revolution.

Silas's sentimental education had taken place in an earlier era, when the spectrum of everyday risks had been very different. His days with Conrad Helier had made him rich, so he now had all the benefits that the best nanotech repairmen could deliver, but his reflexes could not be retrained to trust them absolutely. The bird man was evidently young as well as rich: *authentically* young. Whatever PicoCon's multitudinous ads might claim, the difference between the truly young and the allegedly rejuvenated Architects of Destiny was real and profound.

"Why does the sun look bigger when it's close to the horizon?"

Silas had not heard his guest come up behind him; she was barefoot, and her feet made no sound on the thick carpet. He turned to look at her.

She was wearing nothing but a huge white towel, wrapped twice around her slender frame. The thickness of the towel accentuated her slimness—another product of authentic youth. Nanotech had conquered obesity, but it couldn't restore the full muscle tone of the subcutaneous tissues; middle age still spread a man's midriff, if only slightly, and no power on earth could give a man as old as Silas the waist he had possessed a hundred years before.

Catherine Praill was as young as she looked; she had not yet reached her full maturity, although nothing remained for the processes of nature to do, save to etch the features of her body a little more clearly. The softness of her flesh, its subtle lack of focus, seemed to Arnett to be very beautiful, because it was not an effect of artifice. He was old-fashioned, in every sense of the word, and unrepentant of his tastes. He loved youth, and he loved the last vestiges which still remained to humankind of the natural processes of growth and completion. He had devoted the greater part of his life to the overthrow of nature's tyranny, but he still felt entitled to his affection for its art.

"I don't know," he said, a little belatedly. "It's an optical illusion. I can't explain it."

"You don't know!" There was nothing mocking in her laughter, nothing contrived in her surprise. He was more than a hundred years older than she was; he was supposed to know everything that was known, to understand everything that could be understood. In her innocence, she expected nothing less of him than infinite wisdom and perfect competence. Men of his age were almost rare enough nowadays to be the stuff of legend.

He bowed his head as if in shame, then took a penitent sip from the wineglass as she looked up into his eyes. She was a full twenty centimeters shorter than he. Either height was becoming unfashionable again or she was exercising a kind of caution rare in the young, born of the awareness that it was far easier to add height than to shed it if and when one decided that it was time for a change.

"I gave up trying to hold all the world's wisdom in my head a long time ago," he told her. "When all the answers are at arm's length, you don't need to keep them any closer." It was a lie, and she knew it. She had grown up with the omniscient Net, and she knew that its everpresence made ignorance more dangerous, not less—but she didn't contradict him. She only smiled.

Silas couldn't decipher her smile. There was more than amusement in it, but he couldn't read the remainder. He was glad of that small margin of mystery; in almost every other respect, he could read her far better than she read him. To her, he must be a paradox wrapped in an enigma—and that was the reason she was here.

Women of Cathy's age, still on the threshold of the society of the finished, were only a little less numerous than men of his antiquity, but that did not make the two of them equal in their exoticism. Silas knew well enough what to expect of Cathy—he had always had women of her kind around him, even in the worst of the plague years—but men of his age were new in the world, and they would continue to establish new precedents until the last of his generation finally passed away. No one knew how long that might take; PicoCon's new rejuve technologies were almost entirely cosmetic, but the next generation would surely reach more deeply into a man's essential being.

"Perhaps I did know the answer, once," he told her, not knowing or caring whether it might be true. "Fortunately, a man's memory gets better and better with age, becoming utterly ruthless in discarding the trivia while taking care to preserve only that which is truly precious." Pompous old fool! he thought, even as the final phrase slid from his tongue—but he knew that Cathy probably wouldn't mind, and wouldn't complain even if she did. To her, this encounter must seem untrivial—perhaps even truly precious, but certainly an experience to be savored and remembered. He was the oldest man she had ever known; it was entirely possible that she would never have intimate knowledge of anyone born before him. It was different for Silas, even though such moments as this still felt fresh and hopeful and intriguing. He had done it all a thousand times before, and no matter how light and lively and curious the stream of his consciousness remained while the affair was in progress, it would only be precious while it lasted.

Silas wondered whether Cathy would be disappointed if she knew how he felt. Perhaps she *wanted* to find him utterly sober, weighed down by ennui—and thus, perhaps, even more worthy of her awe and respect than he truly was.

He placed his hand on her shoulder and caressed the contour of her collarbone. Her skin, freshly washed, felt inexpressibly luxurious, and the sensation which stirred him was as sharp—perhaps even as innocent—as it would have been had he never felt its like before.

A practiced mind was, indeed, exceedingly adept at forgetting; it had wisdom enough not merely to forget the trivial and the insignificant, but also that which was infinitely precious in rediscovery.

"It must be strange," she said, insinuating her slender and naked arm around his waist, "to look out on the sea and the sky with eyes that know them so well. There's so much in the world that's unfamiliar to me I can't begin to imagine what it would be like to *recognize* everything, to be completely *at home.*" She was teasing him, requiring that he feed her awe and consolidate her achievement in allowing herself to be seduced.

"That's not what it's like," he said dutifully. "If the world stayed the same, it might be more homely; but one of the follies of authentic youth is the inability to grasp how quickly, and how much, everything changes—even the sea and the sky. The line left behind by the tide changes with the flotsam; even the clouds sailing serenely across the sky change with the climate and the composition of the air. The world I knew when I was young is long gone, and depollution will never bring it back. I've lived through half a hundred worlds, each one as alarming and as alien as the last. I don't doubt that a dozen more lie in ambush, waiting to astonish me if I stay the course for a few further decades."

He felt a slight tremor pass through her and wondered whether it was occasioned by a sudden gust of cool wind or by the thrust of her eager imagination. She had known no other world than the one into which recently acquired maturity had delivered her, but she must have had images in her mind of the various phases of the Crisis. It was all caught in the Net, if only as an infinite jumble of glimpses. Today's world was still haunted by the one which had gone madly to its destruction—the one which Silas Arnett had helped to save.

She smiled at him again, as innocently as a newly hatched sphinx.

It's not my wisdom which makes me attractive to her, Silas thought. She sees me as something primitive, perhaps feral. I was born of woman, and there was a full measure of effort and pain in my delivery. I grew to the age she is now without the least ability to control my own pain, under the ever present threat of injury, disease, and death. There's something of the animal about me still.

He knew that he was melodramatizing for the sake of a little extra excitement, but it was true nevertheless. When Silas had been in his teens there had been more than ten billion people in the world, all naturally born, all naked to the slings and arrows of outrage and misfortune. Avid forces of destruction had claimed all but a handful, and his own survival had to be reckoned a virtual miracle. When Catherine Praill came to celebrate her hundred-and-twentieth birthday, by contrast, nine out of ten of her contemporaries would still be alive. Her survival to that age was virtually assured, provided that she did not elect to waste herself in submission to extravagant and extraordinary risks.

Silas looked up briefly, but the bird man was out of sight now, eclipsed by the green rim of the cliff. He imagined Catherine costumed with brightly colored wings, soaring gloriously across the face of the sinking sun—but he preferred her as she was now, soft and fresh and unclothed.

"Let's go inside," he said, meaning Let's make love while the sunlight lasts, while we can revel in the fleeting changes of the colored radiance.

"Might as well," she said, meaning Yes, let's do exactly that.

Sexual intercourse never left Arnett deflated or disappointed. It never had, so far as he could remember. It might have done, sometimes, when he was authentically young, but in the fullness of his maturity lovemaking always left him with a glow of profound satisfaction and easeful accomplishment. He knew that this seeming triumph probably had as much to do with the gradual adjustment of his expectations as with the honing of his skills but he did not feel in the least diminished by that hint of cynicism. He believed with all sincerity that he knew the true value of everything he had—and his expert memory had scrupulously erased most of the prices he had been forced to pay by way of its acquisition.

Cathy had drifted into a light sleep almost as soon as they had finished, and when her sleep had deepened Arnett was able to disentangle his limbs from hers without disturbing her. He helped the half-reflexive movements which eased her into a more comfortable position, and then he slowly withdrew himself from the bed. Naked, he went back to the open window and on to the balcony.

The sun had set and the wing glider was long gone. Arnett relaxed into the luxury of being unobserved. He put a high value on that privilege, as anyone would who had grown to maturity in a world teeming with people, where the friction of social intercourse had only just begun to be eased by access to the infinite landscapes of virtual reality.

He had chosen the house in which he lived precisely because it was hidden from all its neighbors by the contours of the cliff. The house was not large, and far from fashionable—it was all above ground, its walls as white as the chalkiest aspects of the cliff face, its angles stubbornly square, its windows unrepentant panes of plain glass—but that was exactly why he liked it. It did not blend in with its surroundings; its roots and all its other quasi living systems were hidden away in closets and conduits. It was, after its own fashion, every bit as old-fashioned as he was, although it was no more than twenty years old—almost as young as Catherine Praill.

Silas wondered whether Cathy would quickly drift away now that she had "collected" him, or whether she would attempt to maintain their friendship, seeking further amusement and further enlightenment in the patient acquaintance of one of the oldest men in the world. He didn't want her to drift away. He wanted her to stay, or at least to return again and again and again—not because her slowly evaporating youth was such a rare commodity, but because he had long ago learned to appreciate constancy and to expand his pleasures to fit the time and space that were available for their support.

A movement caught his eye: something which emerged very briefly from the gathering shadows at the foot of the cliff face and then faded back into obscurity.

He was not immediately anxious, even though he guessed that it must be a human being who had descended unannounced into his haven of privacy—but he stepped back from the balcony and went to dress himself.

The bedroom was dark by now, but he had no difficulty finding what he needed. He pulled on the various elements of his suitskin. Their seams reacted to his body heat, joining up with smooth efficiency as if they were eager to begin their cleansing work. He stepped into a pair of slippers, no stronger or more massive than was necessary to protect the suitskin's soles in an indoor environment.

Silas didn't switch on the landing light until the door was safely closed behind him. He didn't want to wake the girl from what he hoped were pleasant dreams. He went swiftly down to the hallway and stepped into the tiny room beneath the staircase. He activated the house's night eyes, bringing a dozen different images to the bank of screens mounted on the wall. He picked up the VE hood, which would give him a far clearer view once he had selected the right pair of artificial eyes—but there was no way to make the choice.

The foot of the cliff, limned in red, was stubbornly bare. The shadows in which he had glimpsed movement were empty now.

One of the screens blanked out, and then another.

That did alarm him; in the circumstances, he couldn't believe that it was a mere malfunction. He lifted the VE hood, but he still had no idea which connection he should make—and if the screens were going down, the hood would be just as useless as they were. Someone was blinding the house's eyes, and must have come equipped to do it—but why? He had no enemies, so far as he knew, and the rewards of burglary had long ago sunk to the level which made the risk unacceptable to anyone but a fool. The quaint outward appearance of the house might, he supposed, have indicated to juvenile vandals that it was poorly protected, but he couldn't imagine anyone scaling the cliff face in the dark merely to do a little gratuitous damage.

He watched, helplessly, as the screens went out. When six more of the night eyes had been blinded without his catching the briefest glimpse of a hand or a face, he knew that it was not the work of children or foolish thieves. He became afraid—and realized as he did so how strange and unfamiliar fear had become.

A rapid dance of his fingertips sealed all the locks that were not routinely engaged, activated all the house's security systems and notified the police that a crime might be in progress. That, at least, was what his instructions *should* have accomplished—but the confirmatory call which should have come from the police didn't arrive; the telephone screen remained ominously inactive. He knew that there was no point in putting the VE hood over his head and he lowered it onto its cradle.

Several seconds dragged by while he wondered whether it was worth running to his study, where the house's main workstation was, but when he emerged from the cupboard he didn't head in that direction. Instead, he stood where he was, watching the door at the end of the hallway. It was obvious that his links with the outside world had been severed, and that the door in question was the only security left to him. He wondered whether the threat might be to her rather than to himself, feeling a pang of bitter resentment because a near perfect day was about to be ruined at the eleventh hour—but that was just a desperate attempt to pretend that the danger wasn't *his* danger.

The simple truth was that his communication systems were very nearly the best that money could buy, and that someone had nevertheless overridden them with ridiculous ease. Whatever reason they had, it couldn't be trivial.

When the door burst in, Silas couldn't quite believe his eyes. In spite of the failure of his artificial eyes and voice he had not believed that his locks could be so easily broken—but when he saw the human figures come through, wearing black clothes and black masks, the outer layers of his patiently accreted, ultracivilized psyche seemed to peel away. He knew that he had to fight, and he thanked providence that he still knew how. In his innermost self, he *was* still primitive, even feral. He had no weapon, and he could see the foremost of the invaders had some kind of snub-nosed pistol in his hand, but he knew that he had to go forward and not back.

His rush seemed to take the intruder by surprise; the man's eyes were still slightly dazzled by the bright light. Silas lashed out with his foot at the hand which held the gun, and felt his slippered toes make painful connection—but the pain was immediately controlled by his internal technology.

The gun flew away. It was the unexpectedness of the assault rather than its force that had jolted it free, but the effect was the same. Silas was already bringing his flattened hand around in a fast arc, aiming for the man's black-clad throat—but the intruder had evidently been trained in that kind of fighting, and was more recently practiced in its skills. The blow was brutally blocked and Silas felt unexpectedly fiery pain shoot along his forearm; it was controlled, but not before he had flinched reflexively and left himself open to attack.

His hesitation probably made no difference; there would have been no time for a riposte and no effective blow he could have dealt. There were three intruders coming at him now, and they hurled themselves upon him with inelegant but deadly effect. He flailed his arms desperately, but there was no way he could keep them all at bay.

With his arms still threshing uselessly, Silas was thrown back and knocked down. His head crashed against the wall and the pain was renewed yet again. The pain was almost instantly contained and constrained, but it could only be dulled. Merely deadening its fury could not free his mind to react in artful or effective fashion. There was, in any case, no action he could take that might have saved him. He was outnumbered, and not by fools or frightened children.

One of the intruders bent to pick up the fallen gun, and he began firing even as he plucked it from the floor. Silas felt a trio of needles spear into the muscles of his breast, not far beneath the shoulder. There was no pain at all now, but he knew that whatever poison the darts bore must have been designed to resist the best efforts of his internal technology. These people had come equipped to fight, and their equipment was *the best.* He knew that their motives must be similarly sophisticated and correspondingly sinister.

It was not until the missiles had struck him and burrowed into his efficiently armored but still-frail flesh, that Silas Arnett called to mind the deadliest and most fearful word in his vocabulary: *Eliminators!* Even as the word sprang to mind, though— while he still lashed out impotently against the three men who no longer had to struggle to subdue him—he could not accept its implications.

I have not been named! he cried silently. *They have no reason!* But whoever had come to his house, so cleverly evading its defenses, clearly had motive enough, whether they had reason enough or not.

While his internal defenses struggled unsuccessfully to cope with the drug which robbed him of consciousness, Silas could not evade the dreadful fear that death—savage, capricious, reasonless death—had found him before he was ready to be found.

Two

Damon Hart had never found it easy to get three boxes of groceries from the trunk of his car to his thirteenth-floor apartment. It was a logistical problem with no simple solution, given that his parking slot and his apartment door were both so far away from the elevator. Some day, he supposed, he would have to invest in a collapsible electric cart which would follow him around like a faithful dog. For the moment, though, such a purchase still seemed like another step in the long march to conformism—perhaps the one which would finally seal his fate and put an end to the last vestiges of his reputation as a rebel. How could a man who owned a robot shopping trolley possibly claim to be anything other than a solid citizen of the New Utopia?

In the absence of such aid Damon had no alternative but to jam the elevator door open while he transferred the boxes one by one from the trunk of the car. By the time he got the third one in, the elevator was reciting its standard lecture on building policy and civic duty. While the elevator climbed up to his floor he was obliged to listen to an exhaustive account of his domestic misdemeanors, even though he hadn't yet clocked up the requisite number of demerits to be summoned before the leasing council for a token reprimand. Unfortunately, he wasn't able to ride all the way on his own; two middle-aged women with plastic faces and brightly colored suitskins got in at the third and traveled up to the tenth, doubtless visiting another of their ubiquitous kind. They pretended to ignore the elevator, but Damon knew that they were drinking in every word. He had never been introduced to either one of them and had no idea what their names might be, but they probably knew everything there was to know about him except his real name. He was the building's only ex-streetfighter; in spite of their youth—and partly because of it—he and Diana had more *real* misdemeanors credited to their law accounts than all the remaining inhabitants of their floor.

He managed to get all three boxes out of the elevator without actually jamming the door, but he had to leave two behind while he carried the third to the door of his apartment. He set it down, ringing his own doorbell as he turned away to fetch the second. When he came back with the second box, however, he found that his ring had gone unanswered. The first box was still outside. Given the number of spy eyes set discreetly into the corridor walls there was no way anyone would take the risk of stealing any of its contents, but its continued presence was an annoyance nevertheless. When Damon had placed the second box beside the first he fished out his key and opened the door himself, poking his head inside with the intention of calling for assistance.

He closed his mouth abruptly when the blade of a carving knife slammed into the doorjamb, not ten centimeters away from his ducking head. The blade stuck there, quivering.

"You bastard!" Diana said, rushing forward to meet him from the direction of his edit suite.

It didn't take much imagination to figure out what had offended her so deeply. The reason she hadn't answered the doorbell was that she'd been too deeply engrossed in VE—in the VE that he'd been in the process of redesigning when concentration overload had started his head aching. Damon realized belatedly that he ought to have tidied the work away properly, concealing it behind some gnomic password.

"It's not a final cut," he told her, raising his arms with the palms flat in a placatory gesture. "It's just a first draft. It won't be you in the finished product—it won't be anything *like* you."

"That's bullshit," Diana retorted, her voice still taut with pent-up anger. "First draft, final cut—I don't give a damn about that. It's the principle of the thing. It's *sick,* Damon."

Damon knew that it might add further fuel to her wrath, but he deliberately turned his back on her and went back into the corridor. He hesitated over the possibility of picking up one of the boxes of groceries he'd already brought to the threshold, but he figured that he needed time to think. He walked all the way back to the elevator, taking his time.

This is it, he thought, as he picked up the third box. This is really it. If she hasn't had enough, I have.

He couldn't help but feel that in an ideal world—or even the so-called New Utopia which was currently filling the breach—there ought to be a more civilized way of breaking up, but his relationship with Diana Caisson had always been a combative affair. It had been his combativeness that first attracted her attention, in the days when *he* had wielded the knives—but he had only done so in the cause of sport, never at the behest of mere rage.

A great deal had changed since then. He had switched sides; instead of supplying the raw material to be cut, spliced, and subtly augmented into a salable VE product, he was now an engineer and an artist. She had changed too, but the shift in her expectations hadn't matched the shift in his. With every month that passed she seemed to want more and more from him, whereas he had found himself wanting less and less from her. She had taken that as an insult, as perhaps it was.

Diana thought that the time he spent building and massaging VEs was a retreat from the world, and from her, which ought to be discouraged for the sake of his sanity. She couldn't see how anyone could *absorb* themselves in the painstaking creation of telephone answering tapes and pornypops—and because every stress and strain of their relationship had always become manifest in her explosive anger, she had developed a profound hatred even for the more innocuous products of his labor.

In the beginning, Diana's habit of lashing out had added a

certain excitement to their passion, but Damon had now reached a stage when the storm and the stress were nothing but a burden—a burden he could do without. He had given up street-fighting; he was an *artist* now, through and through. He had hoped that Diana would share and assist his adaptation to a new lifestyle and a new philosophy—and he had to give her some credit for trying—but the fact remained that their move into polite society had never really come close to working out. Diana even got steamed up when the elevator took leave to remind her of the small print in the building rules.

It's over, Damon told himself again as he picked up the third box of groceries. He was testing himself, to see whether anxiety or relief would rise to the surface of his consciousness.

Diana was all ready to fight when he came back through the door, but Damon wasn't about to oblige her. He put the box he'd carried from the elevator on the floor and stepped back to collect another. She knew that he was buying time, but she let him go back for the third without protest. The expression in her blue-gray eyes said that she wasn't about to calm down, but she hadn't gone back for another knife, so he had reason to hope that the worst was already over.

Once the last box was inside the apartment and the door was safely closed behind him, Damon felt that he was ready to face Diana. Fortunately, her tremulous rage was now on the point of dissolving into tears. She had dug her fingernails into her palms so deeply that they had drawn blood, but they were unclenching now. With Diana, violence always shifted abruptly into a masochistic phase; real pain was sometimes the only thing that could blot out the kinds of distress with which her internal technology was not equipped to deal.

"You don't want me at all," she complained. "You don't want any *living* partner. You only want my virtual shadow. You want a programmed slave, so you can be absolute master of your paltry sensations. That's all you've ever wanted."

"It's a commission," Damon told her as soothingly as he could. "It's not a composition for art's sake, or for my own gratification.

It's not even technically challenging. It's just a piece of work. I'm using your body template because it's the only one I have that's been programmed into my depository to a suitable level of complexity. Once I've got the basic script in place I'll modify it out of all recognition—every feature, every contour, every dimension. I'm only doing it this way because it's the easiest way to do it. All I'm doing is constructing a pattern of appearances; it's not *real.*"

"You don't have any sensitivity at all, do you?" she came back. "To you, the templates you made of me are just something to be used in petty pornography. They're just something *convenient—* something that's *not even technically challenging.* It wouldn't make any difference what kind of tape you were making, would it? You've got my image worked out to a higher degree of digital definition than any other, so you put it to whatever use you can: if it wasn't a sex tape it'd be some slimy horror show . . . anything they'd pay you money to do. It really doesn't matter to you whether you're making training tapes for surgeons or masturbation aids for freaks, does it?"

As she spoke she struck out with her fists at various parts of his imaging system: the bland consoles, the blank screens, the lumpen edit suite and—most frequently—the dark helmets whose eyepieces could look out upon an infinite range of imaginary worlds. Her fists didn't do any damage; everything had been built to last.

"I can't turn down commissions," Damon told her as patiently as he could. "I need connections in the marketplace and I need to be given problems to solve. Yes, I want to do it all: phone links and training tapes, abstracts and dramas, games and repros, pornypops and ads. I want to be master of it all, because if I don't have *all* the skills, anything I devise for myself will be tied down by the limits of my own idiosyncrasy."

"And templating me was just another exercise? Building me into your machinery was just a way to practice. I'm just *raw material.*"

"It's not *you*, Di," he said, wishing that he could make her understand that he really meant it. "It's not your shadow, certainly not your soul. It's just an appearance. When I use it in my work I'm not using *you.*"

"Oh no?" she said, giving the helmet she'd been using one last smack with the white knuckles of her right hand. "When you put your suit of armor on and stick your head into one of those black holes, you leave *this* world way behind. When you're there—and you sure as hell aren't *here* very often—the only contact you have with me is with my appearance, and what you do to that appearance is what you do to *me*. When you put my image through the kind of motions you're incorporating into that sleazy fantasy it's *me* you're doing it to, and no one else."

"When it's finished," Damon said doggedly, "it won't look or feel anything like you. Would you rather I paid a copyright fee to reproduce some shareware whore? Would you rather I sealed myself away for hours on end with a set of supersnoopers and a hired model? By your reckoning, that would be *another woman*, wouldn't it? Or am I supposed to restrict myself to the design and decoration of cells for VE monasteries?"

"I'd rather you spent more time with the *real* me," she told him. "I'd rather you lived in the *actual* world instead of devoting yourself to substitutes. I never realized that giving up fighting meant giving up *life.*"

"You had no right to put the hood on," Damon told her coldly. "I can't work properly if I feel that you're looking over my shoulder all the time. That's worse than knowing that I might have to duck whenever I come through the door because you might be waiting for me with a deadly weapon."

"It's only a kitchen knife. At the worst it would have put your eye out."

"I can't afford to take a fortnight off work while I grow a new eye—and I don't find experiences like that amusing or instructive."

"You were always too much of a coward to be a *first-rate*

fighter," she told him, trying hard to wither him with her scorn. "You switched to the technical side of the business because you couldn't take the cuts anymore."

Damon had never been one of the reckless fighters who threw themselves into the part with all the flamboyance and devil-may-care they could muster, thinking that the tapes would make them look like real heroes. He had always fought to win with the minimum of effort and the minimum of personal injury—and in his opinion, it had always worked to the benefit of the tapes rather than to their detriment. Even the idiots who liked to consume the tapes raw, because it made the fights seem "more real," had appreciated his efficiency more than the blatant showmanship of his rivals.

Because most of his opponents hadn't cared much about skill or sensible self-preservation Damon had won thirty-nine out of his forty-three fights and had remained unbeaten for the last eighteen months of his career. He didn't consider that to be evidence of stupidity or stubbornness—and he'd switched to full-time tape doctoring because it was more challenging and more interesting than carving people up, not because he'd gone soft.

Unfortunately, the new business wasn't more challenging or more interesting for Diana. Watching a VE designer working inside a hood wasn't an engaging spectator sport.

"If you're hankering after the sound and fury of the streets," Damon said tiredly, "you know where they are."

It wasn't the first time he'd said it, but it startled her. Her fists unclenched briefly as she absorbed the import of it. She knew him well enough to read his tone of voice. She knew that he meant it, this time.

"Is that what you want?" she said, to make sure. Her palms were bleeding; he could see both ragged lines of cuts now that she was relaxing.

Damon toyed with the possibility of parrying the question. It's what you want, he could have said—but it would have been less than honest and less than brave.

"I can't take it anymore," he told her frankly. "It's run its course."

"You think you don't need me anymore, don't you?" she said, trying to pretend that she had reason to believe that he was wrong in that estimation. When she saw that he wasn't going to protest, her shoulders slumped—but only slightly. She had courage too, and pride. "Perhaps you're right," she sneered. "All you ever wanted of me is in that template. As long as you have my appearance programmed into your private world of ghosts and shadows you can do anything you like with me, without ever having to worry whether I'll step out of line. You'd rather live with a virtual image than a real flesh-and-blood person, wouldn't you? You wouldn't even take that helmet off to eat and drink if you didn't have to. If you had any idea how much you've changed since. . . ."

The charges were probably truer than she thought, but Damon didn't see any need to be ashamed of the changes he'd made. The whole point about the world inside a VE hood, backed up by the full panoply of smartsuit-induced tactile sensation, was that it was *better* than the real world: brighter, cleaner, and more controllable. Earth wasn't hell anymore, thanks to the New Reproductive System and the wonders of internal technology, but it wasn't heaven either, in spite of the claims and delusions of the New Utopians. Heaven was something a man could only hope to find on the *other* side of experience, in the virtuous world of virtual imagery.

The brutal truth of the matter, Damon thought, was that everything of Diana Caisson that he actually needed really *was* programmed into her template. The absence from his life of her changeable, complaining, untrustworthy, knife-throwing, flesh-and-blood self wouldn't leave a yawning gap. Once, it might have done—but not anymore. She had begun to irritate him as much as he irritated her, and he hadn't her gift of translating irritation into erotic stimulation.

"You're right," he told her, trying to make it sound as if he were admitting defeat. "I've changed. So have you. That's okay. We're authentically young; we're supposed to change. We're supposed to become different people, to try out all the personalities of which we're capable. The time for constancy is a long way ahead of us yet."

He wondered, as he said it, whether it was true. Were his newly perfected habits merely a phase in an evolutionary process rather than a permanent capitulation to the demands of social conformity? Was he just taking a rest from the kind of hyped-up sensation-seeking existence he'd led while he was running with Madoc Tamlin's gang, rather than turning into one of the meek whose alleged destiny was to inherit the earth? Time would doubtless tell.

"I want the templates back," Diana said sharply. "All of them. I'm going, and I'm taking my virtual shadow with me."

"You can't do that," Damon retorted, knowing that he had to put on the appearance of a fight before he eventually gave in, lest it be too obvious that all he had to do was remold her simulacrum by working back from the modified echoes which he had built into half a dozen different commercial tapes of various kinds. While he only required her image, he could always get her back.

"I'm doing it," she told him firmly. "You're going to have to start that slimy sideshow from scratch, whether you pay for a ready-made template or rent some whore who'll let you build a new one on your own."

"If I'd known that it had come to this," he said with calculated provocativeness, "I wouldn't have had to struggle upstairs with three boxes of groceries."

From there, it was only a few more steps to a renewal of the armed struggle, but Damon managed to keep the carving knife out of it. His aim—as always—was to win with the minimum of fuss. He made her work hard to dispel her bad feeling in pain and physical stress, but she got there in the end, without having to bruise her knuckles too badly, or cut her palms to pieces, or even make her throat sore by screaming too much abuse.

* * *

Afterwards, while Diana was still slightly stoned by virtue of the anesthetic effect of her internal technology, Damon helped her to pack up her things.

There wasn't that much to collect up; Diana had never been much of a magpie. She was a doer, not a maker, and it was easy enough for Damon to see, in retrospect, that it was the doer in him that she had valued, not the maker. Unfortunately, he had had enough of doing, at least for the time being; his only hunger now was for making.

When the time came to divide the personal items that might have been reckoned joint property Damon gave way on every point of dispute, until the time arrived when Diana realized that he was purging his life of everything that was associated with her—at which point she began insisting that he keep certain things to remember her by. After that, he began insisting that *she* kept her fair share of things, precisely because he didn't want to be surrounded by things that were, in principle, half hers. In all probability, it was not until then that the reality of the situation really came home to her—but it was too late for her to scrub out the fight and start again in the hope of rebuilding the broken bridge.

The possessions Diana was prevailed upon to take with her filled up the trunk she'd brought when she moved in plus the three boxes Damon had used to transport the groceries and a couple of black-plastic waste sacks. Even though there were two of them to do the work, there was far too much of it not to pose a logistical problem when the time came to take them down to her car. They had to jam the elevator door open in order to load the stuff inside, and they had to compound that misdemeanor with another when they had to tell an old man who stopped the elevator on the eleventh that there wasn't room to fit him in and that he'd have to wait. The elevator gave them hell about *that* one, but neither of them was in a fit state to care.

When they had packed the stuff away in the trunk and rear-seat space of her car, Damon tried to bid her a polite good-bye, but Diana wasn't having any of it. She just scowled at him and told him it was his loss.

As he watched her drive off, muted pangs of regret and remorse disturbed Damon's sense of relief, but not profoundly. When he walked back to the elevator his step was reasonably light. When it came down again the man from the eleventh floor stepped out, scowling at him almost as nastily as Diana, but Damon met the scowl with a serene smile. Although his past sins had not been forgotten, the elevator never said a word as it bore him upward; it was not permitted to harbor grudges. By the time it released him he was perfectly calm, looking forward to an interval of solitude, a pause for reflection.

Unfortunately, he saw as soon as the elevator doors opened that he wasn't about to get the chance. There were two men waiting patiently outside his apartment door, and even though they weren't wearing uniforms he had experience enough of their kind to know immediately that they were cops.

Three

Damon knew that it couldn't be a trivial matter. Cops didn't make house calls to conduct routine interviews. In all probability they'd soon be conducting all their interrogations in suitably tricked-out VEs; if the LAPD contract ever came up for tender he'd go for it like a shot. For the time being, though, the hardened pros who had been in the job for fifty years and more were sticking hard to the theory that meeting a man eye-to-eye made it just a little more difficult for their suspects to tell convincing lies.

One of the waiting men was tall and black, the other short and Japanese. Cops always seemed to work in ill-matched pairs, observing some mysterious sense of propriety carried over from the most ancient movies to the most recent VE dramas, but these two didn't seem to be in dogged pursuit of the cliché. Damon knew even before the short man held out a smartcard for his inspection that they were big-league players, not humble LAPD.

The hologram portrait of Inspector Hiru Yamanaka was blurred but recognizable. Although Damon had never seen an Interpol ID before he was prepared to assume that it was authentic; he handed it back without even switching it through his beltpack.

"This is Sergeant Rolfe," said Yamanaka, obviously assuming

that once his own identity had been established his word was authority enough to establish the ID of his companion.

"Whatever it is," Damon said, as he unlocked the door, "I'm not involved. I don't run with the gangs anymore and I don't have any idea what they're up to. These days, I only go out to fetch the groceries and help my girlfriend move out."

The men from Interpol followed Damon into the apartment, ignoring the stream of denials. Inspector Yamanaka showed not a flicker of interest as his heavy-lidded gaze took in the knife stuck into the doorjamb, but his sidekick took silently ostentatious offense at the untidy state of the living room. Even Damon had to admit that Diana's decampment had left it looking a frightful mess.

As soon as the door was shut Yamanaka said, "What do you know about the Eliminators, Mr. Hart?"

"I was never that kind of crazy," Damon told him affrontedly. "I was a serious streetfighter, not a hobbyist assassin."

"No one's accusing you of anything," said Sergeant Rolfe, in the unreliably casual way cops had. Damon's extensive experience of LAPD methods of insinuation encouraged him to infer that although they didn't have an atom of evidence they nevertheless thought he was guilty of *something.* Long-serving cops always had a naive trust in their powers of intuition.

"You only want me to help with your inquiries, right?"

"That's right, Mr. Hart," said Yamanaka smoothly.

"Well, I can't. I'm not an Eliminator. I don't know anyone who is an Eliminator. I don't keep tabs on Eliminator netboards. I have no interest at all in the philosophy and politics of Elimination."

It was all true. Damon knew no more about the Eliminators than anyone else—probably far less, given that he was no passionate follower of the kind of news tape which followed their activities with avid fascination. He was not entirely unsympathetic to those who thought it direly unjust that longevity, pain control, immunity to disease, and resistance to injury were simply commodities to be bought off the nanotech shelf, possessed in the fullest measure only by the rich, but he certainly wasn't sufficiently hung up about it to become a terrorist crusader on behalf of "equality and social justice for all."

The Eliminators were on the lunatic fringe of the many disparate and disorganized communities of interest fostered by the Web; they were devoted to the business of giving earnest consideration to the question of who might actually *deserve* to live forever. Some of their so-called Operators were in the habit of naming those whom they considered "unworthy of eternity," via messages dispatched to netboards from public phones or illicit temporary linkpoints. Such messages were usually accompanied by downloadable packages of "evidence" which put the case for elimination. Damon had scanned a few such packages in his time; they were mostly badly composed exercises in hysteria devoid of any real substance. The first few freelance executions had unleased a tide of media alarm back in the seventies—a blaze of publicity whose inevitable effect had been to glamorize the entire enterprise and conjure into being a veritable legion of amateur assassins. Things had quieted down in recent years, but only because the Operators had become more careful and the amateur assassins more cunning. Being named by a well-known Operator wasn't a cast-iron guarantee that a man would be attacked—and perhaps killed, in spite of all that his internal technology could contrive—but it was something that had to be taken seriously. It didn't require much imagination on Damon's part to figure out that Interpol must be keen to nail some guilty parties and impose some severe punitive sanctions, *pour encourager les autres*—but he couldn't begin to figure out why their suspicions might have turned in his direction.

"There's really no need to be so defensive," Yamanaka told him. "We find ourselves confronted by a puzzle, and we hope that you might be able to help us to understand what's going on."

The sergeant, meanwhile, had begun to drift around the apartment, looking at the pictures on the wall, scanning the discs on the shelves and eyeing Damon's VE equipment as if its abundance and complexity were a calculated affront to his stubborn fleshiness.

"A puzzle?" Damon echoed sceptically. "Crossword or jigsaw?"

"May I?" Yamanaka asked, refusing to echo Damon's sarcasm. His neatly manicured finger was pointing to the main windowscreen.

"Be my guest," Damon said sourly.

Yamanaka's fingers did a brief dance on the windowscreen's keyboard. The resting display gave way to a pattern of words etched in blue on a black background:

> CONRAD HELIER IS NAMED AN ENEMY OF MANKIND
> CONRAD HELIER IS NOT DEAD
> FIND AND IDENTIFY THE MAN WHO WAS CONRAD HELIER
> PROOFS WILL FOLLOW
> OPERATOR 101

Damon felt a sinking sensation in his belly. He knew that he ought to have been able to regard the message with complete indifference, but the simple fact was that he couldn't.

"What has that to do with me?" he asked combatively.

"According to the official record," Yamanaka said smoothly, "you didn't adopt your present name until ten years ago, when you were sixteen. Before that, you were known as Damon Helier. You're Conrad Helier's natural son."

"So what? He died twenty years before I was born, no matter what that crazy says. Under the New Reproductive System it doesn't matter a damn who anybody's natural father was."

"To most people," Yamanaka agreed, "it's a matter of complete indifference—but not to you, Mr. Hart. You were given your father's surname. Your four foster parents were all close colleagues of your father. Your father left a great deal of money in trust for you—an inheritance which came under your control two years after you changed your name. I know that you've never touched the money and that you haven't seen any of your foster parents for some years, apparently doing your utmost to distance yourself from the destiny which your father had planned out for you—but that doesn't signify *indifference*, Mr. Hart. It suggests that you took a strong dislike to your father and everything he stood for."

"So you think I might do something like this? I'm not that stupid, and I'm certainly not that crazy. Who told you I might know something about this? Was it Eveline?"

"No one has named you as a possible suspect," the inspector said soothingly. "Your name came up in a routine data trawl. We know that Operator one-oh-one always transmits his denunciations from the Los Angeles area, and you've been living hereabouts throughout the time he's been active, but—"

Damon cut him off in midsentence. "I told you—I'm not that kind of lunatic, and I try never to think about Conrad Helier and the plans he had for me. I'm my own man, and I have my own life to lead. Why are you so interested in a message that's so patently false? You can't possibly believe that Conrad Helier is still alive—or that he was an enemy of mankind, whatever that's supposed to mean."

"If you had let me finish," Yamanaka said, his voice still scrupulously even although he was obviously becoming impatient, "I'd have emphasized yet again that you're not under suspicion. Although the local police have an extensive file on your past activities there's nothing in it to suggest any involvement with the Eliminators. I'm afraid this is a more complicated matter than it seems."

Now Damon wondered whether Yamanaka might want to recruit him as an informant—to use his contacts as a means of furthering their investigation. He wanted to interrupt again, to say that he wasn't about to do that, but he knew that the conclusions he'd jumped to had so far only served to slow things down. He figured that if he held his tongue, this might be over much sooner.

"Before going on to the other aspect of our inquiry, however,"

Yamanaka continued, when he realized that he still had the floor, "it might be worth my pointing out that this message has some unusual features. No Operator, including one-oh-one, has ever used the phrase *enemy of mankind* before; *unworthy of immortality* is the customary formula. Nor is it usual for Operators to appeal to kindred spirits to *find and identify* someone. It might be a hoax, of course; one of the nastiest aspects of the Eliminators' game is that anyone can play. Code number one-oh-one has been used a dozen times, and the relative coherency of the attached files has allowed it to build up a certain reputation, but that doesn't necessarily mean that all the messages came from one source. In any case, the message was only the first piece of the puzzle. You know, I suppose, that you're not the only person connected with Conrad Helier living on the Pacific Coast."

"One of my foster parents, Silas Arnett, lives near San Francisco," Damon admitted warily. "Some stupid resort area landscaped to look like the south coast of Old England—or some so-called continental engineer's notion of what the south coast of England used to look like. I haven't seen Silas in years. We don't communicate."

Actually, Silas Arnett was the only one of his foster parents with whom Damon might have communicated, had he been a little less rigorous in his determination to carve out his own destiny. Silas had been far more of a father to him than Karol Kachellek or Conrad Helier ever had, and had made his own escape from the tight-knit group shortly after Damon—but Damon had always had other things on his mind, and Silas hadn't contacted him except for sending dutiful messages of goodwill on his birthdays and at each year's end.

"Silas Arnett has disappeared from his home," Yamanaka said. "According to a witness, he was forcibly removed—kidnapped—the night before last."

Damon felt a stab of resentment. Why hadn't the Interpol man told him this *first,* instead of teasing him with all that crap about the Eliminators? He knew, though, that it was mostly his own fault that the discussion had got bogged down.

"What witness?" he asked.

"A young woman named Catherine Praill. She was an overnight guest at Arnett's house. She was asleep when the abduction took place—she heard the struggle but she didn't see anything."

"Is she involved?"

"We have no reason to think so. There's no evidence of any untoward activity on her part, and no indication of a possible motive." Yamanaka was being very careful, and Damon could understand why. Silas Arnett's house must have had all the standard security systems; it would have been very much easier to bypass them if the intruders had someone inside with direct access to the controls. The police must have gone through Catherine Praill's records very carefully indeed.

"Was she a *very* young woman?" Damon asked.

"There is little to distinguish her from dozens of other guests Mr. Arnett had entertained during the last few years," Yamanaka replied diplomatically—perhaps meaning that if the kidnappers knew Arnett's tastes and habits well enough, it would have been easy enough to get someone inside to facilitate their work.

"You think the people who took Silas also posted that message?" Damon said, pointing at the windowscreen.

"We think that it's an interesting coincidence," Yamanaka admitted. "There's more. Another of your father's contemporaries has an address in San Diego, but he's proving equally difficult to trace."

"Who?"

"A man named Surinder Nahal."

Damon could understand why the pedantic inspector has chosen the word *contemporaries.* Conrad Helier and Surinder Nahal had been in the same line of work, but they'd never been colleagues. They'd been rivals—and there had been a certain amount of bad blood between them. Damon didn't know exactly why; it hadn't been an acceptable topic of conversation among his foster parents.

"Has he been abducted too?" Damon asked.

"Not as far as we know," said Yamanaka, careful as ever.

The inspector's associate had now drifted back to his side, having completed his superficial inspection of the apartment. "Karol Kachellek also claimed that he hadn't seen Silas Arnett for many years," Rolfe put in. "Eveline Hywood said the same. It seems that your surviving foster parents fell out with one another as well as with you."

Damon realized that it would be foolish to swing from one extreme to the other—from taking it for granted that he was a suspect to taking it for granted that he wasn't. The Interpol men were undoubtedly fishing for anything they could catch. "I dare say it's true," he said cautiously. "Silas's decision to retire must have seemed to Karol and Eveline to be a failure of vocation almost as scandalous as my own: yet another betrayal of Conrad Helier's sacred cause."

Yamanaka nodded as if he understood—but Damon knew that he almost certainly didn't. It was difficult to guess Yamanaka's true age, because a man of his standing would have the kind of internal technology which was capable of slowing down the aging process to a minimum, as well as PicoCon's latest cosmetic engineering, but he was probably no more than sixty. To the inspector, as to Damon, the glittering peak of Conrad Helier's career would be the stuff of history. At school the young Hiru Yamanaka would have been dutifully informed that the artificial wombs which Conrad Helier had perfected, and the techniques which allowed such wombs to produce legions of healthy infants while the plague of sterility spread like wildfire across the globe, were the salvation of the species—but that didn't mean that he could understand the appalling *reverence* in which Conrad Helier had been held by his closest coworkers.

"Do you have any idea why anyone would want to kidnap Silas Arnett?" Yamanaka asked Damon with unaccustomed bluntness.

"None at all," Damon replied, perhaps too reflexively.

"Do you have any idea why anyone would want to blacken your father's name?" The follow-up seemed as bland as it was

blunt, but Damon knew that if Yamanaka was right in his estimation of the *interesting coincidence* this might be the key that
tied everything together. A brusque *none at all* would not serve
as an adequate answer. "I was encouraged in every possible way
to see my father as the greatest hero and saint the twenty-second
century produced," Damon said judiciously, "but I know that
there were some who had a very different opinion of him. I never
knew him, of course, but I know there were people who resented
the strength of his views and his high media profile. Some
thought him unbearably arrogant, others thought he got more
credit for the solution to the Crisis than was due to him. On the
other hand, although I couldn't follow in his footsteps—and
never wanted to—I don't disapprove of anything he did, or anything my foster parents did in pursuit of his ambitions. If you
want my opinion, whoever posted this notice is sick as well as
stupid. It certainly wasn't Silas Arnett, and I find it difficult to
believe that it might have been anyone who understood the nature and extent of Conrad Helier's achievements. That includes
Surinder Nahal."

Sergeant Rolfe curled his lip, evidently thinking that this eye-
to-eye interview was turning out to be a waste of valuable time.

"There were several witnesses to the death of Conrad Helier,"
the inspector said matter-of-factly, "and his last days were
recorded, without apparent interruption, on videotape which
can still be accessed by anyone who cares to download it. The
doctor who was in attendance and the embalmer who prepared
the body for the funeral both confirm that they carried out DNA
checks on the corpse, and that the gene map matched Conrad
Helier's records. If the man whose body was cremated on 27
January 2147 wasn't Conrad Helier then the gene map on file in
the Central Directory must have been substituted." He paused
briefly, then said: "You don't look at all like your father. Is that
deliberate, or is it simply that you resemble your mother?"

"I've never gone in for cosmetic reconstruction," Damon told
him warily. "I have no idea what my mother looked like; I don't
even know her name. I understand that her ova were stripped

and frozen at the height of the Crisis, when they were afraid that the world's entire stock might be wiped out by the plague. There's no surviving record of her. At that time, according to my foster parents, nobody was overly particular about where healthy ova came from; they just wanted to get as many as they could in the bank. They were stripping them from anyone more than five years old, so it's possible that my mother was a mere infant."

"It's possible, then, that your natural mother is still alive," Yamanaka commented, with a casualness that was probably feigned.

"If she is," Damon pointed out, "she can't possibly know that one of her ova was inseminated by Conrad Helier's sperm and that I was the result."

"I suppose Eveline Hywood and Mary Hallam must both have been infected before their wombs could be stripped," Yamanaka said, disregarding the taboos that would presumably continue to inhibit free conversation regarding the legacy of the plague until the last survivors of the Crisis had retired from public life. "Or was it just that Conrad Helier was reluctant to select one of your foster parents as a natural mother in case it affected the partnership?"

"I don't think any of this is relevant to the matters you're investigating," Damon said. "The kidnapping is the important thing—the other thing was probably posted simply to confuse the matter."

"I can't tell as yet what might be relevant and what might not," Yamanaka said unapologetically. "The message supposedly deposited by Operator one-oh-one might be pure froth, and there might be nothing sinister in the fact that I can't contact Surinder Nahal—but if Silas Arnett really has been seized by Eliminators this could represent the beginning of a new and nastier phase of that particular species of terrorism. Eliminators already attract far too much media attention, and this story might well become headline news. I'd like to stay one step ahead of the dozens of newsmen who must have been commissioned to start digging—in fact, I *need* to stay at least one step ahead of them because they'll certainly confuse the issue once they begin stirring things up. I'm sorry to have troubled you, Mr. Hart, but I thought it best that I contact you directly to inform you of what had happened. If you think of anything that might help us, it might be to your own advantage to let us know immediately."

He's implying that I might be in danger too, Damon thought. If he's right, and the message is connected to Silas's disappearance, this really might be the beginning of something nasty—even if it's only a news-tape hatchet job. "I'll ask around," he said carefully. "If I discover anything that might help you, I'll be sure to let you know."

"Thank you, Mr. Hart," the man from Interpol said, offering no clue as to exactly what he understood by Damon's promise to *ask around.* "I'm grateful for your cooperation."

When he had closed the door behind his unwelcome visitors Damon pulled the carving knife out of the jamb, wondering what Sergeant Rolfe had made of it. Would Interpol be checking Diana's record as carefully as they had checked his? Would they find anything there to connect her to the Eliminators? Probably not—but how well did *he* know her? How well had he *ever* known her? And where would she go, now that she was homeless again? Might she too become "untraceable," like Silas Arnett and Surinder Nahal? Suddenly, he felt an urgent need of someone to talk to—and realized belatedly that since he had quit the fight game he had gradually transferred all his conversational eggs to one basket. Now that Diana was gone, there was no one who regularly passed the time of day with him except the censorious elevator, which didn't even qualify as a worm-level AI.

All I want is a chance to work, he thought. All I need is the space to get on with my own projects. None of this is anything to do with me. But he knew, even as he voiced the thought within the virtual environment of his mind, that he didn't have the authority to decide that he was uninvolved in this affair. Nor, he realized—slightly to his surprise—was he able to attain the level of indifference that would allow him simply to turn his back on the mystery. In spite of everything that had happened to spoil the relationship between himself and his foster parents, he still cared—about Silas Arnett, at least.

Oh, Silas, he thought, what on earth have you done? Who can you possibly have annoyed sufficiently to get yourself kidnapped? And why have the Eliminators turned their attention to a saint who's been dead for nearly fifty years?

four

D amon knew that there was no point searching the apartment for the bugs that Sergeant Rolfe had planted while he was wandering around. Interpol undoubtedly had nanomachines clever enough to evade detection by his antique sweeper. Nor was he about to ask for help—Building Security had better sweepers but they also had a rather flexible view of the right to privacy that they were supposedly there to guarantee. He had enough demerits on his account already without giving formal notification of the fact that he was under investigation by a high-level law enforcement agency.

Instead, he donned his phone hood and started making calls.

It was, as he'd anticipated, a waste of time. Everybody in the world—not to mention everybody off-world—had a beltpack and a personal call-number, but that didn't mean that anybody in the world was accessible twenty-four hours a day. Everybody in the world also had an AI answering machine, which functioned for most people as a primary status symbol as well as a protector of privacy, and which needed to be shown off if they were to perform that function adequately. The higher a man's social profile was the cleverer his AI needed to be at fielding and filtering calls. Damon usually had no cause to regret the trend—customizing virtual environments for the AI simulacra to inhabit provided nearly 40 percent of his business—but whenever he actually wanted to make urgent contact with some people he found the endless routine of stagy reply sequences just as frustrating as anyone else.

Karol Kachellek's simulacrum was standing on a photo-derived Hawaiian beach with muted breakers rolling in behind him. The unsmiling simulacrum brusquely reported that Karol was busy operating a deep-sea dredger by remote control and couldn't be disturbed. It warned Damon that his call was un-likely to be returned for several hours, and perhaps not until the next day.

Damon told the sim that the matter was urgent, but the as-surances he received in return were patently hollow.

Eveline Hywood's simulacrum wasn't even full length; it was just a detached head floating in what Damon took to be a straightforward replication of her lab. The room's only decora-tion—if even that could be reckoned a mere ornament—was a window looking out upon a rich star field. It was the kind of panorama which people who lived with five miles of atmosphere above their heavy heads only ever got to see in virtual form, and it therefore functioned as a status symbol, even though La-grangists were supposed to be above that sort of thing. The sim's gray hair was trimmed to a mere fuzz, according to the prevail-ing minimalist philosophy of the microgee colonists, but its fea-tures were slightly more naturalistic than those Karol had contrived for his alter ego.

The sim told Damon that Eveline was working on a delicate series of experiments and wouldn't be returning any calls for at least twenty-four hours. Again, Damon told the sim that the mat-ter was urgent—but the sim looked back at him with a cold hau-teur which silently informed him that *nothing* happening on Earth could possibly be urgent by comparison with the labor of a dedicated Lagrangist.

Damon doubted that the news about Silas and the strange de-claration of Operator 101 had reached either of his foster par-ents as yet; unless Interpol had sent someone to see them face-to-face the information would be stuck in the same queue as his own calls, probably assigned an equally low priority by the two AI filtering devices.

Madoc Tamlin's simulacrum had a lot more style, as did the surreal backcloth which Damon had designed for it, with a liquid clock whose ripples told the right time and a very plausible phoenix that rose afresh from its pyre every time the sim accepted a call. The sim gave no reason for Madoc's unavailability, although the expression in its eyes carefully implied that being the kind of rakehell he was he was probably up to no good. Damon knew, though, that its promise that Madoc would get back to him within the hour was trustworthy.

When he lifted the hood again the one thing on Damon's mind was getting to the bathroom, so it wasn't until he'd done what he had to do and emerged again that he saw the envelope lying on the floor just inside the apartment door. The absurdity of it stopped him dead in his tracks and almost made him laugh. *Nobody* pushed envelopes under apartment doors—not, at any rate, in buildings as well supplied with spy eyes as this one.

Damon picked the envelope up. It wasn't sealed.

He drew the enclosed piece of paper out and unfolded it curiously. The words printed on it might have been put there by any of a million near identical machines. They read:

DAMON
IT IS TRUE
CONRAD HELIER IS ALIVE
ARNETT WILL BE RELEASED WHEN HE HAS TESTIFIED
AHASUERUS AND HYWOOD HAVE THE REMAINING ANSWERS
OPERATOR 101

This time, Damon *did* laugh. This made the whole affair seem suddenly childish, like a silly game. He remembered the way Yamanaka had carefully called his attention to the unusual features of the original message, implying that it wasn't *really* an Eliminator who had posted it. This was surely confirmation of the fact—no authentic Eliminator would post personal messages under someone's door. This had to be a joke.

Damon slipped back under the hood and called Building Security.

The call was answered by a real person, just as the lease specifications promised. "This is thirteen four seven," he said reflexively, although she could have read that from the automatic display.

"What can I do for you, Mr. Hart?" said the real person gravely. She had a broad halo of honey blond hair, a superabundance of facial jewelry, and an anxious expression, none of which were properly coordinated with her sober gray uniform.

"Somebody just slipped something under my door—within the last thirty minutes. Could you decant me the spy-eye tape that gives the clearest picture?"

He took her assent so much for granted that he almost severed the connection before she said: "I'm sorry, Mr. Hart, but that won't be possible. We've suffered a slight system failure." She sounded very embarrassed, as well she might. Setting aside such routine antisocial behavior as jamming the elevator open for a couple of minutes, the misdemeanor rate within the building was so low that Security was having a hard time justifying its proportion of the lease tax.

"What do you mean, a *slight system failure?*" Damon asked, although he had a pretty good idea.

"Well," said the blond woman unhappily, "to tell the truth, it's not that slight. In fact, it's fairly general."

Damon considered the implications of this news for a few moments before saying: "General enough to allow someone to walk into the building, take the elevator to the thirteenth, push something under a door, take the elevator back down again, and walk out undetected?"

"It's possible," she conceded, quickly adding: "It's a *very* unusual situation, Mr. Hart. I've never known anything like it."

Damon judged from her tone that she had encountered similar situations several times before, but had been instructed not to admit the fact to the tenants. This wasn't the kind of building that software saboteurs would target, but it wasn't the kind they'd leave alone either. Damon had crashed similar systems in the days when he'd been in training to be an all-around juvenile delinquent and taken pride in it. The only authentically unusual thing about this particular act of sabotage was that someone had taken advantage of it to pay a personal call. The blond woman, who was waiting impatiently for him to break the connection and let her get on with her work, obviously hadn't cottoned on to that.

"Thanks," he said reflexively. He didn't give her time to say "You're welcome," although she probably wouldn't have bothered.

When he'd slipped off the hood, Damon devoted a few moments to wondering who might want to make a joke at his expense, and why. Diana hadn't had time to set it up, and it wasn't her style—although she certainly knew enough amateur saboteurs capable of crashing Building Security. Madoc Tamlin knew many more, and he was one of the few people to whom he'd confided his original surname and his reasons for changing it, but Madoc wouldn't stoop so low.

Eventually, he came around full circle. What if it *weren't* a joke? Interpol seemed to be taking it seriously enough, even though they didn't think it was authentic Eliminator action—and something *had* happened to Silas Arnett.

He wondered whether he ought to tell the police about the note. He had no particular reason to conceal it, although its sender presumably intended it for his eyes only. He decided to keep his options open, at least for the time being, and tackle the matter himself. That had always been his natural inclination— an inclination which, if it was hereditary, had very probably been gifted to him by his long-dead father. He put the envelope in a drawer and the note into the inside pocket of his suitskin. Then he went to get something to eat.

* * *

Just as Damon finished his meal the alarm he'd set to notify him of any response to his various calls began beeping. He ducked under the phone hood and displaced his AI answering machine, which was in the middle of telling Madoc Tamlin that he was on his way. The VE which surrounded them was a lush forest scene whose colorful birds and butterflies were the product of a spontaneous ecology rather than a simple tape loop; it was unnecessarily elaborate but it served as an ad for his VE engineering skills.

"Is this about Diana?" Madoc said—which at least solved the minor mystery of where Diana had gone after storming out of Damon's life. It made sense; she had known Tamlin a good deal longer than she had known Damon, and she was on no better terms with her foster parents than Damon was with his.

"No, it's not," he said. "It's business. Have you heard anything about a kidnap up the coast?"

Madoc raised a quizzical eyebrow. His eyebrows were as black as his hair and as neatly shaped; they made an interesting contrast with his pale eyes, which had been tinted a remarkably delicate shade of green. "Haven't seen the news," he said. "Anyone you know?"

"My foster father. There may be an Eliminator connection."

The quizzical expression disappeared. "Not good," Madoc said—then waited, expecting more.

"I've got a proposition that might interest you," Damon said carefully.

"Yeah?" Madoc knew better than to ask for details over the phone. "Well, I won't be back at the apartment for quite a while, and that might not be a good place, all things considered. You can find me in the alley where we shot your second-to-last fight. You remember where that is, I suppose?"

"I remember," Damon assured him drily. "I'll be there in an hour and a half, traffic permitting."

"No traffic here," Madoc drawled. "You should never have moved so close to the coast, Damie. World's still overcrowded, thanks to you-know-who. Too many people, too many cars, wherever the real estate is in good condition. It'll be a long time before the gantzers get to *this* neighborhood."

"Don't bet on that," Damon said. "The new generation can turn rubble back into walls with no significant effort at all. Around here you'd never know there was ever an earthquake, let alone two plague wars."

"Around the alley," Madoc riposted, "we don't forget so easily. We're conservationists, remember? Preserving the legacy of the plague wars and the great quakes, keeping alive *all* the old traditions."

"I'm on my way," Damon said shortly. He wasn't in the mood for banter.

Tamlin laughed, and might have said more, but Damon cut him off and the forest faded into darkness, leaving nothing visible except the customary virtual readouts, limned in crimson against the Stygian gloom.

He didn't waste any time leaving the apartment and taking the elevator down to the basement. The elevator's voice was back online but it didn't have a word of complaint to utter.

The traffic was bad enough to make Damon wonder whether the twenty-first-century mythology of endless gridlock was as fanciful as everyone thought. At the turn of the millennium the world's population hadn't been much over five billion; the present day's seven billion might be distributed a little more evenly in geographical terms, but people only thought of it as "small" by comparison with the fourteen billion peak briefly attained before the Second Plague War. As Madoc had said, the planet could still be considered overcrowded, thanks to Conrad Helier. The rising curve of the birthrate would cross the declining curve of the death rate again within ten or twelve years, and yet another psychologically significant moment would be upon the worrying world. Los Angeles had been so severely depopulated in the plague wars that it still lay half in ruins, but now that PicoCon had the Gantz patents all wrapped up and the last of the ancient antitrust laws had been consigned to the dustbin by the Wash-

ington Rump it was only a matter of time before the deconstructionists started the long march inland.

The further east Damon went the thinner the traffic became.
He headed straight into the heart of the badlands, where the
Second Plague War had struck hardest once the bugs had moved
out of Hollywood, leaving nothing for the '77 quake to do but a
little minor vandalism—by the time the Crisis arrived some
twenty years later there had been no one around these parts to
care. Soon enough, he was in a region where all the buildings
which hadn't already collapsed were in permanent danger of so
doing: a district which was, in practice if not in theory, beyond
the reach of the LAPD.

In truth, little enough of what Madoc Tamlin and his fellows
got up to out here was unambiguously illegal. The fights were
private affairs, which couldn't concern the police unless a com-
batant filed a complaint—which, of course, none ever did—or
someone died. Fighters did die, occasionally; a lot of the kids
who got involved did so in order to earn the money that would
pay for advanced IT, and some of them didn't advance far
enough quickly enough to keep themselves from real harm. Tap-
ing the fights wasn't against the law, nor was selling them—except insofar as the tapes in which someone *did* get killed might
be counted as evidence of accessory activity—so Madoc's reputation as an outlaw was 90 percent myth. His only real crimes
arose out of his association with software saboteurs and creative
accountants.

Damon's own record was no dirtier, formally or informally. He
had never killed anyone, although he'd come close once or twice.
He really had tried to see the fighting as a *sport*, with its own particular skills, its own unique artistry, and its own distinctive spectator appeal. He hadn't given it up out of disgust, but simply
because he'd become more and more interested in the technical
side of the business—the way the raw tapes of ham-fisted brawls
were turned into scintillating VE experiences for the punters.
That, at least, was what he had told himself—and anyone else
who cared to ask.

Damon found Madoc easily enough. He hadn't been down the alley for more than a year, but it was all familiar—almost eerily so. The graffiti on the walls had been renewed but not significantly altered; all the heaps of rubble had been carefully maintained, as if they were markings on a field of play whose proportions were sacred. Madoc was busy wiring up a fighter who didn't look a day over fourteen, although he had to be a *little* older than that.

"It's too tight," the fighter complained. "I can't move properly." Damon had no difficulty deducing that it was the boy's first time.

"No it's not," said Madoc, with careful patience, as he knelt to complete the synaptic links in the *reta mirabile* which covered the fighter's body like a bright spiderweb. "It's no tighter than the training suit you've been using all week. You can move quite freely."

The novice's fearful eyes looked over Madoc's shoulder, lighting on Damon's face. Damon saw the sudden blaze of dawning recognition. "Hey," the boy said, "you're Damon Hart! I got a dozen of your fight tapes. You going to be doctoring the tape for this? That's great! My name's Lenny Garon."

Damon didn't bother to inform the boy that he hadn't come to watch the fight and he didn't deny that he had been brought in to doctor the tapes. He understood how scared the youngster must be, and he didn't want to say anything that might be construed as a put-down. If he had judged the situation rightly, Lenny Garon was due to be cut up by a skilled knifeman, and he didn't need any extra damage to his ego. Damon didn't recognize the boy's opponent, but he could see that the other wired-up figure was at least three years older and much more comfortable with the pressure and distribution of the *reta mirabile*.

Madoc stood up, already issuing stern instructions as to where the combatants shouldn't stab one another. He didn't want the recording apparatus damaged. "The only way you can make real money for this kind of work," he told the novice, "is to get used to the kit and to make damn sure it doesn't get damaged. Given that your chances of long-term survival are directly proportional to your upgrade prospects, you'd better get this right. It's a good break, if you can carry it off. Brady's tough, but you'll have to go up against tougher if you're to make your mark in this game."

Lenny nodded dumbly. "I can do it," he said uneasily. "I got all the feints and jumps. It'll be okay. I won't let you down."

"We don't want *feints and jumps,*" Madoc said, with a slight contemptuous sneer that might have been intended to wind the boy up. "We want purpose and skill and desperation. Just because we're making a VR tape. . . . Explain it to him, Damon."

Madoc turned away to check the other fighter's equipment, leaving Lenny Garon to look up at Damon with evident awe. Damon was acutely embarrassed by the thought that it might have been using *his* tapes that had filled this idiot with the desire to get into the fight game himself. The cleverer the tapes became as a medium of entertainment, the easier it became for users to forget the highly significant detail that fighters who were doing it for real were not insulated, as VE users were, from the consequences of their mistakes. Even if they had IT enough to blot out their pain, the actual fighters still got stabbed and slashed; the blood they lost was real, and if they were unfortunate enough to take a blade in the eye they lost the sight of it for a very uncomfortable couple of weeks.

"Any advice?" the boy asked eagerly.

Damon was tempted to say: Forget it. Get out now. Make the money some other way. He didn't, because he knew that he had no right to say any such thing. He hadn't even needed the money. "Don't try to *look good,*" he said, instead. "Remember that we aren't making a straightforward recording that will give a floater the illusion that he's going through your moves. We're just making a *template*—raw material. You just concentrate on looking after yourself—leave it to the doctor to please the audience."

"Shit, Damon!" Madoc complained. "Don't tell the kid he doesn't have to give us any help at all. He's just trying to go easy on you, Lenny, with it being your first time and all. Sure, play-acting doesn't do it—it reeks of fake—but you have to show us *something.* You have to show us that you have *talent.* If you want to be good at this, you have to go *all the way . . .* but you have to look after the wiring. No record at all is far worse than a bad one."

The boy nodded respectfully in Damon's direction before turning to face his opponent. The gesture brought it home to Damon that he still had a big reputation on the streets. He might be out of circulation, but his tapes weren't; his past was going to be around for a long time. But that, in a sense, was why he was here. Aspects of his past that seemed even more remote than his fighting days were still capable of tormenting him, still capable of *involving* him.

"Just remember," Madoc Tamlin said as he pushed the boy forward, "it's a small price to pay for taking one more step toward immortality."

Like the Eliminators, street slang always spoke of *immortality* rather than *emortality*—which, strictly speaking, was all that even the very best internal technology could ever hope to provide. Not that anyone expected current technology to guarantee them more than a hundred and fifty years—but in a hundred and fifty years' time, current technology would be way out of date. Those who got the very best out of today's IT would still be around to get the benefit of tomorrow's—and might, if all went well, eventually arrive at the golden day when all the processes of aging could be arrested in perpetuity.

According to the ads, today's young people were solidly set on an escalator that might take them all the way to absolute immunity to aging and disease. As the older generation—who had already aged too badly to be brought back permanently from the brink—gradually died off, the younger would inherit the earth *in perpetuity.* Not that anyone believed the ads implicitly, of course—ads were just ads, when all was said and done.

Five

Damon watched the two fighters square up. Their kit *was* more than a little cumbersome, but very few artificial organics were as delicate as the real thing and you couldn't get template precision with thinner webs. As the two moved together, though, he deliberately looked away at the ruined buildings to either side of the street.

His eye was caught by one of the items of graffiti sketched in luminous paint on a smoke-blackened fragment of wall. It read: Live fast, die young, leave a beautiful corpse. It was an antique, so old that Madoc must have found it in a history book. In fact, he could imagine Madoc chuckling with glee when he discovered it, immediately appropriating it as part of the backcloth for his dramatic productions. No child of today, however dangerously he or she might want to live, would ever have come up with such a ridiculous slogan—although there were plenty of centenarians who might like to believe it of them.

Centenarians loved to see themselves as the survivors of the Second Deluge. Those who had made no effective contribution to the world's survival were worse than those who had, swelling with absurd pride at the thought that they had endured the worst trial by ordeal that nature had ever devised and proved their worth. Such people could not imagine that anyone who came after them could possibly value the earth, or life itself, as much as they did—nor could they imagine that anyone who came after them could be as worthy of *life* as they were, let alone of immortality. No one knew for sure, but Damon's suspicion was that a hundred out of every hundred-and-one Eliminator Operators were in their dotage.

He wondered what the neighborhood must have been like in the bad old days of the early twenty-first century, and what angry words might have been scrawled on the walls by boys and girls who really were condemned to die young. Throughout that century this neighborhood would have been crowded out with the unemployable and the insupportable: one of countless concentration-city powder kegs waiting for a revolutionary spark which had never come, thanks to the two plague wars—the first allegedly launched by the rich against the poor and the second by the poor against the rich. In the short term, of course, the rich had won both of them; it had taken the Crisis to restore a measure of equality and fraternity in the face of disaster. Now the Crisis was over and the New Utopia was here—but the neighborhood was still derelict, still host to darkness and to violence, still beyond the reach of supposedly universal civilization.

When the fight began in earnest, Damon couldn't help looking back. He couldn't refuse to watch, so he contented himself with trying to follow every nuance with a scrupulously clinical eye. The other watchers—whose sole raison d'être was to whip the combatants into a frenzy—weighed in with the customary verve and fury, howling out their support for one boy or the other.

Amazingly, Lenny Garon managed to stick Brady in the gut while the experienced fighter was arrogantly playing a teasing game of cat and mouse with him—which made Brady understandably furious. It was immediately clear to Damon that the older boy wasn't going to settle for some token belly wound as a reprisal; he wanted copious bloodshed. That would be more than okay by Madoc Tamlin, so long as the cuts didn't do too much damage to the recorders. Lenny Garon would suffer more than he had anticipated, perhaps more than he had thought possible, and for far longer—but it probably wouldn't put him off. In all probability, he would be all the more enthusiastic to work his way up to something *really* heavy, in order to pay for the nanotech that would make him as good as new and keep him that way no matter what injuries his frail flesh might sustain.

Madoc had, of course, taken note of Damon's reluctance to join in the loud exhortations of the crowd. "Don't get all stiff on me, Damon," he said. "You may be in the Big World now, but you're still too young to get rigor mortis. Are you worried about splitting with Diana? She's at my place now, but it isn't permanent. I could help fix things up if you want me to." Damon took the inference that Madoc had found Diana's sudden reintroduction into his life burdensome.

"Interpol paid a call on me yesterday," Damon told him, thinking that it was time to get down to business. No one was likely to be listening to them while the fight was on. "Silas Arnett has been snatched by persons unknown. They seem to think that I might be a target too."

Madoc put on a show of astonishment. "I can't believe that," he said. "Eliminators only go after the older generation—and they use bombs and bullets. They're all loners, and losers too. If they had any real organization they'd have been busted long ago. A snatch takes planning—not their style at all. What's it got to do with you, anyhow? I thought you didn't talk to your family."

"I don't, but it *is* Silas—the nearly human one. I don't suppose you know anything at all about a particular loner who calls himself Operator one-oh-one? He's said to be local."

"Not my territory," Madoc said with a shrug. "You want me to ask around, right?"

"It's more complicated than that. The Operator in question named Conrad Helier as an enemy of mankind. When you're through, okay?"

Madoc looked at him sharply before nodding. Even Diana Caisson didn't know that Damon Hart had once been Damon Helier, and Madoc knew how privileged he was to have been let in on the secret. He'd probably have found out anyway—Madoc knew some very light-footed Webwalkers, first-rate poachers who had not yet turned gamekeeper—but he hadn't had to go digging. Damon had trusted him, and obviously trusted him still. Damon knew that he could rely on Madoc to do everything he could to help, for pride's sake as well as anything else he might be offered.

Lenny Garon was in real trouble now. The crowd were baying for blood, and getting it. Damon kept his own eyes slightly averted as Madoc turned back to concentrate fully on the business in hand, but he couldn't turn away. He could feel the stir and surge of his own adrenalin, and his muscles were tensing as he put himself in the shoes of the younger fighter, trying to urge the boy on with his body language.

It didn't work, of course.

A roar went up from the watchers as Brady finally rammed home his advantage. Poor Lenny was on the ground, screaming. The blade had gone deep, but the wound wasn't mortal.

Damon knew that it would all be feeding into the template: the reflexes and convulsions of pain; the physical dimensions of the shock and the horror. It would all be ready digitized, ripe for manipulation and refinement. The tape doctor would take a little longer to tease it into proper shape than the real doctor would take to stitch up the fighters, but once the tape was made it would be fixed and finished. Lenny Garon might never be the same. His wounds would mend, leaving no obvious scars, but. . . .

He abandoned the train of thought. This affair seemed to be feeding an unhealthy tendency to melodrama. He reminded himself of what he'd told Diana about the porn tape. By the time the doctor had finished with the recordings there'd be nothing of *Lenny* left at all; there'd only be the actions and the reactions, dissected out and purified as a marketable commodity. The fighter on the tape might have Lenny's face and Lenny's pain, but it wouldn't be *him*. It would be an artifact, less than a shadow and nothing like a soul.

The whole thing was in rank bad taste, of course, but it was a living for all concerned. For the first few months after he had quit fighting, it had been *his own* living, and it had been based in talents that were entirely and *exclusively* his own, using nothing that Conrad Helier had left to him—in his will, at least.

Damon had wanted then, and he wanted still, to be his own man.

Madoc Tamlin had moved forward to help the stricken street-fighter, not because he was overly concerned for the boy's health but because he wanted to make certain that the equipment was still in good order. Not until the silvery web had been stripped away were the two fighters handed over to the amateur ambulance drivers waiting nearby. Brady got in under his own steam but Lenny Garon had to be carried.

The crowd drifted away, evaporating into the concrete wilderness.

Damon waited patiently until Madoc's gear was all packed up and the produce of the day had been handed on to the next phase of its development.

"Your place or mine?" Madoc said, waving his hand in a lazy arc which took in both their cars. Damon led the way to his own vehicle and the older man followed. Damon waited until both doors had closed before starting to set out his proposition.

"If this thing turns out to be serious," Damon said, stressing the *if*, "I'd be willing to lay out serious credit to pursue it."

"How serious?" Madoc asked, for form's sake.

"I've got some put away," Damon said, knowing that his friend would understand exactly what he meant. He fished a smartcard out of his pocket and held it out. "I'll call the bank in the morning and authorize it for cash withdrawals," he said. "Everything's aboveboard—there's no need to hide the transactions. I'll fix it so that you can draw ten thousand with no questions asked. If you need more, call me—but it had better be worth paying for."

"What am I looking for?" Madoc asked mildly. "Apart from Operator one-oh-one, that is."

"Silas was with a girl named Catherine Praill when he was

snatched. The police don't think she was involved, but you'd better check her out. Interpol also mentioned the name of another biotechnologist by the name of Surinder Nahal, recently resident in San Diego. That might also be irrelevant, but it has to be checked. If you can find Silas, or identify the people who took him, I'll pay a suitable finder's fee."

"I'll see what I can do," Madoc said equably. "Are you going to tell me what Operator one-oh-one has posted, or do I have to go trawling through the Eliminators' favorite netboards?"

"He posted a message saying that Conrad Helier is still alive and calling him an enemy of mankind. He also sent me a personal message, which Interpol might not know about."

Damon took the piece of paper from his suitskin's inner pocket and handed it to Madoc Tamlin. Madoc read it and gave it back. "Could be from anybody," he observed.

"Could be," admitted Damon, "but whoever carried it up to the thirteenth floor took the trouble to crash Building Security. A playful move—but sometimes playful is serious in disguise. Somebody's trying to jerk my strings, and I'd like to know who—and why."

Madoc nodded, carefully furrowing his remarkable eyebrows. "Hywood's another of your foster parents, right?"

"Right. Eveline Hywood. Currently resident in Lagrange-Five, allegedly very busy with important experiments of an unspecified nature. I doubt that she'll return my call."

"It won't be easy to check her out. The Lagrangists don't play by our rules, and they have their own playspace way out on the lunatic fringe of the Web."

"Don't worry too much about that. I can't imagine that Eveline's involved in the kidnapping or the Eliminator messages, even if she does have some relevant information. What do you know about Ahasuerus?"

"The original guy or the foundation?"

"I presume that the reference is to the foundation, rather than the legend," Damon said, refusing to treat the issue as a joke.

"Not much," Madoc admitted. "Been around for the best part

of two hundred years. Major players in the longevity game, funding research here, there, and probably everywhere. Reputation ever-so-slightly shady because of a certain bad odor attached to their start-up capital, although it beats me why anybody should care after all this time. Every fortune in the world can be traced back to some initial act of piracy, isn't that what they say? What was it they used to call the Ahasuerus guy, way back when?"

"The Man Who Stole the World," Damon said.

"Yeah—that's right. Zimmer, was it? Or Zimmerman?"

"Zimmerman."

"Right." Madoc nodded, as if he were the one answering instead of the one who'd asked. "Well, if he *did* steal the world, we seem to have got it back again, don't we?"

Damon didn't want to get sidetracked. "I'll dig up what I can about connections between Ahasuerus and my father," he said, "although it'd be no surprise at all to find that they'd had extensive dealings. Ahasuerus must have had dealings with every biotech team in the world if they've been handing out cash to longevity researchers since the days before the Crash.

Madoc stroked his chin pensively. It seemed that his green eyes now glowed a little more powerfully than they had before. "What that note implies," he said, "is that Arnett was taken because he knows something about Conrad Helier—something dirty. I don't suppose you have any idea what that is, do you?"

"If I did," Damon told him, "I'd probably want to sit on it awhile longer, just in case this business can be wrapped up quickly and quietly—but as it happens, I don't. I was only ever told about Saint Conrad the Savior, in whose holy footsteps I was supposed to follow."

"Were you ever given any cause to think that he might not be dead?"

"Quite the reverse," Damon said. "According to his disciples, it was a major point of principle with Saint Conrad that an overcrowded world of long-lived individuals had to develop an etiquette, if not an actual legal requirement, whereby a dutiful citizen of the New Utopia would postpone the exercise of his—

or her—right of reproduction until after death. If my foster parents are to be believed, my very existence is proof of Conrad Helier's demise; if he were still alive, he'd be guilty of an awkward hypocrisy."

"It's Conrad Helier you're really interested in, isn't it?" Madoc suggested, running his neatly manicured fingernails speculatively back and forth along the edge of the smartcard that Damon had given him. "This Arnett guy is a side issue. You want to know if your natural father really is alive, and if the Eliminators really have grounds for resenting his continued presence in the world."

"Concentrate on finding Silas Arnett, for the time being," Damon said flatly.

Madoc nodded meekly. "I'll put the Old Lady herself onto it," he said. "She doesn't take this kind of work normally, but she likes me. I can talk her into it."

"I don't want you hiring someone just because she's a living legend," Damon told him sharply. "I want someone who can get the job done."

"Trust me," Madoc advised him, with the casual air of a man who was as trustworthy as his own artificial graffiti. "Harriet's the best. I *know* these things. Have I ever let you down?"

"Once or twice."

Madoc only grinned at that, refusing to take the complaint seriously. "How are things otherwise?" he asked as he put the smartcard away. "Honest toil living up to your expectations?" Damon knew that what Madoc really wanted to know was whether he and Diana were washed up for good and all—but it wasn't a topic he wanted to discuss.

"I'm thinking of taking a little break," Damon told him. "I have some digging of my own to do tonight, but if I don't get answers to a couple of calls I might have to take a brief excursion to Hawaii tomorrow."

"What for?"

"Karol Kachellek is there, working out of Molokai. Like Eveline, he's pointedly refusing to get back to me. He won't want to tell me anything, even if he knows what all this is about, but if I go in person I might get *something* out of him. At the very least, I might unsettle him a bit."

Madoc grinned. "You always were good at unsettling people. Is that it?" When Damon nodded, he let himself out of the car.

"Give my regards to Diana," Damon said as Madoc began to walk away. "Tell her I'm sorry, but that it'll all work out for the best."

Madoc nearly turned back in order to follow that up, but he must have judged Damon's mood more accurately than he'd let on. After a moment's hesitation he kept going, answering the instruction with a calculatedly negligent wave.

As soon as the other car had pulled away Damon began to ask himself whether he'd done the right thing. Taking money from the legacy to bankroll Madoc's investigations wasn't really a betrayal of his determination to make his own way in the world—it was surely wholly appropriate that Conrad Helier's money should be used in an attempt to find out what had happened to Silas, especially if it was Silas's association with Conrad Helier that had given his kidnappers their motive. The real problem was whether Madoc's involvement would actually help to solve the mystery, or merely add a further layer of complication. If he found anything damning, he would certainly offer it to Damon first . . . but what might he do with it thereafter? Even if Operator 101 could be thwarted, he might only be the first of many—and if Conrad Helier really had been an enemy of mankind, why should the secret be kept, even if it could be?

Damon checked the alarms on the car's console, just to make sure that their inactivity really was testimony to the fact that neither Karol nor Eveline had replied to his calls.

They were in perfect working order; the silence was real. In fact, now that he was alone at the end of the alley the silence was positively oppressive. The night was clear and the stars were out, but they seemed few and very faint by comparison with the starscape he'd glimpsed in Eveline's phone VE. Each one seemed set in splendid isolation against the cloth of black oblivion—

and he had never felt as keenly as he did now that he was alone himself, a mere atom of soul stuff lost in a desert void.

"You're going soft," he told himself, unashamed of speaking the words aloud. "It was what you wanted, after all. No parents, no girlfriend, no opponents wielding knives. Just you, magnificently alone in the infinite wilderness of virtual space."

It was true. The sense of relief he felt as he raced away from the gloomy badlands toward the welcoming city lights seemed far less ambiguous than what he'd felt when Diana had driven off and left him to his own devices.

irst thing next morning, Damon obtained a reservation on the two o'clock flight to Honolulu. There was no point in taking the earlier flight because he'd only have had to spend an extra two hours in Honolulu waiting for the shuttle to take him on to Molokai.

He called Karol again, to warn him of his imminent arrival; the sim accepted the news impassively, as any AI would have done, but Damon took some small comfort from the fact that Karol would now have cause to regret not having taken the trouble to return his earlier call. Damon reset his own answerphone to make sure that if Karol chose to call back *now* he'd be conclusively stalled. He also put in a second call to Eveline Hywood, but he got the same response as before. In Lagrange-5 no one had to worry about frustrated callers deciding to put in a personal appearance.

It only took his search engine forty seconds to sort through the news tapes and Eliminator netboards for any mention of Silas Arnett, Conrad Helier, Surinder Nahal, or Operator 101, but it took Damon a further hour and a half to check through its findings, making absolutely sure that there was no authentic news. No one of any importance was issuing serious speculations about a possible connection between the Operator 101 posting and

Arnett's kidnapping, although a couple of newswriters had been alerted to Surinder Nahal's unavailability by their search-engine synthesizers. So far, everyone in the public arena was whistling in the dark—just like Interpol.

Damon knew that he ought to do some work, but he hadn't the heart to start the tawdry business of recovering Diana's vital stats for the pornypop tape and the only other worthwhile commission he had on hand was an action/adventure game scenario which required him to develop an entire alien ecosphere. It wasn't the sort of job he wanted to start when he knew he'd have to break off in three hours to go to the airport—especially when he had another option. He knew that it was just as likely to turn into a blind alley as trying to place a call to Eveline Hywood, but he figured that it had to be explored, just in case.

He packed his overnight bag and deposited it in the trunk of his car. Then he instructed the automatic pilot to find out where the nearest offices of the Ahasuerus Foundation were located and offer him an ETA. Given the size of the world—or even the USNA—he could easily have got an ETA that was the day after tomorrow, but the display assured him that he could be there long before noon.

The offices in question were close enough, and in territory familiar enough, for him to take the controls himself, but driving in downtown traffic was bad for his stress level at the best of times, and these were definitely not the best of times. He told the machine to set a course, but he didn't retreat into the safe haven of the VE hood the way most nondrivers did. He just sat back with eyes front, rehearsing the questions he intended to ask, if it turned out that there was anyone prepared to give him some answers. He tilted his seat back slightly so that the traffic wouldn't be too distracting.

The effect of the slight tilt was to fix his eyes on the shifting skyline way ahead of the traffic stream. At first, while the car seemed to be turning at every second intersection, the skyline kept changing, but once the pilot had found a reasonably straight route by which to follow its heading the Two Towers stuck out like a pair of sore thumbs—or a gateway to which the vehicle was being inexorably drawn.

The symbolism of the illusory gateway was not lost on Damon. The whole world was steering a course into the future with OmicronA on the left and PicoCon on the right. Ostensibly archrivals, the two megacorps and their various satellites were an effective cartel controlling at least 70 percent of the domestic nanotech business and 65 percent of the world's. Now that PicoCon had the Gantz patents stitched up, its masters probably had 70 percent of the domestic biotech business too, insofar as it made any sense to separate biotech from nanotech when the distinction between organic and inorganic molecular machines was becoming more and more blurred with every year that went by.

Possession of the Gantz patents entitled PicoCon to the slightly higher tower, so the edifice that reared up on the right was just a little more massive than the one to the left, but both had been forged out of ocean-refined sand and both architects had done their utmost to take advantage of sparkling salt in catching and reflecting the sun's bright light. Although PicoCon was the larger, it wasn't necessarily the brighter. There was a curious defiance about the glow of OmicronA which refused to accept the metaphorical shade—but Damon knew that it was only an optical illusion. As a beacon signaling the advent of tomorrow the two corps were flames of the same furious fire.

Needless to say, the offices of the Ahasuerus Foundation weren't in the same league. Ahasuerus didn't even have its own building—just a couple of floors in one of the humbler structures right across the road from the PicoCon tower. By comparison with its taller neighbor the building looked as if it had been gantzed out of an unusually objectionable mudslide; there was not a glimmer of sea salt about its stern exterior and its windows were tinted brown. Most of its neighbors were equipped for a measure of continuing accretion, so that salt from windblown spray *had* accumulated on their slightly blurred surfaces, giving each of them a curious glittering sheen, but the building housing Ahasuerus had been comprehensively *finished*, and it seemed utterly self-satisfied in its relative dullness—although some observers might have reckoned it sinister as well as stern. Its car park was certainly dimmer and dingier than fashion prescribed.

Damon had already decided that the best course of action was to throw the burden of secrecy onto the foundation's own security, so he simply marched up to the reception desk and summoned a human contact. When a smartly dressed young man eventually emerged from the inner offices Damon gave him the folded note.

"My name's Damon Hart," he said. "I'm the biological son of Conrad Helier and the foster son of Silas Arnett and Eveline Hywood. It might be to the advantage of the foundation if someone in authority were to read this document. It might also be to the advantage of the foundation if lesser mortals—including yourself—refrained from reading it. Personally, I don't care at all; if you or anyone else wants to take the risk of looking at it, you're welcome."

That, he figured, should get the item as far up the chain of command as was feasible without the contents of the enigmatic message becoming common knowledge.

The fetcher-and-carrier disappeared into the inner offices again, leaving Damon to his own devices for a further ten minutes.

Eventually, a woman came to collect him. She had silky red hair and bright blue eyes. For a moment Damon thought that she was genuinely young, and his jaw tightened as he concluded that he was about to be fobbed off, but the hair and eye colors were a little too contrived and a slight constriction in her practiced smile reassured him that she had undergone recent somatic reconstruction of the kind that was misleadingly advertised as "rejuvenation." Her real age was likely to be at least seventy, if not in three figures.

"Mr. Hart," she said, offering him the piece of paper, still folded, in lieu of a handshake. "I'm Rachel Trehaine. Won't you come through."

The corridors behind the security wall were bare; the doors had no nameplates. The office into which Rachel Trehaine eventually led Damon was liberally equipped with flat screens and fitted with shelves full of discs and digitapes, but it had no VE hood. "Perhaps I'd better warn you that I'm only a senior reader," she said as she waved him to a chair. "I don't have any executive authority. I've had an encrypted version of your document relayed to New York, but it may take some time to get a response from them. In the meantime, I'd like to thank you for bringing the matter to our attention—we had not been independently informed."

"You're welcome," Damon assured her insincerely. "I hope you'll show me the same courtesy of bringing to my attention any pertinent matters of which I might not have been independently informed." He winced slightly as he heard the pomposity in his tone, realizing that he might have overrehearsed his opening speech.

"Of course," said Rachel Trehaine, with the charming ease of a practiced dissembler. "I don't suppose you have any idea—if only the merest suspicion—who this mysterious Operator might be, or why this attack on your family has been launched?"

"I thought you might know more about that than I do," Damon said. "You'll have complete records of any dealings between Ahasuerus and Conrad Helier's research team."

"When I say that I'm a senior reader," she told him mildly, "I don't mean that I have free access to the foundation's own records. My job is to keep watch on other data streams, selecting out data of interest, collating and reporting. I'm a scientific analyst, not a historian."

"I meant you plural, not you singular," Damon told her. "Someone in your organization must be able to figure out which particular closeted skeleton Operator one-oh-one intends to bring out into the open. Why else would he have sent me to you?"

"Why would he—or she—have sent you anywhere at all, Mr. Hart? Why send you a personal message? It seems very odd—not at all the way that Eliminators usually operate."

The delicate suggestion was, of course, that Damon was the source of the message—that he himself was Operator 101. As a scientific analyst Rachel Trehaine would naturally have considerable respect for Occam's razor.

"That's an interesting question," Damon said agreeably. "When Inspector Yamanaka referred to the situation as a puzzle he was speaking metaphorically, but that message implies that the instigator of this series of incidents really *is* creating a puzzle, dangling it before me as a kind of lure—just as I, in my turn, am dangling it before you. Operator one-oh-one wants me to go digging, and he's offering suggestions as to where I might profitably dig. Given that Conrad Helier is dead, he can't possibly be the Eliminators' real target—and if their promise that Silas Arnett will be released after he's given them what they want is honest, he isn't the real target either. If the note is to be taken at face value, Operator one-oh-one might be building a file on Eveline Hywood, with particular reference to her past dealings with your foundation."

Rachel Trehaine took a few moments to weigh that up, presumably employing all her skills as a senior reader. Anyone but a scientific analyst might have challenged his conclusions, or at least pointed out the tentative nature of his inferences, but she was content merely to observe and record.

"Have you spoken to Eveline Hywood?" she asked.

"I've tried," Damon told her. "She isn't accepting calls at the moment. There's nothing sinister in that—she tends to get engrossed in her work. She never liked being interrupted. I'll get through eventually, but she'll probably tell me that it isn't my business anymore—that I forfeited any right I might have had to be told what's going on when I walked out on the Great Crusade to run with the gangs."

The red-haired woman pondered that information too. Damon judged that she was under real pressure to make sense of this, or thought she was. However lowly her position within the organization might be she was obviously in charge of the Los Angeles office, at least for the moment. She knew that she might have decisions to make, as well as orders to follow from New York.

"The Ahasuerus Foundation's sole purpose is to conduct research into technologies of longevity," she said sententiously. "It's entirely probable that we provided funding to Conrad Helier's research team if they were involved in projects connected with longevity research. I can't imagine that there was anything in our dealings to attract the interest of the so-called Eliminators."

"That is strange, isn't it?" Damon said, trying to sound insouciant. "The usual Eliminator jargon charges people with being *unworthy of immortality*—a formula which takes it for granted that your researchers will eventually hit the jackpot. In a way, you and the Eliminators represent different sides of the same coin. If and when you come up with an authentic fountain of youth you'll be forced into the position of deciding who should drink from it."

"We're a nonprofit organization, Mr. Hart. Our constitution requires us to make the fruits of our labor available to everyone."

"I looked up your constitution last night," Damon admitted. "It's an interesting commitment. But I also glanced at the way in which you've operated in the past. It's true that Ahasuerus has always placed its research findings in the public domain, but that's not the same thing as ensuring equal access to the consequent technologies. Consider PicoCon's new rejuvenation procedures, for example: there's no secret about the manner in which the reconstructive transformations are done, but it's still an expensive process to carry out because it requires such a high level of technical expertise and so much hospital time. Effectively, it's available only to the rich. It seems highly likely to me that the next breakthrough in longevity research will be a more wide-ranging kind of somatic transformation which will achieve an *authentic* rejuvenation rather than a merely cosmetic one.

Assuming that it requires even more technical expertise and even more hospital time, it's likely to be available only to the *very rich,* at least in the first instance, even if all the research data is in the public domain. If so, the megacorps will still have effective control over its application. Isn't that so?"

"*In the first instance* is the vital phrase, Mr. Hart," she informed him, still carefully maintaining the stiffness of her manner. "The early recipients of such a treatment would be those who could most easily afford it, but it would eventually filter through the entire population. The rich are always first in every queue—but that only means that the poor have to be patient, and in the New Utopia even the poor have *time enough.* Provided that your hypothetical technology of *authentic rejuvenation* were to take the form of a treatment that a person need only undergo once—or even if it needed to be repeated at long intervals—there'd be plenty of time to work through the queue. No one has any interest in delaying our work, Mr. Hart—and that includes the lonely and resentful individuals who have nothing better to do with their time than denounce the follies and failures of their fellow men and urge maniacs to attempt murder."

"I couldn't agree more," Damon said, although he wasn't sure that the matter was as simple as she made it out to be. "As I said, I've read your constitution. It's a fine and noble commitment, even if it was written by a man who made his fortune by turning a minor storm in the troubled waters of the world's financial markets into a full-scale hurricane. But lonely and resentful individuals often nurse paranoid fantasies. Operator one-oh-one might have got it into his head that you've already developed a method of authentic rejuvenation, but that you're keeping it very quiet. Perhaps he thinks that *you're* the real Eliminators, standing by while the people *you* consider to be undesirables peacefully pass away, and saving your immortality serum for the deserving few."

"That's absolutely untrue," said Rachel Trehaine, her bright blue eyes as fathomless as the California sky.

"A paranoid fantasy," Damon agreed readily. "But I did happen to notice, while inwardly digesting your constitution, that although it commits you to releasing the results of the research you fund, it doesn't actually specify *when* you have to do it. You're not the only player in the field, of course—I dare say there's not a single megacorp which doesn't have a few fingers thrust deep into this particular pie—but you've been going for a long time and you have a good deal of expertise. If I were a bookmaker, I'd make you third favorite, after PicoCon and OmicronA, to come up with the next link in the chain that will eventually draw us into the wonderland of true emortality. Some day, someone like you is going to have to decide exactly how and when to let the good news out. Whoever makes that decision runs the risk of making enemies, don't you think?"

The remark about Ahasuerus being third favorite after the biggest players of all was pure flattery, but it didn't bring a smile to Rachel Trehaine's face. "I can assure you," the red-haired woman said, "that the Ahasuerus Foundation has no secrets of the kind you're suggesting. You've already admitted that this mysterious Operator is deliberately teasing you, trying to draw you into reckless action. If that's so, you ought to think very carefully about what you say, and to whom. If Operator one-oh-one has paranoid fantasies to indulge and lies to spread, it might be wise to let him be the one to do it."

Damon would have assured her that he agreed with her wholeheartedly, but before he could open his mouth her attention was distracted. One of her machines was beeping, presumably to inform her that urgent information was incoming. From where he was sitting Damon couldn't see the screen whose keyplate she was playing with, and he didn't try to sneak a peep.

"The Ahasuerus Foundation thanks you for bringing this matter to our attention," the red-haired woman said, reading from the screen. "The Ahasuerus Foundation intends to cooperate fully with Interpol and suggests that you do the same. If the Ahasuerus Foundation can help in any way to locate and liberate Silas Arnett it will certainly do so."

Damon knew that he was being slyly rebuked for not taking

the note straight to Hiru Yamanaka, but he couldn't guess whether the rebuke was sincere or not. He had no way of knowing whether coming here had made the general situation better or worse—or, for that matter, what might count as "better" or "worse." When he saw that she was finished, he rose to his feet.

"I'm afraid I have a plane to catch," he said. He knew perfectly well that he was about to be thrown out, but figured that he might as well seize whatever initiative remained to be seized. "If I hear any further mention of the foundation I'll be happy to pass the news on. I take it that my discretion wasn't necessary, and that you won't mind in the least if I simply use the phone in future?"

"We have nothing to hide," said Rachel Trehaine as she came to her feet, "but that doesn't mean that we don't appreciate your discretion, Mr. Hart. Privacy is a very precious commodity in today's world, and we value it as much as anyone."

Damon took that to mean that she would definitely prefer it if he exercised the utmost discretion in passing on any further information, but that she wasn't about to feed anyone's paranoid suspicions by saying so explicitly.

As soon as he got back to his car Damon checked into the netboard where Operator 101 had posted the notice Yamanaka had showed him, but there was nothing new. There were no messages from Madoc Tamlin or Eveline Hywood awaiting his attention. Having decided that everything else could wait, Damon sent the car forth into the traffic.

He had no doubt that his movements were being monitored by Interpol, and that the fact of his visit to Ahasuerus, if not its content, would be known to Yamanaka. His eastward expedition would also have been observed and noted, but Tamlin could be trusted to evade any surveillance to which he was subject as and when he wished.

While the car made its silent way along the city streets, observing the speed limit with mechanical precision, Damon took out the folded note yet again and scanned the tantalizing lines for the hundredth time. He had expected no more from Ahasuerus than he had got and he had no doubt that he would have got no more from Rachel Trehaine no matter what tack he had adopted in making conversation, but he couldn't help wondering whether he had concentrated on the wrong part of the puzzle. The most remarkable allegation it made was not that Eveline Hywood and the Ahasuerus Foundation knew something significantly shady about Conrad Helier's past but that Conrad Helier was still alive. How could that be, when so much solid evidence remained of his death?

Damon wondered whether the kind of reconstructive somatic engineering that had been used to make Rachel Trehaine look younger than she was could be used to alter a man's appearance out of all recognition. And if some more extravagant version of it *did* exist, if only as an experimental prototype, might it be applied to other applications? Specifically, might it transform the cells of one body in such a way that genetic analysis would conclude that they belonged to an entirely different person? In sum, how easy was it, in this day and age, for a man to fake his own death, even to the extent of providing a misidentifiable corpse? And if it were possible today, what was the likelihood that it had been equally possible fifty years ago?

"Paranoid fantasies," Damon muttered as the stream of unanswerable questions dwindled away. He knew well enough that even if the matters of practicality were not insuperable the question of motive still remained—not to mention the matter of *principle* that he had quoted to Madoc Tamlin.

The car came gently to a standstill and Damon realized that the traffic stream in both directions had ground to a halt. A quick look around told him that every emergency light in sight was on red and he groaned. Some idiot saboteur had hacked into the control system and thrown a software spanner into the works. He sighed and tried hard to relax. Usually, such glitches only took a few minutes to clear—but one of the reasons they had become so common of late was that rival parties of smart and prideful kids were trying just as hard to set new records as the city was.

By the time the car got moving again, Damon was not finding it at all difficult—in spite of his own checkered history—to sympathize with the hypothetical proposition he had put to Rachel Trehaine. Anyone who did come up with an authentic emortality serum might well be tempted to reserve it for the socially conscientious, while allowing all the lonely and resentful individuals who had nothing better to do with their time than fuck things up to fade into oblivion.

'm sorry we couldn't bring flowers," Madoc Tamlin said to Lenny Garon, "but they reckon flowers compromise the sterile regime and promote nosocomial infections. It's bullshit, but what can you do?"

Lenny Garon made the effort to produce a polite smile. Madoc couldn't help contrasting the boy's stubbornly heroic attitude with that of Diana Caisson, who hadn't smiled all day and didn't seem likely to start now. He wouldn't have brought her along if he'd had any choice, but even though the hospital was nearly the last place in the world she wanted to be she'd insisted on tagging along. It seemed that what proverbial wisdom said about misery loving company was true—and when Diana was miserable, she certainly had enough to go around.

"I shouldn't be here," the novice streetfighter said, as if the hospital's insistence on keeping him in were a slur on his manhood. "The intestine's not leaking anymore and the nanotech's taking care of the peritonitis. I was just unlucky that the cut reached my spleen—it was nothing, really. They'll probably let me out in a couple of hours if I kick up a fuss."

"It *would* have been nothing if you'd had IT as good as Brady's," Madoc told him cynically. "Pretty soon, you will. You have talent. It's raw, but it's real. Just a couple more fights and you'll be ready to turn the tables. You hurt Brady too, you know—he might not be in the next bed, but he knows he was in a fight. One day, you'll go even further than he has—if you stick at it."

"Did you give the tapes to Damon Hart?"

Madoc couldn't help glancing at Diana to see what effect the mention of Damon's name had, and was unfortunate enough to catch her eye.

"Why should he give the tapes to Damon Hart?" she snapped at the boy, without taking her accusative eyes off Madoc.

"I thought that's why he came to the fight," Garon retorted innocently.

Madoc had a stoical expression all ready for display. He hadn't had a chance to warn the boy to be discreet, and it was inevitable that the cat would be let out of the bag. Now it was his turn to be stubbornly heroic in the face of adversity. He waited for the storm to break.

"You didn't tell me Damon was there," Diana said, far less frostily than Madoc had anticipated. "What did he want?"

Madoc realized that her anger had been deflected by a false assumption. She assumed that Damon had sought out Madoc in order to talk about *her*. She must be hopeful that he had been consumed by regret and wanted Madoc to act as an intermediary in arranging a reconciliation. Madoc had already divined from the rambling odysseys of complaint he'd been forced to endure that what she wanted above all else was for Damon to "see sense" and realize that life without her was hardly worth living. Unfortunately, Madoc's opinion was that Damon had been perfectly sensible in realizing that life without her *was* worth living. He considered lying about Damon's real purpose in visiting the fight scene, but figured that the web of deceit would probably grow so fast that it would end up strangling him. "He didn't actually come over to watch the fight, Lenny," he said, judiciously addressing the boy rather than Diana. "He doesn't do a lot of that kind of work anymore. He's busy with other things—customized VEs, mostly. You know the kind of thing— for phones, games, cable shows. . . ."

"Pornotapes," Diana cut in acidly.

"Yeah . . . well, it was just business."

"What kind of business?" Diana wanted to know. Now her resentment was building, as much because Madoc was avoiding her eye as because the news wasn't what she wanted to hear. Madoc could see that the boy was curious too, but Diana's curiosity was much sharper and it wasn't going to be easy to fob her off. He felt obliged to try, though, if only for form's sake.

He turned back to the boy and said: "How d'you feel now? The pain control working all right?"

"Oh sure," Lenny assured him. "It was never bad. I felt a little spaced out after the fight—floating, you know. Soon as I got here they shot me up with something real good. Don't even feel dreamy now. Sharp as a tack."

"What kind of business?" Diana repeated frostily.

"Come on, Di," Madoc said. "We're here to see Lenny. The boy took an awkward cut. We can talk about our own things later."

"No," said Lenny helpfully. "You go ahead. You can talk about Damon all you want—I got all his tapes, you know."

Of course I know, you stupid little shit, Madoc thought. Aloud, he said: "He just wanted me to ask around about some things. We're still friends—we do little favors for one another occasionally. It's . . ." He stopped himself saying *a personal thing*, because he knew that Diana would misinterpret it. She misinterpreted it anyhow.

"*Little favors*," she repeated. "Little favors of the kind that you weren't supposed to mention to me."

"No, Di," Madoc said with a contrived sigh. "Actually, it's not to do with you. Something's happened to one of his foster fathers, that's all. The Eliminators may be involved, although it seems to be a kidnap rather than a murder. He just asked me to ask around, see if anyone knew who might have made the snatch or why."

Madoc could see that Diana was having trouble remembering whether she'd ever been told who Damon's foster parents were, but Lenny Garon had no such difficulty. Lenny was a fan, and fans liked to know everything that could be known about their heroes.

"There's no public record of Damon's foster parents," the boy piped up. "I checked . . . a while ago."

"That's because he didn't like to talk about them," Diana said, her wrath dying back into icy frustration. "Madoc is his *friend*, though. It's only natural that *Madoc* knows who they were."

"Can we talk about something else?" Madoc said, because he felt obliged to try. "This stuff is confidential, okay?"

"It's *not* okay," Diana said. "You're supposed to be *my* friend right now, and I don't like the idea of your going behind my back like this—seeing Damon and not even telling me. They were biotech people, weren't they? Damon's foster parents, that is. He fell out with them because they wanted him to go into the same line of work."

"That's right," Madoc said. "But it doesn't mean that he doesn't care what happens to them. I just have to make some inquiries, see what I can find out."

"Can I help?" Lenny wanted to know.

"No," said Madoc. "Nor can you, Diana. It's best if I handle it myself."

"Just because I fell out with him," Diana was quick to retort, with manifest sarcasm, "it doesn't mean that I don't care what happens to him. He's in some kind of trouble, isn't he?"

"No," Madoc said automatically.

"Is he?" Lenny asked curiously. It was obvious to Madoc that his blunt denial had been read as a tacit admission, even by the boy.

"Not *exactly*," Madoc said, immediately retreating to what he hoped was a tenable position. "It's just Eliminator shit. It means nothing. It's not even Damon they're after. Look, can we just let it drop, for now? Damon wouldn't want me to talk about it *here*. Hospital walls have more eyes and ears than most."

That argument was sufficient to make Lenny Garon back off, but it had the opposite effect on Diana.

"I want to know what's going on," she said ominously. "I have a *right* to know. You were the one who saved the news until we were here."

"If you hadn't walked out when you did," Madoc told her waspishly, "you *would* know what's going on. You'd still have been there when the cops came to call."

"All the more reason why you should have told me," she said. "All the more reason why you should tell me now."

Madoc raised his eyes to heaven. "Not *here,*" he said. "Lenny, I'm really sorry about all this. I just wanted to make sure that you were okay."

"You just wanted to make sure that he wasn't about to quit on you when he realized how dangerous your little games can be," Diana came back maliciously. "You have to be careful choosing your so-called *friends,* Lenny. Some of them only want to jerk your strings. People die in those backstreets, you know—far more than Eliminators ever kill. Whatever kind of trouble Damon thinks he's in is nothing compared to the trouble *you're* in. Always remember—Damon *got out* of your line of work and took up making pornypops and phone link frippery. That's the example to bear in mind."

"She's right, Lenny," Madoc said, having been given ample time to replan his strategy while the vitriol was pouring out. "Damon got out, and you should aim to get out too—but Damon didn't get out until he'd *made his mark.* He went out a winner, not a quitter. You can be a winner too, Lenny, if you stick at it."

"I know that," the boy in the bed assured him. "I know I can."

"Let's get out of here," said Diana disgustedly. "You've checked your investment, and it seems to be in working order. They'll let him go home tonight, if he insists."

"I'm sorry, Lenny," Madoc said. "Diana's under a lot of strain just now. I shouldn't have brought her with me." Maybe I shouldn't have let her through the door, he added beneath his breath, and maybe I shouldn't let her in again—except that she might be more of a nuisance out of my sight than she will be where I can keep an eye on her. He followed her out of the room and along the corridor to the elevator.

Diana didn't say a word until they were back in the car, but she didn't waste any time thereafter. When he took the controls himself she actually lifted his hands from the keypad and switched on the AP, instructing it to take them home.

"What's going on?" she wanted to know.

"Damon got a visit from the cops after you left," he said. "Interpol, not his old friends from the LAPD. They wanted to know if he knew anything that could help them find his foster father. He didn't so he asked me if I could use my contacts to find out anything. I'm trying to do that. That's all."

"Where do the Eliminators come in? They don't *do* kidnappings."

"They may have done this one. About the time the foster father went missing some crazy posted a notice about Damon's biological father."

"I didn't know that Damon knew who his biological father was, or that he cared. I don't even know the name of mine—do you?"

"As a matter of fact, I do know my biological father's name, although it was never a matter of great interest to me. Damon's case is different—but he didn't like to talk about it. I guess he wanted to keep all that stuff from cluttering up his relationship with you."

"I guess he did," she said bitterly. "If he hadn't been so determined to keep his stupid secrets, maybe. . . ."

"Maybe nothing," Madoc said wearily. "It's over—let it go."

"It's over when it's over," she told him, trading cliché for cliché. "So tell me—who *was* Damon's biological father? I can find out on my own, you know—I'm no Webwalker, but it has to be a matter of record, if only someone can be bothered to look hard enough. Interpol must have made the connection."

"It's not exactly a matter of *public* record," said Madoc unhappily. He knew, though, that even a rank amateur like Diana could probably turn up the information eventually, if she had motive enough to try. Damon's change of name wasn't likely to confuse her for long. Anything Interpol could find out, anyone could find out—given a reason to make the effort.

"I have friends too," she said firmly. "You know Webwalkers, I know Webwalkers. I bet you've asked that mad cow Tithonia to help out—but who needs *her*? Suppose Damon's *fans* were to find out that there's a mystery which needs solving?"

"One of them already did, thanks to you," Madoc pointed out.

"So tell me what's going on. Maybe I can help you—but I can only do that if you let me in."

"I already let you in," Madoc muttered. "When I opened the door, I didn't know all this was going to blow up, or . . . well, given that it *has* blown up and that I *did* let you in . . . Damon's original name was Helier. His father was Conrad Helier."

Diana thought about that for a full minute. "The Conrad Helier who invented the artificial womb?" she said eventually. "The one who made it possible for us all to be born? The man who saved the human race from extinction?"

"The very same. Except that he didn't exactly *invent* the artificial womb—he just perfected it. It isn't as if the sterility transformers would have put an end to the human race if Helier hadn't been around. One way or another, we'd all have been born. Given the urgency of the demand, someone else was bound to have come up with the answer within a matter of months. Some say that Helier was just the guy who beat the others in the race to the patent office, like Bell with the telephone. A guy named Surinder Nahal reckoned that he should have been there first, and I dare say he wasn't the only one."

"But Conrad Helier *did* get there first," said Diana, who was far from slow when it came to certain kinds of calculation. "Which means that he must have got rich as well as famous. Damon is his biological son—and *knows* that he's his biological son."

"That's right," said Madoc shortly—although he knew that it was useless to try to stop now.

"And he's *your* friend," Diana went on inexorably. "Just like that poor kid lying in the hospital. And he's *still* your friend, even though he doesn't even doctor tapes for you anymore."

"I *do* have friends!" Madoc protested. "*Real* friends. People who know they'll always be let in if they come knocking on my door."

The barbed comment didn't bother her at all. "You've already started digging, haven't you?" she said. "You must have been high as a kite when he *asked* you to do it. You think there's a game to be won here—a *rich* game."

"You don't know me at all, do you?" Madoc retorted bitterly. "You think I'm just a hustler, incapable of genuine loyalty—but you're wrong. Damon knows me better than that."

"Damon doesn't even know what day it is if there isn't someone there to remind him," she sneered. "Without me, he's just an innocent abroad. If I'd only known that he was about to get into trouble. . . ."

If you'd only known that he had millions stashed away, Madoc thought—but he didn't dare say it aloud, and he knew that it would have been unfair. The fact that Diana *hadn't* known, and still felt bad about the split, proved that she loved him for himself, not his fortune. The fortune just added insult to injury.

"Damon knows I can be trusted," Madoc said. "He's known me a long time. He told me who he really was way back at the beginning. It never affected our friendship. I've always respected his privacy and his wishes. I never expected anything like this to come up, but now that it has I intend to play it straight. I'll do everything I can to find out what Damon wants to know, and I would have done the best I could even if he hadn't put up the money. So would the Old Lady, who isn't mad and isn't a cow. You don't understand this, Di. Just let me get on with it in my own way, will you?"

"I've known you longer than Damon has," she pointed out. "I

probably know you better than you know yourself. I want to help. I'm entitled to help. I still have Damon's best interests at heart, you know. Just because he's a pigheaded fool who's impossible to live with, it doesn't mean I don't care."

Before Madoc had a chance to respond to this catalogue of half-truths the car came to an abrupt stop. When he looked around he saw that all the emergency lights in the street had come on, and that they were all blazing red. They were only a couple of hundred meters from home, and the foul-up wouldn't take more than ten minutes to sort out—a quarter of an hour if the crash was a *really* big one—but it somehow seemed like the very last straw.

"Oh *shit*," Madoc groaned, with feeling, "not *again.*"

"It's probably friends of *yours*," Diana opined, not needing sarcasm to ram home the irony of it. "Maybe even fans."

PART TWO

Trials and Tribulations

Eight

Silas Arnett dreamed that he was in a lab somewhere: a strange, dilapidated place full of obsolete equipment. He was hunched over a screen, squinting at meaningless data which scrolled by too fast to allow his eyes to keep up. He was working under pressure, desperately thirsty, with a head full of cotton wool, wishing that he were able to concentrate, and wishing also that he could remember what problem he had been put here to solve and why it was so urgent. . . .

At first, when he realized that he was dreaming, he was relieved.

He was relieved because he felt that he could relax, because the problem—whatever it was—was unreal.

Unfortunately, he was wrong. The consciousness into which he descended by slow degrees was a more complex web of discomforts and restraints than the dream he had fled.

His internal technology was dulling all the nastiest sensations, but there was an awkward tangibility about its anesthetic efforts, as if the nanomachines were working under undue pressure with inadequate reserves of strength and ingenuity. He wondered whether it might be his IT that had been keeping him unconscious—there was only so much the most benevolent nanotech could do without suppressing awareness itself—and why, if so, it had released him to wakefulness now. If the nanomachines had done their work properly, he ought to have been feeling far better than he was and he ought to have been lying down in a comfortable bed.

Without opening his eyes he attempted to take census of the bad news.

His wrists and ankles were pinned by two pairs of plastic sheaths, each at least three centimeters broad, which clasped him more tightly when he struggled against them. There was another sheath lightly gripping the head of his prick and some kind of catheter stuck up his backside. He was in a sitting position but his head wasn't lolling to one side: it was held upright by some device which gently but firmly enfolded his entire skull.

There was light beyond his closed eyelids, but he knew that the device clasping his head had to be a VE hood. When he opened his eyes he would not be looking out upon the world, but into a counterfeit space synthesized from bits of digitized film and computer-generated images.

He supposed that he ought to be grateful that he wasn't dead, but no such gratitude could extricate itself as yet from the morass of his unease and anxiety.

He put out his tongue to test the limits of the thing enclosing his head, and found—as he had half expected—a pair of teats. He tested the left-hand one with his lips, then seized it in his teeth and teased cold liquid out of it. The thirst afflicting him in his dream had been real, and the orange-flavored juice, slightly syrupy with dissolved glucose, was very welcome.

When he finally consented to open his eyes Silas found himself looking out upon a courtroom. It was an impressionistic image, a mere cartoon rather than a sophisticated product of mimetic videosynthesis. The twelve jurors who were positioned to his left were barely sketched in, and the prosecuting attorney whose position was to the right had little more in the way of features than they did. Directly in front of him was a black-robed judge whose image was more detailed, although he didn't look any more *real.* The judge's face had simply been more carefully drawn, presumably in order to allow for more effective animation.

The judge's platform was about a meter above the level of the dock whose caricaturish steel spikes rose in front of Arnett's viewpoint. This allowed its occupant to look down at the prisoner, mingling contempt with hostility.

Silas guessed that he and the "judge" were quite alone within the hypothetical space of the virtual environment. He could not believe that an actual prosecutor and a human jury were going to hook into the shared illusion at some later time. He knew that it must have required a conspiracy of at least four persons—perhaps including sweet, seemingly innocent Catherine—to arrange his abduction, but a real mock trial would require four times as many. There was no shortage of crazy people to be found in the meshes of the Web, but wherever a dozen forgathered in innerspace you could bet your last dose that two would be corpsies and three others potential beanspillers.

For the time being, the counterfeit courtroom wasn't even under the aegis of an active program. Nothing moved except the judge, and that particular icon was almost certainly a mask, reproducing the facial expressions of a real person. Silas tried to take heart from that. Masks need not bear the slightest resemblance to the actual features of the people using them, but their echoes of tics and mannerisms could offer valuable clues to the identity of their users. If the slightly narrowed expression in those coal black eyes and the tension lines etched upon the raptorial face *were* the property of the user rather than the image, he might eventually be able to conjure up an image of the actual eyes and the actual mouth.

"Please state your name for the record," said the judge. His baritone voice wasn't obviously distorted but it was too stagey by half.

"Joan of Arc," said Silas weakly.

"Let the name Silas Arnett be entered in the record," said the sonorous voice. "I feel obliged to point out, Dr. Arnett, that there really *is* a record. Every moment of your trial will be preserved for posterity, and any parts of your testimony may be broadcast as we see fit. My advice is that you should conduct yourself as though the whole world were watching. Given the nature of the charges which will be brought against you, that may well be the case."

"That's Arc with a *c,*" Silas said, trying to sound laconic, "not a *k.*" He wondered whether he ought to be speaking at all. No matter how mad this setup was, there had to be method in it. If he said too much, his words might be edited and recombined into any kind of statement at all. On the other hand, his voice was no secret; if these people could screw up his security systems efficiently enough to remove him from his own home they could certainly plunder the records in his phone hood. He was, in any case, an old man—there must be tens of thousands of recordings of his voice in existence, easily amassable into a database from which clever software could synthesize anything from the Gettysburg Address to a falsetto rendition of "To Be a Pilgrim."

"Perhaps I should begin by summarizing the procedure," said the judge calmly. "This is, of course, merely a preliminary hearing. Your trial will not begin until tomorrow, at which time you will be called upon to give evidence under oath. At that time, no refusal to answer the charges brought against you will be tolerated, nor will any dissimulation. The purpose of the present session is to offer you the opportunity to make an opening statement, free of any pressure or duress. Should you wish to make a full confession now, that would, of course, be taken into consideration when your sentence is determined."

Perhaps I should begin by summarizing the possibilities, Silas thought. The rhetoric suggests Eliminators, but the only reason the Eliminators have remained a thorn in society's side for so long is that they have no organization. The sophistication of the operation suggests that it's a corp with real resources—but what kind of corp would snatch a retired playboy like me, and why?

It was not until he reached this impasse that the implications of what the voice had said sunk in. Tomorrow they would begin in earnest, at which time *no refusal to answer would be tolerated*. That formulation suggested that they could and would employ torture, if necessary. Three days would be the minimum interval required to flush out his internal technology and disable his nanotech defenses against pain, injury, and aging—which implied that he had already been unconscious for at least forty-eight hours.

"Why all the ceremony?" he asked, his voice hardly above a whisper.

"Silas Arnett," the voice intoned with a solemnity that had to be satirical, "the principal charge laid against you is that you were an accessory to the crimes of Conrad Helier, enemy of mankind. There is no need for you to plead, as your guilt has already been determined. The purpose of this trial is to determine the extent of that guilt, and to establish an appropriate means of expiation."

"An *appropriate means of expiation?*" Silas repeated wonderingly. "I thought you people only had one sentence to hand down to those deemed unworthy of immortality: death by any convenient means."

"Death is not the only means of Elimination," said the voice, with a sudden injection of apparent sincerity, "as you, Dr. Arnett, know very well." As the last phrase was intoned, the cartoonish face of the judge hardened considerably—presumably in response to a sudden tension in the features of the man or woman behind it.

Well, at least that tells me what it is they want me to confess, Silas thought, even if it doesn't tell me why. After all these years, he had actually thought that the matter was dead and buried, but in a world of long-lived people—no matter how expert they might become in the artistry of forgetfulness—nothing was ever comprehensively dead and buried. Expertise in forgetfulness, alas, was not the same as generosity in forgiveness.

There was, Silas supposed, a revealing dishonesty in the fact that the Eliminators were almost the only people who talked freely and openly about the expectation of immortality in a world in which everyone hoped—and almost everyone *believed*—that the breakthrough to *real* immortality would happen within his own lifetime. Serious people were required by reason to hedge the issue around in all sorts of ways, always speaking of *e*mortality rather than *im*mortality, always stressing that nobody could live forever even in a world without aging, always reminding their listeners that disease had not yet been *entirely* banished from human affairs and probably never could be, always restating that some injuries were simply too extreme to be repaired even by the cleverest imaginable internal technology, and always remembering—perhaps above all else—that the life of the body and the life of the person were not the same thing . . . but all of that was just pedantry, bluff and bluster to cover up the raw force of underlying conviction that eternal life was truly within reach.

Silas realized that he was struggling reflexively against the straps that bound his wrists and ankles, even though the only effect his struggles had was to make his confinement even closer. Eternal life, it seemed, was no longer within *his* reach, and he was in the process of being cast out of the pain-free paradise of the New Utopia. He was not only mortal but punishable, and his guilt had already been determined.

He was tempted to declare that Conrad Helier had not been an enemy of humankind at all—that he had, in fact, been the savior of humankind—but he had a shrewd suspicion that that kind of defense would be seen by his captor, and perhaps by the larger audience to whom his captor intended eventually to speak, as proof of his guilt.

"You have the right to remain silent, of course," the voice remarked, recovering all of its mocking pomposity. "It would, however, be far wiser to make a free and full confession of your involvement with Conrad Helier's conspiracy." The mask had relaxed again, but it was not unexpressive. Silas tried to concentrate his mind upon its subtle shifts in the faint hope that he might be able to penetrate the illusion.

"I've got twenty-four hours before the last of my protective nanotech is flushed away," Silas said, trying his utmost to keep his voice level. "A lot can happen in twenty-four hours. People must be searching for me. Even if Catherine was working for you the alarm will have been raised soon enough."

"You're right, of course," the judge informed him. "The police are searching for you with more than their usual diligence—Interpol has taken charge of the investigation, on the grounds that the Eliminators are a worldwide problem. Damon Hart's unsavory acquaintances are using their less orthodox methods to search for information as to your whereabouts. The Ahasuerus Foundation is also diverting considerable effort to their own investigation. Were all three to pool their resources they might actually stand a chance of finding you before the trial gets under way—but in a world where privacy is fatally compromised by technology, discretion becomes an instinct and secrecy a passion."

Silas was genuinely astonished by the list of people who were actively searching for him. "Damon?" he echoed suspiciously. "What's Damon got to do with this? Why on earth should the Ahasuerus Foundation be interested?"

"Damon Hart is involved because I took care to involve him," the voice replied with a casualness that was almost insulting. "The Ahasuerus Foundation is interested because I took care to interest them. I omitted to mention, of course, that Conrad Helier will also be doing his utmost to find you—but he is hardly in a position to pool his resources with anyone else."

"Conrad Helier's been dead for half a century," Silas said.

"That's not true," said the judge, with equal conviction. "Although I will admit to some slight doubt as to whether or not you *know* it to be untrue. How soon was he aware, do you suppose, that you would eventually desert his cause? Did he identify you as his Judas before he went to his carefully contrived crucifixion?"

"I only retired from the team ten years ago," Silas said.

"Of course. The burdens of parenthood served to resensitize you to your own old age. You developed a passion for the company of the authentically young: naive flesh, naive intelligence. In a way, they're *all* Conrad Helier's children, aren't they? All born from his womb—the womb he gifted to humankind after robbing them of all the wombs they already possessed. He appointed you to foster his son, but he surely considers your defection as a kind of betrayal."

Unable to help himself, Silas stared at his virtual adversary with a new intensity. He had not seen Conrad Helier for forty-six years, and his memories had faded as all memories did, but he was absolutely certain that Conrad Helier was one of the few people in the world who could come to him masked as artfully as any man could be masked and yet be recognizable.

Whoever his interrogator was, he swiftly decided, it could not possibly be Conrad Helier, or even his ghost.

"Torture can make a man say anything," Silas said, feeling that he ought to say *something* to cover his fearful confusion. "Anything at all. I know well enough how utterly unused to pain I've become. I know that as soon as your nanomech armies have smashed mine to smithereens I'll be utterly helpless. I'll say whatever you want me to say—but it will all be worthless, and worse than worthless. It won't be the truth, and it won't even *look* like the truth. No matter how cleverly you edit your tapes, people will know that it's a fake. Anybody with half a brain will see through the charade—and even if the police don't find you while I'm still alive, they'll find you once I'm dead. This is a farce, and you know it. You can't possibly gain anything from it."

Even as he made the speech, though, Silas realized that it couldn't be as simple as that. Whatever game his captor was playing, it wasn't just a matter of extorting a confession to post on some Eliminator billboard. Damon had been brought into it, and the Ahasuerus Foundation—and Silas honestly couldn't imagine why . . . unless, perhaps, the sole purpose of the crime had been to prompt its investigation by parties sufficiently interested and sufficiently powerful to uncover *real* proof of its motive—proof that would be worth far more than any tricked-up tape of a confession. . . .

"Who are you?" he asked, unable any longer to resist the temptation, although he knew that it would be a pointless admission of weakness. "Why are you doing this?"

"I'm a judge," said the voice flatly. "I'm doing this because *someone* has to do it. If humankind is to be worthy of immortality, it ought to begin with a clean slate, don't you think? Our sins must be admitted, and expiated, if they are not to spoil our new adventure."

"Who appointed *you* my judge and executioner?" Silas retorted, miserably aware of the fact that he was still displaying weakness and terror, even though he had not yet been stripped of all his protective armor.

"The post was vacant," the judge said. "No one else seemed to be interested in taking it up."

Silas recognized the words and felt their parodic force. "Fuck off," he said, with feeling. It seemed, suddenly, to be a direly old-fashioned curse: a verbal formula he had brought with him out of Conrad Helier's ark; a spell which could not have any force at all in the modern world. The existential significance of sexual intercourse had altered since the old world died, and the dirty words connected with it had lost their warrant of obscenity. *Shit* and its derivatives still retained their repulsive connotations, but the expletives which had once been strongest of all had lost their fashionability along with their force. Habit might preserve them awhile longer, at least in the language of centenarians like himself, but for all the effect they had one might as well make reference to God's wounds or the Prophet's beard.

"The charges laid against you are these," said the machine-enhanced voice as the lips of the caricature face moved in perfect sync. "First, that between 2095 and 2120 you conspired with Eveline Hywood, Karol Kachellek, Mary Hallam, and others, under the supervision of Conrad Helier, to cause actual bodily harm to some seven billion individuals, that actual bodily harm consisting of the irreversible disabling of their reproductive organs. Second, that you collaborated with Eveline Hywood, Karol Kachellek, Mary Hallam, and others, under the supervision of Conrad Helier, in the design, manufacture, and distribution of the agents of that actual bodily harm, namely the various virus species collectively known as meiotic disrupters or chiasmalytic transformers. You are now formally invited to make a statement in response to these charges."

"If you had any real evidence," Silas said stiffly, "you could bring the charges in a real court of law. I don't have to answer any charges brought by a caricature judge in a cartoon court."

"You've had seventy years to submit yourself to trial by a legitimately constituted court," said the judge, his mechanical voice dripping acid. "Those who prefer to evade the courts whose legitimacy they acknowledge ought not to protest too loudly when justice catches up with them. This court is the one which has found the means to bring you to trial; it is the one which will determine your fate. You will be given the opportunity to enter your defense before sentence is passed upon you."

"But you've already delivered your verdict, and I doubt that you have it in your power to determine any sentence but immediate execution—which will make you guilty of murder in the eyes of any authentic court in the world."

"Death is not such a harsh sentence for a man of your kind," opined the man behind the mask, "when one considers that you—like the vast majority of those previously condemned as unworthy of immortality—have already lived far longer than the natural human life span. One of the principles on which this court is founded is that whatever society bestows upon the individual through the medium of technology, society has every right to withdraw from those who betray their obligations to the commonweal."

"Eliminators aren't part of society. They're just an ill-assorted bunch of murderous maniacs. But you're no run-of-the-mill Eliminator, are you? You're something new, or something worse. Psychologically you're the same—in perfect harmony with the solitary spiders who get their kicks out of dumping malevolent garbage into the data stream in the hope that some other shithead will take it into his head to start blasting—but you've got an extra twist in you."

It was all bluster, but Silas took what comfort he could from its insincerity. Whoever had come to seize him had come well equipped, and however ridiculous this virtual court might be on the surface it was no joke, no merely amateur affair. Someone was taking this business very seriously—whatever the business in question really was. He had to try to figure that out, even if figuring it out couldn't save him from pain and death. If his sentence were already fixed, and if the police were unable to find him, the only meaningful thing he could do with what remained of his life was to find out who was doing this to him and why—and why *now,* when it had all happened so long ago.

"You still have time to make a clean breast of it," the voice informed him, refusing to respond to his insults. "No one can save you, Dr. Arnett, except yourself. Even if your trial were to be interrupted, you would still stand condemned. We are an idea and an ideal rather than an organization, and we can neither be defeated nor frustrated. When human beings live forever, no one will be able to evade justice, because there will be all the time in the world for their sins to find them out. We really do have to be *worthy* of immortality, Dr. Arnett. You, of all people, should understand that. This is, after all, a world which *you* helped to design—a world which could not have come into being had you not collaborated in the careful murder of the world which came before."

Silas didn't want to engage in philosophical argument. He wanted to stick to matters of fact. "Will you answer me one question?" he asked sharply.

"Of course I will," the judge replied, with silky insincerity. "*We* have no secrets to conceal."

"Did Catherine set me up? Did she rig the house's systems to let your people in?" He didn't imagine that he would be able to trust the answer, but he knew that it was a question that would gnaw away at him if he didn't voice it.

"As a matter of fact," the other replied, taking obvious pleasure in the reply, "she had no idea at all that she was carrying the centipedes which insinuated themselves into your domestic systems. We used her, but she is innocent of any responsibility. If anyone betrayed you, Dr. Arnett, it was someone who knew you far better than she."

Silas hoped that he would be able to resist the lure offered by that answer, but he knew that he wouldn't. *Someone* had set him up for this, and he had to consider everyone a candidate—at least until the time came for him to play the traitor in his turn, when his trial by ordeal began in earnest.

Nine

Damon stood on the quay in Kaunakakai's main harbor and watched the oceanographic research vessel *Kite* sail smoothly toward the shore. The wind was light and her engines were silent but she was making good headway. Her sleek sails were patterned in red and yellow, shining brightly in the warm subtropical sunlight. The sun was so low in the western sky that the whole world, including the surface of the sea, seemed to be painted in shades of crimson and ocher.

Karol Kachellek didn't come up to the deck until the boat was coming about, carefully shedding speed so that she could drift to the quay under the gentle tutelage of her steersman. Kachellek saw Damon waiting but he didn't wave a greeting—and he took care to keep his unwelcome visitor waiting even longer while he supervised the unloading of a series of cases which presumably held samples or specimens.

Two battered trucks with low-grade organic engines had already limped down to the quayside to pick up whatever the boat had brought in. Kachellek ostentatiously helped the brightly clad laborers load the cases onto the trucks. He was the kind of man who took pride in always doing his fair share of whatever labor needed to be done.

Eventually, though, Karol had no alternative but to condescend to come to his foster son and offer his hand to be shaken.

Damon took the hand readily enough and tried as best he could to import some real enthusiasm into the gesture. Karol Kachellek had always been distant; Silas Arnett had been the real foster father of the group to whose care Damon had been delivered in accordance with his father's will, just as poor Mary Hallam had been the real foster mother. If Silas was gone forever, leaving Damon no living parents except Karol and Eveline, then he had probably left it too late to restore any meaningful family relationships.

"This isn't a good time for visiting, Damon," Karol said. "We're very busy." At least he had the grace to look slightly guilty as he said it. He raised a hand to smooth back his unruly blond hair. "Let's walk along the shore while the light lasts," he went on awkwardly. "It'll be some time before the mud samples are ready for examination, and there won't be any more coming in today. Things might be easier in three or four weeks, if I can get more staff, but until then. . . ."

"You're very busy," Damon finished for him. "You're not worried, then, by the news?"

"I haven't time to waste in worrying about Silas. I'm concerned for him, of course, but there's nothing I can do to help and I don't feel that I'm under any obligation to fret or to mourn. I understand that you're bound to think of us as a pair, but he and I were never close."

"You worked together for more than eighty years," Damon pointed out, falling into step as the blond man settled into his long and economical stride.

"We certainly did," agreed the blond man, with a conspicuous lack of enthusiasm. "When you're my age you'll understand that close company can breed antipathy as easily as friendship, and that the passage of time smothers either with insulating layers of habit and indifference."

"I'm afraid I haven't formed those insulating layers yet," Damon said. "You're not worried about yourself either, then? If the Eliminators took Silas they might come after you next."

"Same thing—no time to waste. If we let Eliminators and

their kin drive us to trepidation, they've won. I can't see why Interpol is so excited about a stupid message cooked up by some sick mind. It should be ignored, treated with the contempt it deserves. Even to acknowledge its existence is an encouragement to further idiocies of the same kind." While he talked Karol's stride echoed his sermon in becoming more positive and purposeful, but Damon had no difficulty keeping up. Damon remembered that Karol *always* acted as if he had an end firmly in mind and no time to spare in getting there—it was sometimes difficult to believe that he was a hundred and twenty-two years old. Perhaps, Damon thought, he had to maintain his sense of purpose at a high pitch lest he lose it completely—as Silas seemed to have lost his once Damon had flown the nest.

They quickly passed beyond the limits of the harbor and headed toward the outskirts of the port, with the red orb of the setting sun almost directly ahead of them.

Mauna Loa was visible in the distance, looming over the precipitous landscape, but the town itself was oddly and uncomfortably reminiscent of the parts of Los Angeles where Damon had spent the greater part of his adolescence. Molokai had been one of numerous bolt-holes whose inhabitants had successfully imposed quarantine during the Second Plague War, but when it had tried to repeat the trick in the Crisis it had failed. The new pestilence had arrived here as surely as it had arrived everywhere else. Artificial wombs had been imported on the scale which the islanders could afford, but the population of the whole chain had been dwindling ever since. The internal technologies which guaranteed longevity to those who could afford them would have to become even cheaper before that trend went into reverse, unless there was a sudden saving influx of immigrants. In the meantime, that part of the port which remained alive and active was surrounded by a ragged halo of concrete wastelands.

Because there was so little to see on the landward side save for the lingering legacy of human profligacy, Damon looked out to sea while he walked on Karol Kachellek's right-hand side. The ocean gave the impression of having always been the way it was:

huge and serene. Where its waves lapped the shore they created their own dominion, shaping the sandy strand and discarding their own litter of wrack and rot-misshapen wood. He could just make out the shore of Lanai on the horizon, on the far side of the Kaiohi Channel.

"Why did you come out here, Damon?" Karol asked. "Are *you* scared of the Eliminators?"

"Should I be?" Damon countered—but his fosterer had no intention of rising to that one. "You wouldn't talk to me on the phone," Damon said after a pause. "Eveline hasn't replied in any way at all—as if it would somehow pollute her glorious isolation in the wilderness of space even to tap out a few words on a key-plate."

"She's working. She gets very engrossed, and this is a difficult time for her. She'll get back to you in her own time."

"Sure. Unfortunately, the Eliminators seem to be keeping to their own timetable. Would it inconvenience her that much to take my call while Silas may still be alive?"

"She'll talk to you," Karol assured him. "I would have too, when I could find the time—no matter how much I hate that fancy VE you've got hooked up to your phone."

"If you'd taken the call," Damon pointed out, "we could have met in your VE instead of mine. That's *not* one of my designs. Even if you'd called me, we could have fixed that at a keystroke."

VEs weren't really an issue, and Karol didn't press the point. "Look, Damon," he said, "the long and the short of it is that I didn't call you back because I simply don't have anything to tell you. Your father's dead. He wasn't an enemy of mankind. I have no idea why Eliminators or anyone else should want to kidnap or murder Silas. Eveline would say exactly the same—and she probably hasn't called you because she doesn't see any real need. I think you should let the police take care of this. I don't think it serves any useful purpose for you to start stirring things up."

"Am I stirring things up?" Damon asked. "It's just a social visit."

"I'm not talking about your coming here. I'm talking about

your unsubtle friend Madoc Tamlin and that stupid note you took to the Ahasuerus Foundation. What on earth possessed you to do something like that?"

Damon was startled by the news that Karol knew about his meeting with Rachel Trehaine, and even more startled by the blond man's seeming assumption that he had produced the note himself—but he took due note of the fact that Karol knew more about what was going on than his professed indifference had suggested. Was it possible, he wondered, that Karol and Eveline were trying to *protect* him? Were they refusing to talk to him because they were trying to keep him out of this weird affair? Karol had never been entirely at ease with him, so it was difficult for Damon to judge whether the blond man was any more unsettled than usual, but there was something about his manner which smacked of uncomfortable dishonesty.

I must be careful of seeing what I want to see, Damon thought. I must be careful of wanting to find a juicy mystery, or evidence that my paternal idol had feet of tawdry clay.

"Has Ahasuerus contacted you about the note?" he asked. "You weren't named in it—only Eveline."

"Eveline and I don't have any secrets from one another."

Damon wondered whether that meant that Ahasuerus had contacted Eveline and that Eveline had contacted Karol. "Don't you feel the same way about Eveline as you do about Silas?" he asked. "Isn't she just someone you worked with for so long that habit has bound up every last vestige of feeling? Why shouldn't you have secrets from one another?"

"I'm *still* working with her," Karol replied, again choosing to evade the real question.

"Not directly. She's off-planet, in L-Five."

"Modern communications make it easy enough to work in close association with people anywhere in the solar system. We're involved with the same problems, constantly exchanging information. In spite of the hundreds of thousands of miles that lie between us, Eveline and I are close in a way that Silas and I never were. We're in harmony, dedicated to a common cause."

"A common cause which I deserted," Damon said, taking up the apparent thread of the argument, "in spite of all the grand plans which Conrad Helier had for me. Is *that* why you and Eveline are trying to freeze me out of this? Is that why you resent my trying to *stir things up?*"

"I'm trying to do what your father would have wanted," Karol told him awkwardly.

"He's dead, Karol. In any case, you're not *him*. You're your own man now. You and I are perfectly free to build a relationship of our own. Silas could see that—Mary too."

"Fostering you was a job your father asked me to do," Karol retorted bluntly. "I'd have continued doing it, if there had been anything more I could do. I *will* continue, if there's anything I can do in future—but you can't expect me to forget that what *you* wanted was to get away, to abandon everything your father tried to pass on to you in order to run wild. You ran away from us, Damon, and changed your name; you declared yourself irrelevant to our concerns. Maybe it's best if you stick to that course and let us stick to ours. I don't know why you're so interested in this Eliminator stuff, but I really do think it's best if you let it alone."

Damon didn't want to become sidetracked into discussions of his irresponsible adolescence, or his not-entirely-respectable present. "Why should anyone accuse Conrad Helier of being an enemy of mankind?" he asked bluntly.

"He's dead, Damon," Karol said softly. "Nobody can hurt him, whatever lies they make up."

"They can hurt you and Eveline. Proofs will follow, they say. Whatever they're planning to say about Conrad Helier will reflect on you too—and would even if he were just another colleague you happened to work with once upon a time, to whose fate you were now indifferent."

"Conrad never did anything that I would be ashamed of," Karol said, his voice becoming even softer.

Damon let a second or two go by for dramatic effect and then said: "What if he *were* alive, Karol?"

The blond man had sufficient sense of drama to match Damon's pregnant pause before saying: "If he were, he'd be able to work on the problem which faces us just now. That would be good. He's present in spirit, of course, in every logical move I make, every hypothesis I frame, and every experiment I design. He made me what I am, just as he made the whole world what it is. You and I are both his heirs, and we'll never be anything else, however hard we try to avoid the consequences of that fact." He tried to fix Damon with a stern gaze, but stern gazes weren't his forte.

The blond man paused before a rocky outcrop which was blocking their path, and knelt down as if to duck any further questions. Miming intense concentration, he scanned the tideline which ran along the wave-smoothed rock seven or eight centimeters above the ground. It was a performance far more suited to his natural inclinations than stern fatherly concern.

The wrack which clung to the rock was slowly drying out in the sun, but the incoming tide would return before it was desiccated. In the meantime, the limp tresses provided shelter for tiny crabs and whelks. Where the curtains of weed were drawn slightly apart barnacles had glued themselves to the stony faces and sea anemones nestled in crevices like blobs of purple jelly. The barer rock above the tide line was speckled with colored patches of lichen and tarry streaks which might—so far as Damon could tell—have been anything at all.

Karol took a penknife from his pocket and scraped some of the tarry stuff from the rock into the palm of his hand, inspecting it carefully. Eventually, he tipped it into Damon's hand and said: *"That's* far more important than all this nonsense about Eliminators."

"What is it?" Damon asked.

"We don't have a name for the species yet—nor the genus, nor even the family. It's a colonial organism reminiscent in some ways of a slime mold. It has a motile form which wanders around by means of protoplasmic streaming, but the colonies can also set rock-hard, setting their molecular systems in sugar like sporulating bacteria or algae that have to withstand ultralow temperatures. In its dormant state it's as indestructible as any life-form can be, able to survive all kinds of extremes. Its genetic transactions are inordinately complicated and so far very mysterious—but that's not surprising, given that it's not DNA-based. Its methods of protein synthesis are quite different from ours, based in a radically different biochemical code."

Damon had given up genetics ten years before and had carefully set aside much of what his foster parents had tried so assiduously to teach him, but he understood the implications of what Kachellek was saying. "Is it new," he asked, "or just something we managed to overlook during the last couple of centuries?"

"We can't be absolutely certain," Karol admitted scrupulously. "But we're reasonably certain that it wasn't *here* before. It's a recent arrival in the littoral zone, and as of today it hasn't been reported anywhere outside these islands."

Damon wondered whether *as of today* meant that Karol had reason to expect a new report tomorrow or the day after, perhaps when the mud samples he'd loaded onto the lorry had been sieved and sorted. "So where did it come from?" he asked.

"We don't know yet. The obvious contenders are up, down. . . ." The blond man seemed to be on the point of adding a third alternative, but he didn't; instead he went on: "I'm looking downward; Eveline's investigating the other direction."

Damon knew that he was expected to rise to the challenge and follow the line of argument. The *Kite* had been dredging mud from the ocean bed, and Eveline Hywood was in the L-5 space colony. "You think it might have evolved way down in the deep trenches," Damon said. "Maybe it's been there all along, ever since DNA itself evolved—or maybe not. Perhaps it started off in one of those bizarre enclaves that surround the black smokers where the tectonic plates are pulling apart and has only just begun expanding its territory, the way DNA did a couple of billion years ago—or maybe it was our deep-sea probes that brought it out and gave it the vital shove.

"On the other hand, maybe it drifted into local space from elsewhere in the universe, the way the panspermists think that *all* life gets to planetary surfaces. We have probes out there too, don't we—little spaceships patiently trawling for Arrhenius spores and *stirring things up* as they go. Maybe it's been in the system for a long, long time, or maybe it arrived the day before yesterday . . . in which case, there might be more to come, and soon. I can see why you're interested. How different from DNA is its replicatory system?"

"We're still trying to confirm a formula," Karol told him. "We've slipped into the habit of calling it para-DNA, but it's a lousy name because it implies that it's a near chemical relative, and it's not. It coils like DNA—it's definitely a double helix of some kind—but its subunits are quite different. It seems highly unlikely that the two coding chemistries have a common ancestor, even at the most fundamental level of carbon-chain evolution. It's almost certainly a separate creation.

"That's not so surprising; whenever and wherever life first evolved there would surely have been several competing systems, and there's no reason to suppose that one of them would prove superior in every conceivable environment. The hot vents down in the ocean depths are a different world. Life down there is chemosynthetic and thermosynthetic rather than photosynthetic. Maybe there was always room down there for more than one chemistry of life. Perhaps there are other kinds still down there. That's what I'm trying to find out. In the meantime, Eveline's looking at dust samples brought in by probes from the outer solar system. The Oort Cloud is full of junk, and although it's very cold there now it's not beyond the bounds of possibility that life evolved in the outer regions of the solar system when the sun was a lot younger and hotter than it is now, or that spores of some kind could have drifted in from other secondary solar systems. We don't know—*yet.*"

"You don't think this stuff poses any kind of *threat,* do you?" said Damon, intrigued in spite of himself. "It's not likely to start displacing DNA organisms, is it?"

"Until we know more about it," Karol said punctiliously, "it's difficult to know how far it might spread. It's not likely to pose any kind of threat to human beings or any of our associated species, given the kind of nanotech defenses we can now muster, but that's not why it's important. Its mere existence expands the horizons of the imagination by an order of magnitude. What are a few crazy slanderers, even if they're capable of inspiring a few crazy gunmen, compared with *this?*"

"If it *is* natural," said Damon, "it could be the basis of a whole new spectrum of organic nanomachines."

"It's not obvious that there'd be huge potential in that," Karol countered. "So far, this stuff hasn't done much in the way of duplicating the achievements of life as we know it, let alone doing things that life as we know it has never accomplished. It might be woefully conventional by comparison with DNA, capable of performing a limited repertoire of self-replicating tricks with no particular skill; if so, it would probably be technologically useless, however interesting it might be in terms of pure science. We're not looking to make another fortune, Damon—when I say this is important, I don't mean commercially."

"I never doubted it for a moment," Damon said drily—and turned abruptly to look at the man who was rapidly coming up behind them. For a moment, it crossed his mind that this might be an Eliminator foot soldier, mad and homicidal, and he tensed reflexively. In fact, the man was an islander—and Karol Kachellek obviously knew him well.

"You'd better come quick, Karol," the man said. "There's something you really need to see. You too, Mr. Hart. It's bad."

Ten

The package had been dumped into the Web in hypercondensed form, just like any other substantial item of.mail, but once it had been downloaded and unraveled it played for a couple of hours of real time. It had been heavily edited, which meant that the claim with which it was prefaced—that nothing in it had been altered or falsified—couldn't be taken at all seriously.

The material was addressed To all lovers of justice, and it was titled Absolute Proof That Conrad Helier Is an Enemy of Mankind. It originated—or purported to originate—from the mysterious Operator 101. Karol Kachellek and Damon watched side by side, in anxious silence, as it played back on a wallscreen in Karol's living quarters.

The first few minutes of film showed a man bound to a huge, thronelike chair. His wrists and ankles were pinned by two pairs of plastic sheaths, each three centimeters broad, which clasped him more tightly if he struggled against them. He was in a sitting position, his head held upright by an elaborate VE hood which neatly enclosed the upper part of his skull. His eyes were covered, but his nose, mouth, and chin were visible. His pelvic region was concealed by a loincloth. There were two feeding tubes whose termini were close to the prisoner's mouth, and there was a third tube connected to a needle lodged in his left forearm, sealed in place by a strip of artificial flesh.

"This man," a voice-over announced, "is Silas Arnett, an intimate friend and close colleague of Conrad Helier. He has been imprisoned in this manner for seventy-two hours, during which time almost all of the protective nanomachinery has been eliminated from his body. He is no longer protected against injury, nor can he control pain."

Damon glanced sideways at Karol, whose face had set like stone. Damon didn't doubt that this was, indeed, Silas Arnett; nor did he doubt that Arnett had been stripped of the apparatus that normally protected him against injury, aging, and the effects of torture.

But if they intend to force some kind of confession out of him, Damon thought, everyone will know that it's worthless. Take away a man's ability to control pain and he can be made to say anything at all. What kind of "absolute proof" is that?

The image abruptly shifted to display a crude cartoon of a virtual courtroom. The accused man who stood in a wooden dock topped with spikes like spearheads was a caricature, but Damon had no difficulty in recognizing him as Silas Arnett. The twelve jurors who were positioned to his left were mere sketches, and the person whose position was directly opposite the camera's—presumably the prosecutor—had features no better defined than theirs. The black-robed judge who faced Arnett was drawn in greater detail, although his profile was subtly exaggerated.

"Please state your name for the record," said the judge. His voice was deep and obviously synthetic.

"I'll do no such thing," said the figure in the dock. Damon recognized Silas Arnett's voice, but in the circumstances he couldn't be sure that the words hadn't been synthesized by a program that had analyzed recordings and isolated the differentiating features of the original.

"Let the name Silas Arnett be entered in the record," said the judge. "I am obliged to point out, Dr. Arnett, that there really *is* a record. Every moment of this trial will be preserved for posterity. Any and all of your testimony may be broadcast, so you should conduct yourself as though the whole world were watching. Given the nature of the charges which will be brought against you, that may well be the case."

"I didn't think you people bothered with interrogations and trials," Arnett said. It seemed to Damon that Silas—or the software speaking in his stead—was injecting as much contempt into his voice as he could. "I thought you operated strictly on a sentence first, verdict afterwards basis."

"It sometimes happens," said the judge, "that we are certain of one man's guilt, but do not know the extent to which his collaborators and accomplices were involved in his crime. In such cases we are obliged to undertake further inquiries."

"Like the witch-hunters of old," said Arnett grimly. "I suppose it would make it easier to select future victims if the people you select out for murder were forced to denounce others before they die. Any testimony you get by such means is worse than worthless; this is a farce, and you know it."

"We know the truth," said the judge flatly. "Your role is merely to confirm what we know."

"Fuck you," Arnett said with apparent feeling. The obsolete expletive sounded curiously old-fashioned.

"The charges laid against you are these," the judge recited portentously. "First, that between 2095 and 2120 you conspired with Eveline Hywood, Karol Kachellek, Mary Hallam, and others, under the supervision of Conrad Helier, to cause actual bodily harm to some seven billion individuals, that actual bodily harm consisting of the irreversible disabling of their reproductive organs. Second, that you collaborated with Eveline Hywood, Karol Kachellek, Mary Hallam, and others, under the supervision of Conrad Helier, in the design, manufacture, and distribution of the agents of that actual bodily harm, namely the various virus species collectively known as meiotic disrupters or chiasmalytic transformers. You are now formally invited to make a statement in response to these charges."

Damon was astonished by his own reaction, which was more extreme than he could have anticipated. He was seized by an actual physical shock which jolted him and left him trembling. He turned to look at Karol Kachellek, but the blond man wouldn't meet his eye. Karol seemed remarkably unperturbed, considering that he had just been accused of manufacturing and spreading the great plague of sterility whose dire effects he and his collaborators had so magnificently subverted.

"Karol . . . ?"

Karol cut Damon off with a swift gesture. "Listen!" he hissed

"If you had any *real* evidence," the cartoon Arnett said, while the face of his simulacrum took on a strangely haunted look, "you'd have brought these charges in a *real* court of law. The simple fact that I'm here demonstrates the absurdity and falseness of any charges you might bring."

"You've had seventy years to surrender yourself to judgment by another court," said the judge sourly. "This court is the one which has found the means to bring you to trial; it is the one which will judge you now. You will be given every opportunity to enter a defense before sentence is passed upon you."

"I refuse to pander to your delusions. I've nothing to say." Damon found it easy enough to believe that it was Silas Arnett speaking; the crudely drawn figure had his attitude as well as his voice.

"Our investigations will be scrupulous nevertheless," the judge said. "They must be, given that the charges, if true, require sentence of death to be passed upon you."

"You have no right to do that!"

"On the contrary. We hold that what society bestows upon the individual, through the medium of technology, society has every right to withdraw from those who betray their obligations to the commonweal. This court intends to investigate the charges laid against you as fully as it can, and when they are proven it will invite any and all interested parties to pursue those who ought to be standing beside you in the dock. None will escape, no matter what lengths they may have gone to in the hope of evading judgment. There is no station of civilization distant enough, no hiding place buried deeply enough, no deception clever enough, to place a suspect beyond our reach."

What's that supposed to mean? Damon wondered. Where do they think Conrad Helier is, if he's still alive? Living under the farside of the moon? Or are they talking about Eveline? Are there Eliminators in the Lagrange colonies too?

"The people you've named are entirely innocent of any crime," Arnett said anxiously. "You're insane if you think otherwise."

Damon tried to judge from the timbre of the voice the extent to which Silas's pain-control system might have been dismantled. So far, he gave no real indication of having been forced to suffer dire distress. If there were indeed a reality behind this charade Silas Arnett's body must by now be an empire at war, and he must be feeling all the violence of the conflict. The tireless molecular agents which benignly regulated the cellular commerce of his emortality must have gone down beneath the onslaught of custom-designed assassins: Eliminators in miniature, which had exterminated his careful symbiotes and left their detritus to be flushed out by his kidneys. Even if Silas had not yet been subjected to actual torture he must have felt the returning grip of his own mortality, and the deadly cargo of terror which came with it. Had the terror been carefully expurgated from his voice—or was all this mere sham?

The picture dissolved and was replaced by an image of Conrad Helier, which Damon immediately recognized as a famous section of archive footage.

"We must regard this new plague not as a catastrophe but as a challenge," Helier stated in ringing tones. "It is not, as the Gaian Mystics would have us believe, the vengeance of Mother Earth upon her rapists and polluters, and no matter how fast and how far it spreads it cannot and will not destroy the species. Its advent requires a monumental effort from us, but we are capable of making that effort. We have, at least in their early stages, technologies which are capable of rendering us immune to aging, and we are rapidly developing technologies which will allow us to achieve in the laboratory what fewer and fewer women are capable of doing outside it: conceive and bear children. Within twenty or thirty years we will have what our ancestors never achieved: democratic control over human fertility, based in a new reproductive system. We have been forced to this pass by evil circumstance, but let us not undervalue it; it is a crucial step forward in the evolution of the species, without which the gifts of longevity and perpetual youth might have proved a double-edged sword. . . ."

The speech faded out. It was easy enough for Damon to figure out why the clip had been inserted. Recontextualized by the accusations which the anonymous judge had brought against Silas Arnett, it implied that Conrad Helier had thought of the transformer plagues as a good thing: an opportunity rather than a curse.

Damon had no alternative but to ask himself the questions demanded by the mysterious Operator. Had Conrad Helier been capable of designing the agents of the plague as well as the instruments which had blunted its effects? If capable, might he have been of a mind to do it?

The answer to the first question, he was certain in his own mind, was *yes.* He was not nearly as certain that the answer to the second question was *no*—but he remained uncomfortably aware of the fact that he had never actually *known* his biological father; all he had ever known was the oppressive force of his father's plans for him and his father's hopes for him. He had rebelled against those, but his rebellion couldn't possibly commit him to believing *this.* In any case, he *did* know the other people named by the judge. Karol was awkward and diffident, Eveline haughty and high-handed, but Silas and Mary had been everything he could have required of them. Surely it was unimaginable that they could have done what they now stood accused of doing?

The image cut back to the courtroom, but the moment Damon heard Silas Arnett speak he knew that a lot of time had elapsed. The alteration in the quality of the prisoner's voice left no doubt that a substantial section had been cut from the tape.

"What do you *want* from me?" Arnett hissed, in a voice full of pain and exhaustion. "What the fuck do you *want*?"

It was not the virtual judge who replied this time, although there was no reason to think that the second synthesized voice issued from a different source. "We want to know whose idea it was to launch the Third Plague War," said the figure to Silas Arnett's right—the figure who had always occupied center stage but had never claimed it. "We want to know where we can find incontrovertible evidence of the extent of the conspiracy. We want to know the names of everyone who was involved. We want to know where Conrad Helier is now, and what name he is currently using."

"Conrad's dead. *I saw him die!* It's all on tape. All you have to do is look it up!" Silas's voice was almost hysterical, but he seemed to be making Herculean efforts to control himself. Damon had to remind himself that *everything* on the tape could be the product of clever artifice. He could have forged this confrontation himself, without ever requiring Silas Arnett to be present.

"You did not see Conrad Helier die," said the accusing voice, without the slightest hint of doubt. "The tape entered into the public record is a forgery, and someone switched the DNA samples in order to confuse the medical examiner who carried out the postmortem. Was that you, Dr. Arnett?"

There was no immediate reply. The tape was interrupted again; there was no attempt to conceal the cut. When it resumed, Silas looked even more haggard; he was silent now, but he gave the impression of having exhausted his capacity for protest. Damon could imagine the sound of Silas's excised screams easily enough. Only the day before he had listened to poor Lenny Garon recording a tape which it might yet be his privilege to edit and doctor and convert into a peculiar kind of art. Were he to offer to take on that job Lenny Garon would probably be delighted—and would probably be equally delighted to hear his own screams, carefully intensified, on the final cut.

"It was my idea," Silas said in a hollow, grating voice saturated with defeat. "Mine. I did it. The others never knew. I used them, but they never knew."

"They *all* knew," said the inquisitor firmly.

"No they didn't," Silas insisted. "They trusted me, absolutely. They never knew. They still don't—the ones who are still alive, that is. I did it on my own. I designed the plague and set it free, so that Conrad could do what he had to do. He never knew that the transformers weren't natural. He died not knowing. He really did die *not knowing.*"

"It's very noble of you to take all the guilt upon yourself," said the other in a voice dripping with sarcasm. "But it's not true, is it?"

"Yes," said Silas Arnett.

This time, the editor left in the sound of screaming. Damon shivered, even though he knew that he and everyone else who had managed to download the tape before Interpol deleted it was being manipulated for effect. This was melodrama, not news—but how many people, in today's world, could tell the difference? How many people would be able to say: It's just some third-rate pornotape stitched together by an engineer. It's just a sequence of ones and zeros, like any other cataract of code. It doesn't mean a thing.

Suddenly, Diana Caisson's reaction to the discovery that Damon was using her template as a base for the sex tape he had been commissioned to make didn't seem quite so unreasonable. In using Silas Arnett as the basis of this elaborate fiction the people behind the cartoon judge were not merely exploiting him but destroying him. Silas would never be the same, even if they restored his internal technology. Even if all of this were shown to be a pack of lies, he would never be the same in the eyes of other men—which was where everyone had to live in the world of the Net, no matter how reclusive they chose to be.

The prosecutor spoke again. "The truth, Dr. Arnett, is that at least five persons held a secret conference in May 2095, when Conrad Helier laid out his plan for the so-called salvation of the world. The first experiments with the perfected viruses were carried out in the winter of 2098–99, using rats, mice, and human tissue cultures. When one of his collaborators—was it *you*, Dr.

Arnett?—asked Conrad Helier whether he had the right to play God, his reply was 'The post is vacant. No one else seems to be interested in taking it up. If we don't, who will?' That's the truth, Dr. Arnett, isn't it? Isn't that *exactly* what he said?"

The cartoon Arnett's reply to that was unexpected. "Who are you?" he asked, his pain seemingly mingled with suspicion. "I know you, don't I? If I saw your real face, I'd recognize it, wouldn't I?"

The answer was equally surprising. "Of course you would," the other said with transparently false gentleness. "And I know you, Silas Arnett. I know more about you than you can possibly imagine. That's why you can't hide what you know."

At this point, without any warning, the picture cut out. It was replaced by a text display which said:

CONRAD HELIER IS AN ENEMY OF MANKIND
FIND AND IDENTIFY CONRAD HELIER
MORE PROOFS WILL FOLLOW
—OPERATOR 101

Damon stared numbly at the words; their crimson letters glowed eerily against a black background, as if they had been written in fire across the face of an infinite and starless void.

Eleven

Damon's first thought was that he had to get in touch with Madoc Tamlin, and that he had to do so privately. He was spared the need to apologize to Karol Kachellek because Karol obviously had calls of his own to make and he too wanted to make them without being overheard. Instead of having to cover his own retreat, Damon found himself being bundled out of the room. He ran all the way back to his hotel, but he went to one of the public booths rather than using the unit in his room.

He checked his incoming mail in case there was anything important awaiting his attention, although he had set alarms to sound if Madoc or Eveline Hywood had called. The only name that caused him to pause as he scanned the list was Lenny Garon. He almost took a look at that message, just in case Madoc had decided to send some item of information by a roundabout route for security reasons, but it seemed more sensible to go directly to the source if it were feasible.

Unfortunately, Madoc seemed to be lying low. Tamlin's personal number should have reached his beltpack, but it didn't; the call was rerouted to Madoc's apartment, where Diana Caisson fielded the call. She didn't take it in the VE that Damon had designed, though; she must have had the machine set up so that any call would automatically be switched to the caller's VE. The booth had set the image of Damon's head and shoulders against a simple block pattern—one of the most primitive still in use in the USNA.

"Going back to the basics, Damon?" Diana asked, although she must have had a readout to inform her that he was calling from a public phone in Kaunakakai. After she'd finished the contrived sneer she looked him defiantly in the eye, as if to say that it was about time he made a start on his apologies.

"Never mind the smart remarks, Diana," Damon said. "I need to get hold of Madoc as soon as possible."

"He's out," she said sourly. Her face blurred slightly as she moved back from her own unit's camera, reflexively trying to cover her realization that he hadn't called to talk to her.

"I know that. I also know that he doesn't want to be located, even by me—but I need to get a message to him with the least possible delay. Will you do that for me, please?"

Damon could see that Diana was tempted to tell him where to put his message, but she thought better of it.

"What message?" she asked curiously.

"Can you tell him that in view of recent developments I really need that package we discussed. He'll understand what I mean and why. I've authorized him to draw more cash on the card I gave him, so that he can pull out all the stops. I'll be flying back tonight or early tomorrow, and I need to know what he's dug up as soon as I land. If he can meet me at the airport that would be good, but not if it takes him away from significant investigations. Have you got all that?"

"Of course I've got it," she snapped back. "Do you think I'm stupid or something? What's all this shit about *recent developments* and *the package we discussed*? Why are you trying to hide things from *me*? We had a *row*, that's all!"

Damon had to suppress an impulse to react in kind, but he knew that matching wrath with wrath would only escalate the conversation into a shouting match. Instead, he found the most soothing tone he could and said: "I'm sorry, Di—I'm a bit wound up. I'm not trying to keep secrets from you, but this *is* a public booth. Just ask Madoc to do what he can, and tell him he has extra resources if he needs them to speed things along. I really need you to do this for me, Diana. In a couple of days, if you want to, we can talk—but right now Silas Arnett is in bad trouble, and I have to do everything I possibly can to help find him. Bear with me, please. I have to go now."

"I know what's going on," she said quickly. She didn't want him to cut the connection.

"That's okay, Di," he said reassuringly. "It's no big secret—but it's not something I want broadcast, certainly not in the direction of the news tapes. If you're keeping up with the news, you'll realize why I'm in a hurry."

Her perplexed expression told him that she hadn't been monitoring the Web for new information regarding Silas Arnett, although Madoc must have been alerted to the new Operator 101 package at least as quickly as Karol Kachellek's assistants. Perhaps Madoc had deliberately killed the alarms in the apartment because Diana was there—although it was careless of him, if so, to have allowed his calls to be automatically diverted from his beltpack to his home phone.

"Why didn't you tell me that your father was Conrad Helier?" Diana demanded, still trying to stop him from breaking the connection.

"I was trying to forget it," Damon told her tersely. "It wasn't relevant."

"It seems to be relevant *now*," she said.

"It's Silas Arnett's kidnapping that's relevant to me," he retorted. "I've got to go, Di. I have to talk to my foster father—my *other* foster father. I'll call again, when I can. We *will* talk, if that's what you want."

"I might not be here," she informed him without much conviction. "I have better things to do than provide Madoc's answering service."

"Good-bye, Di," Damon said—and cut the connection before she could string the exchange out any further.

He reached out to the door of the booth, but then thought better of it. He called up the message that Lenny Garon had left for him. It was a simple request for him to call. Still figuring that it might be Madoc's way of steering information around Diana's inquisitive presence in his apartment, Damon made the call.

Lenny answered his own phone, but his machine was also rigged to use the caller's VE—presumably because the boy didn't like to advertize the fact that he didn't have a customized VE of his own. The block-patterned VE didn't bother him at all, though—when his image formed, his eyes were still fixed on the virtual readout telling him where the call was coming from.

"Damon!" he said, as if Damon were someone he'd known all his life. "What are you doing in Kaunakakai?" He stumbled over the pronunciation of the last word, but that was probably because he was excited rather than because he didn't have a clue where Kaunakakai might be.

"Personal business," Damon said. "Why did you want me to call, Lenny?"

"Yeah. *Personal business.* Sure . . . yeah, about that."

"About what?"

"About personal business. Madoc came to see me in hospital today—I got carved up a bit in the fight . . . internal damage. Nothing serious, but . . . well, anyhow, Madoc mentioned you were worried about a snatch—your foster father."

"Did Madoc give you a message?" Damon put in impatiently.

"No, of course not," the boy said. "He didn't want to talk about it at all—but that woman with him wouldn't let up. He wasn't talking about you, Damon, honestly—he just let slip that your foster parents were biotech people. When I got back here a little while ago, it wasn't difficult to put snatch and biotech together and come up with Silas Arnett's name. I'm not trying to interfere or anything . . . it's just that being a fan and all . . . I had no idea that I'd find anything I knew something about . . . but when I did I thought you'd want to know. It may be nothing. Probably is."

"What are you talking about, Lenny?" Damon said as patiently and as politely as he could.

"Cathy Praill," the boy replied, coming abruptly to the point. It took Damon a second or two to remember that Catherine

Praill was the young woman who'd been with Silas when he was abducted.

"What about her?" he asked.

"Well, like I say, nothing *really*. It's just that I know her. Sort of."

"How?"

"Silly, really. It's just that we're the same age—both seventeen, although I guess she's nearer eighteen than I am, probably past her birthday by now. Kids the same age, even approximately, are pretty thin on the ground. Foster parents tend to shop around their acquaintances making contacts, so that the kids can get together occasionally. You know the sort of thing—a couple of hundred adults getting together for a big party so that a dozen kids can *socialize with their peers.*"

Damon did know, but only vaguely. It wasn't the sort of thing his own foster parents had ever gone in for. They'd never worried about his social isolation and lack of peer-group interaction because they thought of him as one of a kind. In their eyes— even Mary's eyes and Silas's eyes—Heliers had no peers. Most groups of foster parents these days, at least in California, were ten or twelve strong, and they usually did their parenting strictly by the book. They took care to ensure that their children had other children to interact and bond with. It was possible that Lenny Garon had at some stage in his brief life made contact with every other person of his own age within a hundred miles.

"How well do you know her?" Damon asked.

"Not that well," Lenny admitted. "It must be two years since I actually saw her—but she was still posting to the Birthdate 2175 Webcore when I dropped out of all that."

She was only just eighteen, Damon thought. Silas was a hundred and ten years older than she was. What on earth was the point . . . ? He strangled the thought. It was obvious what the point was. The fact that they were a hundred and ten years apart *was* the point. "Get to the bottom line, Lenny," he said aloud. "Exactly what have you got to tell me about Catherine Praill?"

"Nothing *definite*—but I tried to get in touch with her. I tried *hard,* Damon. I talked to some of the others—other Birthdate 2175 people, that is. Interpol had already talked to a couple of them, the ones who were her closest friends. Damon, it's not on the news and I can't be *absolutely* sure, but I think *she's* disappeared too. She's not at home, and she's not anywhere else she'd be likely to be. Her foster parents are covering, but it's obvious they're worried. The other Birthdaters said that she couldn't possibly have had anything to do with Arnett being taken by the Eliminators, but they're as certain as I am that her foster parents don't have the slightest idea where she is—and it isn't because she left home to run with the gangs, like I did."

"Does Madoc know this?" Damon asked.

"Probably—but I can't get through to him. I didn't want to say too much to that woman. She doesn't seem to be on your side, even though she says she's your girlfriend."

"That's okay. Keep trying to get through to Madoc, though. He must be in some place where he can't take calls right now, but he's bound to move on. Give him what you can when you can—and thanks for your help. I have to go now."

"Wait!" The boy's expression was suddenly urgent—as if he feared that this would probably be the last chance he ever had to talk to his hero, or at least his last chance to have the advantage of just having done his hero a small favor.

Damon didn't have the heart to cut him off. "Make it quick, Lenny," he said, with a slight sigh.

"I just want to know," the boy said. "Madoc says that I can be good at it—that I show promise, even though Brady cut me up so easily. He says that if I keep at it . . . but he would, wouldn't he? He gets the tapes whether I win or lose, to him it's just *raw material*—but you're a real fighter and you don't have any reason to lie. Just tell me straight, Damon. Am I good enough? Can I make it, if I give it everything I've got?"

Damon suppressed a groan. Even though Lenny had given him little or nothing he felt that he really did owe the boy an answer. In any case, this might be one of the few instances in his life when what he said could make a real difference.

"I can only tell you what I think, Lenny," he said, in what he hoped was a man-to-man fashion. "However good you are, or might become, fighting is a fool's game. I'm sorry that I ever got involved in it. It was just a way of signaling to the world and my foster parents that I was my own person, and that I didn't have to live according to their priorities. It was the clearest signal I could send, but it was a stupid signal. There are other ways, Lenny. I know you think the money looks good, and that the IT it buys will more than compensate for the cuts you take, but it's a false economy—a bad bet.

"If Madoc's given you the same spiel he gave me he'll have told you that the human body renews itself every eight years or so—that all the cells are continually being replaced, on a piece-meal basis, to the extent that there's hardly an atom inside you now that was there when you were nine years old, and hardly an atom that will be still with you when you're twenty-five. That's true—but the inference he intends you to take, which is that it doesn't matter what you do to your body now because you'll have a brand-new one in ten years' time is false and dangerous. That constant process of reproduction isn't perfect. It's like taking a photocopy of a photocopy of a photocopy—every time an error or flaw creeps in it's reproduced, and gradually exaggerated.

"Your internal technology will increase the number of times you can photocopy yourself and still be viable, but the errors and flaws will still accumulate—and everything you do to create more flaws will cost you at the far end of your life. In a few days' time you won't be able to see the scars that Brady's knife left, but you should never make the mistake of thinking that you've been fixed up as good as new. There's no such thing. If you want my advice, Lenny, give it up now. It doesn't matter how good you might become—it's just not worth it."

The expression on the boy's face said that this wasn't the kind of judgment he had expected. He had braced himself against the possibility of being told that he might not be good enough to make the grade, but he hadn't braced himself against this. He opened his mouth, but Damon didn't want to know what he was going to say.

"Don't blow your chance to ride the escalator all the way to true emortality, Lenny," he said. "The ten-year advantage you have over me could be vital—but not nearly as vital as looking after your tender flesh. Maybe neither of us will get there, and maybe both of us will die in some freak accident long before we get to our full term, but it makes sense to do the best we can. Getting the IT a little bit sooner won't do you any good at all if you give it less to work with when it's installed. Nanotechnology is only expensive because PicoCon takes so much profit; in essence, it's dirt cheap. It uses hardly any materials and hardly any energy. Everything goes to the rich first, but after that the price comes tumbling down. The best bet is to look after yourself and be patient—that's what I'm doing now, and it's what I'll be doing the rest of my life, which I hope will be a *very* long time."

Damon knew that the lecture was rushed, but he didn't have time to fill in all the details and he didn't have time to take questions. Lenny understood that; his face had become more and more miserable while Damon spoke, but he was still determined to play it tough. The boy waited for Damon to close the conversation.

"I really have to go, Lenny," Damon said as softly as he could. "I'm sorry. Maybe we can talk again, about this and other things, but not now." He broke the connection. Then he got out of the booth and went in search of Karol Kachellek.

Twelve

Karol Kachellek was still in the workroom where he and Damon had watched the tape of Silas Arnett's mock trial. When Damon came back he was under the phone hood and the room was unlit, but he came out as soon as he realized that he wasn't alone and brushed the light-switch on his console. Damon hadn't managed to catch the last few words Karol had spoken before signing off but he blushed slightly anyway, as if walking into a darkened room were an infallible sign of stealthy intent.

Damon was all set for more verbal fencing, but the bioscientist was in a very different state of mind now.

"I'm sorry, Damon," Kachellek said, with unaccustomed humility. "You were right. This business is far more complicated than I thought—and it couldn't have come at a worse time."

"What's it all about, Karol?" Damon asked quietly. "You do know, don't you?"

"I only wish I did." The unprecedented plaintiveness in his foster father's voice made Damon want to believe that he was sincere. "You mustn't worry, Damon. It will all be sorted out. I don't know who's doing this, or why, but. . . ." As the blond man trailed off, Damon stared at him intently, wondering whether the red flush about his brow and neck was significant of anger, anxiety, embarrassment, or some synergistic combination of all three.

Karol reddened even more deeply under his foster son's steady gaze. "It's all lies, Damon," he said awkwardly. "You can't possibly *believe* any of that stuff. They *forced* Silas to say what he did, if he said it at all. We can't even be sure that it really *was* his voice. It could all have been synthesized."

"It doesn't much matter whether it's all lies or not," Damon told him grimly. "It's going to be talked about the world over. Whoever made that tape is cashing in on the newsworthiness of the Eliminators, using their crazy crusade to ensure maximum publicity for those accusations. The tape doctor didn't even try to make them sound convincing. He settled for crude melodrama instead, but that might well be effective enough for his purposes if all he wants is to kick up a scandal. Why put in those last few lines, though? Why take the trouble to include a section of tape whose sole purpose is to establish the possibility that Silas might have known his captor? What are we supposed to infer from that?"

"I don't know," Karol said emphatically. His manner was defensive, but he really did sound sincere. "I really don't understand what's happening. Who would want to do this to us, Damon? Why—and why *now*?"

Damon wished that he had a few answers to offer; he had never seen any of his foster parents in such a state of disarray. He felt obliged to wonder whether the tape could have been quite as discomfiting if there had been no truth at all in its allegations, but he was certain that Karol's blustering couldn't all be bluff. He really didn't understand what was happening or who was behind it, or why they'd chosen to unleash the whirlwind at this particular time. Maybe, given time, he could work it all out—but for the moment he was helpless, to the extent that he was even prepared to accept guidance from Damon the prodigal, Damon the betrayer.

"Tell me about Surinder Nahal," Damon said abruptly. "Does *he* have motive enough to be behind all this?" He was avid to seize the chance to ask some of the questions he'd been storing up, hoping that for once he might get an honest reply, and that seemed to be the best item with which to begin. Karol was far more likely to know something useful about a rival gene-tweaker than the disappearance of an eighteen-year-old girl.

However far Karol was from recovering his usual icy calm, though, he still had ingrained habit to come to his aid. "Why him?" he parried unhelpfully.

"Come on, Karol, *think,*" Damon said urgently. "Silas isn't the only one who's gone missing, is he? If nothing was wrong, Madoc would have found Nahal by now and let me know. If he isn't part of the problem, he must be part of the solution. Maybe his turn in the hot seat is coming next—or maybe he's the one feeding questions to the judge. How bad is the grudge he's nursing?"

"Surinder Nahal was a bioengineer back in the old days," Kachellek said, with a slight shrug of his shoulders. "His field of endeavor overlapped ours—he was working on artificial wombs too, and there was a difference of opinion regarding patents."

"How strong a difference of opinion? Do you mean that he accused Conrad Helier of obtaining patents that ought to have been his?"

"You don't know what it was like back then, Damon. The queue outside the patent office was always five miles long, and every time a significant patent was granted there were cries of *Foul!* all along the line—not that it mattered much, the way the corps were always rushing to produce copycat processes just beyond the reach of the patents and throwing lawsuits around like confetti. The Crash put an end to all that madness—it focused people's minds on matters of *real* importance. There's nothing like a manifest threat to the future of the species to bring people together. In 2099 the world was in chaos, on the brink of a war of all against all. By 2110 peace had broken out just about everywhere, and we were all on the same side again.

"Sure, back in ninety-nine Surinder Nahal was hopping mad with us because we were ten places ahead of him in the big queue—but it didn't last. Ten years later we were practically side by side in the struggle to put the New Reproductive System in place. There was a little residual bad feeling because he thought he hadn't been given his fair share of credit for the ectogenetic technology that was finally put in place, but nothing serious. I haven't heard of him in fifty years; if I'd ever thought about him at all I'd have presumed that he was retired, like Silas. I can't believe that a man like him could be responsible for all this—he was a *scientist,* like us. It makes no sense. It must be someone from. . . ." He stopped as soon as he had fully formulated the thought in his own mind.

"Someone from what?" Damon asked sharply—but it was too late. The moment of his foster father's vulnerability had passed, killed by the lengthy development of his judgment of Surinder Nahal. Karol had no intention of finishing his broken sentence; he deliberately turned away so that he didn't have to answer Damon's demanding stare. Whatever conclusion he had suddenly and belatedly jumped to, he clearly intended to act on it himself, in secret. Damon tried to make the charitable assumption that Karol had only stopped dead because he was standing in a room whose walls might easily be host to a dozen curious eyes and ears, but he couldn't help feeling that it was a personal slight nevertheless: a deliberate act of exclusion.

"Is it possible," Damon said, trying not to sound *too* hostile, "that the viruses which caused the plague of sterility really were manufactured, by *someone*? Was it really a Third Plague War, as the judge said? Could the Crash have been deliberately caused?" He didn't expect an honest answer, but he figured that if a man like Hiru Yamanaka could set such store by eye-to-eye interrogation, there must be something in the theory.

Karol met his eye again, pugnaciously. "Of course it could," he snapped, as if it ought to have been perfectly obvious. "History simplifies. There weren't two plague wars, or even three—there was only one, and it involved more battles than anyone ever acknowledged. All that stuff about one war launched by the rich against the poor and another by the poor against the rich is just news-tape PR, calculated to imply that the final score was even. It wasn't."

Damon wasn't at all surprised by this judgment, although he hadn't expected to hear it voiced by a man like Karol Kachellek. He was familiar with the thesis that *all* wars were waged by the rich, with the poor playing the part of cannon fodder.

"Are you saying that *all* the new and resurgent diseases were deliberately released?" Damon asked incredulously. "All the way back to AIDS and the superbacs?"

"No, of course I'm not," Karol said, scrupulously reining in his cynicism. "There were real problems. Species crossovers, antibiotic-immune strains, new mutations. There really was a backlash against early medical triumphs, generated by natural selection. I don't doubt that there were accidental releases of engineered organisms too. There's no doubt that the first free transformers were spontaneous mutations that allowed gene-therapy treatments to slip the leash of their control systems and start a whole new side branch in the evolutionary tree. Maybe ninety-nine out of every hundred of the bugs that followed in their wake were products of natural selection—and nine out of ten were perfectly harmless, even benign—but the people who made good transformers by the score were perfectly capable of making not-so-good ones too."

"And they could get paid to do it, I suppose? They weren't too proud to take defense funding."

"*Everybody* took defense funding in the twenty-first century, Damon. Purely for the good of science, you understand—for the sake of the sacred cause of progress. There must have been thousands who wrung their hands and howled their lamentations all the way to the bank—but they took the money anyway. That's not the point. The point is that nobody knows for sure where *any* of the bad bugs came from—not even the ones whose depredations were confidently labeled the First and Second Plague Wars. The principal reason why the Crash wasn't called a plague war at the time was that nobody was excluded from it. No one seemed to have any defense ready; everybody seemed to be a victim. That doesn't mean that no one had any reason to release viruses of that type. As Conrad said in that clip the Eliminator dropped into his little comedy, it *forced* us to do what we'd needed to do for a hundred years but never contrived to do—to bring human fertility under careful control."

"Not so much a war of the rich against the poor, then, as a war of the few against the many."

"No. If it was any kind of plague war at all it was a war to end that kind of warfare. It was humankind against the Four Horsemen of the Apocalypse—the last stand against the negative Malthusian checks."

"So if it *was* deliberate, the people responsible would have had your wholehearted support?"

"You don't understand, Damon," Karol said, in a tone of voice that Damon had heard many times before. "People don't talk about it nowadays, of course, because it's not considered a fit topic for polite conversation, but the world before the Crash was very different from the one in which you grew up. There were a lot of people prepared to say that the population explosion *had* to be damped down one way or another—that if the sum of individual choices didn't add up to voluntary restraint, then war, famine, and disease would remain necessary factors in human affairs. People were already living considerably longer, as a matter of routine, than their immediate ancestors. PicoCon and OmicronA were only embryos themselves in those days, but their mothercorps were already promising a more dramatic extension of the life span by courtesy of internal technology. It was easy enough to see that matters would get very fraught indeed as those nanotechnologies became cheaper and more efficient.

"The world was full of new viruses. A lot of them were arising naturally—more than ten billion people crammed into polluted supercities constitute a wonderland of opportunity for virus evolution—and a lot more were being tailored in labs for use as transgenic vectors, pest controllers, so-called beneficial fevers, and so on. All kinds of things came out of that cauldron, far more of them by accident than by design. It really doesn't matter a damn, and didn't then, how the Crash was *started;* the brute fact of it forced us all to concentrate our attention and energies on the problem of how to *respond* to it.

"We came through it, and we got the world moving again. It's a changed world and it's a better world, and Conrad Helier was one of its chief architects. Maybe you think we made a lot of money out of the world's misfortune, but by comparison with PicoCon, OmicronA, and the other cosmicorps we've always been paupers. What we did, we did for the common good. Conrad was a fine man—a *great* man—and this crazy attempt to blacken his name is the product of a sick mind."

Damon reminded himself that Karol Kachellek had been born in 2071, only four years after Silas Arnett but fifteen years after Conrad Helier. Karol was only thirty years short of the current world record for longevity, but he still thought of Conrad Helier as the product of an earlier generation: a generation that was now lost to history. Conrad Helier had been a more powerful father figure to Karol Kachellek than he ever could have been to Damon.

"Were you actually present when my father died, Karol?" Damon asked quietly.

"Yes I was. I was by the side of his hospital bed, watching the monitors. His nanomachines were at full stretch, trying to repair the internal damage. They were PicoCon's best, but they just weren't up to it. He'd suffered a massive cerebral hemorrhage and there were more complications than I could count. We like to think of ourselves as potential emortals, but we're not even authentically immune to disease and injury, let alone the effects of extreme violence. There are dozens of potential physiological accidents with which the very best of today's internal technology is impotent to deal. Kids of your generation, who feel free to take delight in savage violence because its effects are mostly reparable, are stupidly playing with fire. The proximal cause of your father's death was a massive stroke—but if the lunatic who made that tape intends to build a case on the seeming implausibility of that cause of death he's barking up the wrong tree. If Conrad had wanted to fake his death, he'd have chosen something far more spectacular."

"How did you know he was dead?" Damon asked. He couldn't help comparing the lecture that Karol had just given him with the one he'd given Lenny Garon; the depth of his estrangement from his foster parents didn't seem quite so abysmal now.

"I told you," Kachellek replied, with ostentatious patience. "I was watching the monitors. I also watched the doctors trying to resuscitate him. I wasn't actually present at the postmortem, but I can assure you that there was no mistake."

Damon didn't press the point. If Conrad Helier had faked his death, Karol Kachellek would surely have been in on the conspiracy, and he was hardly likely to relent in his insistence now.

"I'm going back to Los Angeles as soon as I can," Damon said quietly. "Maybe you ought to come with me. The people who took Silas might have designs on you too. Interpol can offer you far better protection on the mainland than they can in a desolate and underpoliced spot like this."

"I can't possibly go to Los Angeles," Karol said mulishly. "I've got important work to do *here.*"

I have work to do too, Damon thought. I know what skills it took to put that tape together, technically and in terms of its narrative implications. Through Madoc I have access to some first-rate outlaw Webwalkers, including Old Lady Tithonia herself. I can get to the bottom of this, if I try hard enough, no matter how insistent Karol and Eveline are in trying to keep me out of it. Maybe I can get to the bottom of it sooner than Interpol. Maybe I can get to the bottom of it quickly enough to take a hand in the game myself.

That bold and positive thought was, however, quickly followed by a host of shadowy doubts. Perhaps he could get to the bottom of the matter faster than Interpol—but might that not be exactly what Operator 101 wanted? Why would the mysterious

Operator bother to push a note under his door unless he was *intended* to take a hand in the game? What, exactly, did the writer of that note want him to do? Might he not be lending unwitting assistance to the persecutor of his foster parents, collaborating in the assassination of his biological father's reputation? Rebel though he certainly was, did he really want to take his rebellion to the point of joining forces with his family's enemies—and if not, how could he be sure that he wouldn't do so simply by uncovering the truth?

The night air was surprisingly cold, given that the day had been so hot. The wind was brisker than it had been earlier, and it had reversed its direction now that the sea was warmer than the land. The palm trees planted in a neat row in the forecourt of the hotel were waving their fronds murmurously.

Once he was back in his room Damon tried to book a seat to Honolulu on the first flight out in the morning, but it wasn't scheduled to leave until eleven and he didn't want to wait that long. He called Karol to ask about the possibility of arranging a charter.

"No problem," Karol said, showing evident relief at the thought that he wouldn't have to face any more of Damon's questions. "Name your time."

Damon was tempted to name first light, but he was too tired. His IT was supposed to have the capacity to keep him going for seventy-two hours without sleep, if necessary, but when he'd tried to use the facility in the past it had brought home to him the truth of the adage that the flesh was not the person. His mind needed rest, even if his body could be persuaded that it didn't. Whatever faced him tomorrow, he wanted to be fully alert and mentally agile.

"Make it eighty-thirty," he said.

"It'll be waiting," Karol promised—and then added: "It *will* be all right, Damon. Silas will be okay. We all will."

Even though he knew full well that the promises were empty, Damon was glad that Karol had taken the trouble to make them.

Eveline Hywood wouldn't have bothered—or, if she had, would certainly have affected an infinitely more patronizing tone.

"Sure," Damon said. "Thanks. I'm sorry I got under your feet—but I'm glad I came."

"So am I," said Karol—and he might even have meant it.

Thirteen

Karol Kachellek took time out from his busy schedule to drive Damon out to a small private airstrip near the southeastern tip of the island. Damon couldn't help thinking, churlishly, that the gesture had less to do with courtesy than a keen desire to see the back of him, but there was no hostility in his foster father's manner now. The Eliminator broadcast had knocked all the stiffness out of the bioscientist, who was visibly anxious as he bounced his jeep over the potholes in the makeshift road. Damon had never seen him so obviously distressed.

"Bloody road," Karol complained. "All it needs is a man with a shovel and a bucketful of gantzing bacs. He could take the dirt from the side of the road—there's plenty of it. Nobody ever admits responsibility without a fight, and when they have to, it's always going to be done tomorrow—the kind of tomorrow that never comes."

"Wouldn't be tolerated in Los Angeles," Damon agreed, with a slight smile. "If the city couldn't take care of it immediately the corps would race one another to get a man out there. OmicronA would be determined to win, in order to demonstrate that PicoCon's ownership of the patents is merely an economic technicality. The staff in the California offices pride themselves on being hands-on people, always willing to get involved in local issues."

"I bet they do," Karol muttered tersely. "Nanotech hands by the trillion, at work in every last nook and cranny of the great showcase of the global village—it's different here, of course. No Silicon Valley–type monuments to the Third Industrial Revolution, no social cachet. We're still the backwoods—the kind of wilderness that isn't even photogenic. Nobody gives a damn about what happens out here, especially the people who live here."

"You live here," Damon pointed out. He refrained from adding an observation to the effect that Karol could have packed his own bucket and spade, pausing to repair the potholes on his way back to the lab. After all, Karol was *very* busy just now.

"Here and hereabouts," Karol admitted grimly.

Damon relented slightly. "Actually," he said, "the corps are selectively blind even on their own doorstep. Until the deconstructionists move into the LA badlands in earnest nobody's going to tidy them up. Filling in a hole downtown counts as an ad—filling one in where the gangs have their playgrounds wouldn't win a nod of approval from anyone. You know how corpthink goes: no approval, no effort."

"If only the world were as simple as that," Karol said sadly. "The real problem is that too many people spend their entire lives sweating blood for the best possible causes and end up being denounced as enemies of mankind."

That was more like the Karol he knew of old, and Damon was perversely glad to see the real man surfacing again, filling in his psychological potholes with great globs of biotech-cemented mud. Karol wasn't sweating yet because the sun was too low in the eastern sky, but Damon knew that he'd be sweating by noon—not blood, to be sure, but beads of good, honest toil. Para-DNA had no chance of keeping its secrets, no matter how fervently it clung to the fugitive backwoods of the global village, and no matter how hard it tried to disguise itself as the detritus of a twentieth-century oil spill. Moves like that couldn't possibly divert the curiosity of a true scientist.

As the jeep lurched onto the lawn beside the strip a flock of brightly colored birds grudgingly flew away, mewling their objections. Damon couldn't put a name to the species but he had no doubt that Karol could have enlightened him had he cared to ask.

The two of them said their good-byes brusquely, as if to make sure that they both understood that their mutual mistrust had been fully restored, but there was a manifest awkwardness in their lack of warmth. Damon suspected that if he'd only known exactly what to say, he might have made a better beginning of the process of reconciliation, but he wasn't certain that he wanted to try. Karol might be showing belated signs of quasi-parental affection, but he hadn't actually told Damon anything significant. Whatever suspicions Karol had about the identity and motives of Silas Arnett's kidnappers he was keeping to himself.

Damon would rather have sat up front in the cockpit of the plane, but he wasn't given the choice. He was ushered into one of the eight passenger seats by the pilot, who introduced himself as Steve Grayson. Grayson was a stocky man with graying temples and a broad Australian accent. Maybe he thought the gray made him look more dignified, or maybe it was a joke reflecting his surname; at any rate, he was certainly no centenarian and he could have had his hair color reunified without recourse to the new generation of rejuvenation techniques. Damon took an immediate dislike to the pilot when Grayson insisted on reaching down to fasten his safety harness for him—an ostensible courtesy which seemed to Damon to be an insulting invasion of privacy.

"We'll be up and down in no time at all," Grayson told Damon before taking his own seat and fastening his own belt. "Might be a little rough in the wind, though—I hope your IT can cope with motion sickness."

"I'll be fine," Damon assured him, taking further insult from the implication that in the absence of his IT he'd be the kind of person who couldn't take a few routine aerial lurches without losing his breakfast.

While the plane taxied onto the runway Damon watched Karol Kachellek jump back into the jeep and drive away, presumably hastening back to the puzzle of para-DNA. Damon had a puzzle of his own to play with, and he had no trouble immersing himself within it, taking up the work of trying to figure out whether there *might* be something in what Karol had said to him that might lead to a fuller understanding of the game that Operator 101 was playing.

He was so deep in contemplation that he took no notice of the plane's banking as it climbed. He watched the island diminish in size until it was no more than a mere map, but even then it did not occur to him that there was anything strange in the course they were taking. Ten or twelve minutes had elapsed before it finally occurred to him that the glaring light which had forced him to raise his left hand to shield his face should not have been so troublesome. Once Grayson had settled the plane on its intended course the sun ought to have been almost directly behind them, but it was actually way over to port.

"Hey!" he called to the pilot. "What's our course?"

Grayson made no reply.

"Isn't Honolulu due west of Molokai, away to the right?" Damon asked. He was beginning to doubt his knowledge of geography—but when Grayson again failed to turn around and look him in the eye, he knew that something was amiss.

He tested his safety harness and found that it was locked tight. The belt which Grayson had advised him to keep locked couldn't be unlocked; he was a prisoner.

"Hey!" he shouted, determined not to be ignored. "What's going on? What are you doing? Answer me, you bastard."

At last, the pilot condescended to turn his head. Grayson's expression was slightly apologetic—but only slightly.

"Sorry, son," he said. "Just take it easy—when there's nothing to be done, that's what you might as well do."

The homespun philosophy was a further annoyance, but Damon still couldn't unfasten the seat belt. Like Silas Arnett before him—and possibly Surinder Nahal, not to mention Catherine Praill—he was being kidnapped. But why? And by whom? The mystery briefly overwhelmed the enormity of the realization, but the brute fact of what was happening soon fought back, insistently informing him that whoever was responsible, he was *in danger*. Whether he was in the hands of Eliminators or not, he was being carried off into the unknown, where any fate at all might be waiting for him.

His years of experience on the streets were supposed to have hardened him against fear and dread, but all that seemed futile now. However mean the streets were—and however one might try to dignify them with titles like "the badlands"—they were only a half hour away from the nearest hospital. As he had explained to Lenny Garon, people did die in knife fights—but if one drew back to consider life less narrow-mindedly, there were still a thousand *other* ways a man might die, even in the New Utopia. It didn't require a bullet or a bomb, or any act of violence at all. A man might drown, or choke, or. . . .

He abandoned the train of thought abruptly. What did it matter what *might* happen to him? The real question was what he intended to *do* about the ugly turn of events.

"Who are you working for?" he called to the pilot.

"Just doing a job," Grayson called back. "Delivering a package. You want explanations, I don't have them—I dare say the man on the ground will have plenty."

"Where are you taking me?"

Grayson laughed, as if he were taking what pleasure he could in holding on to his petty secrets. "You'll see soon enough," he promised.

Damon abandoned the fruitless inquisition for the time being, instructing himself to take more careful stock of his situation.

He could see Maui away to port, and he assumed that if he were seated on the other side of the plane he'd be able to see Lanai as well, but there was nothing directly below but the Pacific. Damon's knowledge of the local geography was annoyingly vague, but he figured that on their present heading—which seemed to be slightly east of south—they'd be over Kahoolawe at much the same time that they ought to have been coming down at Honolulu. If they kept going twice as long they might eventually hit the west coast of Hawaii. How many other islands there might be to which they might be headed Damon had no idea, but there were probably several tiny ones and the plane was small enough to land on any kind of strip.

He tried to make a list of the possibilities. Who might want him out of the way badly enough to bribe Grayson? Surely not Operator 101, who had sent him a note inviting him to investigate—nor Rachel Trehaine, who presumably thought of him as an irrelevance. There was, of course, another and more obvious possibility. Karol Kachellek had hired the pilot—it was most probable, therefore, that *he* had decided that Damon ought to be removed from the field of play until the game was over. Grayson might well have been instructed to take Damon to a place of safety, not merely to keep him from harm but also to keep him from asking any more awkward and embarrassing questions.

Damon had to admit that this was not an unattractive hypothesis, insofar as it suggested that no one was intending to flush out his IT and force him to confess that he was an enemy of humankind, but he felt no relief. To the contrary, as soon as he had convinced himself of its likelihood he felt exceedingly annoyed. The fact that his foster father might think that he had the right, and also the responsibility, to do such a thing was a terrible slur on his adulthood and his ability to look after himself.

"Whatever Karol's paying you," he shouted to Grayson, "I'll double it if you take me to Honolulu."

"Too late, mate," Grayson shouted back. "I'm on the wrong side of the law now—once you cross the border you have to keep on going. Don't worry—nobody's going to hurt you."

"This is for my own good, is it?"

"We all have to lend one another a helping hand," Grayson told him, perhaps faking his malicious cheerfulness in order to cover up his anxiety at the thought that he was indeed beyond the bounds of the law. "If things work out with the IT fountain of youth, we could all be neighbors for a long, long time."

It was difficult to be patient, or even to try, but Damon had no alternative.

It turned out that the journey wasn't that much longer than it would have been had Grayson actually gone to Honolulu, but the plane eventually passed beyond the southern tip of Lanai and missed Kahoolawe too. The pilot headed for a much smaller and more densely forested island top to the west of Kahoolawe. It was dominated by what appeared to be a single volcanic peak, but Damon wasn't convinced that it was genuine.

Back in the early twenty-first century the precursors of today's self-styled continental engineers had enjoyed a honeymoon of fashionability by virtue of the greenhouse effect and the perceived threat of a significant rise in the world's sea level. When global warming hadn't produced a new Deluge, even in Shanghai and the South Seas, they'd deflected the results of their research into building artificial islands aimed at the tourist trade. Such islands had initially had to be anchored to subsurface structures by mechanical holdfasts because Leon Gantz's techniques of biotech cementation hadn't been around in those days, but anyone who cared to employ gantzers on a sufficiently lavish scale could now make better provision. Building mountains underwater was just as easy as building them anywhere else. The ocean hereabouts was full of deep trenches but it wasn't uniformly deep, and even if it were it would only make the task of securing new land more expensive, not more difficult in technical terms.

Even natural islands, Damon knew, had often been personal property back in the buccaneering days of classical capitalism—but *all* the artificial islands had been owned by the corps or individuals who had put them in place, and probably still were. That didn't exclude them from the Net, and hence from the global village, but it made them relatively easy to protect from spy eyes and the like. If there was anywhere on Earth that secrets could be kept in reasonable safety, this was probably one of them.

The plane came down on an airstrip even tinier than the one from which it had taken off, gantzed out of dark earth in a narrow clearing between dense tropical thickets.

When Steve Grayson came back to release Damon from the trick harness he was carrying a gun: a wide-barreled pepperbox. If it was loaded with orthodox shot it would be capable of inflicting widespread but superficial injuries, but it couldn't be classed as a lethal weapon. Were it to go off, Damon would lose a lot of blood very quickly, and it would certainly put him out of action for a while, but his nanomachines would be able to seal off the wounds without any mortal damage being done.

"No need to worry, Mr. Hart," the stout man said. "You'll be safe here until the carnival's over."

"Safe from whom?" Damon asked as politely as he could. "What exactly is *the carnival*? Who's doing all this?"

He wasn't surprised when he received no answers to any of these questions—but the expression which flitted across Grayson's face suggested that the pilot wasn't just tormenting him. Damon wondered whether Grayson had any more idea than he did why he had been paid to bring his prisoner here, or what might be going on.

Damon wondered whether his streetfighting skills might be up to the task of knocking the gun out of the Australian's hand and then kicking the shit out of his corpulent form, but he decided not to try. He didn't know how to activate and instruct the plane's automatic systems, let alone fly it himself, so he had no way of escaping the island even if he could disarm and disable the man.

The air outside the plane was oppressively humid. Damon allowed himself to be guided across the landing strip. A jeep, very similar to the one Karol had used to drive him to the airstrip on Molokai, was parked in the shadow of a thick clump of trees.

A man was waiting in the driving seat of the jeep. He was as short as the pilot but he was much slimmer and—if appearances could be trusted—much older. His skin was the kind of dark coffee color which most people who lived in tropical regions preferred. He didn't have a gun in his hand, but Damon wasn't prepared to assume that he didn't have one at all.

"I'm truly sorry about this, Mr. Hart," the man in the jeep said, in what seemed to Damon to be an overly punctilious English accent, "but we weren't sure that we could persuade you to come here of your own accord and the matter is urgent. Until we can get to the people who have Arnett everyone connected with your family may be in danger." Turning to the pilot he added: "You'd better go quickly, Mr. Grayson. Take the plane to Hilo—then make yourself scarce, just in case."

"Who are you?" Damon demanded as the Australian obediently turned away and headed back to his cockpit.

"Get in, Mr. Hart," the thin man said. "My name is Rajuder Singh. I've known your foster parents for a long time, but I doubt that any of them ever mentioned me. I'm only support staff."

"Did Karol Kachellek arrange this?"

"It's for your own protection. I know how you must feel about it, but it really is a necessary precaution. Please get in, Mr. Hart."

Damon climbed into the passenger seat of the vehicle and settled himself, suppressing his reflexive urge to offer violent resistance to what was being done to him. The jeep glided into a narrow gap in the trees and was soon deep in a ragged forest of neocycads, thin-boled mock conifers, and a dozen other species that Damon couldn't classify at all. The road was narrow but it didn't seem to have any potholes. The island was presumably equipped with a ready supply of men with shovels and buckets, although none was in evidence now.

The forest was quiet, after the fashion of artificially regenerated forests everywhere; the trees, genetically engineered for rapid growth in the unhelpful soil, were not fitted as yet to play host to the overelaborate fauna which ancient tropical forests had entertained before the logger holocaust. A few tiny insects splashed on the windshield of the jeep as it moved through the gathering night, but the only birds whose cries could be heard were seabirds.

"You mustn't blame Dr. Kachellek, Mr. Hart," Rajuder Singh told him blandly. "He had to make a decision in a hurry. He didn't expect you to come to Molokai. Our people should be able to bring the situation under control, given time, but we don't yet know who we're up against and things have moved a little too fast for comfort. He *was* right to do what he did—I'm afraid that you're in more danger than you know, and it might not have been a good idea for you to arrive in Los Angeles on a scheduled flight. I'll show you why in a few minutes' time."

"Who, exactly, are *our people*?" Damon wanted to know.

Rajuder Singh smiled. "Friends and allies," he said unhelpfully. "There aren't so many of us left, nowadays, but we still keep the faith."

"Conrad Helier's faith?"

"That's right, Mr. Hart. You'd be one of us yourself, I suppose, if you hadn't chosen to digress."

"To *digress*? That assumes that I'll be back on track, someday."

Rajuder Singh's only answer to that was a gleaming smile.

"Are you saying that there's some kind of conspiracy involving my foster parents?" Damon asked, unable to keep the aggression from filtering back into his voice. "Some kind of grand plan in which you and Karol and Eveline are all involved?"

"We're just a group of friends and coworkers," the dark-skinned man replied lightly. "No more than that—but someone seems to be attacking us, and we have to protect our interests."

"Might Surinder Nahal be involved with the people attacking you?"

"It's difficult to believe that, but we really don't know yet. Until we do know, it's necessary to be careful. This is a very bad time—but that's presumably why our unknown adversaries chose this particular moment for their assault."

Damon remembered that Karol Kachellek had been equally

insistent that this was a "very bad time." Why, he wondered again, was the present moment any worse than any other time?

The sun had climbed high into the clear blue sky and Damon was finding its heat horribly oppressive by the time the vehicle reached its destination. The destination in question was a sizable bungalow surrounded by a flower garden. Damon was oddly relieved to observe that the roof was topped by an unusually large satellite dish. However remote this place might be it was an integral part of the Web; all human civilization was its neighborhood. The flowers were reassuring too, by virtue of the orderly layout of their beds and the sweet odors they secreted. There were insects aplenty here, including domestic bees.

Rajuder Singh showed Damon through the double door of the bungalow into a spacious living room. When Damon opened his mouth to speak, though, the slim man held up his hand. He swiftly crossed the room to a wall-mounted display screen, beckoning Damon to follow.

"This is the same netboard which carried Operator one-oh-one's earlier messages," Rajuder Singh said while his nimble fingers brought the screen to life.

Damon stared dumbly at the crimson words which appeared there, reading them three times before he accepted, reluctantly, that they really did say what they seemed to say.

He had not known what to expect, but he could never have expected *this*. It was as terrible as it was absurd.

The message read:

> **CONRAD HELIER IS NOT DEAD**
> **CONRAD HELIER NOW USES THE NAME "DAMON HART"**
> **"DAMON HART" IS NAMED AN ENEMY OF MANKIND**
> **FIND AND DESTROY "DAMON HART"**
> **—OPERATOR 101**

fourteen

Madoc Tamlin had had no alternative but to return to his apartment to gather the equipment he needed for his expedition, but he had known that the necessity was unfortunate.

"I want to go with you," said Diana Caisson, in a tone which suggested that she intended to have what she wanted no matter what objections Madoc Tamlin might raise. "You owe me that. *Damon* owes me that."

"I really need someone here to man the phone," Madoc lied. "This business is moving too fast and it's getting seriously weird. If you want to help Damon, here's where you'd be most useful."

"I've been manning your stupid phone for two solid days," Diana told him. "What's the point if you're always out of touch? This is the first time I've clapped eyes on you since we went to visit that idiot boy in the hospital, and I don't intend letting you out of my sight until I get an explanation of what's going on and a chance to help. You owe—"

"I don't owe you anything!" Madoc protested, appalled by her temerity. "Not even explanations. I only let you stay here for old time's sake—you were supposed to be gone by now. You don't have any claim on me at all."

Diana wasn't impressed. "*Damon Hart* owes me explanations. I lived with him for nearly two years. I never knew that he was Conrad Helier's son, and I certainly never knew that he was Conrad Helier himself, and an enemy of mankind. The day after I gave up trying to make our relationship work I found out I'd been living with a trunkful of mysteries, and they've been getting stranger and stranger with every hour that passes. *Two years,* Madoc! I want to know what I wasted my two years on, and if you're Damon's legman in Los Angeles you're the one who has to start paying me off. Wherever you go, I want to go—and whatever you find out, I want to know."

"This wasn't part of the deal," Madoc told her. "I let you stay for a couple of nights when you walked out on Damon—that's not the same as taking you into partnership. One of the things Damon is paying me for is *discretion.* He doesn't want *anyone* knowing what I find out, and he'd certainly include you in that company."

"It's okay for me to carry his messages," she pointed out. "It's okay for me to pass on messages from your pet streetfighter. What's *not* okay for me to know? What is it that your apprentice Webwalkers have turned up that even Interpol isn't supposed to know?"

The problem, Madoc knew, was time. What Interpol didn't know yet, they might very soon find out—and they'd find out all the sooner if he were fool enough to start blabbing to Diana Caisson, even in the privacy of his apartment or his car. It was easier for him to turn up evidence of work done through illegal channels than it was for officers of the law, but this case was now a triple disappearance, with a rich icing of crazier-than-usual Eliminator antics. The police would be making a very big effort now, even if they hadn't before. Whoever had stirred up this hornet's nest had done a thorough job. He had no time to argue with Diana, and the only way to shut her up was to give in on *something.*

Anyway, he rationalized, if he forced her to stay behind that would only increase the danger that she might do something really inconvenient by way of getting her own back—like calling up the LAPD and sending them after him.

"It could be dangerous," he said, knowing that it wouldn't serve as a deterrent.

"It'll probably be less dangerous," she countered, "if we both know exactly what we're trying to do. What have you found?"

Before answering, Madoc collected the last of the crude mechanical tools he'd come back to gather. The men who had broken into Silas Arnett's house hadn't needed cutting gear and crowbars, but Madoc hadn't got the kind of technical backup they must have had, and he was heading for a different kind of house. If it was a fortress, it was likely to be a *brute* fortress, not a sophisticated affair of anxious eyes, clever locks, and mazy software. He was able to shut Diana up with a gesture—but only because the gesture implied that he'd pick up the conversation later.

Finally, he led her to the door of the apartment and let her follow him out. He signaled once again that he couldn't speak, for fear of the eyes and ears with which the walls were undoubtedly sown, and she had perforce to wait until they got into the car. Even then, he insisted on bringing the vehicle out into the street before relaxing slightly.

It was midmorning and the traffic was well below its daytime peak, but it didn't matter—he wasn't headed downtown.

When Diana was certain that he had run out of excuses she repeated her last question, richly salted with seething impatience.

"An address way out east," he told her. "It's not a million miles away from the alleys, but it's not gang turf. Above the ground it still looks derelict, but the word is that some heavy gantzing's been done underneath by way of excavation. The hole's been set up for use as a black-box drop site, supposedly untraceable. Nothing's authentically untraceable, but no one's had a reason yet to send hooks into this one. Harriet's boys tipped her off that something was on, though, and she dug up some background on it, working back from the cowboy contractors who did the gantzing."

"I thought the idea of gantzing was to raise buildings up," Diana objected, "not to dig holes."

"The neobacteria that cement walls together are only part of the gantzing set," Madoc told her wearily. "You have to have others that can unstick things, else you wouldn't be able to shape the product. Moleminers use the unstickers to burrow through solid rock. It's not the ideal way to dig out a permanent cellar or tunnel but it does the trick—and you can use the cementers to harden the walls and ceilings, making sure they'll bear the load. Anyway, that's not the point. Even moonlight labor has to be paid for. The title deeds to the property are locked up tight, but there's a trail leading back from the people who worked on it to one of the people Damon told me to ask about: the one who can't be located in San Diego, Surinder Nahal."

"You think these underground workings might be where Silas Arnett's being held? The Praill girl too?"

"Maybe. Maybe it's something else entirely. All I know is that I need to take a look, and there aren't any spy eyes I can use. The Old Lady dug up some information about the security they installed, but being gantzers rather than silicon men it's mostly solid. Not much of a challenge to a man of my talents, but I guess they didn't want to bring in state-of-the-art stuff because putting a top-quality electronic fence around a supposedly derelict building would look suspicious in itself."

"So we're going to break in and look around?" Diana said, stressing the *we* to make sure that he understood that she had no intention of waiting in the car.

"If we can."

"Suppose *we* get into trouble? Is anybody going to come looking for us? Will anyone know where to look?"

"It's not that kind of deal, Di—but if we *were* to vanish from human ken, the Old Lady would put two and two together. She'd tell Damon."

"Damon? Not the police."

"He's the man who's paying us—and one of the things he's paying for is discretion."

"What else have you found out?"

"Like I said," Madoc retorted obstinately, "one of the things he's paying for is discretion."

"If he'd been discreet enough not to use my body in his porno-tapes, I wouldn't be here," Diana said, "but he did and I am. When he talked to me he said it was no big secret, but that was probably a lie. *Is* Damon really Conrad Helier, like the last notice said?"

"Don't be ridiculous," Madoc said. "I knew him when he was barely starting to shave and I nursed him practically day by day from his first fight to his last. Believe me, I've seen enough of him over the last ten years to know that he isn't a hundred and thirty-seven years old trying to pass for twenty-six. He's exactly what he appears to be—and that includes the fact that he's Damon Hart and not Damon Helier anymore. If Operator one-oh-one wants some lunatic to take a shot at Damon, it's not because anyone thinks he's an enemy of mankind unworthy of immortality—it's because Operator one-oh-one now thinks Damon may be dangerous to *him.* Maybe he knows that the Old Lady and I have been sniffing around—maybe he thinks that I'm getting too close for comfort."

"If he thinks *that,*" Diana pointed out, suffering a sudden attack of logic, "we're probably riding straight into a trap."

"Do you want to get out?" Madoc asked. "If you do, better do it now. The badlands start at the end of the street."

"I'm sticking to you like gantzing glue," she told him stiffly. She didn't believe what he'd said about the Operator getting spooked because he and the Old Lady had got too close. Neither did he—but he'd had to say something, to cover up the fact that he hadn't the slightest idea why anyone would draw Damon into the game and then make a show of setting him up for target practice.

As they passed from the well-tended streets into an unreclaimed district Madoc slowed down slightly and checked for signs of pursuit—but when he found none he speeded up again. If Damon hadn't sent an e-mail canceling the instruction that Madoc should meet him at the airport Madoc would have been in a quandary about whether to delay the adventure, but since

Damon had decided to stay away for a while longer Madoc felt that the whole burden of action was on his shoulders, and that he had to press on as quickly as possible.

"I'm here because I care, you know," Diana said defensively. "I walked out on Damon because he hurt me, but it was as much for his good as for mine—to make him see what's happening to him. I still love him."

"I'd never have guessed," Madoc muttered, with savage irony.

"You don't understand," she said flatly.

"That's a matter of opinion. I should have left you tied and gagged at my place. If I had any sense . . ."

"If you had any sense, Maddie," she told him, "you'd have a nice safe job with PicoCon—an honest job, with prospects. There's no real profit in living on the edge, you know. It might be more fun, but it won't take you anywhere in the long run. The day of the buccaneers is long gone."

This new argumentative tack was even more irritating than the one she'd set aside. "Did Damon tell you that?" Madoc said acidly. "Did you consider the possibility that he might have been trying to convince himself? There's *always* scope for buccaneers. Rumor has it that the best and boldest of the old ones are still alive, if not exactly kicking. Adam Zimmerman never died, so they say—and if Conrad Helier didn't, my bet is that he's sleeping right next door." He realized, belatedly, that he had been so concerned to score the debating point—off Damon rather than Diana—that he had let discretion slip a little.

Diana didn't seem to realize that she'd just got a partial answer to her question about what else he'd found out while digging on Damon's behalf. "Who's Adam Zimmerman?" she asked, attacking the more basic question.

"The guy who set up the Ahasuerus Foundation. Known in his own day—or shortly thereafter—as the Man Who Cornered the Future or the Man Who Stole the World. Born some time before the turn of the millennium, vanished some time after."

"But he'd be more than two hundred years old," Diana objected. "The oldest man alive only passed a hundred and sixty a year or two back—the news tapes are always harping on about the record being broken."

"The record only applies to those alive *and kicking,*" Madoc told her. "Back in the twentieth century, people who wanted to live forever knew they weren't going to make it to the foot of the escalator. Some elected to be put in the freezer as soon as they were dead, looking forward to the day when it would be possible to resurrect them and give them back their youth. Multimillionaires who couldn't take it with them sometimes spent their dotage pouring money into longevity research, stone-age rejuve technologies and susan—that's short for suspended animation. Long-term freezing did a lot of damage, you see—very difficult to thaw out tissues without mangling all or most of the cells. The tale they tell is that Zimmerman tried to ride a susan escalator to the foot of the emortality escalator, commissioning the foundation he established to keep him alive and ageless by whatever means they could, until the time becomes ripe for him to wake up and drink from the fount of youth. Now *that's* bold buccaneering, wouldn't you say."

"And you think Conrad Helier went to Ahasuerus in search of a similar deal?" Diana said, picking up the point which he shouldn't have let fall. "You think he *might* be still alive, and that if he is, that's where Ahasuerus comes in."

"I don't think anything," Madoc said, wishing that he could sound more convincing, "but if there's some kind of interesting link between Ahasuerus and Helier, that would be a candidate. It's impossible to say—Ahasuerus is stitched up very tight indeed. They're *very* keen on privacy. It's partly a hangover from the days when they faced a lot of hostility because of their founder's reputation, but it's more than just a habit. Who knows how many famous men might be lurking in the vaults, sleeping their way to immortality because they were born too early to make it while awake? I'd be willing to bet that there wouldn't be one in ten that the Eliminators would consider *worthy of immortality.*"

For once, Diana had no reply ready. She seemed to be thinking over the implications of this intriguing item of urban folklore, which obviously hadn't come her way before. It hadn't come Madoc's way either, but the Old Lady had a long memory.

It was perhaps as well, Madoc thought, that Diana had finally fallen silent. There was work to be done, and if she intended to play her part she'd need to keep her head.

Madoc stopped the car, then checked the deserted street and its glassless windows very carefully, searching for signs of movement or occupation. There was no sign that anything was amiss. At night there would have been rats, cats, and dogs roaming around, but at noonday those kinds of scavengers stayed out of sight.

He reached under his seat to pick up the bag he'd brought from the apartment, opening it briefly to pull out a couple of the items he'd stashed within it.

"Are we here?" Diana asked—and then, without waiting for an answer, added: "Is that a *crowbar*?" Obviously she'd had her mind on higher things while he'd been getting the stuff together.

"No," he said, "and yes. That is, no, we still have a couple of blocks to walk, on tiptoe—and yes, it's a crowbar. Sometimes scanners and slashcards are second best to brute force. You *do* know how to tiptoe, don't you?"

"I can be as quiet as you," she assured him, "but it seems silly to tiptoe in broad daylight."

"Just go carefully," Madoc said, with a slight sigh, "and carry this." He gave her a flamecutter, refusing to listen to her protest that it was at least three times as heavy as the crowbar and twice as heavy as whatever remained in the bag.

Madoc got out of the car and closed the door quietly. Diana did likewise. He set off along the rubble-littered pavement, treading as carefully as he could. She followed, matching his studied quietness.

When they got to the particular ruin that he was looking for, Madoc set about examining its interior with scrupulous patience. There were no obvious signs of recent gantzing on the crumbling walls, but a host of tiny details inside the shell revealed to Madoc's forewarned eye that this was not the rubble heap it pretended to be. In a corner of the room that was furthest away from the street he found the head of a flight of stone steps leading down into what had been a cellar, and once he'd eased aside the charred planks that were blocking the way down it was easy enough to see that the door at the bottom was perfectly solid. When he'd tiptoed down to it he found that it had two locks, one of which was electronic and one of which was crudely mechanical. Madoc put the crowbar aside for the moment and set to work with a scanner.

It took two minutes of wizardry to release the electronic lock, and five of patient leverage to dislodge the screws holding the mechanical lock. Madoc eased the door open and stepped gingerly inside, checking the corridor within before letting Diana in behind him. No attempt had been made to conceal the fact that the walls had been recently gantzed.

When Diana had pulled the door closed behind her Madoc plucked a flashlight from his satchel and switched it on. The flashlight showed him that the corridor was at least twenty meters long, and that it had another door at the further end. There were several alcoves let into the walls, which might or might not hide further doors. Fixing the field of illumination on the floor ahead of him, Madoc began to move deeper into what now seemed to him to be an unexpectedly complex network of cellars. He figured that all the inner doors would be locked at least as securely as the one through which they'd come, and that it might require considerable effort to locate the one behind which the excavation's real treasures were concealed. As things turned out, however, the first shadowy covert let into the corridor wall turned out to have no door within it—it was simply a portal giving uninterrupted access to a room about three meters by four.

The floor of the room was even more glittery than the sandgantzed exterior of the PicoCon building; it looked almost as if it had been compounded out of broken glass. Stretched out on the gleaming surface, with both arms awkwardly outstretched, was a blackened humanoid shape which Madoc mistook at first for some kind of weird sculpture. It was, in fact, Diana who first leaped to the more ominous conclusion, which Madoc deduced when her sharp intake of breath hissed in his right ear.

"Oh shit," he said. He had seen dead bodies before—he had even seen burned bodies before—but he had never seen human remains as badly charred as these. A little of the ash that had once been flesh had dusted onto the floor, as if the pitch-dipped skeleton had shed an eerie shadow. On the corpse's tarry breast, however, was something innocent of any fire damage: a VE pak, placed atop the dead man's heart. If it had been resting on a tabletop, Madoc would have whisked it away into an inside pocket without a moment's delay, but he hesitated to take it from where it had been so carefully set. It looked uncomfortably like bait in a trap.

"Do you think that's Silas Arnett?" Diana asked. Her voice fractured as she spoke the words, so that the whisper became louder than she had intended.

"I hope not," Madoc said—but he had no idea who to hope it might be instead. He might have hoped that it was an ancient corpse which had lain undiscovered for years, but his nose would have told him otherwise even if the floor on which it lay and the object set upon it had not been products of contemporary technology.

They were both still hovering in the doorless entrance, uncertain as to whether they dared to approach and crouch down to examine the body, when the door at the far end of the corridor opened with a considerable crash. Madoc instantly stepped back, using the flashlight to see what was happening.

Two men had come through the door: men with guns in their hands.

By the time he heard their warnings and recognized the weapons they were holding out before them, Madoc's panic had already been leavened by a certain relief. It could have been worse. It *could* have been the people who had killed the poor bastard stretched out on the floor and torched his corpse. Compared with men capable of such an act as that, the police could only seem gentle. Madoc had been under arrest a dozen times before, and had survived every time.

Obediently, he dropped the flashlight on the floor of the corridor, and the tool kit too. He even raised his hands before stepping back into the room from which he'd just emerged.

"Well," he muttered to Diana, who was trying to see over his shoulder, "you wanted in, and you're in. I only hope you can talk your way out again."

The two cops moved confidently forward to complete the arrest. As soon as they had relaxed, Madoc grabbed Diana, maneuvered her through the empty doorway, and shoved her with all the force he could muster along the corridor toward the oncoming cops. She had raised her own arms, and her hands grappled for purchase as she cannoned into the two men and tried to stop herself falling.

While the cops tried to catch her, and to save themselves from being bowled over, Madoc plucked the VE pak off the chest of the blackened corpse with his left hand while the right groped for the crowbar. Once he had both items securely within his grip he moved forward with a ruthless determination befitting the trainer and master of the best streetfighters in the city.

As he had told Diana, gentler methods were sometimes second best to simple brute force. He hoped that this would prove to be one of those times.

PART THREE

Brute Force and Gentler Methods

Fifteen

During the hours when the last vestiges of his internal technology had tried their damnedest to maintain some semblance of function Silas Arnett had felt like a turtle floating beneath the surface of a stagnant pond. It was as if his self-consciousness had been immersed in murky, cloying depths which lay upon him like a horrid dead weight, compacting his bodily mass.

In the meantime, his weary and leaden eyes had looked out into a very different world: a world that was all light and color and action where there seemed to be no weight at all.

Now, he felt that he was the same turtle rudely stripped of its shell. His frontier with the outer world was exposed to all manner of assaults and horribly sensitive. He could hardly believe that thousands of generations of human beings had lived their entire lives becalmed in flesh as awkward and as vulnerable as this. The novelty of the experience had already worn off—and the process of psychological readaptation was neither as radical nor as difficult as he had feared—but the sensitivity remained.

No matter how still Silas sat, simple existence had become a torrent of discomforts. The straps at his wrists and ankles chafed his skin, but that was not the worst of it. The worst of it was that he could not scratch his itches, although the fact that he could not alter his position save by imperceptible shifts of weight and strain was almost as bad.

It was torture of a kind, but the wonder of it was that it was not *real* torture. No pincers had been applied to his nipples, no electric shocks to his genitals, no hot irons to his belly, no slivers of bamboo to his fingernails. It was as if he had been prepared for the operating theater only to discover that the surgeon had been called away . . . and had left no word as to the likely time of his return. He had been thoroughly insulted, in body and in mind, but no dire injury had as yet been added to the insult.

What made this all the more puzzling was the tape he had been shown of his "trial," whose maker had taken the trouble to include one very audible—and rather realistic—scream, and had made some effort to imply that others had been edited out of the package.

The trial scene was gone now, and Silas was in a very different virtual environment—one which mimicked the texture of visual reality reasonably faithfully. The room in which his prison chair now seemed to be standing was also mostly white. It had white walls and a cream carpet, and its ceiling was uniformly lit by a gentle artificial bioluminescence which had very little color in it.

Silas knew that the universe of virtual reality was overabundantly well-equipped with white rooms. Far too many of the people who specialized in VE design cultivated a thorough understanding of the hardware and software they were using while neglecting the development of their own creative imagination and aesthetic sensitivity. It was becoming routine for software engineers and "interior decorators" to form up into "renaissance teams," although youngsters like Damon Hart always figured that they could do everything themselves. Silas did not assume, however, that this particular white room was a convenient fiction. Life always imitated art, and he could easily believe that the place of his confinement had been decorated in imitation of an elementary VE.

The man who stood before Silas in the white room was not a judge. He was wearing Conrad Helier's face, but any halfway competent VE engineer could have contrived that—there was a vast reservoir of archive film which could be plundered for the purpose of making a template. "Conrad" was wearing a white lab coat, but that seemed blatantly incongruous to Silas. Conrad had never been a man for white coats.

"I don't understand," Silas said. "The trial tape even *looks* like a fake. You didn't need me at all. You could have put that farce together without any of the snippets of actual speech that you borrowed. If you already knew what you were going to put in my so-called confession, why did you bother throwing all those questions at me?"

He knew, even as he made this speech, that it was ridiculously optimistic to suppose that the fact that he had not been hurt *yet* meant that he was not going to be hurt at all, but he was telling the simple truth when he said that he didn't understand.

"It's useful to have some authentic footage on which to build," said the man in the Conrad Helier mask, in Conrad Helier's voice, "but the only thing I *really* needed from you was your absence from the world for the three days which it would take to flush out your IT and reduce you to the common clay of unaugmented human flesh."

"Why have you bothered to do that," Silas wanted to know, "if you didn't intend to use real screams in your little melodrama? *Do* you intend to interrogate me under torture, or are you just making the point that you could have if you'd wanted to?"

"There you are," said the man who was not Conrad Helier. "You *are* beginning to understand. I knew you could. If only you'd been able to understand a little earlier, all this might not have been necessary. The world has changed, you see—a whole century has passed since 2093. It may have been unlike any other century in history, by virtue of the fact that many of the people who really *mattered* in 2093 are still alive in 2193, but it still packed in more extravagant changes than any previous century. Whatever the future brings, it will never produce such sweeping changes again. *You*'ve changed too, Silas. You probably seem to yourself to be exactly the same person you were at twenty-six, but that's an understandable illusion. If you could only look at yourself from a detached viewpoint, the changes would be obvious."

"So what?"

The fake Conrad Helier was already standing at ease, but now he put his hands into his pockets. In the sixty years that he had known him, Silas had *never* seen Conrad Helier put his hands into his pockets.

"It used to be reckoned that people inevitably became more conservative as they got older," the man in the white coat said, with only the faintest hint of irony in his earnest expression. "Young men with virile bodies and idealistic minds, it was said, easily embraced utopian schemes for the radical transformation of society. Old men, by contrast, only wanted to hang on to the things they already had; even those who hadn't made fortunes wanted to hang on to the things they were used to, because they were creatures of habit. The people who spoke out against technologies of longevity—and there *were* people like that, as I'm sure you can remember—often argued that a world ruled by the very old would become stagnant and sterile, fearful of further change. They prophesied that a society of old people would be utterly lacking in potency and progressive zeal, devoid of any sense of adventure.

"They were wrong, of course. Their mistake was to equate *getting older* with *nearing the end.* The old became conservative not because of the increasing number of the years they'd lived but because of the dwindling number of the years that still lay before them. The young, whose futures were still to be made, had a strong vested interest in trying to make the world better as quickly as was humanly possible; the old, who had little or no future left, only wanted to preserve what they could of their old and comfortable selves. Things are very different now. Now, the prospect of true emortality lies before us, like the light at the end of a long dark tunnel. Not everyone will make it all the way to the light, but many of us will and we *all* live in hope. The old, in fact, understand that far better than the young.

"The young used to outnumber the old, but they don't now and never will again; the young are *rare* now, a protected species. Although the future which stretches before them seems limitless, it doesn't seem to them to be *theirs*. Even if they can still envisage themselves as the inevitable inheritors of the earth, the age at which they will come into their inheritance seems a very long way off and likely to be subject to further delays. It's hardly surprising, therefore, that the young are more resentful now than they have ever been before. It is the old who now have the more enthusiastic and more constructive attitude to the future; they expect not only to live in it, but also to *own* it, to be masters of its infinite estates."

"I know all this," Silas said sullenly, wishing that his itches were not so defiantly unscratchable.

"You know it," said the man masked as Conrad Helier, "but you haven't *understood* it. How, if you understood it, could you ever have thought of *retirement*? How, if you understood it, could you waste your time in pointless and undignified sexual encounters with the authentically young?"

"I can live my own life any way I choose," Silas told his accuser coldly. "I'm not just old—I'm also free."

"That's the point," said the ersatz Helier. "That's why you're here. You're *not* free. Nobody is, who hopes and wants to live forever. Because, you see, if we're to live forever, we have to live *together*. We're dependent on one another, not just in the vulgar sense that the division of labor makes it possible to produce all the necessities of life but in the higher sense that *human* life consists primarily of communication with others, augmented, organized, and made artful by all the media we can devise. We're social beings, Silas—not because we have some kind of inbuilt gregarious instinct but because we simply can't do anything worthwhile or be anything worthwhile outside of society. That's why our one and only objective in life—all the more so for everyone who's a hundred and fifty going on a hundred and fifty thousand—ought to be the Herculean task of making a society as rich and as complex and as *rewarding* as we possibly can."

"The only reason I'm not free," Silas replied tersely, "is that I've been strapped to a fucking chair by a fucking maniac."

Conrad Helier's face registered great disappointment. "Your

attitude is as stupidly anachronistic as your language," he said—and went out like a switched-off light, along with the virtual environment of which he was a part. Silas was left entirely to himself.

Silas was stubbornly glad that he had had an effect on his interrogator, but the effect itself was far from rewarding. In the darkness and the silence he was alone with his discomforts, and his discomforts were further magnified by lack of distraction. He was also acutely aware of the fact that he had failed to obtain answers to any of the questions which confronted him—most urgently of all, what would happen to him now that Operator 101 had released his slanders onto the Web?

Mercifully—although mercy may not have been the motive—he was not left in the dark and the silence for long.

His senses of sight and hearing were now engaged by a kaleidoscopic patchwork of fragments excerpted from old and nearly new VE tapes, both documentary and drama. If there was any pattern of relevance in the order in which they were presented to him, he could not discern it—but he became interested in spite of that, not merely in the individual snatches that had been edited together but in the aesthetic experience of the sequence.

He "walked" on the surface of Mars, surveying the roseate desert and looking up into the tinted sky at the glaring daystars. He saw the rounded domes where the human Martians lived and watched the glass facets sparkle and glint as he changed his position. Then, on the horizon, he "saw" the crazy-tale castles of the Mars of obsolete dreams, the skycars riding the imagination-thickened air—and dramatic music crashed through the brief, golden silence. . . .

He saw earth-moving machines on the fringe of the Australian superdesert, laying out the great green starter plane which would begin the business of soil manufacture, bridging the desiccation gap which had deadened the land in spite of all life's earlier attempts to reclaim it. A sonorous voice-over pumped out relentless adspeak about the technical expertise behind the project: glory, glory, glory to the heroes of the genetic revolution. . . .

He saw a gang fight in the derelict suburban wasteland of a city he couldn't name: young men costumed and painted like crazy fetishists, wielding knives and razors, eyes wild with adrenalin and synthetic ecstasy, living on and by the edge. He watched the vivid blood spurt from wounds, and he winced with sympathy because he knew full well that these would-be savages must be equipped with relatively primitive internal technology, which provided elementary protection against permanent injury but left them horribly vulnerable to pain and the risk of death. He heard their bestial cries, their wordless celebration of their defiance of civilization and all its comforts, all its protective guarantees. . . .

It was as if the virtual aspect of the life of modern man were being condensed into a stream of images. Silas couldn't help but feel annoyed about the fact that his captors seemed hell-bent on *educating* him, but the process had a curious fascination of its own. Much of the imagery was, of course, "reality-based"—videotapes of actual events reformatted for VE playback, sometimes in 2-D, sometimes in 3-D—but even in the documentary material, reformatted footage was juxtaposed and mingled with synthesized material produced by programmers. Today's programmers were almost good enough to synthesize lifelike fictions, especially when they used templates borrowed from reality-based footage which could be mechanically animated and subtly changed without losing their photographic appearance.

With only a hood at his disposal, Silas couldn't obtain the full benefit of such illusions, most of which were designed to provide tactile sensations with the aid of a full-body synthesis suit, but the detachment that was heir to limitation made it all the more difficult to tell the reformatted real from the ersatz.

Silas saw himself standing by Conrad Helier's side, listening to the older man saying: "We must regard this new plague not as a catastrophe but as a challenge. It is not, as the Gaian Mystics would have us believe, the vengeance of Mother Earth upon her rapists and polluters, and no matter how fast and how far it spreads it cannot and will not destroy the species. Its advent requires a monumental effort from us, but we are capable of making that effort. . . ."

He saw two women, naked and oiled, caressing one another sinuously, engaged in carefully choreographed mutual masturbation, first with fingers and then with tongues, moving ceaselessly, putting on an ingeniously artful and tantalizing display for voyeurs. The soundtrack was soft music, overlaid by heavy breathing and gasps of simulated ecstasy, and the flesh of the two women seemed to be taking on a life of its own, a strange glow. Their faces were changing, exchanging features; they seemed to flow and merge, as though the two were becoming one as the carefully faked climax approached. . . .

Silas recognized this as one of his foster son's compositions, as crudely and garishly libidinous as one might expect of a *young* man's imagination. He was glad when it was replaced by scenes from a food factory, where tissue cultures were harvested and processed with mechanical efficiency and hygiene by robot knives and robot packagers.

After that there was more Conrad Helier, this time in closeup—which meant that it was probably faked. "We must be sure," the probably fake Conrad was saying, "that our motives are pure. We must do this not to secure an advantage for ourselves, but for the sake of the world. It is time to set aside, for the last time, the logic of the selfish gene, and to proclaim the triumph of altruistic self-awareness. The first children of the New Utopia must be not the children of an elite; they must be the children of everyman. If we ourselves are to have children we must allocate ourselves the lowest priority, not the highest."

The viewpoint swung around to bring Eveline Hywood's face into embarrassingly intimate focus. "It's the privilege of gods to move in mysterious ways," she said laconically. "Let's not tie ourselves down with self-administered commandments that we'll surely have occasion to break and break again."

Conrad Helier's disciples had, in fact, bound themselves with edicts and promises—and had kept them, after a fashion. Silas believed that he had kept them better than most, in spite of the heresies which had crept upon his mind and condemned him, in the end, to confusion. He had kept almost all his promises, if only in order to ensure that whatever else he lost, he would have *clean hands.*

Now he was looking out at the factory again, at the robot butchers working clinically, tirelessly, and altruistically for the greater good of ambitious humankind. He presumed that the image was meant to be symbolic, but he refused to try to figure out exactly what it was symbolic of, and why it had been laid before him now.

The robot butchers tirelessly plied their gleaming instruments for a few seconds more, and then dissolved into a vision of cars racing through city streets, speeded up until they were little more than colored blurs, racing ceaselessly past.

But it is true, he reflected, that some of those of us who are left over from the old world remain anchored to that world by our habits of mind. Some of the old haven't yet become accustomed to the new outlook, and perhaps I'm one of them—but we can't be expected to shed the superficialities of our heritage as easily as a snake sheds its skin. We do evolve—but we can't do it overnight. Conrad would have understood that. Whoever is using his face must be younger than Conrad, and younger than me—but not as young as Damon. He surely belongs to the new old, not to the true old.

The scene changed again; this time it was an episode of some popular soap opera, but the characters were mercifully silent. As they exchanged insults and bared their overwrought souls they were rendered impotent and absurd by silence. A girl slapped a man across the face; without the sound track there was no telling why, but the blow wasn't halfhearted. These days, blows rarely were. Nobody pulled their punches for fear of hurting people, because everybody knew that people couldn't be hurt—even "primitives" had some degree of artificial insulation from actual bodily harm. Hardly anyone went entirely unaugmented in the world, and the prevailing view was that if they wanted to do so, they had to accept the risks.

All the old inhibitions were dying, Silas reminded himself, in an appropriately grim fashion. A radically different spectrum of dos and don'ts was establishing itself in the cities of what would soon be the twenty-third century.

Silas's head, isolated within its own private pocket universe, took off from the cape, mounted atop a huge sleek rocket. His eyes were looking up into the deepening sky, and the sound which filled his ears was a vast, angry, undeniable roar of pure power, pure *might*.

It went on, and on, and on. . . .

In the end, Silas couldn't help but call out to his tormentors, to beg them to answer his questions, even to lecture him like a recalcitrant schoolboy if they felt the need. He knew as he did it that he was proving them right, demonstrating that the limits of his freedom extended far beyond the straps binding him to his ignominy, but he no longer cared. He wanted and needed to know what they were doing to him, and why, and how long it would last.

He wanted, and needed, to *understand,* no matter what price he had to pay in patience and humility and craven politeness.

Sixteen

"The message was dumped shortly after you boarded the plane at Kaunakakai," Rajuder Singh told Damon, when the import of the words displayed on the screen had had time to sink in. "When Karol decided to send you here instead of Los Angeles he couldn't have foreseen anything as outrageous as this, but it's better proof than any he *could* have imagined that his instincts were right."

"If he had such faith in his instincts," Damon said sourly, "why didn't he do me the courtesy of explaining what he wanted me to do, and why?"

"He thought that telling you his plan would make it impossible to carry through. He seems to be of the opinion that you always do the opposite of anything he suggests, simply because it's his suggestion."

Damon could understand how Karol Kachellek might have formed that impression over the years, but he felt that it was an injustice nevertheless. The matters on which he had habitually defied Karol in his younger days had all been trivial; he was now an adult and this was *not* a trivial matter. "It's crazy," he said, referring to the message. "It's completely crazy."

"Yes it is," said the dark-skinned man. "Denials are going out, of course—not just from our people but from Interpol and the doctors who attended the womb in which your embryo developed. Your progress from egg to adult has been mapped as scrupulously as that of any individual in the history of the world. The lie is astonishingly blatant—but that only makes it all the more peculiar. It's attracting public attention and public discussion, I'm afraid. Together with Silas Arnett's supposed confession, it's getting coverage on the worst kinds of current affairs and talk shows. I suppose any man who lives a hundred and twenty years might expect to make a few enemies, but I can't understand why anyone would want to attack *you* in this bizarre way. Can you?"

It occurred to Damon that some of the people he had ordered Madoc Tamlin to investigate might have resented the fact—and might possibly be anxious that the buying-power of Conrad Helier's inheritance might pose as great a threat to their plan as Interpol or the friends and allies of Silas Arnett. All he said to Rajuder Singh, however, was: "No, I can't."

"It'll be a nine-day wonder, of course," Singh observed, "if it even lasts that long. Unfortunately, such slanders sometimes linger in the mind even after convincing rebuttals have been put forward. It really was the best course of action to remove you from harm's way as quickly as possible. We're truly sorry that you've been caught up in all this—it really has nothing to do with you."

"What *has* it to do with?" Damon asked, his voice taut with frustration. "What are you people up to and who wants to stop you? Why is this such a *bad time* for all this to blow up?"

"I can't tell you what we're doing," Singh said, with a note of apology in his voice that almost sounded sincere, "and we honestly don't know why we're being attacked in this fashion. All I can say is that we're doing everything we can to calm the situation. It can only be a matter of time before Silas is found, and then. . . ."

"I'm not so sure of that," Damon said, cutting short the string of platitudes. "Maybe he will be found and maybe he won't, but finding him and catching the people who took him are two different things. This whole thing may look amateurish and stupid—just typical Eliminator nonsense taken to a new extreme—but it's not. That tape of Silas could have been edited to look real but it was edited to *look fake.* All the artlessness in this seems to have much subtler thought behind it—and real power too. The kidnapping itself is a case in point—a confusing compound of the brutal and the clever. The same is true of my involvement: one day I'm getting sly messages pushed under my door, the next I'm being publicly denounced in an incredible fashion. In between times, the girl Silas was entertaining is spirited away—but not until *after* the police have questioned her, investigated her thoroughly, and decided that she's not involved. To add even further to the sum of dissimulation, while Karol Kachellek is busy insisting that there's absolutely nothing for me to worry about he's actually planning to have me bundled up and sent to some stupid mock-volcanic island in the middle of nowhere where even the local ecology is a blatant fake."

"I really am sorry," Rajuder Singh assured him. "Alas, it's not for me to explain matters even if I could. I think that Eveline Hywood might be willing to take your call, though, once we've gone down."

"Down where?"

Damon had so far been under the impression that the room he was in had only three doors, one of them part of a pair. Singh had closed the double doors through which they had entered but two others stood half-open, óne offering a glimpse of a bedroom while the other gave access to a narrow corridor leading to a kitchen. Singh now demonstrated the error of Damon's assumption by going to the wall alongside the kitchen door and pressing a hidden switch of some kind. A section of "wall" slid aside to reveal an empty space—presumably an elevator.

"So the mountain's hollow as well as fake," Damon said incredulously. "Down where the magma ought to be there's some kind of secret laboratory, where my father's old research team is laboring away on some project too delicate to be divulged to the world."

"It's not a laboratory," Singh told him. "It's just a hiding place.

There isn't any legion of white-coated workers conducting secret experiments—although I suppose it's possible that someone thinks there's more going on here than there is. The original setup was built more than a hundred and fifty years ago—long before we acquired it, of course—as a nuclear bunker. It was a rich man's fantasy: a hidey-hole where he and a few friends could wait out the coming holocaust. The plague wars were running riot at the time and the fear of escalation was acute. A hundred years after the bunker was built—still some little time before the island came into *our* hands—someone equally rich and equally paranoid expanded it with the aid of primitive gantzers. I presume that he was more anxious about an asteroid strike or some other natural disaster than about nuclear war, but I don't know for sure. I suppose it would still be capable of fulfilling any of those functions, were the need to arise."

"But *you* aren't interested in anything as absurdly melodramatic as that, of course," Damon said sarcastically.

Singh was standing beside the open door, politely indicating that Damon should precede him into the empty space. Damon stayed where he was, waiting for more answers.

"We're interested in privacy," Singh told him brusquely. "It's an increasingly rare commodity in a world of rampant nanotechnology. We're interested in independence—not political independence, just creative independence."

"And this *we,* I suppose, comprises Karol Kachellek and Eveline Hywood—if she should ever return to Earth—and other old chums of Conrad Helier. Maybe you even have Conrad Helier himself hidden away down there, dead to the world but still slaving away at all the labor of creation that God somehow left undone? Perhaps that's what Operator one-oh-one believes, at any rate."

"Please, Mr. Hart," the thin man said plaintively.

"I'll find out what this is all about eventually," Damon told him, "one way or another." He was wary enough not to let bravado lead him to give too much away, though. It might be inadvisable to boast about Madoc Tamlin's capabilities to people who might be just as reluctant to be found out as the mysterious Operator 101 was.

The words displayed on Singh's screen suddenly disappeared, to be replaced by an urgently flashing message which simply said: READ NOW. The system had presumably been programmed with nets set to trawl the cyberspatial sea for items of a particular kind, and one of them had just made contact.

"You'd better come look at this," Damon said.

Singh was reluctant to come away from the open elevator, but he did come. When he saw the message, though, his suspicious expression cleared. "Excuse me," he murmured, as he moved to obey the flashing injunction.

When the thin man's skeletal fingers brushed the keypad beneath the screen the flashing words were replaced by an image of a man sitting on a perfectly ordinary chair. Damon was not in the least surprised to recognize Silas Arnett. Silas was no longer under any obvious restraint, but there was a curious expression in his eyes, and both of his hands were heavily bandaged. He began speaking in a flat monotone.

Damon knew immediately that the image and the voice were both fakes, derived with calculated crudity from the kind of template he used routinely in his own work.

"The situation was out of hand," the false Arnett said dully. "All attempts to limit environmental spoliation by legislation had failed, and all hope that the population would stabilize or begin to decline as a result of individual choice was gone. We were still winning the battle to provide enough food for everyone, even though the distribution system left seven or eight billions lacking, but we couldn't cope with the sheer physical *presence* of so many people in the world. Internal technology was developing so rapidly that it was obvious to anyone with half a brain that off-the-shelf emortality was less than a lifetime away, and that it would revolutionize the economics of medicine. Wars over lebensraum were being fought on every continent, with all kinds of weapons, including *real* plagues: killing plagues.

"When Conrad first put it to us that what the world needed

more desperately than anything else was a full stop to reproduction—an end to the whole question of individual choice in
matters of fecundity—nobody said 'No! That's horrible!' We all
said 'Yes, of course—but can it be done?' When Conrad said
'There's always a way,' no one challenged him on the grounds of
propriety.

"I couldn't see how we might go about designing a plague of
sterility, because there were no appropriate models in nature—
how could there be, when the logic of natural selection demands
fertility and fecundity?—and I couldn't envisage a plausible
physiology, let alone a plausible biochemistry, but Conrad's way
of thinking was quite different from mine. Even in those days, all
but a few of the genes we claimed to have 'manufactured' were
actually simple modifications of existing genes or the chance
products of lab-assisted mutation. We had little or no idea how
to go about creating genes from scratch which would have entirely novel effects—but Conrad had a weird kind of genius for
that kind of thing. He *knew* that he could figure out a way, using
the somatic transformer packages that were then routinely used
to treat genetic deficiency diseases.

"I wonder, sometimes, how many other groups must have had
conversations very like ours. 'Wouldn't it be great if we could design a virus that would sterilize almost everyone on earth without the kinds of side effects that accompany pollution-induced
sterility?' . . . 'Yes, wouldn't it—what a shame there's no obvious place to start.' Was there anywhere in the world in the 2070s
where bioengineers gathered where such conversations *didn't*
take place? Maybe some of the others took it further; maybe
they even followed the same thread of possibility that Conrad
pointed out to us. Maybe Conrad wasn't the only one who could
have done it, merely the one who hit the target first. I don't
know—but I do know that if you'd put that kind of loaded pistol into the hand of any bioengineer of the period the over-
whelming probability is that the trigger would have been
squeezed.

"We had no desire to discriminate: we set out to sterilize

everybody in the world—and we succeeded. That's what saved the world from irredeemable ecocatastrophe. If the population had continued to increase, so that nanotech emortality spread like wildfire through a world which was still vomiting babies from billions of wombs, nothing could have restrained the negative Malthusian checks. The so-called plague wars had already proved themselves inadequate to cut population drastically in a world of advanced medical care, but there were plenty more and even nastier weapons to hand. The world really was set to go bad in a big way; all that remained for sane men to do was exercise the least worst option, and that's what Conrad Helier did.

"What happened in the last decade of the twenty-first century and the first decades of the twenty-second wasn't a tragedy at all—but the fact that it was *seen* as a tragedy, and a terrible threat to the future of the species, increased its beneficial effects. The Crash was a common enemy, and it created such a sense of common cause, focused on the development of artificial wombs and the securing of adequate supplies of sperms and ova, that for the first time in history the members of the human race were all on the same side.

"We're still living on the legacy of that break in history, in spite of attempts made by madmen like the Eliminators to set us all at one another's throats again. We're still all on the same side, all engaged in the same ongoing quest—and we have Conrad Helier to thank for that. You have no conception of the debt which the world owes to that man."

"You don't regret what you did, then?" asked a whispery voice from off-stage.

"No," said Arnett's simulacrum dispiritedly. "If you're looking for some sign of repentance, forget it. What we did was necessary, and *right.*"

"And yet you've kept it secret all these years," the voice observed. "When you were first accused of having done this, you denied it. When you realized that further denial was useless, you attempted to take sole responsibility—not out of pride, but out of a desire to protect your collaborators. The truth had, in the end, to be extracted from you. Why is that, if you aren't ashamed of what you did?"

"Because there are people in the world like *you,*" the ersatz Silas countered unenthusiastically. "Because PicoCon and the other purveyors of cheap longevity have ensured that the world is still overfull of people whose moral horizons are absurdly narrow and horribly bleak. For every person alive in 2095 who would have understood our reasons, there were half a hundred who would have said 'How dare you do this to *me?* How dare you take away *my* freedom of self-determination, even for the good of the world?' Too many people would have seen sterilization as a theft, as a loss of power.

"Many young people nowadays, born into a world of artificial wombs, find it frankly repulsive that women ever had to give birth like wild animals—but too many members of the older generations still feel that they were robbed, changed without their consent. Karol Kachellek and Eveline Hywood are still doing important work; they never wanted to be sidetracked by the kind of publicity the revelations which you've forced out of me would generate—*will* generate, I suppose."

"What right did you have to make decisions for all mankind?" the second synthetic voice asked, still maintaining its stage-whisper tone. "What right did you have to play God?"

"What gave us the right," Arnett's image replied, the voice as relentlessly dull as it had been throughout, "was our understanding. Conrad had the vision, and the artistry required to develop the means. The responsibility fell to him—you might as well ask what right he had to surrender it to others, given that those others were mostly ill-educated egomaniacs whose principal short-term aim was to slaughter their neighbors. Someone had to be prepared to *take control,* or the world was doomed. When you know that people won't accept the gift of their own salvation, you have only two choices: to force it on them, or to leave them to destruction. It was better for the world to be saved—and it was better for the world to believe that it had been saved by a fortunate combination of miracles rather than by means of a conspiracy of scientists. Conrad always wanted to do what was best for the world, and keeping our actions secret was simply a continuation of that policy."

"What of the unhappiness caused by the frustration of maternal instinct?" asked the interrogative voice, in a tone devoid of any real indignation. "What of the misery generated by the brutal wrench which you administered to human nature? There are many—and not merely those who survived the Crash—who would argue that ours is now a perverted society, and that the reckless fascination with violence which is increasingly manifest in younger generations is a result of the perversion of human nature occasioned by universal sterilization."

"The empire of nature ended with the development of language," the fake Arnett replied. "Ever since then, human beings have been the product of their technology. All talk of human nature is misguided romantic claptrap. The history of human progress has been the history of our transcendence and suppression of the last vestiges of instinctive behavior. If there was any maternal instinct left in 2070, its annihilation was a thoroughly good thing. To blame any present unhappiness or violence on the loss or frustration of any kind of genetic heritage is both stupid and ridiculous."

There was an obvious cut at this point. The next thing Arnett's image said was: "Who told you about all this? It can't have been Karol or Eveline. Somebody must have put the pieces together—somebody with expert knowledge and a cunning turn of mind. Who?"

"That's of no importance," the other voice said. "There's only one more matter which needs to be determined, and that's the identity which Conrad Helier adopted after faking his death. We have reason to believe that he reappeared in the world after an interval of some twenty-five years, having undergone extensive reconstructive somatic engineering. We have reason to believe that he now uses the name Damon Hart. Is that true, Dr. Arnett?"

"Yes," said the voice which sounded like Arnett's, ringing false because his head was bowed and his lips hardly moved. "The person who calls himself Damon Hart is really Conrad Helier. It's true."

The tape ended there.

"I wonder how many other installments there are to come," Damon said.

Singh's lips moved as if he intended to reply, but he choked off the sound of the first syllable as his ears caught another sound, faint and distant.

Damon cocked his own ear, straining to catch and identify the sound. "Helicopters," he said, when he had leaped to that conclusion. Singh, who was evidently a more cautious man than he, had not yet made the same leap—but when Damon said it he was ready to believe it.

"We have to go down," Singh said. "There's no time to lose!"

"They're only *little* helicopters," Damon said, using expertise gained from hours spent watching sportsmen whizz over the beaches of California. "The kind you can fold up and store away in the back of a van. They must be local—they wouldn't have the range to get here from Lanai." Instead of obeying Rajuder Singh's urgent request to go to the elevator he moved toward the window that looked out in the direction from which the noise was coming.

"It doesn't matter how small they are," Singh complained, becoming increasingly agitated. "What matters is that they're not *ours*. I don't know how they got here, but they're not here on any kind of routine business—and if they're after somebody, it has to be you."

Seventeen

Damon knew, deep down, that he ought to do as Rajuder Singh said. The sensible thing to do was to move to the elevator and let it carry him down to the hidey-hole beneath the fake volcano, not merely because that was the way that safety lay, but also because he might find answers down there to some of his most urgent questions. He also knew, however, that Karol Kachellek's estimation of his reflexive perversity had a good deal of truth in it. Obedience had never been his strong suit.

"There's plenty of time," he said to Rajuder Singh, although he knew that there wasn't.

He peered out of the window, looking up at the crowns of the trees that fringed the flower garden. The thick foliage blocked out the greater part of the sky and anything that might be flying there—but not for long.

When the first tiny helicopter finally came into view, zooming over the topmost branches of the nearest trees, Damon's first reaction was to relax. The machine wasn't big enough to carry human passengers, or even a human pilot. The sound of its whining motor was like the buzz of a worker bee, and he knew that the AI guiding it could not be any more intelligent than a worker bee. As it passed rapidly out of sight again, wheeling above the roof of the bungalow, Damon turned back to Rajuder Singh, intending to reassure him—but the expression on the other man's face told him that Singh was not about to be reassured, and his own composure began to dissolve. In a world of rampant nano-tech, small did not mean harmless—far from it.

It occurred to Damon then to wonder where the tiny machine—and its partner, which was already visible—had come from. Such toys had insufficient range to have been launched from Lanai or Kahoolawe, but if they had not come from another island, they must have come from the deck of a ship. What ship? How had it come to be here so soon after his own arrival—unless that arrival had somehow been anticipated?

"Please, Mr. Hart," said the desperate Rajuder Singh, coming forward as he spoke and reaching for a pouch suspended beside his beltpack. Damon guessed immediately what it was the thin man was reaching for, and was struck by the sudden thought that he didn't know *for sure* whose side Rajuder Singh was on. Everything the man had told him had seemed plausible enough—but the fact remained that Steve Grayson had *kidnapped* him and brought him here against his will. What if it had *not* been Karol Kachellek who had given the order? What if Karol Kachellek had sent the helicopters in hot pursuit from the deck of the *Kite?*

As the miniature gun came out of its hiding place Damon reacted with a streetfighter's instinct. He hadn't been able to do anything about Grayson's weapon, but the situation was different now. The blow he aimed with the edge of his right hand was delivered with practiced efficiency, knocking the hand which held the gun aside. That left Singh's midriff wide open, and Damon lashed out with his right foot, ploughing his heel into the thin man's solar plexus. The sudden shock put Singh down, as it would have put anyone down, no matter how efficient his internal technology was. Singh's mouth had been open as he prepared to speak, but all that came out now was a sharp gasp of surprise. Damon pinned the thin man's right arm to the floor with his foot and knelt down in order to pluck the weapon out of his hand.

The gun was a darter, even less powerful than Grayson's pepperbox. It was incapable of inflicting any lethal injury, although its darts were presumably capable of inducing paralysis for several minutes, until his internal technology could rally itself to cancel out the effects of the toxin.

Singh pried his right arm loose and tried to grab the gun, wailing: "You don't understand!"

Damon lifted the weapon out of his captive's reach but didn't hit him again. "Nor do you," he muttered through clenched teeth.

The noise of the whining helicopters was louder now; both machines were hovering close to the house, perhaps coming in to land. They were descending slowly, presumably because the machines were delicate and the available space between the flower beds was by no means generous.

Now there was another sound audible beyond and beneath the whine of the toys: a much deeper drone, of the kind a *real* helicopter might make. There was no possibility that a *real* helicopter could have been launched from the deck of the *Kite*—but there *was* a possibility that the big machine was in pursuit of the little ones rather than complementing their mission. All was confusion, and confusion heaped upon confusion—and Damon had not the slightest idea what he ought to do next. He only knew that he had to make up his mind very quickly.

Under more relaxed circumstances, Damon might have been able to take advantage of Rajuder Singh's obvious distress. He felt that if he were to demand answers to his questions under the threat of further violence, he would probably get them. The thin man's eyes were flickering wildly from side to side, as if he expected to be shot at any moment—but there was no time for questions. Damon had to make his move, and there were only two ways to go: inside or outside.

As he moved toward the double door that would let him out into the tangled forest, the window at which he had been standing mere moments before imploded with a deafening roar. One of the tiny helicopters had shot it out. While Damon and Singh were still ducking away from the blast, arms raised against fly-ing shards, two objects flew through the broken window. As they bounced across the carpet they began pumping out smoke.

Thanks to his misspent youth, Damon was able to recognize the objects and the belching smoke. He knew that he hadn't time to get through both the doors that stood between him and fresh air—but the elevator door was still wide open, less than three meters away. Singh was already headed for it, without even both-ering to come to his feet.

Damon couldn't beat the dark-skinned man to the open door but he managed a tie. He couldn't pull the other man back but he hauled him to his feet so that he could reach out a slender fin-ger and punch the button that would close the door behind them.

They had beaten the smoke, although a little of its stench lin-gered in the trapped air as the elevator began its descent.

Damon still had hold of Singh, and he shoved him up against the back wall of the elevator before pressing the barrel of the darter to his neck. "Don't ever threaten me again, Mr. Singh," he growled theatrically. "I really don't like it."

"I'm s-*sorry,*" the slender man gasped, desperate to spit the words out. "I only wanted. . . ."

"I *know* what you wanted," Damon said, releasing his hold and lifting his hand reflexively to his face, as if to shield his nose and mouth from the few smoke particles that had accompanied them into the elevator. "You'd already *told* me what you wanted."

Singh breathed a deep sigh of relief as he realized that no fur-ther violence would be done to him, and that he had achieved his object in spite of all the difficulties. Damon didn't want him re-laxing too much, so he made a show of pointing the gun at him.

"You're not out of the woods yet," he said grimly. "If there's anything I don't like waiting for us down below, you could still end up with a belly full of needles."

"It's all right," the thin man said quickly. "There's nothing down below but a safe place to hide. I haven't lied to you, Mr. Hart! I just had to get you down below, before you were hurt."

Now that there was time to make the play, Damon pointed the gun at his companion's face and tried to make his own expression as fearsome as he could. "Who are you *really* working for?" he demanded.

"Karol Kachellek," the other said plaintively, with tiny tears at the corners of his frightened eyes. "It's all true! I swear it. You'll see in a minute! You'll . . ."

The agitated stream of words died with the elevator light. The descent stopped with an abrupt lurch.

"Oh shit!" Damon murmured reflexively. This was a development he had not expected. He had assumed—as Singh clearly had—that once the elevator doors had closed they were safe from all pursuit.

"It's impossible," Singh croaked, although it clearly wasn't.

"Is there anyone down below at all?" Damon asked, abruptly revising his opinion as to the desirability of finding a reception committee awaiting his arrival.

"No," said Singh. "It's just . . ."

"A safe place to hide," Damon finished for him. "Apparently, it isn't."

"But the systems are secure! They're supposed to be tamperproof!"

"They might have been tamperproof when they were put in," Damon pointed out, belatedly realizing the obvious, "but this is the age of rampant nanotechnology. PicoCon's current products can get into nooks and crannies nobody would even have noticed twenty years ago. They got to Silas, remember—this is mere child's play to people who could do that. The only question worth asking is how they knew I was here—if it *is* me they've come for. If they have a ship, it must have been here or hereabouts before Grayson took off from Molokai."

The lights came back on again, and the elevator lurched into motion. Unfortunately, it began to rise. Damon immediately began to regret the delay caused by his stubborn perversity. If he'd only come into the elevator when Singh had first invited him, they'd surely have been able to get all the way to the bottom before his pursuers could stop them. Whether that would have qualified as safety or not he couldn't tell, but he was certain that he was anything *but* safe now.

Rajuder Singh must have reached the same conclusion, but he didn't bother to complain, or even to say "I told you so."

Damon ostentatiously turned the gun away from Rajuder Singh, pointing it at what would soon be the open space left by the sliding door. He knew that the room would still be filled with poisonous smoke, and that anyone who had got to the console in the middle of the room in order to send a return signal to the elevator would have to be wearing a gas mask, but that didn't mean that they'd be armored against darts. One shot might be enough, if only he could see a target—and even the larger helicopter which had followed the two miniatures couldn't have been carrying more than a couple of men. If he could hold his breath long enough, there might still be a chance of getting outside and into the welcoming jungle. It was a one in a million chance, but a chance nevertheless.

"They must have been waiting," he muttered to Rajuder Singh. "But they couldn't have known what Karol would do, even if they figured that I'd fly to Molokai. They must have been here because they were keeping watch on *you,* waiting to take action against *you."*

"That's impossible," Rajuder Singh said again. "I'm just support staff."

"But you're sitting on a secret hidey-hole," Damon pointed out. "Maybe there isn't anything down there to interest them—but they don't know that. Maybe they really do think that Conrad Helier's there, directing Karol's operation. Maybe this was always part of their plan, and my presence here is just an unfortunate coincidence. Maybe they don't give a damn about you *or* me, and only want access to the bunker. . . ."

Damon could have gone on. His imagination hadn't even come near to the limit of its inventiveness—but he didn't have time.

The elevator stopped again, although the lights stayed on this time.

Bitter experience had told Damon to take a long deep breath, and that was what he did. As the doors began to open, before the gas could flood in, he filled his lungs to capacity. Then he threw himself out into the smoky room, diving and rolling as he did so but keeping his stinging eyes wide open while he searched for a target to shoot at.

There was no target waiting; the room was devoid of human presence.

His ill-formed plan was to get to the doors that led outside, and get through them with all possible expedition. He managed to make it to the inner door easily enough and brought himself upright without difficulty—but the door was locked tight. He seized the grip and hauled with all his might, but it wouldn't budge. He was fairly certain that Singh hadn't locked it, and he knew that it wouldn't matter whether the thin man was carrying a swipecard capable of releasing the lock. There wouldn't have been time, even if the other had been right behind him—which he wasn't.

Damon immediately turned for the window, even though he knew full well that it wouldn't be easy to exit past the jagged shards of glass that still clung to the frame. His long stride carried him across the room with the least possible delay, but his eyes wouldn't stay open any longer and his nose was stinging too. By the time he reached the window he felt that he couldn't hold on any longer—but he knew that there was fresh air outside.

Damon grasped the window frame with his free hand, steadying himself as he let out his breath explosively. Then he stuck his head out into the open, in the hope of gathering in a double lungful of untainted air, while the hand that held the gun groped for a resting place on the outer sill.

Someone standing outside plucked the dart gun neatly out of his hand. Damon tried his utmost to force his stinging eyes open, but his reflexes wouldn't let go. He never saw who it was that turned the darter against him and shot him in the chest.

The impact would probably have hurt a good deal worse if Damon hadn't sucked in just enough smoke to make him gag and befuddle his senses. As it was, he felt almost completely numb as he reeled backward.

The next breath he took was so fully impregnated with smoke that he must have passed out immediately—or so, at least, it seemed when he woke up with a sick headache and found himself lying prone on a ledge, looking down the sheer slope of an incredibly high mountain.

Eighteen

Damon was no more sensitive to heights than the average man, but the sight confronting him would have shocked anyone into instant acrophobia. He looked downward at a face of bare gray rock that plummeted for miles. The bottom of the chasm was visible because it was lit up like the face of a full moon on a clear night, but it seemed so very far away that the notion of it's being connected to his present station by an actual wall of rock was so incredible as to be horrible.

He felt cold sweat break out on his face as terror grabbed him, and he recoiled convulsively, squeezing his eyes shut and pulling his head back from the rim. He rolled over without even caring what might be behind him, but when he was supine he opened his eyes again to look up, and gasped once again in alarm.

The steep slope extending upward from the left-hand edge of the narrow ledge on which he lay was not as extensive as the chasm that lay to his right, but it posed no threat, but there was a certain sinister malignity in its frank impossibility. The mountain was topped by a building that was lit as brightly and as strangely as the chasm floor, so that every detail of its construction stood out sharp and clear against a cloudless and starless sky.

It was a castle of sorts, with clustered towers and winding battlements, but it was compounded out of crystals, as if it had been gantzed from tiny shards of glass and the litter of a jeweler's workshop. The walls were not transparent, nor were they even straightforwardly translucent; they were shining brightly, but the manner of their shining was an outrage to logic which played tricks with his mind's procedures of visual analysis. As he stared at the amazing structure he saw that its towers were linked by crisscrossing bridges whose spans were impossibly knotted, and that its ramparts were decorated with ascending and descending staircases which faded into one another in perspective-defying fashion. It was magnificent—all the more so because it was so far above him, separated by a slope so sheer and forbidding.

There was no path up the mountain—no way the castle could be approached without climbing several kilometers of hostile rock face. Its existence was no more plausible than that awful abyss, which would have plunged halfway to Earth's molten core had it been in the world he knew: the *real* world.

Damon shut his eyes again. Safe in that darkness, he pulled himself together.

It's just a VE, he assured himself. It's clever, but it's just a VE full of optical illusions.

Carefully, he began to run his fingers over his limbs. His fingers registered the texture of his suitskinned flesh; the muscles of his belly and his thighs registered the passage of his fingers. He assumed that the suitskin must be an illusion and that he must really be wearing a synthesuit delicately wired to reproduce the sensations of touch. It was obviously state-of-the-art, given that the movement of his fingers seemed so very natural, but all such suits had limitations of which he was very well aware.

He put his right forefinger into his mouth, running it back and forth over his teeth and tongue. Then he touched his closed eye and gently depressed the eyeball. Then he passed his hand back over the crown of his head, feeling the texture of his hair and the vertebrae of his neck. Finally, he put his hand inside the collar of the virtual suitskin and shoved his hand into his armpit; when he withdrew it he sniffed his fingers.

None of these sensations were capable of synthesuit duplication, at least in theory. Taste and odor were beyond the present limits of synthesuit sensoria; eyeballs were reserved for confrontation with the screen and couldn't be touched; every synthesuit required input cabling, which was usually situated at the rear of the head or the back of the neck. All four tests had failed to reveal any deception; according to their verdict, everything he had seen was real.

And yet, he told himself, it must be a virtual environment, because no such real environment exists. However improbable it seems, this is a charade. I don't know who has the equipment to play such a trick, or how they're doing it, or why, but it's a trick and nothing more. It's just a trick.

"You can open your eyes, Damon. It's perfectly safe." Damon didn't recognize the voice.

He opened his eyes, hoping that the VE into which he'd woken might have changed into something far more accommodating.

It hadn't. The impossible building still sat atop the impossible mountain, against the backdrop of the impossible sky. He *knew* that he was safe, but it was extremely difficult to believe it. Damon's reflexes fought to shut his eyes again, but his consciousness fought to keep them open. It was a hard fight, but reason won.

During the last five years Damon had spent a great deal of time in VEs of every marketed and marketable kind, searching for better illusions of reality in order that he might become a better architect of artificial spaces. He needed to be able to cope with this—indeed, he needed to come to terms with it, to master it, and, if possible, to find out how it was done and how he could do likewise.

When he was sure that he could keep his eyes open he deliberately moved back to the rim of the ledge and extended his head into the position it had been in when he first opened his eyes. He wanted to look down again. He *needed* to look down again, in order to sustain his credentials as an artist in virtual realities, a virtuoso of illusion.

Vertigo seized him like a vice, but he fought it. Knowledge conquered sensation. He looked into the abyss and knew that he would not fall.

Only then did he move again, coming back from the rim and scrambling into a sitting position. He set his back against the upper cliff face and extended his legs so that his ankles were balanced on the lip he had just vacated. *Then* he turned, to look at the person who had spoken to him.

The figure was as strange as the world which contained him. His shape was human, and recognizably male, but his body was literally mercurial, formed as if from liquid metal. He shone with reflected radiance, but the light which flowed across his contours as he moved was as deceptive as the light which flowed through the walls and spires of the crystal castle, defying all the experience of Damon's educated eyes.

For a moment or two, Damon wondered whether this gleaming silver exterior might be a new kind of synthesuit—a kind which extended into the mouth and nasal cavities as well as covering the eyeball, and which needed no input cable. Could it be a monomolecular film of some kind, as perfectly reflective as a mirror or chrome-plated steel? It was just about plausible, although meetings in VEs usually hid the equipment required to produce and perpetuate the illusion. When he worked on his illusions from within, Damon typed his instructions on a virtual keyplate.

He looked down at his own body, half expecting to see that he too had turned to mercury, but he hadn't. He recognized the blue-and-gray suitskin he seemed to be wearing as one of his own, but it was not the one he had been wearing when Steve Grayson had carried him away to Rajuder Singh's island.

"Who are you?" Damon demanded of the mercury man. The shape of the apparition's face did not seem familiar, although he was not sure that he could have recognized someone he knew reasonably well were their features to be transformed to a fluid mirror in this remarkable fashion.

"I think you can probably figure that out," the other replied.

"My name doesn't matter. It's what I am and where we are that counts. You did very well. Not everyone can learn to cope with worlds like this, and few can adapt so quickly—but the real test will come when you try to fly. That requires genuine artistry and limitless self-confidence."

"So *what* are you?" Damon demanded, determined to take matters one at a time and to follow his own agenda.

"I like to think of this as Mount Olympus," the mercury man told him, ignoring the question. "Up there, the palace of Zeus—impossible, of course, for mere human eyes to figure—where Apollo, Aphrodite, Ares, and Athena have their separate apartments. Down there, the earth, unquiet even by night with the artificially-lit labor and the radiant dreams of billions of men."

"The illusion's magnificent," Damon conceded. "Far better than anything I ever thought *I* could make—but you'll spoil it all if you insist on talking nonsense. You went to a great deal of trouble to bring me here. Why not tell me what it is that you want?"

"Fair enough," said the mirror man agreeably. "I'd like you to get a message to your father. We can't find him, you see—and while we can't find him, it's rather difficult to negotiate with him. We've tried talking to his underlings, but they simply aren't licensed to be *flexible*. We rather hoped he might be hiding out on that artificial island, but he isn't; all we found was you."

"Conrad Helier's dead," Damon said wearily.

"We're *almost* ready to believe that," the apparition conceded, "but not quite. It *is* conceivable that it's only his spirit that lives on and that Eveline Hywood is pulling the strings herself, but you'll understand our scepticism. We live in a world of deceptive appearances, Damon. You only have to look at me to realize why we aren't prepared to take anything on trust."

Damon didn't have any ready answer to that.

"It's the same with the people at Ahasuerus," the mercury man continued. "They're obsessed with the continuation of Adam Zimmerman's plan, and they refuse to see that all plans have to adapt to changes in the world's circumstances. That's why we sent you to them—we figured that we might as well trap both wayward birds with a single net, if we can. There's always the possibility, of course, that the foundation has your father salted away in the same cold place as Adam Zimmerman, but we don't think it's likely. Your father isn't the kind of man to settle for an easy ride to Ultima Thule via suspended animation."

By this time, Damon had found his answer. "If Conrad Helier isn't dead," he said, "he's certainly not disposed to let me know it. Karol doesn't trust me, and neither does Eveline. Even Silas never gave me the slightest reason to think that Conrad Helier is alive. Anyhow, if you think he's still guiding Eveline and Karol, you only have to leave your message on their answerphones."

"It's not as easy as that, as you know very well. When I say that we want you to get a message to him, I mean that we want you to get *through* to him. We want him to listen. We think that you might be the person to do that for us. Karol and Eveline are only his hirelings, and they'll be dead within thirty or forty years. You're his son, and he must at least hope, if he doesn't actually believe, that you might live for a thousand years. I know that he poses as a lover of all mankind, making no discrimination between rich and poor, worthy and unworthy, but he took the trouble to have a son and to deliver that son into the patient care of his most trusted confidants. Doesn't that suggest to you that the plans he makes for the future of mankind are really plans for *your* future—or at least that he imagines you as a central figure, somehow symbolic of the race as a whole?"

"If he did, and if he *were* alive, I'd be a great disappointment to him," Damon said shortly. "I've my own life to lead. I'm not interested in delivering messages for you."

"It's a little late to make that decision," the mirror man observed.

Damon could see what he meant. What his captors wanted, apparently, was to get through to whoever was running Conrad Helier's operation—and Damon had obligingly hopped on a plane to Molokai, calling in on the Ahasuerus Foundation en route. He'd also unleashed Madoc Tamlin—and thus, in all likelihood, every outlaw Webwalker on the West Coast. He'd already collaborated as fully as anyone could have desired in the mission of *getting through* to Karol Kachellek. The only person he hadn't quite got through to, yet, was Eveline Hywood.

"None of this makes sense," Damon complained. "None of it was *necessary*. You're just playing games."

"Perhaps we are," the mirror man admitted, "but we aren't the only ones. Your father started this, Damon—our moves have been made in response to his, and he's still responding to ours. He should have come to the conference table the night we took Silas Arnett hostage, but he called our bluff. I suppose you realize that the second tape of his supposed confessions was theirs, not ours? It was a move we hadn't anticipated—a sacrifice we thought he wouldn't be prepared to make. We didn't anticipate that Karol Kachellek would send you off to the island either, but that may have worked out to our advantage. Naming you was a rather crude response, but the Operator one-oh-one pseudonym was about to become useless and it seemed politic to increase the general confusion. We're suitably impressed by your father's initiative and his fighting spirit, but it doesn't alter the situation. He shouldn't try to keep us out. He *mustn't* try to keep us out, Damon. It's not that we want to stop what he's doing—but we can't let him do it *alone*. The world has changed, Damon. We can't tolerate loose cannons. The day of *little* conspiracies, like your father's and Adam Zimmerman's, is long gone. Now they have to submit to the same discipline as the rest of us."

"I don't have the least idea what you're talking about," Damon said, "and I still believe that Conrad Helier's been dead for nearly fifty years." The latter statement was a straightforward stalling move, intended to slow things down while he tried to fathom the implications of what the mirror man was saying.

"We have confidence in your ability to figure it out," the apparition told him. "We also have confidence in your ability to see reason. You're fully entitled to resent the way we've used you, but we hope that you might be prepared to forgive us."

"I'm not the forgiving type," Damon retorted, although he knew that it wasn't the diplomatic thing to say.

The mirror man ignored the futile threat. "What do you think of the quality of the VE?" he asked.

"It's forced me to revise my estimate of what can and can't be done," Damon admitted. "I didn't think *any* kind of bodysuit would ever get this close to reproducing the minutiae of tactile experience. It makes the kind of work I do seem rather childish."

"It's next-generation technology. Now that you know it *can* be done, can you guess how?"

"Not exactly. I suppose it has to be done with some kind of new nanotech, using a synthesuit that's even thinner than a suit-skin."

"It's an interesting idea, but it's headed in the wrong direction. You're not in any kind of bodysuit. You're lying down on a perfectly ordinary bed, fast asleep. This is a lucid dream."

Damon quelled a reflexive response to deny the possibility. He knew that research into the mechanisms of dreaming had been going on for more than a hundred years, attended all the while by speculations about taped dreams that would one day be bought off the supermarket shelf just like VE paks, but he'd always believed the sceptics who said that such speculations were unreasonably wild, and that the plausibility of the notion was just an accountable illusion, like the plausibility of telepathy. "You're right about one thing," he said drily. "If you can do that, I ought to be able to work out who you are. There can't be more than a handful of research teams who've got within a light-year of that kind of device."

"It's all done by IT," the mercury man told him equably. "It's easy enough to operate the switch in the hypothalamus which prevents instructions to the motor nerves generated in dreams getting through to the body, while preserving the *illusion* that you're acting and reacting as you would in everyday life. Sensory information is filtered through a similar junction whose functions can be just as easily usurped. It doesn't require millions of nanomachines to colonize the entire structure of the brain—it only requires a few thousand to stand in for the neuronal gate-keepers that are already in place. The whole set up isn't that much more complicated than a synthesuit—but it's so much neater to wear the suit inside instead of out, and it saves a small fortune on your electricity bill. As you can see, it gives the VE a texture much more like reality, even if the information is incredible. It also allows the programmers to build in facilities which reproduce things you can sometimes do in dreams but never in real life. As I told you earlier, the *real* test of your psychological adaptability is whether you can step off that ledge believing that you can fly."

Damon was uncomfortably aware of the fact that his chosen career—the design of virtual environments for use with ordinary commercial hoods and synthesuits—had just been revealed to be a blind alley. Unless he could adapt his skills to the coming regime of manufactured dreams, everything he'd ever done and everything he currently planned to do would be consigned to the scrap heap of obsolescence.

"When will this hit the market?" he whispered.

"That's an interesting question," said the mirror man. "In fact, it's a question which cuts to the heart of the emergent philosophy of the new world order. For hundreds of years, people have been developing products *for the market:* for the purposes of getting rich. Even artists got sucked into it, although the motive forces involved in their creativity—as I'm sure you understand very well—usually went far beyond the vulgar necessity of making a living. The sole raison d'être of the so-called mothercorps was to make as much money as possible as rapidly as possible. The defining feature of the Age of Capital was that money became an end instead of a means. The richest of men became so very rich that they couldn't possibly spend what they had, but that didn't stop them trying to make more and more. Money ceased to be mere purchasing power and became a *measuring device*—a way of keeping score of the position and prestige of individuals within the great competition that was the world. Every new discovery was weighed in the balance of the market, assessed according to its power to *make money*. Do you understand why that age is now over, Damon? Do you understand why everything has changed?"

"Has it changed?" Damon asked sceptically. "Maybe the people you know are so rich they no longer bother keeping score, but everyone I know needs all the money they can lay their hands on, because the purchasing power of money is their only hope of staying one step ahead of the Grim Reaper and riding the escalator to eternity."

"Exactly," said the mirror man, as if Damon were agreeing with him rather than disputing what he'd said. "That's exactly the point. Money has retained its power because the ultimate product isn't yet on the market. Until we have authentic emortality at a fixed price, the pursuit goes on and on—and while even the richest of men knew full well that he couldn't take his money with him when he died, all the money in the world could be nothing to him but a means of keeping score. But that's no longer the case, as Adam Zimmerman was the first to understand and demonstrate.

"Now every rich man—perhaps every man of moderate means—understands perfectly well that if he can only hang around long enough for the appropriate technologies to arrive, he *will* have the chance to live forever. *That* becomes the end, and money merely the means. We're already living in a postcapitalist society, Damon—it's just that many of our fellows haven't yet noticed the fact or fully understood its significance. Your father understood the fundamental point long ago, of course— which makes it all the more frustrating that he doesn't seem to be able to grasp its corollaries. I suppose it's because he prides himself on being a scientist, too fine a man to dirty his hands with mere matters of economics. We have to make him take those blinkers off, Damon. We can't let him go ahead with what he's doing while he's still wearing them."

"What *is* he doing?" Damon wanted to know.

"I'd rather not be the one to fill you in on the details," the mirror man told him blithely. "As long as you're curious, I know you'll keep niggling away at Kachellek and Hywood. We might need you to do that if our latest moves don't do the trick. If Helier *still* won't come to the conference table we'll need you to keep nagging away on our behalf until he does."

"And if I won't?"

"You won't be able to help yourself," the mirror man told him, with insulting confidence. "You can't kill curiosity—it has nine lives. In any case, your father will have to take you back into the fold. He can't leave you alone and exposed after all that's happened. We've called attention to you—whatever they believe or don't believe, the Eliminators are interested in you now. Your worthiness is under examination. We don't approve of the Eliminators, of course—not *officially*—but we like the fact that they take things seriously. We like the fact that they raise the important question: *who* is worthy of immortality? That's what this is all about, you see. What kind of people ought to inherit the earth, in perpetuity? What kind of people must we become, if we intend to live forever? Eliminator violence is just childish jealousy, of course—but the question remains to be answered. We don't want to eliminate Conrad Helier, or the Ahasuerus Foundation, but we *do* want them to understand that if they want to play games they have to play by the rules. If we're going to live forever, we all have to play *as a team*."

Damon had found it so uncomfortable to stare into the apparition's reflective face that he had spent most of the conversation staring into space or at his own hands, but now he looked directly at the convex mirrors which were the mercurial man's robotic eyes.

"You don't seem to me to be much of a team player," he said. "You seem to me to be trying to play God, just as you've accused Conrad Helier of doing. 'As flies to wanton boys—' "

"We haven't killed anyone," the mirror man said, cutting him off in midquote. "Like Conrad Helier, we take a certain pride in that. As for playing God—well, there *was* a time when your father could say 'If we don't who will?' but that time is over. This is Olympus, Damon—the place is positively lousy with would-be gods, and that's why we all have to work *together*. That's what your father has to understand. You have to persuade him that it's true, if no one else will."

"I can't."

The mirror man dismissed his stubbornness with a casual gesture. He stood up, his movement impossibly fluid and graceful. No real body could have moved like that. "Are you ready to fly?" he asked, implying with his tone that Damon wasn't.

Damon hesitated, but he stood up without taking the helping hand that the mirror man had extended toward him.

"This is just a VE," he said. "No matter how clever it is, it's just a VE. I can step over that ledge, if I want to. No harm can come to me, if I do none to myself."

"That's right," the mirror man told him. "In this world, all your dreams can come true. In this world, you can do *anything* you have a mind to do." His hand was still extended, but Damon still refused to take it. Had he done so, it would have been a gesture of forgiveness, and he wasn't the forgiving type.

Damon remembered the sermon he'd preached to Lenny Garon, about the danger of believing that all injuries could be mended, and the wisdom of not taking too many risks in life lest one miss the escalator to emortality. He didn't think of himself as a hypocrite, but he knew full well that he hadn't ever practiced what he'd preached—and he hoped that his long practice would come to his rescue now. He wasn't about to let the mirror man's challenge pass unmet, and he wasn't about to accept the mock-paternal helping hand. If he were to fly, he would fly alone.

He stepped to the very edge of the abyss, spread his arms wide as if they were wings, and jumped.

Perhaps he could have flown, if he'd only known how, or even if he'd only had enough faith in himself—but he didn't.

Damon fell into the awful abyss, and terror swallowed him up.

He lost consciousness long before he reached the bottom, and was glad to be received by the merciful darkness.

Nineteen

When Damon awoke he was not in pain, but his mind seemed clouded, as if his brain were afflicted by a warm and clammy mist. He had endured such sensations before, when his internal technology had been required to deal with the aftermath of drink or drugs. In such circumstances, even the most vivid dream should easily have drifted into oblivion, but the unnaturally lucid dream of the mirror man clung tight to memory, and the legacy of that final fall was with him still.

When he finally forced his eyes open he found that he was, as the mirror man had insisted, lying on a bed, wearing neither a hood nor a bodysuit. He looked down at himself to find that he was dressed in the same suitskin he had been wearing when he stepped into the elevator with Rajuder Singh. It was not noticeably dirtier than it had been then, but there was a ragged tear in the middle of his chest that hadn't had time to heal.

He sat up. The bed on which he was lying had a heavy iron frame that gave it the appearance of a genuine antique, although it was presumably there for utility's rather than art's sake. His right wrist was handcuffed to one of the uprights.

It took him a few seconds to realize that his was not the only bed in the room, and that he was not the only prisoner it held. He blinked away the mucus that was still obscuring his vision slightly and met the inquisitive gaze of his companion. She was not as tall as recent fashion prescribed, but he judged that she was nevertheless authentically young. Her blond hair was in some disarray, and she was handcuffed just as he was, but she didn't seem to be in dire distress.

"Who are you?" he asked dully.

"Catherine Praill," she told him. "Who are you?"

"Damon Hart," he replied reflexively—a second or two before the significance of what she had said sunk in. He reached up with his free hand to rub the sleep from his eyes. His hand was trembling slightly.

"Are you all right?" the girl asked. She seemed a little tremulous herself—understandably, if she too had been kidnapped by the man of mercury and his associates.

"Just confused," he assured her. "Do you know where we are?"

"No," she answered. Then, as if fearing that her bluntness might seem impolite, she added: "I've heard of you. Silas mentioned your name."

Damon inferred that she hadn't been in a position to keep tabs on the Eliminator boards, or she'd surely have mentioned Operator 101's last message before recalling that Silas Arnett had "mentioned his name."

"I've heard of you too," he said. "Lenny Garon told me you'd disappeared."

"Lenny?" She was genuinely astonished by the introduction of *that* name. "How did he know? I hardly know him. Didn't he leave home or something?"

"He asked after you when your name came up in connection with Silas Arnett's kidnapping. How long have you been here? Who brought you?"

She recoiled slightly under the pressure of the doubled-up questions. "I don't know anything," she protested defensively. "I was in a car—the police were taking me home after questioning me. I must have dozed off. I've been awake for about an hour but I haven't seen anyone except you. I don't feel hungry or thirsty, so I can't have been asleep very long—but if you think *you're* confused. . . ." She left it at that.

"So you've no idea what day it is, I suppose, or where we might be?" Damon looked around the room for clues, but there were no obvious ones to be seen. There was nothing visible through the room's only window but a patch of blue sky. The patterned carpet that covered the floor looked as old as the bedstead, but it was probably modern. It was faded but quite free of dust and crumbs—which suggested that it had a suitskin capacity to digest waste. A closet door that stood ajar showed nothing but bare boards and empty hangers. There was a small table beside Damon's bed on which his beltpack and sidepouch had been placed, and the only item there which had not been on his person when he succumbed to the gas was a glass of clear liquid. It was easy enough to reach, and he picked it up in both hands so that he could take a sip. It was water.

"I don't know anything at all," Catherine Praill repeated, her voice increasing its note of alarm. "I don't understand why they brought me here. Are they holding us to *ransom*?"

She pronounced the word as if the possibility were almost unthinkable—a revenant crime from a more primitive world. Was it unthinkable, though? Was *anything* unthinkable now? In a world where every child had eight or ten parents, might not the potential rewards of kidnapping-for-cash come to outweigh the risks, especially given the awesome powers which these kidnappers seemed to possess?

"I don't think so," Damon told her. "It wouldn't make much sense. But then—I don't know anything either. It's not for lack of information—I simply can't separate the truth from the lies. I don't know what to believe."

"My foster parents will be worried. I didn't have anything to do with Silas being kidnapped. The men from Interpol seemed to think that I did, but I didn't. I would have helped them if I could."

"It's okay," Damon told her. "Whoever brought us here, I don't think they mean to do us any harm."

"How do you know?" she demanded. "You said you didn't know *anything*."

"I don't—but I *think* they took Silas because they were trying to force two of my other foster parents to abandon some plan they've cooked up, or at least to let them in on it. They thought that if they could attract enough public attention my foster parents would be intimidated—but my foster parents aren't the kind to bend with the wind. I can't figure out who did what, or why, and I can't trust anything that anyone says to me, but . . . well, it wouldn't make sense for them to harm us. I think they want me to do something for them, and I suspect that they only took you to add to the confusion."

"I don't understand," said the blond girl, growing more distraught in spite of Damon's attempt to soothe her fears. "Silas doesn't have anything to do with his old friends—and I certainly don't."

"Nor do I," Damon said, while he tested the handcuffs to make certain that there was no way of slipping out of them. "Unfortunately, the people who've imprisoned us refuse to believe that, of Silas or of me. I really don't think they have anything against *you*, though. You just got caught up in it by accident."

Damon believed what he'd told the girl, but he couldn't help feeling a slight twinge of doubt as to whether all this was actually happening at all. It *could* be another VE, similar to the last although far more modest. How could he ever be sure, now, that he'd really woken up? How could he ever know whether there really had been a mirror man and a miraculous new VE technology, or whether it had all been a product of his own fertile imagination?

Even if this were real, he realized as he pursued the discomfiting thought, he might be snatched back into some such VE without a moment's notice if clever nanomachines really had been implanted in his hindbrain, and if they were *still there*. In today's world, it wasn't only walls and phone links that couldn't be trusted. How could any man know what kind of burden he was carrying around in the depths of his own being? He was carrying his own cargo of watchful nanomachines, charged with the duty of keeping his flesh free from invaders, but who could stand watch over the watchmen? In PicoCon's empire, there could be no ultimate security, no ultimate secrecy—and it appeared that PicoCon's empire was closer to its final conquest than he had ever imagined. What could now stand in its way, save for confusion? In a world where nothing could be sealed away in any kind of vault, everything that was to be hidden had to be hidden in plain view, camouflaged by a riot of illusions.

If Conrad Helier really had faked his death, Damon thought, he really might have returned to public life by pretending to be his own son—but Conrad Helier's son was very definitely, and very defiantly, his own man. Unfortunately, Conrad Helier's son had a brain shrouded in mist, and he felt further away from understanding now than he had been before.

"Did you have any unnaturally vivid dreams while you were asleep?" he asked the young woman.

"No dreams at all," she replied, "so far as I can remember. Why?" Her voice cracked on the last word, as fear broke through. She looked as if she were about to cry. She was immune to the worst effects of pain, but IT couldn't immunize anyone against the purely psychological component of fear.

"Please don't worry," he begged her, although the plea sounded foolish even to him. "I really don't think we're in any danger." He wasn't at all certain that *he* was out of danger. When he had tried to fly, he had only fallen. Either the mirror man had tricked him and mocked him—for no reason Damon could fathom—or the fault had been in himself, in his skill or his courage. Which was worse?

"It's *crazy*," Catherine Praill insisted. "Why would anyone want to kidnap someone like me? What kind of—"

Before she could finish the sentence the door of the room was kicked open and thrust violently back against the wall. A head peered around the jamb, while the barrel of an obscenely heavy gun, clutched in two unfashionably hairy hands, swept the enclosed area from side to side with crude threat.

Once the gunman was sure that the two prisoners were help-less, and unaccompanied by anyone more menacing, he said: "All clear." He didn't come into the room itself, being content to hover in the corridor while a woman stepped past him, pausing on the threshold to survey the scene with calm disdain.

"Oh," she said as her eyes met Damon's. "It's *you.*" Her dis-appointment was palpable.

"Rachel Trehaine," Damon said as lightly as he could. He shook his head but the fog wouldn't clear. "I thought you were just a scientific analyst," he added, knowing that he was only a pale imitation of his old smart-ass self. "I didn't expect to see you in charge of a hit squad."

The expression of disgust on the red-headed woman's face was something to be seen. "I'm not *in charge of a hit squad,*" she said. "I'm just. . . ." She hesitated, obviously unsure as to how her present occupation ought to be characterized.

"They didn't shove a note under your door, by any chance?" Damon meant it as a feeble joke, but when he saw the disgusted expression turn to one of puzzlement he realized that it might have been a lucky guess. He resisted the temptation to giggle and took advantage of his luck to hazard another guess. "You were expecting Silas Arnett, weren't you?"

Rachel Trehaine wasn't in the least amused by his perspicacity. "Call Hiru Yamanaka at Interpol," she said to one of the men waiting in the corridor. "Tell him we've found one of his missing persons. And try to find something in the van that we can use to cut through the chains of those handcuffs."

"How long have I been a missing person?" Damon asked, still fighting the fog.

"I wasn't talking about *you,*" the woman from Ahasuerus said. "I was referring to Miss Praill."

Damon grimaced slightly as he realized that he should have known that. So far as Interpol knew, he was probably still safe and sound on Rajuder Singh's private island. "Where are we?" he asked as mildly as he could. He didn't want to add any further fuel to Rachel Trehaine's understandable annoyance.

"Venice Beach," she told him, with only a slight hint of disgust.

His captors had brought him home—or very nearly home. In retrospect, that wasn't particularly surprising.

"Thanks for coming to fetch us," Damon said meekly. "I'm sorry you had to take the trouble."

"I don't suppose you have any idea why they didn't contact Interpol directly," the woman said wearily. She was looking out into the corridor, waiting for the members of her team to find something that could be used to cut Damon and Catherine free.

"I *think* they're trying to tell you something," Damon said. "Not you personally—the people in charge of the foundation."

"*What* are they trying to tell us?" the data analyst demanded sharply.

Damon didn't want to admit that he was confused, but he wasn't sure that his run of lucky guesses could be sustained. "They seem to think that Ahasuerus and the remnants of Conrad Helier's old research team are loose cannons rolling around their deck," he said tentatively. "I think they want everybody—including Interpol—to know that there's a new captain on the bridge, one who intends to run a very tight ship from now on."

"What on earth is all *that* supposed to mean?" Rachel Trehaine demanded aggressively. She looked at Catherine Praill as if to see whether the younger woman understood it any better than she did.

"I wish I could be more precise," Damon assured her. "I wish *they'd* be more precise. I don't know what to believe. There's too much of it, and it's almost all lies."

The woman from Ahasuerus was still annoyed, but she wasn't entirely insensitive to his distress. She nodded, as if to concede that he'd been through enough for the present. By the time one of the gunmen appeared with a pair of wire cutters she had begun to look thoughtful. Damon didn't suppose she'd been able to find out exactly what Eveline and Karol were playing at in the short time available to her, but she must have found out enough to keep her interested. She probably knew at least as much as

Damon did, and was probably better placed than he was to start putting the pieces together. When Damon thanked her for cutting him free from the bed's head she finally took the trouble to ask whether he was all right.

He assured her that he was, then went to place a reassuring hand on Catherine Praill's arm.

"It's all over now," he told her gently. "The police will want to question you again, but I'm sure they don't suspect you of being involved in Silas Arnett's abduction. It's possible that you carried something into his house without knowing you were doing it, but Interpol must have a reasonable idea by now what kind of game this is. They're being played with exactly as we are."

"That's an interesting observation, Mr. Hart," said a new voice.

Damon looked around to see Hiru Yamanaka, who was coming through the doorway waving his ID card at all and sundry.

"You got here very quickly," said Rachel Trehaine, her eyes narrowing slightly with awful suspicion.

"So we did," Yamanaka agreed. "That's because we weren't very far away. Mr. Hart is right, Miss Praill—we do have some other questions to ask you, but we certainly won't be bringing any charges against you and we'll take much better care of you this time. You, Mr. Hart, are under arrest."

"For what?" Damon demanded, blurting the question out with frank amazement. "You don't *really* think I'm Conrad Helier, enemy of mankind, do you?"

"No, I don't," the inspector said equably. "In fact, I'm certain that you're not, but I do have reason to think that you have information relevant to an ongoing murder inquiry, and perhaps to the whereabouts of a man we're currently seeking in that connection."

Damon felt horror clutch at his stomach. The mirror man had said that his side in the dispute hadn't killed anyone—but there was no way to know how many lies the mirror man had told. "Silas is *dead?*" he said, leaping to what seemed to be the obvious conclusion.

"We still have no information as to the whereabouts or well-being of Dr. Arnett," Yamanaka said, taking no satisfaction from his own punctiliousness. "The inquiry in question is into the murder of Surinder Nahal. We are holding your friend Diana Caisson as a possible accomplice, and we are making every effort to locate our chief suspect, Madoc Tamlin—who is, I believe, currently in your employ."

Damon was lost for words. He didn't know whether to be more alarmed by the fact that Diana was in custody or the fact that Madoc—who evidently wasn't—had somehow been fingered for a murder he surely couldn't have committed. He had thought himself dazed and confused before, but he was doubly so now. "Oh shit," he murmured, in lieu of anything meaningful to say.

Yamanaka was looking at the short length of chain dangling from Damon's wrist, as if regretting that Rachel Trehaine had taken the trouble to have it cut. "Please come with me, Mr. Hart," he said. "I think it's time you told us everything you know about this matter. We're rather tired of people *playing* with us."

For a fleeting second, Damon wondered whether the man from Interpol might be right—but only for a fleeting second. By the time he consented to be led away, he was already rehearsing the half-truths and evasions he would have to deploy. Whatever kind of game this was, he didn't think Interpol could possibly win it. He didn't even think they could be reckoned as serious players, although Inspector Yamanaka obviously didn't see things that way.

Damon was taken to one of two waiting cars. Sergeant Rolfe was beside it, holding the rear door open. While Damon climbed in, Hiru Yamanaka went around the other side and took the seat next to him. Rolfe slammed the door shut and walked away, escorting Catherine Praill to the second car.

"I suppose you got a note pushed under your door too," Damon said to Yamanaka as the car pulled away.

"We put Ms. Trehaine under discreet surveillance after you

went to see her," the inspector told him mildly. "We were taking an interest in all your movements, and the call you paid on Ahasuerus stood out as one of the least expected."

"Where were you when Steve Grayson kidnapped me?" Damon asked sourly.

"Again, not as far away as you might have thought. Unfortunately, we lost sight of you temporarily. We feared for your safety, having seen the message which was put out on the Web shortly after you and Mr. Grayson took off—and even more so when Rajuder Singh satisfied us that you really had been taken from the island by force. Do you wish to press charges against Grayson and Singh, by the way? We didn't have enough evidence to arrest them without your testimony, but we're still keeping an open file on the matter."

"That's okay," Damon said drily. "They thought they were acting in my best interests, and perhaps they were. Best to let it alone—Karol is my foster father, after all." As an afterthought, he added: "They *were* working for Karol, weren't they?"

"I believe so," the Interpol man confirmed. "We checked their records, of course. Rajuder Singh's is unblemished to a degree that's rather remarkable in such an old man. He's an ecological engineer and has been for well over a century. He knew your father quite well, although that was a long time ago."

Damon didn't respond to that item of delicately trailed bait. When the silence had lasted five or six seconds, Yamanaka spoke again in an awkward manner to which he was plainly unaccustomed. "I ought to inform you that there was an unfortunate incident shortly after you left Molokai—an explosion aboard the *Kite*. Rescuers picked up a dozen survivors, but there was no sign of Karol Kachellek."

Damon turned to look at him, feeling that insult was being heaped upon injury. "Karol?" he said helplessly. Numbly, he noted that the Interpol man had said "incident" rather than "accident."

"I'm afraid so," Yamanaka said. "It seems probable that he's dead, although no body has been found."

"Murdered?"

"We don't know that. The investigation is continuing."

"Am I a suspect in that investigation too?" Damon asked abrasively. "Do you think I went to Molokai to plant a bomb on my foster father's boat?" He didn't expect an answer to that and he didn't get one, so he quickly changed tack. "Is Eveline okay?"

"So far as we know," the man from Interpol said, with a slight sigh that might have been relief at the opportunity to impart some good news. "I'm very concerned, though, for the safety of Silas Arnett. If you have any information regarding the identity of the persons responsible for his abduction I implore you to tell me without delay. We've now received several communications from someone who claims to be the *real* Operator one-oh-one, disowning all the recent notices posted under that alias. It's difficult to confirm her story, of course, but given that she's incriminating herself I'm inclined to believe her. It has always seemed to me that this business could not be the work of Eliminators, unless some powerful organization had suddenly decided to commit its resources to the cause of Elimination. I find that hard to believe."

"How old is the woman who claims to be the original Operator one-oh-one?" Damon asked curiously.

"She's a hundred and five now," Yamanaka told him, "but that's a side issue. My most urgent concern is the safety of Silas Arnett. Now that those confessions have been released. . . ."

"They were fakes," Damon told him.

"Painfully obvious fakes," Yamanaka agreed, "which could easily have been made without Dr. Arnett's active involvement. That's what worries me. If his kidnappers didn't actually need *him*, but only needed to remove him from the scene, they might have killed him before they removed him from his house. Now that we've found Dr. Nahal's body, there seems to be more than adequate cause for concern."

"You don't really think I had anything to do with that, do you?" Damon asked gruffly.

"You commissioned Madoc Tamlin to look for Dr. Nahal.

When the local police discovered Tamlin at the murder scene he attacked them with a crowbar and ran away."

"I commissioned Madoc to collect some information," Damon said defensively. "I can't believe he'd involve himself in a murder—that's not his style at all. You *can't* be serious about holding Diana as an accomplice."

The man from Interpol wouldn't confirm or deny his seriousness. Instead, he said: "Dr. Arnett's supposed confession was an interesting statement, wasn't it? Food for thought for everyone—and food which will be all the more eagerly swallowed for being dressed up that way."

"It was rubbish," Damon said.

"I dare say that Dr. Arnett was correct about the effect the Crash had, however," Yamanaka went on. "The way he spoke in his second statement about bringing people together was really quite moving. The idea that for the first and only time in human history all humankind was on the same side, united against the danger of extinction, is rather romantic. The world isn't like that anymore, alas. That's a pity, don't you think?"

"Not really," Damon replied, wondering where this was leading. He knew that the Japanese were supposed to have made a fine art of beating around the bush before coming to the point, but the man from Interpol hadn't previously shown any particular inclination to circumlocution. "A world devoid of conflicts would be a very tedious place to live."

"I take your point," Yamanaka conceded, "but you are a young man, and even I can barely imagine what the world was like before and during the Crash. I wonder, sometimes, how different things might seem to the very old: to men like Rajuder Singh, Surinder Nahal, and Karol Kachellek, and women like Eveline Hywood and the real Operator one-oh-one. They might be rather disappointed in the world they made, and the children they produced from their artificial wombs, don't you think? They were hoping to produce a utopia, but . . . well, no one could convincingly argue that the meek have inherited the world—at least, not yet."

Damon didn't know what the policeman might read into any answer he gave, so he prudently gave none at all.

"Sometimes," Yamanaka added, in the same offhandedly philosophical tone, "I wonder whether *anyone* can inherit the world, now that people who owned it all in the days before the Crash believe that they can live forever. I'm not sure that they'll ever let go of it deliberately . . . and such fighting as they'll have to do to keep it will be mostly among themselves."

He thinks he's figured it out, Damon thought, with a twinge of grudging admiration. He's asking for my help in finding the evidence. And why shouldn't I cooperate, if people are actually dying? Why shouldn't I tell him what I know . . . or what I believe? "My father never owned more than the tiniest slice of the world," he said aloud, by way of procrastination. He was awkwardly conscious of the fact that he had said *my father* instead of *Conrad Helier.* "He was never a corpsman, and never wanted to be."

"Your father remade and reshaped the world by designing the New Reproductive System," Yamanaka replied softly. "The corpsmen who thought the world was theirs to make and shape might well have resented that, even if he never disturbed their commercial empire. Men of business always fear and despise utopians, even the ones who pose no direct threat to them. The corpsmen probably resent your father still, almost as much as the Eliminator diehards resent *them.*"

"He's been dead for fifty years," Damon pointed out. "Why would corpsmen want to waste their time demonizing the dead?" He hoped that Yamanaka might be able to answer that one; he certainly had no answer himself.

"His collaborators are still alive," Yamanaka countered—and then, after a carefully weighed pause, added: "or *were*, until this plague of evil circumstance began."

Twenty

By the time the two cars reached the local Interpol headquarters Damon had decided to continue the strategy that he had reflexively undertaken while chatting informally to Hiru Yamanaka, and which he had employed in all his previous dealings with the police. He proceeded to deny everything. He told himself that his purpose was to conserve all the relevant information he had for his own future use, but he was uncomfortably conscious of his own inability to decide exactly what was relevant.

The strategy was not without its costs. For one thing, Yamanaka refused to let him speak to Diana Caisson—although Damon wasn't certain that he needed to rush into a confrontation as awkward as that one would inevitably prove to be. For another, it intensified Yamanaka's annoyance with him—which would be bound to result in an intensification of the scrutiny to which his life and actions were currently being subjected.

Yamanaka had obviously anticipated that Damon would not respond to his subtle overtures, although he put on a show of sorrow. He soon reverted to straightforward interrogation, although his pursuit of information seemed rather halfhearted. At first Damon took this to be a gracious acceptance of defeat, but by the time the interview was over he had begun to wonder whether Yamanaka might actually prefer it if he were out on the street inviting disaster rather than sitting snugly and safely in protective custody while Interpol chased wild geese.

"The claims made by the so-called real Operator one-oh-one are, of course, receiving a full measure of publicity," Yamanaka told him, with a dutiful concern that might well have been counterfeit. "They have not gone uncontradicted, but would-be assassins might not be inclined to believe the contradictions. Were you to return to your apartment right away, trouble might follow you. Were you to attempt to disappear into the so-called badlands in the east of the city, you might easily deliver yourself into danger."

"I can make my own risk assessments and responses," Damon told him. The fog was lifting now, and he was becoming more articulate by the minute. "You don't have any evidence at all to connect me to Surinder Nahal's death. As far as I can tell, you have nothing to connect Madoc and Diana to it either, except that they found the body before the local police. Maybe Madoc got a bit excited when the cops burst in on him, but that's understandable. It's not as if they did any real damage. Even if you press ahead with the assault charges, the fact that they might have gone to the place where they found the body on my behalf doesn't make me an accessory to the assault. Given that you don't have any charges to bring against me, I think you ought to let me go now."

"I can hold you overnight if I have reason to believe that you're withholding relevant information," Yamanaka pointed out, strictly for form's sake.

"How could I possibly know anything relevant to the assault?"

"Apparently," Yamanaka observed serenely, "you don't even know anything relevant to your own kidnapping. Given that you were unlucky enough to be kidnapped twice in a matter of hours, that seems a little careless."

"Karol's error of judgment wasn't a kidnapping at all," Damon said. "It was just a domestic misunderstanding. As for the second incident, I was asleep the whole time, from the moment I was gassed until the moment I woke up where Rachel Trehaine found me."

"Even so, Mr. Hart," Yamanaka observed, as a parting shot, "you seem to have become extraordinarily accident-prone lately. It might be unwise to trust your luck too far."

Damon didn't want to extend the conversation any further. He accepted a ride back to his apartment building, but the uniformed officer who drove the car didn't attempt to continue the interrogation.

When he'd taken time out to visit the bathroom and order some decent cooked food from the kitchen dispenser, Damon checked his mail. He wasn't unduly surprised or alarmed to find that there was nothing from Madoc Tamlin, although there were three messages from Diana Caisson, all dispatched from the building he'd just come from. There was nothing from Molokai, but there was, at long last, a curt note from Lagrange-5, saying that Eveline Hywood would be available to take his call after nineteen hundred hours Greenwich Mean Time.

Damon subtracted eight hours and checked the clock, which informed him that he had half an hour still in hand. He doublechecked the date to make sure that he had the right one—he'd lost an entire day between the time he'd been snatched from Karol Kachellek's secret hideaway and the morning he'd been picked up in Venice Beach.

By the time he'd changed and eaten a makeshift meal the half hour was almost up. He decided that he couldn't be bothered twiddling his thumbs until the hour struck, so he slipped inside his hood.

It would have been typical of Eveline to refuse the call until the appointed hour actually arrived, but she didn't. It wasn't an AI sim that answered the phone, but that didn't mean that the conversation would be eye-to-eye. The image floating in the familiar VE environment was being directly animated by Eveline Hywood, but it still had to be synthesized to edit out the hood she was wearing. Damon knew that Eveline would be giving no secrets away, in what she said or the way she looked, but he still wanted to hear what she had to say.

"Damon," she said pleasantly. "It's good to see you. I've been very worried about you. Is there any news of Karol or Silas?" Eveline knew perfectly well that if there had been any news it would have been relayed to her instantly, but she was putting on a show of concern. Damon noticed that the last time she had undergone somatic adjustment for her progressive myopia she had had her irises retinted. Her natural eye color was dark brown, but her irises were now lightened almost to orange. Given that the melanin content of her skin had been carefully maintained, the modified eyes gave her stare a curiously feline quality. It was easy enough to believe that she might be the prime mover in whatever plot had caused such intense annoyance to the recently self-appointed overlords of Earth.

"They're still missing," Damon confirmed. "I expect they'll turn up eventually, dead or alive. That's out of our hands, alas. Do you have any idea what's going on, Eveline?" He knew that he'd have to wait a little while for her answer; their words and gestures had a quarter of a million miles to traverse. The time delay wasn't sufficient to cause any real difficulties, and Eveline must be thoroughly accustomed to it, but Damon knew that he would find it disconcerting to begin with. While he waited, he looked at her appraisingly, trying to figure out exactly what kind of person she was. He had never managed to do that while they were living under the same roof.

He wondered why Eveline had designed the VE as a duplicate of her actual environment. Was she underlining the fact that she lived in deep space: the only foreign country left where things *had* to be done differently? In L-5, even a room decked out as simply as possible had to have all kinds of special devices to contain its trivial personal possessions and petty decorations. In space, nothing could be relied upon to stay where you put it, even in a colony which retained a ghost of gravity by virtue of its spin.

"Someone is evidently intent on blackening your father's name," Eveline told him, with an airy wave of her slender hand. "I can't imagine why. These self-appointed Eliminators seem to be getting completely out of hand. There are none up here, mercifully; L-Five isn't perfect, but it's a haven of sanity compared to Earth. I think it's because we're building a new society from scratch, without nations or corporations; because we have no history we feel no compulsion to maintain such ancient traditions as rebellion, hatred, and murder."

Damon didn't bother to question her certainty as to whether L-5 was really Eliminator-free, or corporation-free. It had taken so long to get through to her that he didn't want to waste any time. He knew perfectly well that he wasn't going to get any straight answers, but he wanted to know where he stood, if she was prepared to tell him.

"Why is it happening *now*, Eveline?" he asked softly. "What brought your adversaries crawling out of the woodwork after all this time?"

"I have no idea," she said. Damon had to presume that she was lying, but that was only to be expected, given that this was far from being a secure call. They both had to proceed on the assumption that anyone with any interest in this convoluted affair might be listening in. If she wanted to give him any clues, she would have to do it very subtly indeed. Unfortunately, he and Eveline had been virtual strangers even while they were living under the same roof; they had no resources of common understanding to draw on.

Damon had opened his mouth to ask the next question before he realized that Eveline had only paused momentarily. "You might be better able to guess than I am," she added. "After all, this whole affair is really an attack on you, isn't it?"

"It seems to have turned out that way," he admitted. But it didn't start like that, he thought. That's a deflection, a diversionary tactic—for which you and my father's other so-called friends are partly responsible. You called the bet and raised the stakes. I'm just caught in the crossfire.

"Please be careful, Damon," Eveline said. "I know that we've had our differences, but I really do care about you a great deal."

Damon was glad to hear it. It was an encouragement to continue. Eveline could have shut him out completely, but it seemed that she didn't want to do that—or didn't dare to. "Could it have something to do with this stuff that you and Karol are investigating—these para-DNA life-forms?" he asked, biting the bullet. He expected her spoken answer to be a denial, of course, but he also expected it to be a lie. So far as he could judge, Karol's dabbling with the black deposit on the rocks of Molokai's shoreline was the only thing which could possibly make this a "very bad time."

"How could it have anything to do with that?" Eveline asked, frowning as if in puzzlement—but her synthesized stare was gimlet sharp. A flat denial would have instructed him to let the matter lie; the question was actively inviting further inquiry. Damon knew that he had to select his words very carefully, but he felt slightly reassured by the fact that his foster mother *might* be making a vital concession.

"I'm not sure," he said, in a calculatedly pensive manner. "Karol said there were two possibilities regarding its origins: up and down. He was looking at the bottom of the sea while you're looking for evidence of its arrival from elsewhere in the solar system." But he had a third alternative in mind when he said it, Damon left unsaid, and there is a third alternative, isn't there? The third alternative was sideways, and he searched Eveline's steady gaze for some confirmatory sign that she knew what he was driving at.

"That's right," Eveline said conversationally. "We're expecting two of our probes to start relaying valuable information back from the outer solar system within a matter of days. Karol's people will continue to work on the seabed samples, of course, but my own estimate of the probabilities is that they're unlikely to find anything. I think the Oort Cloud is the likelier source—but I've always had panspermist leanings, as you know. It's very difficult to be perfectly objective, even when you've been a scientist for more than a hundred years."

"It would be more interesting, in a way, if it had come from one of the black smokers," Damon said, hoping that she would not mind being challenged. "For one planet to be able to produce two different forms of life suggests an authentic creative verve. I always thought panspermia was a rather dull hypothesis, with its suggestion that wherever we might go in the universe we'll only find more of the same."

"Sometimes," Eveline said, "the truth *is* dull. You can design virtual environments as gaudy and as weird as you like, but the real world will always be the way the real world is." She looked around as she said it at the scrupulously dull and slavishly imitative VE with which she had surrounded herself.

"Speaking of dull truths," Damon said, "I suppose you and my late father didn't really cause the Crash?"

"No, we didn't," she answered predictably. "When they find Silas, he'll put the record straight. He didn't really say any of those things—it's all faked. Just another virtual reality, as fantastic and ridiculous as any other. It's all lies—you know it is." Her eyes weren't fixed on his now; if he was reading her correctly, she was dismissing this topic and asking him to move on.

"Do you think there might be a new plague?" he asked mildly. "Might this para-DNA invader throw up something just as nasty as the old meiotic disrupters and chiasmalytic transformers?"

"That's extremely unlikely," she answered, just as mildly. "So far as we can tell, para-DNA is entirely harmless. Organisms of this kind will inevitably compete for resources with life as we know it, but there's no evidence at all of any other kind of dangerous interaction and it would be surprising if there were. Para-DNA is just something which happened to drift into the biosphere from elsewhere—almost certainly from the outer solar system, in my opinion. It's fascinating, but it's unlikely to pose any serious threat."

"Are you absolutely sure of that?" Damon asked, watching the luminous eyes.

"You know perfectly well that there's no absolute certainty in science, Damon," Eveline answered equably. "Investigations of this kind have to be carried out very carefully, and we have to wait until we have all the data in place before we draw our ultimate conclusions. All I can say is that there's no reason at present to believe that para-DNA is or could be dangerous."

"Of course," Damon said in a neutral tone. "I do understand that. It's interesting, though, isn't it? A whole new basis of life. Who knows what it might have produced, out there in the vast wilderness of space? I asked Karol whether it might be the gateway to a whole set of new biotech tools. Have you had much interest from the corps?"

"A little," Eveline said, "but I really can't concern myself with that sort of thing. This isn't a matter of *commerce,* Damon—it's far more important than that. It's a matter of *enlightenment.* I really wish you understood that—but you never did care much for enlightenment, did you?"

There had been a time when a dig like that would have stung him, but Damon felt that she was fully entitled. He was even prepared to consider the possibility that she might be right.

"A lot of people will be interested," he predicted, "even if there are no fortunes to be made. The corps will want to investigate the possibilities themselves. Para-DNA doesn't actually *belong* to you, after all. If you're right about its origins, it's just one more aspect of the universe—everybody's business."

"Yes it is," she agreed, looking sideways at the window which offered them both a view of the magnificent starfield. *"Everybody's* business. Anything we discover will be freely available to anyone and everyone. We're not profit minded."

"Nor is the Ahasuerus Foundation," Damon observed. "You and they have that in common—but I met a corpsman not long ago who contended that even the corps aren't really profit motivated anymore. He suggested to me that the Age of Capital was dead, and that the New Utopia's megacorps have a new agenda."

"The problem with corporation people," Eveline said, with the firmness of committed belief, "is that you can never believe a word they say. It's all advertising and attention seeking. Science is different. Science is interested in the truth, however prosaic it might be." Again she looked sideways at the star field, which was not in the least prosaic, even in the context of the virtual environment.

"You would say that, wouldn't you?" Damon pointed out. "After all, you've given a lifetime to the pursuit of scientific truth, dull and otherwise. But I will try to understand, Eveline. I think I'm beginning to see the light. I wish you luck with your inquiries—and I hope that the kind of misfortune which seems so rife down here can't reach out as far as Lagrange-Five."

"I hope so too," Eveline assured him. "Take care, Damon. In spite of our past disagreements, we all loved you and we still do. We'd really like to have you back one day, when you've got all the nonsense out of your system." Her eyes were still uncommonly bright. They shone more vividly than he'd ever seen them shine before, or ever thought likely—but they didn't shine as brightly or as implacably as the stars that she could always look out upon, whether she were in her actual laboratory or its virtual simulation.

I know you'd like to have me back, Damon thought. I only wish you weren't so certain that there's nothing else I can do. All he said out loud was: "I'll be careful. Don't worry about me, Eveline. I understand that you've got more important things to do."

After he'd broken the connection Damon found that two images still lingered in his mind's eye: Eveline's eyes, and the star field at which she'd glanced on more than one occasion. Eveline wasn't one for idle sidelong glances; he knew that she'd been trying to make a point. He even thought he knew what point it was that she had been trying to make—but it was just a guess. Beset by confusions as he was, there was nothing he could do but guess. Unfortunately, he had no idea what reward there might be in guessing correctly, nor what penalty there might be if he jumped to the wrong conclusion.

In a way, the most horrible thought of all was that it might not matter in the least what he came to believe, or what he tried to do about it. The one thing he wanted more than to be safe and sound was to be *relevant*. He wanted to be something more than Catherine Praill; he wanted a part to play that might *make a difference*, not merely to his own ambitions but to those of his foster parents and those of the stubbornly mysterious kidnappers. If there were people in the world who thought it possible, reasonable, and desirable to play God, how could any young man who was genuinely ambitious be content to play a lesser role?

Twenty one

Madoc Tamlin waited patiently while Harriet, alias Tithonia, alias the Old Lady, watched the VE tape that he'd found on the badly burned body. She sat perfectly still except for her hands, which made very slight movements, as if she were a pianist responding reflexively to some inordinately complicated nocturne that she had to memorize.

Madoc knew that the Old Lady was concentrating very intently, because she wasn't just watching the recording; she was also watching the code that reproduced it, whizzing past in a virtual display-within-the-display. Over the years, Harriet had built up a strange kind of sensitivity to code patterns which allegedly allowed her to detect the artificial bridges used to link, fill in, and distort the "natural" sequences generated by digitizing camera work.

Madoc had never been admitted into Harriet's lair before; on the rare occasions when they'd met they'd done so on neutral ground. She'd made an exception this time, but not because he was on the run from the LAPD after clobbering one of their finest with a crowbar. She'd let him in because she was *interested* in the business he'd got mixed up in.

That was quite a compliment, although Madoc knew that it was a compliment to Damon rather than to him. It was Damon's mystery, after all; he was only the legman.

In order to get into the Old Lady's lair he'd had to undergo all the old pulp-fiction rituals: a blindfold ride in a car, followed by a blindfold descent into the depths of some ancient ruin in the Hollywood hills. Most people still avoided Hollywood, associating it with the spectacular outbreak of the Second Plague War rather than the long-extinct film industry, but Harriet wasn't like most people. There were hundreds of thousands—maybe millions—of centenarians in the USNA, but she was nevertheless unique.

Most people who lived to be a hundred had bought into IT in the early days; the brake had been put on their aging processes when they were in their thirties or forties, way back in the 2120s. No one knew exactly what Harriet had been doing in those days, but it certainly hadn't been honest or profitable. She'd been part of the underclass that had absorbed all the shit flying off the fan of the genetic revolution. In the previous century her kind had provided both plague wars with the greater part of their virus fodder, but Harriet had been born just late enough to miss the longest-delayed effects of those conflicts. Circumstances had dictated, however, that she continue to age at what used to be the natural rate until she was well into her seventies and the calendar was well into the 2150s. Apart from the usual wear and tear she'd had multiple cancers of an unusually obdurate kind—the kind that didn't respond to all the usual treatments. Then she'd been picked up by PicoCon as a worst-case guinea pig for the field trials of a brand-new fleet of nanomachines.

PicoCon's molecular knights-errant had gobbled up the Old Lady's cancers and stopped her biological clock ticking. They had snatched her back from the very threshold of death, and made her as fit and well as anyone could be who'd suffered seventy-odd years of more-than-usual deterioration. Nine hundred out of a thousand people in her situation would have been irredeemably set on the road to premature senility, and ninety-nine out of the remaining hundred would have keeled over as a result of some physical cause that the nanomech hadn't entirely set aside, but Harriet was the thousandth. Gifted with the poi-

soned chalice of eternal old age, she'd gone on and on and on—
and she was still going on, nearly forty years later. She was a
walking miracle.

In a world full of old ladies who looked anywhere between
forty and seventy years younger than they actually were, Harriet
was *the* Old Lady, Tithonia herself. Madoc knew, although most
of her acquaintances did not, that her second nickname came
from some ancient Greek myth about a man made immortal by
a careless god, who'd forgotten to specify that he also had to stay
young.

Even as a walking miracle, of course, Harriet *alias* Tithonia
would have been no great shakes in a world lousy with miracles.
PicoCon had a new one every day, all wrapped up and ready for
the morning news, with abundant "human interest" built in by
the PR department. Harriet had taken it upon herself to become
more than a mere miracle, though; she'd become an honest-to-
goodness legend. Almost as soon as she was pronounced free of
tumors she'd reembarked on a life of crime, mending her ways
just sufficiently to move into a better class of felonies.

"If *I* can't live every day as if it were my last, who can?" she
was famous for saying. "I'm already dead, and this is heaven—
what can they do to me that would make a difference?"

Madoc supposed that if the LAPD had *really* wanted to put
Harriet out of business, lock her up, and throw away the key,
they could probably have done it twenty years ago—but they
never had. Some said that it was because she had powerful
friends among the corps for whom she undertook heroic missions of industrial espionage, but Madoc didn't believe that. He
knew full well that any powerful friends a mercenary happened
to acquire were apt to be out of the office whenever trouble
came to call, while the powerful enemies on the other side of the
coin were always on the job. Madoc's theory was that the LAPD
let Harriet alone out of respect for her legendary status, and because a few notorious adversaries on the loose were invaluable
when it came to budget negotiations with the city.

Either way, Madoc and everyone else figured that it was a

privilege to work with the Old Lady. That, as much as her efficiency, was why she was so expensive.

Harriet finally finished her scrutiny of the VE tape and ducked out from under the hood. Her face was richly grooved with the deepest wrinkles Madoc had ever seen and her hair was reduced to the merest wisps of white, but her dark eyes were sharp and her gaze could cut like a knife.

"The body had been burned, you say?" she questioned him—not because she didn't remember what he'd said but because she wanted it all set out in neat array while she put the puzzle together.

"Thoroughly," he confirmed. "It must have been covered in something that burned even hotter than gasoline, then torched." It was easy enough to see what Harriet was getting at. Whoever had committed the murder had had *time*. They could have torched the VE pack along with the body if they'd wanted to, or they could simply have picked it up and put it in a pocket. If they'd left it behind they had done so deliberately, in order that it would be found. The only hitch in that plan, Madoc assumed, had been that it was he and Diana who had found it instead of the police. Madoc, naturally enough, had brought it to the Old Lady instead of to Interpol.

"We're supposed to believe that the tape explains why the guy was killed," Harriet concluded.

"That's the way I figure it," Madoc admitted. "If that really is the original tape that was used as a base to synthesize Silas Arnett's confessions—or the first of them, at any rate, it identifies Surinder Nahal as the kidnapper in chief."

Madoc had inspected the tape himself before giving it to Harriet for more expert analysis. It contained a taped conversation between the captive Silas Arnett and another man, easily identifiable in the raw footage by voice as well as appearance as Surinder Nahal. Various phrases spoken by both men—but especially those spoken by Nahal, carefully distorted to make recognition difficult—had been used in the first of Arnett's two "confessions," but nothing Arnett had said on *this* tape amounted to an admission of guilt regarding *any* crime, past or present. On the other hand, there was no evidence on *this* tape that he had been tortured, or even fiercely interrogated.

"Insofar as the discovery points a finger at anyone," Harriet went on, "it implies that Arnett's friends took swift and certain revenge against Surinder Nahal because he tried to set them up, and left the VE pak on his body to explain why they killed him."

"Thus setting themselves up all over again," Madoc pointed out. "I think it stinks, but I'm not sure where the odor originates. How about you? Is the tape genuine? Is it really raw footage, or is it just a slightly less transparent lie than the one they dumped on the Web?"

"That's an interesting question," Harriet said.

"I know it is," Madoc said, trying not to let his exasperation show. "What's the answer?"

"I'll be honest with you, Madoc," Harriet said. "The tape's a fake. It's not a crude fake, but it's definitely a fake. Even Interpol could have determined that—probably. The fact that Silas Arnett still hasn't turned up would have alerted them to the same stink that reached your sensitive nostrils."

"So why the hesitation?" Madoc wanted to know.

"The thing is," the Old Lady said, "that I'm not sure how much deeper we ought to dig into this. You see, if Arnett's friends *didn't* kill the man whose body you found, then someone else did—and it certainly wasn't some dilettante Eliminator."

"I don't get it," Madoc said. "You're supposed to be the only ace Webwalker in the world who doesn't give a damn what she gets involved with. You're supposed to be utterly fearless."

"I am," she told him coldly. "This isn't a matter of watching *my* back, Madoc—it's *you* I'm worried about. Nobody's going to come after me, and I doubt that they intend to harm Damon Hart, but you're not part of the game plan. You might easily be seen as a minor irritation best removed from the field of play with the minimum of fuss. If this tape was really intended to fall into Interpol's hands rather than yours the people who left it might be a trifle miffed, and they're not the kind of people you want to have as enemies. It's one thing to set yourself up as an outlaw, quite another to become a thorn in the side of people who are above the law."

Madoc stared at her. "Do you know who's behind all this?" he asked sharply.

"I don't *know* anything," she told him, "but I'm absolutely certain that I can make the right guess."

"Is that why you called it an *interesting* problem?"

"Yes it is—but what interests me is *why,* not who. It's the *why* that I can't fathom. The how has its intriguing features too, but I think I understand pretty well how the moves came to be played the way they were—I just can't figure out why the game's being played at all."

"Well," said Madoc a little impatiently, "what interests *me* at present is that Damon has disappeared. When I first got you involved, I admit, it was mainly a matter of money—Damon's money. I was just doing a job for him. I don't really care about Arnett, or Nahal, or Kachellek—but I *do* care about Damon."

"Damon's back," Harriet replied, raising her white eyebrows a fraction, as if she had only just realized that he didn't know. Maybe it hadn't occurred to her that a young man on the run couldn't keep his fingers on the pulse of things quite as easily as an old lady in hiding.

"Since when?" Madoc asked.

"Since this morning. That tap I put into Ahasuerus told me— not that they were trying to keep it a secret. As soon as Trehaine found out that it was Damon she'd been sent out to find she called Interpol. Catherine Praill was with him. She's probably irrelevant, but the people who took Damon clearly wanted him back in play as soon as possible. That's why I'm fairly sure they won't hurt him. It's possible that he now knows far more than I do. Interpol will have him under a microscope, of course—it won't be easy for you to get to him without being picked up."

"I've got to get the tape to him," Madoc said, "and anything else you can give me. Who's doing this, Harriet? Who's jerking us all around?"

Harriet shrugged her narrow shoulders. "PicoCon," she said flatly. "OmicronA might be in it too, but PicoCon's board likes to keep these little adventures in-house. It's a matter of style. What I can't figure out is what they're so *annoyed* about and why they're tackling it in such a roundabout way. Compared with their irresistible juggernaut, Eveline Hywood's organization is a mere ant, which could be crushed underfoot on a whim. Ahasuerus might be a flea, but it's a flea that's already in their pocket, moneywise. This can't be everyday commercial competition, and it must be something that they find *interesting*, or they'd just stamp on it—but if it isn't about money. . . ." She left the sentence unfinished.

"PicoCon," Madoc repeated wonderingly. *"PicoCon* kidnapped Silas Arnett and tried to frame Conrad Helier for causing the Crash? *PicoCon* blew up Kachellek's boat, torched Surinder Nahal's body, and strewed forged tapes and Eliminator bulletins all over the Net?"

"They're also handily placed for pushing messages under people's doors hereabouts—but for what it's worth, I don't think PicoCon did *all* of that. They just started the ball rolling. This business with the burned body and the VE pak is a counter-punch. I think Hywood's people did that—and I think they rigged the second confession too. They were supposed to roll over and beg for mercy, but they fought back instead. You have to admire them for it, but it might be unwise. Just because Pico-Con used gentler methods first time around it doesn't mean that they won't use brute force to settle the matter. That's why I'm worried about you. If Kachellek really was blown up, you might be next on the list."

"I can't believe that cosmicorps play games like this," Madoc said wonderingly. "PicoCon least of all—they've got more than enough real work to occupy them."

"That's a matter of perspective," Harriet told him drily. "You could say that there's a point at which any successful corporation becomes so big and so powerful that the profits take care of themselves, leaving the strategists with nothing to do *but* play games. Serious games, but games nevertheless. Attacking Conrad Helier's memory seems a trifle unsporting, though—terrible ingratitude."

"Ingratitude? Why? Helier's team was always strictly biotech, as far as I can work out. I thought PicoCon's fortune was based on inorganic nanotech. What did he ever do for them?"

"He gave them the world on a plate. PicoCon may be the engine churning out the best set pieces nowadays, but the New Reproductive System stabilized the board for them. The Crash put a belated end to unpoliced population growth, but Helier's artificial wombs made certain that the bad old days would never come back again. If Helier hadn't got the new apparatus up and running in time to become the new status quo, some clown would have engineered a set of transformer viruses to refertilize every woman under the age of sixty-five and we'd have been back to square one. You probably think the Second Plague War was a nasty affair, but that's because you read about it in the kind of history books which only tell you what happened and skip lightly over all the might-have-beens. If it hadn't been for Conrad Helier, you'd probably have had to live through the *third* round of the Not-Quite-Emortal Rich versus the Ever-Desperate Poor—and PicoCon would have spent the last half-century pumping out molecular missiles and pinpoint bombs instead of taking giant strides up the escalator to *true* emortality."

Madoc had to think about this for a minute or two, but he soon saw the logic of the case. New technologies of longevity were an unqualified boon in an era in which population had ceased to grow, even though access to them was determined by wealth. In a world whose poorer people were still producing children in vast numbers, those same technologies would inevitably have become bones of fierce contention, catalysts of all-out war.

"You don't suppose," he mused, "that Hywood and Kachellek might have done just that—engineered a set of viruses to refertilize the female population?"

"No, I don't," said Harriet. "Even if they were silly enough to work on the problem, they'd have the sense to bury their results. Anyway, the world now has the advantage of starting from a position of relative sanity instead of rampant insanity—if some such technology did come along I think ninety-nine women in every hundred would have the sense to say no. It would be interesting to know what Hywood and Kachellek *have* done— but it might be safer not to try to find out. As I said before, if they really did blow Kachellek's boat to smithereens with him in it. . . ."

"If?" Madoc queried.

"It really is a *game*, Madoc. Bluff and counterbluff, lie and counterlie. The one thing of which we can be certain is that nothing is what it seems to be—not just on the surface but way down through the layers. PicoCon is making a big issue out of the possibility that Conrad Helier is only *playing* dead. Maybe Kachellek's playing dead too. Maybe Surinder Nahal is only playing dead."

"If that burned body really was his," Madoc murmured, "he was putting on a very convincing act."

"That might be the whole point of the exercise. Do you want me to get a message to Damon for you?"

"Can you do that? Without the cops knowing, I mean."

"I think so—but you can't bring him here. I've used up so much borrowed time that I'll be dying way beyond my means whenever I go, but I still like to be careful. It's a matter of professional pride. You'll have to figure out a safe place—and he'll have to figure out how to get there without dragging Interpol in his wake. I'll set it up for you—but if you want my advice, you'll tell him to put the rest of his money back in the bank and call it quits, so that you can start playing Three Wise Monkeys. We're out of our league here. Nobody can fight PicoCon and win."

If you never play out of your league, Madoc thought, you never get promoted. All he said aloud, though, was: "Okay—I need to get a meeting set up as soon as possible. Damon will want the tape, and everything else I've got, whether he intends to fight or not."

"Don't be too sure of that," Harriet advised him soberly. "Things have moved fast—he might not be in the same frame of mind as he was when he sent you off on this wild goose chase. Now that he's had his little holiday, he might want to play Three Wise Monkeys too, and he might be prepared to cut you adrift and leave you to PicoCon's tender mercies—or to the LAPD's."

Her concern seemed genuine, but Madoc couldn't imagine that he needed it. You might know PicoCon, Old Lady, he thought, but you don't know Damon. He'd never change sides on me. Madoc was as certain of that as he needed to be—and even if he hadn't been, what choice did he have?

PART FOUR

Movers and Shakers

Twenty-two

After sitting through the second tape of his "confessions," Silas Arnett found himself looking out upon a pleasant outdoor scene: a wood, like the ones to the south of his house. A rich carpet of leaf litter was delicately dappled by sunlight streaming through the canopy. The gnarled boughs of the trees offered abundant perches to little songbirds whose melodies filled the air. It was a simulation of an ancient woodland, whose design owed more to nostalgia than historical accuracy.

Unfortunately, the pleasantness of the surroundings found no echo within his body. In the VE he was a mere viewpoint, invisible to himself, but that only served to place more emphasis on his sense of touch, which informed him that the conditions of his confinement were now becoming quite unbearable.

The subtle changes of position he was able to make were no longer adequate to counter the aching in his limbs. The chafing of the straps which bound his wrists and ankles was now a burning agony. It did no good to tell himself that by any objective standard these were very minor pains, no worse than those which constituted the everyday condition of millions in the days before IT. He, Silas Arnett, had grown fully accustomed to being able to control pain, and now that he could no longer do it he felt that he might easily die of sheer frustration.

A human figure came through the trees to stand before him.

It was dressed in a monk's habit, and Silas inferred that it was supposed to be male, but it was a modern secular monk, not a member of any religious order that might have been contemporary with an ancient forest. The ornament the monk wore around his neck was not a cross but a starburst: a symbol of the physicists' Creation rather than the redemptive sacrifice of the Christ whose veneration was now confined to a handful of antiquarians.

The man pushed the hood back from his forehead and let its fold fall upon his shoulders. Silas didn't recognize the exposed visage; it was a handsome, serene face which bore the modest signs of aging that most monks considered appropriate to their station.

Silas wasn't fooled by the appearance. He knew that the mind behind the mask was the mind of his tormentor.

His "tormentor" had not, in the end, resorted to any very violent torture, but in his present condition Silas found it impossible to be grateful for that. Even had he been more comfortable, any gratitude he might have felt would have been tempered by the knowledge that even though he had not been cut or burned he had certainly been imprisoned, maligned, mocked, and misrepresented.

"That one looked even worse than the first one," he said, gritting his teeth against his discomfort and hoping that talk might distract him from his woe. "It really doesn't add anything. I can't see why you bothered."

"I didn't," said the monk. "That was someone else's work. I presume that your friends did it—you noticed, I dare say, that the underlying message was that what you and Conrad Heller did was both necessary and justified. On the surface, it begged to be identified as a mere lie, a vicious but half-baked slander, but that was double bluff. The subtext said: *Even if it were true, it wouldn't be in the least terrible. Even if Conrad Heller did cause the Crash, he did it for the noblest of reasons, and it desperately needed to be done. He was a hero, not an enemy of mankind.* When the original Operator one-oh-one indignantly blew her cover, by the way, she objected strenuously to my use of that particular phrase. She thinks that I should have said 'enemy of humankind.' She's of an age to be sensitive about that sort of thing—and I suppose a man of your age can probably sympathize with her."

Silas wasn't in the least interested in the authentic Eliminator's retention of outdated radfem sensibilities. "I suppose the subtext of that habit and starburst you're wearing," he said, "is that what you're doing to me is being done for the noblest of reasons— even though you won't deign to explain what they are."

"Nobility doesn't come into it," the monk told him. "I simply want Conrad Helier to come out of hiding. You were the bait. To be perfectly honest, I'm a little disappointed in him. Dumping that tape was a distinctly weak-kneed response to my challenge. The tape I left with the burned body was much cleverer—as we would all have had the chance to appreciate if Damon's troublesome friend hadn't got to the scene before the police and removed the evidence. I wish I knew whether your friends' failure to rescue you is a matter of incompetence, laziness, or a sacrifice move. They might actually have abandoned you to whatever fate I care to decide. Perhaps they think that it might inconvenience me more if nobody actually came to rescue you at all."

"Fuck this," Silas said vituperatively. "All this may be just a game to you, but I'm *suffering*. If you've done what you set out to do and don't intend to kill me, isn't it about time you simply let me go?"

"It's certainly time that someone came to get you," the monk admitted. "I'm truly sorry that Conrad Helier hasn't bothered to do it. Alas, I can't simply *release* you. This VE's fitted to a telephone, and I'm calling from elsewhere. The mechanical devices holding you in position require manual release."

"Someone was here earlier—actually in the room. You took care to let me know that when I first woke up."

"Everything had to be set up, and manually operated devices have to be put in place manually. As soon as you were secure, however, my helpers made themselves scarce. You've been alone for some time, excepting virtual encounters. You mustn't worry, though. I may have overestimated Conrad Helier's resources or willingness to respond, but if he doesn't come for you soon Interpol or Ahasuerus will. That wouldn't suit my purposes nearly as well, but I suppose it might have to do."

"The reason you overestimated Conrad's resources and his *willingness to respond*," Silas snarled, "is that you simply can't bring yourself to accept that he's dead and buried."

"No," said the monk, "I can't. I know how he did it, you see—and I've proved it by repeating the trick. He's not too proud to repeat it himself, it seems. Karol Kachellek's gone missing, supposedly blown up by a bomb planted on the *Kite* by persons unknown. The implication, of course, is that whoever took you has also gone after Kachellek—but I didn't do it. I dare say a dead body will turn up in a day or two, suitably mangled but incontrovertibly identifiable by means of its DNA. By my count, that makes three men who are supposed to be dead but aren't. Where will it all end? It's beginning to look as if Helier is determined to call my bluff and sit tight no matter what."

It seemed to Silas that the only one who was *sitting tight* was him. He wriggled his torso, deliberately pushing against the back of the padded chair in the hope of countering the aches generated within his muscles. He dared not move his arms or legs in the same way because that would have made the restraining cords contract and cut into his raw flesh. It helped a little.

"I'd hoped, of course, that Helier might be hiding out on the artificial island," the monk went on, "but that was overoptimistic. He's off-world—probably a lot further from Earth than Hywood. Not that that's a bad thing, from my point of view. If Kachellek joins them the whole core of the team will be up, up, and away. I'd be prepared to settle for that—always provided that if they ever want to play in *my* sandpit again they'll accept *my* rules. Heaven forbid that we should ever succeed in crushing the spirit of heroic independence, when all we actually need to do is send it into space. If Conrad Helier does eventually come to get you, Silas, tell him that's the deal: he can follow his own schemes in heaven, but not on Earth. Anything he does down here has to be checked out with the powers that be, and if it isn't authorized it doesn't happen. He'll know who the message is from."

Silas remained stubbornly silent, although he knew that he was supposed to respond to this instruction. The twittering of virtual birds filled the temporary silence. Their voices seemed oddly insulting; the cycles of their various songs were out of phase, but the programmed nature of the chorus was becoming obvious. Damon Hart, Silas felt sure, would have used an open-ended program with an elementary mutational facility for each individual song, so that the environment would be capable of slow but spontaneous evolution.

As if he were somehow sensitive to Silas's thoughts, his captor said: "It begins to look as if Damon Hart's the only worth-while card I've got. You really should have taken better care of that boy, Silas—you've let him run so far that you might never get him back. Do you suppose Conrad Helier might be prepared to sacrifice him as well as you?"

"You're crazy," Silas said sulkily. "Conrad's dead."

"I understand that you feel the need to keep saying that," the monk reassured him. "After all, you're still on the record, even if no one's ever going to play it back but me. You'll forgive me if I ignore you, though. Helier *will* have to have come out eventually, if he wants to deal. I really don't want to foul his operation up. I admire his enterprise. All I want is to ensure that we're all playing on the same team, planning our ends and means together. We *are* all on the same side, after all—we'll get to where we're going all the sooner if we all pull in the same direction."

"Where *are* we going?" Silas asked. "And who's supposed to be doing the pulling? Exactly who *are* you?" Unable to resist changing the position of his legs he tried to do so without moving his ankles, but he was no contortionist. He gasped as the ankle straps clutched at him.

If the real man behind the image of the monk could hear evidence of Silas's distress he ignored it. "Please don't be deliberately obtuse, Silas," he said in the same bantering tone. "We're going to the land of Cokaygne, where all is peace and harmony and everybody lives forever. But there can't be peace unless we find a peaceful way of settling our differences, and there won't be harmony unless we can establish a proper forum for agreeing on our objectives and our methods. That's all I want, Silas—just a nice, brightly polished conference table to which we can *all* bring our little plans and projects, so that they can all receive the blessing of the whole board of directors. As to who's doing the pulling, it's everyone who's making anything new—and those who make the most are pulling the hardest."

When the flaring pain in his ankles died down of its own accord Silas felt a little better. "Conrad never liked that kind of corpspeak," he growled, "or the philosophy behind it. If he were alive—which he isn't—you'd never get him to knuckle under to that kind of system. He always hated the idea of having to take his proposals and projects to panels of businessmen. He did it, when he needed finance—but he stopped doing it the moment he could finance himself. He'd never have gone back to it. Never in a million years."

"That's because he was a child of the old world," the monk said. "Things are different now, and although it's a little ambitious to start talking in terms of a million years I really do believe that we have to start thinking in terms of thousands. If Conrad Helier hadn't decided to drop out of sight, he'd be in a better position to see how much things have changed. If he participated in the wider human society even to the limited extent that Hywood and Kachellek do he'd still have his finger on the pulse of progress, but he seems to have lost its measure. I think he's fallen victim to the rather childish notion that those who desire to plan the future of the human race must remove themselves from it and stand apart from the history they intend to shape. That's not merely unnecessary, Silas, it's downright *silly*—and we can't tolerate it any longer."

Silas was busy fighting his anguish and couldn't comment. The other continued: "We don't have any objection to vaulting ambition—as I said before, we admire and approve of it—but Helier and his associates have to realize that there are much bigger fish in the pool now. We're just as determined to shape the future of the world as he is, and we have the power to do it. *We don't want to fight,* Silas—we want to work together. Helier is being unreasonable, and he must be made to see that. The simple fact is that if he can't be a team player, we can't allow him to play *here.* That goes for Eveline Hywood and Karol Kachellek too. People can't make themselves invisible by pretending to die, any more than they can exclude themselves from their social obligations by refusing to answer their phones. We have to make them see that—and in this instance, *we* includes *you.*"

"I don't want to play," Silas told the man of many masks flatly. "I'm retired, and I intend to stay that way. All I want is out of here. If you want me to beg, I'm begging. Tell your machine to give me back my IT. At the very least, tell it not to grab me so hard every time I twitch. I couldn't break free if I tried."

"It won't be long now," the monk said. "If I'd realized in advance that Helier would play it this way I'd have made things easier for you. My people could have found you two days ago, and I didn't want to make it *too* easy. I really am sorry. I'll give Helier two more hours, and if nobody's found you by then I'll tip off Interpol. They should be able to get the local police to you within twenty minutes—it's not as if you were way out in the desert."

"Two fucking hours may seem like nothing to you," Silas muttered hoarsely, "but you aren't sitting where I am."

"Oh, pull yourself together, man. You're not going to die. You've got sore wrists and ankles, not a ruptured ulcer. I'm trying to make you understand something *important.* I could almost believe that you really *have* retired."

"I have, damn it! I got heartily sick of the whole fucking thing! I'm done working night and day in search of the biotech Holy Grail. I'm a hundred and twenty-six years old, for God's sake! I need time to rest, time to let the world go by, time without *pressure.* Eveline and Karol might have been entirely swallowed up by Conrad's obsessions, but I haven't. I watched Mary die and I watched Damon grow up, both of them so tightly bound by those obsessions that they were smothered. Damon had a life in front of him, but the only way Mary could break free, in the end, was to die. Not me. I *retired.*"

"You really don't see, do you?" said the fake monk patronizingly. "You've never been able to break free from the assumptions of the twenty-first century. In spite of all that IT has achieved, you still take death and decay for granted. You think that your stake in the world will end in ten or twenty or fifty years' time, when the copying errors accumulated in your DNA will have filled out your body with so many incompetent cells that all the nanomachines in the world won't be able to hold you together."

"It's true," Silas growled, surprising himself with the harshness of his voice. "Even men fifty or a hundred years younger than I am are being willfully blind if they think that advances in IT will keep pushing back the human life span faster than they're aging. Sure, it's only a matter of time before rejuve technology will cut a lot deeper than erasing wrinkles. It really will be possible to clear out the greater number of the somatic cells which aren't functioning properly and replace them with nice fresh ones newly calved from generative tissue—but only the greater number. Even if you really could replace them all, you'd still be up shit creek without a paddle because of the Miller effect. You *do* know about the Miller effect, I suppose, even though you're not a biologist by trade or vocation?"

"I know what the Miller effect is," the monk assured him. "I'm thoroughly familiar with *all* the brave attempts that have been made to produce a biotech fountain of youth—even those made way back at the dawn of modern history, when Adam Zimmerman was barely cold in his cryonic vault. I know that there's a fundamental difference between slowing aging down and stopping it, and I know that there's an element of paradox in every project which aims to reverse the aging process. I'm not claiming that *anyone* now alive can become truly emortal no matter how fast the IT escalator moves. I might have to settle for two hundred years, Damon Hart for two-fifty or three hundred. Even embryos engineered in the next generation of Helier wombs for maximum resistance to aging might not be able to live much beyond a thousand years—only time will tell. But that's not the point.

"The point, Silas, is that even if you and I won't be able to play parent to that new breed, Damon's generation will. Conrad Helier and I must be reckoned *mortal* gods—but the children for whom we hold the world in trust will be an order of magnitude less mortal than we. The world we shape must be shaped *for them,* not for old men like you. Those who have had the role of planner thrust upon them must plan for a thousand years, not for ten or a hundred.

"Conrad Helier understands that well enough, even if you don't—but he still thinks that he can play a lone hand, sticking to his own game while others play theirs. We can't allow that. We aren't like the corpsmen of old, Silas—we don't want to tell you and him what to do and we don't want ownership of everything you and he produce, but we do want you both to join the club. We want you both to play with the team. What you did in the Crash was excusable, and we're very grateful to you for delivering the stability of the New Reproductive System, but what Conrad Helier is doing now has to be planned and supervised by all of us. We have to fit it into *our* schemes."

"Exactly what *is* it that you think Conrad's followers are doing?" Silas asked curiously.

"If you don't know," the monk replied tartly, "they must have been so deeply hurt by your decision to retire that they decided to cut you out entirely. Even if that's so, though, I'd be willing to bet that all you have to do is say you're sorry and ask to be let back in. You really should. I can understand that you felt the need to take a holiday, but people like us don't retire. We know that the only way to make life worth living is to play our part in the march of progress. We may not have true emortality, but we have to try to be worthy of it nevertheless."

"Cut the Eliminator crap," Silas said tersely. "You're not one of them."

"No, I'm not," the monk admitted, "for which you should be duly thankful. I do like the Eliminators, though. I don't altogether approve of them—there's too much madness in their method, and murder can no longer be reckoned a forgivable crime—but I like the way that they're prepared to raise an issue that too many people are studiously avoiding: who *is* worthy of immortality? They're going about it backwards, of course—we'll never arrive at a population entirely composed of the worthy by a process of quasi-Darwinian selection—but we *all* need to think about the myriad ways in which we might strive to be worthy of the gifts of technological progress. We are heirs to fabulous wealth, and the next generation will be heirs to an even greater fortune. We have to make every effort to live up to the responsibilities of our inheritance. That's what this is all about, Silas. We don't want to eliminate your estranged family—but they have to acknowledge the responsibilities of their inheritance. The fact that they played a major role in shaping that inheritance doesn't let them off the hook."

"And if they won't?" Silas wanted to know.

"They have to. The position of God isn't vacant anymore. The privilege of Creation has to be determined by negotiation. Conrad Helier may be a hundred and thirty-seven years old, but he's still thinking and still learning. Once we get through to him, he'll understand."

"You don't know him as well as I do," Silas said, having finally become incapable of guarding his tongue so carefully as never to let any implication slip that Conrad Helier might not be dead.

"There's time," his captor assured him. "But not, I fear, for any further continuation of this conversation. I don't know who, for the moment, but *somebody* has finally managed to locate you. I hope we'll meet again, here or in some other virtual environment."

"If we ever meet in real space," Silas hissed with all the hostility and bravado he could muster, "you'd better make sure that your IT is in good shape. You'll need it."

The woodland blanked out, leaving him adrift in an abstract holding pattern. He heard a door crash inwards, battered down by brute force, and he heard voices calling out the news that he was here. He felt a sudden pang of embarrassment as he remembered that he was nearly naked, and knew that he must present a horribly undignified appearance.

"Get me out of this fucking chair!" he cried, making no attempt at all to censor the pain and desperation from his voice.

The hood was raised from his eyes and tilted back on a pivot, allowing him to look at his cell and his rescuer. The light dazzled him for a moment, although it wasn't very bright, and he had to blink tears away from the corners of his eyes.

There was no way to identify the man who stood before him, looking warily from side to side as if he couldn't believe that there were no defenders here to fight for custody of the prisoner; the newcomer's suitskin had a hood whose faceplate was an image-distorting mask. He was carrying a huge handgun that didn't look like a standard police-issue certified-nonlethal weapon.

"I think it's okay," Silas told the stranger. "They left some time ago. Just cut me loose, will you?"

The stranger must have been looking him directly in the face, but no eyes were visible behind the distorting mask.

"Who are you?" Silas asked as it dawned on him belatedly that his troubles might not be over.

The masked man didn't reply. A second man came into the room behind him, equally anonymous and just as intimidatingly armed. Meanwhile, the first man extended his gun—holding its butt in both hands—and fired at point-blank range.

Silas hadn't time to let out a cry of alarm, let alone to feel the pain of the damage that must have followed the impact or to appreciate the full horror of the fact that without his protective IT even a "certified-nonlethal" shot might easily be the death of him.

Twenty-three

Damon was intending to call Interpol anyway, so the fact that his phone hood lit up like a firework display commanding him to do exactly that didn't even make a dent in his schedule. It did worry him, though; no one got a five-star summons like that unless there was something far more important on the agenda than his ex-girlfriend's bail bond.

Hiru Yamanaka took Damon's incoming call personally. Interpol's phone VE was stern and spare but more elaborate than Damon had expected. Mr. Yamanaka was reproduced in full, in an unnaturally neat suitskin uniform, sitting behind an imposing desk. The scene radiated calm, impersonal efficiency—which meant, Damon thought, that it was as inaccurate in its implications as the most blithely absurd of his own concoctions.

"What's happened?" Damon asked without preamble.

"Thank you for calling, Mr. Hart," the inspector said with a determined formality that only served to emphasize the falseness of his carefully contrived inscrutability. "There are several matters I'd like to discuss with you." The inspector's eyes were bleak, and Damon knew that things must have taken a turn for the worse—but he also knew that Yamanaka would want to work to a carefully ordered script. The inspector knew that Damon was holding out on him, and he didn't like it.

"Go on," Damon said, meekly enough.

"Firstly, we've received the medical examiner's final report on the body discovered in the house where Miss Caisson was arrested. DNA analysis confirms that it's the body of Surinder Nahal. The ME estimates that the time of death was at least two hours before Miss Caisson and Madoc Tamlin arrived on the scene, so we're certain that they didn't kill him, but it has become a matter of great urgency that we see the VE pak which your friend removed from the scene. We have reason to believe that it might contain valuable evidence as to the identity of the real killer and the motive for the crime."

What reason? Damon wondered. "I'd be very interested to see it myself," he countered warily. "Unfortunately, I haven't been able to contact Madoc. I presume, then, that you'll be releasing Diana immediately?"

"I'm afraid not," Yamanaka told him. "The local police are still considering the possibility of charging her with illegal entry—and she was of course an accessory to the assault."

"So charge her and bail her out."

"I'm reluctant to do that until I've talked to Madoc Tamlin," the inspector told him.

"You can't hold her hostage, Mr. Yamanaka."

"I wouldn't dream of it," Yamanaka assured him, "but until Tamlin and the VE pak are safely in my hands, I can't be sure of the exact extent of her culpability." The virtual atmosphere was still heavily pregnant with some vital item of information that Yamanaka was carefully withholding.

Damon fought to suppress his annoyance, but it wasn't easy. "You must know as well as I do that the VE pak is an ill-wrapped parcel of red herring that's already begun to stink," he told the inspector waspishly. "The same is probably true of its resting place."

Yamanaka didn't raise an eyebrow, but it seemed to Damon that the policeman's synthesized gaze became more tightly focused. "Do you have any evidence to support the conjecture that the body is *not* that of Surinder Nahal?" the inspector asked sharply.

"No, I don't," Damon admitted, "but the evidence that it *is* could have been cooked up by a biotech team with the necessary expertise just as easily as a fake VE tape. If whoever is behind the kidnapping really is convinced for some reason that Conrad Helier faked his own death, it would be only natural for him to hire a bioengineer with a similar background to repeat the trick. Ask yourself, Inspector Yamanaka—if you were in that position, who would *you* have hired to do the job?"

"I'm a policeman, Mr. Hart," Yamanaka reminded him. "However difficult it may be, my job is to collect evidence and build cases. You, on the other hand, are a citizen. Your duty, however you might resent it, is to obey the law and give what assistance you can to my investigation. That VE pak was taken from a crime scene, which makes it evidence—and I'd be very annoyed if anyone tampered with it before handing it in."

"If I can get the VE pak for you," Damon said bluntly, "will you drop all the charges against Madoc and Diana?"

"That's not my decision," Yamanaka replied unyieldingly.

Damon gritted his teeth and paused for a few seconds, instructing himself to remain calm. "What else?" he asked. "What's happened to heat things up?"

"We've found another body," the inspector told him bleakly.

"Karol's?" Damon asked, although he knew that was the lesser of the two probable evils.

"No—Silas Arnett's. He was found in a body bag dumped in the middle of a road up in the Hollywood Hills. Police officers conducting a routine search of the neighborhood found a chair identical to that displayed in the first broadcast tape in a house nearby. There were bloodstains on some recently severed straps that had been used to bind a man's wrists and ankles to the chair. There were several spy eyes in the walls of the room, all of them on short loop times. The tapes we've recovered show Arnett being shot in the chest while still confined. The man in the body bag died from exactly such a gunshot—without his internal technology, he had no effective defenses against such an injury."

Damon was silent for a few moments, absorbing this news.

"Does the tape show the shooter?" he asked.

"Yes, but he's unidentifiable. His suitskin had a face mask. He had a companion, similarly masked."

"But you think they're Eliminators—and you suspect that the VE pak left on the burned body will be a similar record of an execution."

"The body bag was presumably placed in the road in order to draw attention to the house, and to the tape," Yamanaka said. "That seems consonant with the hypothesis that the shooting was the work of Eliminators."

Damon couldn't be sure whether the careful wording was routine scrupulousness, or whether Yamanaka was laying down a red carpet for any alternative explanation Damon might have to offer. Damon had already laid the groundwork for a rival account by suggesting that the burned body Madoc had found wasn't Nahal's at all but merely some dummy tricked out to *seem* like Nakal's, possibly designed by Nahal himself—but Silas Arnett's body hadn't been burned to a crisp.

We haven't killed anyone, the mirror man had said—but he had certainly exposed the people he had named to the danger of Eliminator attack. Now Karol's boat had been blown up, and Silas Arnett had been shot. If Conrad Helier had faked his own death, perhaps he had faked those incidents too—but that *if* was looming larger by the minute. Nor was Silas the only one who had been exposed to possible Eliminator wrath by the mirror man's stupid broadcasts. Damon was the only one alive who had been forthrightly condemned as an "enemy of mankind."

There was still a possibility, Damon told himself, that this was all a game, all a matter of carefully contrived illusions piled up tit-for-tat—but if it weren't, he could be in big trouble. The question was: what did he intend to do about it?

"Your people always seem to be one step behind, Mr. Yamanaka," he observed, by way of making time to think.

"So it seems," the inspector agreed. "I think it might help if you were to tell us *everything* you know, don't you? Surely even you must see that the time has come to give us the VE pak."

It was the "even you" that did it. Damon felt that he had troubles enough without insult being added to injury.

"I don't have it," he snapped. "I don't have *anything* that you could count as evidence."

Yamanaka's image didn't register any overt trace of disappointment or annoyance, but the lack of display had to be a matter of pride. Yamanaka still had one card up his sleeve, and he didn't hesitate to play it in spite of its meager value. "Miss Caisson is *very* anxious to contact you, Mr. Hart," he said. "I'm sure she'd be grateful if you'd return her calls."

"Thanks for your concern," Damon said drily. "I'll do that. Please call me if you have any more news." He broke the connection and immediately called the number Diana had inscribed on his answering machine in letters of fire that were only a little less clamorous than Interpol's formal demand.

The LAPD's switchboard shunted him into a VE very different from the one Hiru Yamanaka had employed: a pseudophotographic image in which Diana was seated in a jail cell behind a wall of virtual glass. Fortunately, she seemed more relieved than angry to see him. She hadn't forgiven him anything, but she was desperate for contact with the outside world.

"I've just been talking to Yamanaka," Damon said, by way of preemptive self-protection. "I told him to charge you and bail you if he wasn't prepared simply to release you, but he won't do it. He's got dead bodies piling up all over the place, and he wants Madoc badly. He'll be forced to let you go eventually, but you'll have to be patient."

"This is crazy, Damon," Diana complained. "They must know that we didn't kill the guy. We didn't even know the body was there."

"They know you didn't kill him," Damon reassured her. "What on earth possessed *you* to go there? Why was Madoc fool enough to let you?"

"I was only trying to help," Diana said defensively.

"Thanks," Damon said, for diplomatic reasons. There was no point in contradicting her, even though it was a blatant lie. "I'm sorry you got involved in this, Di—but I'll do my best to make sure that you get out clean."

"If the Eliminators are after you," she told him sharply, "I'm hardly likely to stand idly by and let them get you, am I? Just because we fell out over private matters doesn't mean that I want you hurt."

For the sake of eavesdroppers, Damon said: "As soon as Madoc contacts me I'll tell him to turn himself in and hand the VE pak to Interpol. I'll pay for his lawyer and any fine he incurs. Neither of us ever intended our investigation to overstep the limits of the law, and I'll make certain that there are no further transgressions."

"And what then?" she asked, presumably hoping that he might have an olive branch ready to extend to her.

"I might have to go away for a while," he said.

"Where?" she wanted to know. She was trying hard to cling to a forgiving mood—or at least the appearance of one—but all her resentments were still bubbling away beneath the surface.

"I don't know. I've been out of touch with my family for too long; it might be a good idea to rebuild some bridges. If Karol and Silas really are dead I ought to see Eveline, even if it means a trip into space. There's just the two of us now, it seems—and I hear that one can get a very different perspective on things from L-Five. One that helps a lot of things become clear."

Diana looked at him as if she thought he might be taunting her. In her view, the first person he ought to be seeing with a view to putting things right was her. "And *then* what?" she said, not bothering to apply the brake to the escalation of her anger.

"I don't know, Di," Damon said, refusing to be drawn. "I haven't thought any further ahead than that. Just sit tight for a while, okay? You'll be out soon."

As soon as she realized that he had no intention of sticking around for a row, her rising anger melted into mere anxiety. "Don't go," she said swiftly. "We really need to talk, Damon— to straighten things out."

"*Those* things are already straightened out," he said as gently as he could. "None of this concerns you, Di. I didn't know you'd gone to Madoc when I asked him to help me. I suppose I'd have asked him anyway, because he was the one who seemed best placed to help me out—but to be honest, Di, your involvement is a complication I could well do without. Let's leave things as they are, shall we?"

"You ungrateful bastard!" she howled as the anger returned in full force. "After all I've done for—"

"I don't have time for this, Di," Damon said brutally—and broke the connection.

He remained silent and still in the ensuing darkness for a few moments while he collected himself, and then he returned himself to one of his own customized VEs: one which made it appear that he was imprisoned within a vast multifaceted gem. He set up his other messages on a virtual lectern and began to scroll through them tiredly, fearful of finding some Eliminator threat that would further intensify his confusion and anxiety. Mercifully, nothing of that kind seemed to be lurking among the more usual junk.

Had he been in a more conventional holding pattern Damon would have noticed the flicker earlier, but it hardly showed up against the dazzling crystalline background and its first effect was to communicate an unfocused and near-subliminal awareness that something was slightly out of kilter. He glanced around anxiously for a moment or two, wondering whether there was some kind of glitch in his code reader, before he realized what was happening—at which point he returned his attention to the lectern and tried to look as if he were engrossed in the routine business of informational triage.

Having dumped all the electronic junk and sorted the scant remainder, Damon called Karol's base at Molokai, to ask for news of the men injured in the explosion aboard the *Kite*. The man summoned by the AI answerphone to take the call evidently knew who Damon was, although Damon didn't recall seeing him on Molokai, but he seemed to have classified Damon as an outsider, if not a hostile witness. He gave a brusque rundown of the injuries sustained by crewmen Damon had never met but said that Karol hadn't yet been found, dead or alive.

Damon put on a show of profuse apologies and deep concern, in the course of which he asked his impatient informant for permission to switch the call into one of his own VEs. When the other shrugged his shoulders Damon decanted them into a pleasantly moonlit meadow. The signal hidden within the flicker was easier to read there, but Damon carefully gave no indication that he was paying attention to anything other than the tense features of Karol's associate.

He learned nothing of interest except that Rajuder Singh had made a full recovery from his "accidental injuries" and had joined in the search for Karol—or for Karol's body. His informant didn't react to the news that Silas Arnett had been found dead.

"Have you got the centipedes out of the island's systems?" Damon asked mischievously. "It must have been very inconvenient to have the elevator out of commission."

"Everything is under our full control once again," the other informed him brusquely, "but we still have a great deal of work to do. I must go now."

"I've a lot to do myself," Damon assured him, having made his own decisions. "I'll call again for further news of Karol."

When he came out from under the hood Damon immediately went to the bathroom and took a shower. He scrubbed himself as thoroughly as he could, although he knew full well that there were bugs on the market nowadays that no amount of scrubbing could remove. He had to hope that the people who'd taken him to the foothills of Olympus and lied to him about his ability to fly hadn't been able to see any reason for getting under his skin— or that if anything *had* been planted under his skin his own internal technology had been able to take care of the intrusion.

He went into the bedroom to put on a fresh suitskin, but he didn't take his beltpack or sidepouch from the bedside table where he'd laid them down. The only things he picked up were two swipecards that had been lurking at the back of a drawer let into the beside table; these he placed in a pocket in the lower element of the suitskin.

After leaving the apartment Damon stopped the elevator at street level instead of going down into the car park. He went out into the street, nodding politely to Building Security's desk man as he passed by, and ambled along the crowded pavement, checking the reflections in a number of plate-glass windows just in case he was dealing with people who thought that the unsophisticated approach was best.

By the time he'd taken three turns he had identified the man who was following him. It seemed infinitely more likely that the tail was one of Yamanaka's men rather than an Eliminator, but Damon knew that no one could prove that he had even considered the possibility, and he wasn't feeling much better disposed toward the forces of law and order than he was to crazy assassins.

Damon took another turn down a service alley cluttered with recycling bins that had been richly fed with the litter of a dozen stores and businesses. He had plenty of time to duck out of sight behind the second bin before his pursuer turned the corner.

The man who moved furtively into the alley, anxiously craning his neck for some sign of his target's passage, was at least five centimeters taller than Damon and eight or ten kilos heavier. Damon knew that if he *were* a cop he'd also have taken lessons in the art of self-defense—but Damon had a much more extensive education in the art of attack. When his follower reached the dump bin Damon went for him without delay, aiming his first kick at the inside of the man's knee and the first upward sweep of his hand at the Adam's apple.

Damon didn't pause when his opponent went down. He kicked again and again, as hard as he could. He knew that the man's IT would take care of the damage, but that didn't figure in his calculations. He was glad of the opportunity to hit back at his persecutors, knowing that this time there would be no gas grenades to interrupt him.

Until he had laid the man unconscious, Damon had not known how much anger and frustration had been pent up in him; but the exhilaration of the whirlwind action had hardly begun the work of purging it. He felt a perverse stab of disappointment when no one else appeared in the alley's mouth to provide a further challenge.

He knelt down beside his victim and checked the pouches in the man's beltpack. There was nothing to identify him; like Damon, he was carrying no identifiers save for a gnomic set of unmarked swipecards. Damon picked these up by the edges, wondering whether it might be worth keeping the swipecards to see what might be retrieved electronically therefrom. He knew, though, that if the man *were* a policeman it wouldn't be a good idea to be found in possession of stolen goods. In the end, he replaced the cards in the pouch.

Before Damon went on he landed one last gratuitous kick on the side of the stricken man's head, just in case he deserved it: one which would leave an ugly and very noticeable bruise.

As soon as he had put a safe distance between himself and the alley, Damon went into a clothing store. He bought a new suitskin off the peg and left his own behind in the fitting room, transferring nothing to the new garment except the two swipecards. After leaving the store he booked into a public gym and took another shower, just in case his hair or skin had picked up any stray nanomachines while he had been getting rid of the inconvenient follower. Madoc had always advised him that the cleverest bugs were the ones that infected you *after* you figured that you'd purged them all.

As soon as he was finished in the gym Damon moved away from the busier streets toward ones which were less well-equipped with eyes and ears, taking shortcuts whenever they became available and changing direction five times to make any attempted analysis of his movements virtually impossible. Then he called into a bar so that he could look up Lenny Garon's address on the customers' directory terminal.

He thought it best to move once more before getting down to

the serious business of the day, so he slipped out into the street again and wandered into a run-down mall which had a row of terminal booths. All of them were empty.

Damon slotted one of the swipecards and immediately set to work, his fingers flying over the keyplate. He knew that he had less than two minutes in which to make his mark, and that he wouldn't be able to do much more than five minutes' worth of sabotage—but the evening traffic was already building up and five minutes would be enough to store up a wealth of trouble.

When he emerged from the mall again every traffic signal for at least a kilometer in all directions was on green, and the jams were building up at every intersection.

He'd estimated that five minutes of downtime ought to be enough to snarl up at least twenty thousand vehicles, creating a jam so tight that it would take at least an hour to clear. The pavements were jamming up almost as badly as the gridlocked vehicles, and tempers were soaring in the late afternoon heat with amazing rapidity.

Damon kept on ducking and dodging until he was certain that he was free and clear of all humanly possible pursuit, and then he began the painstaking business of making his way across town to his destination—the destination that had been coded into the flicker affecting his domestic VEs.

That flicker had used a code which he and Madoc Tamlin had worked out seven years before, so that they might exchange information while under observation, using their fingers or any object with which a man might reasonably fidget. It was a crude code, but Damon still remembered every letter of the alphabet.

L-E-N-N-Y, the flicker had spelled out.

There was only one Lenny the signal could possibly refer to, and only one reason why Madoc might want him to visit the Lenny in question. Whether Madoc was with him or not, Lenny Garon had to have the VE pak which Madoc had stolen from under the noses of the LAPD—the one piece of the mirror man's carefully constructed puzzle which had been prematurely swept from the field of play.

Damon didn't imagine for a moment that whatever the VE tape had to show him would be any more reliable than the VE tapes of Silas Arnett's bogus confessions, but just for once he wanted to be a step ahead of all the people who were trying to push him around. Just for once, he wanted to be able to do things *his* way—whatever his way turned out to be, when he'd had time to think and time to make a plan.

Damon knew that he had to advise Madoc to turn himself in, but he had told Diana the truth when he said that he might have to go away, perhaps even to rebuild bridges linking him to his estranged family. Everything depended on what Madoc had found out about Silas's kidnappers and about what had *really* happened to Surinder Nahal.

Twenty-four

The capstack in which Lenny Garon lived was not one of the more elegant applications of gantzing technology—as was only to be expected, given that it dated back to a time before PicoCon had acquired the Gantz patents and begun the synergistic combination of Leon Gantz's exclusively organic technology with their own inorganic nanotech. In those days, gantzers had looked for models in nature which their trained bacteria might be able to duplicate without too much macrotech assistance, and they had come up with the honeycomb: six-sided cells laid out in rows nested one on top of another.

The pattern had the strength to support tall structures—Lenny's stack was forty stories high—but the resultant buildings had zigzag edges that looked decidedly untidy. The individual apartments came out like long square tubes with triangular-sectioned spaces behind each sidewall, into which all the supportive apparatus of modern life had to be built. Bathrooms and kitchens tended to be consigned to this inconvenient residuum, so that the square section only needed one dividing wall separating living room and bedroom.

All this might have seemed charming, in a minimalist sort of way, had it not been for the fact that the entire edifice in which Lenny Garon lived had been gantzed out of pale gray concrete rubble and dark gray mud. Beside the more upmarket blocks that had been tastefully decorated in lustrous pigments borrowed from flowering plants or the wing cases of beetles, Lenny's building looked like a glorified termite mound.

"Thanks for coming, Damon," Lenny said, anxiously blinking his eyes as he checked the corridor while letting Damon into a capsule that was only slightly more squalid than the rest. "I really appreciate your giving me the benefit of your experience."

It took Damon a moment or two to realize that the boy was putting on a show for the eyes and ears that even walls as shabby as these must be expected to contain, in case anyone should ever consult them with a view to identifying accessories to a crime. He didn't bother to add his own line to the silly charade.

"Thanks, Lenny," Madoc said to the anxious streetfighter, once Damon was safely inside. "Now take a walk, will you. I'll pay you a couple of hundred in rent, but you'll have to forget you ever saw us, okay?"

Lenny was evidently disappointed by the abrupt dismissal, but he was appropriately impressed by the notion that he could sublet his apartment by the hour for real money. "Be my guest," he said—but he dawdled at the door before opening up again. "I hear you're an enemy of mankind now, Damon. Good going—anything I can do, you only have to ask."

"Thanks," Damon said. "I will."

As the door slid shut behind the boy Damon looked around the room, wondering why people still chose to live this way in a city full of empty spaces. While the greater part of Los Angeles slowly rotted down to dust—whole counties ripe for redevelopment by today's more expert gantzers—it was preference rather than economic necessity which kept its poorer people huddled together in neighborhoods full of high-rise blocks, living in narrow rooms with fold-down beds, kitchens the size of cupboards, and even smaller bathrooms.

Perhaps, Damon thought, people had grown so completely accustomed to crowding during the years before the Crash that their long-lived children had had the habit ingrained in their mental pathways during infancy, and there simply weren't enough children in Lenny Garon's generation to start a mass migration to fresher fields. That kind of explanation seemed, at any rate, to make more sense than oft-parroted clichés about buildings needing services and the proximity principles of supply and transport.

"I suppose you heard what happened?" Madoc said miserably.

"Yamanaka gave me the brute facts," Damon admitted. "I talked to Diana, but she had other things on her mind and it wouldn't have been a good idea to tell me anything the cops didn't already know. You found a VE pak—have you had a chance to play it through?"

"Sure. I took it all the way to the top—the Old Lady herself—so that we could play it through without anyone else looking in. It shows Silas Arnett being questioned by Surinder Nahal, giving answers very different from those he gave on the tape that was dumped on the Web. Do you want to see it? The Old Lady says it's just another fake, probably cooked up for Interpol's benefit."

"It doesn't show Nahal being killed?"

Madoc was infinitely more willing than Hiru Yamanaka to display his surprise. "No," he said, raising his eyebrows. "Why would it?"

"That's what Yamanaka's expecting. They found Silas dead and a tape that shows him being shot—as if it were an execution."

"Eliminators?" Madoc asked.

"That's what it looks like," Damon said with a sigh, "but we live in a very deceptive world. Unfortunately, the fact that it's only one more fake cooked up for his benefit won't make Yamanaka any less anxious to get his hands on the VE pak. Avoiding loss of face is just about the only thing left to him—he must know by now that the people behind this are out of reach. The police might think they're maintaining the law of the land, just as the Washington Rump still thinks it's in charge of making it, but the whole system is exhausted. When all appearances can be manufactured, the concept of *evidence* loses its meaning."

Madoc released the VE pak from where he'd loaded it into Lenny Garon's console and passed it over to Damon. "Do you know who's behind this?" he asked.

"I haven't the faintest idea," Damon admitted. "According to a dream I had when they snatched me away from Karol's friends, it's someone who claims to be speaking on behalf of the entire world order, but that might be megalomania or simple over-statement."

Madoc was so enthusiastic to say what he had to say that he didn't bother to query Damon's reference to a dream. "The Old Lady says that it's someone from PicoCon. Someone high up in the corp structure." He met Damon's eyes anxiously, looking for a reaction.

"That would make sense," Damon conceded. "It has to be someone with access to cutting-edge technology, and PicoCon is the edge beyond the edge. I'm sorry I got you into this, Madoc— I thought at first that it was just a petty thing. Nobody expects to go after an Eliminator Operator and run into the full might of PicoCon."

"The cops know that I didn't kill the guy whose body we found, don't they?" Madoc queried uneasily.

"Sure. Yamanaka knows that the corpse was torched several hours before you got there. His own surveillance team gave you a perfect alibi. If you say the cops spooked you—came in without a proper warning or whatever—you might excuse the blow with the crowbar as a reflexive response. The LAPD will want to pay off some of their grievances against you, but a decent lawyer ought to be able to persuade a judge to take a reasonable view of the matter."

"Who did kill him, do you think?" Madoc asked cautiously. "PicoCon?"

"I'm not sure that anybody did. I suspect that the orchestrator of this little pantomime is trying to establish that in today's world a body, an autopsy, and a DNA analysis don't add up to proof that someone is actually dead. The people behind this are convinced that Conrad Helier's alive, and they refuse to be told that he's not."

"Where did they get a body with Surinder Nahal's DNA?" Madoc wanted to know.

"Tissue-culture tanks that turn out steaks the size of a building could turn a half a liter of blood into a skeleton with a few vital organs and a covering of skin, without even needing rejuve technology to stretch the Hayflick limit. If Karol's body ever gets fished out of the Pacific, I suspect it'll be just as thoroughly beaten up and just as fake. None of which would prove anything about my father, who died in bed of natural causes—*his* cadaver would have gone to the medical examiner with every last anatomical detail in its proper place. As for Silas . . . well, it looks as if he really *might* be dead, but I don't know what to believe anymore. What else have you got for me?"

"Not much," Madoc admitted with an apologetic sigh. "The way the latest round of false testimony is being set in place, it *looks* as if this guy Nahal had some kind of grudge against your father and his cronies that he'd been nursing for a hundred years. It *looks* as if Nahal had Arnett snatched, and that he put out the counterfeit Operator one-oh-one stuff himself—although the word is already out that the woman who built up the Operator one-oh-one name and reputation has turned herself in to prove that her name's been taken in vain. If you want stand-up proof that the *real* movers and shakers are PicoCon people, I don't have any—and I don't think you or I could ever come up with any. Do you think *they* killed Arnett so he couldn't retract his confessions?"

Damon shrugged. "I haven't been idling around while you've been battling it out with the LAPD," he said. "I got kidnapped twice—once by Karol's hirelings and once by some people who didn't want Karol's hirelings to put me away. The second crowd introduced me to the VE to end all VEs—a manufactured dream, of the kind the industry's been trying to develop for a century and more. It might have been a trick, and I suppose it *might* have been a real dream—but if it wasn't the spokesman for the movers and shakers gave me a message to pass on to my dead father. Then they stuck me in a derelict house with Lenny's friend Cathy to wait for the bloodhounds." After a slight pause he went on: "The Old Lady has to be right. No one but PicoCon could have access to VE tech that far ahead of the market—although the guy I talked to, whose image was all tricked out like some chrome-plated holovid robot, spun me some line about products not being made for the market anymore."

"Lenny told me about Cathy," Madoc said. "Was she in on Arnett's kidnap?"

"I don't think so—although they probably planted the centipedes that disabled Silas's defenses in her luggage when they found out he'd invited her to stay. Her abduction was just a red herring. Whoever's doing this—and I mean the individual in charge of the operation, not the corp—believes in having his fun while he works."

"What was the message to your father?" Madoc asked curiously but tentatively. He obviously half expected to be told that it wasn't his business.

Damon didn't see any need to keep that particular secret. "Stop playing God," he said bluntly. When Madoc raised his eyebrows, expecting further elaboration, he added: "Apparently, everybody who's anybody wants to play God nowadays, and the *big* gods way up on Olympus are trying to figure out a set of protocols that will allow them all to play together. They want everybody to abide by the rules. If the story I was told can be taken seriously, this thing got started because my foster parents turned churlish when they were invited to join the club. So did the people at Ahasuerus. The alleged purpose of this little game is simply to force them to play ball, but the fact that it's being formulated as a game certainly doesn't mean that it's harmless. You know what they say: '*As flies to wanton boys are we to the gods; they kill us for their sport.*' "

"What's that supposed to mean?" Madoc demanded obligingly.

"It means that self-appointed gods inevitably begin to see *everything* as a game," Damon told him. "When you can do anything at all, you can only decide what to do at any particular moment on aesthetic grounds. Once you get past the groundwork of Creation, what is there to do with what you've made but play with it?"

Madoc picked up the thread of the argument readily enough. "Is that what your foster parents are doing? Playing a game with the world they made?"

Damon shrugged his shoulders. "If they are," he said, "they're being very secretive about it. Karol dropped a few hints, but the guys he hired to remove me from the action were giving nothing away. I suppose it's only natural that after I dropped out they'd want me to get down on my knees and beg before they let me in again."

"But you don't want to get back in. You've got a life of your own now."

"It's not that simple anymore," Damon said.

"It is if you want it to be."

"I suppose I can simply refuse to play messenger no matter how hard I'm pressed," Damon conceded, working through that train of thought. "I could go home, get back into my hood and pick up where I left off, building Planet X for those game players, designing phone tapes, putting Di into the pornotape and taking her out again, using her and then erasing all the recognizable aspects of her individuality. I *could* just get on with my work and hope that I'll be allowed to get on with it in peace—except that after my little trip to Olympus, I'm no longer sure that kind of thing is worth doing. The chrome-plated cheat who told me I could fly was lying—but I think he was trying to persuade me that if only I were willing to come aboard I might be able to *learn* to fly."

Madoc couldn't follow that, but Damon was too preoccupied with his own train of thought to pause for fuller explanations. "The trouble is," he went on, "that when you've looked up at Olympus and down into the ultimate abyss, it puts everything else into a new perspective—even though you know full well that it's only a VE, just one more small step on the way to realizing *all* our dreams. That's who the *real* movers and shakers were supposed to be, in the original poem: not statesmen or corpsmen, but dreamers of dreams."

"Realizing our dreams is a long hard road for people like you and me," Madoc pointed out. "Our kind of work might look a little shabby compared with PicoCon's, but how else are people like us to work our way up? Unless, of course, you've decided that now you've broken into your father's money you might as well use it all. You don't have to—just because you're not a virgin anymore it doesn't mean you're a whore." He sounded genuinely concerned for the matter of principle that seemed to be at stake.

"I want to *know*, Madoc," Damon said softly. "I want to know *exactly* what's going on—and you can't find out for me. PicoCon has all the answers; maybe I *should* try to get aboard."

"A corpsman? Not you, Damon. Not *that*."

Damon shrugged again. "Maybe I should go to Lagrange-Five, then, and make my peace with Eveline. She might have been a lousy mother, but she's the only one I have left . . . and *she* must know what all this is about, whether my father's alive or not."

"Nobody needs mothers anymore," Madoc opined. "All that went out with the sterility plagues—but if you choose your friends wisely, they'll be with you all the way. Whether you use the money or not, you can still be Damon Hart. If you and I stick together, we can still take on the world."

Damon knew that they were talking at cross-purposes—that Madoc's anxieties weren't connecting with his at all. Even so, the underlying substance of Madoc's argument was closer to the heart of the matter than Madoc probably knew.

Damon was still trying to figure out what his next step ought to be when the door buzzer went.

"Shit!" said Madoc, immediately moving to hit a combination of keys on the console of Lenny Garon's display screen.

The camera mounted in the outside of the door dutifully showed them two men standing in the corridor, waiting for an answer to their signal. Damon couldn't put a name to either one of them, but one of them was unusually tall—and he was sporting an ugly and very obvious bruise.

Damon echoed Madoc's expletive.

"Who are they?" Madoc asked, having picked up the note of recognition in Damon's tone.

"Probably cops," Damon said. "The big one followed me from my building. I thought I'd put him out of it—I hit him hard enough to stop any ordinary man tailing me. Must be tougher or smarter than I thought."

The man with the bruise was already growing impatient. "Mr. Tamlin?" he said. "It's all right, Mr. Tamlin—we're not the police. We just want—"

Mr. Tamlin? Damon echoed silently, wondering why on earth they were addressing themselves to Madoc rather than to him. Before he had time to focus on the seemingly obvious inference, however, the tall man's attempted explanation was brutally cut short. Something hurtled into him from beyond the limits of the picture frame and sent him cannoning into his companion.

"Oh, *shit!*" said Madoc, with even more feeling than before—but he was already diving for the door to wrestle it open.

Damon, for once, was much slower to react. He was still trying to piece together the logic of what was happening.

Lenny Garon had obviously not gone far when Madoc had suggested that he take a walk. Indeed, he had evidently taken it upon himself to stand guard somewhere along the corridor. As soon as he had seen the two strangers press his door buzzer, he had decided that Damon and Madoc were in dire need of his protection—and he had thrown himself at the two visitors with little or no regard for his own safety. If they were telling the truth about not being the police, Lenny might be in very grave danger indeed; he didn't have the kind of IT which could pull him through a *real* fight.

Madoc had the door open by now, and he hardly paused to take stock of the situation before throwing himself at the tall man's companion, who was already struggling to his feet.

The man with the bruise had knocked Lenny aside, but wasn't going after him. Instead, he was backing up toward the far wall of the corridor, holding his arms out as if he were trying to calm everything down. He had opened his mouth, probably to shout "Wait!" but he choked on the syllable as he looked into the open doorway and caught sight of Damon. The shock in his eyes seemed honest enough. He really had come looking for Madoc Tamlin, not knowing that Damon would be here too.

Damon still hesitated, but Lenny Garon didn't. Lenny had already committed himself and he was sky-high on his own adrenalin. The boy went after the tall man like a ferret after a rat, and his adversary had no alternative but to turn his placatory gesture into a stern defense.

Cop or not, the man with the bruise was certainly no innocent in the art of self-defense, and he had already been knocked down too often to tolerate being put down again. He blocked Lenny's lunging blows and hit the boy, then grabbed him and smashed him into the wall as hard as he could—hard enough to break bones.

That made Damon's mind up. He went after the tall man for a second time, determined to amplify the bruises he had already inflicted. As he charged through the doorway he didn't even look to see what had become of Madoc and the second man; he trusted Madoc's streetfighting instincts implicitly.

Again the man with the bruise tried to avoid the fight. He backed up the corridor as rapidly as he could, and this time he actually managed to shout: "Wait! You don't—"

Damon didn't wait for the "understand"—he kicked out at the knee he'd already weakened in the alley. The tall man yelped in agony and dropped to one knee, but he was still trying to scramble away, still trying to put a halt to the whole fight.

Damon figured that there'd be plenty of time for discussion once he and Madoc had the two men safely under control in Lenny's capsule, so he didn't stop. He slashed at the man's throat exactly as he had done before, and made some sort of connection before something slammed into his back and pitched him forward onto his knees.

His instinct was to lash out backward, on the assumption that someone had charged into him, but there was no one there—and the pain in his back grew and grew with explosive rapidity, giving him just time to realize that he had been shot yet again: hit by some kind of dart whose poison was making merry hell with his nervous system. His IT was undoubtedly fighting the effect, and the pain soon slackened to crawling discomfort—but he didn't lose consciousness. His rigid body hit the ground with a sickening thud, but the dart hadn't been loaded with the kind of poison that would force his senses to switch off.

As the two men snatched him up and scuttled toward the stairs, though, he began to wish that it had.

Twenty-five

Damon never did lose consciousness, but the consciousness he kept had little in reserve for keeping track of what was happening to his paralyzed body. He knew that he had been loaded into the back of a car which roared off at high speed, and he knew that when the car eventually stopped he was taken out again and bundled into a helicopter—but the only part of the journey that really *commanded* his attention was the time they tried to force his paralyzed limbs into a different configuration so that they could strap him into one of the helicopter's seats. He heard a great deal more than he saw, but most of what he heard was curses and oblique complaints from which he wouldn't have learned anything worth a damn even if he'd been able to concentrate.

What he *was* conscious of, to the expense of almost everything else, was the battle inside his body for control of his neurones. He knew that the sensation of being occupied by hundreds of thousands of ants burrowing their way through his tissues wasn't *really* the movement of his nanomachines, but it was hard to imagine it any other way. It wasn't especially painful, but it was severely discomfiting, both psychologically and physically. He was reasonably certain that he would come through it safely and sanely, but it was an ordeal nevertheless.

Damon found a little time to wonder whether the two hit

men—which was what they presumably were, given that they certainly didn't seem to be cops—knew what effect the weapons they carried might have on moderately IT-rich victims, and whether they cared, but it wasn't until he began to recover fully possession of himself that he was able to pay close attention to their conversation. By that time, the thrum of the helicopter's rotors had bludgeoned them into taciturnity—a taciturnity that might have lasted until they landed had not the man he'd ambushed in the alley noticed that Damon was recovering from the effects of the shot. That was enough to restart the catalogue of complaints; his luckless pursuer obviously had a lot of grievances to air.

"You've got a real problem, you know that?" the tall man said. "You hear me? A real problem."

Damon fought for the composure necessary to move his head from side to side and blink his eyes. When he eventually succeeded in clearing his blurred vision, he was surprised to see that the bruise on the man's face was in better condition than it had any right to be. Somewhere along the line, he'd slapped some synthetic skin over it to provide his resident nanotech with an extra resource. The expression surrounding the bruise was one of whiney resentment.

Damon was sitting in a seat directly behind the helicopter's pilot. The shorter man who'd come to Madoc's apartment with the man with the fading bruise was sitting beside the pilot; the copter only had the four seats. Reflexively, Damon moved his reluctant hand toward the lock on his safety harness, but the tall man reached out to stop him.

"Careful!" he said. "You got me in enough trouble as it is. Anything else happens to you, I'll be out of a job for sure. *Please* sit tight. None of this was supposed to happen. If you'd just given me time to *talk* . . . like I said, you got a real problem, lashing out like that all the time. It's crazy!"

Damon felt an impulse to laugh, but he wasn't yet in any shape to act on it. He tried to edge sideways so that he could look out of the porthole beside his seat, but the effort proved too much.

Beyond the pilot, though, he could see dark green slopes and snow-capped peaks as well as sky. He thought he recognized Cobblestone Mountain directly ahead of the copter's course, although it was difficult to believe that they'd come so far in what had not seemed to be a long time.

"It isn't funny," the tall man complained, having deciphered the attempted laugh. "I guess I might have asked for it, the first time, waiting till you were in the alley before I tried to catch up and not realizing you'd gone in there to jump me—but what was all that stuff at the kid's apartment? We *told* you we weren't the police. Stupid kid could have got himself badly hurt."

By the time this speech was finished Damon had got his head far enough up to take a peep through the porthole, but it didn't tell him anything he didn't already know. They were in the hills, heading for the Sespe Wilderness.

"What happened to Madoc?" Damon asked weakly.

"We left him laid out on the kid's bed, with the VE pak cradled in his arms. The police will have them both by now—and don't blame us for having to do it that way. All we wanted was to get the tape to where it was always supposed to go. We would have let Tamlin go his own way if you hadn't practically started a war. The kid's in hospital again, but he'll be okay. You'll have to talk to him about his attitude—he doesn't have the IT for that kind of action."

"You didn't know I was there, did you?" Damon whispered, just to make sure. "I *thought* I left you in no shape to follow me."

"Damn right. Dirty trick, kicking a guy in the head when he's down. When I woke up I had to get new instructions. I was told to go get the tape, so that we could deliver it to Interpol, just as we intended when we left it with the burned-out body. You really are a nuisance, you know that? Thanks to you, I am having the worst day of my *life*. All I wanted to do was *talk* to you—and now you've *really* messed things up."

"You followed me into the alley because you wanted to talk to me?"

"Sure. Once you'd got rid of Yamanaka's bugs my employers

figured it was safe to have a private word. You could have had it in town and been free and clear by dinnertime, if you hadn't taken it into your fool head to start a shooting match in a public corridor."

"*You* started a shooting match," Damon pointed out. "Lenny only started a brawl."

"Either way," the tall man said in an aggrieved tone, "the cops will have dug out every bug in the walls by now and run the tapes. Your face, my face . . . and the face of my colleague here, who had no option but to pull his gun before your friend carved him up. All you had to do was let us in, but you had to wade in and we had to defend ourselves any way we could. Violence escalates—and now we're *all* in Yamanaka's file. You could have cost us our *jobs.*"

"How sad," Damon muttered. "Who exactly *is* your employer?"

"I can't answer that," the tall man complained. "All I wanted was a quiet word, and now I'm up for kidnapping. They have my *face*. They never got my face before, but who knows what'll happen now? I could be in real trouble."

"Why?" Damon wanted to know. "How many kidnappings did you do *before* they got a picture of your face?"

His captor wasn't about to answer that one either.

"Why didn't your *employer* have his quiet word before he turned me loose last time?" Damon demanded, allowing his tone to declare that *he* was the one who had the serious grievance, even though he no longer felt as if he were a fleshy ants' nest. "Why come after me again, after a mere matter of hours?"

"Something else went wrong," the tall man muttered. "You Heliers are absolute hell to deal with, I'll give you that."

"What?"

The man with the bruise shrugged his shoulders impatiently. "We were monitoring an eye at the place we left Arnett," he said. "We were expecting hugs all round when your people came to get him—but that wasn't the way it went. They shot him! Can you believe that? They *shot* him. Next thing we know, he's been dumped in the road!"

"Are you sure they *killed* him?" Damon asked sharply.

The tall man hesitated before he shrugged again, which suggested to Damon that it was a recognized possibility that Silas hadn't been killed and that the body dumped in the road might have been the same kind of substitute as the body left for Madoc to find. "His nanotech had all been flushed," the man with the bruise said eventually. "They must have known that if they watched the tape we put out on the Web. Maybe they were just knocking him out—but they had no reason to do that if they were *your* people. Who'd ever have thought Eliminators could be that smart, that well organized?"

"Who are *my* people supposed to be?" Damon asked him. "You mean Conrad Helier's people—except that Conrad Helier's dead. So is Karol Kachellek, except that you probably don't believe that either. So who's supposed to be running things, given that Eveline Hywood's a quarter of a million miles away in lunar orbit? Me?"

The tall man shook his head sadly. "All I wanted was a quiet *talk*," he repeated, as if he simply could not believe that such an innocent intention had led to brawling, shooting, and kidnapping—all of it dutifully registered on spy eyes that the police would have debriefed by now.

"Where are we going?" Damon asked.

"Out of town," the tall man informed him gruffly. "Your fault, not mine. We could have sorted it out back home if you hadn't blown it. Now, we have to take it somewhere *really* private."

The Sespe and Sequoia Wilderness reserves had supposedly been rendered trackless in the wake of the Second Plague War—by which time its chances of ever getting back to an authentic wilderness state were only a little better than zero—but Damon knew that closure against wheeled vehicles didn't signify much when helicopters like this one could land in a clearing thirty meters across.

"You can't get more private than Olympus," Damon said—but as he looked out again at the nonvirtual mountains which were now surrounding the helicopter he realized that he had actually contrived to force his adversaries to take a step they had not intended. This time, there was a record of his abduction in Interpol's hands. This time, Interpol could put faces and names to his captors, or at least to their foot soldiers. He knew that he could claim no credit for the coup—it was all the result of a chapter of accidents and misconceptions—but the fact remained that the game players had finally been taken beyond the limits of their game plan. They had been forced to improvise. For the first time, PicoCon—assuming that it *was* PicoCon—was losing its grip.

"Your boss is scared," Damon said, working through the train of thought. "He thinks it really might have been the Eliminators who got to Silas, after the people he expected to collect him never showed up. One minute he was convinced the message Silas was supposed to deliver was home and dry, the next he was unconvinced again. You're right—if Silas *is* dead you could be in real trouble, especially now that Interpol has two faces in the frame. Mr. Yamanaka doesn't like the way you've been running rings around him. He'll come after you with such ferocity that you'll be very lucky indeed to get away with only losing your job. How much damage could you do to PicoCon, do you think, if you and your partner decided to talk?"

The tall man didn't react to the mention of PicoCon. "All you had to do was *listen,*" he complained. "You could have saved us all a hell of a lot of trouble."

"If you were the ones who took Silas in the first place," Damon pointed out, "and posted that stupid provocative note under my door, you went to a hell of a lot of trouble yourselves, all because you *wouldn't listen* when we told you that Conrad Helier is dead."

"Sure," said the tall man scornfully. "Helier's dead, and para-DNA is a kind of extraterrestrial tar, just like Hywood says. *All you ever had to do was listen*—but now it's getting ugly and it's all *your* fault."

"*What* does Eveline say about para-DNA?" Damon wanted to know.

"If you spent more time listening to the news and less playing cloak-and-dagger, you'd know. She made an announcement to the entire world, press conference and all. Para-DNA is extraterrestrial—the first representative of an entirely new life system, utterly harmless but absolutely fascinating. We are not alone, the universe of life awaits us, etcetera, etcetera. Now we know where you got your impulsive nature from, don't we?"

"Are you saying that para-DNA *isn't* extraterrestrial—or that it isn't harmless?"

"I don't *know*," the tall man informed him, as if it were somehow Damon's fault that he didn't know. "All I know is that if it's on the news, it's more than likely to be lies, and that if the name Hywood's attached to it then it must have something to do with our little adventure. I may be only the hired help but I'm not *stupid*. Whatever all this is about, your people aren't responding sensibly. It doesn't take a genius to figure that Hywood was supposed to talk to my employers before she started shooting her mouth off to the whole wide world, but she decided to kick off early instead. The whole damn lot of you are so damn *touchy*. Must be hereditary."

Damon didn't bother to point out that Eveline Hywood wasn't his mother. Conrad Helier *was* his real father, and Conrad Helier's closest associates had provided the nurture to complement his nature. It had never occurred to him before that his contentiousness might be a legacy of his genes or his upbringing, but he could see now that someone considering his reactions to this strange affair alongside those of his foster parents might well feel entitled to lump them all together.

The helicopter now began its descent toward a densely wooded slope which, while nowhere near as precipitate as the slope of the virtual mountain where he had talked to the robot man, nevertheless seemed wild enough and remote enough to suit anyone's idea of perfect privacy.

It was just as well that the helicopter could land in a thirty-meter circle, because the space where it touched down wasn't significantly bigger. The tall man undid Damon's safety harness before he could do it himself and said: "Can you get down?"

"I'm fine," Damon assured him. "No thanks to you. You're not coming?"

"I'm far from fine—and that's entirely down to you," the man with the bruise countered. "*We* have to disappear. It wasn't exactly a pleasure meeting you, but at least I'll never see you again."

"You know," said Damon as the pilot reached back to open the door beside him, "you really have a problem. Apart from being an incompetent asshole, you have this moronic compulsion to blame other people for your own mistakes." He got the distinct impression that the tall man would have hit him, if only he'd dared.

"Thanks," said Damon to the pilot as he lowered himself to the ground. He ducked down low the way everybody always did on TV, although he knew that he was in no real danger from the whirling rotor blades.

There was a cabin on the edge of the clearing that looked at first glance as if it must have been two hundred years old if it were a day—but Damon saw as soon as he approached it that its "logs" had been gantzed out of wood pulp. He judged that its architect had been a relatively simple-minded AI. The edifice probably hadn't been there more than a year and shouldn't have been there at all. Given that the nearest road was halfway to Fillmore, though, it was certainly private; it probably had no electricity supply and no link to the Web. It was a playpen for the kind of people who thought that they could still get back in touch with "nature."

The man who was waiting for Damon stayed inside until the helicopter had risen from the ground, only showing himself in the doorway of the cabin when no one but Damon could see his face. Damon saw immediately that he was an *old* man, well preserved by nanotech without being prettified by rejuve cosmetology. His hair was white and he was wearing silver-rimmed eyeglasses. Nobody had to wear spectacles for corrective purpose anymore, so Damon assumed that he must have become used to wearing them in his youth, way back in the twenty-first century, and had kept them as a badge of antique eccentricity.

"Are you the Mirror Man?" Damon asked as he approached.

The ancient shook his head. "The Mirror Man's off the project," he said, evidently untroubled by the admission he was making in recognizing the description. "I've been appointed in his stead, to tidy things up—and to calm things down. Come in and make yourself at home." He pronounced the final phrase with conscientiously lighthearted sarcasm.

"I'm a prisoner," Damon pointed out as the other stood aside to let him pass, "not a guest."

"If you'd only paused to listen to what the man had to say," the old man replied mildly, "we'd have offered you a formal invitation. I think you'd have found it too tempting to refuse. You can call me Saul, by the way." It wasn't an invitation to intimacy; Damon guessed that if the man was called Saul at all it would be his surname, not his given name.

"Stay away from the road to Damascus," Damon muttered as he surveyed the room into which he was being ushered. "Revelations can really screw up your life."

The cabin's interior was more luxurious than the exterior had implied, but it had a gloss of calculated primitivism. Authentic logs were burning within the proscenium arch of an inauthentic stone fireplace set upon a polished stone hearth. There were three armchairs arranged in an arc around the hearth, although there was no one waiting in the cabin except the old man.

There was a stick of bread on the table, together with half a dozen plastic storage jars and three bottles: two of wine, one of whiskey. Damon almost expected to see hunting trophies on the wall, but that would have been too silly. Instead there were old photographs mounted in severe black frames: photographs taken in the days when the wilderness had only been half spoiled.

"Are we expecting somebody else?" Damon asked.

"I hope so," said Saul. "To tell you the truth, I'm rather hoping that your father might drop by. If he's still on Earth, he's had time to reach the neighborhood by now. If he's stranded out in space, though . . . well, we'll just have to wait and see."

Damon didn't bother with any tokenistic assertion of his father's membership of the ultimate silent majority. Instead, he said: "Nobody came in response to your other invitations. Why should anyone come now?"

"Because the cat's out of the bag," the old man told him. "Eveline Hywood hurried the announcement through, in spite of everything. When the grim satisfaction has worn off, though, she'll remember that this is only the beginning. Your father's shown us that he won't be bullied, and that he's more than willing to fight fire with fire, tape for tape and appearance for appearance—but he can't move to the next stage of his plan without clearing it with us because he now knows that we know what that next phase will be—and that if we think it's necessary, we'll close the whole thing down."

"Who's *we?*" Damon wanted to know—and was optimistic, for once, that he might be told.

"All of us. Not just PicoCon, by any means. Your father may think that he made the world, and we're prepared to give him due credit for saving it, but we're the ones who *own* it, and we've already made *our* peace. If he's absolutely determined to return to the days when we were all on the same side, that's fine by us—just so long as it's *our* side that everybody's on."

Damon pulled one of the armchairs back from the fire before sitting down in it. He'd thought that he had recovered well enough from the shot in the back, but once he'd taken the weight off his feet he realized that nobody could get shot, even in today's world, without a considerable legacy of awkwardness and fatigue. He stirred restlessly, unable to find a comfortable posture.

Saul drew back the neighboring chair in the same careful manner, but he went to the table instead of sitting down. "You want food?" he said. "You haven't eaten in quite a while."

Damon knew that he was being offered waiter service, but he didn't want to take it. "I'll help myself, if you don't mind," he said.

"Somehow," said the old man, peering over the rim of his spectacles, "I just *knew* you were going to say that."

Twenty six

I never delivered your message," Damon said when he'd finished licking his fingers. He was sitting more comfortably now—comfortably enough not to want to get up for anything less than a five-star emergency. Saul was still standing up, hovering beside the table while he finished his own meal.

"Yes, you did," the old man countered. "Hywood's more sensitive than you give her credit for. You got through to her, far better than you got through to Kachellek."

"Is Karol really dead?"

"I honestly don't know. I doubt it very much. The business with Silas Arnett took us aback a bit, but I sincerely hope that it was merely a matter of playing to the grandstand: tape for tape, as I said, appearance for appearance. *Our* fake body's better than *your* fake body *and* we got our tape to Interpol while you let yours go astray, so up yours. That *has* to be your father, don't you think? Eveline's as clever as she's stubborn, but she isn't angry or vengeful. But *you'd* have done it all, wouldn't you? You'd have lashed out as soon as you came under attack—and even when you thought you'd won, you'd still have put out one last kick in the head for good measure. You're Conrad Helier's son all right."

"The only father I ever had was Silas Arnett," Damon said, trying to sound offhanded about it. He sipped from his glass. It was only tap water; he'd thought it best to avoid the whiskey and the wine.

"Was it Silas you ran away from?" Saul countered. "Is it Silas you're still kicking against? I think he's just your big brother, who happened to baby-sit a lot. Dead or not, in *that* household` Conrad Helier was always your one and only father. He still is."

That was too near to the knuckle to warrant any response. .

"Why would you send the hired help to invite me up here?" Damon asked. "You already had me not forty-eight hours ago and you threw me back into the pond. You didn't *really* need me to get your message across to Eveline."

Saul smiled. "The Mirror Man thought that we did," he said. "In any case, we had to let you go before we could invite you to join us in a suitably polite fashion. We *are* inviting you to join us, by the way. Partly because it would give us a link to the Lagrange-Five biotech cowboys, but mainly because we think you're good. Now you've seen what virtual reality technics can really do, it's time for you to get properly involved, don't you think?"

"You're offering me a job?"

"Yes."

"With PicoCon?"

"Yes. You could go to OmicronA if you'd prefer—it comes to the same thing in the end."

"I'm not sure I'm ready for that," Damon said slowly.

"I think you are," Saul told him, finally condescending to take the seat opposite Damon's, leaving the one in between for whoever might turn up to take it. "I think you're as thoroughly frustrated with a life of petty crime as Hiru Yamanaka is with the business of catching petty criminals. You must understand by now what drew you into that life—and if you understand that, you must understand how pointless it is."

Damon said nothing to that. Saul didn't press him for an answer but simply settled back in his chair as if he were preparing for a long heart-to-heart talk.

"We live in a world where crime has become much easier to

detect than of old," Saul observed. "A world so abundantly populated by tiny cameras that hardly anything happens unobserved. These ever present eyes are, of course, unconsulted unless and until the police have reason to believe that they might have recorded something significant, but everyone tempted to commit an antisocial act knows that he's *very* likely to be found out.

"If our New Utopia really were a utopia, of course, its citizens wouldn't want to commit antisocial acts, but the sad fact is that almost all of them do. In many cases, the desire to commit such acts is actually *increased* by the awareness that such acts are so readily detectable. In operating as a deterrent, the high probability of detection also acts as a challenge. Everyone knows that spy eyes can be evaded and sometimes deceived—and everyone is ready to do it whenever an opportunity arises. No matter how intensive and efficient Building Security becomes, petty thefts will still occur—not because people need to steal, or because they're avid to acquire whatever it is that they happen to be stealing, but simply because stealing proves that they're still *free* and that the spy eyes haven't *got the better of them.* That's natural, as an immediate reaction, but it's no agenda for a lifelong career."

"Tell that to the Eliminators," Damon said. "They're the ones who take it to extremes—extremes you're not too proud to exploit if it suits you. The Mirror Man *likes* the Eliminators."

"It's not a view I share," Saul told him with a slight sigh. "I do understand them, because I'm of the same generation as most of them, but I think they're foolish as well as wicked. They know that they've been condemned by evil fate to die, while some of those who come after them will be spared that necessity, so it's not entirely surprising that some say to themselves: *murderers were once condemned to die for their crime; why should I, who am condemned to die, refrain from murder? Why should I not enjoy the privilege of my fate? Why should I not accept the opportunity to make the only contribution I can to the coming world of immortals—the exclusion of someone who is unworthy of immortality?* It's not surprising—but it *is* wrong, and ultimately self-destructive.

"Operator one-oh-one, I gather, is rather looking forward to her day in court, in anticipation of being able to plead the Eliminator cause with all due eloquence before a large video audience. Perhaps you ought to watch her—and find a little of your own futility mirrored in hers. It's time to set bitterness and its corollary hostility aside along with other childish things, Damon. Even present technology will give you a hundred and fifty years of adulthood, if you'll only condescend to look after yourself. The technology of a hundred years hence might give you three hundred years more. Think what you might do, if you began now; think what you might help to build, if you decide to become one of the builders instead of one of the vandals."

Damon knew that it all made sense, but he'd had a few thoughts of his own on the matter in spite of the hectic pace of the last few days, and he wasn't ready to roll over just yet. "A little while ago," he said, "I talked to a boy named Lenny Garon. You probably taped the conversation. I told him exactly what you've just told me: to look after himself, to keep his place on the escalator that might one day give him the chance to live forever. Afterwards, though, I got to wondering whether I might be taking too much for granted.

"We've all grown used to the familiar pattern, haven't we? Every couple of years PicoCon or OmicronA pumps out a new fleet of nanotech miracles, which slow down the aging process just a little bit more or take rejuve engineering just a little bit deeper, chipping away at the Hayflick limit and the Miller effect and all the other little glitches that stand in the way of true emortality. Each new generation of products works its way down through the marketplace from the rich to the not-so-rich, and so on, every expansion of the consumer base adding cash to the megacorp coffers. But what if someone *already has* the secret of true emortality? What if the upper echelons of PicoCon already possess a nanotech suite which, so far as they can judge, will let them live forever? What if they decided, when they first obtained the secret, that it was a gift best reserved for the favored few rather than put on general release? After all, even under the New Reproductive System the stability of the population relies on people dying in significant numbers year after year, and megacorp planning depends on the steady flow of profits feeding a never-ending demand, a never-ending *hunger*. I could understand the temptation to hoard the gift away, couldn't you?

"The only trouble is that everyone who was in on the secret—and everyone who subsequently discovered it—would have to be trustworthy. They'd have to be *in the club*. The men in control couldn't have loose cannons threatening to go off at any moment, with no way of knowing where the blast would go. If there were a person like that around, the gods would have to silence him—but they'd have to find him first. As you've so carefully pointed out, a person like me can easily be exposed to thoroughgoing scrutiny in a world where every wall has eyes and ears . . . but some people really can stay out of sight, if they know where the darkest shadows are.

"It's interesting to follow these flights of fancy occasionally, isn't it, Mr. Saul? I still don't know for sure why PicoCon is so desperate to locate a man who's been dead for fifty years, do I?"

"That's an interesting fantasy, Damon," Saul replied. "Isn't it a trifle paranoid, though? The idea that big corporations hold back all the best inventions in order to maintain their markets is as old as capitalism itself."

"We live in a postcapitalist era, Mr. Saul," Damon said earnestly. "The market isn't everything—not anymore. We have to start thinking in terms of millennia rather than centuries. Gods have nobler goals in mind than vulgar profits—and you can spell *profits* any way you like."

Saul laughed at that, and there didn't seem to be anything forced about the laughter. "I suppose that sophisticated biotechnics and clever nanomachinery are so similar to magic that we *have* begun behaving rather like the magicians of legend," he admitted. "We have a tendency to be jealous and secretive; some of us, at least, have learned to love deceit for its own sake. Has your father's team behaved any differently?"

"I think Eveline would argue that your end is merely her means," Damon countered. "She'd say that what the Mirror Man told me—and what you're telling me now—is just advertising, bait on a line to reel me in. She'd argue that you don't really have any long-term objectives except preserving your advantages and maintaining your comforts—that you're obsessed about controlling things because you couldn't bear to *be controlled.* She sees the megacorps as an anchor holding progress back rather than a cutting edge hastening its progress forward."

"And she'd be echoing Conrad Helier every inch of the way—but she'd be wrong. The point is, what do *you* think?"

"I think that you and the Mirror Man really do believe that you're the new gods and I think you're as jealous as any god of old. You want to plan the future, and you want to make sure that everyone will play his allotted part in the plan—or at least that no one's in a position to put a spoke in your wheel."

"I didn't ask you what you think I believe. I asked you what *you* think."

Damon had known exactly what he was being asked—but he wasn't sure that he'd made up his mind about that. "I doubt that you'll ever get *everyone* to agree about the objectives of the game," he ventured. "I think it might be healthier if you didn't even try. After the last couple of days, though, I think one thing you *do* need to get settled is that the game shouldn't be played with real bullets—even certified-nonlethal ones. There's a lot to be said for conflict, if it maintains the dynamic tension that generates social change. There's even something to be said for combat, so long as it isn't mortal, but the distinction between cuts that heal and cuts that don't isn't as easy to make as some people imagine. I don't approve of Elimination either, but I don't want a two-tier system. Everybody should get a chance at real life, whether they're team players or not."

Damon never found out what Saul's reply to that would have been, and he wasn't sorry when the interruption came. He needed time to think about the offer Saul had made him, and he knew that there was vital information that he still didn't have. When the cabin door opened behind him, he was grateful for the respite.

The newcomer looked very tired—as well he might, given that there had been no sound of rotor blades. He'd come on foot, at least for the last kilometer or so.

Damon figured that Saul would be disappointed not to see Conrad Helier, but on his own account he was profoundly glad that the man standing in the doorway was Silas Arnett, very much alive.

"It's very good of you to come, Silas," Saul said with only a hint of mocking irony. "Do join us."

As Silas came forward Damon jumped to his feet and ran to meet him. It wasn't a five-star emergency, but it was a five-star opportunity. Silas seemed slightly surprised, but he accepted the hug before wincing under its pressure.

"Mind my stigmata," he muttered. The wound in his chest was overlaid by his suitskin, but the cloth clung so tightly to the contours of his chest that Damon could see the outlines of the swelling.

"I thought it really might have been the Eliminators who got to you first," Damon said.

"It really might have been," Silas agreed sourly. "As it was, they came too close for comfort to being *accidental* Eliminators. It seems that Karol thought it would be a good idea to declare me dead, just in case I decided to deny that heartfelt confession he put together on my behalf when I returned to public life. As you've probably found out, leaving the group means that they're *very* reluctant to trust you in future. Is this the piece of shit who was judge and prosecutor at my trial?"

Damon could feel the tension in Silas's arms, and he knew that an affirmative answer was likely to call forth an immediate and violent response. He was sorely tempted to say yes, but Saul had softened him up just enough to make him hesitate. "He says not," he said in the end. "He says we can call him Saul, but he didn't say whether it's his first name or his last."

Silas obviously wasn't immediately convinced by the first item of information, but he extricated himself from Damon's embrace and looked hard at the seated man. "Oh *shit!*" he said eventually. "It really is you, isn't it?"

"It's been a long time, Silas," Saul said evenly, "but everyone remembers the spectacles. You really didn't know the man who conducted your interrogation, in spite of that teasing coda he tacked onto the broadcast tape. That was just to prepare the way for the VE pak that went astray—the one that falsely implied that the supposedly late Surinder Nahal was your captor."

"Whereas, in fact," Damon put in, "Surinder Nahal is presumably heading up PicoCon's own zombie biotech team, in direct opposition to yours. Who is this guy, Silas?"

"His name really is Saul," Silas admitted. "Frederick G. Saul was his favored signature way back when—but that was in the days when everybody knew what the G stood for without having it spelled out. I thought he was long dead, but I should have known better."

"I never pretended to die," the bespectacled man observed drily. "I just faded out of view. Would you like something to eat, Silas?"

"I've eaten," Silas replied brusquely.

"To drink?"

Silas looked at Damon's glass. "Just water," he said. He let Saul go to the bathroom to get it while he studied Damon. Saul didn't hurry.

"You all right?" Silas said. "I heard they shot you too."

"Twice," said Damon. "My own fault—the first time I wouldn't lie down for the gas and the second time I wouldn't wait for a polite invitation. I'm fine—and still alive by everyone's reckoning, including the Eliminators who have me down as an enemy of mankind. What *does* the G stand for?"

"Gantz," Silas told him, watching the bathroom door at which

Saul had not yet reappeared. "He's Leon Gantz's grandson, nephew of Paul and Ramon—and his other granddaddy was one of the insiders in the Zimmerman coup. He's one of the last best products of the Old Reproductive System."

Damon said nothing while he mulled over the possible significance of this revelation.

"How's Diana?" Silas asked, groping for a topic of conversation more suited to an emotional reunion between a foster father and his estranged child.

"We split up," Damon told him. By way of retaliation he asked: "How's Cathy?"

"She thinks I'm dead. I haven't decided yet whether to let her in on the secret."

"But you're going to keep it from the rest of the world?" Damon asked, with one eye on the third party who had just reemerged from the bathroom.

Silas shrugged as he accepted a tumbler of water from Frederick Gantz Saul's steady hand; his own was trembling slightly. "Between them, PicoCon and Karol haven't left me a lot of choice, have they? I'm flattered that Eveline wants me back, but it would have been nice to have a less pressured decision to make."

"*Is* it just Karol and Eveline?" Damon asked. "Or is there someone else jerking *their* strings?"

It seemed that Silas couldn't quite meet Damon's eye, so he looked sideways at Saul, as if to say that there were secrets that still needed to be kept.

"He's been told a thousand times," Saul said, "but he still won't believe it. He even tried to imply that it was *you* he was rebelling against, because you were the only real father figure he had. You're the one who owes it to him to explain that flesh and blood do not a father make."

"Clever bastard, isn't he?" Silas said to Damon. Then he sighed theatrically. "We lied to you, Damon. We lied to the world. Conrad's alive. Not on Earth, mind—but he *is* alive. I didn't want to lie to you, but by the time I was ready to break ranks I wasn't sure I could tell you without also telling the world."

It was no longer a surprise, but it *was* a shock of sorts. Damon had to sit down again, and this time he looked into the fire, at the glowing ash flaking from the half-consumed logs.

Silas took the seat next to him: the seat that had been reserved for him all along. "What else do you want to know?" he said quietly. "Saul knows it all by now, I suppose—but he might not have given you a straight account of it. I'm not here to negotiate with him, or to set the seal on any agreements. I'm just here to acknowledge that we've taken note of his concerns."

"So he really is playing God," Damon said, meaning Conrad Helier. "Even to the extent of moving in mysterious ways."

"We're not interested in playing God," Silas countered. "That's *Saul*'s way of looking at the world. The man who taunted me while he made up that fatuous tape mistook the meaning of that quote he flung in my face. We never aimed to *occupy* the vacant throne of God—we just decided that we had to do our bit to help compensate for its vacancy. We're not interested in moving into Olympus—we never have been."

"You'd be happier in the palace of Pandemonium, no doubt?" Damon suggested sarcastically.

"Damon, I don't want to be a god and I *certainly* don't want to be a devil. I'm a man, like other men. So is Conrad."

"Except that you're both supposed to be dead. I couldn't believe that my father had faked his death, even though the Mirror Man seemed so very sure. Even after the Mirror Man had shown me that if anyone in the world had the technical resources to *make* sure, it was him, I wouldn't concede. I couldn't believe that Conrad Helier could be so hypocritical—to preach the gospel of posthumous reproduction as forcefully as he did, and then go into hiding while his friends brought up his own child. If you and he are men like other men, how come there's one law for the rest and another for you?"

"Conrad did back himself into a corner," Silas admitted. "Sometimes, when you change your mind, you have to figure out how best to limit the damage. Being men like other men, Conrad and I don't always get things right. If you live as long as you might, Damon, you'll make plenty of errors of judgment along the way."

"Like designing the viruses which caused the Crash? You did that too, I suppose?"

"We designed one of them. To this day, I don't know for sure who designed the others, although we always suspected that Surinder Nahal must have made at least one—and it wouldn't surprise me in the least if Frederick G. Saul had a hand in it somewhere, even if the hand in question was only clutching a thick wad of cash. It's possible that some of the transformers really did arise naturally—in which case we needn't have bothered—but I always thought the Gaian Mystics were fools to insist beforehand that Ma Nature would find a way, and even bigger fools to insist afterwards that she had. The arguments in the second of my fake confessions were good ones: we didn't kill anybody; we just took away a power which should never have been claimed as a right. When the multiplication of the species reached the point at which the ecosphere stood in imminent danger of irreversible injury, the increase had to be halted, and the reproduction of individuals had to be limited in the interests of the whole community. The Crash had to happen. Conrad tried to make it as painless as possible. If you'd been in his place you'd have done it too."

"So why not take credit for it? Why not admit it, instead of letting the despised Gaian Mystics credit it to the Earth Mother? Why let it hang over your reputation like the sword of Damocles, waiting for a rival megacorp or a maverick Eliminator to cut it loose?"

"The fallout would have interfered with our work. If Conrad had tangled himself up with the necessity to plead his case in the media, he wouldn't have been able to get the New Reproductive System up and running so quickly. Sometimes, hypocrisy is unavoidable."

Damon curled his lip righteously. "And it still is, isn't it?" he said. "Otherwise, Conrad would be able to stand up and take due credit for his latest parlor trick. *He* designed para-DNA, didn't he? Eveline's so-called discovery is just one more Big Lie—a lie that Mr. Saul's friends were trying to nip in the bud. That's what the whole pantomime was intended to do: squash *your* plan before it had a chance to interfere with *theirs.*"

"I don't know anything about that," Silas said sourly. "As soon as I retired, I was out of it. After that, neither Eveline nor Karol would give me the time of day. You'll have to ask Saul for *recent* intelligence of Conrad's plans."

Saul had taken his own seat by now. "You're too modest, Silas,," he said. "You knew the way things were heading. Isn't that why you left?"

"G for Gantz," Silas repeated. "Is that *really* what this has all been about? Keep your sticky hands off *my* toys?"

"No, it isn't," Saul replied sharply. "It isn't a *petty* matter at all. I only wish your friends had realized that."

"You're losing me," Damon observed.

Saul said nothing, stubbornly waiting for Silas to take the responsibility. "You're right, Damon," Silas said eventually. "Para-DNA is a laboratory product. We worked on it for years: a non-DNA life system capable of forming its own ecospheres in environments more extreme than the ones DNA can readily cope with. At first we were talking in terms of bridging the gap between the organic and the inorganic—a whole new nanotech combining the best features of both. The early talk about applications was all about seeding Mars and the asteroids, perhaps as a step in terraformation but not necessarily. Conrad was disappointed about the failure of our probes to find extraterrestrial life, and doubly disappointed by the fact that all the pre-Crash arks that set out in search of new Ararats seemed to have failed in their quest. It was another little flaw in the universal design which Conrad set out to correct. He didn't think of it as playing God—merely compensating once again, in a wholly *human* way, for the vacancy of the divine throne."

"But that was only the *first* plan, wasn't it?" Saul put in.

"Yes," Silas admitted. "Eventually, Conrad began considering other possible applications. There were a lot of people who were glad that the probes and the arks hadn't turned up anything at all: people who'd always thought of alien life in terms of competition and invasion, as a potential *threat*. Conrad despised that kind of cowardice—but there's something about the view of Earth you get from Lagrange-Five and all points farther out that gives people a jaundiced view of the people at the bottom of the gravity well. You've probably seen it in Eveline, if you've talked to her lately—and Mr. Saul is unfortunately correct in judging that Eveline's not much more than Conrad's echo.

"Anyway, for whatever reason, Conrad became increasingly disappointed by the development of the utopia which the New Reproductive System was supposed to have produced. He felt that the old world still cast too deep and dark a shadow over the new. He thought he'd put an end to the old patterns of inheritance, but he was overoptimistic—as you can readily judge from the fact that men like Frederick Gantz Saul are now safely ensconced in the uppermost echelons of PicoCon. For a brief while, when the viruses seemed to have the upper hand, everyone was on the same side—or so it appeared to Conrad—but when the menace had been overcome and the NRS was up and running, the old divisions soon reappeared."

"Remember, though," Saul put in, "that Conrad Helier was a backslider too. You're the living proof of it, Damon. Even he couldn't live up to the highest principles of the utopia he'd sketched out on his drawing board."

Silas ignored that. "Conrad became convinced that Earth had lost its progressive impetus," he said dully. "He became very fond of going on and on about new technology being used to preserve and reproduce the past instead of providing a womb for new ambition. It was mostly hot air, I thought—that was one of the reasons why we fell out. He came to believe that the only way to get things moving here on Earth in a way that would give proper support and encouragement to the people out on the frontier—the Lagrangists and their kin—was to get everyone back on the same side, united against a perceived threat. He came to think that Earth was in need of an alien invader: an all-purpose alien invader which could turn its hand to all kinds of tasks."

Damon shook his head. "Para-DNA," he said. "Utterly harmless but absolutely fascinating, etcetera, etcetera—until more and more of it turns up and it begins to reveal its true versatility. And what then, Silas? Conrad can't possibly be backslider enough to start killing people."

"No," Silas said unhappily. "But he doesn't have any compunctions at all about destroying *property*. That, I assume, is what attracted the attention and fervent interest of Frederick *Gantz* Saul and the present controllers of the Gantz patents. Hence the warning shots fired across our bows. Hence this meeting, in the course of which Mr. Saul will no doubt commission both of us to explain to Conrad and Eveline that the fun's over: that Eveline's preemptive move to established the extraterrestrial credentials of para-DNA has to be our last. I assume he's about to tell us that if the plan goes forward one more inch he and his friends will come after us *hard,* with authentically lethal force."

Damon looked at Saul, who was still looking at Silas. "You shouldn't have retired, Silas," Saul remarked. "You should have stayed on the inside, to maintain a bridge to sanity."

"Conrad's not mad," Silas was quick to retort. "His anxieties were real enough. He's afraid that the earthbound majority of the human race is on the brink of exporting its spirit of adventure to virtual environments, by courtesy of PicoCon's VE division and all the bright young men of Damon's generation. The fashionability of VE games, VE dramas, and telephone VEs is already helping to move a substantial part of everyday human existence and everyday communication into a parallel dimension where artifice rules—and the cleverer the VE designers and the AI answering machines become, the more secure that reign will be.

"Conrad thinks that people shouldn't be living in the ruins of the old world, contentedly huddling together in the better parts of the old cities, binding themselves ever more tightly to their stations in the Web like flies mummified in spider silk. Nor does he think it's rebellion enough against that kind of a world for the disaffected young to use derelict neighborhoods as adventure playgrounds where they can carve one another up in meaningless ritual duels. He thinks that if we can't maintain some kind of historical momentum, we'll stagnate. He thinks that we have to build and keep on building, to grow and keep on growing, to expand the human empire and keep on expanding it, to *make progress.* If people need a spur to urge them on, he's more than willing to provide it. I don't say that's right, but it's not *mad.*

"Like the viruses which caused the Crash, Conrad intends para-DNA to be nonlethal weaponry—nothing more than a nuisance. It's supposed to attack the structure of the cities and the structure of the Web; it's supposed to make it impossible for the human race to dig itself a hole and live in manufactured dreams. It wouldn't attack people, and it certainly wouldn't murder people wholesale, but it would always be *there:* a sinister, creeping presence that would keep on cropping up where it's least expected and where it's least welcome, to remind people that there's nothing—*nothing,* Damon—that can be taken for granted. Long life, the New Reproductive System, Earth, the solar system . . . all these things have to be managed, guarded, and guided. According to Conrad, we ought to be looking toward the *real* alien worlds instead of—or at least as well as— synthesizing comfortable simulacra. Whatever you or I might think of his methods, he's *not mad.*"

"I can see why PicoCon thinks it's necessary to rein you in, though," Damon observed. "I can understand why the people who actually *own* the earth and all the edifices gantzed out of its surface would like the right of veto over schemes like that."

"Maybe," said Silas. "But I think Conrad *might* argue that the current owners of the Gantz patents ought to be down on their bended knees thanking him for introducing an element of built-in obsolescence to their endeavors. Mr. Saul would presumably prefer it if the meek inherited the earth, because he thinks that a meek consumer is a good consumer. He and his kind are interested in what people *want,* and the more stable and predictable those wants become, the better he'll like it—but Conrad's more interested in what people *need.*"

Damon looked at Saul, who seemed quite untroubled by anything Silas had said.

"At the end of the day, though," Damon pointed out, "Pico-Con calls the shots, here *and* in outer space. The secret couldn't be kept—and now that it's out, Conrad, Eveline, and Karol have no alternative but to abandon the plan."

"That's not for me to decide," Silas said obdurately. "I'm not here to negotiate."

"Of course not," said Saul with a hint of malicious mockery. "But you can carry an olive branch, can't you? One way or another, now that you've joined the ranks of the unsleeping dead, you'll be able to transmit our offer of a just and permanent peace to Conrad Helier?"

"Just and permanent?" Silas echoed, presumably to avoid giving a straighter answer.

"That's what we want," Saul said. "It's also, in our opinion, what we all *need.* We don't want to bludgeon Conrad Helier—or the Ahasuerus Foundation for that matter—into reluctant and resentful capitulation. We really would like them to see things our way. That's why we're mortally offended by their refusal even to *talk* to us. Yes, we do have the power to impose our will—but we'd far rather reach a mutually satisfactory arrangement. I think Conrad Helier has seriously mistaken our position and our goals, and the true logic of the present situation here on Earth."

All Silas said in reply to that was: "Go on."

"Your anxiety regarding the possibility of people giving up on the real world in order to live in manufactured dreams is an old one," Saul said mildly. "The corollary anxiety about the willingness of their effective rulers to meet the demand for comforting dreams is just as old—and so is Conrad's facile assumption that the best way to counter the trend is to import new threats to jolt the meek inheritors of Earth out of their meekness and expel them from their utopia of comforts. Frankly, I'm as disappointed by Conrad's recruitment to such an outmoded way of thinking as I am by the Ahasuerus Foundation's retention of *their* equally obsolete attitude of mind.

"I can understand the fact that you don't approve of me, either personally or in terms of what I represent. One of my grandfathers was part of the consortium which funded Adam Zimmerman's scheme to take advantage of a worldwide stock-market crash—one of the men who really did *steal the world* or *corner the future,* according to your taste in clichés. The other was the man whose pioneering work in biotechnological cementation made it possible to build homes out of desert sand and exhausted soil that were literally *dirt* cheap, thus giving shelter to millions, but you probably think that the good he did was canceled out by the enormity of the fortune that flowed from the generations of patents generated and managed by his sons—my uncles. I am the old world order personified: one of a double handful of men who really did own the world by the end of the twenty-first century.

"Oddly enough, the fact that we still own it today has a good deal to do with Conrad Helier. Had he not put the New Reproductive System in place so quickly, the devastations of the Crash might have extended even to us; as it was, his efficiency allowed rather more of the old world order to be saved than he might have thought ideal. Nor has he put an end to the ancient system of inheritance, as his own legacy to Damon clearly demonstrates. When I and my fellow owners die—as, alas, we still must, in spite of all the best efforts of the Ahasuerus Foundation—we shall deliver the earth into safe hands, which can be trusted to keep it safe for as long as they may live. Eventually, there will arise a generation who will keep it safe forever.

"You may think it terrible that effective ownership of the entire earth should remain forever in the hands of a tiny Olympian elite, but ownership is also stewardship. While the earth was effectively common land it was in the interest of every individual to increase his own exploitation of it at the expense of others—and the result was an ecocatastrophe which would have rendered the planet uninhabitable if the Crash had not been precipitated in the nick of time.

"We cannot and will not tolerate further threats to the security of Earth, because Earth is too precious to be put at the smallest risk. Our news of the arks is old, and the news sent back by our more ambitious probes is hardly less recent, but the fact is that we have so far found no sign of any *authentic* extraterrestrial life. There is no threat in that discovery, but there is no *promise* either: no promise of any safe refuge should any extreme misfortune befall Earth. The pre-Crash ecocatastrophe might well have caused the extinction of the human species, and nothing like it can ever be permitted to happen again. If our outward expansion into the universe is to continue—and I agree with Conrad Helier that it ought not to be the exclusive prerogative of clever machinery—then it must continue in response to *opportunity,* not to threat.

"True progress cannot be generated by fear; it has to be generated by *ambition.* You may well dread the prospect of a wholesale retreat into artificial worlds of custom-designed illusion, but it's pointless to try to drive people from their chosen refuges with whips and scorpions; they'll only try all the harder to return. The *real* task is to offer them real-world opportunities that will easily outweigh the rewards of synthetic experience."

"When your new nanotech VEs hit the marketplace, that isn't going to be easy," Damon observed. "Or did the Mirror Man's little lecture about products not being made for the market mean that you intend to bury the technology?"

"What my colleague was trying to explain," Saul said, "is that we're not developing such technologies solely with a view to putting new products in the marketplace. We have much broader horizons in mind, but we're not going to bury *anything*—not even para-DNA. We have more faith in humankind than Conrad Helier does. We don't believe that the people of Earth, however meek they may become, will want to retreat into manufactured dreams twenty-four hours a day. We don't believe that people will settle for cut-price contentment when they still have the prospect of real achievement before them—and we *do* believe that they still have the prospect of real achievement. We think Conrad Helier's aims can better be served by a carrot than a stick—and *that*'s why we're so very anxious to bring him to the conference table. We never wanted to bury para-DNA; what we'd really like to do is to investigate the contribution it might make to our own methods of breaking down the distinction between the organic and the inorganic."

"You want to *buy* it?" Silas said in a tone which implied that he didn't believe that a man like Conrad Helier—unlike the inheritors of the Gantz patents—would ever sell out to PicoCon.

"Not necessarily," said Saul wearily. "In fact, I have grave doubts as to whether it has any potential at all that our own people don't already have covered—but I do want to talk about its potential, and its appropriate uses. It's not impossible that we might actually be able to assist in Conrad's great crusade. In fact, I think it's more than likely that we can. If only he would condescend to listen, I think we can show him a future far brighter and infinitely more promising than the one he presently has in mind."

Damon could see that this was not what Silas had expected. He had had no clear idea what to expect on his own account, but he had to admit that Saul's line of argument had taken him by surprise. Like Silas, he had been thinking entirely in terms of threats—who could blame either of them, after the violent farce of the last few days?—and he was not quite willing to believe, as yet, that there was nothing within the iron glove but a velvet fist. He was, however, prepared to listen—and so, it appeared, was Silas, both on his own behalf and that of Conrad Helier.

"All right," said Silas, flushing slightly as he glanced at Damon—as if he were in search of approval, or at least of understanding. "Tell me what you're offering. If it seems worthwhile, I'll do everything within my power to make sure that Conrad, Eveline, and Karol pay proper attention—but it had better be good."

"It is," said Frederick Gantz Saul. "It certainly is."

Twenty-seven

Damon eased his car through the midmorning traffic, which was flowing normally through well-behaved control lights. He couldn't help feeling a slightly exaggerated sense of his own mortality, in spite of the profuse official denials that had been issued to confirm that he was *not* Conrad Helier, enemy of mankind. While there were people around who worked on the assumption that everything on the news was likely to be a lie, such denials were likely to be less effective than sly denunciations of the kind that Saul's people had put out while they were still playing rough.

He knew that it was well within the capability of any twelve-year-old or hundred-and-twelve-year-old Webwalker to discover his address and car registration. He knew too that one of the problems of longevity was that it preserved a substantial fraction of the madness to which people were subject alongside the sanity which only the majority achieved. The downside of efficient IT was that it did a far better job preserving the body than it did preserving the mind—and some kinds of madness, albeit not the nastiest kinds, really were *all* in the mind.

At present, that downside was limited; the most powerful nanotechnologies were so recent in their provenance that even under the New Reproductive System less than a sixth of the population of California consisted of centenarians. In fifty years' time, however, that percentage would have trebled, and most of the 15 percent of current centarians would still be alive. Nobody knew how many of those would still be compos mentis; Morgan Miller had been dead for nearly a hundred and eighty years, but the effect named after him had not yet revealed the full extent of its horror. True emortality required more than the continual revitalization of somatic cells; it required the continued revitalization of the idiosyncratic neuronal pathways that were the foundation of every individual self, every unique personality.

According to Frederick Gantz Saul, there would be crazy people around for some time yet—but not forever. In time, according to Saul, sanity would prevail; foolishness, criminal behavior, and disaffection would fade into oblivion and everyone would be *safe*. Damon still had not made up his mind whether to believe that, let alone whether to believe Saul's further assertion that the sanity and safety in question would not be a kind of stagnation.

The heightened sense of mortality should have worn off once he was off the street, but it didn't. It accompanied him in the elevator and didn't let up when he stepped out into the LA offices of the Ahasuerus Foundation. Damon hadn't made an appointment, and he wouldn't have felt utterly crushed if he'd been told to go away by the AI receptionist; but Rachel Trehaine didn't even keep him kicking his heels for the customary ten minutes of insult time. He had expected to find her in a frosty mood, but she was positively welcoming—presumably because she was curious.

"How can I help you, Mr. Hart?" she asked.

"I hoped that you might be able to offer me an expert opinion," he said. "I'm not sure that I have anything to offer in trade, but you might be interested in some of what I have to say."

"I can't speak on behalf of the foundation," she was quick to say. "I'm only . . ."

"A humble data analyst," Damon finished for her. "That's okay. You've heard, I suppose, that the three men Yamanaka arrested have pleaded guilty to all the charges—kidnapping, illegal imprisonment, conspiracy to pervert the course of justice, etcetera. They'll be put away for at least twenty years—but I dare say that when they come out of suspended animation they'll walk straight into jobs with PicoCon, who'll bear the full responsibility and cost of their rehabilitation. There won't be a full trial, of course—just a formal hearing to determine the sentence."

"I'm sure that Inspector Yamanaka is very grateful to you," the red-haired woman said. "If you hadn't resisted so valiantly when they came after you a second time. . . ."

"Actually, it was all Lenny Garon's doing. When he heard them say that they weren't police, he leaped to the conclusion that they were Eliminators enthusiastic to execute an enemy of mankind. Hero worship eclipsed his sense of probability for a few vital moments. I'm grateful to him, of course, but I think Inspector Yamanaka still has a lurking suspicion that he's been fobbed off with a few disposable scapegoats. He doesn't believe that it was all their own idea. On the other hand, he doesn't really want to look *too* hard for evidence of the involvement of a man like Frederick Saul, in case his career runs onto the rocks."

"People who *have* careers do have to be careful, Mr. Hart," she pointed out.

"True—and I certainly don't want to jeopardize yours. In fact, I rather hoped that you might be able to help me out with my own career decisions. I seem to have reached something of a crossroads."

"The Ahasuerus Foundation isn't interested in employing you," she told him.

"PicoCon is."

"In that case," she said, "you should count yourself very fortunate."

"I've heard that they have a great future ahead of them," Damon admitted, "but I'm not sure that their optimism would be shared—at least not wholeheartedly—by an unbiased observer."

"I'm flattered that you consider me an unbiased observer," she assured him, "but I'm not sure that I have enough facts at my disposal to make a reasoned analysis of your career prospects with PicoCon or any other company."

"But you do know something about the Saul family, don't you? One of the men who financed the foundation was a Saul, wasn't he?"

"The Ahasuerus Foundation was set up by Adam Zimmerman, entirely funded from his own resources."

"Resources which he earned, if *earned* is the right word, by masterminding a coup which turned a stock-market crash into an economic holocaust—and left a few dozen men with effective possession of two-thirds of the earth's surface. The possession in question then made inexorable progress to the point at which those men's heirs—who are even fewer in number than they were—are now the effective owners of the whole earth."

"That's a slight exaggeration," Rachel Trehaine protested.

"I know," Damon said. "But the point is that it's only *slight*. As long as they're united, and as long as they can keep buying up innovators like PicoCon and OmicronA, the gods of New Olympus really do own the earth—and they're busy reinventing the laws of trespass."

No reply was forthcoming to that observation, but Damon hadn't expected one. "I looked at the background material Madoc dredged up for me," he said. "Adam Zimmerman's so-called confession is a remarkable document—as remarkable, in its way, as the charter he set up for the foundation. His *penultimate will and testament* poses an interesting philosophical question, though. You're supposed to bring him out of suspended animation when you have the technology available to make him young again and keep him that way forever—barring the usual accidents, of course—but what would qualify as reasonable grounds for believing that the latter criterion had been achieved? Some might argue that a man of his age—he was forty-eight, wasn't he, when he was consigned to the freezer?—already has a good chance of riding the escalator all the way, but you'd undoubtedly take the view that he'd want the benefit of *much* better rejuve technology than the current market standard—technology that could be *guaranteed* to beat the Hayflick limit and the Miller effect."

"With all due respect," said the red-haired woman, "the internal affairs of the foundation are none of your concern."

"I understand that. I'm only talking hypothetically. I'm intrigued by the question of how we could ever *know* that we were in possession of a technology of rejuvenation that would stop aging *permanently*, preserving the mind as well as the body. How could we ever know that a particular IT suite was good for, say, two thousand years, without actually waiting two thousand years for the results of the field tests to come in? What sort of data analysis would allow us to reach a conclusion regarding the efficacy of the technology ahead of time?"

"It wouldn't be easy," Rachel Trehaine admitted warily. "But we now have a very detailed knowledge of the biochemistry of all the degenerative processes we lump together as *aging*. At present, we arrive at estimates of projected life spans by monitoring those processes over the short term in such a way as to produce an extrapolatable curve. That curve has to be adjusted for rejuvenative interruptions, but we can do medium-term experiments to monitor the effects of repeated rejuvenative treatments."

"Do you still use mice for those experiments?" Damon asked.

"We use live animals in some trials," she countered rather stiffly, "but most of the preliminary work can be done with tissue cultures. I assume that what you're driving at is the impossibility of getting rid of the margin of uncertainty which arises from dealing with any kind of substitute for human subjects. You're right, of course—we'll never be sure that a treatment which multiplies the lifetime of a cell or a mouse by a thousand will do the same for a human being, until we've actually tried it."

"As I see it," Damon said, "we'll *never* be able to tell the difference between a technological suite that will allow us to live for a long time and one which really will allow us to live *forever*. Most people, of course, don't give a damn about that—they only want the best there is—but *you* have to decide when to wake

Adam Zimmerman up. You have to decide, day by day and year by year, exactly how to balance the equation of potential gain against potential risk—because you can't leave him in there indefinitely, can you? Nor can you keep waking him up to ask his advice, because every journey in or out of susan multiplies the risks considerably, and even the nanotech you pump into him while he's still down and out can't fully compensate for the fact that the first susan technology he used was pre-ark."

"You're right," she admitted. "For us, if for no one else, nice statistical distinctions are important. What's your point?"

"For a long time, Ahasuerus must have been field leaders in longevity research. Your heavy investment in biotech put you on the crest of the wave—and you presumably had a healthy and mutually supportive relationship with other researchers, all the way from Morgan Miller to Conrad Helier and Surinder Nahal. You were all on the same side, all trading information like good team players. Then PicoCon and OmicronA came at the problem from a different angle, with a different attitude. They're the field leaders now, aren't they? While they've been forming their own team, yours has broken up. Nowadays, it must require serious industrial espionage to discover what the boys across the street are up to, and exactly how far they've got."

"The Ahasuerus Foundation is not involved in industrial espionage," she informed him as stiffly and as flatly as she was bound to do.

"It's not simply a matter of there being a new team in town, is it?" Damon went on softly. "The real problem is that they're trying to redefine the game. They're moving the goalposts and rewriting the rules. They're worried about your willingness to play by the new rules because they're worried about the terms of your charter—about the responsibility you owe to Adam Zimmerman. Is it possible, do you think, that they're anxious that letting Adam Zimmerman out of the freezer might be tantamount to letting the cat out of the bag?"

"What's that supposed to mean, Mr. Hart?"

"Let me put it this way, Dr. Trehaine. It might well be that the people with the very best internal technology would consider it desirable, or even necessary, to play down its power: to maintain the belief that what people insist on calling immortality not only isn't immortality but isn't even true emortality. It might well be that the people who control the IT megacorps consider it desirable or necessary to persuade their would-be heirs that patience is still the cardinal virtue—that in order to inherit the earth they only have to wait until their elders lose their memories, their minds, and, in the end, their *lives*. If that reality were mere appearance and illusion—if all the patience in the world wouldn't be enough to allow the young to come into their inheritance—what hope would there be for people like me? What is there to wait for, if my generation can *never* become the inheritors of Earth?"

"If you think that we already have true emortality, Mr. Hart," Rachel Trehaine said drily, "you're mistaken. I can say that with certainty."

"I'm not sure how much your certainty is worth, Dr. Trehaine," Damon told her bluntly, "but even if you're right—what about the escalator? If IT really is advancing quickly enough to put true emortality in the hands of people now alive, what will it be worth *to the young*? While each generation thinks that it has a chance to be the first to the top of the mountain, the philosophy of Elimination will remain the province of outsiders—but as soon as it becomes generally known that the summit has been claimed, and claimed in perpetuity, the Eliminators might become a valuable asset to those whose uneasy heads are only a few funerals away from the crown.

"You're the professional data analyst, Dr. Trehaine—you're in a far better position than I am to balance all the variables in the equation. How do *you* like the Eliminators? How far away are we, in your estimation, from an undeclared war between the young and the old? And what, if you were a rising star in the Pico-Con/OmicronA constellation, would you want to do about it?"

"I think you're being ridiculously melodramatic," said Rachel Trehaine calmly. "We live in a civilized world now. Even if everyone knew that they were truly emortal, they'd have better sense than to go to war for ownership of the world. They'd know perfectly well that any such war might easily end up destroying the prize they were fighting for. Wouldn't it be better to live forever, happily and comfortably, in a world you didn't own than to risk death in order to possess a handful of its ashes?"

"You might think that," Damon said, "and so might I—but we've moved in rather different social circles during the last twenty years, and I can assure you that there are plenty of people out there who are willing to kill, even at the risk of being killed. There are plenty of people who value real freedom over comfort and safety—people who would never be content to live in a world they have no power to change."

"There are other worlds," Rachel Trehaine said mildly. "Now that we've saved Earth, the new frontiers in space are opening up again. The arks launched before the Crash are still en route—and if Eveline Hywood and her panspermist friends are right, the galaxy must be full of worlds that have ecospheres of their own, including many that are ripe for colonization."

"That's the optimistic view," Damon agreed. "As far as we know for sure, though, there isn't an acre of worthwhile real estate anywhere in the universe outside of Earth. As far as we know for sure, this world is *the* world. No matter how many people decide to live in glorified tin cans like the domes of Mars and Lagrange-Five, *Earth* might be the only inheritance that has any real market value—the only thing worth fighting for."

"Perhaps your years as a streetfighter have given you an unduly jaundiced view of your fellow men, Mr. Hart," said the data analyst. "Perhaps you haven't yet become sufficiently adult to realize how utterly juvenile such boys' games are."

"I realize that you don't much like playing games, Dr. Trehaine," Damon countered, "but you must have noticed that not everyone shares your distaste."

"What, exactly, do you want from me?" she asked.

"An opinion. An *honest* opinion, if you're willing to provide it, regarding Frederick Gantz Saul's argument that no one should fight the world's present owners for control of the world."

"What *is* his argument?" she countered, although Damon had already judged—on the basis of their eye-to-eye contact—that she knew perfectly well what Saul was offering the independent thinkers who hadn't yet fallen in line with his plans for the remaking of the world.

"He says that the nanotech revolution has only just begun, and that it can't be carried forward to its proper conclusion by the forces of commercial competition. He says that the future of the world now needs to be planned, and that too many cooks would undoubtedly spoil the broth. He reckons that the world has always underestimated the true potential of gantzing biotech because of its historical association with the business of building elementary shelters for the poorest people in the world. Cementing mud, sand, and all kinds of other unpromising materials into solid structures may seem crude and vulgar to us, but in Saul's estimation it's the foundation stone of a true bridge between the organic and the inorganic.

"We already have biotech which will transform animal egg cells into huge tissue cultures of almost any design the gene-tweakers can dream up, and modify viable organisms in thousands of interesting and useful ways. If research like yours eventually bears fruit, we'll be able to modify human beings in exactly the same way, engineering ova in artificial wombs so that they won't need elaborate IT to provide all the extra features—like emortality—that we consider necessary and desirable. According to Saul, that revolution will be completed by gantzing biotech/nanotech hybrids, which will enable us to work miracles of transformation with any and all *inorganic* structures.

"Saul calls himself a true Gaian—not a Gaian Mystic, but someone with a *real* understanding of the implications of the Gaia hypothesis. The whole point of that hypothesis, according to Saul, is that it's wrong to think of the inorganic environment as something *given,* as a framework within which life has to operate. Just as Earth's atmosphere is a product of life, he says, so are its oceans and its rocks: *everything* at the surface is part of the same system—and when we take control of that system, as we very soon will, it won't simply be a matter of juggling Earth's biomass; we'll have more transformative power than the so-called continental engineers ever dreamed of. Earth's crust will be ours to sculpt as we wish—or, rather, as Earth's *owners* wish.

"But that, according to Saul, is only the beginning. As below, he says, so above. Give him gantzers powerful enough and a few hundred years, and he'll change the faces of Mars and Venus. Every asteroid in the belt will be an egg patiently awaiting gantzing sperms to transform it into a star-traveling monster, bigger than a thousand arks and infinitely more comfortable. Only give them the time, he says, and the owners of Earth will give the whole universe to the rest of us. Only give them time, and they'll show us what *ownership* really can mean, by demonstrating that there is no matter anywhere which needs to be considered inert or useless. Only give them time, and they will bring the entire universe to life—and all they ask in return is Earth, their own precious corner, their own legitimate heritage.

"That's what Frederick Gantz Saul offered Conrad Helier, in exchange for effective ownership and control of para-DNA. That's what he must have offered your employers in order to bring them meekly into line. It's what he'll offer everyone who ever looks as if they *might* be getting out of line—but I'd be willing to bet that he'll always be prepared to show them the stick before offering the carrot, just to make sure that he has their full attention. So what I need to know, Dr. Data Analyst, is: *is it true?* Or is it, perhaps, just a clever line of patter, intended to defuse all opposition to a state of affairs that puts Saul and his friends in almost total control of what might—so far as we know for sure—be the only world there is or ever will be."

"And you want an honest opinion?" Rachel Trehaine challenged him. "*My* honest opinion, as an individual rather than an employee of the Ahasuerus Foundation."

"If you think I've given you enough in exchange," he said, "I'd be very grateful."

"Unfortunately," she said, "you've already put your finger on the root of the problem. However expert we may be as data analysts, we can't possibly know for sure how good our extrapolations are. Only time will tell whether Saul's promises can be redeemed. In the meantime, they're pie in the sky. On the other hand, what other choice have you got? If you don't buy into *his* dream, all you have is the prospects of a teenage streetfighter permanently engaged in a rebellion he can't win. If you don't want to work directly for PicoCon you can always join Eveline Hywood in Lagrange-Five, or make your way to whichever far-flung hidey-hole your father found for himself, but you know better than to think that they can continue to avoid toeing the line. They're old enough to know better—and so are you."

Damon had kept his eyes locked on hers while she delivered this speech, but he let them fall now.

"What did you expect me to say?" she asked him not unkindly. "What else *could* I say?"

"I thought I ought to make sure," Damon told her, trying to sound grateful for her effort. "I didn't know how far out of line Ahasuerus was. I suppose I was wondering whether there was something you knew that I didn't, or something you might see that I'd missed—something which would put the matter into a less dismal light."

"If Saul's right," she told him, "the light's not dismal at all. You may not be able to have a substantial share in the earth, but how many people ever could? The point is that you—or your heirs—might still be able to claim a substantial share of the universe. For all his faults, Saul tells a hell of a story—and it *might* be true. Shouldn't we at least hope that it is?"

"I suppose we should," Damon admitted grudgingly.

Twenty-eight

Madoc Tamlin went out onto the bedroom balcony and lifted his face to bathe in the light of the afternoon sun. The breakers tumbling over the shingle had just begun their retreat from the ragged line of wrack and plastic that marked the high tide. In the distance, he could see Lenny Garon and Catherine Praill walking together, making slow but methodical progress in the direction of the house.

High above the house a young wing glider was wheeling in search of a thermal. His angelic wings were painted like a flamingo's, each pink-tinted pinion feather brightly outlined. Madoc had never seen a real flamingo, but he knew that they were smaller by far than the bird boy. Natural selection had never produced a bird as large as the human glider, but modern technology had taken over where mutation had left off, in every sphere of human existence.

Madoc smiled as he watched the glider swoop low and then soar, having found his thermal. He willed the flier to attempt a loop or some equally daring stunt, but the conditions weren't right and the boy hadn't yet obtained the full measure of his skill. In time, no doubt, he would dare anything—flirtation with danger was at least half the fascination that attracted men to flight.

Damon was lucky to have inherited a house like this, Madoc thought—all the more so if, as Damon continued to insist, Silas

Arnett's death had been no more real than Surinder Nahal's. It was a pity that Damon didn't seem to appreciate what he had—but that had always been Damon's problem.

"Who was on the phone?"

Madoc hadn't heard Diana Caisson come up behind him; her bare feet made no sound on the thick carpet.

"Damon," he said, without turning to look at her. He knew that she would be wearing nothing but a bath towel.

"When's he coming?"

Still Madoc wouldn't turn to face her. "He's not," he said.

"What?"

"He's not coming."

"But I thought. . . ." Diana trailed off without finishing the sentence, but *she* wasn't finished. Madoc watched her cheeks go red, and he saw her fist clench harder than any streetfighter's fist. He'd seen her draw blood before, and he didn't expect to see anything less this time.

Madoc knew what Diana had thought. She'd thought that Damon had offered them temporary use of the house he'd inherited from Silas Arnett as a roundabout way of fixing up a meeting. She was still waiting for Damon to "see the light": to realize that he couldn't bear to be without her and that he had to mend his ways in order to win her back. When Damon had returned the full set of master tapes which he'd plundered for his various VE productions, she'd recklessly assumed that it was the first step on the way to a reconciliation: a gesture of humility.

Madoc knew different. Damon had never been one for seeing the lights that other people suspended for him. He liked to chase his own fox fires.

"What *did* he say?" Diana asked.

Madoc thought for a moment that she might be trying—unsuccessfully—to suppress her annoyance, but then he realized that it was just a slow buildup. He didn't suppose he had any real chance of heading her off, but he felt obliged to try. "He said that we should relax and enjoy ourselves. He said that we could stay as long as we want, because he doesn't anticipate using the house at all. It's on the market, of course, but it could take weeks to sell, or even months."

"Will he be coming later in the week?"

"No, Di. When he says that he doesn't intend using the place at all, that's exactly what he means. He's busy."

"Busy!" Her voice had risen to a screech. "He's just inherited two small fortunes, to add to the one he already had but somehow never got around to mentioning. He doesn't have to make any more telephone tapes, or any more game tapes, or any more fight tapes, or any more pornotapes . . . not that he ever did, it seems. He can do anything he damn well likes!" Diana had not yet begun to accept that she was fighting a losing battle, because she hadn't yet begun to understand why she had never had a chance of winning it.

"That's right," Madoc told her as gently as he could. "He can do anything he *likes*—and what he likes, as it happens, is setting himself up in business."

"He could have done that in Los Angeles!"

"He thinks Los Angeles is way too crowded. There's no real privacy here. If he were going to stay here, he said, he might as well take the job that PicoCon offered him. He wants to work where he can feel free."

"And what, exactly, is he going to work *at*?" Her fingernails were drawing blood now, and were sinking even further into her flesh in response to the anesthetic ministrations of her IT.

"I don't know. Not VE, he says. Biotech, I suppose—that's what he was trained for, before he ran away to join the circus. As to what kind of biotech, I wouldn't know."

Diana had no reply to that but curses—and the curses rapidly turned to violent action. For a moment, Madoc thought she might actually try to take it out on him, but she turned and hurled herself upon the bed instead, tearing at the quilt with her bloody hands, lacerating its surface as easily as she had lacerated her own flesh. The filling came out in flocculent lumps which rose into the air as she beat the bed in frustration.

Madoc wondered, as he always did, whether he ought to slap

her about the face the way people sometimes did in antique movies, but he had never believed that it would work. It might conceivably have worked *then,* but it wouldn't now. The world was different now, and so was the quality of Diana's hysteria. Madoc couldn't believe that the hysteria was authentically destructive, let alone self-destructive. He couldn't believe that it was anything more than a performance, whose safety was guaranteed by courtesy of her IT—but it wasn't a performance he wanted to get involved in.

Damon had had something of the same fierce reactivity in him once, but Damon's had drained away. Damon had made a kind of peace with the world, and Diana's inability to make a similar peace had driven them apart.

"It's pointless, Di," Madoc said, going forward as if to take her arm when her fury had abated a little.

She lashed out at him from a prone position, but it was a half-hearted blow. He caught her arm easily enough, turned her over, and then caught the other so that he could look into her face without fear for his eyes.

She was weeping, but she wasn't sobbing.

"Give it up, Di," he said as softly as he could. "It's not worth it. *Nothing*'s worth that kind of heartache, that much frustration."

Diana shook away his constraining hands, then shoved him aside and walked past him to the balcony. She barely glanced at the boy with the flamingo wings, or at the approaching figures of Lenny and Catherine. She was lost inside herself.

"I'd have gone with him, if he asked," she said in a tortured voice. "To the ends of the earth, if necessary. A new start might be exactly what we need. I wish he could understand that. I wish. . . ."

"He isn't going to ask you, Di," Madoc said. "He isn't even going to ask *me.* Damon's always been restless. He has to keep moving on."

"He shouldn't be in such a hurry," Diana said, still shivering with resentment. "The one thing nobody needs to do in today's world is *hurry*. There's time enough for everything. He really ought to slow down. I think he's running away, and I don't think it'll solve anything. Running never does. Nobody ever really *solves* anything until they can settle down and sort out exactly what it is they want. He *needs* me—he's just too stubborn to admit it."

"Maybe he is running away," Madoc said, "but not from you. Whatever he wants, you're simply not included. He doesn't mean to hurt you; he's just doing what he thinks he needs to do. Let him go, Di, for your own sake."

Madoc knew that he wasn't getting through to her, but Lenny and Cathy were close enough by now to see her face, and she still cared enough about appearances to want to hide the true extent of her despair from them.

"Why do *they* get the big bedroom?" she demanded, fixing her angry gaze on their fellow guests but holding her bloody hands behind her back, where only Madoc could see what she'd done.

"Because that's what Damon wanted," Madoc muttered. "He thinks he owes Lenny a favor, even though it was all a stupid mistake. I owe him one too, I suppose—if Yamanaka hadn't had the other guys to stamp on, I might not have got off with a fine. Try to relax, will you. You might actually begin to enjoy yourself."

There was a slight pause before she said: "I can't." Her voice was barely above a whisper, but it was no less bitter for that— and she was only keeping her voice down because Lenny and Catherine were almost within earshot. Madoc suppressed his annoyance and put a protective arm around her bare shoulders.

"Time heals," he said, "and as you say, we have plenty of it."

"Sure," she said, continuing in the same conspicuously weak but bitter tone. "We have a hundred years, or maybe two. We have legions of little robocops patrolling our veins and our nervous systems, ready to take care of any pain that might happen to catch us by surprise. We're superhuman. Except that there are some pains that all the nanotech in the world can't soothe, some sicknesses that all the antiviruses in the world can't cure. At the end of the day, it's what you feel in your *heart* that counts, not what you feel in your hands and feet—and *there*, we're as frail and feeble as we ever were. What use is eternity, if you can't have what you want?"

"What use would eternity be if we could?" Madoc countered, knowing that it was exactly what Damon would have said. "If there were nothing we needed so badly it made us sick, and nothing we wanted so avidly that it made us wretched, what would draw us through today into tomorrow . . . and tomorrow and tomorrow and tomorrow?"

"That's good," said Lenny, standing below the balcony and waving up at them. "That's really good. You sound exactly like Damon."

"I taught him everything he knows," Madoc said, offhandedly. "He got it all from me. He may think he doesn't need me any-more, but I'll always be with him. In his mind and in his heart, there'll always be something of me. And you too, of course, Di. We mustn't forget your contribution to the making of the man."

Diana had already turned away, unwilling to expose the soreness of her distress to two mere children who couldn't possibly understand. She didn't look back to acknowledge Madoc's sarcasm.

"One day," said Cathy, looking up at the glider, "I'm going to get a pair of wings like that. Not in pink, though. I want to be a falcon, or a bird of paradise, or a golden oriole . . . or all three, and then some. I want to fly as high as I possibly can, and as *far* as I possibly can."

Diana made a sound like a kitten in pain, but she was still determined to keep the full extent of her anguish from the boy and the girl.

"You will," Madoc said, looking down at the silken crown of Cathy's head and wondering whether Lenny could possibly be persuaded that an older and more passionate woman might be far more useful to his sentimental education than a girl his own age. "Once *you've* learned to fly, even the sky won't be the limit."